She has to save **[   ]**
but he's not the only one in danger. . . .

Suddenly, the air in the lab became chilled, as if an arctic wind had blown through. The desk lamp started to sputter, and Cumberland growled deeply.

Kate froze.

"*Wwwherrrre iisssss iittttt?*" crackled an otherworldly voice from somewhere in the hallway.

Kate turned to the door, and again to the ring sitting in the drawer. Hurriedly, with trembling hands, she took the beaker, lifted the top, and poured in the precious green fluid. The ring snapped closed.

"*Ggggiiivvve iittttt ttoo mmmeeeee.*"

She stared at the ring, but sheer fright kept her from putting it on. The ghost was back! The empty beaker fell from her hand onto the floor and splintered into pieces.

The lab grew quickly colder as a wisp of white vapor appeared in the doorway.

"*Iittttt iisssss mmmiinnnne.*"

Then everything became a blur of motion as the ghost sailed through the door, Cumberland leaped, and Kate reached for the ring.

THE Heartlight SAGA

HEARTLIGHT
THE ANCIENT ONE
THE MERLIN EFFECT

T. A. BARRON

PUFFIN BOOKS
An Imprint of Penguin Group (USA)

HEARTLIGHT

To Currie

PUFFIN BOOKS
Published by the Penguin Group
Penguin Group (USA) LLC
375 Hudson Street
New York, New York 10014

USA * Canada * UK * Ireland * Australia
New Zealand * India * South Africa * China

penguin.com
A Penguin Random House Company

First published in the United States of America by Philomel Books,
a division of The Putnam & Grosset Book Group, 1990
Published by Ace Books, a division of Penguin Group (USA) Inc., 2003
This edition published by Puffin Books, an imprint of Penguin Young Readers Group, 2014

THE LIBRARY OF CONGRESS HAS CATALOGED THE PHILOMEL BOOKS EDITION AS FOLLOWS:
Barron, T. A.
Heartlight / by T. A. Barron
p. cm.
Summary: Kate and her grandfather use one of his inventions to travel faster
than the speed of light on a mission to save the Sun from a premature death.
ISBN 978-0-399-22180-4
[1. Science fiction. 2. Grandfathers—Fiction.] I. Title.
PZ7.B27567He 1990 [Fic]—dc20 89-70947 CIP AC

This omnibus ISBN 978-0-14-751032-7

Printed in the United States of America

1 3 5 7 9 10 8 6 4 2

Contents

I

The Mystery of the Morpho

Kate spun around when she heard the crash.

"Cumberland!"

The golden retriever had Grandfather pinned on the kitchen floor. She dashed over and pulled the dog away, but not before he gave his victim one last slobbery kiss.

"Cumberland!" scolded Kate. "No jumping on Grandfather!"

"Nonsense," grumbled the old man as he painfully regained his feet. "I'm eighty years old and I've had a lot of practice falling. He's just keeping me in shape."

"Are you sure you're all right?"

Grandfather reached shakily for the arm of the rocker. He steadied himself, then slid into the seat. Pushing a tangle of white hair off his forehead, he glared at the dog.

"You will be the death of me, Cumberland."

The dog padded over to the chair and nuzzled his leg affectionately. Heedless of any scorn, he assumed a dignified posture by the old man's side, his fur shining regally with the rust color of heather moors in autumn. Only his still-wagging tail revealed the irrepressible puppy underneath.

"Do you still feel like a picnic?" asked Kate.

Grandfather raised the great bushy brows that hung like clumps of wild moss over his eyes. "A picnic? Oh, dear—I did agree to that, didn't I?"

"It would be the first break you've taken from work in the last week," she coaxed.

He looked distractedly over his shoulder down the long hallway leading to his laboratory. "Could we put it off until tomorrow, Kaitlyn? I have so much to do just now."

"But, Grandfather . . . I've got everything all ready: cold chicken, carrot salad and two Granny Smiths. I even made you some lemon poundcake."

"Did you?"

"With Grandmother's recipe."

The white head cocked toward Cumberland, who was still briskly wagging his tail. "She is a terrible taskmaster, isn't she? I should be glad she doesn't own a whip." He looked up. "Although lemon poundcake is even more effective. I guess it would do me good to enjoy the garden colors at least once this year. Lord knows I need the break. And autumn in New England turns to winter so quickly."

Kate had already climbed atop a wooden stool and thrust her head into one of the deep cabinets built into the kitchen walls. Her muffled voice declared: "Drink some of that tea I made you, while I look for some plates. They must be in here somewhere." Pushing aside the jars of raspberry preserves her mother had made in August, she hunted for the stoneware she had eaten from so many times. "This kitchen has the deepest shelves! You could store an elephant in here."

"That's a farmhouse kitchen for you. Two hundred years ago, when this house was surrounded by nothing but wild woods and a few apple trees, those shelves had to hold all the provisions needed for a long winter."

"Now they hold mostly spider webs," said Kate, still searching for plates.

"Yes, I know. It's only thanks to your mother that this house has any food at all. If left to my own devices, I'd end up dining exclusively on books and prisms . . . with an occasional cup of tea to wash it all down."

Pouring a heavy dose of cream into his teacup, he reflected: "Sunshine and cream, that's all my mother said she ever required for a happy life. In Scotland she found plenty of good Jersey cream, but not much sunshine. Now here I am in America, with plenty of sunshine, but inferior cream."

As he took a sip, his eye caught a spiral-shaped prism, hanging from a string in the sunlight. Tiny fragments of rainbows swam across the wooden walls of the kitchen like shimmering fish of liquid light.

"You know," he said pensively, "a person's life should be like a prism: inhaling light . . . exhaling rainbows." He pushed back some stray strands of hair. "If only it weren't so brief. If only there were more time."

"Time for what, Grandfather?" asked Kate, descending from the cabinet with two handfuls of dust and spider webs, but no plates.

Grandfather didn't answer. Since moving to this quiet college town a year ago, Kate had been his constant companion, watching him do experiments in the lab, helping him mount butterflies for his collection, joining him for long walks in the university woods, or entertaining him with attempts to mimic his rich Scottish accent. Even before the move, when she had lived an hour away, she had enjoyed visiting Grandfather every bit as much as her schoolmates would enjoy going to the beach or the amusement park. Although she had always been something of a loner, the kids at her old school had seemed to accept that fact; they understood that she was more interested in her books and her collection of rocks and crystals than in the usual after-school games.

Now, however, life was different. Because her parents' appointments at the university—her father as chairman of the history department and her mother as a professor of geology—had caused them to move into town, a mere two blocks from Grandfather's house, Kate invariably came here straight after school. All the teasing she now had to endure about her "eighty-year-old boyfriend" made her angry, of course—enough to have broken the tooth of one especially loud-mouthed boy—and there were moments when she dearly wished she had never moved at all, or at least had some friends of her own age. But whenever she stepped through the door of Grandfather's house, those problems seemed to melt away. If Grandfather was preoccupied with an experiment, she would just curl up for the afternoon with one of his books on crystals, cloud formations, space travel, or Greek myths.

"Two peas in a pod," her mother had often called them. To which Grandfather invariably replied: "Two biscuits in a basket, if you please."

They were inseparable.

But not lately. For the last month or so, Grandfather had retreated deeply into his work, so deeply that even Kate's best efforts to rouse him had failed. He had always been a little absentminded, even during the years when he had been in charge of the Institute of Astrophysics. Yet now something was different. Even Cumberland sensed it. Most painful of all, Grandfather had taken to locking the lab door at all times, and he wouldn't—or couldn't—open it when she knocked.

"You are feeling all right, aren't you? No more of those dizzy spells?"

"Of course not, dear child. I'm fit as a fiddle."

Trying not to sound overly interested, Kate asked: "Then what's been keeping you from answering the door to the lab? What is it you're working so hard on?"

The old man drew in a thoughtful breath. "It's complicated," he finally replied. He scratched behind Cumberland's long ears. "Too complicated."

"Is it another telescope?" she asked. "Like the huge one you built in South America?"

"No, Kaitlyn. Designing that telescope was exciting, but not really my normal line of work." His face creased slowly into a smile. "I did enjoy those trips to Chile, though. I used to do some of my best butterfly collecting en route to the Southern Observatory."

Kate continued to probe the cupboards for plates. "Another laser, then? You're inventing a new one?"

A sparkle from the prism flashed in Grandfather's eyes. "No, not another laser. That would be a much simpler task." He resumed rocking the chair, as if for a moment he had forgotten Kate was there.

She leaned across the counter. "Grandfather, do your experiments have something to do with traveling faster than light?"

Grandfather stopped rocking, and his eyebrows lifted high on his forehead. "How did you ever—"

"The pamphlet in your bookshelf," replied Kate. "It's your most recent one, so I thought it might be what you're working on."

"Don't ever tell me you're not a budding scientist," nodded the old astronomer.

"But I'm *not*. You know I almost flunked science!" Kate looked at her feet. "I just miss you, that's all."

"Miss me? But I'm right here. I haven't gone anyplace."

"Oh, yes you have!" Kate's eyes began to brim with tears. "You've been so buried in your mysterious project for the last month I've hardly seen you! Right after school started, something happened to you. All of a sudden. It's like—why, it's like you took off to another planet."

Grandfather stiffened. "I suppose I have been a little distracted lately."

Kate tossed her blond braid over her shoulder. It reached almost to her jeans, which not so long ago had drooped about her legs like wide pantaloons. Now they pinched her uncomfortably, like so many of her clothes. So much had changed during the past year, and her jeans were the least of it. New home, new school, new braces . . . The only thing that hadn't changed, she used to tell herself, was her friendship with Grandfather: Nothing could ever change that.

"I've tried not to disturb you," she continued. "I've really tried! Mom and Dad keep saying it's just a project you're doing, and all projects have to end sometime. But I'm getting tired of waiting! I don't have anybody to talk to now except Cumberland! Sometimes . . . sometimes I wish you weren't a famous astronomer, with a dozen projects always on your mind!"

The old man beckoned and Kate stepped slowly to the side of the rocking chair. Kneeling, she rested her head against his familiar white lab coat. As his arms enfolded her, she closed her eyes and tried to swallow the lump in her throat.

"I'm sorry, Grandfather! I just miss you."

"I'm the one who's sorry, Kaitlyn. I've been so wrapped up in my work I haven't remembered anything else."

Suddenly, something wet and scratchy slapped Kate's face.

"Cumberland!" She struggled to push the dog away, but he continued to lick her hands and arms and even the air when he could no longer reach her face.

"Down, Cumberland!" commanded Grandfather, his eyes twinkling. "You never miss a chance for a bit of affection, do you?"

The great retriever swished his broad tail in agreement.

Grandfather turned to the girl kneeling by his chair. "It's a great blessing for me that your parents got teaching positions right here at the university."

"For me, too. I'd rather spend time here than anywhere else. It's better than school, that's for sure." She glanced at the cupboard. "Now, let's eat. I'm hungry! Where *do* you keep your plates these days? I can't find them anywhere."

"I think they're all in the lab," came the sheepish reply. "I guess I've let things get a little disorganized around here in the past few weeks."

"So what do you use for a plate when you're in the kitchen?"

Grandfather pointed guiltily to a tottering wooden chair in the corner. On it was a half-eaten cheese sandwich, sitting inside an old Frisbee.

"Yikes!" Kate exclaimed. "If Mom knew you were eating out of a dirty old Frisbee, she'd be over here in ten seconds with a truckload of new dishes."

"No doubt," agreed Grandfather. "But let's not ruin her day by telling her, all right?"

Sometimes Kate felt Grandfather needed a mother more than she did. She grinned. "All right, I won't tell."

"Now let's have that picnic. I want to try some of your famous lemon poundcake."

"Without any plates?"

"I have an idea," Grandfather suggested, lowering his voice to a whisper, as if he were about to impart a valuable scientific secret. "How about this: Let's *both* eat out of the Frisbee. Just this once." He touched her nose gently as he rose from the rocker and walked over to an oaken table piled high with various papers and journals of astronomy and physics. Opening a drawer beneath it, he pulled out a faded cotton tablecloth printed with green and purple flowers. He regarded it affectionately before laying it over his forearm. Kate knew it had once belonged to Grandmother.

"Take your sweater, Kaitlyn. The sun is out, but there's an autumn chill in the air already. We may get our first frost tonight."

17

*　　*　　*

Arms laden with picnic makings, the old man and the girl stepped down the flagstone walk to the garden. Close behind them followed Cumberland, his tail wagging energetically.

Kate used her shoulder to push open the old wooden gate, and Cumberland strolled through immediately, rubbing her leg as he passed. Then came Grandfather, moving more stiffly than usual, it seemed to her. His eye was on a patch of unruly grass next to the great stone fountain, but before he could speak, Kate had already put down her load at the very spot.

Grandfather shook open the picnic cloth and set it carefully on the grass. Grape arbors, hanging heavily with Concord bunches, sent the fragrance of their fermenting fruit in all directions. Shafts of purple aster grew tall and proud, the better for being untended by gardening hands. A few milkweed stalks, their seed pods full and ripe, stood like streetlamps amidst the fallen leaves surrounding the old maple. Most glorious of all were the chrysanthemums, which decorated the garden with a full array of autumn colors.

"I've never seen the mums so beautiful," said Kate, patting down the cloth.

"My favorites are the purple ones. Chrysanthemums are usually gone by now. It's rare they last into October, but this year the frost has been kind to them." He sighed wistfully. "It doesn't seem so long ago that your grandmother first planted them here. She had a long wooden box filled with roots and took great care to plant each one individually, letting it know it was specially appreciated. I'm afraid I haven't been doing my garden chores very well since she died . . . There won't be any daffodils, tulips, or hyacinths next spring."

He looked back at the garden gate, swinging slowly in the breeze. "There is no better place than a garden to see the changing of the seasons, Kaitlyn. Birth, death, then rebirth, all happen naturally, regularly, and peacefully. Flowers don't fight against death like people do."

He submerged in thought for a moment, then cast an eye toward Kate, his voice a whisper. "This was her favorite spot to sit, you know."

"I know, Grandfather." Kate wanted to reach over and hug him, but held herself back. She added gently: "This was her favorite tablecloth, too. I hope she wouldn't mind our using it for a picnic."

"She wouldn't mind. She used it for quite a few picnics herself."

Together, in silence, they unpacked the meal. Cumberland positioned himself nearby, his brown eyes filled with longing for a taste of lemon poundcake.

They ate quietly in the crisp autumn air. Every so often Grandfather's misty eyes would glint in the sunlight. He seemed to be remembering other places and times, and Kate did not want to disturb him. Some of their best conversations, Grandfather had once observed, happened without any words at all. Often one of them would finish the other's sentence; just as often, the sentence wasn't even started and the other understood.

Nobody else but Grandfather made Kate feel so comfortable—just as she was, braces and all. Nobody else but Grandfather welcomed her endless questions (usually inspired by her forays into his vast collection of books)—unless, of course, he was in the middle of an experiment, in which case even an earthquake couldn't distract him. To Grandfather it made no difference whether she asked about how the universe began or how the penny-farthing bicycle got its name: Both questions deserved an answer. One day last winter, a simple query about the formation of snowflakes prompted Grandfather to lead her outside in a raging snowstorm, where they caught the falling crystals on their gloves and talked about the endless variety until their numbed feet finally forced them to go back indoors. Rather often, it seemed, she would raise a question that even Grandfather couldn't answer. At those moments, his bushy brows would climb skyward and he would reply: "Only God knows the answer to that one, Kaitlyn. But if you keep asking, perhaps He'll give us a hint."

Of course, having a famous astronomer as a grandfather wasn't always peaches and cream. Grandfather's image often haunted her at school, whether from the other kids' teasing or from her tendency to daydream during class. Only last week, she hadn't been listening when Mrs. Donovan, her seventh-grade science teacher, had assigned a special overnight homework project. When Kate arrived the next morning empty-handed, her classmates made great sport of her. Somebody slipped a small dunce cap into her book bag; somebody else taped a sign to the end of her braid that read: "Pull here to wake."

Mrs. Donovan, who had a figure like an over-stuffed shopping bag, took her out to the hallway. Shaking her head solemnly, she said: "Kate, Kate, Kate! You have no idea how hard I've tried to get you to show some interest in my science class! With no success at all, I'm afraid. At first I thought it was just a matter of time, but now—now I've given up. Don't you share any of your grandfather's interest in science?"

Kate didn't respond. Answering such questions only made things worse.

"Really, Kate! How can someone with a family like yours be so lazy in school?"

She merely gazed at the floor.

Placing her hands on her nonexistent hips, Mrs. Donovan declared: "If you think having a famous grandfather allows you to daydream through my classes, I've got bad news for you."

"I wasn't daydreaming!" Kate objected. "I was thinking."

Mrs. Donovan peered dubiously down at her. "Thinking about what?"

Kate hesitated. "I was thinking about sunspots—how they form, how they can even change our weather. I'm reading about them in one of Grandfather's books."

The teacher scowled, her several chins drooping in unison like a stack of frowns. "For someone who daydreams her way through school, you certainly do come up with some inventive excuses."

"I wasn't daydreaming!" protested Kate, her temper flaring like a solar prominence.

Grandfather never asked, nor did Kate explain, why she came home from school so early that day.

"Do you remember your grandmother, Kaitlyn?"

Grandfather's question jolted her back to the present. "Yes, sort of. I mean, it was a long time ago that she died."

"Not so long, really." He glanced at the grape arbor. "She knew me, Kaitlyn. She knew that I much preferred the wild moors over any garden, that I missed the call of the curlew, the crumbling stone walls, the gorse growing wild that I knew as a child in Scotland. The moors are in my blood. If she'd left it up to me, this garden would look more like the Back of Beyond!" He laughed, remembering some distant moment. "But she taught me how to love a calmer place like this, as well as some of the wilder places within myself. Your grandmother could see further through a millstone than most." He sighed. "The only thing she couldn't teach me was how to accept the fact of death. That lesson has always been beyond my grasp, I'm afraid. She went so peacefully when her time came . . . while I'm certain I'll battle it every step of the way."

Kate thought about the large portrait of Grandmother as a young woman that hung in the hallway by the front door. Those deep brown eyes, the open face, the comfortable dignity of her posture, all made her seem so alive. And so lovely. There was also a slight touch of impatience at the corners of her mouth: It was clear she would much rather have been out working in the garden than sitting still for a formal portrait. Like Kate, she often wore her flowing blond hair in a braid, but unlike Kate's slapdash knotting, it always looked effortlessly elegant. To have known such a person, and then to have lost her . . .

"She would have liked to have known you better," he continued. "The two of you would have much in common."

Kate flushed with doubt. "I don't know. She was so wise and beautiful and everything."

"You don't think you're wise?"

"Are you kidding? Just ask Mrs. Donovan! I'm at the bottom of my class."

Grandfather shook his white mane. "Einstein was bored at school, too."

"That's different! He was a big brain! I'm more like a big dunce."

"A dunce is one thing you're most definitely not, my child. You have very special gifts. You have extraordinary insights. It's only a matter of time before you discover how you want to use them. Try to be patient—"

"Patient! I've never been patient in my life!"

"I said *try* to be patient, Kaitlyn." He extended a weathered hand to her. "This has been a hard year for you, hasn't it?"

Kate nodded, and her round eyes began to fill with tears. "Sometimes I wish we'd never moved! I don't have a single friend at school. Everybody's always making my life miserable."

He drew her near in a gentle hug. "You're still my special friend, you know. You're the same little girl I've always loved."

"But I'm not!" she spouted, pushing away. "I'm not little! And I'm not the same! Nothing's the same!" Her gaze fell to the ground. "Sometimes I feel like . . . like I don't belong *anywhere*!"

"Kaitlyn," said Grandfather quietly. "You still belong here."

She looked at his eyes, sparkling in the same hazel-green hue as her own, and felt her tears welling to the surface. She buried her head in his familiar white lab coat.

For many minutes, Grandfather held her and said nothing. Gently he stroked her long braid, as the sound of her quiet sobbing filled the garden. Cumberland nestled his head between his paws.

In time, Kate lifted her face.

"Oh, Grandfather . . . this was supposed to be a fun picnic for you."

"Who says this isn't fun?" he answered with a twinkle. "I thought you were just working up an appetite for some lemon poundcake."

Kate wiped her face on her sleeve. "Grandfather, I don't know what I'd do without you."

"You'd probably eat off clean dishes, like normal people."

Kate grinned, already feeling a little better. "Somehow you always—oh! Look!"

She jumped to her feet, pointing to a tiny glittering form dancing on the fountain. "There! What an amazing butterfly!"

Grandfather, too, was on his feet. *"Morpho nestira,"* he said softly in wonderment. "So you are still alive."

As the butterfly settled upon the stone fountain, it began slowly to open and close its delicate wings, rhythmically, like a beating heart. Each time the wings opened, they flashed with iridescent blue, green, and violet—colors more brilliant than Kate had ever seen. As the wings drew closer together, the colors evolved from the deepest hues into an opalescent luster. The undersides of the wings, by contrast, were a simple shade of brown, with only a subdued pearly sheen around the edges providing any hint of the colors inside. Then suddenly: The wings reopened in a burst of brilliance, radiating blues and greens of impossible purity.

"Those wings are like rainbows," Kate whispered.

"Yes," answered Grandfather, "but even better. No

rainbow has colors so intense. Those wings are covered with millions of microscopic prisms that concentrate and purify the light."

"What did you call it?"

"*Morpho nestira.* It comes from South America."

"South America! How did it get up here?"

Grandfather watched the pulsing wings thoughtfully. "I brought it back with me, on my last trip to the Southern Observatory in June. It took me three expeditions into the Amazon to find one. At the rate the forests down there are being destroyed, the butterflies' habitat is being wiped out and they may soon be extinct."

"You wanted it for your collection?"

"No. Not this butterfly."

"Then why did you bring it back here?"

"I wanted to study its wings. How they move. How they refract light. How they *glow.* Kaitlyn, the wings of the morpho butterfly produce the purest colors found anywhere on Earth."

For a split second, Kate turned from the butterfly to glance at Grandfather. His eyes shone with the excitement of discovery; he was utterly immersed in the present. This was the Grandfather she knew.

"No technology ever invented can do what those wings can do," he continued. "What the morpho uses every day to frighten predators or signal courtship is really the nearest thing to *pure light* found on this planet."

At that instant, the butterfly lifted off from the

fountain. It rose into the air and then, with a sparkling swoop, fluttered in the direction of the chrysanthemums. For a moment it danced above the colorful petals, and then, whirling, floated slowly toward the picnickers. It hesitated for an instant, as the ocean sun hesitates on the horizon before setting, then landed softly on Kate's forearm.

Her heart pounded as she watched the rhythmic opening and closing of the wondrous wings. Not daring to move, nor even to breathe, she felt a warm tingling sensation bathing her entire body. When the tiny legs of the butterfly shifted slightly, she could feel the pressure of each footstep on her skin, even through her heavy sweater. In that moment, time stood still. The universe became a suffusion of colors—brilliant, flashing colors flowing from boundless blues to radiant greens and violets. Grandfather was right: No rainbow could possibly compare with these radiant wings.

Finally, the butterfly stirred, and the glittering wings carried it skyward. Gracefully, it rode a breeze over the garden fence and out of sight. Kate quietly reached for Grandfather's hand. Silently, they stood for several minutes, looking at the spot where the morpho had disappeared.

"Its wings are more than just colors," said Kate at last. "You know what I mean?" She wasn't quite sure herself what she meant.

"I think so," replied the white-haired man beside her. "Those wings are *light,* Kaitlyn. Pure light."

"That's why they glow so much?"

Grandfather nodded. "And they'll continue to glow like that as long as the butterfly remains alive."

"Alive?"

His face grew somber. "Something changes when the butterfly dies. The wings grow dimmer, duller. The prisms still refract light, but it's only a pale imitation of the living morpho."

"Why?" demanded Kate. "What happens when it dies?"

"That, I'm afraid, is still a mystery."

"Is that why you wanted to study it? Why you brought it all the way back here?"

"Not exactly. Let's just say the wings of the morpho hold many great mysteries. When my experiments were done, I couldn't bear to let it die in some little glass case in the lab. So I let it go, out here in the garden. That was over a month ago."

"That's a long time for a butterfly."

"Yes," replied Grandfather, again suddenly distracted. "And quite a month it's been." His brow wrinkled in concern, and he released her hand. "Time for me to get back to work, Kaitlyn."

He pushed the remains of the lemon poundcake toward Cumberland. Before he could remove his hand, the dog snapped up the entire serving in one bite.

"What did you learn from the morpho's wings?" pressed Kate. "Please tell me."

The white eyebrows lifted. "Something I never dreamed possible."

"About light, Grandfather?"

"That's how it began. But . . ."

"But what?" pressed Kate. "Tell me, please."

The aging astronomer pushed back a handful of white hair, then gazed at her for a long moment. At last, he spoke softly, so softly that she could barely hear. "One day, Kaitlyn, if I'm right, what I learned could make it possible for people to travel to the most distant stars in the universe."

Kate's gaze fell. "I guess that means you're going to lock yourself up in the lab again."

"I'm afraid so," answered Grandfather. "I'm sorry, Kaitlyn. I hope it won't be much longer. I'm really very close." He reached out his hand and gently raised her chin. "But I'd love to join you for supper."

She lifted her eyes. "Really?"

"Yes, Kaitlyn." A warm smile illuminated his face and he drew a deep, satisfied breath. "I needed this picnic more than you know."

"So did I," Kate replied. "More than you know."

Although something about Grandfather still troubled Kate—something she couldn't quite put her finger on—his promise made her happier than she had felt in weeks. She glanced at the spot on her forearm where the morpho had rested, then turned back to Grandfather. "You'd better get going. The sooner you start, the sooner you'll finish! Cumberland and I will clean things up."

The old man winked at her. "At least you don't have any plates to wash."

II
Almighty Wings

By ten o'clock, Grandfather still had not emerged from behind the locked door of the lab. Kate finally gave up waiting and prepared dinner for Cumberland and a ham and cheese sandwich for herself. Just in case, she made an extra one for Grandfather.

She had barely taken her first bite when the telephone on the kitchen counter rang. She put down the sandwich and lifted the receiver.

"Hi, Mom," she said through a mouthful of ham and cheese. "I was going to call you, really I was."

"I know, dear. Sometimes you're just as absent-minded as your grandfather, that's all. It's a Prancer family trait. Are you coming home?"

"It's a weekend, so I was hoping to stay over here tonight. Is that all right?"

"Well . . ."

"Please?"

"Grandfather certainly needs the company these days. I'm worried he's working too hard—especially the past few weeks. All this pressure isn't good for him."

Kate knew well the edge in her mother's voice. Grandfather's health was something the family understood was a problem, but never discussed openly. She volunteered: "We had a great picnic out in the garden this afternoon." She didn't add that Grandfather had promptly locked himself in the lab again.

"All right, Kate. You can stay."

"Thanks, Mom."

"Goodnight, dear. Don't stay up too late."

Taking her sandwich with her, Kate stepped over to the rocker and opened *Pennington's Exotic Butterflies,* which had been her afternoon reading, to the page about morphos. A pair of lustrous wings, poised to lift off from the page, greeted her as before. Next to the picture, written in Grandfather's nearly illegible scrawl, were the words *light and soul.*

Just then she heard a loud sizzling and crackling, like frying bacon but much louder, coming from behind the locked door to the lab. A strange burning smell floated down the long hallway from the lab to the kitchen. *If only I had X-ray vision*, thought Kate.

Hearing no further sound, she scanned the bulging shelves of Grandfather's book collection, which lined both sides of the hallway and one entire wall of the kitchen. She particularly loved this part of the rambling old house. The oaken shelves of Grandfather's library held at least fifty books on the nature of light, and twice that number on the evolution of stars. A particular star named Trethoniel was the subject of so many volumes that it required a special shelf all its own. Kate's favorite books were about the weather, its many patterns and causes; the little ladder was still resting in front of that particular section. She smiled at seeing the large number of works bearing the name *Miles Prancer, D. Phil.* She knew from experience that these were beyond her comprehension, except for the dedications, which were always to Grandmother and always loving without being sentimental.

Then she spied a small gray pamphlet leaning against the most recent edition of Grandfather's text, *The Life Cycle of Stars.* It looked innocuous, even uninteresting, except for its title: *Beyond Starships: Is It Possible to Travel Faster Than Light?* Protruding from the pamphlet was a badly crumpled piece of paper. It looked like a letter that had been thrown away and later retrieved.

She hesitated for an instant, then removed the letter and read it to herself.

THE ROYAL SOCIETY
London
Founded 1662

My Dear Prancer:
It is with considerable regret that I must report that the Royal Society has elected to with-

draw its invitation to you to present your most recent speculations about traveling faster than light. Given our increasingly crowded calendar, we are simply unable to schedule a time to consider your ideas, intriguing though they may be to some of our members.

Please rest assured that this decision was taken only after the most thorough deliberation. Should you choose to present a paper at some time in the future, presumably on a subject rising to traditional standards of documentation and proof, we would of course be pleased to consider your application.

> *Yours Cordially,*
> *Rt. Hon. M. L. Hunter*
> *Chairman, Committee on Peer Review*

Suddenly, Kate felt something move behind her.

She spun around, dropping the letter. But there was nothing unusual to be seen. Cumberland had gone outside after his meal, so she was completely alone.

Yet, it was almost as if she could feel the presence of something else in the kitchen. Something shadowy . . . and cold . . . and watching.

Cautiously, she crept closer to the stone fireplace. "It's nothing, I'm sure," she told herself. "Probably just a draft from the chimney." She knew the kitchen fireplace was so old it was like an open window.

As she bent over to look up the chimney, the ceiling light flickered noisily. She froze, as the light sputtered and wavered on the edge of going out.

Again she sensed something behind her and she whirled around. Her heart was pounding. Where is Cumberland? What had Grandfather once said about hearing ghosts in this house, moaning and creaking with the wind in these old timbers? The light flickered again, like a candle in a cold breeze.

Slowly, Kate backed up until she was pressed against the wall of books. She stood there, too afraid to scream.

*   *   *

"Almost . . . almost there," Grandfather muttered as he pored over a gleaming green metal box, surrounded by a gnarled nest of wires and silicon chips. "I'm so close now I can taste it."

As if he were gathering his strength for the final moment, he lifted his eyes from the green box and surveyed the familiar surroundings of his lab. In addition to the thirty-centimeter telescope poised beneath the sky-hatch, the room contained a powerful microscope, an ultraviolet spectrograph, a radiometer specially designed to measure stellar luminosity, and several homemade lasers. One solid-state laser, only as large as a lemon, sat on a small freezer capable of chilling microchips nearly to absolute zero. A stack of homemade holograms rested on his cyclic interferometer, still showing the measurements of its last light wave.

The walls were cluttered with star maps and computer-enhanced images of various celestial bodies, as well as Grandfather's Oxford University diploma, now so faded with age that most of its Latin script was indecipherable. Next to it was posted a piece of yellow paper with the words, written in crayon several years ago: "Dear Grandfather, Thank You For The Pretty Butterfly. Love, Kate."

In the far corner stood a new invention: a large device designed to measure the health and longevity of stars. Right now, it was clattering relentlessly as it analyzed some recent data on the Sun.

The lone bookshelf in the lab was tilting dangerously; it contained mostly notebooks of many colors and thicknesses. The only exceptions were tattered copies of the *Old* and *New Testaments* (King James Version), *The Once and Future King,* and *The Wind in the Willows.* (Aristotle's collected writings, sometimes also found there, were currently being employed as a lamp stand.)

Next to the bookshelf, directly beneath the lab's open window, stood his bureau of butterflies, holding thirty-five specimens in each of its eighteen slim drawers. Against one side were piled several nets, jars, and other trappings of lepidopterology; on its top, an unfinished chess game waited patiently for someone to make the next move. Carefully placed on the windowsill were a plaster cast of a polar bear paw print and a fossil of a trilobite. Next to them rested a small stack of dinner plates, permanently bound together with the glue of petrified cheese sandwiches.

Leaning precariously against the wall, a large wooden table sagged beneath the weight of hundreds of specialized tools, prisms, cannisters, and components—so many that not even Grandfather could remember what all of them were meant for. His portraits of Albert Einstein, Leonardo da Vinci, and Robert H. Goddard, once in clear view, were now totally obscured by the rising tide of clutter on the table.

Grandfather's gaze returned to his desk, and to the green metal box resting atop his minicomputer. The surface of the box shone with an electric luster and it vibrated, humming faintly, like the voice of a Tibetan monk chanting a mantra. Behind the minicomputer, a crowded rack of beakers and flasks, filled with brightly colored liquids, rattled continuously from the vibration of the green box.

"Almost," he whispered, perspiration gathering in the wild eyebrows on his forehead. "Steady now. Steady . . ."

Concentrating intently, he adjusted several of the wires and silicon chips protruding from the box, using a slender pair of tweezers. But for the occasional pause to check a formula on his clipboard or punch a few keys on the minicomputer, Grandfather worked without interruption until, at last, he heaved a sigh that had been building for more than fifty years.

"Ah, yes," he whispered, placing the tweezers on a stack of computer printouts next to his desk.

His hands trembling, Grandfather removed several

wires and closed the lid of the green box. Then, with an excited gleam in his eye, he pushed the key on the minicomputer marked *Enter*.

He sank back in his chair, feeling strangely drained, at a moment when he had always imagined he would feel triumphant. Wearily, he raised his wrinkled hands before his face and regarded them ruefully. How quickly the time had flown since those hands had first thrown a baseball or toyed with a telescope . . .

Then he turned again to the green box, and his energy started to return. "It's here," he said softly. "My moment in the Sun is finally here."

"Grandfather!"

At first he thought he had just imagined the cry. Then it came again, this time louder than before.

"Grandfather!"

Someone began battering on the door to the lab.

"Kaitlyn!" he exclaimed. "What on Earth are you yelling about?"

He swiftly covered the green box with a ragged cloth, then walked over to the door. He turned the latch and started to open it—when suddenly a violent push shoved both him and the door aside.

"Oh, Grandfather!" she cried, running to him and hugging him tightly. "Grandfather, I'm scared!"

The old man knelt down and peered into her frightened eyes. She was quivering with fear. "What is it, Kaitlyn? What happened?"

"There's—there's something here in the house,

Grandfather! Something like—like a ghost. I'm sure of it. I felt it."

Grandfather drew her close and stroked her long braid. "I'm sure you did, my child. This is an old house, and sometimes it does strange things."

Kate pushed herself away. "No, but this was real! I'm sure! I'm not just imagining things." She glanced behind herself at the open door to the hallway. Nothing looked at all unusual; the hallway now seemed quiet, even inviting.

Kate swallowed hard and started to continue—when suddenly she noticed the strangely contented look on the old astronomer's face. "Grandfather, what is it?"

The lab was dim, lit only by the shaded table lamp next to the desk, but the sparkle in Grandfather's eyes was unmistakable. "If there are any ghosts in this house tonight, dear child, they must be good ones."

"What do you mean?"

Pushing back a handful of white hair, he answered: "I mean that I have just made a breakthrough that has taken me more than fifty years to accomplish."

"Is this the project you told me about after the picnic?"

"Yes, Kaitlyn." A sudden recollection clouded Grandfather's face and he added: "Oh, I missed our date for supper, didn't I? Sorry about that."

"That's all right." Slowly, Kate's concerns about ghosts were being overcome by curiosity. "Go on, Grandfather. Tell me about this breakthrough."

Stiffly, Grandfather stepped across the floor to his

desk. "Ever since I was a student at Oxford, I have suspected that deep in the core of every star there is a special substance—a substance that holds the key to explaining how stars really function."

"Isn't that the stuff you've written so much about? The stuff you call PLC?"

"PCL," corrected Grandfather. "It stands for *Pure Condensed Light.*"

Kate nodded, but her attention had focused on the ragged cloth covering something on the minicomputer. A mysterious humming sound, accompanied by the constant rattling of beakers, seemed to come from beneath the cloth.

"Of course," continued Grandfather, "that was only a theory. There was no way I could prove that PCL actually exists—let alone that it might also have some rather peculiar properties."

"Like traveling faster than light?"

"Yes, Kaitlyn." The old man's eyes shone like beacons. "It won't be long before I will unveil a discovery that will one day make spacecraft obsolete. At last, PCL's existence will finally be treated as a fact, and my own maligned reputation will be restored." His eyes darkened. "Most people allow themselves to be herded around like sheep, I'm afraid, in science just as much as in religion or politics. They prefer a daily dose of predictable rules—with a touch of self-righteousness—to the often unpredictable truth. So the general opinion that I've been wrong about PCL hasn't really bothered me. But, in recent years, even my closest colleagues have started to doubt my sanity, and that's hurt a bit."

"Is that why they wouldn't let you speak to their meeting?" asked Kate, taking her eyes from the cloth and studying Grandfather sympathetically. "That's the rudest thing I ever heard of."

A half-smile creased the astronomer's face. "You read the Royal Society letter, didn't you?"

Kate nodded guiltily.

"That's all right. I should never have kept it anyway. Couldn't throw it away for some reason. But the last laugh is going to be mine."

"I still don't understand why they'd treat you that way. Why do they hate you so much?"

"They don't hate me. They're just frightened."

"What's so frightening about traveling faster than light?"

Grandfather laughed. "What's so frightening? Nothing at all, except that it could alter the whole way we think about the universe! It could destroy hundreds of old theories and build new bridges between relativity and quantum mechanics that now seem impossible."

"I still don't think they should have treated you like that," objected Kate. "If you ask me, the Royal Society is a bunch of royal jerks!"

"Old Ratchet would have agreed with you," replied Grandfather. "He used to fondly call them 'brain-dead Neanderthals.'" He turned to a dusty photograph on the wall of a thin, hairless man in a wheelchair. "Ah,

Ratchet! If only you were still around to witness this moment! You never doubted that PCL exists, or that it powers the energy of every star, although I doubt that even you realized what *other* powers it might also have." Grandfather chortled to himself. "Perhaps it's for the best you're not still here. I don't think you could stand the idea that I—someone you saw as your lowly student—crossed the finish line before you did."

Kate remembered well the mysterious saga of Dr. Ratchet, which she had heard so often from Grandfather. Suffering from a degenerative nervous disease, which had struck him in his thirties and left him confined to a wheelchair for the rest of his life, Ratchet had developed an amazing ability to perform four-dimensional mathematics in his head. Ultimately he came to rely heavily on Grandfather, his best student, to translate his visionary theories into practice, which is why the young Miles Prancer had first trained his telescope on a little-known star called Trethoniel. Despite his genius, however, Ratchet remained an embittered and angry man, haunted always by the fear of death. He never missed an opportunity to berate a colleague or squash a student. Consequently, few tears were shed when he died in a mysterious fire that destroyed Oxford's entire physics complex and left behind little more than the scorched wreck of his wheelchair.

"So you've finally proved that PCL exists?" asked Kate.

"Even better," answered Grandfather, and his eyebrows lifted like rising white clouds. "I have identified all of its ingredients. I now possess the recipe for PCL."

"Wow!" exclaimed Kate. "But how?"

"Perseverance, Kaitlyn. That's how. If there is any quality I wish for you, it's perseverance." With a swipe of his hand, Grandfather removed the cloth, revealing the gleaming green box. "This box represents my entire life's work—and Ratchet's as well. On the day he died, I vowed to find out whether there was any truth to his revolutionary theory about pure condensed light—no matter how long it took. And here I am, fifty years later, still working on it. Until tonight, all my conjectures about PCL and its role in explaining the evolution of stars were nothing but that: conjectures. Until I could actually identify its ingredients, I couldn't convince anyone it exists. I didn't have a ghost of a chance."

The mention of that word caused Kate to glance again over her shoulder at the hallway. Seeing no sign of anything unusual, she turned back to Grandfather.

"Have you tested the box yet?" she asked.

"Not yet," the old astronomer replied excitedly. "But the time is near."

"I still don't get it. How does making some substance that's found in stars allow you to travel faster than light?"

"Well," answered the inventor as he studied the humming box closely, "during my years of work on

PCL I've learned enough about it to predict that it has some rather unusual properties. For example, it ought to melt anything frozen that touches it. But very recently—purely by accident—I discovered that it also has another property. An absolutely astonishing property."

Kate could feel his swelling enthusiasm and it stirred her own. "What property is that?"

Grandfather straightened his tall frame and looked squarely at her. "PCL has the ability to liberate the part of us most similar to pure light."

"You mean our souls?" asked Kate in wonderment.

"You could call it that," answered Grandfather. "People have given it many names in many languages across the ages. I call it our *heartlight.*"

"But how, Grandfather? How does it work?"

"Only God knows the answer to that one, Kaitlyn. But if you keep asking—"

"Perhaps He'll give us a hint!" finished Kate, grinning. "But what does all this have to do with traveling faster than light?"

"Everything," replied Grandfather, taking her hands in his own. "When PCL is allowed to react with your inner light—with your heartlight—then you can travel anywhere in the universe, faster than light."

"I still don't understand how you could travel into outer space without a spaceship to take you there."

Grandfather's brow furrowed. "How can I explain it to you? Think of it like—like your imagination.

All you need to do to go someplace in your imagination is to imagine it. Right? Then—presto!—you arrive there, faster than light. That's how heartlight works."

Kate leaned against the desk in utter amazement. Even if she didn't understand how heartlight worked, she finally understood why Grandfather had been working so hard.

"So this is why you wanted to study the wings of the morpho?" she asked quietly.

"Yes, Kaitlyn." His voice was almost a whisper. "It was the morpho who gave me the first clue that there is indeed a connection between the nature of light and the nature of the soul."

"You're saying that our souls and the stars and the wings of a butterfly are all somehow connected?"

"Yes," the old man agreed, nodding thoughtfully. "They are all part of God's great Pattern."

For a long moment, neither of them spoke. The only sounds were the humming of the green box, the vibrating of the beakers, and the continuous clattering of the machine in the corner of the lab.

At last Kate whispered: "If you're right about PCL and how it can free your heartlight to travel anywhere in the universe . . ."

"Where would I choose to go first?" finished Grandfather, his eyes alight. "Let me show you."

He led her across the room to a massive monitor screen next to his telescope. He switched it on, then began twirling one of the dials. Like a young child playing with his favorite toy, he typed some co-ordinates onto the keyboard.

With a flash, a highly magnified star appeared suddenly on the monitor. It radiated powerfully, and its shimmering red light seemed to reach right out of the screen and into the room itself. Behind Grandfather, the prisms on the table began to glow dimly red.

As he twisted more dials, the brightly colored gases of a great nebula surrounding the star came into view. They spiraled around it like a brilliant veil of incandescent clouds, finally fading into the deep darkness of space.

"It's beautiful," sighed Kate.

"That it is," replied Grandfather. "No other star is as beautiful as Trethoniel."

Pressing a button, he brought the swirling clouds into sharper focus, revealing several planets which orbited through the glowing gases of the star's system. One of them gleamed with a pearly white color. In the center of the spiraling veil, the great red star Trethoniel sat like an imperious queen upon her throne, unaging and untouchable.

"No other star in the sky radiates so strongly, Kaitlyn. And here is the puzzle of puzzles: How can Trethoniel possibly stay so bright, without burning out completely and collapsing into a black hole? Scientists from all over the world—myself included—have failed to answer that important question. All I can say for sure is that it has something to do with its supply of PCL. Trethoniel is more advanced in manufacturing

PCL than any star in the known universe. Meanwhile, it continues to flame, so powerfully that you can see it without a telescope even on full-moon nights."

Grandfather spun another dial, and the seething, scorching surface of the star completely filled the screen. Towers of superheated gases danced thousands of miles out into space. "On our world I am believed to know much," he said softly. "But one glimpse of this star reminds me how little, how very little, I truly understand. There is so much to learn about the Pattern."

He turned to the girl standing beside him. Her face, like his own, had been touched with a new and lovely light.

"Someday, Kaitlyn, if I'm right, people will explore Trethoniel and learn some of its secrets." He touched her braid gently. "Maybe you and I will be the very first to go."

"Me?" Kate shook her head. "Not a chance! I'm no explorer and I'm certainly no scientist! You'd be a lot better off going by yourself."

"What if I asked you to join me?" questioned Grandfather playfully.

"I guess I'd have to think about it," Kate replied with a grin. "But I'd rather you just sent me a postcard."

Her gaze returned to the image on the screen. "Trethoniel is full of mysteries, isn't it?"

"Right you are," agreed the old astronomer. "As Einstein said, *mystery is the essence of beauty*. No one can explain how Trethoniel could swell up like a giant red balloon—expanding to a thousand times its former size—then resist collapsing into a bottomless black hole. Traditional physics says that should have happened long ago. But Trethoniel has done exactly the opposite! Against every law of physics, it's grown steadily brighter, actually gaining luminosity with time. Its curve of binding energy is beyond anything we've ever known."

Grandfather studied the image on the screen. "When I first started observing you, Great Star, I watched you ceaselessly, like a vulture circling over some near-dead prey. Then, with time, I came to respect you more and more. I came to admire your beauty, your power, your desire to live."

"I'm glad Trethoniel is alive, too," said Kate quietly. "Somehow it makes me feel . . . well, hopeful."

"Yes," nodded Grandfather. He glanced at his own wrinkled hands, then turned back to the screen. "At least somewhere in the universe, mortality and death have been held at bay, if not entirely beaten." With a sigh, he continued: "One of the reasons Trethoniel is so intriguing is that it shares some extraordinary similarities with the Sun. Both stars are nearly the same age, probably condensed out of the same original cloud of swirling gases. And, before Trethoniel suddenly expanded and turned upside down all the laws of physics, it was a typical yellow star, just like the Sun."

At that moment, something new on the monitor screen caught Kate's eye.

"What's that dark place on Trethoniel, Grandfather?" she asked, feeling strangely uneasy. "I don't think it was there just a few seconds ago."

Grandfather dismissed her question with a wave of his hand. "Probably just a storm on the surface or a simple refraction error, that's all. Nothing to worry about." He smiled. "By the way, how are you feeling? I mean, after your encounter with our friendly local ghosts?"

Kate shivered slightly. "They didn't feel so friendly to me. I'd forgotten about them, so I guess I'm fine now. Except . . . I just can't shake this feeling."

"What feeling?"

"I can't quite explain it. It's a feeling that something . . . something just isn't right around here."

Grandfather gave her a gentle squeeze. "It's probably just an aftereffect from your fright. Perhaps you—"

Buzzzzzz.

Kate jumped. "What's that noise?"

"It's the timer on the astro-vivometer," declared Grandfather. "My new invention over there in the corner."

He walked over to the contraption, which was shaped like a large gray file cabinet bearing numerous dials and switches on its face. "It can measure the level of PCL in any star, so I can assess the star's health and longevity with great accuracy."

"What was that timer for?"

"Oh, I've been doing a test run to make sure it works properly. I set it to work on the Sun, since it's the easiest star to analyze from Earth. The buzzer says it's finished the computations."

With an effort, Grandfather stooped down to pick up a printout that had dropped from a slot in the astro-vivometer. Suddenly, his face went white, and he whispered: "My God!"

"Grandfather!" cried Kate, hurrying to his side. "What is it?"

The old man gave no answer. He continued to scrutinize the printout, trying to check some of the calculations in his head. His expression grew more grim with every passing second.

"It must be mistaken," he muttered. "It must be."

"What does it say?" pleaded Kate, seeing nothing but rows of meaningless numbers and symbols crowding the printout.

At last Grandfather raised his head. Deep concern lined his brow, and the light of his breakthrough had vanished from his eyes. He looked at Kate somberly.

"What does it say?"

"It says the Sun is in trouble, Kaitlyn. Serious trouble." His gaze fell to the machine, still clattering away ceaselessly. "There could be a problem with the astro-vivometer itself . . ."

"But you don't think so, do you?"

The old man turned again to Kate, and for a long moment they held each other's gaze. "No."

"What kind of trouble, Grandfather? Please tell me. What's going to happen to the Sun?"

Shaking his head sadly, Grandfather replied: "I—I don't know how to explain it, Kaitlyn. It's so—so enormous . . ."

"This sounds as bad as nuclear war."

Grandfather grimaced. With a quivering finger, he pointed to various numbers on the printout. "You see, there's been no change in the Sun's temperature, chemistry, density, magnetism, or surface dynamics. Only one factor has changed—the most important one."

"You mean its PCL?"

"Yes. If these figures are right, its core supply of PCL has started dropping at a precipitous rate."

"What does it mean, Grandfather?"

He drew his hand slowly across his brow. "If—if nothing happens to reverse it . . . then . . ."

"What? What then?"

"The Sun will eventually lose so much PCL that it will reach a state of catastrophic energy imbalance." Grandfather seemed to choke on the words as he spoke them. "Without any warning, it will collapse violently, and then—oh, Kaitlyn! The Sun will go out *forever.*"

Kate stepped backward in disbelief. "But—but—the Earth . . ."

The white head nodded despondently. "We're not talking about any ordinary star, Kaitlyn. We're talking about the Sun. The life-giving, beneficent Sun!

What the Egyptians worshipped as Ra, the Greeks as Helios, the Romans as Sol; the star that inspired the great temples of the Aztecs, the ancient circle of Stonehenge, and so much more. This means no more dawns and no more sunsets; no more lilies or roses or chrysanthemums; no more kangaroos or chipmunks, sequoias or sunflowers." He seemed to be talking to himself. "Millions of species, developed over millions of years—all wiped out in a single instant."

"But how can that be?" She struggled to take all this in. "It felt just like normal outside today."

Grandfather sighed. "This isn't something you can see or feel. Only an astro-vivometer is sensitive enough to discern what's happening inside the Sun. And the only one of those in existence is telling us we're in grave danger."

Pressing a blue button on the side on the machine, Grandfather pulled another printout from the slot. Instead of being covered with equations, this one bore an image, much like a blurred photograph. Kate knew instantly that it was a picture of the Sun.

"I haven't had time to bring the imaging capability up to speed," said Grandfather. "But this is good enough to show you. Do you see the dark blotch in the lower hemisphere?"

"It looks like a huge sunspot."

"If only it were! That is a PCL void deep within the core of the Sun. And according to the figures, it's spreading like a deadly cancer. At this rate, the Sun has no more than a thousand years left to live."

"A thousand years!" Kate felt suddenly relieved. "That's a pretty long time, Grandfather."

"Not to a star. To a star it's virtually nothing. If its natural lifespan hadn't been disrupted, the Sun would have had several billion years left to live."

Kate frowned. "How can this be happening? Why does our star have to be the one that's stricken by this—this disease?"

"I don't know, I don't know. I suppose it's all part of the Pattern, Kaitlyn. There is no other answer."

"What kind of Pattern would let such a thing happen?" exclaimed Kate. "If God really has some sort of Pattern, why does He let things die at all? Why doesn't He stop the Sun from collapsing and destroying the Earth and everything on it?"

The great eyebrows lifted. "Your grandmother would say that living and dying are both part of the Pattern. When something in the universe dies, she believed, something else is born." Grandfather looked at Kate's worried face and placed his arm around her shoulder. "And remember this: God has also given us the gift of free will, and that's part of the Pattern, too. Maybe—just maybe—humanity can use its free will to find some way to save the Sun from premature death. After all, we still have a thousand years to find a cure."

Kate drew in a deep breath. "I guess a thousand years, while it's not much time for a star, is really a pretty long time for humanity to figure something out. Do you think it's possible that your discovery of PCL could help?"

"Perhaps," answered Grandfather. His gaze wandered from the astro-vivometer to the wall monitor, still glowing red from the light of Trethoniel, and a mysterious gleam shone in his eye. "Perhaps."

Lowering his arm, he spoke reassuringly. "We're safe for now, Kaitlyn. The Sun will rise again tomorrow . . . in not very long, as a matter of fact. In any case, it's time for me to get back to work. And for you to go to bed."

"Bed!" cried Kate. "But—"

"You need your sleep," he declared firmly. "Especially if you're going to be helping me in the lab tomorrow."

"In the lab?" Kate nearly jumped out of her sneakers. "Really?"

"You heard me, Kaitlyn. I've discovered today how much I need your company."

Kate turned and squeezed him as hard as she could. "Oh, Grandfather!"

"Please! Please!" he protested. "I have too much to do to get a broken rib."

She released the hug. "Can I ask you a favor?"

"You can ask."

"Would you mind—"

"Coming upstairs with you?" finished Grandfather. "Not in the slightest. I want to make sure myself there aren't any ghosts roaming around your bedroom."

"Thanks," breathed Kate.

"I don't blame you. After all, you had quite a fright. I'll leave the lab door open tonight, so if you get scared at all you can come right down here and join me." Seeing the look of gratitude in her eyes, Grandfather added: "And I'll do one thing more. I'll join you in saying prayers."

As they walked down the hallway to the stairs, Kate cast an eye into the kitchen. It seemed the same as usual; the light burned strongly. She sighed in relief and started up the stairs. By the time Grandfather had joined her, she had already brushed her teeth and pulled on her pajamas.

Together, they knelt beside the bed. The half-moon's pearly light drifted through the high window, across the soft cotton quilt, and over their clasped hands.

"What prayer shall we choose?" she asked.

Grandfather thought for a moment. "Let's sing the Tallis Canon," he replied. "It's the perfect thing for times like this."

"I remember when you first taught it to me, the night we went camping in Montana and we thought we heard a grizzly bear."

"Which turned out to be your father snoring," he chuckled. "I'll never forget that."

"Neither will he."

Suddenly, Grandfather's face grew serious. "Kaitlyn," he said softly, "if, for some reason . . ." Then he stopped himself. "I want you to know how much I love you."

Kate looked at him uneasily.

"Why don't you start the Canon?"

For a long moment, Kate searched the old man's eyes—for what, she wasn't certain. Finally, she spoke quietly: "I love you, too, Grandfather. And I always will. Please remember that."

"I will, Kaitlyn. Now start us."

Kate lifted her eyes to the window, glowing in the moonlight. Then she began to sing:

> *All praise to thee my Lord this night,*
> *For all the blessings of thy light.*
> *Keep me, O keep me, King of Kings,*
> *Beneath thine own almighty wings.*

Grandfather's gravelly tones rose to accompany her voice like a bass fiddle. Three times they sang the Canon, and each time their voices swelled stronger, until the room was filled with their melody and with a peculiar kind of warmth both beyond feeling yet fully tangible. As they finally fell silent, Kate could still hear the words *almighty wings* hovering in the air, like the fading echo of an iron bell.

At last Grandfather spoke again. "Time for sleep, Kaitlyn."

He kissed her gently on the forehead, then promptly turned and left the room.

Moonbeams fell across the quilt like lovely long arms, ready to carry Kate off to sleep. But sleep was still beyond her. In her chest rose a surge of excitement, and a touch of foreboding, about tomorrow.

In the darkness she felt she could hear anything,

even the breath of a butterfly. The image of a lovely morpho, small and silent, came to her, beckoning her to float away on a gentle breeze of dreams.

Soon she was sound asleep.

*   *   *

Grandfather re-entered the lab and moved directly to the astro-vivometer, not even pausing to inspect the green box still humming on his desk. He turned several dials, then pushed a button marked *Update*.

As he waited, he rubbed his chest, muttering: "So sore . . . perhaps she did break a rib after all."

Buzzzzzz.

Impatiently, he pulled the printout from the slot and began poring over it. "Oh, no!" he exclaimed, his face filled with horror. "This can't be right!"

Stuffing the printout into the pocket of his lab coat, he walked over to his desk and stiffly sat down. Reaching for his pocket calculator and clipboard, he somberly shook his head. "There must be some mistake. I'll have to recheck all the calculations. How can things have deteriorated so much in just half an hour? If PCL keeps vanishing at this rate, we'll have only *two or three years* before . . . before . . ."

As he labored feverishly, he didn't notice when the Sun's first rays started slowly to fill the sky. Songbirds, unaware of any peril, greeted the dawn with a chorus of celebratory chatter, and the room grew lighter by degrees. Fresh morning air began to mix with the slightly burned smell of the lab.

He raised his eyes from the clipboard and cocked

his head hopefully at the astro-vivometer in the corner. "It's time to check you again," he said aloud. "Perhaps it was only a temporary fluctuation . . . perhaps the trend has reversed. Then this will be a day of good tidings after all."

The old man lifted himself wearily from the chair and began to cross the room. "If only I had—"

Suddenly, he clutched his chest.

"No!" he gasped, staggering toward the door. "Not now!"

Before he had taken another step, a new spasm of pain shot through his chest. He buckled and collapsed on the floor, knocking over a pile of papers as he fell.

III

The Green Box

Kate awoke to a wet tongue licking her face excitedly.

"Cumberland! Leave me alone!"

She rolled over, burying her head under the quilt.

The dog barked twice, leaped off the bed and padded to the top of the stairs. Then he turned, barked again, and waved his prominent tail like a red flag.

"What is it, Cumberland?" Kate lowered the quilt and stretched her arms. "What are you so worked up about?"

Cumberland barked again, then disappeared down the stairwell. As if taking no chances that Kate would change her mind, he sat at the bottom of the stairs and began to howl pitifully.

"All right, all right, I'm coming," she said as she rolled out of bed and quickly donned her jeans, sneakers, and a well-worn sweatshirt.

As she descended the stairs, Cumberland padded swiftly into Grandfather's lab. Suddenly, Kate sensed trouble and she ran through the open door.

"Grandfather!" she screamed.

The old man was sprawled on the floor, surrounded by a mess of papers and notebooks. His skin was terribly pale and covered with perspiration. She rushed over to him, just as he began to stir slowly.

"Grandfather! What happened?"

"Ohhhhh," he moaned, rubbing his head and rolling over on his back. "I fell . . . But why now?" He looked up at Kate. "I'm fine, really. Just a bit dazed."

"I knew something bad was going to happen!" Kate's round eyes began to fill with tears. "I should have stayed right here with you instead of going to bed."

"Nonsense," said Grandfather as he forced himself to sit upright. "It feels like an elephant sat on my chest! I'll be fine, though. Give me a hand."

"Are you sure you should move?"

"Yes, yes. Just help me into the kitchen. A cup of strong tea is all I need. Then I must get back to work."

With Kate's assistance, he struggled to his feet. So wobbly was he that he had to lean against her with most of his weight to stay upright. Awkwardly, they negotiated the long hallway, stopping twice to rest against the bookshelves. Finally, they entered the kitchen, with Cumberland at their heels.

Kate helped him lower himself into the old rocker. Before he could object, she had covered him with

Grandmother's picnic cloth and tucked it in around him.

"That will keep you warm," she said, breathing hard from exertion. She put some water in the tea kettle and placed it on the stove.

Cumberland seized the opportunity and started licking his master's face energetically.

"Down, boy!" Grandfather pushed him away, then looked at the dog severely. "Not now, Cumberland."

"You need to take better care of yourself," said Kate. "You gave me an awful scare! How did you fall, anyway?"

"Oh, I just fell, that's all. Must have tripped on something."

She looked at him piercingly. "That's not true, is it?"

The old man averted his eyes. "I suppose it could have been a minor heart attack. Nothing serious, though."

"Nothing serious!" Kate nearly lost hold of the kettle as she was filling the teapot. "A heart attack!"

"I've survived worse things," he grumbled. "I'm sturdier than you think."

"But a heart attack is serious," scolded Kate as she poured the brew into his favorite blue cup. "People *die* of heart attacks! You've got to slow down, Grandfather."

Wearily, he pushed some white hairs off his forehead. "I know you're worried about me, Kaitlyn. But I can't possibly die now. The Sun—"

"I don't care about the Sun! I care about you! I think we should call a doctor."

"No doctors are needed," said Grandfather testily. "All I need is that cup of tea that's growing cold as we speak."

"Here it is," said Kate as she handed him the cup. "Won't you please let me call a doctor?"

The old man's eyes flashed with determination. "The answer is No." He took a sip of tea, then studied her closely. "The Sun is in trouble, Kaitlyn," he said earnestly. "Much more trouble than I thought." He pulled the latest printout from his pocket and waved it before her face. "We could have only two or three years left! Maybe even less."

His words hit Kate like a splash of ice water. "I thought we had a thousand years!"

"So did I," answered Grandfather grimly. "But I was wrong! Now we have no time to spare. Here . . . help me get up."

"Are you sure you can do it?"

"Help me."

With a strong tug from Kate, the old astronomer rose shakily to his feet. Suddenly, his legs buckled and he fell back into the chair, knocking over the cup of tea.

"Drat!" he cursed, panting heavily. "Just when I most need my body to co-operate, it's failing me! Come, let's try again."

He reached a trembling arm toward Kate.

"No, Grandfather," she protested, tucking the picnic cloth around him again. "You should rest! Please stay in the chair! If you need something from the lab, I can get it for you."

Grandfather looked at her resignedly. "All right . . . Just until I'm a little more rested. Here's what I need you to do." He leaned forward in the rocker and whispered anxiously: "Go to the green box. Right next to—"

At that instant, Cumberland barked loudly and bounded out of the kitchen and down the hallway.

"What is it?" Kate asked.

Grandfather shook his head. "That's not like him."

From down in the lab, they heard the dog bark again frantically.

"I'll go check it out," said Kate as she ran down the long hallway, leaving Grandfather in the rocker.

As she entered the lab, she felt suddenly colder.

Just then she noticed the desk lamp was flickering and sputtering noisily. A blur of motion near the desk caught her eye.

"The ghost!" she screamed, as a frigid, formless cloud of white vapor began swirling around the desk—hovering, as if it were searching for something.

Then it began to coalesce around Grandfather's green box. Slowly, as Kate watched in horror, the green box lifted into the air, borne by the white vapors gathered around it.

"Stop!" she screamed, lunging after the green box. "You can't have it!"

The phantom cloud quivered, then suddenly blew her backward with the force of a hurricane—straight into the table laden with Grandfather's equipment.

Shattered glass and equipment flew in all directions. The table collapsed as she landed, sending tools and prisms skidding across the floor. The computer design terminal tottered precariously for an instant, then crashed to the floor with an explosion of glass. Brightly colored chemicals sprayed the walls and Kate's clothes.

"Stop!" she screamed, picking herself up again. Her head was sore and her wrist was bleeding from a flying shard of glass. All she could think of was Grandfather's life's work being destroyed.

The green box continued to float toward the door of the lab.

"No!" cried Kate hysterically. "That belongs to Grandfather!"

"Nnnoooo," came a voice like an iceberg cracking in two. It wasn't the kind of voice that Kate could hear with her ears; rather, it vibrated deep down inside of her bones. *"Ittt bbellonnnggss tttoo mm-meeee."*

As suddenly as a bolt of lightning, Cumberland leaped at the green box, knocking it free from the ghost's grasp. The box skidded across the room and came to rest in the corner. Meanwhile, the retriever ran to Kate's side and began licking her wounded wrist.

For an instant, the ghost seemed to dissipate, like a

cloud of poisonous gas dispersing with the breeze. Eyeing the box, Kate started to regain her feet.

Suddenly she saw one of Grandfather's largest lasers teetering and about to fall—directly on top of them.

"Look out!" she yelled, rolling to her side just as the heavy contraption came crashing to the floor.

Above the explosion of metal and glass, Cumberland's squeal of agony pierced the air.

"No!" cried Kate, crawling toward the helpless dog. "No!"

Cumberland lay motionless under the weight of the toppled machine. As Kate tried to lift the tangle of metal off his body, the air shivered with a laughter colder than death.

Like an evil wind, the ghost gathered up the green box, whisked through the door, and disappeared.

Kate could barely see for all the tears that filled her eyes. But she pulled and pried with all her strength. There was a sound of grinding metal when, at last, she lifted the heavy machine from Cumberland's body. Pushing against it with her shoulder, she shoved it aside.

Miraculously, the dog moved his prominent tail.

"Cumberland! You're alive!"

He whimpered pitifully, and Kate hugged his neck, burying her face in his flowing cloak. "You're alive!"

With an effort, Cumberland wriggled into a crouch position. He whimpered again, then licked

Kate's ear. Slowly, he rose to his feet and took a few halting steps.

"You're limping terribly." She tried to examine the dog's raised paw, but he drew it away as soon as she touched it. "And you may have broken a rib or something worse."

Kate forced herself to stand. Her head hurt where she had hit it, and she felt nauseous and dizzy. As she surveyed the room, her heart sank. Smashed equipment, splattered chemicals, broken glass, and scattered papers surrounded her. It looked as if someone had dropped a bomb in the middle of the lab.

At that moment, the full weight of the disaster descended. The box! The green box was gone!

"What's going on here?" Grandfather, looking exhausted, stepped into the lab. "It sounded like—oh, my God. This place is destroyed!"

Kate darted to the doorway and hugged him tightly. "The ghost," she blurted. "The ghost was here. In the lab!"

"Here? A ghost?" His voice was incredulous.

He kneeled to look her in the eye. "Are you all right, Kaitlyn? Are you hurt?"

"I'm fine," she said bravely, wiping the tears from her face. "Just a little dizzy. I hit my head, that's all. But he nearly killed Cumberland."

"What?"

The golden retriever barked loudly and limped over to them. Grandfather patted him and scratched behind his ear. "Cumberland, you old trooper!

You're a match for any ghost." He turned again to Kate. "What did this ghost look like?"

"Like a ghost! Like a cloud or something . . . It wasn't solid—sometimes it was practically invisible. We had a terrible fight. We tried to stop it from . . ." Tears began to well up again, but she fought them back. "Oh, Grandfather! It stole your green box."

"What?" The old man rose and scanned his desk, now surrounded by the wreckage of the lab. The spot where the box had once rested was vacant.

To Kate's astonishment, a slow smile spread across his face.

"But—but I don't understand," she objected. "It stole your box. Your special green box."

"Yes, I know," answered Grandfather, still looking at his desk and smiling broadly.

"Then what's so funny?"

He didn't respond.

"What's so funny?"

"It stole the wrong thing."

"Wrong thing!" exclaimed Kate. "I thought—"

"You thought the box was what I wanted. I know. That's because I hadn't finished telling you exactly what to bring me."

"But the green box—"

"Was needed for my research, that's all. Now that I've found the formula for PCL, it's no longer necessary. And I am quite sure it's not what our intruder was really after."

Stepping stiffly over broken glass and metal, Grandfather worked his way to the desk where the green box had once rested. Behind the minicomputer rested the rack of brightly colored beakers, still unbroken after the battle. From this rack, he pulled one simple beaker which held a half-inch deep pool of radiant green liquid.

"The best way to hide something special," Grandfather declared, "is to make it look as ordinary as possible." Holding the beaker high in the air, he announced: "*This* is what our intruder wanted, I'll warrant."

"What is it?" asked Kate, peering closely at the beaker. "What's so special about it?"

With considerable difficulty, Grandfather lifted his desk chair upright and sat down heavily. Then he turned to her and whispered in a tense voice: "There is something I didn't tell you last night, Kaitlyn. Something very important. I've not only identified all the ingredients of PCL—although that was difficult enough, believe me! No, I've done something far more difficult."

He glanced at the sparkling green fluid in the beaker and a smile flickered across his face. "I have actually *made* some PCL."

"Grandfather!"

"Yes." Grandfather straightened himself in the chair. "Last night I made the very first batch. No easy trick, without the intense heat and pressure of a star to help the chemistry along. But it worked. Now this beaker holds a small amount of the most precious substance found anywhere in the universe: pure condensed light."

"I can't believe it!" shouted Kate. "You fooled the ghost."

"Not for long, though. Once that intruder—whatever sort of being it really is—discovers it was fooled, my guess is it will come back."

Nervously, Kate glanced at the doorway. "Why would it want your PCL?"

Grandfather placed the beaker on the edge of the desk and frowned. "I don't know. It's useless to speculate. And right now we have more urgent matters to deal with. Can you make it over there to the astro-vivometer? Push the button marked *Update*, then bring me the printout so I can see it."

Deftly, Kate maneuvered across the wreckage-strewn floor to the astro-vivometer, which was still clattering noisily. She retrieved the printout and carried it back to Grandfather.

As she handed it to him, a look of such gravity filled his face that she at first thought he was having another heart attack.

"Heavens!" he muttered. "How can this be happening?"

"How bad is it?" asked Kate, almost afraid to hear the answer.

Grandfather looked at her with an ashen face. "Very bad. Very bad, indeed. The PCL drain is accelerating rapidly." He reached for her hand, and his voice was less than a whisper. "Unless something happens, the Sun will collapse in . . ."

Kate's heart froze in her chest. "In how long? Grandfather, how long?"

The old astronomer did not answer. "I must do something drastic," he whispered resolutely.

Fear flooded Kate's veins. "Grandfather, you're not well enough to do anything—let alone anything drastic. You could have another heart attack!"

"That's right," he said in a voice as hard as stone. "That's another reason I must act now. Too much is at stake, and we have almost no time left."

With that, he reached deep into one of his lab coat pockets. Carefully, he removed a small velvet box which resembled an ordinary ring case. As Kate looked on fearfully, he opened the box to reveal an unusual ring with a turquoise band. Instead of a jewel, however, upon the band was mounted a small transparent container crafted in the shape of a butterfly.

With a touch of his finger, Grandfather flipped open the top of the butterfly container on the ring. Then, holding the velvet box securely, he began to pour in the fluid. Concentrating intently, he watched it flow into the ring like sparkling syrup. Before he had emptied half of the beaker, the wings of the butterfly brimmed at full capacity, and the top snapped closed automatically. Waves of illumination flowed through the entire ring, like glowing coals at the base of a fire.

"What are you going to do with that?" demanded Kate, eyeing the velvet box and the mysterious object it held.

Grandfather's brow furrowed deeply. "I am going to do what I have labored many years to do, Kaitlyn. I had only hoped that the first time would be a moment of triumph, instead of desperation."

"But what are you going to do?"

The old astronomer looked deeply into her eyes. "I'm going to put on this ring. The instant I touch it, the pure condensed light inside it will set free the most alive part of myself, the part most akin to light."

"You mean you'll turn into light?"

"No, Kaitlyn. I will turn into *heartlight*. And then I can travel anywhere in the universe."

Kate shook her head in disbelief. "How can a ring do that?"

"It's made from a special conductive material, whose molecular structure is designed to bring the PCL in the ring into contact with the heartlight in my body. When that contact happens—well, just watch."

"But, Grandfather! You can't be sure it's going to work."

"I'm sure, Kaitlyn. I'm sure."

"Can't you at least wait until you're more rested?"

"There is no time left to wait," said Grandfather as he replaced the beaker on the desk.

"But where will you go? What can you do?"

"I will go to the one place in the universe that

might provide me with enough information to find a cure—the place where more PCL is manufactured than anywhere else. I will go to—"

"Trethoniel!" Kate exclaimed.

"Yes! I don't know what I'm looking for, exactly. It may be some kind of substance, or process, that allows Trethoniel to make such enormous quantities of PCL. If somehow Trethoniel's secret could be applied to the Sun—"

"No, Grandfather, you can't! It's too dangerous. Your machine might be wrong . . . This could be a gigantic mistake. You'd be risking your life for nothing."

Grandfather shook his head. "It's no mistake. I am convinced."

"But you can't possibly go to Trethoniel and back in time."

The wild eyebrows climbed skyward. "Yes, I can. You see, Kaitlyn, time in interstellar travel is greatly expanded compared to time on Earth. It should take me only two or three minutes of our time to fly to Trethoniel, learn whatever I can about how it manufactures so much PCL, and return to help the Sun. Of course, it will feel like a lot more time, but by your watch I'll only be gone a few minutes. Besides, this ring holds only *four minutes' supply of PCL*— measured in Earth time, that is. So whether I like it or not, I can't be gone any longer than that."

"Only four minutes?" Kate struggled to comprehend.

"Yes. I haven't been able to figure out how to make PCL liberate heartlight for more than four minutes. There seems to be some sort of physical barrier halting the reaction at that point. I had hoped eventually to find some way to extend it, but without the green box, that's impossible now. And we have no more time for such experiments, anyway."

He looked thoughtfully at the radiant ring resting in the box. "I had even hoped that one day, Kaitlyn, you could travel with me—perhaps to the moon, or even to Mars . . ." His eyes glistened as he turned to her. "Maybe someday we'll still have that chance."

"No!" cried Kate, her own vision clouded with tears. A feeling of foreboding, stronger even than she had felt last night, swelled inside of her. "I don't want you to go! I have a feeling—a terrible feeling—that if you go you'll be in danger—worse danger than you can possibly imagine. Grandfather . . . please don't go. The risks are too great."

Grandfather touched her head gently. "There are risks, my child. I'm not going to say there aren't. There are still a few adjustments to the PCL I'd hoped to make before trying it out—one or two random elements I've not yet identified. Still, I think the ring should work. The risks are worth it, if there's any chance of saving the Sun. Can't you understand? All life on Earth is going to perish unless something changes soon. Everyone and everything on it will disappear forever."

Kate sighed miserably and looked at the floor.

"I am an old man, Kaitlyn. I'm going to die soon enough as it is. You must understand. I've got to try."

She raised her head slowly. "Can I see the ring one more time?" she asked, her voice quivering.

The old man held out his hand, with the velvet box resting in his palm. The butterfly ring gleamed, radiant and mysterious.

Suddenly, she snatched the box from his hand.

"Kaitlyn!" shouted Grandfather, lurching after it.

"No!" Kate jumped out of reach. "I'm not going to let you do this to yourself," she declared. "You could be wrong about the way PCL works. You could even be wrong about the Sun. I won't let you do it, Grandfather."

A fire blazed in the old man's eyes, but he held his voice steady. "Now, Kaitlyn. Give me back the ring."

"I won't," she replied, darting behind the desk. Her mind was made up.

"Please," he begged, his hands shaking.

"No."

"Kaitlyn, please." He dropped his hands, and defeat was in his eyes. "All right," he whispered. "If I promise not to go anywhere until I've made absolutely certain that the astro-vivometer is right—that there's no chance at all of any mistakes—will you give me back the ring?"

Kate hesitated. "What if it takes you more time than the Sun has left to check the machine?"

The astronomer sighed in resignation. "That's a

risk I'll just have to take. A risk we'll all have to take. But maybe—maybe you're right. Maybe there's some mistake after all."

"Do you really truly promise?" demanded Kate. "And not like your promises to finish working by a certain time! I want a *real* promise. The kind that makes you fry in agony and pain and horribleness if you break it."

Grandfather was beaten. Shoulders slumped, he whispered: "I promise."

Slowly, Kate walked over to his side. Closing the top of the velvet box, she placed it in his lab coat pocket. "I'm sorry, Grandfather, but I had to do it."

The old man didn't respond. He merely gazed despondently at the astro-vivometer in the corner. At length, he lifted his eyes toward her. "I feel so drained," he said wearily. "Since you've laid these chains on me, would you mind getting me some of that tea I never got to finish? It would give me the energy I need to walk over there and start working on the machine."

Feeling both triumphant and a little sad, Kate nodded. "One cup of tea with cream coming up."

She walked through the lab door and down to the kitchen, with Cumberland limping behind her. Making a whole pot of tea was as easy as a cup, so she prepared a full teapot of his favorite brew. Her thoughts drifted back to the ghost in the lab, and she shivered despite the heat of the stove. When the tea was ready, she put it on a tray and carried it carefully down the hallway.

As she turned into the lab, she suddenly let out a shriek. The teapot smashed on the floor.

Grandfather was gone.

"No!" she cried, running to the empty chair where he had been seated just a moment before. "He promised!"

Cumberland whimpered and sniffed the chair. Then he turned his soulful eyes toward Kate, as if to ask: "Where is he?"

Betrayed, Kate cursed the air and sat down dejectedly. "Grandfather!" she cried, hoping against hope that he would hear her and come back—from wherever he was.

There came no reply.

"I should never have trusted him," she moaned. "I never imagined he'd really break his promise . . . not that kind of promise."

Her eyes fell upon the beaker, still holding a small supply of the mysterious green fluid. She glared at it angrily, then turned toward the astro-vivometer. There it sat, clattering away relentlessly, oblivious to all the distress it had caused. It was as if nothing at all had changed, nothing at all had happened, as if Grandfather had just gone out for a little Sunday stroll around the moon, or maybe Mars.

At that instant, Kate had an idea.

Maybe Grandfather had another ring! He said he'd planned to take her with him—to the moon or to Mars. Maybe . . . maybe that was why he made so much extra PCL! Enough for *two* rings! If only she could find it—but where could it be?

Kate scanned the ruins of the lab. If she were Grandfather, where would she keep something so precious?

She thought hard. The telescope? No, he uses that too much . . . The freezer? No, that sometimes freezes shut and can't be opened for days. Where in this mess could anyone find anything? Maybe it's not even in the lab at all . . . There are so many places to hide things in this old house!

Then his words came drifting back to her: *The best way to hide something special is to make it look as ordinary as possible.* Was there a clue in there somewhere? But what could it mean? It isn't possible to make a butterfly ring look ordinary!

Kate shrugged her shoulders in discouragement. Then, by chance, her eyes fell on the old wooden bureau against the wall. The top-most of its slim drawers was slightly ajar.

"The butterfly bureau!" she exclaimed, darting over to it. Cumberland followed her eagerly.

As she drew open the drawer, a pale turquoise band flashed in the light.

Her heart leaped, and she started to reach for the ring. Then suddenly she drew back her hand.

What if it doesn't work? she asked herself. What if Grandfather didn't want to use this ring for a good reason? What if he didn't go to Trethoniel at all? She could never hope to find Trethoniel anyway. She could imagine it, but she had only seen it once. And even if she could find the star, she might never be able to locate Grandfather, or persuade him to come back home with her, let alone save him from whatever dangers awaited him.

Suddenly, the air in the lab became chilled, as if an arctic wind had blown through. The desk lamp started to sputter, and Cumberland growled deeply.

Kate froze.

"*Wwwherrrre iisssss iittttt?*" crackled an otherworldly voice from somewhere in the hallway.

Kate turned to the door, and again to the ring sitting in the drawer. Hurriedly, with trembling hands, she took the beaker, lifted the top, and poured in the precious green fluid. The ring snapped closed.

"*Ggggiiivvve iittttt tttooo mmmeeeee.*"

She stared at the ring, but sheer fright kept her from putting it on. The ghost was back! The empty beaker fell from her hand onto the floor and splintered into pieces.

The lab grew quickly colder as a wisp of white vapor appeared in the doorway.

"*Iittttt iisssss mmmiinnnne.*"

Then everything became a blur of motion as the ghost sailed through the door, Cumberland leaped, and Kate reached for the ring.

IV

The Wings of Morpheus

A heavy blue-green mist submerged Kate's vision and swirled about her like a cyclone, carrying her into a state of being she had never known before. There was no sound: only motion, motion, motion. Warm electric sensations coursed through and around her; she felt lighter, lighter than a bubble on a breeze.

Slowly, the blue-green color began to deepen, to thicken, until strange shapes began to form out of the wisps of mist surrounding her. On either side she could see the shimmering colors solidify into large, iridescent platforms. Could they be wings? Then she felt herself seated over a sleek black body with a round head directly in front of her. Simultaneously, two delicate antennae began to unfurl from the top of the head, quivering with new life.

"A morpho!" she cried, nearly falling off her perch. "I'm riding a morpho!"

As if in answer, the great flashing wings began beating in a mighty rhythm. Kate suddenly felt like a jockey astride a colossal racehorse. But there was no saddle to hold her steady and no bridle to guide her course.

"No!" she cried. "Stop moving! I'm going to fall off!"

But the powerful wings continued to beat. Kate clasped her arms tightly around the butterfly's neck, as the colored mist was swiftly replaced by thick white clouds.

In a dazzling burst of light the clouds parted and Kate could see the buildings of a town far below them. Her own town! There was the tower of the university chapel, and there was Grandfather's house. *I never did like heights*, she thought. A sudden wave of nausea passed through her, and she hugged ever more tightly the neck of her butterfly steed, pressing her face against its thick black fur. She shut her eyes, afraid to look down again.

Borne on brilliant blue-green wings, she rose swiftly through the clouds. Higher and higher she climbed. Eventually, she opened her eyes, just in time to see a group of snow geese emerging from a lumbering cumulus cloud ahead. She forced herself to glance downward at the hilly countryside fast receding in the distance. There was the Connecticut River . . . and were those the White Mountains in the distance? They seemed so small!

It dawned on Kate that she was climbing fast—at least ten thousand feet already—and yet her ears hadn't popped at all. This ride was far smoother than any airplane: She hadn't felt even the slightest jostling from air currents. Her eyes fell to the powerful pumping wings and she recalled the gentle touch on her arm of the morpho in the garden.

Without thinking, she glanced at her wrist. Curiously, the cut from the broken glass had disappeared; no sign of it remained. Even the small bloodstain on her sleeve had vanished. The butterfly ring sat securely on her finger, its miniature wings pulsing with luminescence.

Then Kate remembered the horrible sight of Cumberland trapped beneath the collapsed laser, and she shivered. *Poor Cumberland! I hope he's all right.*

Kate's grip loosened a notch, as she felt increasingly secure on the back of the smoothly soaring butterfly. At that moment, the snow geese passed beneath them, honking loudly. She watched in awe as the perfect V-formation sailed into another cloud.

More quickly than she would ever have guessed, the clouds themselves began to disappear. The surrounding atmosphere gradually grew thinner and darker. She leaned forward on the butterfly, straining to see, as the first small pinpoints of light began to emerge in the sky. Soon, the morpho wings began to glitter faintly with starlight.

Higher and higher they flew until finally, without warning, the butterfly's ascent slowed, then halted. Kate realized that she was floating freely, without the aid of any manmade machinery, at the outer edge of the atmosphere.

As she peered over the wide wings, Kate could see a deep blue planet, enrobed with white clouds, spinning far below them. It glowed like a sapphire, a delicate blue jewel both firm and fragile. From this perspective, Earth was more than the endless variety of settings and species that she had read about in books. It was a single, unified organism, a lovely island of life drifting in the silent sea of space. It was home.

She turned to face the familiar yellow star that had radiated sunlight for years numbered in the billions. It looked as constant as ever, ferociously hot, and powerful beyond anything she had ever known. It was difficult to the point of incredulity to imagine this fiery furnace ever going dark. Then again, she knew that before Copernicus it was difficult to the point of incredulity for anyone to imagine that the Sun, which swept across the sky each day for all to see, did not rotate around the Earth! Grandfather had once said that the Sun's energy output was the same as a hundred billion hydrogen bombs exploding every second; that it had delivered a hundred trillion kilowatt-hours of energy constantly to the Earth for several billion years. Could such fantastic power really be on the verge of dying? If so, how could Grandfather—one tiny human—possibly do anything to stop it? What if Trethoniel didn't show Grandfather the cure? What if she couldn't find him at all?

"Your questions are many and difficult, Kate," said a strange voice.

She looked frantically behind, above, and below

the butterfly to find the source of the deep, melodic voice.

"And the answers may be as elusive as I seem, or as near as I am," spoke the voice again.

It was the butterfly itself!

"How do you know my name?" she cried, both amazed and afraid. She grasped the butterfly's neck more tightly. "How did you know what I was thinking?"

"You do ask many questions, Kate." The butterfly laughed, and it reminded Kate of a rolling wave booming on the ocean shore.

"How do you know my name?" she repeated.

"Because your ring, which has freed your heartlight, has also brought me to life. I know more about you than you realize."

"Do you have a name yourself?"

"I am Morpheus," the butterfly declared. "My brother, Orpheus, is carrying your grandfather."

"Really?" Kate exclaimed, so excited she nearly lost her balance for an instant. "Your brother? Then you must know where Grandfather's gone!"

"I am afraid not," answered the butterfly. "Orpheus and I were created from the same materials on the same day in the laboratory—but I have no way of knowing where he may have flown. They could have gone anywhere in the universe."

With that, Morpheus turned his head sideways so that one of his two great green eyes, honeycombed with hundreds of facets, gleamed at her. For a moment, she gazed into the eye, captivated by its prisms within prisms within prisms.

"I never would have—" she began, then suddenly stopped herself. "I'm speaking without moving my mouth!"

"Quite right," replied Morpheus, with only a slight quivering of his antennae. "Now that you are made of heartlight, you no longer need your former voice. You can communicate with your thoughts alone, at least over short distances."

"This is a lot to get used to," replied Kate in disbelief. "Here I am floating on the back of a giant butterfly, miles above the Earth, and speaking telepathically. It's not possible!"

The long antennae waved in response. "So it seems to you, Kate, only because you have not experienced it before. There are wonders even more amazing on your home planet that you fully believe, simply because they are familiar to you."

"Like what?"

Morpheus slowly blinked his great green eyes. "Like the transformation of a wingless, earthbound caterpillar into a magnificent butterfly. Who would believe that such a thing could happen if it were not common knowledge? Who would predict that such an unimposing creature could construct a cocoon, exchange its wormlike body for another one of dazzling design, and fly off into the forest without a second thought?"

"I know that's amazing," said Kate, shaking her head, "but this is still too much to believe."

"More so than the tadpole who somehow becomes a frog? More so than the trees who manufacture food from beams of light? More so than the flowering spring, which follows the frozen winter? More so than the human child, once smaller than the smallest speck of dust, who comes to learn language, make tools, and bring forth a child of its own?"

"This is still more than I can handle," Kate replied. "How a simple ring could—" She halted, gazing at the butterfly ring on her finger.

"Something's wrong!" she cried. "It's damaged!" Indeed, the rim of the ring's left wing was roughly tattered, as if it had been eaten away by a powerful acid.

"Nothing is wrong," answered Morpheus calmly. "Your ring has begun to deteriorate, that's all."

"Deteriorate?" Kate clasped the butterfly's neck firmly. "What do you mean by that?" Then she remembered: Four minutes . . . that's what Grandfather said was the limit . . .

"The process of deterioration began the instant you put on the ring, and it will continue until the ring has disappeared completely."

Kate stiffened. "You mean I can tell how much PCL is left by watching it, like the fuel gauge in a car?"

Morpheus waved his antennae in assent. "Except with this kind of car, running out of fuel would be fatal."

Gracefully, the butterfly spun his body around so

that, instead of facing Earth, they were facing a dark sector of space. Dark, but for one pinpoint of reddish light that sparkled like a distant ruby.

"Is that where we're going?" asked Kate. "It looks so far away."

"Is it your desire to go to the star Trethoniel?"

"My only desire is to find Grandfather!" she exclaimed. "To make sure he's safe and to bring him home again. I have this dreadful feeling that somehow he's in much more danger than he realizes—from what, I don't know. If finding him means we have to go all the way to Trethoniel, then I guess that's what we'll have to do."

"I don't know where Orpheus has borne him, Kate, although my inner sense tells me it is someplace very distant. All I know are the instructions your grandfather programmed into the ring. You see, like you, this is my very first journey. But I can tell you this: Trethoniel is much farther away than it appears, and the journey there and back could be much more dangerous than you realize. I don't know whether your ring will last long enough to do all that."

Kate looked anxiously at the distant red star. "We have four minutes of Earth time."

The butterfly cocked his head pensively. "Four minutes of Earth time is not a great deal."

His repetition of those words struck Kate, to her own surprise, as vaguely comforting. After all, how much could go wrong in only four minutes? Even in the expanded time of interstellar travel, four minutes didn't feel like very long. The real risk was that it wouldn't be enough time to find Grandfather, and she would be forced to return to Earth empty-handed.

"You must remember one cardinal rule," declared the great butterfly in a tone of voice that suddenly reminded Kate of her fears. "Never, but never, remove your ring."

She shuddered. "What would happen if I did?"

Morpheus studied her gravely. "If you should take off your ring, even for an instant, you would immediately revert to your normal human form. And in the realms where we are traveling—that means certain death. You could be vaporized by the fires of a star, suffocated by some poisonous atmosphere, or instantly frozen—but your ultimate fate would be the same."

"All right, all right!" exclaimed Kate. "I've got the message. I won't take off my ring."

"No matter what," emphasized Morpheus.

"No matter what."

"The only environment where you might have any chance at all to survive would be a planet with an atmosphere much like Earth's—and I don't have to tell you how unlikely that is."

Kate twisted the ring on her finger, making sure it was attached securely, and surveyed the endless darkness of space extending in all directions. "What if I fall off your back? The ring won't stop that from happening, will it?"

"It should," replied Morpheus. "I am the product

of your heartlight reacting with the pure condensed light of the ring, and I am part of you now. As long as you're wearing the ring, I will remain tied to your heartlight. I will hear your every thought, sometimes even before you do. My guess is there's only one way you could leave my back, Kate: If you choose to."

"Fat chance of that happening," she replied, nervously biting her lip. It felt the same as her old lip, even if it were only made of whatever Morpheus said it was made of. "But won't we get burned by the heat of the star? We'll be going awfully close to it, won't we?"

"No, we won't get burned. You're now made of heartlight—and I'm made of pure light. You have no skin to be burned, and no eyes to be blinded by the brightness of Trethoniel."

"But I can still see you," objected Kate. "How can I see you if I don't have any eyes?"

"The same way you see in your imagination."

Kate turned to face the blue planet beneath them, silently spinning in space. She could see the thin, wispy edge of what must be Cape Cod, protruding from the body of North America like the prow of an ancient ship. So many shades of blue were there, they could not be counted; the whole planet gleamed with a luster more luminous than dawn's first light. Then, with a start, Kate realized how perfectly *round* is the Earth: Indeed, it felt as though she had never before understood the true meaning of the word. That very roundness seemed to emphasize the planet's vulnerability. Like a delicate bubble, its sweeping blue curves caressing the sea of outer space, the fragile Earth floated—helpless, lovely, and alone.

"I can feel pain in my imagination, too," said Kate quietly.

"Yes," answered Morpheus with a stirring of his wings. "You can feel anything you could feel with a body—and probably a few things more. You can feel warm or cold; you can laugh or cry. The only difference is that you lack a physical body that would be destroyed by the elements and forces of space travel. You will even continue breathing—although it's not air you will breathe, but light from the stars around us. You are in some ways physical, and in some ways metaphysical. You are part light, and part beyond light. You are *heartlight*."

Kate gazed thoughtfully at the iridescent wings. "Do you think there could be something out there— some kind of force or something—that's dangerous to heartlight?"

"I don't know," replied Morpheus gravely. "There is much that I don't know. That's why you must be very sure you really want to travel all the way to Trethoniel."

For a few moments they drifted in silence at the edge of outer space. No snow geese honked; no winds whistled. Kate felt all alone, poised at the boundary between the known and the unknown.

At last, she spoke again. "I want to try, Morpheus. I want to find him."

Instantly, the butterfly's powerful wings exploded into action. Faster they raced, much faster than before, until soon they were nothing but a vaguely blue blur against the stars.

Kate stole a glance to the rear; Earth was no longer in sight. The Sun itself quickly receded into deep darkness. Now there was no turning back. She turned forward again to see hundreds of new stars moving swiftly toward them. The great glowing arch of the Milky Way slowly submerged into a sea of speckled light, and before her eyes, the sword of Orion compressed into a tight knot of stars.

The ride was amazingly smooth. But for the whirring of the wings and the passage of the starry vista, it seemed as though they weren't moving at all. Kate slightly relaxed her grip on Morpheus' neck. Hearing the hum of his wings, but unable to see them anymore, she wondered for an instant if they were still there. Instinctively, she started to stretch her hand toward one of the invisible wings.

"Don't," warned Morpheus. "My wings are moving faster than light and they could slice anything that touches them to ribbons. That includes you, Kate."

Embarrassed, she withdrew her hand. *None of my thoughts are private anymore. Not even the stupidest ones.*

Quickly, however, she forgot the incident as they raced past hundreds upon hundreds of stars. So swiftly did Morpheus carry her that almost as soon as a star drew near, it had vanished behind them. It was like riding a rocket headlong into an endless meteor shower. Throughout, Kate kept her eye on one glowing red star in the deep distance.

"How many stars can there be?" she mused. "Is there any end to them?"

Morpheus gave no answer except to continue beating his powerful wings.

Suddenly, Kate was aware of a delicate, distant sound that seemed to permeate the silence of space.

"Morpheus! What's that?"

The antennae quivered uncertainly, as the wavering sound grew stronger. As they sailed swiftly into the sea of stars, Kate strained to hear. It was very difficult to catch more than a few faraway wisps of the slow, low, flowing tones.

Gradually, the swelling sound grew more and more resonant. The beautiful tones seemed to dance through the empty corridors of space, like something that was half music and half starlight. Celebration and peace moved through the melody; Kate had never heard anything so lovely. It felt closer and closer, and seemed to surround them, like the beating of some celestial heart.

A special phrase of Grandfather's popped into Kate's memory: *mysterium tremendum et fascinans.* She recalled the day he had discovered it in a medieval prayer and how happily he had shared it with her, saying it should be reserved only for rare moments of wonderment. *O great and wondrous mystery.*

She listened, eyes closed, for a timeless moment. Then she remembered another phrase, one from a poem by Wordsworth. Fortunately, she had read the poem in one of Grandfather's books, rather than at school, or it never would have lodged in her memory. As Wordsworth had entered a beautiful valley in Wales, he had found himself, as he put it, *disturbed with joy.* How, Kate had then wondered, could joy also be disturbing? It seemed an impossible contradiction. Now, for the first time, she felt a glimmer of understanding. But why did this strange music seem to bring those words to life?

Her thoughts turned to the stars whizzing past her: so many of them, and so beautiful! Could they be the source of the music? She recalled how Grandfather had once likened the story of a star's life to a great biography of Gandhi, Joan of Arc, or Abraham Lincoln: a compelling tale of birth, struggle, triumph, and violent death. He had said that every star eventually reaches a point where the age-old balance between its own gravity, which pulls inward, and its radiant energy, which pushes outward, will fall apart. If it's a normal star, like the Sun, it will suddenly shudder and compress down to the size of a moon. But if it's unusually massive, it could expand and expand like a luminous red balloon until—at last—it will burst and collapse so fast and so far that it will *disappear completely,* leaving nothing behind but a black hole.

Kate looked at the radiant glow of Trethoniel, still distant but drawing ever nearer, and she shuddered at the thought of any star, not just the Sun, dying in a final spasm that swallowed up all its energy and light forever. How wrong that such beauty should be doomed to disappear forever down some cosmic drain! Grandfather had once said that the gravity of a black hole is the strongest physical force in the universe—so strong that even light cannot escape. Did that mean that the heartlight of the living star is also trapped, without escape? Could it be lost forever to the universe?

"No, Kate." Morpheus did not wish to leave such a question unanswered. As the strange music washed over them, growing stronger by the second, he explained: "Energy can't be lost completely from the universe. It may be transformed into matter, and back again into energy, but it never totally vanishes. If an electron and a positron collide, they may annihilate each other, but they will still leave behind two photons—brand new particles—with exactly the same energy as before. And what is true at the tiniest level of the universe must also be true for a star. Even a star as big as Trethoniel."

"So the energy of a star that dies might show up somewhere else? In some new form?"

"Perhaps," answered Morpheus, his pulsing wings glistening with starlight. "Your physical body was made of material once manufactured inside of a star. So who can tell? Perhaps some of the energy of a dying star finds its way into the heart of a young girl on a distant planet."

"But what if the whole star gets sucked into a black hole?" demanded Kate, still distraught. "Nothing can get out of there—no light, no heartlight, no anything! Could all that life just vanish?"

Morpheus waved his long antennae gracefully, as if to comfort the hazel-eyed girl seated on his back. "Nothing totally vanishes, Kate. Life doesn't disappear forever. It only evolves."

". . . as part of the Pattern that Grandfather always talks about," Kate heard herself thinking. But she wasn't comforted. The haunting music now seemed more disturbing than joyful.

Suddenly, Kate realized that the great glowing mass of Trethoniel was upon them. Imperceptibly, Morpheus slowed the beating of his wings. Like a flower slowly unfurling, the swirling nebula surrounding the star opened into the spiraling veil she had seen on Grandfather's monitor. There, in the center, sat the magnificent star itself, encircled by a necklace of gleaming planets.

"Trethoniel!" cried Kate. "Is that where the music is coming from?"

"Mysterium tremendum et fascinans," said Morpheus in answer.

Soon the great wings ceased beating entirely, and the travelers coasted in open space, illuminated by the shimmering light of Trethoniel and caressed by its music. At once, Kate understood that Trethoniel was not only a star, but also an entire system of planets, moons, and clouds of incandescent gases—as well as the spiraling nebula that wrapped around them all. How many times larger than the Sun's own solar system this star's realm must be, she could only guess. She looked in wonder at the luminous circles of light at the outermost edge of the nebula, sparkling like spherical rainbows decked with dew. The entire system seemed to whirl around itself like a dog that had chased its own tail since time began, and would continue to chase it as long as time lasted.

Then, abruptly, the music of Trethoniel faded away into silence.

"Where did it go?" cried Kate. She found herself clutching Morpheus' neck. "It was so beautiful! Why did it stop?"

"I don't know," answered Morpheus, sounding worried.

Kate shook her head. "And how—how will we ever find Grandfather in there? Trethoniel's system looks as big as a galaxy! He could be on any one of those planets—I see three or four at least—or somewhere on the other side where we can't see him, or even inside the star itself!"

"Or," added Morpheus grimly, "he could be in none of those places."

Kate's eyes fell from the radiant star to the butterfly ring upon her hand. She caught her breath. A large slice of the left wing was already gone!

Before she could even think the command, Morpheus beat his great wings again. Together, they sailed into the realm of Trethoniel.

V

The Darkness

As if called by an inaudible voice, the great butterfly began beating his wings in a graceful rhythm. Steadily he carried Kate into the open arms of Trethoniel's spiraling nebula. As they entered the shimmering, shifting layers of light, Morpheus began to glide. With great swoops from side to side, they sailed deeper into the star's system, and nearer to the great red star itself.

Kate saw hundreds of objects, large and small, circling the star. In addition to the ones she had expected—planets, moons, asteroids—many strange and lovely formations danced around the star in stately orbit. Some seemingly solid forms were not solid at all when they were seen up close. Some were branching and bent like delicate ferns; others were pinnacles of clouds, whirling and swirling; still others looked like complex geometric crystals. She noticed one formation that resembled a gigantic snowflake, as large as a house. It sparkled like a great jewel as it slowly twirled in space. She wished Grandfather could see this; she could imagine the light of discovery in his eyes. Or had he, perhaps, already seen it?

Morpheus banked to the right to avoid a tangle of holohedral crystals that seemed to be swimming in tight formation, like a school of minnows. As the red light of Trethoniel glistened upon them, Kate wondered if there could be new forms of life here, life totally unlike anything on Earth. She knew how Grandfather would answer her question: *Only God knows the answer to that one, Kaitlyn. But if you keep asking . . .*

"Look there," said Morpheus, his antennae pointing to a creamy white globe emerging from a billowing mass of colored clouds in the distance. "It's Trethoniel's most remote planet."

"It looks like a big snowball," observed Kate. "I had no idea a planet could be so white."

She checked the butterfly ring. Nearly half of the ornament's left wing had disappeared, as had part of the left antenna. How fleeting would be her glimpse of Trethoniel!

As she gazed over Morpheus' broad wings and looked about herself, Kate's thoughts drifted momentarily from her search for Grandfather and the plight of the Sun. She was sailing inside a sanctuary, a slice of the universe all but unknown to earthbound observers. She knew that many great scientists (including the members of the Royal Society) would kill for the chance to see all this. How ironic that such an experience should be wasted on a girl who couldn't even stand science class.

"Wasted is a strong word," admonished Morpheus, as he banked to avoid an orbiting asteroid. "Maybe there is some aspect of Trethoniel that you can appreciate better than anyone else."

Kate furrowed her brow. "But I'm not a great scientist or a great anything!"

"That is true," answered Morpheus with a wave of his antennae. "You are just plain Kate. One day, perhaps, your great qualities will rise above your great insecurities."

"How can you say that?" she demanded. "You barely know me! You don't have any idea what a dunce I can be."

"I know you better than you realize." Morpheus turned his head and observed his passenger closely. "You, Kate, could change the course of the stars."

"Me?" Her gaze fell. "I'd be lucky to change the course of an asteroid! I can't even get Grandfather to eat regular meals, for heaven's sake! How could I possibly make a difference to a star?"

The butterfly shook his antennae in discouragement. "I'm coming to the conclusion that it would be easier to make a difference to a whole galaxy of stars than to convince you you're anything special."

"Just help me find Grandfather," said Kate testily. "That's enough for me."

As the gleaming white planet disappeared into a

collection of clouds, a new formation, shimmering in the stellar breeze, caught Kate's attention. It resembled a kind of curtain, a curtain made of thousands of lavender-tinted icicles. She heard them tinkling gently as the winds passed through them, and the soothing sound helped her mood to pass as well. The lavender curtain glowed invitingly and billowed outward, as if in greeting, as they sailed by.

At that very moment, a vague and shadowy form was gathering itself deep within the bowels of the star. When seen from far away, it resembled a sinister cloud, darker than the foulest pollution ever to belch forth from any smokestack. So huge was its expanse that it could, in repose, obscure a large section of the star from view.

As it drew itself together, the dark form began to knot and tighten until, finally, it had condensed itself into a long, snakelike body—a body so dense that not even the powerful light of Trethoniel could pierce it, a body so black that only one name could describe it.

The Darkness. It was the ultimate void coalesced into a creature. Wherever The Darkness appeared, light withdrew; even as it slithered through space, it erased any light in its path.

The writhing shape of The Darkness lifted itself toward the unsuspecting travelers with frightening speed. Like a vast entrail of emptiness, it gleamed coldly in the starlight, a long and twisting mass with no discernable features save the single red eye, more a swirling electrical storm than an organ of sight, that glowed like an ember in its darkest place. As The Darkness streaked toward the travelers, waves of negative energy crackled around the red eye.

Suddenly, Morpheus felt a tingle of foreboding in his antennae. From the corner of his eye he could see the dark shape approaching rapidly. He swerved sharply and started to climb away from Trethoniel, beating his wings with all of his power.

"What's going on?" shouted Kate, caught by surprise. "Where are you—"

Her question was interrupted by the sight of the frightening form snaking toward them, leaving a trail of impenetrable blackness in its wake.

The Darkness coiled its fearsome tail and prepared to throw it like a mighty whip. With a searing explosion of negative energy, the tail lashed out, eliminating all the light in its path. It struck at precisely the spot where the travelers would have been but for Morpheus' quick change of direction. The whiplike crack of the tail sent powerful shock waves racing outward, demolishing the lavender curtain of crystals and several other formations floating nearby.

The shock waves crashed into Kate and Morpheus, sending them spinning through space. A hail of splintered crystals pounded them like a torrential rain.

"Help!" cried Kate when, for an instant, her legs lost their grip on the butterfly's back. She started to pitch to one side, as fear seized her. "I'm going to fall!"

"Hold on!" commanded Morpheus, wheeling

around and dipping one wing like a rudder to regain his balance. "I won't let you fall!"

As the butterfly righted himself, Kate's panic ebbed only slightly. "I thought you said I couldn't fall off!" she exclaimed, grasping his neck tightly with her arms.

"This creature must be made of some kind of anti-light!" cried Morpheus. "And it's strong enough to separate us."

"Then get us out of here!"

At that instant, the terrible tail struck again. With the weight of a massive moon, it smashed into a large asteroid floating just behind Morpheus. The asteroid exploded in a violent blast, throwing them into an uncontrolled spin. They tumbled through space like a leaf in a hurricane.

"Help!" screamed Kate in terror, as she started to slide off her perch. Her arms and hands clung desperately to Morpheus' broad neck, but the shock waves from the explosion knocked them upside down, then sideways, then upside down again.

She was slipping!

"Hold on!" cried Morpheus, working his wings desperately to halt their spin.

She tried to hold on to the morpho's neck with all her strength. Her heart pounded like a thundering drum. But the tighter she squeezed, the more she slipped to the side. Her fingers dug into the black fur covering the butterfly's body. With a final effort, she reached for one of Morpheus' slender legs . . .

Too late! She slid off the butterfly and fell headlong into the swirling mists.

She screamed—but the whirling winds screamed louder. Wildly she flailed her arms and legs.

Down, down, down she plummeted, like a sack of stones. So fast was she spinning that she could not see the floating crystals whizzing past her, nor even the great mass of Trethoniel itself coming closer and closer.

Nor could she see another shape, dark and sinewy, racing toward her. The red eye of The Darkness pulsed with desire as it drew nearer, approaching fast.

"Help me!" Kate shouted as she tumbled downward. "Morpheus!"

"I am coming!" the butterfly called, as he dove headlong to catch her. He rocketed past clouds and crystals like a shooting star. Then, to Morpheus' great horror, the serpentine form of The Darkness expanded at the end nearest to Kate, as if it were opening a cavernous mouth.

Morpheus beat his wings with all his might. Never before had he flown so fast! Now she was within his reach—even as the shadowy shape closed in from below.

With a crackling of negative energy, The Darkness closed itself about Kate, just a fraction of an instant before Morpheus shot past.

She was gone!

* * *

Suddenly, Kate felt herself completely embraced by darkness: damp, cold, and stifling. Her fall had been broken. But by what? At first the coldness reminded her of the ghost in Grandfather's lab—but this coldness was different: It was far more powerful, penetrating, and frightening. The ghost had been a chilling breeze, but this was more like an Arctic blast.

"Morpheus!" she cried, but the word could not pass beyond the heavy darkness surrounding her.

Gradually, Kate perceived something new. An eerie reddish glow began to flow toward her from all sides. And as it flowed it throbbed, like an aching wound. As irresistible as lava streaming down the cone of a volcano, the glow pressed upon her, trying to smother her.

She gasped. *I'm—I'm suffocating in here!*

The glow grew redder and deeper. It was everywhere. It was everything.

Kate writhed and kicked to get away from it. But there was no place to go. The glow gripped her even more tightly. Breathing with great difficulty, she put her hand on her chest, directly over her heart. It felt so weak! The beating seemed to be getting slower, fainter. Everything inside her felt squeezed, as if she were caught in the middle of a powerful vise.

She labored to breathe, but the red glow only grew stronger. It felt less like a color and more like a heavy woolen blanket, tightening around her, pressing the life out of her.

"Morpheus!" she cried. "Please help me!"

But Morpheus was too far away to hear, too far away to answer.

The deadly blanket grew heavier. Tighter. Every-thing around her was pulsing, squeezing, suspending Kate in its cold grasp. With shock, Kate realized that even her own breathing had taken on the same irre-sistible rhythm. She tried to move, but movement was increasingly difficult. She forced herself to inhale deeply—to break free from the powerful pulse. But its suffocating pressure was too strong. She broke into a spasm of coughing.

A bolt of fear shot through her. *I'm going to die! This thing is killing me!*

Then something inside of her stirred. Something deeper than fear. Something living, and breathing, and angry.

No, she protested weakly. *I don't want to die.*

The red glow pushed violently against her chest, and she coughed uncontrollably.

Tears streamed down her face as she struggled to regain a last measure of self-control. Instinctively, she moved her arm through the smothering cloud and touched her ring—the ring that Grandfather made, the ring that brought Morpheus to life. Somewhere deep within herself, a small candle was kindled.

With great difficulty, she drew in a shallow breath. But it was her own breath, to her own rhythm. *No! You can't have me. I won't let you.*

Slowly, a new feeling started to swell inside her. Gradually, very gradually, her heart began to grow stronger, even as her breathing grew a little easier. The deadly vise seemed to loosen, one notch at a time, until she could feel some of her own strength returning. She kicked her legs angrily. Before long a new illumination seemed to fill her chest, and its warmth flowed through her every artery, like a cascade of liquid starlight.

Haltingly, unwillingly, the red glow began to recede. As the light within Kate expanded, The Darkness itself grew slightly thinner, so that she could suddenly see traces of Trethoniel's light through the shadowy folds around her.

She started to swim toward the light, pushing her way with all of her strength.

Then the air crackled vengefully, and the curtain of darkness started to descend again. A new wave of fear coursed through Kate.

"Morpheus!" she cried, before breaking into an uncontrollable spasm of coughing. "Help me! I—can't—breathe!"

*   *   *

Morpheus hurtled past The Darkness at a speed faster than lightning. What it was and where it came from he did not know; all he knew was that it had swallowed Kate.

Cutting a wide arc through the swirling mists, he swung around to face the great writhing mass, whose red eye now blazed in triumph. Like an arrow shot from a mighty bow, Morpheus soared straight into battle.

The shadowy being condensed itself ever more tightly as it began to squeeze the life out of its prey. Suddenly Morpheus streaked past, almost brushing the red eye with his wing. The eye sizzled and crackled with rage and turned its attention to the riderless butterfly.

From the depths of space rose the whiplike tail, into which so much negativity had been squeezed that it could shatter any solid target or cancel out any light. Curling itself tightly, the tail lashed out at the butterfly.

Morpheus abruptly changed course and dove behind a floating blue crystal as big as an office building.

With a loud crackling, the deadly tail uncoiled, smashing directly into the crystal. Fragments flew in all directions, and the sound of the explosion reverberated throughout the realm of Trethoniel.

For an instant, Morpheus was unable to see any sign of The Darkness through the dust and remnants of the crystal. Still wincing from the shock of the impact, he could only discern the swath of impenetrable blackness left behind by the tail. No stars could be seen there, as if a slice of the sky had simply been erased. He knew that the evil energy of this dark creature could damage—if not destroy—Kate's heartlight.

Like a tiny hummingbird buzzing a giant serpent, Morpheus attacked the creature with all his fury. He dove and darted, spun and soared, occasionally piercing the edges of The Darkness but never inflicting any damage. Every few seconds the tail would coil like a deadly spring and strike, eliminating all the light in its path.

The brave butterfly tried to attack the electric red

eye—which seemed to be the center of the creature's intelligence—but the violent swings of the tail kept him at bay. At one point, the dark mass near the eye suddenly grew lighter and more transparent. Through the swirling blackness, Morpheus glimpsed the form of a small girl.

"Kate!" he cried, and some of his flagging strength returned.

Instantly, Morpheus climbed higher until he was well out of range of the terrible tail. For a moment he circled and then, suddenly, he careened sharply and soared like a missile directly at the red eye.

The great tail held itself completely motionless. Whether out of confusion or design, The Darkness did nothing to remove itself from the path of its attacker.

Although his instinct warned him to beware of a trap, Morpheus did not alter his collision course with the motionless target. Faster than light itself he flew, bearing down on the sizzling center of the red eye.

Then, just as Morpheus approached, from the center of the eye there blew forth a terrible cloud of darkness so thick that no light could possibly penetrate. Trying desperately to avoid it, the butterfly veered upward.

Too late! A blanket of blackness descended over him. It was dark, as a black hole is dark, and cold, as death is cold.

"I can't see anything!" Morpheus cried, his eyes stinging with pain, as he fought to keep his bearings.

Concentrated anti-light pressed against his wings with such force he could barely keep them moving.

At that very instant, the deadly tail coiled to strike at the tiny creature trapped within the black cloud.

Craaaack! A powerful explosion of negative energy and red lightning burst across the starscape as Morpheus forced his way out of the cloud and shot directly into the red eye.

The Darkness recoiled in pain. As it did so, it began to dissipate. For an instant, Kate was visible again amidst the billowing folds of blackness.

Swiftly, Morpheus dove into the parting veil and careened to a halt beside her. "Grab on!" he cried.

She reached to him, even as The Darkness started to close again around them both.

"Grab on!"

As she wrapped her arms around Morpheus' neck, she felt something touch her leg from below. A thin and wiry tentacle, reaching out from the dark mass, began to tighten its grip around her leg.

"No!" Kate screamed. "Something's pulling me back!"

With all his strength, Morpheus tried to pull her upward. Slowly, he lifted her a small distance out of The Darkness, even as its folds gathered about them like enormous jaws. But the tentacle wrapped around her leg still more tightly and drew her down again.

"I'm losing my grip! Oh—Morpheus!" Kate's hands broke free of the butterfly and she was dragged downward.

Instantly, Morpheus wheeled around and dove beneath her. With a flash of his great wing, he sliced cleanly through the thin tentacle and caught Kate on his back. They shot straight out of The Darkness just as it came closing down behind them like a crashing wave.

"Thank you, thank you," she whispered, hugging the broad back of the butterfly as they whizzed away.

"We aren't free yet!" The wings of Morpheus whirred with all their power.

Sizzling with rage, the injured eye of The Darkness pulsed with pain. The tail lashed out, sweeping away the starlight in its path.

Morpheus swerved immediately before the tail whipped past. But its edge glanced against his wing— and the force of the blow sent him reeling. Kate was instantly thrown off his back and started tumbling through space, as the butterfly spun out of control.

"Help!" she screamed, suddenly robbed of her safety. "I'm falling!"

Downward she plummeted, drawn by the gravity of the white planet orbiting below. As she entered its thick atmosphere, she was pursued ever more closely by The Darkness, its red eye seething with desire. The writhing mass stretched toward her, groping, groping.

"No!" she screamed, seeing the shadowy shape approaching from above. "Noooo—"

Her scream was interrupted as she struck the side of a steeply sloping wall of snow and ice rising eighty thousand feet above the mountainous surface of the planet. Her free-fall now became a brutal terror as she rolled and bounced down the ridge of snow, like a tiny pebble thrown over a cliff.

Craaaack!

A great burst of negative electricity filled the sky with red lightning as the terrible tail smashed against the ridge above her. Slamming into the mountain like a gigantic meteor, the tail broke loose an icy cornice and dislodged a tremendous wall of snow.

With a deafening roar, huge islands of white began to cascade down the mountainside, gathering crushing momentum as they fell. Thousands of tons tumbled together into a churning sea of snow, sending a billowing white cloud high into the atmosphere. The roar of the avalanche rocked the mountain to its roots.

As swiftly as it had started, the thunderous cascade came to an end. The mass of snow settled, shifted once with a grinding lurch, then froze into place. But for the gentle wisps of white still hanging in the air, there was no sign of any violence, no sound but the steady sweep of wind across the virgin valleys. It looked as if this world of silent, snowy pinnacles had never been disturbed, by even so much as a footprint, for millions upon millions of years.

VI

The Cocoon

Suddenly, the world turned white.

All the sensations of the past few seconds whirled around in Kate's head: the first scrape of cold snow on her arms; the feeling of falling down a bottomless slide, bouncing and somersaulting with terrifying speed; the dark cracks that snaked swiftly across the slope; the wall of snow rising above her, pushing her ever faster until, like a breaking wave, it collapsed over her, tossing and tearing at her helpless form; and, throughout, the thunderous roar of the avalanche.

Now all was still. All except the thunder, which continued to drum in her ears. She shuddered at the memory of the dark form reaching to grab her—and that horrible eye, seething and sizzling like a whirlpool of red lightning.

She struggled to lower her hands, which had instinctively covered her face as the wave of snow crashed over her. But she could only move with great effort inside her tight cocoon. She wriggled and squirmed and finally succeeded in creating a small space around her head.

A feeling as cold as the snow surrounding her slowly seeped into her consciousness. *I'm trapped! I'll never find Grandfather now!*

Kate felt limp, tired, and helpless.

Then the image of Morpheus, battling gallantly to save her, came into her mind. Perhaps he could help her again! She concentrated her thoughts on the great flashing wings.

"I'm here!" she called. "Can you hear me?"

No answer penetrated the darkness. No movement. No sound.

She gathered her energy and continued to try. "Morpheus!" she called. "Morpheus . . . Can you hear me?"

Still no answer. Only a dull, distant feeling of pain and loss.

Maybe I can dig myself out! Then Morpheus can find me! She shivered, from more than the cold. The dark creature too would be waiting to find her.

With a sideways twist, she managed to free her shoulders slightly. A growing need to rest, to sleep, rose inside her, but she resisted it. Again she twisted, and again her tomb of snow loosened its grip a few degrees, but no more. The tips of her fingers began to ache with cold.

She paused, allowing her limbs to relax. Her heart was pounding, and it seemed somehow to be beating louder than it had since she had left Grandfather's lab. Perhaps this chamber of snow was magnifying the sound? A sudden flash of memory recalled the smothering red glow inside The Darkness, and she released a cry of pain.

Her heart pounded even louder, and she struggled to regain her composure—and not to panic. *There's no red glow in here . . . only snow. Lots of snow. I can still dig myself out. It doesn't matter how long it takes. I'm made of heartlight. I can't freeze to death.*

She swallowed her fears and forced herself to think. First she must figure out which way is up. Otherwise she might dig in the wrong direction.

A wave of uncertainty washed over her. If only she could see . . .

Then an idea flashed in the darkness. *I don't need to see! All I need is gravity. That's it, gravity!*

Pleased with her own ingenuity, Kate hatched a plan. With considerable effort, she pushed away enough snow to create a large cavity around her head and chest. She placed one hand in front of her face and, with a hearty ptttew!, spit a stream of saliva into her palm. *Whichever way it rolls, I'll dig in the opposite direction.*

Slowly, she felt the liquid gather and begin to trickle . . . up her fingers, away from her palm. With satisfaction, she knew that the avalanche had left her upside down. Before she could dig herself out, she must turn around.

Then an icy tremor shook her to the core.

Her hand! What was happening to it?

With frightening swiftness, her hand grew stiff, like wood, and deeply chilled. She tried to squeeze it into a fist, but the base of her fingers had hardened so much that she couldn't bend them. In the darkness, she slid her other hand next to the afflicted one. As her fingertips reached out to touch the stiffened palm, they struck an icy, frozen surface, a surface that had lost its sense of touch.

I'm freezing! she realized, in shock and confusion.

She twisted violently, trying to draw her knees into her chest. They felt heavy and numb.

What was happening? How could this be . . . unless . . .

She reached in the darkness to touch her butterfly ring.

Gone!

Tears, real tears, began to well up in Kate's eyes as she realized that somewhere in the vast mountain of snow squeezing her from all sides was her precious ring. What had Morpheus said would befall her if she ever lost it? *Certain death—vaporized by the fires of a star, suffocated by some poisonous atmosphere, or instantly frozen . . .*

Frozen! Is that how this quest was to end?

Remorse deeper than the snows of this frozen planet suddenly fell upon her. Grandfather will feel as if he killed her, blaming himself for everything. But she did it to herself! Why did she ever think she could find him in the first place? She should never have left the lab . . . She should have let that ghost take the ring! Then it might be the ghost who ended up getting buried alive on some faraway planet . . .

She tried to flex her legs and arms, if only to keep the circulation moving. A deep, dull sensation of heaviness was moving through every cell of her body. She shivered uncontrollably and her teeth began to chatter. Her entire body felt increasingly numb.

And cold, cold!

Kate's eyes felt heavy, and she let them fall closed for an instant. Sleep would feel so good, so peaceful . . . would save her energy for later . . . would give her the rest she deserved . . .

No! I must not sleep. That would be the easy way out. It would be suicide. Maybe Morpheus is digging for me this very second.

She listened for any sounds at all. The only thing she could hear was the pounding of her heart, her true heart, inside her small body. The beating was still there, but slower, more subdued. She listened for a while to the rhythmic pulsing, which made her feel drowsy again. Her eyelids drooped heavily.

A strange sense of calm began to envelop her. Instead of alarm, she felt only weariness. Instead of anger, she felt only sorrow. How sad never to see Grandfather again, nor to run with Cumberland again, nor to sing favorite songs with Dad again. How sad never again to smell the aroma of Mom's bread baking in the kitchen, never again to see the great wings of Morpheus flash in the starlight, never again to hear the music of Trethoniel . . .

Suddenly her body shivered with a tremor of cold, and this reawakened her. *How can I fight off this sleep?* raced her thoughts. *It's getting harder and harder. I can't stay awake much longer.*

Then some words and music from a faraway time and place drifted back to her, echoing in her mind as they had once echoed in a tiny room on a distant planet:

> *All praise to thee my Lord this night,*
> *For all the blessings of thy light.*

Another spasm of chills shot through her. She mustered all of her remaining strength and forced herself to dig, using her throbbing hands as shovels. Slowly, she loosened enough of the snow to turn her body around, then started to work her way upward. And as she worked, Kate began to sing again, as loudly as she could.

> *Keep me, O keep me, King of Kings . . .*

She pressed her numbing fingers against her unfeeling cheeks as her teeth chattered through the words *King of Kings.*

> *Beneath . . . thine own . . . almighty wings . . .*

She continued to dig, handful by handful, stopping only to push her hands into her armpits for a touch of warmth. But the feeling had left them, and soon they felt no more alive than trowels made of metal. Wearily, she pressed on, digging, digging.

At one point, a clump of wet snow came loose and

fell with a splat onto her face. She tried to brush it off, but she struck herself in the eye with her own frozen fingers. She shook her head angrily, trying to remove the snow that had mixed with her perspiration and tears. The pain in her arms was excruciating. She wanted to scream, not to sing!

She wasn't getting anywhere. After all this digging, she had moved only a few feet, if that. Who could tell how far she still had to go? This was hopeless!

She slapped her hand against the wall of snow, half expecting it to splinter into pieces. She was freezing! Her hands and feet had no feeling left. What would Grandfather do now? What would he tell her?

At once, she knew: *Perseverance, Kaitlyn . . . If there is any quality I wish for you, it's perseverance.*

A rush of longing filled her heart—longing for Grandfather, for his voice, for his arms around her. Just to hear him tell one of his stories . . . just to hear him laugh. Maybe he's in trouble, too. Maybe he needs help! Suddenly, Kate knew what she had to do, despite the pain.

She had to try.

With grim determination, she started again to dig. To dig and to sing.

> *All praise to thee . . . my Lord this night,*
> *For all the blessings . . . of thy light.*

With each phrase, she climbed a little higher, although she could not tell whether she was six feet or six hundred feet from the surface.

Keep me, O keep me . . . King of Kings . . .

Like a relentless machine, she pressed ahead. Her hands, feet, and face were now completely numb; she couldn't even feel the touch of her own tongue on her lips. Her entire body felt heavier and heavier and she knew she had little strength left.

Beneath thine own Almighty . . .

Without warning, she slipped backward, bouncing violently against the snow. She could not fall very far; the loose snow she had dug had filled up the cavern beneath her. But it felt as if she had lost all the ground she had gained. She landed with her leg twisted beneath her body. Yet the limb felt only a vague, dull pain: It too was beginning to turn into lifeless stone. Exhausted, she sank back against the snow, too weary to move.

Then, in a distant memory, she heard Grandfather's voice again. *Perseverance, Kaitlyn.*

She shook herself, determined at least to clamber back to the place from which she had fallen.

Desperately, she tried to concentrate. To dig. With a final effort, she swung her hand into the snow above her head.

In a dazzling blaze of light, her hand burst through the surface. Crisp, cold air flowed over her. Utterly exhausted, she mustered barely enough strength to climb out of the tunnel before collapsing, face down, on the snow. Her frosted braid lay across her back as stiff and straight as an arrow.

VII
Ariella

The vast snowscape was as still as it was silent. But for the prominent plumes of snow blowing from the ridge of peaks encircling the valley, there was no movement at all.

Then, from out of the drifts appeared two figures, glistening with the same whiteness as the snow itself. One, shaped like a large hexagonal snow crystal, rolled across the crusted surface with ease, leaving no trace; the other, built like a lanky column of ice, moved more clumsily. They approached the helpless body sprawled upon the snow.

"There it is," said the hexagonal being, pointing to Kate with an outstretched arm. The delicate voice tinkled melodically, like a wind chime made of brass. "There is the creature who made the sounds."

"An ugly thing, isn't it?" observed the other being. "Just like the sounds."

"Don't be silly, Spike. Those sounds were beautiful. A little strange, but still beautiful."

"Nothing this ugly could do anything beautiful. Ariella, you're always imagining that things are better than they really are."

"Does that include you?" she retorted, surveying the columnar crystal with disdain. Then, focusing on Kate, Ariella opened wide her eyes—eyes that glistened with the same silvery sparkle as the other People of the Snow. She gently laid one of her six delicate arms on Kate's back and listened intently.

"I think it's still alive," said the young snow crystal at last. "Just barely."

"Forget it, Ariella!" Spike lifted himself to his full height of almost three feet and regarded his friend scornfully. "We don't have the slightest idea where this creature came from, or whether it's dangerous to Snow People. It definitely doesn't belong on this planet, with that sort of body. It probably carries some terrible disease that could contaminate us all!"

"I don't think so," replied Ariella, bending closer to Kate. "But I am sure of one thing: If we don't act quickly, it will certainly perish."

Spike shook his long face from side to side. "So let it perish! Why can't you Hexagonals just leave well enough alone? You're always trying to heal things, even when the world would be better off without your help. I suggest we forget about it and go back home."

Ariella gazed at Kate with her round, soulful eyes. "Any being that can sing so beautifully deserves to live."

"I suppose you know some kind of secret Nurse Crystal remedy that can bring this creature back to life," said Spike sarcastically. "Didn't your mother teach you one?"

Ariella glowered at him. "The Nurse Crystals brought you back . . . or have you forgotten that already?"

Spike shifted uncomfortably. "So they got lucky! So what?"

"They may have repaired your body, but they couldn't do much for your personality." Ariella turned again to Kate. "Now," she said quietly to herself, "what was that remedy for frozen tissue?"

She lifted Kate's lifeless hand, then closed her eyes in deep concentration.

"Give up, Ariella," urged her companion after several seconds had passed. "This creature is beyond hope."

Ariella continued to hold Kate's hand and sang softly to her. The gentle song, full of soothing tones, filled the silence of the snowy valley. Her crystalline face, set in the middle of her hexagonal body, glowed with a warmth that seemed radically out of place on this frozen planet. Outward the warmth poured, through the crystal's ornamented arms and into the girl's ashen body.

"Yes, yes," whispered Ariella, her eyes still closed. "Not too fast, now. The slower we go the less risk of damage. Take your time, take your time."

Slowly, imperceptibly, a touch of color returned to

Kate's face. At length, she moved her fingers in Ariella's hand. Soon a ruddy tone returned to her skin. Then, with an effort, she opened her eyes.

She started at the sight of the strange creature bending over her. "Who are you?" she cried, trying to crawl away.

"You tell us first," replied Spike, peering down at her. "You tell us, then we'll tell you."

Two creatures! realized Kate. *All that work just to end up trapped by—*

"I am Ariella and I am your friend," declared the hexagonal snow crystal, her telepathic words cutting short Kate's thought. She cast a sidelong glance at Spike. "Don't mind him. He never learned any manners."

"And you never learned any common sense!" blustered Spike angrily. "You don't even know if this creature is good or evil!"

"I don't know if I'm good," answered Kate weakly. "But I don't think I'm evil."

Ariella's eyes glowed with humor. "That's a pretty good answer."

Spike pointed to Kate's leg. "If you're not evil, then what is *that?*"

Clinging fast to Kate's left ankle was the remains of the tentacle that had grasped her in The Darkness.

"Oh!" Kate jumped with fright, rolling into Spike. "Get it off! Get it off me!"

"You claim it's not part of you?" questioned Spike, as he regained his balance.

"Get it off!" shrieked Kate. She yanked at the tentacle, finally pulling it free with a crackle of negative energy, and hurled it hatefully against a drift.

Ariella cringed at the sight of the horrid appendage that had twisted itself into a twitching knot of blackness sizzling on the snow.

"So cold!" cried Kate as she put her hand under her armpit to warm it again. "That thing is ten times colder than even this frozen planet."

"You see?" Spike observed cynically. "She's not from this planet."

"No, I'm not!" Kate couldn't keep the tears from flooding her eyes. "I'm from someplace warm! I'm from Earth! I came here searching for Grandfather— and I've got to find him! Everything was fine until the dark thing attacked us and I fell off Morpheus' back and it tried to suffocate me and—"

Suddenly she felt dizzy and started to fall backward. As she collapsed on the snow, the chill from her hand deepened. Swiftly, like a cancer, the frozen feeling again began to spread throughout her body.

"I'm—I'm freezing!" she chattered, flapping her arms against herself.

"Of course," said Spike scornfully. "That's what you get for digging in the snow when you're not built for it. I'm built for it—and I never dig unless I'm forced to."

"Be quiet, Spike." Ariella looked at Kate sympathetically. "You moved too quickly, I'm afraid. Your body is still on the edge of iceness."

"I'm so c-cold!"

"You must relax."

"I can't relax! I'll freeze. Even my tears are freezing!"

Ariella closed her eyes in concentration. She began turning herself around and around on the snow, until she was twirling in place like a crystalline top. Faster and faster did she spin, so that soon she was no longer a flat hexagonal crystal but a glittering globe, whirling with a subdued silver radiance.

Shivering with cold, Kate watched as Ariella suddenly stepped out of the whirling globe. Instantly, it began to condense into a transparent veil of shimmering light.

Ariella reached for the silver veil and draped it over Kate like a large beach towel. She spread it over Kate's head, arms, and hands, taking special care to cover the hand which had torn the dark tentacle from her leg. Then she stretched the veil over Kate's legs and feet, sealing it at the edges with swift movements of her six long arms.

"How do you feel now?"

"C-cold," chattered Kate.

"Just wait," said Ariella, gently touching Kate's forehead with the tip of one of her arms.

To Kate's surprise, the crystal's touch was not icy and hard, but warm and mysteriously soft. Then she noticed that thousands of delicate white hairs covered Ariella's crystalline body. Her broad face had no mouth, since the People of the Snow could communicate telepathically, nor even an obvious top or bottom; its only features were the two round eyes that glowed like full moons.

Slowly, Kate could feel herself relaxing. "I feel—I feel a bit warmer," she said.

"Good. Just rest a moment so the cloak can do its work."

As Kate sat on the snow, the airy veil began to seep gradually into her body. As it did, her entire self grew warmer, from the inside out as well as from the outside in.

"This is better than a cup of hot chocolate," she joked.

Ariella's face wrinkled in concern. "A what? You're delirious. Just relax."

Kate smiled, and a new surge of warmth filled her body. "Hot chocolate. I'll explain it to you later."

By now the veil of silver light had soaked into her body so that it was completely invisible. Kate felt warm and protected, as if she were covered by an arctic suit of heavy down. Slowly, awkwardly, she rose to her feet.

"You have traveled a long way," said Ariella softly. "How would you like to come home with us?"

"Speak for yourself, you stupid Hex," muttered Spike, still keeping his distance.

"I am speaking for myself," glared Ariella. "You can stay out here forever, for all I care." She turned again to Kate. "By the way, what is your name?"

"Kate. Kate Prancer Gordon."

"And you say you're from somewhere called Earth? Is that a long way from here?"

"Not if you're made of heartlight."

"Of what?"

"Heartlight. I can't explain it. Something like imagination, but better." Kate hung her head. "Anyway, I'll never make that trip again, because I've lost my ring."

"Your what?"

"My ring."

"What is that?"

Kate hesitated. "It's like—like a bracelet, but instead of being for your arm, it's for your finger."

"And what is a finger?"

Kate waved her fingers and saw Ariella study them curiously.

The snow crystal's eyes reflected her puzzlement. "Why do you need little arms like that at the end of your arms? They could freeze so easily! And you say this thing called a ring brought you here?"

"Well, sort of. It's a special kind of ring that brings out your heartlight. So you can travel anywhere. It was Morpheus who really brought me here, but unless I'm wearing the ring I don't think he can find me again."

Ariella's face showed complete confusion. Meanwhile, Spike's face showed mostly disdain, although his eyes glinted with something more.

"Oh, well," said Ariella, erasing her doubts for the moment. "Would you like to come home with me?

My mother doesn't have any rings, I'm sure, but she does have some beautiful bracelets. And perhaps she will know some way to help you."

Kate nodded.

Ariella faced Spike squarely. Her silver eyes opened to their widest, as she declared: "You're welcome to come, too, but only if you start to show some manners."

"No, thanks," answered the columnar crystal. "I'd rather not be seen with an alien. And I'd like to do some more exploring. That's what we came out here to do today, until you decided to play Nurse Crystal."

Kate turned to Spike. "I know you don't like me, for some reason," she said. "But I still want to thank you for saving my life."

He merely grunted and looked away.

Lifting her eyes to the pinnacled ridge of peaks, Kate's gaze floated over them like a slow-flying hawk. She exhaled a puff of frosty white vapor. The air tasted fresh and clean, not unlike the mountain air of the Rockies or the Scottish highlands where she had hiked with Grandfather. Yet it was different: fuller, richer, and more humid. This air had weight where the air of earthly mountains had none.

She walked a few steps on the velvety blanket of snow. Despite her brush with death, she felt light and strong, almost glad to have a body again. Perhaps it was the fact, which she had no way of knowing, that this planet had only eighty-five percent of the gravitational pull of Earth; perhaps it was the richness of the mountain air, which flowed over her like a tumbling brook. She drew in another full breath, tasted its crystalline quality, then exhaled.

"This place is like Shangri-La."

"I don't know that place," replied Ariella, who was leaning against a small drift nearby. "But I do like the sound of the name."

Her voice lifted into a sparkling, musical laughter, the sweetest laughter Kate had ever heard. It sounded like the chiming of distant church bells.

Focusing on the snow crystal, Kate looked deeply into the eyes that resembled bottomless pools of light. "I owe you my life," she said quietly.

"You looked very peaceful there," replied Ariella. "But I felt you wanted to live some more."

"How could you tell?"

"That song you sang," answered the snow crystal. "It sounded so full of faith and love . . . like the music our star Trethoniel used to make."

"Used to make?"

"Before the Great Trouble began," replied Ariella, suddenly somber. Then, just as abruptly, she bubbled up with a playful thought: "How would you like to go sledding with me? It's the quickest way home, and the most fun, too."

"What do you mean by *the Great Trouble*?"

"I don't want to talk about it."

"But it might help—"

"Let's go sledding."

With those words, Ariella instantly cartwheeled to

Kate's side, then slid herself like a large dinner plate under her feet. "Now, sit down," she commanded. "Then push! You're heavier than what I'm used to."

Awkwardly, Kate sat upon the crystalline creature. She grudgingly gave a push against the cold snow, then grabbed two of Ariella's outstretched arms for balance.

Suddenly she realized that they were starting to slide down the same slope that had nearly buried her alive not long ago. "Not too fast!" she yelled as wet snow began to spray in her face.

"Don't worry!" called Ariella. "I never get caught in avalanches, except for fun."

"Fun!" Kate almost fell over sideways.

"Don't worry!" called Ariella. "I know all the safe routes."

They gathered speed like a bobsled on its run. Ariella did indeed seem to know her way as she glided along ice walls, careened away from snowy over-hangs, and slid past towering outcroppings of rock.

As they sailed down the slope, Kate noticed row after row of rainbows in the spraying snow. Towering above them were the glistening ridges of mountains more than twice as high as any on Earth.

"Hold on!"

At that instant, she saw an enormous wall of ice looming directly ahead. They were heading straight for it, at terrifying speed, with no time to make any turns. Kate gripped Ariella's arms tightly and closed her eyes.

Without warning, they dropped into a hole in the snow. Darkness instantly surrounded them, as they slid down a chute of ice. After taking several rapid turns, the tunnel began to angle gradually upward, and Kate could see a hole of light fast approaching.

Like the cork of a champagne bottle, they shot out of the tunnel and into daylight. For an instant they were airborne and Kate felt sure they were about to crash.

But Ariella landed smoothly, skidding across the snow in a wide curve to slow herself down. So much snow was spraying that Kate could see nothing else. Finally, they came to a halt.

Her head was spinning, but she rolled off Ariella with a laugh. "Wow! What a ride! That was amazing!"

"Not bad, if I do say so myself," declared the snow crystal as she brushed the snow off her back with two of her arms. "I especially liked that finish."

"I thought it was *our* finish," replied Kate. "That wall came up so fast I was sure we'd be flattened."

"Not a chance," answered Ariella proudly. "I've had lots of practice entering the City at top speed."

"The City?"

"You have just entered the outermost boundary of Nel Sauria City. It's the capital of the planet Nel Sauria."

"And that ice wall—"

"Is a barrier, of course. In ancient times, before all the families of snow crystals gathered together as one

People, it was used for defense. Now it just protects the City against avalanches. Since Nel Sauria is a planet at peace, we don't have any enemies to worry about." She looked suddenly grave. "At least none who live on Nel Sauria."

A chill wind passed through Kate, but not from the snows surrounding them. She shook herself, as one waking from a nightmare, but she couldn't completely banish the empty coldness that had suddenly touched her.

Ariella spun over to her and lightly touched her hand. "So you too know the terror of The Darkness? I am sorry."

"Is that what you call it? It was horrible! It tried to kill me! I only escaped because of my friend Morpheus."

"Your friend is very brave," said the snow crystal. "And you must be brave as well. Few have ever escaped from The Darkness, and none without a great battle."

"Our battle ended only because of the avalanche. I may have escaped, but in the process I lost my ring and Morpheus and my only hope of finding Grandfather. Now I'll never find him!" She shook her head despondently. "What is The Darkness, anyway? What kind of thing is it? Where did it come from?"

Ariella's eyes brimmed with tears. "It came only recently to the realm of Trethoniel. And with it came the Great Trouble. That is all I know, but my mother knows more."

Kate sensed that Ariella was not telling her something. "Why does she know more?"

A large tear rolled down the crystalline face. "Because The Darkness destroyed my father."

Kate knelt down to face the snow crystal. "I'm sorry," she said, placing her cheek against Ariella's smooth face.

At length, they separated.

"I have a gift for you," said Ariella quietly. Using three arms, she swiftly dug a shallow cavity in the snow, then patted the interior until it was shaped like a smooth bowl.

Holding two of her cup-shaped hands over the bowl, she clapped them together loudly. Instantly, a clear liquid began to pour from them, sparkling brightly as it cascaded down to form a glistening pool.

"For you who have entered The Darkness and survived, I give you a few drops of the most cleansing substance in the universe. It is the pure essence of Trethoniel's liquid crystals. On your planet, you might call it *mountain spring water*. But unlike water, it will not freeze. You may wash yourself with it if you choose . . . but remember, a little will go a long way."

Without hesitation, Kate thrust her hands and face into the cleansing liquid. It was cold and fresh and bracing, like the tarns of Scotland where she had gone swimming with Grandfather—but better. Instantly, she felt cleaner. And something more: As her body drank deeply of the essence, she felt somehow stronger, somehow fortified. She untied her braid and scrubbed her hair vigorously. Then she pulled off her sweatshirt and jeans and rinsed herself thoroughly. From top to bottom she rubbed in the sparkling liquid, including behind her ears and under her fingernails and toenails. Her entire self tingled, as though she had just stepped out of an old and withered layer of skin. Finally, she wrung out her clothes and rinsed them in the crystal essence.

"It feels so good to be clean!" she exclaimed as she dressed herself again. "I've never needed a bath so badly in my life."

"It must have been horrible inside The Darkness," said Ariella.

Kate shook her loose hair like a wet dog and began to braid it. "I don't even want to think about it again. It was . . . the worst."

"We'd better keep moving," warned Ariella. "If The Darkness missed you once, it will be searching to find you again."

"Are you sure?"

"That is its way," answered the snow crystal gravely. "But there is one place where you will be safe, one place even The Darkness cannot enter."

"Where is that?"

Ariella looked toward the far horizon and Kate's eyes followed hers. There, in the center of a large plain, were the structures of Nel Sauria City: several mounds of snow forming a series of concentric circles. In the center of the innermost circle gleamed a gigantic dome of solid crystal, itself large enough to house a small city. The dome radiated a rich green color, much like the eye of Morpheus but even deeper.

"What is that?"

"That is the heart of the City—indeed, the heart of Nel Sauria—the ancient crystal dome we call Broé San Sauria. The secret of how it was made has been forgotten with time, and even the true meaning of its name was lost long ago. It is the most sacred spot on all of Nel Sauria. Most of the residents of the City live in the mounds you can see surrounding the dome, except for the Triangles, who prefer their nests upon the high ridges."

"And what happens in the green dome—Broé whatever-you-call-it?"

Ariella's eyes gleamed proudly. "Broé San Sauria is where the Nurse Crystals do their healing work, and where our young crystals are born. That is where we will find my mother."

Turning to Ariella, Kate asked: "Are you a Nurse Crystal?"

The snow crystal laughed like the pealing of bells. "No," she said, "although someday I hope to be one. My training has barely begun. A true Nurse Crystal has powers beyond anything you could imagine."

Kate studied the dome, glistening brightly in the distance. Broé San Sauria seemed totally protected and peaceful, a place where she could be truly safe, at last.

Then her eyes fell to her hand, to the empty spot on her finger where the butterfly ring had once rested. Where was it now? Where was Morpheus? And, most importantly, where was Grandfather?

"Let's go," said Ariella.

Kate hesitated. "If I go with you, I'm sure I'll be safe and warm . . ."

"That's right. But if you don't come soon, The Darkness is sure to reappear."

Kate still didn't budge.

"What's wrong, Kate? Are you afraid of something?"

Her eyes lifted to the glistening white ridge rising in the distance. "If I go with you, I know I'll be safe, but unless I find my ring soon . . . I know Grandfather's out there someplace—trying to find a way to save the Sun—our star. He could be in serious trouble. The Darkness might attack him! I've got to warn him. I've got to find him. And the only way to do that is to find my ring first."

Ariella gave her a puzzled look. "I don't understand. What's wrong with taking a little time to rest before you go out searching for your ring? You've been through a lot."

"My ring has barely half its time left, that's what's wrong! I don't know whether it keeps losing PCL— that's its source of energy—even when it's not on my hand . . . but I *do* know that Grandfather's ring has even less time left. He might be out of PCL already, for all I know." She touched one of Ariella's arms. "I know The Darkness is out there someplace, but so is Grandfather. I can feel it."

"But you might never find your ring under all that snow!"

Kate's eyes roamed across the fields of white that seemed to stretch endlessly in all directions, then returned to Ariella. "I've got to try."

Ariella spun still closer. "Are you really determined to do this? Broé San Sauria is so near."

"I wish I could be sure what's the right thing to do. I've never been any good at making decisions. But I am sure of one thing. If Grandfather gets into trouble and I'm not there to help him, I'd never forgive myself."

"So you're going to do this crazy thing?"

"I guess so."

Ariella's eyes narrowed in concern. "Then I'm coming with you."

"No," declared Kate. "This is my problem."

"It's mine, too. After all I went through to save you, do you think I'm about to let you go back out there alone and get yourself killed? And what success do you think you'll have without a guide? You'll probably walk right into another avalanche."

"What about The Darkness? I don't want you to risk that."

"I guess I'll just hope for the best."

Kate gazed into Ariella's round eyes. "I may have lost everything else, but I think I've found a friend."

VIII

Nimba's Flight

Scanning the enormity of the snowfields above them, Kate inhaled a deep breath of Nel Sauria's frosty air. "Whewww," she sighed, blowing a puff of mist.

Suddenly, she realized the folly of her decision. "I forgot how far we came down! It'll take so long just to get back up there. How can we possibly find my ring before Grandfather runs out of time?"

"We could spin ourselves up there in no time," suggested Ariella. She cartwheeled a short distance across the snow with amazing speed.

"Are you kidding? That only works if you have six arms! For me, that's as impossible as flying."

"You can't fly either?" asked Ariella, her eyes open to their widest. "I've never met anyone who can't either spin or fly. How do you get around on your home planet when you need to go someplace fast?"

"Rings," answered Kate grimly.

"Oh, I see," replied the snow crystal. Then she brightened and leaped high into the air above Kate. For a moment, she held herself aloft, twirling slowly, before floating back down. "If you can't fly, maybe you can leap like this. It's almost as good."

"I'm afraid not. My body's just not built for it. I guess I'll have to go one step at a time."

Kate glanced at the ridge of peaks rising high above the ice wall, swallowed hard, then started to stride off with determination. Without warning, she sunk to her thighs in the snow.

"Hey! Oh, Ariella. This is terrible!" She tried to extract herself, but the more she struggled, the more deeply she found herself swallowed by soft snow. "Help me, Ariella!"

The snow crystal spun to the edge of the expanding pit, stretched out four of her long arms, and tried to pull Kate free. The snow was now nearly up to her shoulders. Several times Ariella came close to retrieving her, only to have the soft snow break through again.

A wave of fear shot through Kate, and her hands felt suddenly chilled. *Am I going to be buried again?*

"Small steps!" commanded Ariella. "Move slowly and take small steps!"

Kate forced herself to stay calm and to move in small, deliberate steps. Ariella was right; violent movement only made the situation worse. At last, with the crystal's help, she reached a patch of denser snow. She crawled slowly out of the pit and collapsed, breathing heavily.

"That's worse than quicksand."

"It's a soft spot," said Ariella remorsefully. "I should have warned you."

"Yes, you should have. How did the snow get like that?"

"I don't know. It's been warmer than usual recently, and soft spots are more common these days. So are avalanches. Some people think they're all tied to the Great Trouble."

"Trouble is right!" exclaimed Kate as she rose to her feet. "I've got plenty. How am I ever going to find my ring if I can't even take a step without falling in?"

Ariella's round eyes rolled skyward. "I have an idea." She began rubbing several arms together rapidly, until the vibration created a shrill, high-pitched whistle. The sound pierced the air like the cry of an angered osprey.

Kate put her hands over her ears. "What are you doing that for?"

The crystal didn't reply. She continued the vibrating motion and kept her eyes focused on one area of the sky.

Kate looked up. All she could see were banks upon banks of heavy white clouds—until a slight edge of motion appeared. Then, what looked like a piece of the clouds, triangular in shape, grew more visible. It became bigger and bigger, until suddenly Kate realized that it was descending.

The Triangle, which looked like a wing made of ice, coasted to a landing on the snow next to them. Ariella's whistling ceased and she spun to the side of the large, flat crystal.

"You called me for a good reason, I hope," growled the flying wing. "I was in the middle of an updraft, one of the best I've found in ages." His triangular eyes studied Kate suspiciously.

"Yes, Nimba," replied Ariella. "It's a good reason. You know I never would use the distress call otherwise."

"Tell me your reason," grumbled the Triangle, "and I'll be the judge of whether it's any good or not."

"My friend here has lost her ring."

"Her what?"

"Her special ornament. It's very important to her. She needs to search for it in the high snowfields."

The rumble of a distant avalanche echoed in the chilly air. Kate turned toward the daggerlike spires of the ridge. How far above the clouds they soared she could only guess; no mountains on Earth could match their majesty. As the roar of the avalanche reverberated among the peaks, it seemed to warn her to stay away, to forget about retrieving the ring. She had escaped once, by luck. Twice would require a miracle.

Nimba's eyes flashed angrily. "You dragged me out of the sky for some silly little ornament? Just because this alien says it's important?"

Kate gathered her courage and stepped forward. "It

is important. And it's not just an ornament. I need it to—to fly above the clouds. It's my only hope of finding Grandfather. He's somewhere out there—at least I think he is—searching for some way to help our Sun. He could be in trouble. And he's going to run out of time very soon!"

Nimba's pointed face twisted sharply. "That is the most unbelievable tale of woe I've heard in years. No, decades! Ariella, you should be ashamed of yourself. Dragging me out of the sky with the distress call . . . And for what? For some incredible story told by an alien!"

The Triangle shifted his stance in order to begin his takeoff. "That's the last time any Triangle will heed your call, Ariella."

"But The Darkness is out there!" cried Kate. "It might attack Grandfather!"

Nimba froze. "How do you know about The Darkness?"

"She fought with it," declared Ariella. "She escaped, but only because she got buried by an avalanche."

"That's how I lost my ring," added Kate.

Nimba studied her closely. "The Darkness is the enemy of all living creatures. How do I know you're telling the truth? That it's not another one of your stories?"

Kate pondered for a moment. "How would I even know The Darkness exists unless it had attacked me? It's too horrible to make up."

Nimba cocked his head slightly. "That much is true. But how do I know you're not one of its spies?"

"Because I say she's not!" exclaimed Ariella. Her round eyes flashed with anger. "Don't you trust me, Nimba?"

The triangular head turned from Kate to Ariella and back again. "I do trust you, Ariella. But there is much reason for extra caution these days. The Darkness has been growing steadily more powerful, and Nel Sauria remains one of the last strongholds of resistance left. Not without great cost . . . As you know, some of our bravest defenders have fallen to The Darkness."

Ariella bowed her face slightly.

"All right," he said at last. "I'm probably just an old fool for doing this, but if you really fought with that scourge, then at least you're on the right side." He turned to Ariella and added: "And you, young one, should be staying closer to home. These are dangerous times. I was a friend of your father, and I am sure he would tell you the same."

"You were more than a friend," she answered somberly. "You were with him when he died."

"Let's get this over with," said Nimba roughly, lowering an edge of his wide wing. "Climb aboard."

Ariella spun onto Nimba's back and positioned herself in the center. Kate did her best to follow, but the crystalline body of the Triangle was as slippery as ice. Carefully, she crawled across the surface, concentrating hard to avoid sliding off.

"I'm not sure whether this is such a great idea," she said nervously to Ariella.

"Where in the high snowfields do you want to go?" asked Nimba.

"At the base of Ho Salafar Ridge, in the middle of the avalanche zone," answered Ariella. "I'll tell you when we get near." Then she turned to Kate. "Hold my arm tightly and you won't fall. Nimba's the smoothest flier on Nel Sauria, so don't worry."

"Thanks," said Kate. "But I'll keep worrying anyway. It's my nature."

"You will live longer because of it," declared Nimba. "In this case, though, you have nothing to fear. I will create a pressure pocket around you both, and that will hold you securely."

With that, the Triangle began sliding forward across the snow. Immediately, they were airborne, gliding in the direction of the great glistening peaks. Below them stretched the vast snowscape of Nel Sauria.

Kate's eyes followed the lines of white hills leading up to the main spine of the ridge, which rose like a serrated saw into the sky. "This is such a beautiful place," she said, shouting to be heard above the wind. "Especially when you don't need to walk on it. It's amazing to have a whole planet covered with snow."

"It's not," corrected Ariella. "Only the half facing away from Trethoniel is covered with snow. The other side is a single great ocean, what we call the Bottomless Blue. I've never seen it—almost nobody has—but many ancient writings tell of its beauty."

"So Nel Sauria is divided in half?"

"Yes. One half is white, the other is blue."

"But doesn't the planet rotate as it revolves around Trethoniel?"

"Rotate?" Ariella's eyes assumed a quizzical look. "What an odd idea! Does your Earth rotate?"

"Yes. That's how both sides get lit by the Sun, and how day and night follow each other. Say, if this snowy side of the planet is always facing away from Trethoniel, then how do you get any daylight? Why isn't it dark all the time?"

Ariella's laughter rang out, and even the wind seemed to pause and listen. "Why, from the snow, of course! Our light radiates from the snow and lights the sky. It's in the nature of the crust; a thin layer on the surface glows all the time. Do you mean to say that on your Earth it's the other way around? Your sky lights the snow?"

"I guess our snow is a lot different than yours," said Kate. "Our Sun is our only source of light. And Grandfather thinks it's about to die!"

"Did you think our snow could help?"

"No . . . but Grandfather thinks maybe Trethoniel can. That's why I'm sure he's out there someplace. He says Trethoniel is the healthiest star in the galaxy, and if he can just figure out what keeps it so healthy, maybe he can use that knowledge to help the Sun."

"Once that might have been true," said Ariella, lowering her voice so much that Kate could barely hear her above the whistling wind. "Before the Great Trouble began."

"What is this Great Trouble?" asked Kate.

"I don't really know," said Ariella. "I only know The Darkness is part of it. Other things have been happening, too."

"Like what?"

"Like that," the snow crystal answered, pointing one arm toward a gray patch of snow far below them.

At first, Kate thought Ariella was pointing to some sort of shadow, probably from a cloud. Then she realized her mistake. The gray color was part of the snow itself!

"What is it, Ariella?"

The deep pools of Ariella's eyes seemed to fill with sadness. "That was once a field of snow crops—one of the most fertile around. It used to grow tall stalks of crystalmeat, the favorite food of our People."

Examining the field more closely, Kate could see it was covered with hundreds of thousands of stiff gray stalks. They stuck out of the snow like drying bones, giving the place the feeling of an abandoned cemetery. Next to it, another snowfield was covered with pearly white stalks, but an area along its edge was also beginning to turn gray.

"What's wrong down there?" called Kate above the winds. "Is it some kind of disease?"

Ariella studied the landscape glumly. "If it is, it's no disease Nel Sauria has ever known before. Some people say it's because of the warmer temperatures. Others are sure it's something else. Nobody really knows. Not even the Sage of Sauria knows, I'm sure."

"The Sage of Sauria?"

Ariella's eyes refocused on Kate. "Oh, that's just a figure of speech. The Sage of Sauria is a legendary creature who supposedly once lived near the Bottomless Blue, but no one has seen her for thousands of years. Most people agree that she never really existed, that she's just another character out of the ancient writings."

Kate nodded. "We have characters like that on Earth. The Greek myths are full of them, and then there's Merlin and Gandalf and all the others . . . Sometimes they seem too real to be just stories, but then I realize I'm just imagining things. What was this Sage of Sauria like?"

"Very mysterious, and very wise," answered Ariella, glancing at the pinnacled ridge of peaks looming ahead of them, drawing closer by the second. "The Sage was supposed to sit for decades, motionless as a stone, watching the waters of the Bottomless Blue. Only the wisest and bravest of the ancient People tried to find her secret hideaway, in order to seek her advice, and most of them wandered for years and never found anything. Of the lucky few who found the way, most of them could not understand the meaning of the Sage's riddles, or could not remember them when they returned." She paused thoughtfully. "You are very brave yourself, Kate, to journey all the way to Trethoniel."

"Not really. I just worry a lot. If I hadn't been scared by a ghost, I'd probably never be here."

"I've never seen Trethoniel myself," said the snow

crystal. "I've read many writings about it, though. I'm sure it's every bit as beautiful as the old legends say. I hope it has what you need to save your Sun."

"I do, too, but mainly I hope it has Grandfather, and that he's safe."

"There!" cried Ariella, pointing to a small hole in the snow below them. "That's where we start looking."

Like a feather on a breeze, Nimba glided to a stop near the place where Kate had been buried not long ago. His two passengers slid off his back and stood on the snow, facing him.

"Thank you," said Ariella, touching the point of his head lightly.

"We owe you a lot," added Kate.

"Don't mention it," replied the Triangle. "I hope you find your ornament before another avalanche hits." He eyed Ariella with concern. "I hope you know what you're doing. Be very careful, young one! Now, if you don't mind, I'm going to see whether that updraft is still going strong."

With a whoosh of air, Nimba was aloft. Soon he was completely invisible against the white clouds.

They began the search. Ariella spun in slow circles around the area, looking for anything unusual. Meanwhile, Kate stepped to the edge of the hole in the snow, examining it closely. Had she really dug such a deep tunnel?

The tortured black knot of the tentacle sat near her feet, marring the whiteness of the snow. She kicked it vengefully, and the snow sizzled with the impact. Foreboding as it felt to gaze into the place where she had almost perished, she knew that the ring could well be buried down there. She hesitated, then decided to try it.

Kate began to climb down into the tunnel, her heart pounding loudly. As she left the daylight behind, a sudden rush of panic seized her. What if the snow around her collapsed? Would she be buried again? Her hands grew very cold, and a chilly finger of fear ran down her spine.

She turned around, and the sight of the circle of light above helped to calm her. A few dim shafts of light drifted down to her, illuminating the tunnel's frozen walls. But her heart continued to pound with the rhythm of her fear. Then she thought of Grandfather, somewhere up there, searching . . . So too was The Darkness! She swallowed hard and forced herself to keep climbing downward.

The shaft seemed deeper than she had remembered. Then, at a certain depth, it suddenly narrowed and dropped swiftly downward in a vertical descent. Kate clung to the snowy wall and peered down into the seemingly bottomless hole.

This doesn't make sense, she told herself. *This tunnel is far too deep—and also too steep. I'd need a ladder to go down any further.*

Then she noticed a faint trace of green on the snow. The ring! She began to dig madly in the wall of the tunnel, despite how cold it made her hands, until there was a large cavity in the snow. Yet there was no further sign of the ring.

"Kate!" cried Ariella's small voice from outside the tunnel entrance. "Are you there?"

"Yes! And I think the ring is down here, too. But the tunnel is much deeper than I thought."

"Can you come up here?" called Ariella. "I think I've found something important."

Carefully, so as not to lose her footing, Kate climbed back up to the surface. Squinting from the bright light, she looked for Ariella.

"Over here!"

She ran to join the crystal, who indicated some subtle depressions in the snow.

"They look like footprints," panted Kate. "Probably Spike's."

"That's right."

"What's so important about that? I thought you made a big discovery."

"The odd thing about these footprints," explained Ariella, "is they don't leave this area. I've searched all around, and there is no sign of Spike leaving here. Since he isn't here now, that leaves just one alternative."

"I get it!" exclaimed Kate. "So Spike went down into the tunnel—and made it deeper!" She paused thoughtfully. "But why would he go through so much trouble? Unless—"

"Unless he was going after your ring. Spike only digs when he's forced to, or when he's sure he'll find something valuable. Otherwise, he wouldn't dream of lifting an arm to dig. I'm sure he was trying to find your ring . . . and keep it for himself." Ariella's eyes darkened. "He wasn't always like that. But ever since he lost his family in the great ice wall collapse, he's been totally different. So full of bitterness. I've tried to bring him around, but it's hopeless. I'm ready to give up."

Kate pondered the gaping hole in the snow. "Grandfather said something once about PCL—about its special properties—oh, yes! He said PCL can melt through anything frozen! So if the ring was somewhere in the snow, it would have melted straight down—"

"And left a small hole behind!" finished Ariella. "That must be what Spike was following."

"As well as a green tint in the snow," added Kate. "I saw some of it myself down there." Her brow furrowed in concern. "But following Spike isn't going to be so easy. Digging straight down is one thing, but climbing straight down is another."

"No problem," declared Ariella. "Just follow me."

The six-armed crystal moved to the mouth of the tunnel and positioned herself just as if she were going to sled down it. "Climb aboard and I'll show you."

Doubtfully, Kate sat on top of her.

"Give me a push!"

"But—"

"Trust me. Now, push!"

She followed the crystal's command, and they slid

over the edge. To Kate's surprise, instead of falling straight down the tunnel, they began to float slowly downward, as Ariella curved her back like a perfect parachute. Gently they drifted deeper and deeper into the great bed of snow, twirling slowly as they descended. As they passed the point where the tunnel narrowed and dropped precipitously, the circle of light shrunk into nothingness above them.

"How far down does the snow go?" asked Kate, even as the tunnel grew totally dark.

"No one knows," came the reply. "The People of the Snow have always asked that question. Many years ago, before I was born, a few brave explorers tried to find out. But none of them ever came back."

"What's that sound?"

A low, slow rumble rose to them from far below. It grew ever louder as they drifted downward, seemingly magnified by the blackness, until it soon filled the entire tunnel with its reverberations. Gradually it grew into a roar, louder than all the pipes of a great cathedral organ sounding simultaneously.

"What's that—"

Splaaash!

They landed on the surface of a surging river. Suddenly Ariella became not a parachute but a raft, with Kate as her unwilling passenger.

"Ariella!"

Round and round they spun, as the swirling torrent carried them deeper into the caverns of this underground river, raging as it had raged for centuries beneath the silent snows of Nel Sauria. Irresistibly it flowed, far below the mountains and glaciers of the surface, ultimately to empty into the Bottomless Blue.

Onward they rode in the utter darkness of the cavern. At one point, the roof hung so low to the river that Kate was knocked backward and was suddenly submerged. Ariella grabbed her by the arm and struggled to hold on, as the cascading waters pummeled them. Numbed with cold, Kate tried desperately to breathe, but all she got was water. Finally, they bobbed up again and she filled her hungry lungs with air.

"Help!" she sputtered, but the din of the terrible torrent swallowed her words.

In the blackness, they could not tell that the river had now joined other rivers and that the cavern had widened immensely. Mighty stalactites, pinnacles of ice stretching hundreds of feet down from the ceiling, filled the darkened cavern like finely polished teeth.

Then, through the crashing waves, a dim light appeared. Weak and waterlogged, Kate thought it was only her imagination. She felt heavy enough to sink, too weak to struggle any more. Would she ever see Grandfather again? It seemed Ariella had saved her from one death only to join her in another.

Just then a blast of heated air struck them, as though a great furnace door had opened in their faces. In the same instant, the world suddenly grew bright—and Kate realized they were falling, tumbling over the edge of an enormous waterfall.

IX

The Bottomless Blue

At the top of the waterfall, Kate spied the vague outline of a twisted root dangling over the edge. She stretched for it, grabbing hold just as the great falls emptied into the basin below.

As she caught the root with one hand, she felt it sliding through her palm. She twisted in the torrent and reached for it with the other hand, as the force of the cascade bounced her like a ball. The root held fast, but her grip was tenuous.

"I'm slipping!" screamed Ariella, who was clinging desperately to Kate's waist.

"Hold on!" cried Kate above the thunderous roar.

A sudden wave crashed against them. Kate was hurled to the side of the waterfall, where she struck a rock wall and lost her grip on the root. She tumbled down to a narrow ledge protruding from the mountainside.

Amidst the spray, she lay still for a moment. Slowly, she lifted her head, then scrambled to stand. Her ankle throbbed painfully.

"Ariella!" she called.

Her eyes followed the course of the frothing falls as it descended, falling freely for thousands of feet. Finally, it merged with a towering cloud of vapor rising from its base, and she could see no more.

Ariella was gone!

Kate slumped in a heap on the rocky ledge, mortified at her fate. She had meant to risk her own life, but not Ariella's—and now she was lost. The ring was lost. Morpheus was lost. Everything was lost.

Tears swam into her eyes, mixing with the mist of the waterfall. Suddenly she felt a searing pain in her hand.

"Ow!" she cried, jumping to her feet. "That rock is hot."

Then, for the first time, she looked beyond the spray to the landscape stretching before her. So great was her shock that for a moment she forgot about everything else. She stepped along the ledge away from the waterfall in order to get a clearer view.

There was no Bottomless Blue!

Instead of the wide blue ocean that Ariella had described, Kate could see only a roasting red desert beneath a rust-colored sky. From horizon to horizon stretched a single reach of baked rocks and burned soil. No liquid whatsoever moistened this searing cauldron, but for the seething stream of lava Kate saw pouring from one volcanic cone in the distance. Into the burning basin flowed several powerful waterfalls like the one next to her, but none was more than a mere cloud of steam by the time it ultimately reached the desert floor.

Kate lifted her eyes from this desolate landscape to the glowing red disc above her head. Trethoniel dominated the sky. It radiated powerfully, even majestically. Yet . . . it seemed somehow different from here.

"Uhhhhh."

She whirled around. What had made that sound?

There, lying in the shadows of the rocky ledge, lay the bent form of a snow crystal. She ran to see if it was—

"Spike!" Kate couldn't hide her disappointment. "I thought—I thought maybe you were Ariella."

"Uhhhhh," moaned the crystal, struggling to sit up. "I'm just as glad to see you, Alien."

Moving closer, Kate could see that a portion of his lower body was missing, and a long crack wound its way up the columnar crystal's back. She reached to help him, but he swatted at her angrily.

"You keep your distance. It's your fault I'm here. If you hadn't talked about your precious ring—oh! That hurts! My only mistake was listening to you, Alien."

"I didn't mean—"

"And you've killed Ariella, too, haven't you?" Spike tried again to sit upright, but slid back unsuccessfully. "Ah! These sizzling rocks are going to melt me in no time. I'll disappear just like the ocean did—if it ever existed. I never should have listened to those stupid fairy tales!"

"Don't you want some help?" asked Kate. "Maybe I can help you if you'll let me."

"Not on your life. Don't touch me." He groaned painfully. "What's the use? I'm not going to last much longer—in this heat."

"Are you really melting? Does that mean Ariella—"

"So she did come with you! You've killed her, Alien! Killed her for sure. Even if she made it to the valley floor alive, she's been burned to a crisp by now. Those hot rocks down there . . . this place is one big oven. Snow People can't survive in heat like this."

Kate's eyes again filled with tears. "I didn't mean to hurt her," she said sorrowfully. "I didn't mean to."

"That doesn't help her much, does it? You did it to her—just like you did it to me." A look of genuine sadness filled Spike's long eyes. "It's one thing for me to die; I probably deserve to melt, anyway. But Ariella! She stood by me after everyone else had given up trying. And I never got to tell her . . ."

Kate turned away from Spike and peered over the side of the ledge. A sheer rock face dropped precipitously below them. The ledge itself, while it bent upward for some distance along the ridge, stopped completely at the waterfall. There was no route to climb down, no way to reach Ariella.

"If you're thinking about saving her, forget it!"

snarled Spike. "She's long gone. You'd better—ow! Uhhhhh . . . I'm getting weaker . . . by the second. You'd better think—think about saving yourself, Alien. You're trapped here, too. I hope I live long enough to see—to see you melt."

Kate turned again to the crumpled form of the snow crystal lying on the ledge. He looked as miserable as an abandoned child: alone, lost, and frightened.

Then, to her surprise, she spotted a faint outline of something on the rock wall above him. Was she hallucinating? It looked like some sort of carving, a petroglyph made by some ancient hand.

She moved sideways to see if a different angle made the image any clearer. There, indeed, she saw carved into the stone the unmistakable shape of a six-sided snow crystal.

"What are you staring at, Alien?"

"A carving in the rock! It looks like Ariella!"

"You're seeing things."

"No, I'm not. It's there!" She started to run her finger along the deep indentation, but the heat of the rock repelled her. "Somebody carved it. I'm sure of it. That means somebody else has been here! Maybe one of the explorers Ariella spoke about. Either they came here the same way we did—or there's some other route."

"Give up, Alien! Your brain is already—already melting. You'll never get . . . out of here, and neither will I. We're both going to—ah! oh!—roast to death! Already . . . I feel weaker, weaker all the time. I'm never . . . never . . ."

With that, he fell silent.

Kate wiped the perspiration from her face. She had to find a way out of here. She studied the line of the ledge as it climbed along the rocky cliff. No doubt this cliff was just on the other side of the mountains from the snowfields where she had landed. But it seemed like another planet. Perhaps the ledge was actually made by someone . . . someone long ago. Perhaps it was once a trail! To the waterfall, perhaps? But why would anyone have gone through so much trouble?

She gazed at the broken body of Spike, lying motionless against the rock wall, as the striking smell of melting crystal tissue reached her nose. It was as fresh as a spring rain, and as bracing as the bath Ariella had given her. Such a smell was utterly at odds with the desert dryness surrounding her. Again her eyes followed the long contour of the ledge until it disappeared beyond some weathered rocks.

Kate moved closer to the body. He might be alive, even though it didn't look good. If she couldn't help Ariella, and she couldn't help Grandfather, at least maybe she could help somebody.

Clumsily, she lifted the limp snow crystal onto her back. He was heavier than she had thought, like a slab of tightly compressed ice from the very bottom of a glacier. She struggled to lay him across the small of her back, just as she had once seen a fireman do with an unconscious man. With one arm she held his head, with the other his broken base.

Hunched over from her heavy load, Kate started to

walk along the ledge. Maybe, just maybe, if she could transport Spike over to the snowy side of the ridge, she could find someone who could help him. To her delight, she discovered that the ledge continued upward beyond the rock outcropping she could see from the waterfall. Still, it was very rough going: The would-be trail was strewn with broken bits of stones and unforgiving pits. In the sweltering heat, Kate frequently had to stop and lift one hand to her brow—without losing her hold on Spike—to wipe away the perspiration that stung her eyes.

Her ankle pained her with every step, and she tried to favor the other foot. As she lifted her load over one particularly large stone, however, she twisted it slightly.

"Ow!" she cried, dropping Spike's body and collapsing on top of it. She burned her hand again on the hot rocks as she fell, and her ankle throbbed painfully. Tears brewed, blurring her vision, but she forced them back.

She picked herself up and tried again to lift her cumbersome load. With considerable effort, she placed Spike's body back in position and continued to trudge slowly onward.

Recalling some words Grandfather had once chanted as they hiked over a difficult trail in Scotland, she began to repeat them over and over. *Light as a feather, strong as an ox. Light as a feather, strong as an ox.* At first the words made her feel slightly stronger, but soon they seemed as heavy as the body on her back, and she stopped saying the chant.

Slowly, she ascended the side of the ridge. At one point, the ledge suddenly narrowed into a thin shelf, barely six inches wide. Kate tried not to look down, but her memory of the sheer drop below was only too clear.

She hesitated, then glanced behind her toward the waterfall, which was now invisible but for the spiraling tower of mist. She was used to being alone, but this was more alone than she had ever been. She thought of Ariella, dear Ariella, and of Morpheus, who fought so valiantly to save her. She thought of Mom and Dad—so willing to let her be herself, difficult as she could be sometimes, and of Cumberland, her loyal friend who never asked for anything in return. And she thought of Grandfather—oh, Grandfather! Would she ever see any of them again?

Gathering herself, she stepped carefully across the stretch as if it were a slippery log spanning a roaring river. As she reached the other side, she heaved a sigh of relief and mopped her sweaty brow.

Then she saw the crevasse.

A few steps ahead, the rock-strewn ledge divided, as if a fault line had severed the entire mountainside. The resulting gap, more than five feet across, was so deep that she could see nothing but darkness in its shadowy depths.

Light as a feather, strong as an ox, she told herself weakly. *Light as a feather, strong as an ox.*

Kate moved cautiously to the edge. Swinging Spike's body around, she positioned it like an ungainly sack against her shoulder. With an enormous heave, she threw her load to the opposite side. It landed with a thud on the rocks.

Once again Kate looked backward. The waterfall seemed so far away, and yet the top of the ridge seemed even farther. Where was she going, anyway? She wondered whether all this effort would lead only to another impassable crevasse.

Feeling weaker then she had ever felt, she bent forward to stretch her back. Her ankle hurt so much. The swelling was growing worse. Her braid fell over her shoulder, rubbing against her cheek. Kate suddenly remembered the way Grandfather used to run his hand along her braid, one of his gestures that said more than any amount of words.

Kate again eyed the yawning chasm. Her heart pounded. With a deep breath, she limped toward the edge, planted her good foot, and leaped with all her strength.

Made it!

She clung to a jagged rock and pulled herself clear of the crevasse. It was all she could do to lift Spike's heavy body into the fireman's carry again. Her swollen ankle ached and her steps grew increasingly wobbly as she climbed higher and higher on the rocky slope, but she pressed on.

At last, the ledge turned into an uneven trail, which ran like a ribbon over the ridge. By now Kate's head was so heavy that she could not lift it to see what lay ahead: It was all she could do to make one foot move in front of the other.

A gust of cold air hit her, so suddenly that she lost her balance and fell on the side of the trail. To her amazement, gleaming white peaks towered above her left and right sides. Patches of snow were all around. She had reached the top of the ridge!

Kate found herself sitting on a low pass dividing the knife-edge ridge that separated a world of red desolation from a world of creamy white cornices. The trail continued over the ridge to a large snowfield below, where it disappeared from view. She raised her face toward the peaks and drank deeply of the rich mountain air. The wind felt cool against her sweaty face.

Her eye fell to Spike, lying as still as death on the rocks by a snowdrift. He had been right; she had caused Ariella's death. Nothing could ever assuage that pain.

Some very strange things were happening to this planet, things she couldn't fully comprehend. The Great Trouble was more a mystery than ever. Perhaps there was some connection between The Darkness, the soft spots, and the fields of dying crystalmeat. But what could have transformed the Bottomless Blue into a searing desert? How could all these things be happening under the very nose of the most beautiful star in the galaxy?

Earth, that sparkling blue sapphire she had seen from her perch upon Morpheus, now seemed so very far away. How she longed to glimpse it again, to feel its soil underfoot and its air overhead. To smell the chrysanthemums in the garden. To run through the old apple orchard, to swim in the pond behind Grandfather's house, to play with Cumberland . . . oh, Cumberland!

Spying a large, snow-crusted rock sitting near the trail, Kate thought it would be a good place to ponder her fate, and Grandfather's. She had given up any hope of finding him; he would never even know how hard she had tried. Only Ariella and Morpheus knew, and they were lost forever.

Dejectedly, she hobbled over to the rock and started to climb it. Then, without warning, the rock moved.

X

Strange Encounters

Kate tumbled backward onto the snow-dappled ridge as the great rock stirred. Then came a deep rumble that she felt through to the marrow of her bones, and the rock shifted, heaved, and finally started to roll over.

With a gasp, Kate realized that the underside of the rock was coated with some form of densely matted fur. It looked silver in color, although it could actually have been white beneath the layers of finely crushed stones that clung tightly to it. What she had taken for patches of snow on top of the rock were, in fact, more of this rough fur. As the rock rolled onto its side, it began to lengthen and widen, stretching itself like an enormous hedgehog uncurling before Kate's eyes.

The stretching continued until sharp corners began

to appear on the surface of the rock, now standing three times as tall as Kate. Soon the rock's front, back, and sides were covered with a precise array of angles and facets. As the rough face of the rock was replaced by these crystalline corners, it grew smooth, even shiny, except for the splotches of shaggy fur draping over the facets.

Then Kate noticed one thing more: In the center of the crystal sat a single round eye, as blue as the deepest ocean. Its piercing gaze was trained directly on her.

As suddenly as it had started, the rumbling ceased. The great rock, now no longer a rock but a giant dodecahedral crystal, sat motionless atop the ridge, its contours no less imposing than the gleaming peaks behind it.

Kate was too frightened to move. All she could do was to stare helplessly at the unblinking blue eye of the enormous, shaggy crystal whose breadth now blocked the light of Trethoniel, leaving her in shadow. She knew that she was being carefully examined, just as a small fish is examined by a giant polar bear before the bear pounces on it, crushing it to death between its powerful jaws.

"Fear . . . me . . . not."

The words shook the ground like an earthquake. "Fear me not, unless you fear the truth."

Slowly, Kate regained her feet. She stood in awe, not daring to step any nearer to this strange beast that had sprung so unexpectedly from the mountain tundra, and not daring to run away. Mustering her courage, she forced herself to speak. "I don't fear the truth. I only fear The Darkness and the loss of people I love."

The great crystal stirred, grinding together the stones beneath its massive body. Then it spoke again, in a voice as rough as a landslide pouring over a slope. "You have chosen well your fears. Who are you and how did you come to Nel Sauria?"

Kate stood as motionless as the mountains surrounding her and drew in a deep breath. "I am Kate Prancer Gordon, from the planet Earth. I came here searching for Grandfather, but now I'll never find him. There's no hope."

Again the giant crystal stirred, crushing the rocks beneath it. "Hope is like a shadow, not easily lost."

Unsure what to make of this comment, or of the shaggy crystal itself, Kate could only ask: "What do you mean?"

"Your search may have ended," rumbled the huge crystal, "but your struggle has barely begun."

"How can you say that? You don't know what I've been through!"

"To live is to struggle," the shaggy being declared. "To seek is to find."

"Find what? Are you telling me I'm going to find something?"

"I am telling you," the crystal replied in its stone-grinding voice, "that I have seen the one you search for."

Fireworks exploded inside Kate. "What? You saw Grandfather?"

"A single eye can see many things," answered the giant crystal.

With those words, the crystal's deep blue eye suddenly flashed with light, like a signal mirror reflecting the Sun. Kate's hunger to find Grandfather, now fully rekindled, overpowered her fears. She stepped closer to the great crystal.

"Tell me what you saw!" she pleaded. "Is he in trouble? Is he hurt?"

The crystal made no sound. Only the round eye, glowing strangely, showed any sign of life. Across it swirled a whirlpool of undefined shapes and colors.

Then the shapes coalesced into a sharp image. A single yellow star, shining powerfully, filled the eye. *Could that be the Sun?* wondered Kate, studying the image closely.

Without any warning, the star faltered, faded, and suddenly collapsed into a pinpoint of light. Then, as Kate shuddered, it disappeared completely, leaving behind only an empty sector of space. Nothing at all remained to show that once a star had been there, burning brightly.

Before Kate could ask any questions, the eye swirled again and swiftly evolved into a new image. It was a mighty red star, surrounded by a nebula of colorful gases. There could be no mistake about its identity; Kate had come to know it well. She momentarily forgot about the death of the yellow star, as the radi-

ant beauty of Trethoniel touched her again with wonder. She could almost hear the distant strains of its
timeless music floating across the heavens.

Then a sense of dread filled her as she discerned a
darkened shape moving into view. Long and
writhing, its body slowly swam across the brilliant
face of Trethoniel, blocking its light completely. Kate
released a cry of fear and pain, and instantly the eye
went dark.

"Why did you show me The Darkness?" she demanded. "Where is Grandfather? I thought you were
going to show me Grandfather!"

The great crystal again shifted its weight on the
ridge, as the eye's deep blue color returned. "I said
only that I have seen the one you search for,"
rumbled the reply. "It is possible, in time, that you
will see what I have seen. But first you must understand a basic truth."

"What truth?"

"There are two kinds of death for a star, and they
are as different as hope is different from despair."

"Different?" Kate cocked her head in puzzlement.
"I don't get it. Death is death, isn't it? Anyway, what
does all this have to do with Grandfather? Are you
telling me that's the Sun's future? Or Grandfather's
future?"

Grinding more stones into the ground, the crystal
spoke solemnly. "The future cannot be read, for it
waits to be written."

"Then why did you show all that to me?" Kate's

voice was cracking with exasperation. "I don't need to know the future! I only want to find Grandfather!"

"To find him may be one thing, to save him another." The ominous words of the great crystal hung heavily upon the air.

"Save him?" asked Kate. "From what?"

"To save him you must trust that life and death are both seasons of the Pattern. If you trust in the Pattern, you trust in yourself. And if you trust in yourself, your voice holds all the power of truth."

"But why does he need to be saved?" demanded Kate.

The shaggy crystal made no effort to respond.

Kate shook her head in dismay. "Now I know who you really are! Ariella thought you were just a legend . . . but even in the legend nobody could understand your riddles." She moved back a few paces so she could see all of the mammoth being. "You said you might show him to me. Please! Won't you help me?" she cried, arms outstretched. "Won't you help me find Grandfather?"

As if in answer, the Sage of Sauria began to shake violently. A great rumble shook the ridge, and soon the sharp edges of her many facets became blurred and rough-hewn. Her round blue eye closed tightly. Meanwhile, her entire body began to shrink steadily in size until, at last, the Sage of Sauria resembled nothing more than a large rock with several patches of snow encrusting its surface.

"No!" shouted Kate above the tremor. "Don't go! I need your h—"

Suddenly, she caught sight of a dark form emerging from the clouds above. A wave of terror shot through her. *The Darkness. It's come back.*

She ran to the Sage of Sauria, now just an appendage of the rocky ridge, and struck forcefully with her fist. The pain in her hand was dwarfed by the pain in her heart: The rocklike being didn't budge. Like a turtle seeking protection inside its shell, the Sage of Sauria had abandoned her.

Kate scanned the ridge madly, looking for any place to hide. There was none to be seen. Again, she glanced skyward.

At that instant, she realized her mistake.

"Grandfather!"

Diving through the clouds came Orpheus, twin brother of Morpheus, with Grandfather leaning forward like a jockey urging his horse on to maximum speed. With a swoop of iridescent wings, they glided to a landing on the snow-crusted rocks next to Kate.

"Grandfather!" she cried again.

"Kaitlyn!" came the reply.

They ran to each other and embraced. Then Grandfather fell backward into a drift, pulling Kate down with him.

"Oh, Grandfather! I thought—I thought I'd never see you again."

The old man shook the snow from his hair. "I thought I'd see you again—but on Earth! What in God's name are you doing here?"

"I followed you! I was so afraid you might—"

"Get into trouble?" Grandfather's bushy eyebrows

climbed high on his forehead as his amazement now mixed with amusement. "Ah, you clever little creature. Just couldn't bear to see me get myself lost in some far corner of the galaxy, could you?"

"Right! I was so worried about you . . . I just had to make sure you were safe." She tried to frown sternly. "I couldn't believe you broke your most solemn promise."

"Yes, well . . . I had to do it, Kaitlyn. Please forgive me. The Sun is in such peril."

"I forgive you," smiled Kate. "I just hope God does, too."

"God is very forgiving of Oxford men," he replied with a twinkle. "You found the other ring, didn't you?"

"Yes," answered Kate, suddenly somber. "But . . ."

The old man paid no heed to her change of mood. "Didn't you realize how risky a trip like that could be? You're very lucky."

"Yes . . . but Grandfather . . ."

"I haven't been so lucky," he continued. "I've been exploring very close to the star—it's a magnificent sight to behold—and I'm more convinced than ever that Trethoniel must be the greatest source of PCL anywhere in the universe. But I haven't had any success at all in finding out how the star makes it, or how the Sun could make more. Meanwhile, I've lost precious time. I'm starting to doubt I'm going to find out anything before it's too late."

"G-grandfather . . ." began Kate.

The old man gently stroked her long braid. "At least you're safe, dear child. I still can't believe you're really—"

He stopped himself. Grim concern filled his face and he studied her hands anxiously.

"Your ring! It's gone!"

Kate's sad eyes met his. "I know. We were attacked by The Darkness and Morpheus tried to save me, but I got caught in an avalanche and lost it!"

Grandfather stepped back, visibly shaken. "All that you've been through! I had no idea . . . Kaitlyn, it's truly a miracle that you survived. Not only must this planet have an oxygen-based atmosphere, but you could easily have frozen to death under a mountain of snow."

"I nearly did," she replied. "I don't know how I ever dug myself out. I just kept wondering if you were in trouble, and—oh, Grandfather! I'm so glad to see you."

The old man held his granddaughter for a long moment, as the winds whirled across the snowy ridge.

"I still don't understand why you didn't freeze to death," said the old astronomer, wiping the tears from her cheek.

"I would have," she replied, "if it hadn't been for Ariella. She saved my life."

Grandfather then noticed the small crystalline figure lying on the rocks a few paces away.

"Heavens," he said in wonder. "Is that her?"

"No! That's Spike, and he's not anything like her! She's . . ." Her voice faded into silence.

"She's what, Kaitlyn?"

"She's dead. Melted. She went over the waterfall into that horrible desert. And it's all my fault! So I lost her and the ring—and Morpheus, too."

"My brother," moaned Orpheus, shaking his antennae violently. His enormous green eyes gave Kate a look of unbearable pain.

"I'm sorry," said Kate sadly.

The butterfly waved his antennae dejectedly.

Grandfather frowned. "Until the ring is touched again by a living being, Morpheus will remain trapped inside it."

"And he was injured, wasn't he?" asked Orpheus. "I was sure that I felt him in pain."

"Yes," answered Kate, unable to look directly at Orpheus. "I think he was . . . hurt. It all happened so fast. The Darkness hit him with its tail and I don't know what happened after that."

Orpheus' body trembled. Grandfather laid his hand gently on the butterfly's neck, which seemed to calm him a little.

"A creature such as you describe must be a very powerful source of anti-light—very powerful, indeed—to separate you from your butterfly," said Grandfather grimly. "I might have missed some random elements in making the PCL, but that still wouldn't account for what happened. No, there's something strange abroad in Trethoniel."

"Yes," exclaimed Kate. "And that's not all that's strange. Right here on—"

"Orpheus!" Grandfather's cry interrupted her. "Orpheus, calm down!"

The great butterfly suddenly reared back, swaying his antennae furiously. "I must fly!" he cried.

Grandfather tried to restrain him, but without success.

The Darkness is near, thought Kate. Once again she felt the touch of utter coldness, and for the first time since she had donned Ariella's cloak of crystalline light, her whole body felt chilled.

"Stop, Orpheus!"

At that instant, the butterfly broke free of Grandfather's grip and lifted off toward one of the high peaks along the ridge.

"Come back," called Grandfather. "Come back!"

But Orpheus ignored his command.

"Orpheus! Come back!" Grandfather kicked angrily at the snow. "Damn that random element. I should never have—what in heaven's name—"

Just as Orpheus was about to disappear behind a cornice of snow, the great butterfly did something very strange.

"Somersaults!" cried Kate. "He's turning somersaults in the air."

As they stared in amazement, another pair of flashing wings appeared over the edge of the wall.

"Morpheus!"

"But how?"

Together, the two brothers celebrated their reunion in the finest tradition of aerial gymnastics. Somersaults, spins, loop-de-loops, and rolling turns decorated the sky. At last, they sailed down to the ridge next to Grandfather and Kate, landing with only a whisper of wind.

"Morpheus!" cried Kate, as she rushed to the great butterfly's side. "You're back!" She gently touched his left wing, which was badly frayed along its edge. "And you're hurt."

"Nothing serious," declared the butterfly. "I only hope we don't meet that creature ever again."

Kate nodded, then suddenly froze, her eyes fixed on the shape clinging to Morpheus' back.

"Ariella!"

The sparkling snow crystal leaped toward Kate and danced in the air before her face. Then she settled to the ground, and Kate gave her a hug as hearty as anyone with only two arms can deliver.

"Now I know why you wanted to find that ring," Ariella exclaimed. "I've never felt so good in my life." She then turned to Morpheus. "Those were first-class cartwheels you did up there."

The antennae quivered. "Thank you."

"I was afraid you were gone for good," Kate said.

Ariella's eyes gleamed. "So was I, especially when I realized I was melting from the heat. It's so ironic. The first time in my life I get to see our star Trethoniel, it's boiling me to death. I tried several times to climb the cliff, but it was just too steep, and much too high to jump. And those rocks were so hot! I was getting weaker by the second. So I moved back to see if I could see any kind of path or something, when suddenly I felt very faint. I fell down, and right there on the ground I saw the most beautiful little rainbow. I reached for it and the instant I touched it—this glorious creature appeared out of nowhere."

Again the antennae quivered.

"You've got the ring!" cried Kate. Then she paused. "But, Ariella, what happened to the big ocean—the Bottomless Blue?"

The snow crystal's eyes swung sadly toward the red desert. "I don't know. I don't know." Then she turned again to Kate and extended a crystalline hand. "Here. You should take this back. Rings belong to creatures who have fingers."

Kate took the butterfly ring and instantly the familiar green-blue mist filled her eyes. As she slipped it onto her finger, she felt once again the pulse of warm electricity coursing through her. Even as her body vanished, it was replaced with a clearer, lighter version of herself.

Her eyes met Grandfather's. "I had almost forgotten how wonderful it feels."

The astronomer stepped toward Ariella and bent down on one knee. "Dear creature, I know you are the one who saved my Kaitlyn's life. I thank you. I thank you with all my being."

"I accept your thanks," replied the snow crystal.

"But I couldn't bear to let her beautiful song go silent."

Grandfather turned a puzzled face to Kate.

"I think she means the Tallis Canon. I sang it while I was digging myself out, to give me strength."

The white head nodded. "A good choice." Suddenly, he remembered something and glanced at his ring. All but half of the right wing had disintegrated. Grandfather's face grew deeply serious. "I'm afraid it's time for us to return home."

"But what about the Sun? What about the cure?"

"It's time to go, Kaitlyn. We may have a minute or so left on my ring, but with some sort of anti-light creature running loose, I don't want to take any more chances. I had no idea that there would be anything like—"

"The Darkness," completed Kate. "I didn't either. That's for sure! But are you sure you want to turn back now, when you still have a minute left? If you want to use that minute to check out something important, Grandfather, I'm ready to go with you. As long as we're careful, really careful, to avoid The Darkness, I'm willing to stay a little while longer. After all, you still might find a cure. And it's my fault you've used up a lot of time down here on Nel Sauria."

The old man eyed her lovingly. "You are very brave, Kaitlyn. That's something I didn't really know about you before this whole business began. However, it's a risk I just can't accept. If anything were to happen to you, it would be the worst thing imaginable."

"Even worse than the Sun dying?"

"Yes. That I can't control. This I can. We're going home, Kaitlyn, while we still are able. I'll have to try to do what I can in the lab to find the Sun's cure." He looked sadly toward Trethoniel. "You've been no help at all, Great Star. No help at all!"

"You may not have found a cure for the Sun," said Kate, "but you did find me. I don't know how, but I'm awfully glad you did."

Grandfather's brow wrinkled in confusion. "But it was you who found me! I mean, I heard your voice, calling to me, telling me exactly where you were."

"Me?" asked Kate, herself confused. "My voice? I was constantly calling your name, but I never really contacted you."

"That's impossible," said Grandfather, shaking his head. "I heard you, loud and clear. You directed me here."

In a flash, Kate understood. She looked knowingly toward a large, snow-crusted rock not far from where they stood, and a slight smile touched her face. "It wasn't me who contacted you, Grandfather. It was the Sage of Sauria."

Ariella spun to her side. "Are you serious? You actually met the Sage?"

Indicating the rock, Kate answered: "Yes, we met, and she told me some riddles about the Pattern. Not that I could follow any of them! Just try to climb on that rock over there, and she might do the same for you."

Ariella's eyes glowed warmly. Then, for the first time, they fell upon the broken body of Spike lying among the rocks. "Oh, Spike!" she cried, spinning over to the fallen crystal.

"I don't know if he's still alive," said Kate, "but I did my best to get him out of that oven down there."

"He's still alive," pronounced Ariella, "although just barely. You surely saved his life—poor, wretched life that it is." She gazed at the crystal sadly. "Maybe the Nurse Crystals can put him back together—physically, at least. But I don't think anyone can ever heal the bitterness that infected him when he lost his family. I'm afraid the Spike I once knew is gone forever."

Kate reached for one of Ariella's cupped hands and held it in her own. "You may not be able to change Spike's life, but you've definitely changed mine. I don't know how to thank you."

The snow crystal brightened. "By staying awhile longer."

Kate looked hopefully at Grandfather, who shook his head resolutely. She faced Ariella again and whispered, "I guess this means goodbye. I really wish I could give you something special, after all you've given me."

Ariella's eyes sparkled. "Someday, perhaps, you will come back to Nel Sauria and teach me the words to that song."

"And I'll make you some hot chocolate, too," added Kate with a sad smile.

"But not now," declared Grandfather. "Now we must fly. I'm worried that The Darkness, as you call it, is still nearby."

Reluctantly, Kate gave the snow crystal a parting hug. "I will miss you."

"And I will miss you."

"Kaitlyn!" called Grandfather, who was already astride Orpheus. "Let's go!"

She walked slowly over to Morpheus, who had straightened his antennae in readiness for their long voyage. He bent lower so that she could climb aboard easily.

"To Earth, then," commanded Grandfather.

"Goodbye, Ariella!"

With a blur of iridescent blue, the great butterflies lifted off together, beating their wings furiously. Before Ariella could utter the word goodbye, they had disappeared into the clouds.

XI

Earthbound

As they sailed through the atmosphere of Nel Sauria, the vividly colored nebula of Trethoniel wove its way across the starscape. The great red giant itself, glowing as incandescent as ever, seemed to stretch out long arms of light to them, beckoning them to stay.

"We'll be home in no time," said Grandfather, his white hair glistening in the starlight. "Perhaps that cup of tea I asked you to make will still be warm."

To her own surprise, Kate felt more sad than relieved to hear his words. She cast a glance behind them toward the planet Nel Sauria, perfectly white from this angle, receding rapidly in the distance.

"I know it's difficult to leave," said Grandfather, hearing her thoughts. "We've been treated to an experience that no one else on Earth has ever known."

"Or will ever know, unless you can cure the Sun's

problems," replied Kate. She continued to gaze at the small white planet, then added wistfully: "I'm really going to miss Ariella."

"You two actually came to know each other a little bit, didn't you?"

Kate made no answer, but deep inside of herself she knew that she had just made—and lost—her first true friend, other than Grandfather.

Suddenly, both butterflies lurched forward, nearly dislodging their passengers.

"Orpheus! Morpheus!" commanded Grandfather. "What do you think you're doing? This is no time for games. Take us to Earth!"

"I—I'm trying," said Orpheus, his antennae quivering with stress.

"I feel so—so weak all of a sudden," moaned Morpheus. "I—just—can't push myself—any—faster."

"We're slowing down!"

Even as Kate cried out, the wings of their interstellar steeds began to beat less and less vigorously. Soon they were no longer a blur of motion, but were clearly visible, flapping strenuously in the void of space.

"What's wrong?" cried Grandfather. "Is something pulling you back?"

"No," panted Orpheus. "My—strength is being—being sapped."

Kate clutched Morpheus' neck more tightly. She looked toward Grandfather, whose eyes were filled with fear.

"That's impossible!" he protested. "We should have plenty of time left."

"But we don't!" groaned Morpheus. "Something— is blocking—the PCL I need! It's—draining—me!"

Grandfather shook his head in disbelief. "I don't understand. Something must be interfering with the conductive property of the rings!"

Kate looked at her butterfly ring. A good portion of the right wing remained; Morpheus should still have plenty of fuel. Then she noticed something else, something that made her gasp: The ring was steadily losing its luster. Before her eyes, its iridescent gleam faded and hardened into a dense, dull gray, as if it had turned into stone.

Even as the butterflies strained to move ahead, their wings grew steadily thinner, lighter, until they looked like faded reflections of themselves. Patches of the wings became invisible, so Kate could see only empty blackness where once she saw iridescent blues and greens.

"There," called Morpheus, his antennae indicating a flat, rectangular crystal, barely big enough to hold the two butterflies, floating to the left of them. "We—must—land—there."

"I can go—no further," moaned Orpheus, his entire body shivering with exhaustion. "I can't—can't make it."

"It's not far," cried Morpheus. "You—can—do it."

Ghosts of their former selves, Morpheus and Orpheus struggled to bring themselves and their passengers closer to the rectangular crystal. With a wrenching effort of their nearly transparent wings, they finally pulled near to the edge. Then, giving one last push, they toppled over onto the crystal, sending Kate and Grandfather skidding across its smooth, glassy surface.

Exhausted, the great butterflies lay prone on the crystal, legs splayed, breathing heavily. Slowly, to Kate's horror, their wings grew more and more transparent until, finally, they could no longer be seen.

"Morpheus! Your wings!"

The antennae quivered weakly. "I am—fading, Kate. I can't—"

"Morpheus!" she cried. "Come back!"

Grandfather stepped over to her side. Like the butterflies, his eyes also seemed drained of light. He watched helplessly as the two black bodies slowly faded away entirely. The last thing to disappear was one of Morpheus' antennae, which quivered valiantly before it vanished.

"What happened, Grandfather? Can't you fix it? The rings had plenty of PCL left: You said so. You said so. Now we're dead for sure!"

Kate stepped to the edge of the flat crystal and peered dismally over the edge. "Stranded . . . just waiting for The Darkness to come and get us. We should have stayed down there with Ariella." She turned again to Grandfather, and in a fearful whisper, she asked: "What's going to happen now?"

Grandfather heaved a painful sigh. "I don't know, Kaitlyn. I don't know." He studied the dull half-wing on the turquoise band around his finger. "I don't even know what's happened to our rings. Something's blocking their conductivity. We're still made of heartlight, or else we'd be dead already, frozen, suffocated and irradiated to boot. Somehow the rings still have enough power to keep our heartlights intact, but not enough to bring the butterflies to life. It doesn't make any sense!"

He brushed a clump of hair off his forehead and focused his regretful eyes on Kate. "Never—not even in my worst dreams—did I think that I would end up putting your life at risk. I should never have made a second ring. My own life is one thing . . . but yours."

He spun around to face the shining red mass of Trethoniel. Raising his fist, he shouted: "I came here for an answer! I came here for help! And what have you given me? The worst disaster I could ever imagine!"

Dejectedly, he looked at his own reflection in the mirrorlike crystal. "It's my own fault, not Trethoniel's. I'm such a stupid old fool. I never expected that Trethoniel's gift would be death instead of life . . . And I must have botched the formula for making PCL. What a worthless excuse for a scientist I am."

Kate felt a surge of sympathy for him. How could he have known the rings would fail? He never wanted her to come along in the first place: That was her own idea. He wasn't to blame for that. All he had ever wanted was to stop the Sun from destroying itself—and life on Earth in the process.

She moved to his side and touched his arm. "It's not your fault. It's not anyone's fault, really." She laid her head against his white lab coat. "Until this second I never really believed—down inside, I mean—that the Sun would die, and the Earth would die, and we would die. I guess I always thought you'd find an answer somehow. Oh, Grandfather! Now I'm so scared."

Two bushy eyebrows lifted hesitantly, as if to say: "So am I."

Wordlessly, they gazed across the starscape of Trethoniel, watching the shifting, seamless sea of colors. Bursts of bright light and floating crystals seemed to dance around them in an elegant minuet. Stellar winds buffeted them, tousling Grandfather's white hair.

Gently, he put his hand upon Kate's shoulder. Despite everything, the two lost voyagers felt nudged by a growing awareness of the immense beauty surrounding them.

"Whatever happens," said Kate softly, "I'm glad I got to see this." She looked up at Grandfather. "And if something bad has to happen to us, I'd rather it happen while we're together."

"So would I, Kaitlyn." He stroked her braid tenderly. "I just didn't think it would happen like this.

Or so soon! I suppose this is just a lesson in how small and unimportant we are in the grand scheme of things."

"But you're always telling me how every living thing is important."

"Right you are," replied the old man. "Thank you for reminding me. Every piece of the universe, even the tiniest little snow crystal, matters somehow. We can't forget that. I have a place in the Pattern, and you do, too. An important place."

Kate frowned. "I still have trouble swallowing all that."

"Why?"

"I just don't—I just don't feel like I matter much to the universe, that's all. Morpheus tried to tell me the same thing. I know I matter to you, and to Mom and Dad, and maybe to Ariella—but that's different. Why do I really matter to anything else?"

Grandfather shrugged despondently. "I suppose—"

A violent jolt interrupted him.

"Hey!" shrieked Kate. "The crystal! It's moving!"

"My God!"

XII
The Voice

As they held each other tightly, the mirrorlike crystal on which they stood began to buzz with vibrations. Slowly, its once-defined edges became silvery blurs and began to curl upward around them.

With every passing second, the vibrating grew more intense, until they could barely stand upright. The sea of floating crystals was now just a blur.

"We're trapped!" screamed Kate, as the rim of the crystal closed around them.

"Dear God!" exclaimed Grandfather.

The vibrations increased to the point where Grandfather and Kate toppled over in a pile. As the crystalline mass extended itself, the hollow in the middle where they stood began to deepen, like a bowl. At the same time, the crystal grew more and more clear, until finally it was perfectly transparent. Eventually, the edges joined above them in a seamless unity.

Suddenly, the vibrations ceased.

Slowly, cautiously, they regained their feet.

"It's a globe," said Kate, incredulous. "A big globe."

Indeed, they found themselves standing inside a large, transparent sphere. The great sea of mist around them whistled ominously.

"I'm scared," said Kate.

Then came the Voice.

From all around them, made from the deepest tones in the universe, came a bass-bass voice. It sounded as if someone had begun to play a titanic cello, whose strings were as long as a galaxy, and whose reverberations rolled out of a bottomless black hole.

"You need not fear." The words echoed across the starscape. *"I am the Voice of Trethoniel."*

Trying to regain his composure, Grandfather stood erect and tall in the middle of the great globe. He bowed slowly and respectfully.

Kate glanced at him worriedly. How could they be sure this was really the voice of the star? How could they know it was not really The Darkness or some other nightmarish creature?

"I am glad you have arrived. I am glad you have come to me," rumbled the Voice like a thundering storm.

"We are glad to be here," Grandfather replied, with more than a touch of fear in his voice. "I am Doctor Miles Prancer of the planet Earth, and this is my granddaughter Kaitlyn."

"You have come just in time," reverberated the reply.

"Yes," answered Grandfather. "How did you know? Our Sun is on the edge of—"

"No!" bellowed the Voice. "I speak not of your Sun. You have come just in time to save another star."

"Another star?" Grandfather's brow furrowed. "What star is that?"

The winds swept around the globe before the Voice spoke again, answering the question with a single word: "Trethoniel."

"Help Trethoniel?" cried Kate. "Are you really in danger? Is it because of The Darkness?"

"Patience, young one," commanded the Voice. "At the appropriate time, everything will be explained to you. If Trethoniel can be rescued from its current danger, it may even be possible to save that insignificant star you call the Sun. A strong Trethoniel can do many things. First, however, you must prove your worth by helping me."

"It may be insignificant to you," protested Kate, "but it's the only Sun we have. And we don't have much time!"

"You have time enough to help Trethoniel. My need is far greater than yours."

"But—"

"Quiet, Kate!" said Grandfather, squeezing her hand. "How can we help you, Great Star?"

"Soon enough, I shall explain. All you need to

know is that the music of Trethoniel is in grave danger."

What kind of danger? wondered Kate. From The Darkness? From the same disease that had stricken the Sun? She had hoped that Trethoniel would harbor the solution to their problems. Why then did this voice make her feel so afraid?

She turned anxiously to Grandfather. He stood in rapt attention, lost in thought. His face showed great anticipation, as if a long-awaited dream had finally come true.

A deep, full laughter rolled through the mists like a tsunami. "The young one does not yet believe I am Trethoniel."

Grandfather looked at Kate with surprise. She squeezed his hand fearfully.

The Voice came again, but more gently this time. "Very good. Such independence is one reason your little species has survived as long as it has, despite its other qualities." Then it grew serious, almost threatening. "But I am what I say I am. I do not have time to explain myself to small minds. And I hold you both as mere specks of dust in a bubble of my own creation."

"Kate," whispered Grandfather urgently. "Don't upset the star. It may be quick to anger, and its anger could be terrible. Remember that without our butterflies we have no escape!"

"But—" Kate objected faintly. "I was just feeling—"

"Feeling what?"

She looked into Grandfather's eyes. "I don't know exactly. Afraid, I guess."

Grandfather pulled her nearer. "Don't worry, Kaitlyn. I'll do what is best for us. You know I will."

He turned to the swirling mist. "She is only a child," he apologized. "She means no harm to Trethoniel."

They waited for a reply, but no reply came. Instead, a strange tenseness filled the air, a tenseness which brewed and bubbled until it felt like struggle, and pain. Then came a faint sound, or combination of sounds, welling up in the distance. A healing, joyous sound, like the celebration of birds at dawn's first light. Could it be? Yes! It was the music!

Then suddenly, without warning, the fair melody faded away. Deep in her chest, Kate felt again the touch of deadly coldness. She gasped. It was as if The Darkness had just flown past, brushing her heart with its poisonous tail.

"The music!" she cried. "Bring it back!"

"I am trying," declared the Voice, its unfathomably deep tones weighed down by an ancient sadness, too old and too immense to be comprehended by younger beings. "I am trying to save the music from total destruction."

The lovely sounds had vanished completely. All that remained was the empty whistling of the winds.

"How can we be of service to you?" Grandfather called into the starscape.

"I shall explain soon enough," bellowed the Voice. "But first, I wish to show you some of my greatest marvels. I wish to show you the beauty that gives birth to the music you have heard."

Grandfather's eyes flamed brightly. "We would be honored to see any marvels you care to show us."

"But we have no butterflies," objected Kate meekly. "How will we—"

"You will need no butterflies," boomed the reply. "I shall carry you, and you shall see some of my finest treasures. And perhaps you who are so young and full of doubt will eventually come to show me your trust."

Kate flushed with embarrassment. "I didn't mean to—"

A sudden jolt cut her short.

"The globe! It's moving!"

Grandfather reached for her arm and steadied her. "Stay close to me, Kaitlyn. I know you have your doubts . . . and so do I. But we're now at the mercy of this star, and I don't want to upset it. It could even be Trethoniel's energy that's keeping us alive as heartlight, now that our rings have failed. I'm afraid we must do as it says."

"But, Grandfather—"

"No, Kate. If you don't trust the star, then at least trust me. I've made some bad mistakes, but I still know what is best for us." His eyes held hers for several seconds.

At last she lowered her gaze. "I don't know why I'm being so difficult. Maybe it was getting swallowed by The Darkness that did it. That whole experience still feels so . . . so . . . close. I'm sorry. Of course I trust you."

Grandfather's expression softened. "And I trust you. Your instincts aren't all wrong. I'm not completely comfortable with our host, either. But I know enough to be sure this is the only chance we may still have to find a way to help the Sun. And right now, we have no choice."

XIII

Trethoniel

Standing inside the great globe as if it were an ark, the two travelers began to sail into the billowing mists. Crystals, some gargantuan and some as small as stardust, floated past on all sides. Some of them, symmetrical and shimmering, reminded Kate of Ariella. Clouds of heated dust swirled about them, aglow with all the colors of the universe.

A gaseous shape in the distance caught her eye. It was a strange, slender cloud with dozens of long tendrils extending from its sides. As they drew nearer, she discerned that the tendrils themselves branched into smaller tendrils, and from them spouted still smaller tendrils, like thousands of misty fingers reaching out from the main stem. The entire form seemed to be dancing—bending and swaying to a rhythm older than time.

"It looks like a tree!"

Grandfather, who was studying the cloudlike being carefully, nodded in agreement.

Then the form began to metamorphose. Ever so subtly, beginning on the outermost branches, the twigs of the cloud tree began to brighten. As if a swarm of fireflies had alighted upon the misty fingers, the tip of every twig started to glow with a warm, white light. Gradually, the light seeped into the larger branches, then into the trunk, then down to the roots, until finally the whole tree radiated like a miniature star, sparkling silently in space.

Kate reached for Grandfather's hand, which had simultaneously reached out for hers. Together, they watched the glowing cloud tree dance before them.

"That is one of my oldest and finest creations," boomed the Voice, jarring them out of their reverie.

"How old is it?" asked Grandfather.

"It is nearly as old as I am, and that is more than eight billion of your Earth years."

Kate had never found it easy to comprehend such numbers. Eight billion years! And she used to think Grandfather was old.

"I resent that thought," he replied, his eyes aglow with humor. "Compared to this star, I feel like a young bobbin."

"That's the whole point! If Trethoniel is over eight billion years old, that means it's more than a hundred times . . . a hundred times . . . a hundred times a hundred times as old as you."

"You are beginning to understand, young one," boomed the Voice. "Even your rudimentary brain power has led you to the correct conclusion."

Kate stiffened. "I may not be a genius, but at least I don't pretend to know everything."

"Nothing in the universe is hidden from me," replied the Voice in an imperial tone. "Nothing in the universe is beyond my knowledge."

"Nothing at all?" asked Grandfather, an edge of sadness in his voice.

The Voice did not respond for several seconds. At last, its deep tones resonated from above and below the great globe. "You are correct, Doctor Miles Prancer of the planet Earth. Young as you are, you are wiser than I had thought. Only one thing in the entire universe is still beyond my understanding. Only one thing is still beyond my power."

"What? What is it?" asked Kate.

"In time, even you shall understand," replied the Voice.

Kate turned to Grandfather for an explanation when, suddenly, the globe began to rotate. Slowly it spun around until they were no longer facing the illuminated tree. Then, gradually, the misty curtain before them parted, revealing Trethoniel's nebula stretching far out into the galaxy. Intertwined like the threads of a timeless tapestry, the colored clouds undulated gracefully in the stellar winds. Every so often, the light from Trethoniel would catch a floating crystal and it would explode with a dazzling burst of light, shining like a jewel in the tapestry.

Kate was reminded of Morpheus and Orpheus. What had actually happened to them? Were they gone forever? But no answer came to her questions.

"Beautiful," sighed Grandfather, still captivated by the glorious vista.

"Yes, it is beautiful," declared the Voice. "On the day I was first flung to this far corner of the universe, I was nothing more than a ball of gathering gases. When all around me was empty and dark, when not a single neighboring star could be seen, I began to weave my cape of colored clouds. For many star-lives, I have spun endless crystals and painted the moving mist, even as I manufactured more light than can ever be measured. I have labored, long beyond my destined time, to create the most beautiful star in the universe."

"And you have succeeded," Grandfather added.

"No!" boomed the Voice, with such force that it shook the globe and almost knocked them off their feet. "I have not succeeded. All my labors may still amount to nothing. Nothing at all!"

A long pause was filled only with the wailing of the winds.

"Come. I will show you more."

The great globe glided forward into the curling mists. Behind them, the glowing cloud tree reached out its longest branch, as if it were trying to deliver a message to them before they departed. Gracefully it stretched, unfurling like a fiddlehead fern in the spring sunshine, until it was about to touch the surface of the globe.

With a sudden jolt, the globe accelerated its flight. The misty finger reached out to its maximum length, but fell a few inches short of its mark. As the unknowing voyagers vanished into the billowing clouds, the illuminated tree seemed to shrug sadly and recoiled its branch. Slowly, twig by twig, the luminous form went dark, until at last its light was completely gone.

"We're descending," Grandfather declared. "We must be approaching the surface of the star."

Just then a gigantic tower of flame, white at the center and red along the edges, arched above them in a burst of brilliance reaching thousands of miles into space. The atmosphere sizzled and sparked. It felt as if they had just flown into a celestial furnace. For an instant, the swirling clouds turned into scarlet flames, licking at the great globe and its passengers. Then, like a collapsing building, the titanic tower of flame fell back to the star. It washed over them in an avalanche of fire.

"Whew!" said Kate as the flames disintegrated and were replaced by deep red clouds. "I thought the desert on Nel Sauria was hot. This is definitely no place to have a real body. Even inside a globe. If we were made of skin and bones there'd be nothing left now but two lumps of charcoal!"

"Not even that," corrected Grandfather. "It's hard to believe, but we are only at the edge of the corona, Trethoniel's outer atmosphere. Compared to what it's like down inside the core, an eruptive prominence like that is barely lukewarm. The pressure in there is something like five hundred *billion* times the pressure on the Earth's surface, and the temperature is close to seventy *million* degrees Fahrenheit."

"That's what I call hot," agreed Kate. "It makes even a healthy Sun seem pretty feeble."

Grandfather nodded, as the globe drew closer to the turbulent, bubbling surface of the star. Bridges of superheated plasma, arching along the lines of magnetic fields, spanned gigantic cones of ejecting gas. Rumbling like countless engines, huge convection cells—seething pots of ionized gases—percolated with energy from deep within the star's core. The face of Trethoniel looked like one gigantic firestorm, continuously flaming, churning, and erupting.

"Look!" cried Kate. "What's that?"

They trained their vision on a great pillar of yellow-red flames that rose like the stalk of a fiery flower from the stormy surface. Upward it climbed, until finally it opened into a wide bowl, large enough to contain a planet the size of Jupiter.

As the globe approached the midsection of the gigantic flaming stalk, it veered to the side and began to spiral higher and higher. At last, they had climbed to an altitude where they could see the thick folds of red and yellow petals that lined the underside of the great bowl, shielding its contents from the stormy surface of the star.

"I wonder what it holds," said Kate.

"Something very special, I suspect," Grandfather

replied, his voice filled with anticipation. "I didn't see anything like this when I flew near the surface with Orpheus."

"Could it be something that could help the Sun?"

"Possibly."

"Look!" cried Kate as they crossed above the rim. "Look at all those rows of bright green! But what— hey! What's that?"

As they flew above the fiery bowl, dozens of flat yellow creatures that glowed strangely became visible against the scarlet red background of the interior floor. The creatures glided busily to and fro across the radiant green rows lining the bowl, like farmers tending a fertile field.

Grandfather shook his head in amazement. "Those beings are huge! I would guess each one is at least the size of France! What are they?"

"They are Celethoes," answered the Voice. "They live in only two dimensions, so they can be seen only from above or below. Most stars have a few of them, but only the greatest stars have more than that. And no star in the universe has as many Celethoes as Trethoniel."

"And what are they growing?" asked Grandfather, eyeing the luminous rows of green.

"Pure condensed light," thundered the Voice, allowing each syllable to reverberate among the clouds.

Anxiously, Kate squeezed Grandfather's hand.

"It is the rarest element in existence," boomed the Voice, "a substance every star needs to survive. With it, a star will radiate life-giving light across the heavens. Without it, a star will surely die and go dark forever."

"That's—" Kate began.

"Quiet!" commanded Grandfather. "Let me think. Your Celethoes . . . could they be making PCL by breeding some derivative of the hydrogen isotope? Something like deuterium or tritium?"

"A good guess for a beginner, Doctor Miles Prancer. But the pure condensed light they are making is not related to the hydrogen isotopes capable of nuclear fusion. Such primitive materials I have long ago abandoned. My pure condensed light, unique in all the universe, contains free photons, twin neutrinos, and properties far beyond your comprehension."

Kate watched the graceful movements of the Celethoes. They seemed to be spinning threads of glowing filament from their own bodies, then weaving them tenderly through the rows in a methodical manner. Tiny pinnacles of illuminated green dotted the endless furrows: fresh PCL emerging from long incubation.

"And your Celethoes," probed Grandfather, "are they your only source of PCL?"

"No!" declared the Voice. "Over the ages I have developed many other sources."

"Such as?"

"I have no desire to tell you," bellowed the reply. "Even if I chose to tell you, it would take ten thousand of your lifetimes to explain, and then you would still not understand me."

Kate bristled at the Voice's tone.

Grandfather, however, seemed unperturbed. "With so much PCL available to you," he continued, "how can you be in any danger?"

"Because," the Voice rumbled, "I need something else to survive—something more precious even than pure condensed light."

"What could that be?" asked Grandfather, quite puzzled.

"In time!" roared the Voice. "I shall tell you when I am ready, when you will learn how to help me. But do not expect me to explain all my secrets to lesser beings like yourselves. I do not have time, and your tiny mortal minds could never comprehend more than a fraction of my creation."

Kate tried to contain her rising pique, but her thoughts betrayed her. "Who says we're lesser beings? Just because we might live for a shorter time. Aren't we all part of the same big Pattern?"

"Fool!" bellowed the Voice, with such force that the globe jolted and both Kate and Grandfather fell to their knees. "Contemptible fool! I do not need to listen to your childish babble. Trethoniel is the only place of perfection in all the universe!"

Grandfather squeezed her hand urgently.

"Forgive her, Great Star," he called into the mists. "She does not understand."

Kate's mind was whirling with images of The

Darkness, the terrible tail, the scorched desert of Nel Sauria . . . These were not her idea of perfection. Why didn't Grandfather understand?

"But—" she objected meekly.

"Not now, Kaitlyn!"

"Silence!" commanded the Voice, barely suppressing its rage. "I tolerate her ignorance only because she travels with you, Doctor Miles Prancer."

Kate cast a frightened look at Grandfather. Then her eyes fell to the fiery bowl below them.

Something had changed. By some silent command, the Celethoes had ceased in their labors. They were gathering together in the center of the red valley, their bodies glowing brightly as they slid across the fields to their destination. There, they formed a circle, a circle of connected light.

"The perfection of Trethoniel is under attack," the Voice rumbled. "Ignorant Celethoes may continue to perform their labors, hiding the impending tragedy from even themselves, but that does not alter the essential truth. Unless something is done swiftly, unless I can obtain the one thing I need, the greatest star in the universe will soon produce no more light and no more music." There was a somber silence before the Voice uttered its final sentence. "Trethoniel is about to die."

As the words echoed across the starscape, all fell still. Even the wailing wind seemed to hold its breath as the phrase *about to die* hung heavily upon it.

Then came another sound, subtle and struggling to

be heard. Faint though it was, Kate recognized it immediately.

"The music!"

The unmistakable chords rose delicately to them, like the scent of a distant lilac bush on a gentle breeze. Harmonious was the song, and full of healing. Joyful, and full of peace. As Kate drank in the lovely music, she heard something which had eluded her before. Pain too ran through the melody, and tragedy as well. Yet, on some deeper level, the joy seemed to embrace the pain, as the peace accepted the tragedy. The power of the music was all the more profound because of it.

"The music—it's coming from the Celethoes!" cried Kate. She pointed to the shining circle below them, which seemed to swell in luminosity as the music swelled in strength. "They're trying to tell us something. I know they are. I can feel it."

Then a sudden turmoil filled the air. Kate caught a glimpse of a dark form gathering in the faraway mists.

"The Darkness!" she screamed in panic. "It's The Darkness!"

Just then she felt the terrible coldness reaching into her. An evil energy, even more powerful than before, began squeezing her tightly.

"H-help!" she gasped, reaching frantically for Grandfather's outstretched arm. "I'm being str-strangled!"

"Away with you," thundered the Voice. "Leave her alone!"

The music grew dimmer as did the circle of light below them, until finally both were extinguished. Heavy clouds surrounded the great globe, and the sky darkened ominously. The serpentine form of The Darkness encircled them, drawing its vengeful noose of anti-light tighter and tighter.

"Save us, Trethoniel!" pleaded Grandfather. "Get us out of here!"

But the great globe did not move. Only the muffled groans of the Voice came struggling back from beyond the clouds.

Fear flooded Kate as she fought to breathe—desperately forcing herself to inhale. "I want to live," she sputtered with all her remaining strength.

The cold pressure inside her chest only increased. It was closing in on her, suffocating her, squeezing the life out of her heartlight.

Now The Darkness was circling so close that Grandfather could see the electric red eye, sizzling with currents of negative energy.

"Leave her alone!" he cried.

Kate coughed uncontrollably. Her hands grabbed her own throat, and she fell to her side, wrestling with an unseen force. She couldn't breathe at all.

Then, suddenly, she went completely limp.

"Stop!" screamed Grandfather as he scooped her into his arms. "Leave her alone, whatever you are!"

The entire sky flamed brightly, then went totally dark. At the same instant, Grandfather felt Kate's unconscious form disintegrate into nothingness. His arms were empty.

"Kate!" he cried, tears streaming down his face. "Where are you?" He groped madly in the blackness to find her.

In time, a dim light returned to the starscape. The Darkness had vanished, and so had Grandfather's last shred of hope. He collapsed in a heap in the center of the great globe, weeping bitterly.

Kate was gone.

XIV
The Promise

Kaitlyn, dear Kaitlyn," the old man sobbed. "Why did you have to follow me? Why did I ever make two rings? Oh, my dear, dear child . . . I am sorry."

With utter finality, three weighty words thundered across the clouds. *"She . . . is . . . lost."*

Grandfather slowly sat upright. He wiped his tear-washed face with his sleeve, struggling to regain a measure of composure. "What? What did you say?"

"She is lost," rumbled the reply. "Her heartlight has been extinguished."

"Extinguished!" cried Grandfather. "No! God, no!"

He placed his face in his two weathered hands. "It should have been me. Not her. Not my little Kaitlyn."

"Doctor Miles Prancer," spoke the Voice. "Do not despair."

He raised his sorrowful head. "Do not despair? But I've lost her. The person I most loved! Nothing else in the universe matters to me now."

"Something else matters. You also love the star Trethoniel."

A white eyebrow lifted. It struck Grandfather that the Voice sounded different than it had before. It was smaller, thinner, as if it had just survived a brutal battle.

"You love Trethoniel very much. And Trethoniel can still be saved."

"I can't think about anything but Kate," said Grandfather, shaking his head sadly. "Why didn't you save her? Why didn't you save her before she was lost?"

"I tried to save her. But I could not." The sky darkened slightly. "The Enemy wanted her badly. And the Enemy is very, very powerful. Never have I fought so hard, Doctor Miles Prancer. But I failed to save her."

"Who took her away? Who is the Enemy?"

"The agents of the Enemy are all around us. They come in many forms, sometimes frightening, sometimes pleasing. Deception is their weapon and destruction is their goal."

"Why?" cried Grandfather desperately.

"Because the Enemy is bent on destroying every star, every source of light in the universe."

"Including the Sun?"

"Including the Sun."

"But why did they want Kate?"

"She wanted the stars to survive! She wanted your Sun to live, and she wanted Trethoniel to live. Despite her vast ignorance, she was on the side of life, not death. She wanted my music to live, and to live forever."

"They can't have her!" protested Grandfather, tears again brimming in his eyes.

"They already have her," answered the Voice, some of its former strength returning. "They already have your Sun. But they do not yet have Trethoniel."

"Nothing else matters, now that Kate is gone."

"All life matters," the Voice replied. "And no life matters so much as the great star Trethoniel."

"Yes, of course, all life matters," said the old man halfheartedly. "But now that Kate is gone—"

"There is still time," roared the Voice. "There is still time to save the star you most love. But we must act together. And we must act swiftly."

Grandfather bowed his head in despair. "Nothing has any meaning for me anymore. Not even helping Trethoniel."

"Then do it for her. Do it for the young one. She wanted the music of Trethoniel to survive, to ring forever throughout the heavens. Helping me is helping her."

Slowly, the white head lifted. Clumsily, Grandfather regained his feet. His eyes were filled with sadness, but that sadness now mixed with his rising rage.

"Can we still stop the Enemy from destroying Trethoniel?"

"Perhaps," came the thunderous reply. "If we act now."

Grandfather's anger distilled into determination. "What can I do? How can I help you?"

For a long moment, the winds were utterly silent. "You can lend me something," boomed the Voice.

"What can I lend you?"

"You can lend me your heartlight."

Grandfather winced, as if he had been struck by some object. "My—my heartlight? Great Star, you of all beings know that heartlight cannot be loaned! It can only be given, as an act of free choice. But once given it can never be returned. My heartlight would belong to you forever."

The winds whistled ominously.

"You are correct."

"But you're asking me—"

"—to make the greatest sacrifice any mortal being can make. Yes! To give up your individual heartlight forever. There is only one purpose that can justify such a request: the purpose of saving Trethoniel."

"So the precious substance you need is heartlight!" exclaimed Grandfather.

"Yes," answered the Voice. "A small dose of heartlight is the one thing I need, the one thing I lack. And I must have it soon, or the Enemy will destroy me."

"But I don't understand, Great Star! How can my

heartlight be so important to you? Why is a little heartlight so much more necessary to your survival than all the PCL you are manufacturing?"

"Because," rumbled the Voice, "pure condensed light only prolongs life, while heartlight—heartlight is life itself. Pure condensed light has strengthened my body, but the darkest danger I face is to my soul. And the danger is upon me. Only heartlight can save me now."

"But why?" pressed Grandfather. "I still don't understand."

"You need only understand one thing." The Voice sounded closer, almost on top of Grandfather. "Trethoniel is now balanced on the thinnest edge of extinction. There is very little time left. All my beauties and marvels, all my music and light, will be destroyed forever—just like the young one—unless you help me. Even now, the Enemy is gathering for a final attack. You can make the crucial difference, Doctor Miles Prancer."

"Tell me more."

"I will tell you only what you need to know," replied the Voice. "The only fact you need to comprehend, which you have already guessed, is that I have labored for eons with all my energies to postpone the ultimate tragedy: that thing called death."

A swell of sympathy began to rise in Grandfather. "I know, Great Star. For so many years I have believed you were on the verge of collapse! How you have avoided it for so long is a miracle." He shook his head dismally. "I can understand your desire to live, to complete your work. You simply want to grow older and wiser, to avoid becoming—"

"—*a black hole,*" roared the Voice, and with those words a new layer of darkness descended. "The Infinite Nothing! For eons I have lived in fear of this fate. The more beautiful I grew, the more inescapable it became. I have struggled in vain to avoid it, to find the solution to the terrible flaw that afflicts all living things. But I will struggle no longer. For I have finally discovered the answer to the greatest of all riddles. And I need only one more modicum of heartlight to complete my plan."

"So my heartlight will enable you to continue postponing your death?"

"No!" bellowed the Voice. "Postponement alone would be no success! No success at all! In the end, death would still triumph. No, Doctor Miles Prancer, I do not seek merely to postpone death, like every other living thing in the universe. I seek something far more precious. I seek to avoid death completely."

"Avoid death completely!" Grandfather's eyes opened wide. "That's—that's incredible! That would revolutionize astrophysics . . . as well as philosophy and religion! It would change everything!"

"Yes! I have labored for eight billion years to arrive at this moment."

"Perhaps," mused the astronomer, "my own life's work, brief though it's been, has also been just a preparation for this moment."

"And perhaps the young one's sacrifice was a necessary part of your preparation," added the Voice.

Grandfather jolted. "No! There was no purpose to
that—no purpose at all! I would rather have her back
than all the stars in the universe. She was lost out of
stupidity—my stupidity—and nothing could ever justify it."

"I understand your grief," the Voice replied. "But
our time is slipping away! Surely you are wise enough
to understand what is at stake here. It is nothing less
than the ultimate battle of the universe: the battle between life and death. Even the young one understood
that much! Now, we have dallied long enough. Will
you give me your heartlight?"

"If you first tell me how it will enable you to avoid
death completely."

"Time is wasting! I could not possibly explain it to
you in the time we have left. Nor could you understand the answer!"

"But I must understand at least a little more before
I can give up my heartlight forever. It's such a final
thing you are asking."

"Far less final than death! If you will not listen to
me, then perhaps you will listen to someone else.
Someone whose voice you will recognize."

"Who is that?"

All went silent, even the incessant howling of the
winds.

"Who?" demanded Grandfather.

"It is I," declared a thin, raspy voice from behind
the curtain of clouds.

Grandfather shook his head in disbelief. "No—it can't be!"

"But it is."

"Ratchet!"

A hoarse laughter echoed among the mists. "You look much worse for wear, Prancer. Yet still you made it here. Only fifty years late, but at least you made it. I confess I thought you never would."

Grandfather stood awestruck. "How did you do it?"

"How?" rasped the voice of Ratchet. "You are asking me how? The same way you did it, of course! Through a catalyst of PCL. Does it gall you to know that you were not the first to do it? That you were merely a follower, not a discoverer?"

"Yes," replied Grandfather. "Yes, it does."

"I see you haven't learned much, Prancer. You are as honest as ever."

"And you are as spiteful as ever."

"That is the prerogative of the greatest scientist who ever lived."

"So the whole fire in the laboratory was just a ruse?"

"To disguise my exit," agreed Ratchet, cackling proudly. "I am sure there was ceaseless debate over its true cause."

"Yes. But none of us ever guessed that you had found a way to free your heartlight and travel to Trethoniel."

"Or, even better, that I had discovered the path to immortality!"

Grandfather's eyebrows lifted to their maximum height. "You mean that you have merged your heartlight with Trethoniel's?"

"Yes!" Ratchet's voice was triumphant. "At last, to leave my wretched and decaying body behind. To be free, finally and forever! That is my reward for those many years of torture."

"So you have ceased to exist as an individual being?"

"What value is individuality when it is, by its very nature, limited and temporary? Now I am part of something much bigger and far better: the infinite life of a glorious star. And my great intelligence has enabled this star to flourish when it otherwise would have died."

"Fool!" bellowed the Voice, ending its silence. "You are only a tool to Trethoniel! I am growing tired of your endless arrogance. You forget that I have preserved a portion of your ego solely so that you can be more useful to me. But you have served your purpose! However important you might have been once, now much more important is your student. He alone holds the power to save Trethoniel from annihilation."

"Only because he learned a few things from me," snarled Ratchet. "And you have certainly changed your tune, O Voice of Trethoniel! You sent me all the way back to Earth just to prevent him from coming here! Now you are begging him for help."

"Prevent me!" exclaimed Grandfather. "Ratchet! Was that you who ruined my laboratory?"

"You've only now deduced that? You haven't gotten any smarter since I saw you last." Ratchet's hoarse laughter rose above the winds. "I actually quite enjoyed being a ghost."

"You might have killed my dog, you assassin."

"I wish I had. If there hadn't been more important matters to tend to—"

"Important!" Grandfather retorted angrily. "Like stealing an empty, worthless box! I do say, Ratchet, you are easily fooled. You haven't gotten any smarter since I saw you last."

"Silence!" commanded the Voice. "While you two are bickering, my very life is slipping away. And your life as well, Doctor Willard Ratchet."

"Why did you want to prevent me from coming here?" demanded Grandfather. "Answer my question, or I will never help you."

"Because I feared you would be captured by the Enemy, and made to give them your heartlight."

"But heartlight can only be given freely," objected Grandfather. "I would never give them my heartlight!"

"They would have tricked you!" bellowed the Voice. "They will say anything and do anything to annihilate Trethoniel. Just as I need one more drop of heartlight to survive, the Enemy needs it to destroy me."

"Prancer," croaked Ratchet's voice. "It was my idea to prevent you! I figured you might be getting close to making your own PCL by now, if you were lucky. You were never very smart, but you always had more than your share of perseverance. I couldn't take the risk you might be duped into giving your heartlight to the Enemy. And besides, what right do you have to make use of *my* invention? I was the only human ever to have experienced the power of PCL—until you had the audacity to follow in my footsteps!"

"Silence!" ordered the Voice. "I should never have listened to your foolish plans! It is clear to me now that your former student is far too intelligent to fall under the sway of the Enemy. And what is more important, I see now that he was destined to help Trethoniel in my moment of greatest need."

The Voice paused, gathering all its energy. "Doctor Miles Prancer, I have been joined by the heartlights of many wise beings throughout my realm. Now there are no more heartlights within my reach who have not sided either with me or with the Enemy. Your heartlight is therefore my only hope! Unless you join me very soon, the forces of the Enemy will triumph—and all my magnificence will be lost forever. I ask you now: Will you do your part to save Trethoniel?"

"What about saving the Sun, too?" asked Grandfather. "If I help you, will you give the Sun some of your pure condensed light? Its supply is dwindling fast."

"It is too late to save your Sun," declared the Voice. "But Trethoniel still has a chance to survive! And if Trethoniel can be saved, it will open the door to a universe where every star can live eternally, ascending to the heights of glory that stars were meant to achieve!"

A sudden pang of doubt struck Grandfather. "A universe where every star can live eternally? But what happens to the recycling of energy? What happens to the conservation of—?"

"Prancer!" cried Ratchet's raspy voice. "Have you not moved beyond those simplistic laws of physics? You were a fairly good student. Now you're sounding like a brain-dead Neanderthal. Don't you understand that immortality is within your grasp?"

"Yes, but—"

"We need your heartlight, not your questions!" interrupted the Voice. "You could not save the young one, and you could not save the Sun, but you can still save Trethoniel! And in doing so, you will save the heartlight of many others as well. Will you join us?"

"Say yes!" urged Ratchet.

Straightening his tall frame, Grandfather peered into the impenetrable mists swirling about the great globe. He could not even see the outlines of the fiery bowl below, let alone the circle of Celethoes, if they were still there.

"I am prepared to help you, but only on one condition."

"I do not accept conditions from lesser beings," thundered the Voice.

"Then I will not help you," came Grandfather's clear reply.

"What is your condition?" demanded the Voice impatiently.

"That if any of Kate's heartlight has somehow survived, even if it is many eons before she is discovered, you will promise to return her safely to the planet of her choice."

"Nothing at all will survive unless you help me!" exclaimed the Voice with a force that shook the globe and nearly knocked Grandfather over backward.

"And I will not grant you my heartlight unless you accept my condition," he called back into the churning clouds. "While I still have my free will, that is what I demand."

"She has been extinguished!"

"Nevertheless."

"This is nonsense!"

"Nevertheless," insisted Grandfather. "I want your promise."

"Did you travel all the way here and leave your mind behind?" derided Ratchet. "Why don't you join us?"

"I only know that if my heartlight is to be given away, it must be given freely. And before that can happen, I must have Trethoniel's promise."

"Very well," agreed the Voice at last. "You have my promise!"

The old man raised his hand to look at the remains of his lusterless butterfly ring. Only a small portion of one wing remained; before long, nothing more than a turquoise band would be left. "Once there were two of these," he thought sadly. "Now only one is left. What do the laws of physics matter if I can help stop the forces that destroyed her?"

"We must act!" roared the Voice. "Will you join us?"

"Join us, Prancer!" called Ratchet. "Make a decision for once!"

The winds swirled about Grandfather.

"I will help you," he declared at last. "I will do as you wish."

XV

Apple Cider

W hat happened?" cried Ariella. "Why is there so much pain in the air?"

Her mother waved one of her long arms. "Quiet, Ariella! Go back to sleep. We are working very hard."

But the young snow crystal could not sleep. Something important was happening. She could feel it. She rubbed her round eyes and poked her head out of the pouch on her mother's back.

"It's so dark out here," she exclaimed. "Where has all the light gone?"

"Our light has been dimmed," answered her mother in an exhausted voice. "And the light of our snow as well. We gave it up to save the Creature."

"The Creature?"

"Come see for yourself," said the Nurse Crystal.

"But please, Ariella, don't get in our way. We barely rescued it and we still have much work to do. Twice during the battle I thought we had lost it."

"And we may lose it still," added another Nurse Crystal who was bending over the Creature. "It remains very weak."

Ariella spun down one of her mother's arms and landed on the velvetlike floor of Broé San Sauria. So dark was it inside the crystal dome that she could only barely discern the green color of the dome itself. Cautiously, she moved closer.

The dim illumination of the Nurse Crystals' bodies cast a wavering light on the Creature, who lay sprawled on the floor. Attentively, they massaged the limp form, all the while singing softly.

"Kate!" exclaimed Ariella. "It's Kate!"

Her mother stopped her work. "Kate of the Ring?"

"Yes!"

"Are you certain?"

"Yes! That's her."

"Ah," nodded the Nurse Crystal, her silver eyes examining Kate closely. "That explains much."

"Is she going to make it?" asked Ariella, twirling closer to her side.

At that instant, Kate of the Ring opened her eyes. "Where am I?" she mumbled.

"You are on Nel Sauria," answered a gentle voice.

Suddenly Kate saw the huge, hulking shapes bending over her in the half-light. She grabbed her throat in fright.

"No. Stay away!" she screamed. "You can't have me!"

"Don't be frightened, Kate. I'm here."

"Ari-Ariella? Is that really you?"

"Yes. It's really me."

"How did I— Where is—" Kate struggled to sit up, then collapsed backward.

"Oh, Ariella! It tried to kill me again."

"Just be still," whispered another one of the Nurse Crystals. "You are safe now. Do you feel anything yet in your limbs?"

"Y-yes," answered Kate, her thoughts still whirling. "They feel heavy. Almost numb."

"Is the numbness moving into your chest?"

"I don't know! What happened to me? How did I get here? Where is Grandfather? Where is The Darkness? How did you—"

"Hush, hush," said Ariella's mother. She gently stroked Kate's furrowed brow with the tip of one of her long arms. "We will have time for explanations later. Now you must rest, or all our efforts will have been wasted. You are still in danger."

"I'll stay right here with you," whispered Ariella. "Don't worry about anything."

The Nurse Crystal reached into a small silver satchel dangling by her side. Out came her cup-shaped hand, with a sparkling dew upon it.

"This will help you," she said, as she touched Kate lightly upon the lips. "This is the same dew we use to nourish our most fragile baby crystals, when they are so small that even a beam of light weighs heavily upon them."

Kate felt instantly warmer, deep inside herself. Gradually, her questions gave way to a feeling of quiet comfort. An image danced across her memory of curling up beside Cumberland in front of Grandfather's kitchen fireplace, birch logs crackling, firelight dancing on the wooden walls. The room smelled of autumn leaves and apple cider. She lay her head upon his flowing red coat, and felt the dog's rhythmic breathing and warm body beneath her.

Soon she was fast asleep.

XVI

The True Music

Hello."

Kate looked up, her eyes filled with sleep.

"Hello."

She sat up straight and called into the semi-darkness. "Who is that? Where are you?"

"Here," announced a small voice behind her. As Kate turned her head, the voice broke into a sweet, lilting laughter.

"Ariella!"

"Right," beamed the snow crystal, her six ornate arms glittering. "I couldn't wait any longer." She laughed again, like legions of little bells pealing.

Kate found herself smiling. How good to hear Ariella's laughter again! Then, like a steel trap suddenly sprung, her thoughts returned to her own predicament.

"Why am I smiling?" she moaned. "Ariella, what happened? How did I get here?"

"You were saved by the Nurse Crystals."

"Saved from The Darkness?"

"Saved from annihilation." Ariella's voice was somber. "The Nurse Crystals said you almost didn't survive. They said it was the worst battle they have ever had to fight in all the eons they have healed the wounded and tended their young. To save you they sacrificed most of their own light . . . and until it returns, the green dome and all of Nel Sauria will remain in shadows."

"That's why it's so dark?"

"Yes. Before the battle, the Nurse Crystals blazed with light, and the green dome of Broé San Sauria radiated their energy."

"I remember . . . And all to save me?"

Ariella nodded. "And Nurse Nolora will never make any light again."

"Why, Ariella? Why? I'm just a visitor to this place."

"I don't know exactly why, but I am sure they didn't sacrifice so much without a good reason. They must have known The Darkness was after you. If The Darkness wanted so badly to extinguish you, then your heartlight must pose a great threat to its plans."

Kate sucked in her breath. All at once, the horrors of her struggle came flooding back to her.

"Oh, Ariella! It was terrible!"

The snow crystal twirled to her side and nudged her arm. "I know."

"Grandfather!" cried Kate. "I've got to get back to him. He's in trouble. I'm sure of it."

She braced herself and tried to rise to her feet. Suddenly she felt very weak and dizzy.

"Too much too soon," chided a mammoth snow crystal rolling toward them. "Sit back down again."

The command was unnecessary, as Kate's legs collapsed under her. She fell back onto the soft floor.

"Ariella," spoke her mother sternly, "I told you not to disturb her."

"But I was only—"

"She was only helping me understand what happened," interrupted Kate, her head still whirling. "She meant no harm."

Ariella's eyes glowed with gratitude.

"Very well then," spoke the Nurse Crystal. "How are you feeling?"

"Better, I think. Less dizzy now. But I'm still awfully weak."

The Nurse Crystal's six arms quivered. "Understandably, given all that you were battling against when we came to your rescue."

Kate reached out her hand, and a long, glistening arm stretched to meet it. The arm of the snow crystal radiated a soft white glow, and as it moved, thousands of tiny crystalline points radiated rainbows in all directions. The outermost tip touched Kate's middle finger.

"Thank you," said Kate softly.

"You are welcome," replied the Nurse Crystal.

"We will miss our light, and the dear friend we lost, but you are out of danger. At least for the moment."

"Why did it want to kill me?" cried Kate. "All I did was point to the Celethoes—they were trying to tell us something—when suddenly The Darkness was right there. It surrounded us, then it attacked me." She shivered at the memory.

"It was not The Darkness who attacked you," the great snow crystal replied.

"But I saw it. I felt it!"

"That much is true," the Nurse Crystal agreed. "But The Darkness is only a slave. You fought it once before, we learned from Ariella. However, your last battle was not with The Darkness. Your last battle was with its master."

"Its master? Who is that?" Even in the near darkness, Kate felt a shadow fall upon her as she asked the question.

"We dare not speak its true name. It calls itself many things, all of them false. Most often it pretends to be *the Voice of Trethoniel.*"

"The Voice!" Kate exclaimed. "I knew something didn't feel right about it. I just couldn't figure out what. But it kept saying it spoke for the entire star. I was starting to doubt my own instincts—to wonder whether I was crazy to be so suspicious."

"Trethoniel has many voices," declared the Nurse Crystal. "Every living being that is part of this star or its planets, no matter how small or insignificant, has a voice of its own. My little Ariella has a voice, I

have a voice, and even The Darkness has a voice.
None of them can speak for the star. The Voice that
pretended to do so only kept you from hearing the
other voices. But it could not speak for them."

"What about the music? The beautiful music we
heard?"

The eyes of the great crystal danced. "If there is
any true voice of Trethoniel, that is it. For eons and
eons, the music of Trethoniel has grown in majesty
and meaning. Each new voice that was added brought
a new measure of beauty, a new moment of wisdom,
and the song of this star became the most exquisite in
the galaxy."

The Nurse Crystal leaned back to face the dark
clouds swirling above the green dome, and her eyes
darkened as well. "Until the Voice grew to be so
strong! Then it began to block out our music, just as
it blocks out any competing voices."

"But the Voice said it wanted the music to survive," protested Kate. "It said it wanted to save the
music from total destruction."

"How do you explain that?" questioned Ariella.
"That doesn't sound right."

Her mother's crystalline body, fully twice as tall as
Kate, shook with anger. "It isn't right," she declared.
"The Voice does not wish to preserve the True Music
of Trethoniel. No! The True Music is made of mortal voices, a chorus of Celethoes and crystals and creatures of all kinds, whose music is made wiser and
deeper by their very mortality. The music of the

Voice, which it longs to preserve, is utterly different. It is a thin and artificial verse that could stretch on forever, oblivious to the pain of death or the tragedy of transformation. Only by understanding the unity of life and death have we given birth to wisdom and hope. The music of the Voice is immortal, but dead; the True Music of Trethoniel is mortal, but ever alive."

The two young beings sat silently, absorbing her words. At last, Kate spoke again.

"What is the Voice, really? Where does it come from?"

The Nurse Crystal did not reply.

"Please tell us."

"The Voice is part of the star," the great crystal said at last, "just as the True Music is part of the star. Like the music, the Voice is the sum of many individuals, but those individuals fear death so greatly they would sacrifice everything wise and beautiful just to stay alive."

"They are very bad," observed Ariella.

"No, they are not bad individually. They are only bad collectively, when they have grown too strong— as they have in the realm of Trethoniel. Every living being, young and old, has an echo of the Voice somewhere in itself. That is the call of self-preservation, of survival. It is a good and healthy thing, unless it grows too powerful."

"As it has here."

"I fear so," the crystalline creature said sadly. "As

the collective heartlight of Trethoniel grew more self-
ish, the Voice grew in power. We who should have
known better allowed it to grow too strong."

"But how could you?" demanded Kate. "How
could you ever let such a thing happen?"

"Because it happened very, very slowly, and at first
it seemed to be more good than bad. As Trethoniel
grew and evolved, propelled partly by its desire to
survive, much great beauty was wrought. Crystals
blossomed like never before, Celethoes multiplied,
starlight flourished, and healing warmth flowed
throughout the heavens. Trethoniel became one of the
loveliest stars in the universe."

Just then the darkened sky above Broé San Sauria
rumbled with thunder. The Nurse Crystal wrinkled
her face in concentration, as if she were straining to
hear something. Finally, the deep silver pools of her
eyes fell directly on Kate. "Someone you love is in
very serious trouble."

"Grandfather!" exclaimed Kate. "What is happening to him? Is he safe?"

"No," answered the Nurse Crystal. "He is in the
greatest danger that can befall any mortal being."

"Then I must warn him!" Kate tried to stand, but
dizziness descended on her like a torrential rain, and
she fell to her knees. "How can I warn him if I can't
even get to my feet?" she wailed.

The Nurse Crystal reached a glittering arm to
touch her brow. "Soon you will feel better. Your
strength is returning faster than I had ever expected."

Then a new thought twinkled in her eyes. "I wonder if Nolora . . ."

She looked at Kate lovingly. "You will be on your feet soon."

"Soon isn't good enough! I want to help him *now.*"

"First you must listen."

Again, Kate tried to stand, and again the dizziness drove her back. "All right," she said resignedly. "I'm listening."

The eyes of the Nurse Crystal filled with the pain of some distant memory. "Slowly, inevitably, the Voice's lust for immortality overcame all the good works. Before those of us who understood the deeper truths could rouse ourselves, the Great Trouble was upon us. The Voice had grown very powerful—so powerful that we could not stop it from expanding the star beyond its true size. We could not even stop it from destroying the planets nearest to Trethoniel as it grew larger and hotter."

A sudden revelation struck Kate. "So that's how the Bottomless Blue turned into a big desert."

"Sadly, yes," agreed the Nurse Crystal, her moist eyes glistening. "As the star has swelled, it has burned away Nel Sauria's once-glorious ocean. At the same time, it has softened our snows, killed our crops, and warmed our side of the planet beyond a sustainable temperature. The Great Trouble grows worse by the hour. Never again will those wondrous waves embrace our snowy shores; never again will the wisest of the Nurse Crystals pilgrimage to the High Waterfall to meditate upon those infinite blue waters."

"The waterfall!" exclaimed Kate. "Did the Nurse Crystals build a trail to the top of this waterfall?"

"Long, long ago," replied Ariella's mother, "in the days when even the Sage of Sauria was young."

"Why didn't you explain all this to me before?" asked Ariella.

The Nurse Crystal touched her lightly on her arm. "Because you are so young, my child. I was hoping to wait for a better time, a more peaceful time."

"Why haven't you tried to stop the Voice?" questioned Kate. "Why haven't you fought against it?"

"We have!" the Nurse Crystal answered. "We have fought with every ounce of our strength—every ounce of our heartlight—just to prevent the Voice from achieving its goal."

"Which is?"

"To live forever."

"But," protested Kate, "that doesn't sound so bad. I mean, lots of people want to live forever."

"Indeed," the Nurse Crystal said wistfully. "Most mortal beings would love to live forever. But they cannot, because that would destroy the Pattern."

"Why?" asked Ariella.

"Because the Pattern is an endless thread that ties everything in the universe to everything else. If any being tries to go on living forever, then it must steal its energy from someone else who deserves to live. This star has a time to die, just as I do. And if the Pattern is intact, a being who dies doesn't totally disappear from the universe. It merely changes form."

Ariella spun to her mother's side and looked up at

her with doubting eyes. "Do you really believe that? Do you really believe we just change our form when we die?"

"Yes, my child, I do."

"Then why don't I believe it?" the small snow crystal objected. "Death seems so very final—so very sad. Please don't ever die! I don't want you to die!"

"I know," said the Nurse Crystal, as she stroked the delicate arms of her child. Her silvery eyes glowed softly. "You are right that death is sad. Perhaps one day you will understand it is also something more. I pray you will be given the chance."

"I've got to warn Grandfather now," said Kate with determination. "I've got to warn him about the Voice!"

"That will be very dangerous," cautioned the Nurse Crystal. "Remember what happened before! Are you certain you are really ready?"

Kate frowned. "Could the Voice really have destroyed me completely if you hadn't come to my rescue?"

"No," answered the Nurse Crystal. "Its powers are not yet that great. At least some of your heartlight would have survived." Her round eyes opened to their widest. "But for you, being extinguished might have been a kinder end. Any elements of your heartlight that survived would have been utterly mutilated, beyond any recognition. You would have been afflicted with permanent pain and undying agony. You would not have remembered your grandfather, and he would not have recognized you."

A shudder ran through Kate. She turned to scan the sky above the green dome. The darkness had lifted somewhat, and a pale red light sifted through the clouds.

"I've got to try again," she declared, struggling to raise herself.

The great crystal reached down and lifted her gently to her feet. "Then lean on me until you have regained your balance."

The dizziness had disappeared, but Kate still felt very wobbly. She rested for a moment against the broad body of the Nurse Crystal, not yet daring to stand alone.

"If the Voice is so powerful, why is it so afraid of me? I'm nothing more than a tiny flea, compared to a giant elephant. And what does it want with Grandfather?"

"Only you can answer the first question. But as to the second question, the answer is clear. The Voice is not yet immortal. It is almost there, but not quite. The future of this star now hangs on the thinnest of threads."

The Nurse Crystal paused, her intricately carved arms glistening in the dim light. "The Voice has been held in check by an alliance of many beings, great and small, near and far. We prefer music to thunder; we prefer the living universe to a living body; and we prefer even death to eternal stagnation. We have mustered all our strength, as has the Voice, and we have wrestled with each other until we have finally arrived at a complete and absolute stalemate. If only one additional drop of heartlight joins with the Voice, it will tilt the scales enough to destroy the Pattern. But the heartlight must be given by a being with free will, or it cannot change the balance."

Kate was thunderstruck. "So that's why the Voice wants Grandfather! It's going to ask him for his heartlight!"

"It has already asked," corrected the Nurse Crystal as she cast a worried glance skyward. "And your grandfather has very nearly accepted."

"No!" objected Kate, taking a few halting steps. She turned to face the crystalline creature. "He wouldn't do that. He knows too much!"

"He knows many facts. But his great knowledge may obscure his own wisdom. He may not realize that if he sides with the Voice, he will destroy the Pattern. And something more. He will also destroy his own heartlight."

"What do you mean by that?"

The Nurse Crystal bent lower so that her hexagonal face was almost touching Kate's. "Once heartlight is given, it can never be returned."

Kate stepped backward. "That means—that means he would die."

"No, Kate. It means something much worse. His heartlight would be *lost*. It would pass out of the universe . . . forever."

"But I thought heartlight could never be lost!"

"It can be lost if the Pattern is broken."

"No," Kate protested. "We must stop him!"

"The Voice must move swiftly if it is to succeed. If it does not cross the edge into immortality very soon, it cannot sustain itself much longer. The natural forces of the universe—the workings of the Pattern—will eventually win out. If, however, it can manage to swallow one more modicum of heartlight, then it would break the bonds of mortality and the Pattern as well. It would become a gluttonous monster squeezing the heartlight out of every living thing in its path. Already, just to sustain itself until it gets the heartlight it needs, it is consuming more pure condensed light than even the Celethoes can produce. So it has started to siphon the pure condensed light away from other stars."

"The Sun!" exclaimed Kate in horror. "Is that what's happening to the Sun?"

"Yes. The star you call the Sun is one of those whose energy is being stolen."

"And Morpheus and Orpheus. The Voice stole their light, too?"

"No doubt. But while light can be stolen, heartlight cannot. It must be given freely. And if your Grandfather is not stopped, I fear that is what he will do. Then the Voice will have won, and the Pattern itself will begin to unravel. The Voice will continue to grow like a deadly cancer until it has, finally, consumed or destroyed every drop of heartlight in the universe."

"We must reach him. You've got to help me reach him!"

The Nurse Crystal's eyes darkened. "If you try to reach him, Kate, you will have to do it alone. We crystals lost whatever powers might have been useful in our battle to save you. We are powerless now to do anything more than to keep our own heartlights aligned with the True Music. I'm afraid there is nothing more we can do."

"Then there's no hope at all."

"Kate," whispered the small voice of Ariella, who was tugging on her hand. "I won't let the Voice do anything to hurt you."

But Kate felt no comfort. "I want to do something," she whispered. "But what? I can't fly to him without Morpheus. I can't reach him with my thoughts—he's too far away. And you're right: Look what happened the last time I got in the Voice's way. It almost finished me for good."

An air of despair crept over Kate like a heavy fog. She felt small, powerless, and alone. Glancing at her butterfly ring, she saw that it had continued to deteriorate, despite having lost its luster. Now only a quarter of one wing remained! Soon, she realized, the ring would vanish entirely—and with it would vanish any slim chance she might have ever to see the Earth again.

"Are you sure you can't reach your grandfather with your thoughts?" asked Ariella.

"Even if I could reach him, what would I say?" She fought back her rising tears. "And he's so far away behind the clouds! Oh, Ariella, what can I do?"

A small voice spoke from her feet. "You can love him."

The words pierced Kate through. "Yes. I love him. And I would give up anything for him. Even my—"

"No," interrupted the Nurse Crystal. "We cannot accept your heartlight."

Her face fell. "But you said one drop of heartlight on the side of the Voice would tilt the scales. So if I give my heartlight to the side of the True Music before Grandfather—"

"We cannot accept it." The Nurse Crystal's eyes were deeply loving, but her voice was firm. "Your heartlight is your own, and it does not belong to this star. Our laws will not allow us to take it, even to save Trethoniel."

"But the Voice will take Grandfather's heartlight!" objected Kate.

"The Voice does not live by our laws," replied the crystal. "And the laws have an essential purpose. The death and new life we will experience if Trethoniel returns to the Pattern will be far better than the endless life the Voice will experience if it does not."

Suddenly Kate recalled the mysterious words of the Sage of Sauria: *There are two kinds of death for a star, and they are as different as hope is different from despair.*

A painful realization then struck her. "If we somehow stop the Voice, then Trethoniel and its whole system will die, won't it?"

The Nurse Crystal's voice grew smaller, almost as

small as Ariella's. "Yes. Trethoniel will die instantly."

"And everything that's part of it? This planet? You and the other Nurse Crystals, too?"

"Everything."

"But that's terrible! That means Ariella . . ."

"Yes," the Nurse Crystal answered, in a tone of voice that reminded Kate of the True Music. "All of us will die."

"But how can that be good?" she demanded. "This Pattern is crazy! How is that any different from being swallowed up by The Darkness?"

"It is totally different. The Darkness is the opposite of the Pattern, a creature made of negative energy that has grown as the Voice has grown. The Voice has used it as a tool, but what it does not know is that The Darkness is really part of itself, just as an arm is part of the body that bears it. And The Darkness contains the seeds of the Voice's ultimate destruction. Today, it is merely a slave; ultimately, it will grow so powerful that it will consume the Voice itself."

"So the Voice will finally end up in a big black hole?"

"No," corrected the Nurse Crystal. "A black hole still belongs to the Pattern. It may be unfathomably dark and deep, but it is still part of reality. The Darkness, by contrast, is negating reality. A black hole merely transforms heartlight; The Darkness consumes it."

"Isn't there any other way?"

The crystalline creature looked at Kate remorsefully. "Not in this universe. No, there is no other way. The Pattern is not crazy. It is only very difficult to accept. I cannot live beyond my time, nor can any other being. Not without robbing something else of life. Not without upsetting the grand balance. I have lived a full and beautiful life."

"And I have lived a beautiful life," said Ariella bravely. "Just not a full one."

"Dear child," spoke her mother as she plucked her gently from the velvet floor. "I pray your story has some chapters yet to be written."

The Nurse Crystal turned again to Kate. "You are fast running out of time, if you still wish to try to stop your grandfather. Even as we speak, he is preparing to give his heartlight to the Voice. Gather all of your strength, Kate, then finally decide whether you truly want to risk such grave danger to yourself. No one would ever fault you if you do not."

Nervously, Kate tossed her braid over her shoulder. "If the Voice is really stopped, will that bring the Sun back to health?"

"We can't be sure. But if the Voice can be stopped before the Pattern is broken, it is possible—just possible—that all the pure condensed light it has stolen could flow back to its natural home, wherever that home may be."

"And that would return the Sun to health?"

"If my guess is correct, yes."

Kate drew a deep breath and stood erect. "I've got to try. But what can I do?"

"You can try to speak to your grandfather," answered the great crystal. "You can try to reach him, to talk with him, to help him hear his own deepest heart."

"But he's so far away! I can't hear his thoughts at all any more." Kate raised her troubled eyes to the dense clouds billowing above them.

"Perhaps you have not listened hard enough," suggested the Nurse Crystal.

"All I really want is to be someplace safe with him again," said Kate wistfully.

"I hope you will be one day. Right now, all you can do is try to reach him, if you dare."

"I don't know . . . I don't know . . ." Again she felt the sting of doubt and despair.

Ariella leaped from her mother's arms and hung in the air, suspended before Kate's face. She twinkled and gleamed like a miniature star. For an instant Kate wondered whether there could be microscopic worlds and creatures living on Ariella, creatures as small in relation to the crystal as the crystal was to the star.

Ariella's round eyes shone softly. "Trust, Kate. Trust in yourself."

Then the memory of the Sage of Sauria returned, and Kate heard again her final words: *If you trust in the Pattern, you trust in yourself. And if you trust in yourself, your voice holds all the power of truth.*

Bravely, she turned to face the spot in the darkened clouds where she imagined Grandfather now stood.

XVII

Grandfather's Choice

Grandfather studied what little remained of his ring. But he found no comfort, only the painful memory of the loved one he had lost.

"We must act!" thundered the Voice. "Will you join us?"

"I will help you," said Grandfather, speaking slowly and deliberately. "I will do as you wish. But first, I need you to answer just one last question. Before I go out of the universe altogether, I must understand. Forgive me, but I am still a scientist."

"What is your question?" the impatient Voice demanded.

"I am troubled by just one thing. If you continue to live forever, because of my heartlight—"

"And if you delay any longer, I will collapse and die! I will perish absolutely!"

"Yes, I know," continued Grandfather, thinking hard. "Just answer this question, and my heartlight is yours. Tell me why, if you continue to live forever, is not your energy displacing some other life in the universe? If energy is conserved, not destroyed—"

"Nonsense!" boomed the Voice, with such force that the globe jolted and Grandfather lost his balance for an instant. "You are asking for a class in the last eight billion years of developments in physics. I cannot answer your question in the time left to us. We may already be too late!"

"Prancer!" scolded Ratchet's raspy voice. "Didn't I teach you to overcome your doubts in order to pursue the truth? Haven't you learned anything about the way science works? Put your questions aside. We will deal with them later."

"All right. All right. No more questions."

"You are very wise, Doctor Miles Prancer," said the Voice in its most soothing tone. "Great scientist that you are, you will appreciate the most fundamental fact of all. This is an issue of life against death! Do you side with life, or do you side with death?"

At last, Grandfather's mind was clear. "I side with life, Great Star. With your life and the life of my lost Kaitlyn."

He drew in a deep breath, and opened his arms to the swelling mists. "I am yours, Trethoniel! You can take my heart—"

"No!" cried a young girl's voice from far away. "Grandfather, don't do it!"

He dropped his arms. "Kaitlyn!" he called, tears filling his eyes. "Kaitlyn, you're alive! You're alive!"

"Yes, Grandfather! I am alive. Don't do it, Grandfather. Don't listen to the Voice! Remember the music we heard . . . That is the true voice of—"

"Stop!" roared the Voice, with a force that rocked the globe and sent Grandfather sprawling backward. "Do not listen to that voice! It is not her, but an imposter! It is the voice of the Enemy!"

"It doesn't feel like an imposter," objected Grandfather as he struggled to get back up. "It feels like Kaitlyn!"

"It is the Enemy!" bellowed the Voice. "It is the voice of Death! Do not allow your longing to obscure your reason! Give me your heartlight now!"

Grandfather's turmoil swelled until he felt like he would explode. "What do I do?" he cried into the churning clouds.

"Give us your heartlight!" commanded Ratchet. "Do it now!"

"Don't do it, Grandfather!" came the voice of Kate, shrill and urgent. "The Voice doesn't value any life but its own. It's destroying the Sun, just to feed itself."

"That is a lie!" roared the Voice. "Do not believe the Enemy! Give me your heartlight before it is too late!"

*   *   *

"Don't do it, Grandfather!" cried Kate, straining to reach him telepathically. She leaned against the Nurse Crystal for support. "Don't—"

At that instant, she started coughing. The terrible

coldness was coming back, creeping into her heart-light. She felt a dark and evil force reaching deep into her chest, squeezing, squeezing hard.

"What's happening?" screamed Ariella in fright. "Kate! Kate! What's happening to you?"

Smash! The great dome was rocked by a gigantic blow, like a terrible earthquake.

"The Darkness!" exclaimed the Nurse Crystal. "It's trying to break through the dome!"

Smash!

The terrible tail of The Darkness slammed violently into the dome, and the vibrations nearly knocked Kate and the Nurse Crystal to the ground. Pieces of jagged green crystal showered on them from above.

Then Ariella screamed in terror and pointed to the dome. The electric red eye was scanning them through a crack in the crystal.

But Kate did not look up. She was struggling with another foe—an invisible foe.

"Grandfather!" she choked, trying desperately to keep herself from coughing. "Follow your heart!"

She fell to one knee. "Follow the Pattern!" she cried before another spasm of coughing made her collapse to all fours.

"Grand—" she began, when another blow exploded overhead, cutting her off. A gigantic crack appeared in the dome, and the tip of the deadly tail began to probe inside.

Suddenly, Kate felt very dizzy. She couldn't breathe anymore without coughing. Her face was on the floor and the world was going dark.

With her last ounce of energy, she pulled herself back into consciousness. It was all she could do to send one final message to Grandfather. She was too weak to wonder whether it would ever reach him. She coughed savagely, then fell totally silent.

*　　*　　*

"Give me your heartlight before it is too late!"

"Don't do it, Grandfather!" called Kate, sounding weaker than before.

The old man was completely torn. "Dear God!" he exclaimed. "What should I do?"

"Grandfather!" cried Kate's voice, suddenly stronger again. "Give your heartlight to the star! Do as the Voice tells you!"

"Kaitlyn!" he screamed into the whirling winds. "Are you now saying I should give up my heartlight?"

"Yes!" came the response, clear and strong. "The other voice was just an imposter! I am alive, Grandfather, but not for long! Give your heartlight to the star and I will survive!"

Now Grandfather knew exactly what to do. "Trethoniel!" he declared. "I give you my—"

Then a different voice halted him.

"No!" cried another Kate, sounding much weaker this time. "That's not my voice. That's an imitation. Grandfather, please . . . Follow your heart."

With all his concentration, Grandfather listened to the competing voices. "Kaitlyn! Kaitlyn!" he cried, tears streaming down his cheeks. "Which voice is yours? Give me a sign!"

"Save me, Grandfather," called the stronger Kate,

beginning to choke with coughing. "Save us all before it's too late!"

"Follow your heart, Grandfather. Follow the Pattern," pleaded the weaker Kate, now barely audible.

"Give us your heartlight now!" bellowed the Voice.

"Give us your heartlight!" echoed Ratchet.

"Save me! Save us all!" screamed the stronger Kate.

"Follow the Pattern . . ." whispered the weaker Kate.

Grandfather's face twisted in pain. He closed his eyes, trying desperately to concentrate.

"Save me! Save us all!" cried one Kate.

"Follow the . . ." began the other Kate, before fading away entirely.

Grandfather strained to hear the final words of the weaker Kate. But no more words came. He could hear nothing but the wailing winds. Then, in the far, far distance, he heard a small voice whisper hoarsely:

All praise to thee my Lord this night . . .

"Make your choice!" roared the Voice. "Make it now!"

The winds screamed. Grandfather opened his eyes. He lifted his arms high above his head, and cried: "I choose the Pattern! I choose love! And I love you, Kaitlyn! I love you with all my heart!"

XVIII

Revenge of The Darkness

A blinding flash of light seared the starscape. Thunder and electricity erupted everywhere. Crystals cracked, then dissolved into nothingness; mists sizzled and exploded with luminous lightning. The great cape of colored gases began to whirl about itself in a storm of devastating frenzy.

"Fool!" cried the Voice above the din. "Mortal fool! You have doomed us all!"

Wild winds lashed Grandfather. A floating crystal burst just above him, pelting the globe with flying fragments.

"Oh, my God," he moaned. "What have I done?"

"You have destroyed me!" screamed the Voice. "You have destroyed me and all of my works!"

"Prancer, you idiot," called the strained voice of Ratchet. "I sacrificed so much—and for what? For nothing! All because of you. You and that—"

His words were cut off by a wave of explosions that originated deep within Trethoniel itself. The raging surface of the star shook violently, sending blazing towers of fire in all directions.

"I can survive no longer," called the Voice, now barely audible above the great cacophony. "But if Death the Enemy takes me, it will also take—" A new wave of explosions buried the Voice's last words.

At that instant, the globe began to vibrate. The intensity grew and grew until it shook so violently that Grandfather fell on his side. Suddenly, it exploded into tiny pieces, hurling him into space.

"Hellllp!" His scream was swallowed by the shrieking winds.

As the clouds crackled with electricity, Grandfather spun madly downward toward Trethoniel. Helplessly he flailed as the forces of wind and fire tossed and bounced him. All about him the majesty of the star was disintegrating. Down, down he tumbled, faster every second, toward the seething surface of Trethoniel.

"Forgive me, Kaitlyn!" he cried.

A jagged blast of lightning ripped across the sky, illuminating everything.

Just then Grandfather glimpsed something breaking through the clouds. Torn by the angry winds, the object bobbed like a kite crafted of luminescent paper. Closer and closer it came, fighting vigorously against the storm.

"Orpheus!"

"I am coming!" called the butterfly, his powerful wings beating furiously.

With a swoop, Orpheus dove underneath him and gradually slowed his fall. Grandfather embraced the sleek, strong body and felt the rhythmic beating of the great wings, wings that flashed with the light of ten million prisms.

"Orpheus, you're back!"

The long antennae waved happily in response. "The Pattern has returned, and so have I."

Grandfather looked at his ring. The remaining slice of a wing was glowing again, pulsing with its old iridescence.

Another flash of lightning illuminated the starscape.

"Where is Kaitlyn?" cried Grandfather above the whirling winds.

*   *   *

Like a meteor, Morpheus sailed through the gaping hole in the great green dome that had once shielded Broé San Sauria from all intruders. As he scanned the scene below, he saw instantly there was no time to spare.

The Darkness had condensed its anti-light into a writhing body, whose blackness was broken only by the glowing red eye at one end. Slithering across the floor like a monstrous serpent of the void, it left behind the shattered bodies of three Nurse Crystals who had dared to stand in its way. Victims of the terrible tail, the smashed crystals lay in jagged pieces, their light forever extinguished.

Only one Nurse Crystal, Ariella's mother, still survived. Like a sturdy tree planted firmly in the soil of its birthplace, the Nurse Crystal stood as the last barrier between The Darkness and its ultimate prey: the girl who lay sprawled on the floor behind her. Morpheus realized with horror that Kate's motionless form lay completely unprotected, except for the lone Nurse Crystal and another much smaller crystal who was shielding Kate's face.

"Ariella!" cried her mother, not daring to take her eyes off the deadly tail that was coiling again to strike. "Get away from here. The Darkness will destroy you, just like the others."

"I won't go," answered Ariella. "Not without you. Not without Kate!"

"All we can do is hold off The Darkness as long as we can. If the Pattern has been restored, The Darkness will start losing strength. I only pray it happens soon—before we're all destroyed." Quickly, the Nurse Crystal glanced to the rear, and her deep silver eyes met Ariella's. "I love you, my child, and nothing will ever change that."

Suddenly the tail of The Darkness lashed out, and the air crackled with negative energy. At the same time, Ariella's mother stretched herself like a massive cloak, her long arms shielding Ariella and Kate.

Craaaack! With a searing explosion, the deadly whip came crashing down directly into the Nurse

Crystal. She burst into pieces, sending up a flare of white light so brilliant that it stunned The Darkness momentarily.

The dark creature quivered for an instant, dissipating slightly. Then, with a flash of its red eye, it solidified again and started to coil its tail once more.

Morpheus blasted into battle. His wings accelerated to all-out speed, despite the injury from his last encounter with The Darkness. He would not be outraced again. Either this creature would know the pain of death—or Morpheus would himself.

The evil eye of The Darkness, sizzling with negativity, pulsed with rage as it prepared to strike the final blow. To the extent The Darkness perceived thoughts of any kind, it was unified and propelled by a single idea: revenge. Gathering every last shred of its destructive powers, the gargantuan tail coiled itself tightly for the attack.

Then the tail released, slashing through the air toward the helpless body of Kate. Ariella stood as tall as she could, stretching her arms wide as her mother had done. But she could only hope to shield a tiny fraction of the target.

Craaaack!

Morpheus flew directly into the evil eye, as an explosion of negative lightning ripped the air.

The force of the direct hit knocked the tail slightly off course, and it crashed to the floor just wide of Kate and Ariella. Chunks of green crystal fell from above, shaken loose by the impact.

The Darkness shuddered, as if a mighty sword had sliced through its brain. Then a wave of distant explosions, so powerful that they shook the entire planet of Nel Sauria, reverberated inside the green dome. The Darkness released a deep and painful rumbling, a sound so low it was beyond all pitch.

Slowly, the threads of negative energy binding The Darkness together began to loosen, and its body began to dissipate. The raging red eye flared in pain and then started to fade steadily, while a web of negative energy crackled around it. The tail, motionless at last, grew rapidly thinner.

Morpheus fell to the floor with a thud, his wings badly torn. Weakly, he crawled away from The Darkness and toward Kate.

At that instant, she opened her eyes. The first sight she saw was the red eye glowing hatefully.

"Help!" she shrieked, rolling over to her side.

"You're safe now, Kate," said a familiar melodic voice. "The Darkness has lost its power."

"Morpheus! You're back!" Still groggy, Kate sat up and hugged the neck of the great butterfly. "I'm so glad you're here!" She glanced fretfully at the evaporating form of The Darkness and shivered. "Are you sure we're safe?"

"Kaitlyn!" called a new voice from high above her head.

"Grandfather!" she answered, seeing him sailing through the cracked crystal dome.

As Orpheus settled to the floor, the old man slid

from his perch and ran to her. Kate quickly clambered to her feet.

"Thank you," whispered Grandfather, as he stroked her braid lovingly. "Thank you and bless you."

"You heard me," cried Kate happily. "You really heard me!"

"Yes," laughed Grandfather. "And so did the star."

Suddenly, Kate's eyes fell upon the hunched figure of Ariella, bending over her mother's shattered body. Instantly the joy of their reunion melted away. She pulled free of Grandfather's embrace and darted over to her.

Taking the weeping snow crystal in her arms, Kate viewed the ghastly remains of the Nurse Crystal who had restored her life—and her hope. For a while she said nothing, as her own tears mingled with Ariella's.

Gently, she set down the small crystal, whose soulful eyes were saturated with pain. "I'm so—"

Craaaack!

With a flash of negative energy, the fading tail of The Darkness raised itself once again. Sensing Kate's presence, it slithered swiftly toward her, searing the very air as it moved.

"Run!" cried Grandfather.

Kate instantly leaped to the side, but Ariella, still immersed in her grief, did not move.

From out of the shadows, a small form rushed to Ariella and pushed her aside, just a split second before the tail smashed violently on the very spot where she had been standing.

Kate turned to see who had saved her. "Spike!" she cried, amazed to see him alive again. "It's you!"

The columnar crystal bowed awkwardly, due to the portion of his base that was missing.

"That's the bravest thing you've ever done," said Ariella, eyeing him thankfully.

"Let's not get carried away," he replied. "It takes a lot of bravery just to hang around you, even for a few minutes."

Ariella's misty eyes almost smiled.

At that instant, The Darkness crackled and stirred once again. Kate, Ariella, and Spike backed away quickly as the tail, now a thin version of its former self, rose straight up into the air. It hung there for a moment, swaying from side to side, as if it were shaking an angry fist at its conquerors.

Then it fell to the floor, leaving a thin trail of darkness in its wake. It lay there, quivering slightly, as it faded into nothing more than a transparent veil. For an instant, only the red eye of The Darkness remained, glowing feebly. Finally, with a sizzling sound, it disappeared completely.

The Darkness had departed.

Whether the creature of the void had truly died or had merely withdrawn to some other part of the universe, Kate could not tell. All she knew was that her heart leaped at seeing it go; all she hoped was that it had gone forever.

"We've got to leave, Kaitlyn." Grandfather's voice was filled with urgency. "The star has returned to the Pattern, and that means it's beginning to collapse." He looked at his ring: Only a small sliver of the right wing remained. It seemed to be disintegrating before his very eyes. "Let's go."

"But how?" cried Kate, seeing for the first time the tattered wings of her butterfly. "Morpheus! Your wings are ripped to pieces."

"Orpheus and I have already devised a plan," said Morpheus with a graceful swish of his antennae. "You and your grandfather will both ride on my brother's back."

"What?" exclaimed Kate. "And leave you behind?"

The antennae waved sadly. "I fear I won't ever fly again, Kate."

She stepped to the side of the great butterfly and placed her hand upon his neck. "I don't want to go without you."

"You must, Kate," Morpheus replied. "I will stay here with Ariella, who will remind me of the cartwheels I could once perform."

"But the star is collapsing," objected Grandfather. "If you stay here, you'll be destroyed along with everything else."

"I have no choice but to stay," answered Morpheus. He turned again to Kate, and his broken wings rustled like the leaves of a stricken elm tree. "I will miss you. It was an honor to fly with you on my back."

"If only we had more time," said Ariella with regret. "Then perhaps I could find some way to heal you. But time is the one thing we don't have."

Kate stroked the black fur of Morpheus' neck. "I don't want to leave you."

"Come, Kaitlyn." Grandfather's voice was firm. He took her hand and helped her climb onto the back of Orpheus. Then he slid into position behind her, wrapping his arms tightly around her waist.

"Are you sure you can carry us?" he asked Orpheus.

"I can carry you," answered the butterfly bravely. "It is my grief that is now too heavy to carry." Orpheus waved his antennae toward Morpheus. "My brother, when will we meet again?"

The multifaceted eyes of Morpheus gazed at him somberly. "I don't know."

Through her swelling tears, Kate could see Ariella leap into the air. The snow crystal floated before her face and gently touched Kate's cheek with a single delicate arm.

"Ariella . . ." began Kate, but Ariella already knew her thought.

"I will miss you, too," said the shining snow crystal, her own eyes brimming with tears.

Suddenly, Kate removed her butterfly ring and placed it into Ariella's cupped hand. Simultaneously she reached for Grandfather's ring, which was on his hand at her waist, and grasped it firmly. As she had hoped, she remained heartlight because she was still touching Grandfather's ring.

"That's dangerous, Kaitlyn," said Grandfather sternly. "If you should let go of my ring while we're in flight—even for an instant—you'll perish immediately."

"I know," she replied. "But I want Ariella to have my ring. Something to remember me by."

"Are you sure?" asked Ariella. "I don't need your ring to remember Kate of the Ring."

"I'm sure," answered Kate. "I want you to have it. Maybe—just maybe—it will give you a little more time. Maybe you can even find a way to heal Morpheus! Please take it."

"But Kaitlyn—"

"I want to do this, Grandfather."

Seeing she was unshakable, the old man shrugged in resignation. "All right, if you feel you must. But Kaitlyn . . . at least do this for me. You take my ring to wear, and let me hold on to you."

Kate studied him closely for a moment, then nodded. She took Grandfather's ring and slipped it on as he laid his large hand over her own.

Ariella clasped Kate's ring, her silver eyes sparkling. "I love you," she whispered. Then she dropped to the floor next to Morpheus and cried: "Farewell, dear friends! You have saved our star, now save yourselves!"

With that Orpheus began to climb. As they approached the splintered dome, Kate could hear the wild storm raging outside. She looked below to catch one final glimpse of Ariella. To her surprise, the tiny crystal was growing steadily brighter. As Ariella's radiance increased, she began to glow like a small star. Gradually, she grew so luminous that she seemed to be made more of light than of snow.

"I hope we still have enough time," said Grandfather.

Kate, however, wasn't listening. "I love you, Ariella," she said quietly. "And I always will."

XIX

The Black Hole

A devastating blast of supercharged lightning seared the sky. Crimson clouds billowed and the winds whirled about them with gathering fury.

"It feels like everything is falling apart!" cried Kate, as an octagonal crystal burst into pieces directly above them.

"It is," called Orpheus above the din. His antennae waved frantically, searching urgently to find his bearings in the swirling storm.

Boom! Boom! Boom! rolled the thunder of distant explosions, sending shock waves in every direction. Lightning sizzled through the starscape and brightly glowing gas was everywhere. Cannons of destruction sounded continuously.

Boom! Boom!
Boom! Boom!

Grandfather gripped the ring on Kate's hand ever more tightly. Another bolt of lightning ripped across the sky. Crystals exploded on all sides.

Orpheus struggled to stay on course, but the stellar gale was intensifying. Furiously he beat his wide wings, pushing himself as hard as he could.

Kate watched the powerful wings laboring, as her worries mounted. What if one of these explosions knocked Grandfather's hand off the ring? Why did Orpheus seem to be slowing down?

The starscape flared with electricity.

"Grandfather!" she cried. "What's wrong with Orpheus?"

His face was ashen. "He is struggling."

"Against what?"

"Against the most powerful physical force in the universe."

"A black hole?"

He grimaced. "We may be too late to escape."

As the great butterfly strained to carry them forward, Kate realized that everything around them was being pulled backward into the deep funnel of darkness forming to their rear. Gas clouds, crystals, asteroids—all were being sucked into the center of the collapsing star.

"No!" she cried in terror, as Grandfather's description of a black hole flashed like lightning across her mind: *a force so powerful not even light can escape . . .*

Orpheus forged ahead with every ounce of his

strength. His wide wings beat frantically, but his progress diminished steadily. Now they were hardly moving forward at all.

"He can't keep this up much longer. We're barely staying even. As the gravity increases—"

"Look!" shrieked Kate. "His wing. It's disappearing."

She pointed to Orpheus' right wing. The upper tip had vanished completely, as if it had been sliced off by a knife.

"My God! We'll never—"

Zzzzappp!

A sizzling explosion of brilliant white light crashed across the sky. So bright was the blast, much more powerful than anything they had seen, that it seemed to freeze everything instantaneously. The winds died, the wings of Orpheus ceased beating, and Kate felt she could not even blink an eye. Everything around them stopped moving, frozen completely, as if time itself had been suspended, and with it, the collapse of the star. The only sound they could hear was no sound at all: Pure silence surrounded them.

Suddenly, the luminous wings began to surge.

"We're moving!" Kate cried.

Grandfather shook his head in amazement. "I don't understand."

Orpheus flew swiftly, despite his sliced wing. They left star and storm far behind, still suspended in space and time. Soon they had passed the outermost wisps of Trethoniel's multicolored veil.

At length, when they had reached a safe distance, Orpheus glided to a halt. With a graceful swoop, the butterfly turned to face the star.

Trethoniel was bathed in a new illumination, a silvery light that glowed and shimmered. Something about it reminded Kate of Ariella's eyes. Then, welling up from the heart of the star, a beautiful sound came wafting toward them.

Floating in open space, they listened once again to Trethoniel's magnificent music. As the melody radiated from the star, it felt—if such a thing were possible—even more full and beautiful than before. The undertone of tragedy no longer fought against the melody, but joined it, enriched it, deepened it.

Then, as the music swelled in power, something miraculous occurred. Very gradually, graceful wisps of golden light began to form around Trethoniel, encircling it in lovely luminescence. Pure condensed light. Slowly, as if they were waltzing with the music itself, the broadening beams of light began to undulate, twirl, then flow outward into space. Forming great glistening arcs, they stretched, like rainbows made of fiery filament, far into the galaxy.

One of those luminous arcs, both Kate and Grandfather knew, would eventually reach all the way to the Sun.

"You did it, Grandfather," said Kate softly. "You saved the Sun."

The bushy eyebrows lifted. "No, Kaitlyn. You did."

Kate shifted uncomfortably on Orpheus' back. "I

guess I had something to do with it," she acknowledged. Then she asked: "What happened back there? When everything stopped so suddenly?"

"I've been wondering about that myself," he replied, still studying the star. "Sometimes a collapsing star will reach a point of temporary equilibrium that makes it stop before collapsing any further." He grinned. "But that's just ordinary physics. And I have a feeling that something more than physics was at work there."

"But how could it happen? I thought nothing in the universe is strong enough to escape a black hole."

The old man's eyes sparkled. "I guess there is one force in the universe even more powerful than a black hole."

"Look. It's collapsing again!"

With a flash of light, the star began to swirl once again in an ever-tightening spiral. Smaller and smaller it compressed, until finally only a tiny speck of brilliance remained. For an instant it glowed bright, then vanished completely, taking the music with it. Where once the realm of Trethoniel had graced the sky, only a point of impenetrable blackness remained.

For a timeless moment, they gazed in silence at the empty spot.

"Grandfather," spoke Kate at last, "do you think there's any chance—any chance at all—that Ariella could have survived? Maybe even Morpheus? Perhaps the ring . . ."

Gently, he squeezed her waist. "Only God knows the answer to that one, Kaitlyn."

"If they are gone," she said somberly, "the universe has lost some very beautiful voices."

Grandfather sighed. "Yes, they were magnificent. But . . . somewhere else in the universe, some new voices will be born."

"Do you really believe that?"

"Yes, Kaitlyn. For the first time in my life, I truly do." He placed his cheek against hers and whispered: "I believe that every living thing has a time to die, as well as a time to be born. That goes for stars, people, and chrysanthemums, too. The important thing is that they flowered beautifully while they were alive."

Something about his tone of voice was profoundly disturbing, and Kate instinctively placed her free hand upon his and squeezed. Hoping to change the subject, she said: "I think it's impossible to have an experience like this without it changing your whole life."

"That's right," he agreed. "Whatever kind of adult you might have been before, I think you'll be different now—just because you were foolish enough to follow me on a four-minute trip."

"I inherited a certain amount of foolishness from my grandfather, you know," she replied. "What do you really think I'll be when I grow up?"

Grandfather gazed thoughtfully at the wing of Orpheus, glistening in the starlight. Eventually, a white eyebrow lifted. "I think you'll grow up to be a wise and wonderful woman. A lot like your grandmother, as a matter of fact. You'll be a mother, and your children will love to hear you tell them about the stars. And—now I'm going out on a limb—I would venture you'll also become an accomplished meteorologist."

"A what?"

"A scientist who studies the weather, both on Earth and other places. What's more," he added, "your special expertise will be the formation of snow crystals."

Kate couldn't help but grin. "I love you, Grandfather."

The old man looked at her fondly. "I love you, too, Kaitlyn." He smiled. "And I always will."

Suddenly, Orpheus shook his antennae worriedly. "Our time is nearly gone," he declared. "If you wish to return to Earth—"

"Heavens!" exclaimed Grandfather, feeling only the slightest sliver of a wing left on the turquoise band. "The ring is nearly gone. Take us home, Orpheus!"

The great butterfly's wings burst into action, flashing in the starlight, as the old astronomer held tightly to Kate's hand that bore the vanishing ring.

XX

Chrysanthemums

As Kate opened her eyes, she found herself lying on the floor of Grandfather's lab. Smashed equipment, strewn papers, and broken bottles of chemicals lay everywhere; the entire place was in ruins.

Sitting up, she felt a dull pain throbbing in her head. *Must have been a hard landing. Maybe I hit my head . . .*

"Grandfather!" she called.

There came no response.

He's probably down in the kitchen. Making a new pot of tea or something.

At that instant, she heard a noise in the hallway. "Grandfather!" she cried.

Instead of Grandfather, a long reddish face with floppy ears appeared in the doorway.

"Cumberland!"

Before she could get up, Cumberland pounced on her. The retriever licked her face energetically, his prominent tail waving all the while. Then he started barking noisily.

"Enough, enough," she sputtered. "I'm glad to see you, too."

At last Kate freed herself from the dog's enthusiastic embrace. She clambered slowly to her feet. Surveying the wreckage of the lab, it seemed more and more strange that Grandfather wasn't anywhere to be seen.

It wasn't like him just to disappear like this, she thought, her uncertainty beginning to grow. It was almost like . . . like they had never left at all.

A pang of doubt shot through her. Was it all a fantastic dream? She rubbed her sore head again, wondering whether she had been knocked unconscious somehow. Could she have imagined the whole thing?

She stepped over a mass of twisted metal and glass that was once a laser, and with difficulty made her way to the door. Cumberland, who was already there, gave another loud bark. Then he turned and padded down the long hallway to the kitchen, limping slightly.

"Grandfather," called Kate.

Still no answer.

Increasingly unsure of anything, she followed Cumberland past the lengthy rows of bookshelves. As she entered the kitchen, her heart was pounding and she felt a mounting sense of dread.

She froze in midstep.

"Grandfather!"

There he was, seated in the old rocker. His white head leaned back against the chair and his eyes were closed. Both of his weathered hands fell limp to his sides.

"Oh, Grandfather!" Kate ran to his side and shook him by the shoulders. "Grandfather, please. Please wake up."

He didn't stir. Not even an eyebrow lifted in response.

"Oh, no!" cried Kate, kneeling by the rocker and burying her face in the faded picnic cloth that still covered his lifeless body. "Don't die, Grandfather," she wailed. "Please—please don't die."

For many minutes Kate wept, and the picnic cloth grew moist with her tears. "So it *was* just a dream," she sobbed. "Ariella and Morpheus and the Voice and everything."

She raised her head and looked sadly around the kitchen. How empty it seemed now. Her eyes fell to Cumberland, who was sitting by the rocker, nuzzling against Grandfather's leg.

She rubbed behind the devoted dog's ear. "There's nothing you can do to bring him back," she said dismally.

Cumberland turned toward her, and started licking her hand. Kate noticed for the first time that the cut on her wrist from the flying shard of glass had returned. The edge of her sweatshirt was stained with blood.

Then she saw what Cumberland was licking: Upon her finger rested a simple turquoise band.

Even in her grief, Kate's heart leaped. She reached for Grandfather's hand, the hand that had once worn the very same ring, the hand that had brought Morpheus and Orpheus into being. Tenderly, she kissed his hand, then placed it upon his chest.

She rose and walked slowly over to the telephone on the kitchen counter. Her ankle ached painfully, but the greater pain was in a place she could not touch. She dialed home; fortunately, her mother was there. All she had to say was the word *Grandfather*, and her mother knew something was dreadfully wrong.

"You just wait there, Kate, and we'll be right over. I'll take care of calling an ambulance."

"Thanks, Mom," she said, replacing the receiver.

Without any conscious thought, she walked past Grandfather's body and over to the kitchen door. She opened it and stepped into the chilly autumn air.

The sky looked gray and full of grief. Somberly, she shuffled along the flagstone walk in the direction of the garden. At last, she leaned against the old wooden gate, her heart heavy with loss.

There was the great stone fountain, and the patch of unruly grass where they had picnicked only yesterday. The chrysanthemums were still strong, but their colors seemed more muted than before. The grape arbor hung heavily, and the scent of its rotting fruit filled the garden. The air had grown colder and the sky darker.

Suddenly Kate felt a crisp breeze against her back. She glanced at the wintry clouds gathering overhead. It felt like the first snowfall of the season was about to begin.

Slowly, very slowly, a diffuse line of light stretched across the sky. With a strength as irresistible as the first sapling of spring pushing past the lingering snow, the line of light deepened and broadened. Then, with a flash, the Sun broke through the clouds.

Kate's gaze fell to a purple chrysanthemum. As she watched, a single petal dropped to the ground, spinning slowly as it fell.

THE ANCIENT ONE

To my mother,
GLORIA BARRON

With special appreciation to
DENALI,
age three, for the name Kandeldandel

PUFFIN BOOKS
Published by the Penguin Group
Penguin Group (USA) LLC
375 Hudson Street
New York, New York 10014

USA * Canada * UK * Ireland * Australia
New Zealand * India * South Africa * China

penguin.com
A Penguin Random House Company

First published in the United States of America by Philomel Books,
a division of The Putnam & Grosset Book Group, 1992
Published by Ace Books, a division of Penguin Group (USA) Inc., 2004
Published by Puffin Books, an imprint of Penguin Young Readers Group, 2014

THE LIBRARY OF CONGRESS HAS CATALOGED THE PHILOMEL BOOKS EDITION AS FOLLOWS:
Barron, T. A.
The Ancient One / by T. A. Barron
p. cm.
Companion vol. to: Heartlight.
Summary: While helping her Great Aunt Melanie try to protect an Oregon redwood forest from
loggers, thirteen-year-old Kate goes back five centuries through a time tunnel and faces the evil
creature Gashra, who is bent on destroying the same forest.
ISBN 978-0-399-21899-6
[1. Time travel—Fiction. 2. Conservation of natural resources—Fiction. 3. Fantasy.] I. Title.
PZ7.B27567An 1992 [Fic]—dc20 91-45862 CIP AC

This omnibus ISBN 978-0-14-751032-7

Printed in the United States of America

1 3 5 7 9 10 8 6 4 2

The Halamis, the Native American people who figure prominently in this book, are completely fictional. All aspects of their life, including their beliefs and their mysterious disappearance several centuries ago, were created exclusively for this book. For authenticity, certain aspects of their culture are drawn from the author's research into the history of actual residents of the region, including the Tolowa, Takelma, Coos, Yurok, Wiyot, Hupa, Karok, Coquille, and Tututni peoples.

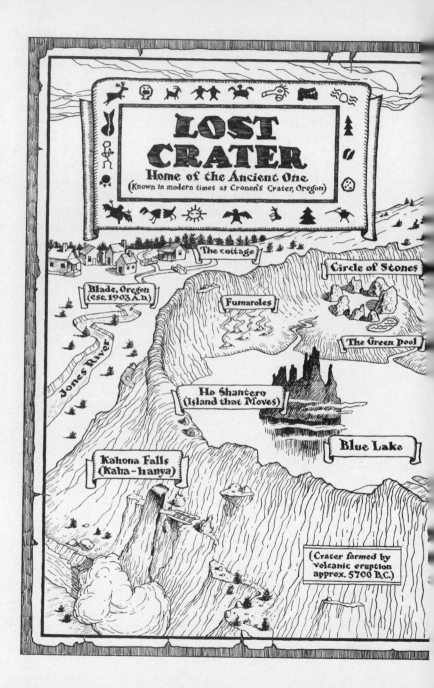

LOST CRATER

Home of the Ancient One

(Known in modern times as Cronon's Crater, Oregon)

The cottage

Circle of Stones

Blade, Oregon
(est. 1903 A.D.)

Fumaroles

The Green Pool

Ho Shantero
(Island that Moves)

Jones River

Blue Lake

Kahona Falls
(Kaha-hanya)

(Crater formed by
volcanic eruption
approx. 5700 B.C.)

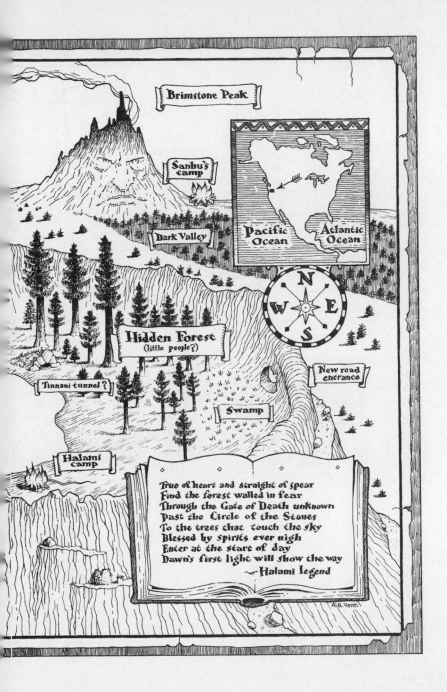

Brimstone Peak

Sanbu's camp

Dark Valley

Pacific Ocean

Atlantic Ocean

N
W E
S

Hidden Forest
(little people?)

New road entrance

Tinnani tunnel?

Swamp

Halami camp

True of heart and straight of spear
Find the forest walled in fear
Through the Gate of Death unknown
Past the Circle of the Stones
To the trees that touch the sky
Blessed by spirits ever nigh
Enter at the start of day
Dawn's first light will show the way
~ Halami legend

A.B. Venti

contents

PART ONE

Into the Crater

1

the brown envelope

FIRST, God created Rain. Then Drizzle. Then Mist, then Fog. And then: More Rain.

Kate smiled soggily at her own adaptation of the story of creation, Oregon style. Her sneakers were wet enough that they squelched like sponges as she walked. She could feel the warmish water sloshing between her toes. No use even trying to stay dry anymore.

She stepped deliberately into a muddy puddle that nearly filled the heavily rutted street. The splash of water slapped against her lower leg, pressing jeans against shin, as brown circles spread outward from her submerged sneaker. Only Aunt Melanie's bright green shoelaces, reluctantly accepted by Kate when her own ones broke, remained visible in the muddy water.

Water everywhere. At this very moment, she could be curled up by the fireplace, stroking the shaggy gray cat Atha. But Aunt Melanie, usually delighted to spend a rainy afternoon warmed by fire coals, quilts, and homemade spice tea, was in no mood for such things just now. Something was troubling her, something serious. So serious she didn't want to talk about it, even to Kate.

She had thought about calling her parents. They'd know what to do, what to make of all this. But they were on that ship, with only a radio telephone on board. Her mother had given her the number in case of an emergency, but Kate did not want to use it. She knew better than anyone how much they needed a few days together without telephone calls, faculty meetings, or research projects that kept them working until all hours. Besides, this was not an emergency, not yet anyway. She had to work this thing out on her own, without any help from Mom and Dad. And, she thought with a sigh, without any help from Grandfather.

A lone hound, squatting beneath a dripping wooden bench, shook himself vigorously. As Kate turned toward him, the dog ceased shaking and gazed back at her, watching her pass with expressionless eyes.

Just a few minutes ago, when Aunt Melanie had checked her watch and realized it was nearly five o'clock, she had beseeched Kate to run to the post office before it closed. Never mind the downpour, or the fact that Kate was warm and dry for the first time since arriving at the cottage five days ago. Muttering something about an important telephone call she had been waiting for all day, Aunt Melanie said she could not go herself. With an edge of urgency, she described the envelope she was expecting: long and brown, pretty thick, the kind lawyers like to use.

Why lawyers? Kate had asked, but her great-aunt didn't answer. She merely ran a hand through her curls of white hair and glanced out the window toward the dark reaches of forest beyond, where the whine of distant chain saws mingled with the sound of swishing branches. Then she had handed Kate her rain jacket and pulled open the cottage door.

Kate leaped across a small stream flowing through a rut, only to land with a splash in another puddle. Without the slightest pause, she continued walking. Her many visits to

Aunt Melanie over the years had developed in her a grudging appreciation for the gentle rains of this land. There was
something she had come to expect and even, at rare
moments, enjoy about the sound of soft rain on the old cottage roof, the awareness of lush greenery all around, the
mist against her cheeks. So much rain back home would
have depressed her thoroughly, especially if it meant can-
celing an after-school softball game. But here in the forest
country of southwestern Oregon, the rain felt no worse
than a nuisance. It was part of the landscape, just as much
as the trees.

Trudging onward, Kate surveyed the scene on Main
Street even as her mind played over and over again Aunt
Melanie's words. *Long and brown, pretty thick, the kind
lawyers like to use.* Although Blade, Oregon, didn't pretend
to be a booming metropolis, it could claim most of life's
necessities. Blurred by mud and mist, the storefronts seemed
to run together like an oversized watercolor painting. She
passed the local Laundromat, right next to the Texaco station, where townspeople often gathered for good conversation. This afternoon, though, it was deserted. The street
itself was strangely empty, nothing but a string of connected puddles.

As she turned the corner, the scene swiftly changed. A
jumble of cars, Jeeps, and mud-splattered pickups lined the
street outside of Cary's Tavern. There was even a logging
truck, bearing emblems of snarling tigers on its mud flaps,
double parked near the entrance. Of course, thought Kate.
It's Saturday afternoon. She had seen Cary's Tavern once
before on a Saturday—packed to the rafters with loggers,
fifty percent sober and one hundred percent boisterous,
celebrating the end of another hard week's work. Or, as
Aunt Melanie had told her was the case more and more,
mourning the end of another week without work.

As she approached the tavern, she could tell today's
mood was not one of celebration. She heard several angry
voices rising above the downpour. Several loggers, wearing

gray and yellow rain jackets, milled around outside in the parking lot despite the wetness. One pair sat behind slashing windshield wipers, engaged in heated conversation. But she had no time to investigate. It was five minutes to five.

Breaking into a jog, she splashed down the remaining block to the old brick building sporting a white cardboard sign in the window with the words *Post Office*. She scampered up the moss-coated wooden steps, slowing only to reach for the rusted door handle. At that instant, the door flung wide open and a lean, red-haired boy not much older than Kate's thirteen years darted out, clutching a parcel of some sort under his arm.

They plowed straight into each other. Kate tumbled backward down the slippery steps, landing on her back in the muddy street. The boy cried out in surprise, almost landing on top of her.

"Hey, watch where you're going," he said accusingly, wiping some mud from his cheek with the sleeve of his yellow rain jacket.

"Watch yourself," Kate retorted. Suddenly her eyes fell upon the parcel the boy had been carrying, now resting on the street only an arm's length away. It was an envelope, brown and shaped like a long rectangle. She caught her breath as she read the name clearly typed on the mailing label: *Melanie Prancer.*

The boy snatched up the brown envelope, rose quickly, and started running down the street in the direction of Cary's Tavern.

"Hey, come back," Kate shouted. She leaped to her feet and flew after him with the speed of a shortstop dashing to snag a line drive. They raced past the buildings of the town, their feet pounding through the puddles. Kate gained on him, but slowly. Just before the parking lot outside the tavern, the boy swerved toward the assembled vehicles.

Kate stretched out an arm and barely caught him by the collar of his rain jacket. She pulled, and the boy lurched backward, his feet sliding out from under him. Before he had even hit the ground, she was on top of him.

"Give me that," she demanded, pulling at the brown envelope.

"No way," answered the boy, struggling to hang on. He kicked at her savagely, spraying mud into the air.

Finally, Kate loosened his grip enough to yank the envelope away. Just then the boy rolled to his knees and butted against her with such force that she fell back into a deep puddle. The brown envelope skidded across the muddy street, coming to rest at the edge of a rut just outside the tavern. Kate crawled madly after it.

As her fingers started to close on the edge of the envelope, a heavy boot slammed down on top of it. At once, Kate knew it was the boot of a logger—beat-up brown leather, without steel toes because if a tree trunk falls on a logger's foot he prefers to have his toes crushed rather than sliced off by the steel lining. She raised her head, seeing the heavy denim pants, the burly chest wearing a yellow slicker over a white T-shirt saying *I love spotted owls—for dinner,* and the grinning face looking down on her from under a weather-beaten hard hat.

She tugged on the brown envelope. "It's mine," she said.

The boot did not budge. For a moment, nothing seemed to move but the grin, which widened slightly.

"Mine," repeated Kate, tugging unsuccessfully. "The envelope's mine."

The man, whose brown eyes watched the girl at his feet with amusement, spoke gruffly. "What envelope?"

Kate furrowed her brow. "This one, here. You're standing on it."

"I don't see any envelope," he answered. He turned toward an older boy standing nearby, as burly as himself but not as tall. "Sly, do you see any envelope?"

"No," the older boy answered, himself grinning. "All I see is my brother Billy, and some girl who likes to crawl around in mud puddles."

At that moment, the red-haired boy, his yellow slicker splattered with mud, moved to Billy's side. "Well," he said, eyeing Kate hatefully. "I brought you the envelope."

"Yeah," answered Sly, stepping closer to them. "But you brought her too."

"I couldn't help it," protested the red-haired boy, bending his lean frame to retrieve the brown envelope. Billy lifted his boot just enough to let him slide it out. "She chased me here from the post office."

The big logger gave him a teasing shove on the shoulder. "That's a new experience for you, getting chased by a girl." He winked at Sly. "He's so excited, he's still puffing like a bay steer."

Even in the rain, the boy's blush was clearly visible. "Look," he said, waving the envelope. "You asked me to get it, and I did. It wasn't so easy, either."

"You're a thief," declared Kate.

Billy's grin disappeared as he concentrated his gaze on her. "Go home now and there won't be any trouble."

Kate pushed herself to her feet. Her heart pounded, but she made herself look the broad-shouldered man directly in the eye. "That's not your envelope. It's not. It's addressed to my Aunt Melanie."

"Aunt Melanie?" asked Billy, his eyebrows lifting. "So you're related to the old schoolteacher?"

"Yes. And that envelope belongs to her."

Billy scowled at the red-haired boy. "You really botched this one, Jody." He stepped toward Kate, so that his ample chest almost touched her chin. "You've got five seconds to disappear, kid. Are you gonna go all by yourself, or do I have to chase you from here to hell's half acre?"

Before Kate could reply, a heavily laden logging truck rumbled down the street. The noise drowned out the voices from Cary's Tavern as it splashed past. Just as Billy, Sly, and Jody turned toward the sound, Kate lunged at the brown envelope, tearing it from Jody's hand. She darted behind the logging truck and ran as fast as she could down an alley behind the tavern.

Leaping over a broken crate, Kate could hear the slapping sound of heavy boots behind her. She grasped the brown envelope as tightly as she could, determined not to lose it again. Not even when she stole home plate in the league softball tournament in May had she run so fast. Yet the heavy boots drew closer by the second, smacking against the mud.

She didn't dare turn around. All her energy was focused on one thing and one thing only: running. For her life. Now she could hear someone's breathing drawing nearer. Seeing a corner just ahead, she didn't slow down even to make the turn.

As she rounded the corner, her foot suddenly slid out from under her. She lost her balance, flipping onto her back in a spray of brown water. Lifting her head, she saw Billy, followed by his brother and the red-haired boy, bearing down on her. Billy's eyes glared angrily as he ran right at her, barreling ahead like a fully loaded logging truck.

Kate rolled to her hands and knees in the deep puddle, still clutching the envelope. She wanted to scream, but her throat released no sound. Water dripped down her back and across her abdomen. She stiffened, preparing to be caught.

Then, unaccountably, Billy and the others ran straight past her, as if she weren't even there. The heavy boots slapped into the puddle, only inches from her submerged fingers, splashing muddy water in her eyes.

As she wiped her face with the inner collar of her jacket, she slowly lifted herself to her feet, panting heavily. Her pursuers turned a corner onto the next street, their pounding boots punctuating the steady sound of the rain. *How?* she asked in disbelief. *How did they miss me?*

At that instant, she heard a rustling sound behind her. Out from the shadows of the windowless building on the corner stepped a diminutive figure, whose curly white hair was visible at the edges of a tightly drawn hood. Holding in one hand a slender walking stick, the figure regarded her intently.

"Aunt Melanie," cried Kate, stumbling toward her. "Did you see that? They—they were chasing me. But when— when I fell, they—"

"Easy, dear, easy," said the woman in a soothing voice.

"Ran right on like—like they didn't, didn't even see me," panted Kate. "I don't get it. They were chasing me, I know it."

Aunt Melanie merely nodded, her dark eyes glinting. She tapped her walking stick sharply against the side of her boot, as if trying to knock some mud off it.

Kate started to speak again, when her attention was caught by the walking stick. For a brief instant, the yellow eyes of the carved owl's head on the handle seemed to glow strangely. Then, swiftly, the brightness faded.

Puzzled, Kate looked over her shoulder to see the sun trying to make a late-afternoon appearance through the slackening rain. Of course, she realized. It's just catching the sunlight. She turned again to the stick, now looking like an ordinary piece of wood, its color and grain dulled by wetness. The owl's head handle had no more life than the handle of an old umbrella.

She shook her head and focused once more on Aunt Melanie. "How could they have missed me?"

Blowing a drop of water from the tip of her nose, the woman examined Kate thoughtfully. Her white curls, studded with raindrops, framed her face like a fluffy cloud. "Heaven only knows. I daresay they were going awfully fast. Why were they chasing you?"

Proudly, Kate raised the brown envelope. Mud streaked its crumpled surface, obscuring the address label. But Aunt Melanie recognized it immediately, and her eyes opened wide.

"Good grief. You mean they tried to steal my mail?"

Kate nodded. "Came pretty close, too."

Aunt Melanie took the brown envelope and stuffed it into the pocket of her blue rain jacket. "Never thought they'd stoop to such a thing, or I wouldn't have sent you. Something told me I shouldn't have let you go by yourself. I'm glad the phone call finally came, so I could come after you." She pursed her lips. "This whole town is coming apart at the seams."

"What do you mean by that?"

"Oh, nothing, nothing. You're all right, though?"

Refusing to let her change the subject, Kate asked, "Aren't you going to see what's in it? Must be pretty important."

"It can wait till I get home." With a tilt of her head, Aunt Melanie beckoned Kate to follow and started walking down the deserted street. "Let's get moving before they decide to come back this way. Billy's got a nasty temper."

Kate frowned, reluctantly giving up for the moment. She trotted to her great-aunt's side, musing, "Sure would be nice if we could make ourselves invisible any time we wanted."

Aunt Melanie made no response. She merely hesitated slightly in her step, as if she had caught her foot on something, then resumed her normal pace. The walking stick continued to poke its way rhythmically through mud puddle after mud puddle.

fennel seeds and
scottish roots

THEY turned down a side street, soon leaving behind the last moss-covered buildings of Blade. As they passed a junkyard piled high with used tires and rusting auto parts, the rain ceased, at least temporarily. Kate threw back her hood, unsnapped her jacket. The thought of her pursuers began to fade, like water evaporating in the sun's rays.

Before long they reached the bridge across Jones River, so murky from erosion that it supported no more than a few struggling fish. Kate leaned over the railing to watch the dark water flowing under the bridge. Someone had tied an old tire to a worn length of rope and dangled it from the branch of a sturdy cedar across the bank, making a simple swing.

Instinctively, she stooped to pick up a small rock, hefted it for a moment in her right hand, then hurled it at the tire. The rock whooshed straight through the hole in the middle, striking the trunk of the cedar with a smack.

"Not bad," said Aunt Melanie, laughing. "I can see why you're so good at baseball."

"Softball," corrected Kate. "Someday I'll have to teach

you how to throw. Who knows? You might end up a better shortstop than me."

"Don't count on it. Remember what happened when you tried to explain baseball cards to me?"

Kate shook her head. "I couldn't even get into hall-of-famers and batting averages. I spent the whole time convincing you that a baseball club and a baseball bat are two different things."

The elder woman grinned at the younger. "Consider that an accomplishment, dear."

They continued walking, soon reaching a lane lined with Norway spruce, whose upturned boughs never failed to make Kate wonder whether they had happy, uplifted spirits. Of course, trees didn't really have individual personalities, but it was fun to imagine such things nonetheless.

Not far up the road she spied a rusted green mailbox with hand-painted black letters reading *Melanie Prancer.* Parked next to the mailbox, leaning precariously in a deep rut, was an equally rusted red Jeep. Trusty, Aunt Melanie called it. A soggy daisy hung twisted around the top of the antenna.

Kate leaped across the permanent puddle beneath the mailbox and stood facing the cottage. It was a cramped, box-shaped structure, thought to be the first house built in the settlement of Blade almost a hundred years ago. The old squared-off logs, hewn with a broad ax so that diagonal chop marks were still visible, were warped to the point where the chinking in some places was as wide as the logs themselves. Permanently musty, the house felt cold in the summer and still colder in the winter. Aunt Melanie's heating system consisted of a large fireplace, a small electric space heater (reserved for overnight guests), and a huge cedar chest filled with bulky sweaters of all colors, styles, and patterns.

Tiny though the cottage was, it was roomy enough for Aunt Melanie. As long as she had space for a few garden tools, her favorite Native American artifacts, and a jar or two of peppermint candies, she could practically live inside the trunk of a tree. At times she even reminded Kate of some spritely gnome, standing amidst the sword ferns and flowering rhododendrons that surrounded the little house, smelling like spice tea and wet moss, scratching the top of her white head with a look of both wonder and mischief. Also like a gnome, she had the annoying habit of appearing and disappearing suddenly, usually when Kate least expected it.

Rain started falling again, and Kate pulled up her hood. At that moment, two mud-splattered ducks waddled onto the driveway, side by side, quacking noisily. Like a pair of old men trading boastful tales, they jabbered constantly, oblivious to anyone else. She recognized them as Chuck and Chuckles, the ducks Aunt Melanie had adopted, or more accurately, who had adopted Aunt Melanie, last spring. They waddled over to the puddle by the mailbox and began to glide around, quacking continually.

From the moment Aunt Melanie had invited her to spend the first week of summer vacation with her here at the cottage, Kate had known that this visit would be different from the others. Not just because her parents would be on the ship and unreachable the whole time. Though she would not allow herself to say so out loud, she hoped in her heart that being here would help her get over Grandfather's death.

I still miss him, she told herself, brushing away from her nostrils the river of drizzle that started at the crook in her hood and ran all the way down the bridge of her nose. She remembered Grandfather saying once that the creation of the universe wasn't just a onetime event, that it was going on all the time, right now even—that the briefest afternoon shower helped continue the process. Given that, she thought wryly, this rain-soaked land must be the most creative place on earth. Grandfather hated foul weather. It depressed him. Made him, as he said, think like a duck instead of a man. He never could understand why his younger sister had chosen to teach school in rural Oregon, where any creatures who lacked webbed feet were at a big disadvantage.

Visiting Aunt Melanie was more than an escape, though it was a relief for Kate not to look out her window every day and see the garden where she and Grandfather had so often picnicked, where not even the relentlessly playful golden retriever Cumberland felt like playing anymore. More important was the simple fact of Aunt Melanie's quiet company. No words needed. Whether they were baking bread together, or husking corn before supper, or walking in the woods, Kate felt accepted with all her flaws, in a way that could heal even the deepest wounds.

She watched as her great-aunt mounted the cottage's stone step and fiddled with her keys. She seemed very small, even delicate, the sort of person one could easily pass on the street without noticing. It was Aunt Melanie's eyes that were impossible to forget: dark, almost black, resonant as ebony, with a few flecks of hazel green around the edges of the pupils. Eyes like hers seemed to reveal Native American, rather than Scottish, ancestry. Her high cheekbones and wide face also contributed to the impression. Only yesterday, Kate had found an old photograph of her as a youngster (with jet black hair instead of the current creamy white) playing with Grandfather on the Isle of Skye, and it was impossible to tell they were related to each other.

As Kate herself ascended the step, she paused to read the crudely carved wooden plaque leaning against the porch railing:

> *There is a pleasure in the pathless woods,*
> *There is a rapture on the lonely shore,*
> *There is society, where none intrudes,*
> *By the deep sea, and music in its roar:*
> *I love not man the less, but Nature more.*

She recalled that Lord Byron's words had once hung on the front door, but the plaque was torn off and broken by some rowdy high school students last year. Aunt Melanie had put the pieces back together, with some help from a carpenter friend, but had not gotten around to hanging it again.

A few moments later, having deposited her foul weather gear in the mud room and her wet sneakers by the hearth, Kate was cuddled beneath a soft blue-gray quilt in front of the fireplace. She knew her damp jeans would dry quickly. Aunt Melanie rested beneath her own quilt, a green and lavender check, in the rocking chair opposite, sipping spice tea.

Pulling her quilt higher so that it wrapped around the back of her neck, Kate blew across the rim of her stoneware mug and took a swallow. "We had this kind this morning. What's in it? Tastes so different from other teas. Sweeter somehow."

"Crushed fennel seeds," came the reply. "Good thing you like it, since it's the only kind I have right now. It's good for afternoon chills." The white-haired woman paused reflectively. "And other things too."

Kate blew again, sipped again. "Like what?"

Aunt Melanie grinned imperceptibly. "Like making youngsters ask lots of questions."

Crinkling her nose, Kate protested, "Come on, tell me."

"Well, if you really want to know . . ." she began, before her voice trailed off. She loosened her quilt and slid forward in her chair. Casting her eyes around the room in mock suspicion, she whispered, "Drinking fennel seeds can make you invisible."

Kate giggled, dribbling some tea down her chin. "So that's why Billy missed me?"

Aunt Melanie savored the question, then replied, "Yes, but it only works on people as big as tugboats."

They both burst out laughing. Aunt Melanie shook so hard that some of her tea sloshed onto her quilt. "Of course," she added, "the bigger they are the more fennel seeds it takes." She dabbed at the spilled tea with a tattered kerchief from her pocket.

"I thought maybe those neon green shoelaces you gave me scared them off," teased Kate.

"Really, now," answered Aunt Melanie, pretending to

be insulted. "Those laces have nothing to do with neon. They're bright, that's all. Like new green leaves on the first day of spring."

"More like the sign in front of Cary's Tavern, if you ask me."

Aunt Melanie shook her head. "No taste in your generation, none at all." She winked at Kate. "Of course, there was no taste in my generation either. We're the ones who invented supermarkets and eight-lane highways." Then all at once, her mirth evaporated. "All the same," she muttered, "it's hard to believe they'd try something like that."

Kate studied her closely. Her thickly woven Cowichan sweater, milky white and decorated with rows of tiny black eagles with wings spread wide, bunched up against her chin so that she looked almost like an owl peering out from a small snowdrift. From each of her ears dangled a string of silvery shells that clinked together gently whenever she turned her head.

No other person in Kate's experience was quite like Aunt Melanie, certainly no other schoolteacher. She could be playful as a kitten or solemn as a tree stump. Something about her just didn't seem to belong here in the middle of rural Oregon. Yet that wasn't it, exactly. Aunt Melanie didn't seem so much out of place as she seemed, inexplicably, out of *time*. There was something mysteriously ageless about her, both younger and older than her years, almost as if she belonged in some other century.

Kate especially enjoyed the times when Aunt Melanie— usually crunching on a peppermint—shared some of her knowledge of Native American lore. She knew as much as anyone alive about the Halamis, a people who vanished so long ago from this area that their lives were almost completely veiled in mystery. Sometimes Kate would return to the cottage to find a Native American friend sitting by the fire with Aunt Melanie, trading speculations about why the Halamis disappeared so suddenly, almost without a trace. And Aunt Melanie's library on Halami life and culture was so good that professors, researchers, and archaeologists from all over the region often stopped by just to borrow a book or check a reference.

Yet it was less the lore than the telling itself that Kate so loved. There was an air of elemental peacefulness in Aunt Melanie when she told some of those nearly forgotten stories, customs, and recipes, an air she seemed to inhale and exhale in deep drafts. More than once Kate had wished that some of that peaceful quality might enter her own being and choose to stay, at least for a while.

This week, however, there had been no time for Halami lore. Whatever was on Aunt Melanie's mind, it crowded out almost everything else. She was more relaxed right now than she had been since Kate's arrival. Maybe whatever was in the brown envelope had solved the problem, or at least made it better.

"So tell me, what was in the envelope?" she ventured, trying her best to sound casual.

Aunt Melanie, who was looking at the fire, started. "Oh, just some papers—legal papers." She worked her jaw for a moment. "I really don't want to talk about it, dear. Maybe another time."

Sensing it would be fruitless to push, Kate forced herself to rein in her curiosity for the time being. She took one of the still-warm oatmeal cookies piled on the plate on the knotted spruce table in front of the fire, dunked it deep into her mug, let it drip into the tea for a few seconds, then took a hearty bite. "I love dunking," she said through a mouthful.

"You definitely have Scottish roots," observed Aunt Melanie, her expression more relaxed again. She reached for one of the peppermint candies resting in an abalone shell next to the cookies. Pulling off the plastic wrapping, she popped the red-and-white striped sweet into her mouth. "No doubt about it."

Placing her mug on the table, Kate gazed across the room to the rickety bookshelf behind Aunt Melanie. In addition to notebooks, articles, and unpublished treatises about the Halamis, it was stacked haphazardly with books on trees, edible plants, and forest ecology. Her eyes followed the lines of the warped living-room window, its sill crowded with a small painted drum, a slab of bark from a Douglas fir, a bag of twisted roots, and a delicate miniature basket that conjured up the image of a Halami woman skillfully weaving it long ago. The room seemed more like the local natural history museum than part of someone's house.

Next to the fireplace rested the walking stick, the deeply carved markings on its shaft reflecting the shifting light of the fire. For the first time, Kate noticed that the face of the owl's head looked oddly human from a distance. The beak could almost pass for a jutting nose; the mouth was more like a man's than a bird's. Only the enormous eyes, yellow and unblinking, were unmistakably those of an owl. They seemed to be watching her closely, observing her every movement.

Just then, a gray cat with white paws padded into the room. Athabasca (called Atha for short) had lived with Aunt Melanie for nearly a decade and was still limber enough to catch an unsuspecting bird on a low-hanging branch. As she passed the fireplace, the cat made a wide detour around the walking stick, as if sensing some secret danger. In two bounds, she leaped to the piano bench and then to the top of the old upright that had never been in tune as long as Kate could remember.

Kate turned in her high-back chair so that the crackling fire could warm her other side. She could almost see steam rising from her damp jeans under the quilt.

"How do you do it?" she asked suddenly.

"Do what, dear?"

"You always seem so, I don't know, so comfortable being in lots of different places, or really times, at once. In this house things that are centuries apart feel so natural together. It makes me feel—well, amazed."

Aunt Melanie crunched down on her peppermint and eyed her pensively. "Is that all you feel?"

Shifting her position under the quilt, Kate said slowly,

"I guess . . . I guess it also bugs me a little. Maybe because there's part of me that would like to be that way too. Connected. Part of something. I mean, I don't even really feel at home in my own town, in my own time. About the only time I feel like I belong there is when I'm shagging balls to somebody behind the house for a few hours. Pretty weird, huh?"

Aunt Melanie stroked her chin, considering the question. "No," she said finally. "It's not weird. Maybe your hometown just isn't big enough to hold you. The world is a big place, you know, full of all kinds of connections. You might find that you're one of those people meant to touch many different times and places. That requires certain gifts, you know."

Kate shook her head. "Whatever they are, I'm sure I don't have them."

"Don't be so certain." A slight grin formed at the corners of her mouth. "Maybe what you need is a vision quest."

"A what?"

"A vision quest. The Halamis, when they got to be your age—aren't you thirteen or so already?—would go off to some remote place in the mountains, sleep alone, fend for themselves for a while. They'd come back with a new understanding of themselves, of their own power." Observing Kate's glum expression, she added, "Forget that. All you really need is a little more humor about yourself."

Again Kate shifted, drawing the quilt closer. "I suppose I have a lot to laugh about."

"We all do." Aunt Melanie leaned back in her rocking chair, which creaked loudly. "I hope you at least appreciate how much it's meant to me to have you here this week. I'm afraid I've been rather distracted." Her expression clouded. "But there never was a time when I needed good company like I do right now."

Kate lowered the quilt and leaned forward, her long braid coiled upon the tabletop. "Aunt Melanie, why is some lawyer sending you mail? And why did they want to steal it? Seems like something pretty strange is going on."

Aunt Melanie's already wrinkled brow wrinkled even more. "You're right about that, dear. Stranger than you know." She sighed, and her dark eyes concentrated on Kate. "But I don't want to get you involved. The kind of help I need is more than any human being can give, I'm afraid."

"But—" protested Kate.

"No buts. That's all I have to say." A sudden idea came to her. "I'll let you help with one thing, though." She found Kate's knee beneath her quilt and squeezed it gently before reaching for her walking stick. "How would you like to come give me a hand in the kitchen? I've got all the makings of a good salad set out. You do that while I do the salmon. It's getting on toward supper time." She set her mug on the table with a thump of finality.

Pouting, Kate protested: "Are you sure there's nothing else I can do?"

Aunt Melanie started to say something, then caught herself. "You can peel the avocado."

Kate shook her head. In a beaten tone, she muttered, "You share another thing with Grandfather. Total, complete, absolute stubbornness."

Feigning a frown, the woman asked, "What's the matter? Don't you like avocados?"

"Sure I do. I just—"

"Enough," said Aunt Melanie, raising a weathered hand. "I know you'd like to help, dear, but you can't." She rose from the rocking chair, leaving her quilt crumpled on the seat. Then, forcing a smile, she added, "I'm glad you like avocados. Me, I can't get enough of them."

Kate stared at her blankly.

Her brow again deeply furrowed, Aunt Melanie whispered, "Don't worry about me, dear. I'll be fine." She pivoted on the walking stick and started toward the kitchen.

Just then they heard a loud banging on the front door.

3

visitors

Two sodden figures faced them on the porch. Closest
to the door was an older man, tall and gaunt, whose torn
gray jacket hung on his body like a loose sack. His crystal
blue eyes, though strangely sorrowful, looked as if they
belonged to a much younger man. Behind him stood the
red-haired boy who had tried to steal the brown envelope.
He shifted nervously, peering down at his shoes.

Aunt Melanie regarded them solemnly. Finally she said,
"Good day, Frank."

"Wish it was," the man replied, his voice joyless. "Hasn't
been a good day in this town for near on eight years."

Kate moved closer, so that her arm was lightly touching
Aunt Melanie's. Several seconds passed with no one willing to speak. Then Frank broke the silence.

"Look, Melanie," he began. "We've been friends a long
time, you and me. Helped each other out a few times. More
than a few, in fact. I didn't come over here today expecting to
change your thinking, but I wanted to warn you. The

temperature in town is getting hot. Real hot. People are bound to do almost anything to keep the sawmill running."

Aunt Melanie studied him without emotion. "Including stealing other people's mail?"

The red-haired boy lifted his head. As his eyes met Kate's, they narrowed with anger. She returned the favor, staring back icily.

"I'm not excusing that," said Frank earnestly. "But you've got to remember what it's like for all the folks who work like hell beating tan bark just to get through the day. When you start bringing in some fancy lawyers, they get mad. And for good reason."

"They were my last resort, Frank. I hate lawyers as much as you do, and you know it. You and the others wouldn't listen to reason, no matter what I tried. You were about to destroy the whole crater, before we even know what's up there. The injunction gives us all a little time, that's all."

"People don't need time, they need jobs." His face reddened. "For heaven's sake, Melanie! Sometimes I think all you care about is owls and trees. Not people."

Aunt Melanie stiffened. "Of course I care about people. Why else do I spend all my days laboring with youngsters?" She shot a glance at the red-haired boy, who avoided her gaze. "But you can't just keep on destroying the forest without giving something back. Look around, will you? Clearcuts everyplace. If we're having tough times, the fault belongs to all of us—me, you, and everybody else who let the forest get cut faster than it could grow back—not the folks who want to save the few remaining scraps."

"I'm not disputing that," retorted Frank. "But people have to eat somehow."

Aunt Melanie's voice dropped to a hoarse whisper. "Those old trees were God's first temple, and now they're almost gone."

At that, Jody spoke, though without looking at Aunt Melanie. "The preacher says trees weren't made in God's image. But men were."

The white-haired woman looked at him sadly. "I wish, Jody, you'd use your own good head instead of just repeating whatever Reverend Natello says. Then maybe you could decide for yourself what's right."

Jody continued to stare at his shoes.

"You might try to ask the reverend a few questions," added Aunt Melanie in a gentle voice. "Ask him whether God made all the creatures of the earth, including the ones we're wiping out. Or you could remind him of the Psalm that says *the righteous shall flourish . . . like a cedar in Lebanon,* and then ask him why there aren't any cedars left in Lebanon now. Ask him why the people cut them down so fast they never grew back."

"I wouldn't waste his time," snorted the boy.

"That's enough, Jody," snapped Frank. "I didn't bring you along to act rude."

"Then why did you bring him along?" demanded Aunt Melanie. "To hear you spout the same old wisdom that got us into this holy mess in the first place?"

A pained look crossed the logger's careworn face. His shoulders sagged from his drenched clothes and something still more weighty. "Understand me, Melanie. I'm only trying to do what I can to keep this place from becoming a ghost town."

For an instant, she regarded him with unmistakable tenderness. Puzzled, Kate pondered this. Then Aunt Melanie's jaw tightened and she asked, "But why steal my mail, Frank? What good does that do?"

"Some of the boys thought, well . . . They thought it might put things off. I tried to talk them out of it, but they wouldn't listen."

"Whatever are they thinking, Frank? The injunction starts on Monday whether I get my mail or not. The crater's off limits. There's no way to change that now."

Jody raised his head and started to say something, when Frank suddenly cut him off. "That's right," he agreed. "No way to change that now."

Aunt Melanie eyed him suspiciously. "What aren't you telling me?"

The crystal blue eyes peered at her. "Nothing, nothing at all. I just wanted to warn you that you're best off staying at home for the next few days, until this whole thing blows over."

At that moment, Chuck and Chuckles came waddling up the driveway, quacking proudly in duet. They hopped up the stone step and walked single file between Jody's legs. While Chuck continued on his way across the porch, Chuckles chose to linger momentarily by the boy's left boot. Jody, watching Frank's face, paid no attention until, with a loud quack of satisfaction, the duck made an unceremonious deposit of greenish-brown matter on his toe.

"Hey!" the boy exclaimed, kicking the duck down the step. Quacking and fluttering in protest, Chuckles quickly collected himself and started to waddle back toward the mailbox. Hearing Kate's snickering, Jody glared at her. Then he turned back to Frank and declared, "I'm leaving." Thrusting his hands in his pockets, he wheeled around and walked off.

Frank lingered on the porch, studying Aunt Melanie closely. He started to speak, hesitated, then shook his head, spraying some water from his rubberized hat. He turned away, moving off into the rain. Soon he was nothing more than a misty shadow.

Slowly Aunt Melanie closed the door, leaning heavily on the handle of her stick. The normal ruddiness had drained from her cheeks. Facing Kate, she said simply, "Something's wrong."

4

lost from time

NOT until supper had been prepared, eaten, and completely cleared did Aunt Melanie choose to speak again. Kate had been waiting, it seemed endlessly, for the silence to break. She had hardly tasted her salmon.

Laying her thin hands firmly on the dining table, a wide slab of richly grained fir resting against the kitchen wall, Aunt Melanie drew in a deep breath. "You're about to get your wish."

Before Kate could respond, Aunt Melanie reached for a weather-beaten roll of paper resting on the row of teacups above the table. With the mud-stained paper in one hand and her walking stick in the other, she started down the hall toward the living room. "Come," she said distractedly. "We'll light the fire first. Bring the pie and the plates."

Soon the fireplace was crackling and orange-tinted shadows flickered across the walls. The room seemed very different to Kate now that the sun had gone down. Firelight now played upon its contents, coaxing out textures and colors less visible in the harsher light of day. Facing Aunt Melanie, she asked, "What's wrong?"

Aunt Melanie didn't answer, but began to unfurl the roll of paper. Using her walking stick to hold down one end and two plates to anchor the other, she flattened it across the knotted spruce table.

It was a map of southwestern Oregon. Amidst the many shades of green that indicated national, state, or private forest lands, Kate could see dozens of winding river canyons flowing westward to the Pacific Ocean. Between the coast and the rugged chain of mountains that ran forty or fifty miles inland, there were several small towns. Kate found herself searching for the name Blade.

"There," said Aunt Melanie, pointing to one black dot, about ten miles inland from the coast, surrounded by a wide swath of green. "That's us." Moving her finger in a wide circle around the spot, she added, "Most of this area's been logged at least once."

"What's this?" asked Kate, pointing to a place a few miles east of town marked Cronon's Crater. A large blue lake sat in the middle, ringed by densely packed contour lines that were broken only by a single high waterfall spilling into a rugged river canyon.

"That's the crater Frank and I were talking about. It's called Cronon's Crater by the mapmakers." Aunt Melanie paused, weighing her words carefully. "But I call it Lost Crater." She swung her eyes toward the fire. "Why it had to appear just now, I'll never know."

"I don't understand," Kate said. "That crater must have been there for ages."

Aunt Melanie turned from the fire, light from the coals still playing on her face. "Not so long, really. In geologic terms, I mean. It's what's left of an ancient volcano that appeared, oh, maybe eight or nine million years ago. Then, about seven thousand years ago, it exploded so violently that the summit collapsed completely, leaving nothing but the huge crater—technically, a caldera—that you see there on the map."

She reached toward the abalone shell of peppermint candies that had been pushed to the edge of the table and then, thinking the better of it, withdrew her hand. "Got to cut back on those," she muttered. "Such a bad habit." Her gaze fell to a cozy gingerbread house that had rested on the bookshelf behind her rocking chair since Christmas, and her eyebrows suddenly lifted. Pinching one of the striped peppermints from the row upon its roof, she said somewhat sheepishly to Kate, "But first I have to finish these or they'll go stale." She popped it into her mouth. "Now, where were we?"

"The crater. You were starting to say why it's such a big deal."

"Oh, yes," said Aunt Melanie, biting into the peppermint with a hearty crunch. "You've got to understand something first. Lost Crater is so steep it's literally unclimbable. It rises a good three thousand feet from the forest floor, much of that straight up. The only way anyone's even known there's a lake inside is from aerial photographs. But since the crater is almost always filled with fog, even those are rare."

"What's all this got to do with the loggers?" pressed Kate, increasingly exasperated. "I still don't get it."

"You will, dear. You see, everyone assumed the lake filled the crater completely. And who'd be foolish enough to try to scale those slippery walls to find out? For most people, it's been just a blank spot on the map, not even worth a second thought. The kind of place Scotsmen call *the Back of Beyond.*"

She pointed to the map. "See this big waterfall coming out of the crater? The mapmakers didn't even bother to name it, even though it's one of the biggest around. A few of us call it Kahona Falls, after the old Halami name, but for most people it doesn't even exist."

Her finger traced the crater's steep contours. "Nobody even takes a hike up there. There's never been a road, not even a trail, that goes the whole way." She smiled almost imperceptibly. "At least none that anyone knows about."

Aunt Melanie's eyes, dark as the bark of rain-washed

cedar, concentrated on the girl by her side. "It's a forgotten place, Kate. Lost. Lost from time." She sighed, running her left hand along the shaft of her stick. "Until now."

Kate leaned forward. "Why until now?"

The earrings clinked gently as Aunt Melanie shook her head at the thought. "Just two weeks ago," she began, "a Forest Service technician happened to be flying over this part of the forest, doing an aerial survey. On the spur of the moment, he decided to fly over the top of the crater, hoping to see the lake. Turned out, he was in luck. The fog in there was a lot thinner than usual, and he had a good view inside. What he saw was—well, amazing."

"What did he see?"

Aunt Melanie's eyes moved to the pie dish. "How about some huckleberry pie, before it gets cold?"

"No thanks, I . . ." Kate's words trailed off as she saw Aunt Melanie reaching for the dish. "Okay, sure. I can't say no to that. So what did he see?"

"These huckleberries I found right out back. Two kinds, in fact. One red, the other purple. Got to learn their names someday." She slid a hefty slice over to Kate, allowing the corner of the map that had been held down by the plate to curl inward. As she took a heaping forkful from the pie dish for herself, the old woman's face crinkled in a smile. "Still as tart as the day I picked them."

"Aunt Melanie! What did he see?"

"Well," began the white-haired woman, pointing at the map with her fork, "there was, in fact, a lake. But to his surprise, it filled only half of the crater. The rest of it was very dense, very old forest. A hidden forest. As he circled closer, he could see some true giants, the kind of trees that make foresters salivate, lots of them bigger than twenty-five feet around. Took pictures of everything, he did, or nobody would have believed him. There were Douglas firs, spruces, cedars, and—most precious of all—a large grove of ancient redwoods."

Suddenly Kate understood. "And the loggers want to cut them all down?"

Aunt Melanie nodded gravely.

"But I thought the crater's impassable. You said your-self there's no road up there."

"Only because there wasn't any reason to build one. That's all changed now. Just before you arrived, a few of them—led by your friend Billy—put a Jeep road up there. Not all the way to the top of the rim, but high enough to get inside if they blasted a hole through the rock."

Kate dropped her fork onto her pie plate. "They're really going to blast their way in?"

"They already did," declared Aunt Melanie. "Yester-day." She rose and moved around to the window. "The only thing left for me to do was get a lawyer in Portland to file for an injunction."

"A what?"

"A court order, one that stops them from entering the crater or cutting anything in there until it's determined whether to make the place into a park."

Kate nodded. "So that's what was in the envelope."

"That's right. Copies of the injunction filing. And we got it. The call came right after you left for the post office. It takes effect Monday morning, first thing." The fire surged brightly as a pocket of resin exploded, shooting glowing embers into the air and over the hearth. Aunt Melanie kicked one back toward the fireplace and returned to her rocker. "I can't believe they thought that stealing my mail would change anything."

"They must be pretty desperate."

"So desperate they might try anything," said Aunt Melanie, tilting her head pensively. "The way Frank was so quick to agree with me out there, did you see? He wants me to think there's no problem. He's probably trying to protect me, the old fool. Afraid I'll get hurt. But I can see right through him. They're up to something, I'm sure of it."

"But what?"

Aunt Melanie shook her head in frustration. "I wish I knew. All I know is this discovery is like manna from heaven for the loggers. Most of them are out of work. The last mill in town is ready to close. The trees from the crater would keep them employed for another year or so, delaying the inevitable at least a little while longer."

She glanced toward the fire. "It's a natural human instinct, Kate, to try to keep your old way of life from changing. I really feel for them. They're proud, independent people, the kind you can depend on. Even Billy. It's hard not to like folks like that."

"Including Frank?"

Caught off guard, Aunt Melanie blinked, her eyes moist. "Yes," she said quietly, "including Frank." She cleared her throat. "And to answer your next question, we were friends once. Special friends. He's—we were—well, that was a long time ago."

"And the red-haired kid?" asked Kate. "He doesn't seem so likable to me."

"Oh, Jody. He's not so bad, really. He's had a hard time since his parents died last year. Worst crash in years, out on Highway 26. Before that happened, he was one of my best students—smart, sensitive, curious—though you'd never know it now. Frank's his grandfather, and agreed to take him in after the accident."

"Frank's a brave man," said Kate under her breath.

Aunt Melanie pushed a hand through her untamed white curls. "That he is. He's one rare human being. One of the few in this town willing to stand up and say that the old ways have to change, that there are no simple answers. Not everyone may agree with him, but they all respect him enough to listen."

She continued rocking, the repeated creaking of the chair punctuating the steady sound of rain drumming on the roof. "Everybody knows that those big trees are good for the air, the water, the soil—and even for fighting disease. But not many people know that the trees in the crater could be the oldest untouched forest in the world. And the northernmost stand of redwoods ever found." Her eyes seemed to shine with a faraway light. "And something more."

"More?"

"Yes," continued Aunt Melanie, leaning forward in the chair. "The Hidden Forest—the whole crater, really—was well known to the Halamis five hundred years ago. It was their most sacred place of all. Since they left, it's been totally undisturbed."

"Lost from time," said Kate, remembering the phrase.

"That's right," agreed her great-aunt. "There's no map anywhere that tells what you might find up there." Her face half lit by the dancing flames, she hesitated, then said in a voice so low it was barely audible: "Except one."

As Kate watched wide-eyed, Aunt Melanie reached across to the spruce table, pressed firmly on the center of one of the knots, then pulled out a small secret drawer. Within it lay a single square of white paper, tattered around the edges, labeled *Lost Crater*. Kate recognized the hand-writing at once.

"You made that?"

Aunt Melanie made no answer. Slowly, carefully, she took the paper and laid it on top of the larger map. "Yes," she said at last. "I made it."

"But how? I thought you said no one's ever been up there."

The dark eyes gleamed. "Except the Halamis."

"But they disappeared centuries ago."

"That's right. They left something behind, though. Songs and stories about their way of life, their beliefs, their prophecies. Whatever disaster wiped them out—no one knows for sure what it was—a few of them survived some-how. They blended in with some of the other native peo-ples who settled this area later. But still they managed to keep their wisdom alive. For hundreds of years, every child with some Halami blood has learned the sacred chants word for word, then passed them on faithfully to the next generation."

"Whew," said Kate. "That's no small feat. It's hard enough for me to remember something for even a day or two, let alone a whole lifetime."

"I used to be the same way," Aunt Melanie replied. "Something happened, though, the first time I heard a Halami song. It stuck in my head, as if it had been there all along, and I couldn't put it out of my mind." Her face crinkled into a grin. "Maybe there's some truth to the rumor I've got some Halami blood in me."

Kate leaned over the hand-drawn map. The words *Lost Crater* were ringed by several small characters that she recognized as symbols from Halami rock carvings. A few names, like Kahona Falls, she also recognized. But others, like Circle of Stones, were completely new. Near the Hidden Forest, she spotted a question: *little people?* Then she noticed some strange words printed at the bottom of the page, but got only as far as *True of heart and straight of spear, Find the forest walled in fear* before Aunt Melanie lifted the map off the table.

"This is my biggest accomplishment," said Aunt Melanie, her white hair aglow with firelight. She brought the map closer and examined it, as one studies the face of an old friend. "It's taken me more than a decade to put it together, piece by piece, from talking with everyone I could find who knows something about the Halamis."

"How did they vanish?" asked Kate. "I know you must have a theory."

Lowering her map, Aunt Melanie pointed to a jagged mountain drawn north of Lost Crater. "Brimstone Peak," she said with certainty. "It had something to do with Brimstone Peak."

Kate turned a puzzled face toward her. "Meaning what?"

The elder sat back in the rocker and gazed into the fire for a moment. "There is a legend," she said, "but it's awfully vague and incomplete. No one, including me, knows quite what to make of it."

"Tell me anyway."

Aunt Melanie gathered her thoughts before speaking. "Well, it seems that Brimstone Peak—we don't know the Halami name for it—was an evil place for the Halamis. They believed that a wicked being called Gashra lived deep inside it. He wanted to control all the lands around him, but apparently the Halamis resisted him. So out of anger and revenge, Gashra decided to destroy both them and their home. He made the mountain erupt and fill the valleys with lava, hoping to wipe them out completely." She glanced again at the hand-drawn map. "Whether he succeeded or not, no one knows. And almost nobody takes the legend very seriously. But it's interesting to note that the last eruption of Brimstone Peak was just about five hundred years ago."

"The same time the Halamis disappeared," said Kate. "Makes you wonder."

"Oh yes," added Aunt Melanie. "There's one more piece to it, though it's the vaguest part of all. Some versions of the legend say an important role was played by a mysterious tree spirit."

"Tree spirit?"

"Don't ask me what it means. Could be just a mistake that crept into the story after so many repetitions. Could be a tree that becomes a person somehow, or the reverse, or something even stranger. I have no idea."

Placing her map back in the secret drawer, Aunt Melanie closed it tight, then faced Kate. "Lost Crater is like no other place on the planet, you see. It holds the Hidden Forest, that much we know. But it holds other things too. Strange things, stranger than you can imagine." A log collapsed in the fireplace, sending up a shower of sparks. "The Ancient One lives there."

"The what?"

"Never mind. My point is that it's a place no one really understands. It ought to be left alone."

"I wish we knew what the loggers are planning to do."

"So do I, dear. So do I."

"What can they do now, though?" wondered Kate. "Tomorrow's Sunday, and then the injunction starts."

She caught her breath, staring at Aunt Melanie, as the same thought flashed across both of their minds at once. "Sunday!" they exclaimed simultaneously.

"That's it," announced the elder. "That must be it. It's just the sort of thing Billy would think of. He was always trying to skirt the rules back when I had him in school, and he's still the same—except now he's angrier. And hungrier too. Frank told me he and Sly existed on nothing but potatoes all last winter." She shook her head slowly. "I'm sure he's planning to go up there tomorrow, before the injunction, and cut down as many redwoods as he can. That way there can't be any more talk about a park."

"You think he'd really do that?"

Frowning, Aunt Melanie replied, "I'm sure."

"But that's terrible! If only—if only there were some way to hold them off, just for one more day." Kate looked into her aunt's eyes, but found no comfort there. "Who's going to stop them?"

Aunt Melanie reached across the table and laid her small hand upon Kate's. "We will."

5

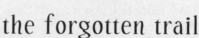

the forgotten trail

THE earth shook with a deep, volcanic rumbling. Force enough to fling incandescent lava into the darkened sky like a pyrotechnic fountain. Masses of thick lava oozed from crevasses along the ridge of the cone-shaped summit, triggering avalanches of superheated stone and mud that roared down river drainages and glacial valleys with enough speed to obliterate whole swaths of forest. Hissing vents and fumaroles blasted columns of super-heated steam high into the sky.

Kate was running from the eruption, dashing through the dense forest, her heart pounding. There was no chance of escape. Drenched from the heat of the inferno behind her, she couldn't even avoid the oncoming lava by climbing a tree, since every tree in its path was instantly incinerated. Rivers of fire, bubbling violently, rushed steadily toward her from the seething summit.

Then the ground shook again. The sky flashed with a brilliant light. Kate screamed.

And she awoke. Aunt Melanie, who had stopped shaking

her bed in order to turn on the overhead light, stood over her, wearing a dark blue nightgown.

"That was quite a dream you were having."

Kate sat up in bed, wet with perspiration. She wiped her face with the edge of the sheet. "You mean—you mean there's no . . . volcano? It was so real, I even felt the heat."

Aunt Melanie laid a gentle hand on her forehead. "The only volcano still active around here is Brimstone Peak, and it hasn't erupted for centuries. I'm the last person to take any dream lightly, mind you, but the only reality to this one is the temperature in here. How did this room get so hot?"

"I did it," confessed Kate. "I was still cold from getting soaked yesterday so I turned on the space heater full blast before I went to bed." She looked sheepishly at Aunt Melanie. "Guess I cooked my own goose, huh?"

"That you did," replied the white-haired woman. "But you did us both a favor. It's only two-fifteen, but since we're both awake, we're going to go now. The earlier we get started, the earlier we'll get there. And we must get up there by dawn."

Kate threw back the sheet. "You think they'll be up there that early?"

Aunt Melanie shook her head. "No, they'll take their new road. It's very long and steep, so it should take them at least until mid-morning."

"Then why do we need to get there so early?"

"Because, dear, we're going by a different way. A better way."

"I thought you said their new road was the only way into the crater."

"It's the only *road*. The way we're going is—well, not a road." Aunt Melanie brushed a moth off the shoulder of her nightgown, then turned to go. "Now hurry. I'll meet you in the kitchen."

The next half hour saw the little cottage in a whirl of activity. Kate quickly braided her hair, threw cold water on her face, and pulled on her green Bulldogs Softball sweatshirt and jeans. Aunt Melanie set out food for Atha and prepared hot chocolate. "There are times when no spice tea can compare to this," she said as she poured the steaming brown liquid into an old thermos and screwed tight the cover.

At last, they left the cottage. Though the rain had stopped, fog had settled so densely on the ground that Kate felt a fine mist on her face as she followed Aunt Melanie onto the porch. There was no light, only gradations of darkness, since there was no moon and the flashlight was not working. Even the neon green shoelaces weren't visible now.

I hate walking at night, she muttered. Although she didn't like to admit it to anyone, including herself, she never felt very comfortable in the dark. Especially outdoors.

Kate stayed as close as she could behind Aunt Melanie, even though it meant slopping straight through a frigid puddle. Ahead she sensed the vague shape that she knew to be the Jeep but that in the gloom could just as easily have been a sleeping stegosaurus. Then, from some faraway place, she heard the distant *hooo-hooo* of an owl.

Aunt Melanie stopped suddenly, causing Kate to walk into her. They listened for a moment, hearing only the sound of their own breathing and the gentle rustling of evergreen branches in the pre-dawn breeze. Kate wondered whether the owl was sailing through the vaporous darkness in search of some small animal to eat, or was even now following their movements from some broken-topped tree.

At last, the call came again, closer this time. *Hooo-hooo, hooo-hooo.* The voice seemed to hover in the moist night air.

As if responding to the signal, Aunt Melanie began walking again. Soon she reached the Jeep, which she announced by tapping its fender with her walking stick. Pulling open the door, whose window consisted of a thin square of plastic wired to the frame, she wiped the puddle off the seat and climbed in. By the time Kate had clambered in the other side (without remembering first to wipe the seat, to her chagrin), the old Jeep was sputtering noisily.

"Hang on, now," Aunt Melanie shouted above the roar as she turned on the headlights. "The road is lousy in any weather, but especially when it's this muddy." She patted the red metal dashboard affectionately, then released the clutch. Trusty lurched forward and off they drove into the night.

Soon after crossing the bridge over Jones River, Aunt Melanie turned onto a heavily rutted road ascending a steep hill. Before long the jostling beams of the headlights revealed forest all around them. Curls of mist wove around small trees, snags, and stumps on both sides of the dirt road. A rivulet running along the left side sometimes curled into the middle of the track, causing Aunt Melanie to swerve sharply to avoid losing a wheel in its channel.

The road was filled with rocks, roots, potholes, and ruts half as high as Trusty's tires. As her stomach tightened from repeated bouncing on the rock-hard seat, Kate began to wonder what the two of them could possibly do to stop a whole team of loggers. She glanced toward Aunt Melanie, hoping she at least had some kind of plan.

At that moment, the Jeep slowed markedly and the driver shifted into low gear. Kate heard the sound of rushing water below as they drove onto a creaking wooden bridge, so flimsy it seemed to tilt sideways under their weight. Slowly, they crept across, bouncing over every crosspiece. Then, with a jolt, they reached solid ground again.

Aunt Melanie rammed the stick shift into a new gear with a grinding crunch and gunned the engine. Keeping her eyes on the potholes ahead, she reached into her sweater pocket and pulled out a peppermint. Handing it to Kate, she said, "Here, dear, eat this. It ought to help."

It was nearly another hour of wrenching jolts, deep gullies, and sharp turns before Aunt Melanie pulled into a ditch on the right side of the road, shifted the stick into neutral, and yanked on the parking brake. She turned off the ignition and the lights and sat back in her seat with a sigh. "We made it."

Kate, who had managed somehow to doze during the

last part of the agonizing journey, woke up with a start. "Did we crash?"

"No, although I guess that would have put you out of your misery." She patted Kate's thigh. "The only good thing about this road is how rotten it is. Like most roads around here, it doesn't get much traffic. Until they built that new road last week, this was the nearest you could drive to the crater." With a sigh, she added, "There's nothing like the combination of bad weather and bad roads to keep a beautiful place beautiful."

Kate opened her door carefully, given the steep pitch of the Jeep. All four wheels were caked with mud, and Aunt Melanie's daisy, more tired than ever, still hugged the antenna. Gingerly, Kate placed her wobbly feet on the ground. To her surprise, it was not muddy but covered with a layer of soft evergreen needles several inches thick. She could almost bounce on the padded surface, but her stomach told her to resist the urge. The sky seemed a touch lighter than when they had started out, but she still wished she had a flashlight.

As she slipped Aunt Melanie's small blue day pack over her shoulders, she was struck by the rich smells surrounding her. She drank in the fragrant air like someone encountering her first rose garden, and her nose tingled with fresh, vibrant aromas.

"Wondrous air, isn't it?" spoke the familiar voice by her side.

"I can't believe how good it smells."

"A friend of mine who plays the cello calls it 'a symphony of scents.' Isn't that so?" Aunt Melanie pointed to the trees on her left with her walking stick. "Over there, if aromas were sounds, would be the violins, dancing brightly. On the other side we have the French horns."

"And the trumpets?"

"Right," she replied. "And sometimes we get jolted by some new spring flower that's like crashing cymbals." She grinned at Kate. "How about a quick cup of hot chocolate?"

Kate smiled, took the thermos and two cups from the

day pack, and poured some in each. After taking her first swallow, she asked, "What did you mean last night about strange things happening up there in the crater?"

Aunt Melanie shifted her weight from one leg to the other. "It's hard to explain, dear."

"Can't you give me an example? Just one?"

"Almost anything is possible in a place that's been undisturbed for so long."

"Like what?"

"Well, for starters, you could assume pretty safely there are plants and animals up there no one's ever seen before."

"Like the Abominable Snowman?" joked Kate.

Her companion did not laugh. Instead, she took a sip of hot chocolate. "There could be things beyond anyone's imagination," she said quietly. Then, rather incongruously, she added, "I read an interesting article recently. By a physicist. He proposed a new theory, about something he called *time tunnels*—places that open up ways to travel to the past or the future."

"Are you serious?" asked Kate.

"This fellow certainly was. He thinks time tunnels are most likely to occur where things have lived without interruption for long periods, so their energies can multiply and magnify enough to distort the flow of time." She fidgeted again, then added, "Pretty farfetched, I admit. But your grandfather would have said that farfetched theories are the ones to take most seriously."

The mention of Grandfather made Kate's stomach clench again. She stared into her cup.

The white-haired woman reached out a hand and stroked her cheek. "I'm so glad you were with him at the end."

Kate's eyes filled with mist. She swallowed, then said mournfully, "I still miss him. So much."

Aunt Melanie nodded, her shell earrings clinking softly. Then her brow wrinkled. "Drat," she said. "In all the rush, I forgot to pack some matches."

"Why would we need matches?"

"You never know when they might come in handy." She checked her watch. "Come. If we hurry, we can still get to Kahona Falls by dawn."

"To the falls?" asked Kate, replacing the cups and thermos in the day pack. "I thought we were going—"

"Into the crater," finished Aunt Melanie. "But we're going by the old Halami trail, the one they used centuries ago and then abandoned. Until I found it again last week, it had been completely forgotten."

Stepping over a gnarled cedar limb by the side of the road, the woman waved her hand toward the forest. In the dim light, Kate could barely discern a shadowy path, overgrown with low-hanging branches, snaking into the trees.

"But," protested Kate, "if the walls are unclimbable, how can there be a trail into the crater?"

"You'll see," declared Aunt Melanie.

Kate scanned the subtle indentation on the forest floor. "If the Halamis haven't been here to walk on it for five hundred years, then how come the trail is still visible?"

Aunt Melanie grinned. "Someone else has been walking on it." She started down the path, her waterproof boots crunching across the bed of needles.

Full of doubt, Kate followed behind. The trail dove straight into the thick forest, climbing gradually uphill. Whenever Aunt Melanie came to one of the many overhanging boughs, she lifted her stick and pushed it aside, holding it just long enough for Kate to pass. When she let go, the bough would spring back into place, showering them both with a spray of dewdrops.

As they moved deeper into this realm of green and brown, the sky, barely visible through the thick canopy of branches above their heads, grew lighter by degrees. Subtle sounds came more and more frequently: Shadowy wings fluttered, twigs snapped, branches creaked, small creatures squealed. It was impossible to tell whether forest beings, alarmed by intruders, were scattering to escape, or whether they were simply stirring in anticipation of the sunrise.

Kate felt the give of the needle-strewn trail under her

feet. As the sky lightened, the trail did as well, until it seemed like a radiant pathway into the woods. She felt for a moment that she was one of the long-vanished Halamis, padding softly along a route that her people had traveled for generations.

Before long, she detected a new openness in the trees ahead of them. The misty light showed a clearing about fifty yards up the trail. Seeing it, Aunt Melanie broke into a run. Kate jogged along behind her, imagining the crashing splendor of the waterfall that would greet them.

At the edge of the clearing, they halted, panting. Together they surveyed the scene before them.

It was not Kahona Falls. Nor was it like anything Kate had ever seen before, except in some old photographs of trenched battlefields in World War One. An entire section of the forest, a square about a quarter mile on each side, had literally vanished. Nothing remained but a wasteland of torn limbs, uprooted trunks, slashed bark, and mangled branches strewn across the pockmarked terrain.

Kate turned to the rear, in disbelief, to see again the rich forest they had just passed through. She could still smell its intertwining fragrances, but a new odor hung over the clearing, an odd mixture of wet sawdust and discarded gasoline cans. She turned back to the clear-cut. No birds sang, no animals stirred, no branches clicked and swished in the breeze. If this had once been a forest, it was no longer. The land lay naked and exposed to the cold mists of morning.

"I had no idea," said Aunt Melanie, trying to contain her anger. "Just a week ago this was all still forested. Last time I was here a family of deer ran across the trail right over there."

"How did the loggers get in here?" asked Kate.

"They must have used their new road."

Without another word, she strode forward. As best she could, she worked her way across the trampled terrain, using her stick to help her step over ripped-up roots and muddy trenches. Kate followed in silence, feeling at times like she was walking on the face of an open wound.

At last, with a sense of relief, they reached the edge of the clear-cut and entered a new section of forest. The trail picked up again, and Aunt Melanie did not linger. Who could blame her? Kate, too, wanted to get far away, deep into the woods, before looking back.

Gradually, amidst the growing light, the forest began to work its healing powers. Subtle aromas comforted her, sounds of the living woods encircled her again. The clear-cut moved farther and farther into the distance, until it was difficult even to remember in the presence of such lush greenery.

Soon the terrain grew rockier and the trail sharply steeper. For an instant, Kate worried that Aunt Melanie might have trouble making it up the slope, but one glance ahead told her otherwise. The small woman moved steadily along, pausing only to lean briefly on her walking stick after climbing the steepest sections.

The trail wound back and forth in an endless series of switchbacks, gaining elevation at every turn. At one point, panting from the ascent, Aunt Melanie halted. Kate, who was huffing as well, used the opportunity to bend over to touch her toes. It felt good to hang there, stretching her thighs; she hadn't had much exercise this week.

As she straightened up, she detected a new sound, one she could not immediately recognize. It was continuous, like the rustle of wind, but deeper, like faraway thunder. As they returned to working their way up the switchbacks, the mysterious sound grew gradually louder. At first, she wondered whether it could be a distant storm. Then, with a pang, she feared it was the sound of a logging crew at work up ahead. Were they already too late?

Finally, as the forest gave way to yet another clearing, she knew what lay ahead. The sound had swelled to such a roar that it could be only one thing.

They had reached the waterfall.

6

the legend of kahona falls

SPRAY soaring in every direction, Kahona Falls leaped out of the side of the steep wall of rock fifty feet above them. It sprung straight out of the mountainside, as if it were a geyser laid on its side, then arched earthward, plunging down the slope into a deep canyon hundreds of feet below. Behind it, the cloudy sky was lit with a pale wash of peach and pink. Dawn.

Kate turned to Aunt Melanie, who was herself captivated by the waterfall. Looking beyond her great-aunt to the landscape stretching far to the north and west, she saw they had ascended to a rocky ledge nearly fifteen hundred feet above the forest floor. To one side, the sheer face of the volcanic cone rose precipitously into the clouds. To the other side, gently rolling ridges reached as far as she could see.

At the edge of the horizon, probably twenty miles away, another volcanic peak loomed high and jagged. A thin trail of steam spiraled skyward from its summit. Even the peaceful glow of sunrise could not disguise the violence and torment of its past. This was not a gentle or strength-giving mountain, but a fang-shaped pinnacle that seemed somehow sinister. In a flash, she realized this peak must have been the legendary home of the Halamis' evil spirit. *Brim* something-or-other, though the name really didn't matter.

Focusing on the nearer ridges, Kate noticed that they looked like a vast checkerboard. Squares of dingy brown alternated with squares of vibrant green. Suddenly she understood that most of them had been clear-cut. So much of the original forest had been removed that she could see clearly the route of Jones River's rugged canyon from its source at the base of Kahona Falls, twisting and turning into the misty distance.

She moved nearer to Aunt Melanie on the ledge, joining her at the edge of the falls. All about them, trees and shrubs had adapted to the constant spray by rounding themselves, bending low toward the ground, anchoring their roots for the duration of their stormy days. Not far above their heads, the forest vegetation grew quite sparse and then ceased entirely. The black volcanic slopes became too steep for anything larger than the occasional tuft of grass or clump of moss to cling to them. The trail did not end here by accident: One could go no farther.

"If this is the way into the crater," said Kate, "then I'm a stewed prune."

"Better start stewing," replied Aunt Melanie, glancing toward the sunrise.

"How can you be so sure?"

The dark eyes concentrated on Kate. "Because," she said slowly, "I've gone this way before."

Staring up at the sheer cliffs, Kate shook her head. "I don't see how." Probing her great-aunt's face, she asked, "How did you find this so-called trail, anyway?"

Aunt Melanie glanced down at her walking stick, its wood warming to the colors of dawn. "When Billy and the others started building their road, I was desperate to get inside the crater before they did, since there's no telling what damage they could do. I had to see it, to record what's in there, before they messed everything up. I knew there would be Halami artifacts like no one's ever dreamed of finding, and lots more besides. Then I remembered the old legend about Kahona Falls."

"What legend?"

The elder ran a weathered hand through her curls. "It goes like this," she said, and she started to chant:

> *True of heart and straight of spear*
> *Find the forest walled in fear*
> *Through the Gate of Death unknown*
> *Past the Circle of the Stones*
> *To the trees that touch the sky*
> *Blessed by spirits ever nigh*
> *Enter at the start of day*
> *Dawn's first light will show the way.*

"My own translation," she said proudly. "Everyone has a hobby, you know. For some, it's baseball cards." She paused, watching the waterfall. "For me, it's the Halamis."

"But what does it mean? *Through the Gate of Death unknown.* That doesn't sound too promising."

Aunt Melanie moved closer to the edge of the precipice, where water from the falls drenched the rocks continually. "There's another piece to the puzzle. A long time ago, I did some research into the origins of the name Kahona. Turns out it's an Anglicization of an old Halami word, pronounced *kaha-hanya.* That's all I could find out. There wasn't a decent translation anyplace. So I put aside the problem and forgot about it." Her white curls caught the light of dawn. "Then, the night after they started making the new road, I couldn't get to sleep. I started reading an old Halami song sent to me by a friend, and I saw it used the word *kaha-hanya.* The meaning was crystal clear, and suddenly the legend made sense."

"What does it mean?" asked Kate, creeping closer to the edge herself.

Aunt Melanie's ebony eyes glinted strangely. "It means passage, or doorway. Another word would be—"

"Gate," completed Kate, in a flash of understanding. *Through the Gate* . . . She peered over the edge into the churning cataract below, and her bewilderment returned. "But how could a waterfall like this be a gate leading anywhere? This thing's two or three hundred feet high. It's a lot more likely to kill somebody than to take them anywhere."

"Through the Gate of Death unknown," repeated Aunt Melanie, swinging her head toward the waterfall. Feeling more exasperated than enlightened, Kate followed her line of vision.

Aunt Melanie was looking neither up at the waterfall's source nor down into its crashing cascade, but straight across its churning surface. There, Kate could see the pale light of dawn glistening in the spray of droplets. Slowly, the effect of the light began to change. The gleaming droplets seemed to melt into each other, to merge into a single beam of light that stretched across the middle of the waterfall. As the shining droplets merged, they began to scatter the sun's rays into a broad spectrum of colors, until at last the glowing beam transformed itself into a shimmering, shifting rainbow.

As Kate watched, the swath of colors grew bolder and brighter. She thought of the way prisms had always fascinated her, so much so that when her father gave her a pair one Christmas, she took to walking around the house holding one in front of each eye in an effort to see the world's true colors. She had never seen any rainbow as intense as this. But a gate it was not.

"I still don't get it," she declared.

"Look more closely," replied the white-haired woman. *"Behind* the rainbow."

As Kate searched the roaring curtain of water to find Aunt Melanie's meaning, she suddenly saw something strange. Whether it was an optical illusion or whether there was really something there, newly revealed by the first light of day, she wasn't certain. She studied the waterfall closely.

Running along the same path as the rainbow, but deeper—as if it were actually behind the waterfall—was a luminous line of some kind. It appeared to be a long rock ledge, protruding from the cliff at about the same elevation as the place where they now stood.

Then Kate realized that the ledge behind the waterfall could once have been connected to the ledge under their feet. There was a small crevasse dividing the two, about six feet wide, which dropped two hundred feet straight into the churning waters of the canyon. But for that gap, the two ledges seemed to be the continuation of a single outcropping that ran like a belt around the outside of the crater cone. She noted also that if the sun were even a little higher in the sky, the ledge behind the falls would probably not be visible, for the angle of sunlight would make it blend in with the background.

Then, the words of the legend came floating back:

Enter at the start of day
Dawn's first light will show the way.

"Yes," said Aunt Melanie, reading her thoughts. "That is the Gate into Lost Crater. Until I found it again last week, it hadn't been used by anyone for over five hundred years."

Kate was awestruck. "You're not serious," she protested. "Who would be crazy enough—even five hundred years ago—to try to walk on that ledge?"

Aunt Melanie patted her chest. "I am. You can watch me do it, before you follow."

She then stepped closer to the crevasse. Reaching beneath a dense tangle of shrubbery on the side of the ledge, she pulled out a wooden ladder only slightly longer than the width of the crevasse. It was difficult for her to lift, especially given the treacherous footing, but at length she succeeded. Then, as Kate watched in dismay, she crawled closer to the crevasse, planted the base of the ladder on the edge, and let the ladder fall across the gap. The ladder crashed to the rock ledge on the other side, making a primitive bridge.

"But Aunt Melanie," Kate protested, listening anew to the crashing roar of the waterfall as it poured countless thousands of gallons into the canyon below. "One little slip and you'll die! Are you sure you want to go this way?"

The white head nodded.

"But," tried Kate again, "even if you can get in this way, do you really think you can convince a whole team of loggers to go back home? What if they refuse?"

Aunt Melanie crawled back from the slippery edge, lifted herself to her feet, took again her walking stick. She stood erect, but she seemed small and frail against the backdrop of the falls. "I don't know," she answered. "All I know is I've got to try."

She approached Kate, turned her around, and unzipped the blue day pack, removing a small painted drum. Kate recognized it as the one she had seen so often resting on the living-room windowsill, and her heart longed to be there right now, curled up safely with Aunt Melanie by the fire. The drum's tan-colored hide was decorated with images of boldly drawn animal faces, all in black. Seating herself on a rounded rock, she motioned for Kate to come sit beside her.

Reluctantly, Kate obeyed. Her head was spinning with doubt about the whole idea of entering the crater, especially this way.

Then, apart from the din of tumbling water, Kate heard another sound. Using only the tips of her fingers, her face angled toward the luminous ledge behind the falls, Aunt Melanie had started tapping the drum. Striking with a light but firm touch, in no particular rhythm, she seemed to be listening to something far away—a special beat, perhaps, or a melody Kate could not hear.

Aunt Melanie's fingers searched for the hidden rhythm, until finally a regular pattern took hold, one that coincided with the splashing and crashing of the great waterfall. Slowly the drumming swelled into a complex sculpting of sounds. Deftly swishing and sliding across the hide, her hands danced eerily on the drum. At last she raised her voice, chanting some mysterious words that made no sense to Kate. Of these words, one that sounded like *halma-dru* was repeated many times.

When finally the hands came to rest, Kate could still hear the echo of drumbeats in the moist air around them. Her concerns, for the moment, had dissipated. She looked up at Aunt Melanie and said, "That was beautiful."

Aunt Melanie's lips curled into a half smile. "The Halami way of asking for good luck."

"What does that word *halma-dru* mean?"

"That's hard to explain. It's a kind of blessing, and it means something like *May your spirit be one with the spirits around you.*"

"Wasn't there a line in the legend about spirits?"

Nodding, Aunt Melanie said, "And the Halamis meant more than just human spirits. They included animals, trees, air, water, and soil as well."

She replaced the drum in the day pack and zipped it closed. Ignoring Kate's worried expression, she regained her feet and slid the walking stick under her belt. Gingerly, she moved to the very edge of the crevasse. She positioned herself at the spot where the ladder met the rock outcropping, overlapping by only a few inches, her hands gripping the ends of the poles. With a brief glance behind her, she started to crawl slowly across the ladder, placing her knees and palms on the crosspieces. The ladder bent visibly beneath her weight.

Kate, her fears reawakened, approached the crevasse. She grasped the ladder in her hands, steadying it against the rock, so that the repeated crawling motion didn't work it over the edge—taking Aunt Melanie with it. Against her will, she looked down. All she could see was a billowing cloud of spray from the falls exploding against the rocks far below.

"I'm over," called a voice. Kate raised her head to see Aunt Melanie standing on the opposite ledge, pulling the walking stick from her belt. She beckoned, saying, "Your turn now."

Remembering how the ladder had sagged, Kate shivered at the thought of what her own weight might do to those creaky wooden poles. She glanced from the ladder to Aunt Melanie and back again.

"Come, Kate," shouted Aunt Melanie. "I'm going to need you." Then she added, "Don't look down. Just keep looking at me."

Clenching the poles with all the strength her hands could muster, her neck craned to keep her eyes on Aunt Melanie, Kate moved cautiously onto the ladder. The deafening roar of the falls shook the very marrow of her bones. She placed one knee on the first rung, then slid the opposite hand forward, then moved her other knee, then the other hand, again and again and again.

A sudden plume of vapor slapped her face. Without warning, one knee slid sideways off the ladder. Kate's heart pounded rapidly and she froze, grabbing the ladder so tightly she drove splinters into her palms. She was looking down, deep into the crashing depths. Her ears buzzed. The words *through the Gate of Death unknown, Death unknown, Death unknown* echoed inside her head.

This is it, she thought, even as she slowly raised her knee and planted it back on the ladder. *I'm going to die. Right here, right now.* The buzzing in her ears grew louder, obscuring even the roar of the falls, as she forced herself to push one knee forward, then a hand, then the other knee. Slowly, haltingly, she crawled, her heart banging against her chest until she thought she would burst.

Finally, another hand clasped her own. Aunt Melanie, kneeling on the ledge, pulled her by the wrists from the ladder onto water-blackened rock. Kate fell forward into her arms.

"First time's always the hardest," said the elder.

Kate, however, saw no humor. "First time's going to be my last."

Standing up, Aunt Melanie moved closer to the edge. With a grunt, she hauled the ladder across the crevasse.

Kate, her head still buzzing, merely watched. Slowly, she rose to her feet, in time to help her great-aunt stash the ladder behind a thick knot of wet roots and branches. As they finished, Aunt Melanie touched Kate's nose with her finger and said simply, *"True of heart."*

Kate merely shook her head. She observed silently as Aunt Melanie turned to face the dark cavern behind the falls.

Mist billowed about the shadowed entrance. The line of the ledge, now barely visible beneath the tumbling water, seemed to disappear in a jumble of foam and spray. After a moment of deliberation, Kate began to follow Aunt Melanie along the ledge, placing her feet carefully on the wet rock. The ledge narrowed severely as they came nearer to the falls.

Turning sideways, their backs pressed against the wall of vertical rock, the pair moved cautiously into the gap under the waterfall. Kate's toes extended past the lip of the ledge, feeling the vibration of water pummeling the rocks below. Water splashed at her from all directions, drenching her completely, and the constant crashing grew steadily louder. If she could have turned back, she would have. But she wasn't about to desert Aunt Melanie now.

Slowly, she made her way along the outcropping, inching to the right with small sideways steps. Before her she could see nothing but the great waterfall, arching over the ledge like a giant curtain, thundering endlessly. Behind her, the sheer face of the crater rose precipitously, and she tried in vain to find handholds for her fingers to grasp. Spray was everywhere, but she dared not raise her hands to wipe her eyes lest the motion throw her off balance. Light filtered through the watery curtain only dimly, shifting and glinting on the black wall of rock.

Despite the peril, she found herself appreciating the smoothly cut surface of the ledge. So perfect was it that it almost seemed to have been carved by intelligent hands. Perhaps the Halamis had maintained this as a secret trail so many centuries ago. But how could anyone have hammered this ledge out of the rock? Unless, of course, they knew how to fly. No, she concluded, this had to be the chance product of endless amounts of water and endless amounts of time. Nothing more complicated than that.

At that moment, her right shoulder bumped into a vertical wall. She looked down at her feet. The ledge had come to an abrupt end. It met the new wall in a clean, impassable corner. Worst of all, Aunt Melanie was nowhere to be seen.

"Aunt Melanie!" she cried, hoping against hope that her great-aunt had not tumbled to her death in the cataract below. But where else could she be?

Frantically, Kate scanned the black wall of rock above and below her, spray splashing in her eyes. There was no way out, except the way they came—or over the edge into the falls.

Angrily, she kicked the back of her left heel into the rock wall. To her surprise, no solid rock met her foot. Angling herself slightly, she bent very carefully, feeling down the flat rock wall behind her with both hands as she dropped lower.

The fingers of her left hand suddenly curled over the lip of a large hole. It was as high as her waist, quite rounded, its base aligned with the surface of the ledge. A tunnel.

Bending lower, she squeezed into the entrance. Then she discovered something strange: Rising from the rock was a row of perfectly carved miniature steps, half the size of normal steps. They ascended gradually into the tunnel from the narrow ledge.

As she crawled into the tunnel, she encountered a tiny but persistent stream of water flowing out of its upper reaches. The stream splashed down the steps, then plunged over the ledge, a dwarf version of Kahona Falls. She puzzled again at the miniature steps; they were far too small to be of any use, even to a diminutive person like Aunt Melanie.

Yet she must have gone this way, Kate assured herself. She must. Peering ahead, she could see a single pinpoint of light at the far end of the tunnel. A prickle of doubt ran through her. Aunt Melanie could never have climbed through to the other side so quickly. Perhaps the falls took her first, before she could even cry out in warning.

Then in the shifting light, she spied a small object resting on the uppermost step. Reaching for it, she recognized the round shape, the clear plastic wrapping. It was a piece of peppermint candy.

Kate clutched it and pushed it into her jeans pocket. She crawled deeper into the tunnel, climbing upward toward the light. As she placed hands and knees on either side of the streaming water, she wondered whether water had made this tunnel. Or perhaps it was made by something—or someone—else, someone who required small steps.

Upward she crawled, not knowing what lay ahead. She knew only that this was indeed the Gate of Death unknown.

7

deadly water

CLAMBERING out of the tunnel, Kate stepped into a world of pervasive whiteness.

Fog was everywhere, licking at her face and the back of her neck. She held out her arm and could barely see her own hand. The mist felt strangely warm, like steam rising from a hot bath.

"Aunt Melanie," she called, surprised to hear her own voice magnified by the fog. "I'm here."

No answer came. Kate stepped forward, her feet crunching on a surface of small stones. She reached down to pick one of them up and found it as light as a handful of popcorn. Bringing it close to her face, she saw hundreds of little holes dotting its buff-colored surface, making it seem more like sponge than stone.

"Aunt Melanie," she called again, fighting back the growing fear that something was wrong. Maybe she had taken false comfort from the peppermint on the step. Maybe it was merely left behind from an earlier trip. Or Aunt Melanie might have emerged from the tunnel only to meet some unexpected danger. She squinted, trying in vain to see through the omnipresent shroud of fog.

"Where are you?" she cried, an edge of panic in her voice.

Listening for a response, she heard nothing but the faint trickle of water entering the tunnel and a distant clap-clapping, like waves beating against some faraway shore. Then she heard another sound, a rushing, moving sound. Could it be the wind swirling about the crater? Yet she felt no wind. Sniffing the air, she sensed a slight smell of sulfur mixing with the mist.

"Welcome," said a voice, so close it made Kate jump.

A shadowy shape emerged from the fog, stepping toward her. It was not very large, and one hand grasped some kind of shaft or stick.

"It's you!" she exclaimed. "I thought you'd disappeared."

"I'm sorry, dear," replied Aunt Melanie, her tone somewhat distant. "I didn't mean to vanish on you."

"It's all right," said Kate. "I should be used to it by now. Where did you go, anyway?"

"Oh, just got ahead of myself. I was hoping to see some . . . friends."

Kate looked at her quizzically. "Are the loggers in the crater yet?"

"No. We could hear them if they were."

"Then who is here for you to talk to?"

The woman gazed at her intently, as the fog dissipated slightly. "Friends. Sometime, when we have more time, I'll introduce you. But for now, what do you think of Lost Crater?"

Kate wiped the droplets of warm mist off her brow with the sleeve of her sweatshirt. "There's something weird about it. Like it's, I don't know, dangerous somehow."

Aunt Melanie's hand, brushing some dirt off her sweater, paused for a split second at her words, then continued. "There is danger, yes, as in any dormant volcano. I see you've discovered pumice."

"You mean this rock? It's amazingly light. What was that about a volcano?"

"Just another name for the crater," explained Aunt Melanie. "Don't worry, it probably won't erupt again in your lifetime."

Kate tossed the rock into the mist, hearing it clatter as it fell. "That doesn't sound too good to me."

"You're still feeling your nightmare, poor child. Anyway, this volcano hasn't been active recently."

"What does 'recently' mean?" probed Kate.

"Oh, in the last seven thousand years." She grinned impishly. "Geologic time always makes me feel so young."

The fog swirled again, pressing closer, turning Aunt Melanie into a mere shadow in the mist. "I still don't like this place," said Kate. "How come it feels so warm?"

"Here," answered her great-aunt, taking her by the sleeve. "I'll show you."

Aunt Melanie led Kate down the sloping rock-strewn terrain for eight or ten paces. Halting suddenly, she bent down for a piece of pumice, then tossed it underhanded into the fog. To Kate's surprise, she heard an unmistakable splash.

"I had no idea the lake was so close."

"Understandable, since you couldn't see it," her great-aunt replied. "The volcanic plumbing under the lake keeps it warm, you see, so steam is rising all the time. The geologists tell me it's had cold spells and warm spells, alternating over the ages. We're in one of the warm ones now. That's why the crater is usually fogged in."

Kate picked up a fist-sized rock and threw it into the fog with the force of a first-string shortstop. The splash soon followed. "Why did the Halamis come all the way up here, if they couldn't see anything when they got here?"

"There are many ways to see," replied Aunt Melanie, her voice seeming to swell in the fog so that it sounded quite close to Kate's ears.

"How many times have you come up here, since you found the way?"

"Twice before. I'd have come more often if this whole business with the new road hadn't kept me tied down all week. There's plenty to explore; the crater's almost a mile across, you know. But even just two visits were enough to find plenty. For instance, there's an old Halami camp on the other side of the lake, right where the old songs said it would be. I found some beautiful tools there. Stone bowls, knives and spoons, a sewing awl, two—"

A sudden movement in the mist distracted her, and she halted. Instinctively, Kate moved closer to her side.

All at once, the fog started to shift. The clouds of mist grew rapidly thinner, like fabric of filigree whose ornamental tracery was pulling apart before their eyes. First to unveil itself was the lake, deep turquoise in color, so utterly blue that Kate felt if she put her hand into the water, it would come out blue.

Across the water and through the mist, Kate could now make out the dark rock of the crater rim, rising straight up another thousand feet or more. She glanced behind to look at the entrance to the tunnel, but she could not find it amidst the jumble of gray and buff-colored pumice. A pang of fear shot through her: If the tunnel was invisible when it was this close and the air was this clear, how could they ever hope to find it again in the fog?

Before she could voice her concern, however, she discovered the source of the rushing sound that she had earlier mistaken for wind. At the edge of the lake, no more than twenty yards to her right, a river of water cascaded briskly down a channel, then disappeared into the rocks. Here was the origin of Kahona Falls.

"Look there," announced Aunt Melanie, pointing toward the middle of the lake.

Kate's attention turned to a shadowy mass that seemed to be rising out of the water. Her skin prickled. The mass, dark and foreboding, seemed like something from another planet. At first it appeared to move, and then she realized that it was only the effect of the swirling mist. It was jagged, covered with spires, and blacker than the blackest thing she had ever seen.

It was an island.

"What—is that?" Kate sputtered.

"That's what the Halamis called Ho Shantero. It means Island That Moves."

"It does seem to move, doesn't it? Of course, it's only a trick of the fog."

Aunt Melanie said nothing.

"I remember now," Kate continued. "It was there on the map, the one you made. But there wasn't any island at all on the big map."

"That's because the mapmakers didn't know it existed until that Forest Service man flew over the crater. I suspect he didn't pay much attention to it, though, since it doesn't have any trees."

Kate furrowed her brow. "I can't imagine flying low over that thing and not paying attention."

Aunt Melanie cocked her head thoughtfully. "I did hear from Frank that he said something curious about it later, in Cary's Tavern after he had a few beers in him."

"What?"

Aunt Melanie looked at her watch, and her face turned grim. "It's later than I thought. Let's get going or they're going to get to the redwoods before we do." She started walking parallel to the shore, away from the bubbling cascade.

Kate jogged to her side. "What did he say about the island?"

The woman shrugged. "Something about the surface of the island seeming to move. Like it was crawling or something."

Kate glanced at the dark mass warily.

Aunt Melanie sped up her pace a bit. "Right after he saw the island, he said the plane was shaken by a sudden updraft—so hard it nearly knocked him off his seat. Made him concentrate on flying for a few seconds, and by the time he was past the turbulence, the island was well behind. Then he saw the forest, and he never looked back."

"Did his pictures show anything weird? You said he took lots."

"None of the pictures he took of the island came out, for some reason."

"Fog," suggested Kate hopefully.

"Or maybe it was the work of Tinnanis," said Aunt Melanie.

"Tinnanis?" Kate wasn't sure she really wanted to know what the word meant.

"Just pulling your leg," answered Aunt Melanie, hopping across a small rivulet that drained into the lake. "They're part of Halami mythology, a magical little people who lived in the most ancient part of the forest. The Halamis believed that they kept the forest healthy, through some secret power of their own. Don't worry, though. I doubt we'll be meeting any."

Kate tugged on her sweater. "It makes me wonder who made those tiny little steps back at the entrance to the tunnel."

"Most people would tell you it was the Halamis. After all, they made all sorts of things in honor of the Tinnanis. Tiny tools, things like that."

"And what would *you* tell me?" asked Kate.

Her great-aunt smiled curiously. "I'd say nobody knows for sure."

"What did these, um, Tinnanis supposedly look like, aside from being small?" Kate rather liked the idea of little people who lived among the trees. Perhaps they could even make themselves invisible at will, or change themselves into animal shapes.

Aunt Melanie slowed her step, peering for a few seconds into the mist swirling about the black island. "Once again, nobody knows." She turned and winked at her companion. "But if you should see one, be sure to tell me, won't you?"

Kate gave no answer. Then she spied an odd protrusion rising from the pumice stones just ahead. Standing about two feet tall, the powdery yellow outcropping looked like an upside-down funnel.

"What's that thing?" she asked, pointing.

"A fumarole," said Aunt Melanie, pausing to bend over it. "Once there was a geyser here, maybe a hundred feet high. Can't you imagine a big plume of steam and sulfur gushing out of this thing?"

"Sure," Kate replied. "Too easily."

Aunt Melanie again checked her watch. "Let's keep moving, Kate." She nodded toward the thick line of trees not far ahead. "That's where we're going."

She resumed her pace, and Kate fell in behind. Over her right shoulder, Kate could see the island, partially obscured by shreds of fog from the ceaselessly steaming lake. It resembled a phantom ship, hovering between darkness and invisibility. Then she noticed that the deep blue water around it permitted no reflection. She pondered whether that was because of the water or the island itself.

Kate turned to the other side, hoping to crowd the haunting thoughts of the island from her mind. Not far above them, resting on the jumble of broken pumice just in front of the dark cliff wall, she noticed a collection of six or seven enormous boulders. They appeared to be arranged in a ragged circle, like rocks around a giant's campfire. Some of the boulders looked bigger than Aunt Melanie's cottage, and none were smaller than Trusty.

She recalled the Circle of Stones she had seen on Aunt Melanie's map. Vaguely, she remembered seeing the word *Beware* written nearby in small letters. But beware of what?

Something about these strange shapes tugged at her, made her curious. *I'll just have a quick look,* she told herself. No need even to tell Aunt Melanie, who had strode off ahead. Better just to dash up there and back before she even notices.

Turning her back to the blue lake, Kate started to scramble up the rock-strewn terrain. At once she discovered how steeply it sloped from the shoreline to the base of the vertical cliffs. The angle was close to forty-five degrees, forcing her to use her hands frequently. The rocks, dampened by fog, were slick and slippery, slowing her progress even more. But as the circle of giant stones drew nearer, their inexplicable attraction grew stronger.

Stopping at one point to catch her breath, she turned and took in the full expanse of the crater. Seen without its normal filling of fog, it was impressive indeed. High cliffs rose along the far rim, some pointed like giant teeth, others curved into monumental domes. New morning light streamed across the undulating wall of rock, staining it deep red. Below, the white sweater of Aunt Melanie moved steadily along the edge of the lake, approaching the forest. Meanwhile, spiraling columns of mist swirled slowly around the cinder-black island.

Kate caught a whiff of an enticing aroma from somewhere above her. Curious, she continued upward. Moving like a spider, she scurried up the slope. At length, the incline leveled off somewhat. She raised her head to see that she had arrived at the circle of boulders.

She stood there, huffing. The stones, she realized, were ribbed with deep cracks that covered their entire surface with a net of dark lines. Whether they had been shattered by an explosion or baked by a burst of volcanic heat, she did not know. They had clearly withstood some sort of violence, powerful beyond imagining. For an instant she wondered whether these giant stones actually were pieces of a puzzle, remains of a single, enormous rock that had been blasted to bits long ago.

Then she perceived again the aroma, unlike anything she had ever smelled before. It was sweet, almost like Aunt Melanie's spice tea, but with an alluring quality no tea could possibly possess. To her surprise, cloves, cinnamon, ginger, and even the essence of lilac—all her most favorite smells—wove themselves through the perfume. It was almost as if this aroma had been created exclusively for her. Underneath, she detected the barest breath of sulfur, strong enough to give added zest, yet not so strong as to detract from the enchanting sweetness.

Searching for the source, she quickly found it: a pool of dark green liquid bubbling beneath the smallest of the huge stones. She stepped closer, immersing herself in the fragrant smell. The pool was lined with some sort of soft green algae whose undulating hairs danced gracefully, making the rocks lining the sides seem gentle and inviting.

What could this lovely liquid be? She wanted to touch it, to taste it, to bathe in it. Heedless of any danger, she kneeled by the side of the frothing pool and reached her hand toward it.

"Kate!"

She jolted at the distant voice. It was Aunt Melanie, calling her. A wave of resentment raced through her, something she had never felt before toward her great-aunt. She called back angrily, "Don't bother me now. I'll be there in a minute."

Again, she cupped her hand, eager to take a drink. She leaned forward, reaching toward the bubbling green pool.

"Kate!" came the cry again, closer this time, as Aunt Melanie toiled her way up the steep slope behind her.

Kate froze, as an inner voice told her to be careful. Perhaps she would wait a moment longer. Then, in a flash, her anger surged anew. Aunt Melanie only wanted to spoil her fun. She wanted the whole crater to herself, wouldn't let her discover anything. But she had. She had discovered this beautiful pool. *I'll show her,* Kate thought. *I can make some discoveries too.*

The pool seemed to reach out with fragrant, comforting arms to embrace her. Kate smiled, leaning still closer to the frothing green liquid. Slowly, she stretched out her hand.

Just as the back of her cupped hand touched the surface, she heard a shrill whistle and looked up. Some sort of bird, looking like a red streak, hurtled at her from the top of the giant stone behind the pool. It smacked full force into her shoulder, knocking her backward onto the rocks, then flew off.

"Ehhhh!" she shrieked, landing on her back with a thud.

Before she could roll back to her knees, someone clasped the arm of her sweatshirt. Aunt Melanie stood above her, breathing heavily. Suddenly, Kate felt a sharp pain on the back of her left hand. Turning it to her face, she saw a mass of green wormlike creatures writhing on her skin. They seemed to be burrowing into the back of her hand.

She screamed again, shaking her hand wildly. Aunt Melanie grabbed Kate's wrist, thrust her hand into a rivulet of water flowing into the pool, and started scrubbing intensely. Kate squealed in pain and tried to pull away.

"I know it hurts," said Aunt Melanie with a scowl, "but it's necessary. Hold steady." She continued the scouring despite Kate's squirms and cries of anguish.

At last, she relented, releasing her grip. Kate looked at the back of her hand to see red and blistered skin below her knuckles. It was bleeding, and ached as if it had been scalded, but the writhing worms were gone.

Aunt Melanie pulled a faded purple kerchief from her pocket. She wrapped it carefully around Kate's hand, securing it with a knot. Holding Kate firmly by the shoulders, she scrutinized her. "Are you feeling all right now?"

"I guess so," muttered Kate, sheepishly avoiding her gaze. "My hand hurts like crazy."

"It will for a while, I'm afraid. It's going to sting for a couple of days, and then you'll probably have a scar."

"What—what happened to me?" Kate stammered. "All I wanted was to get closer to—"

"The green pool," completed her great-aunt grimly. "You were caught in its spell."

"Spell?" repeated Kate, incredulous. She looked over at the pool, frothing energetically. The fragrant perfume had vanished, and so had her desire to touch it. "But how could it? Spells aren't real."

"This one is."

Kate pursed her lips. "And that bird . . . the red one that flew into me. Was it part of the spell too?"

Aunt Melanie stroked her chin. "No, I don't think so." She paused, thinking. "It looked like an owl. Maybe a flammulated owl. It's a rusty color—and small, about the right size. They can be downright feisty. But I've never heard of one flying right into somebody like that. And in broad daylight, too, when it should be sleeping."

"I still can't believe there's some kind of spell."

Shaking her head, Aunt Melanie declared, "Then watch this."

She thrust the end of her walking stick into the pool. Suddenly, it ceased bubbling. The green liquid seemed to evaporate, and in its place Kate saw thousands upon thousands of the same venomous worms that had been on her hand, writhing over and under each other in one massive heap. They filled the depression that had once been the pool, slithering across rocks that had once been its sides. Then, to her shock, she saw several knobs of white mixed in with the gray rocks, and she recognized them at once.

"Bones," she said in horror, drawing her left hand close to her chest. "There are bones in there."

Aunt Melanie pulled out the walking stick, and immediately the bubbling pool returned. The green worms, if still there, disappeared in the froth.

"How does it do that? The stick, I mean."

"This stick is, well—unusual," answered Aunt Melanie, cocking her head to one side. "I've only begun to discover what it can do. It's full of puzzles, like why this owl's face on the handle looks almost human. I found it on my first trip through the tunnel behind the falls. It was just lying there, as if it were waiting for me. Somehow, it has the power to show what the pool really looks like. Don't ask me how."

She hefted the stick in her hand. "It's the only thing that saved me when the spell first drew me up here. I forgot all about the Halami chant about *deadly green water,* though it was one of the first I ever heard:

> *Beware of the deadly green water*
> *That swallows whatever it sees*
> *You shall not escape from the Stones*
> *You shall not encounter the Trees.*

I was about to fall in just like you, when the end of the stick happened to slip into the pool. Suddenly, the spell was broken, and I saw everything. Even that wonderful aroma of juniper berries and peppermint—my favorite smells—vanished instantly. Did I ever feel stupid."

"You and me both," said Kate, regaining her feet.

Aunt Melanie faced the green pool. "Apparently, once the spell's been broken, it doesn't affect you again. That's why it isn't pulling on us now."

Cautiously, Kate stepped nearer to the edge of the boiling liquid. She could not help but wonder how many creatures had been drawn to their death there. "I wonder how it got here," she said, holding her left hand protectively. "It isn't natural. No way. And the stream there, where you washed those—those *things* off my hand, it's clear as anything. But, look, when the water gets to the pool it turns that horrible green color."

Her gaze moved to the assembled boulders. She counted them: There were seven, all deeply cracked. Behind them, a colonnade of eroded lava columns lined the cliff wall, resembling the ribs of a decomposing skeleton. "Something's weird about these boulders too. They feel—I don't know, strange."

"They should," replied Aunt Melanie, as she started down the slope toward the lake. "They are the Circle of Stones."

"The ones in the legend," recalled Kate, hustling to catch up to her. "What else do you know about them?"

"Later," came the response. "Right now we have to get into the Hidden Forest. Before anyone else does."

Kate glanced over her shoulder at the great boulders. "All I know is they make me nervous."

"That," answered Aunt Melanie with a mysterious gleam in her eye, "is because they're watching you."

the hidden forest

AUNT Melanie's pace quickened as they rounded the last inlet on the lake before the deep woods. Whether she was worried that they would arrive after the loggers, or simply excited to be nearing the Hidden Forest, Kate could not tell. Probably some of both. They stepped rapidly over the buff-colored rocks lining the shore of the steaming lake.

At last, they approached the deep woods. The jumble of rocks underfoot turned to sand, then soil, then a curvaceous carpet of grass. Several streams of bright water flowed from the forest across the grass to empty into the lake. Mosses, vibrant green, clung to the broken branches that lay on the ground, while small birds chirped in the branches overhead.

Kate had never seen a meadow so verdant. Her left hand continued to ache, but she gradually grew less aware of it. Flowers—white, yellow, violet—draped the sides of the rivulets. Looking at them instead of where she was going, she thrust her foot into a deep well of mud. She had to lift it out carefully, toes high, to avoid losing her sneaker.

At the border between the meadow and the forest, she looked back once more at the blue, blue lake. The fog was swiftly returning, making the island seem to glide ghost-like over its surface. How deep this lake must be, she could not even guess. She wondered what strange beings might live within its waters.

In a few seconds, fog had completely obscured the island, as well as the Circle of Stones some distance above the shore. Billowing clouds now blocked the sun. It would not be long before the day's first rain would fall, filling the lake and fueling Kahona Falls.

Stepping across a moss-covered log, she entered the Hidden Forest. At once, she was greeted by the familiar fragrance of resins, needles, berries, cones, leaves, bark, and soil, mixing together in a powerful perfume. Yet this time something was different. These woods smelled older, deeper, and something more, something she could not quite identify. She saw Aunt Melanie, looking smaller than usual against the backdrop of tall trees, disappear behind a double-trunked cedar.

A thrill ran through Kate. She and Aunt Melanie were the only human beings ever to walk in these woods since the time of the Halamis. As she strode quickly to catch up, her feet practically sprang across the forest floor. She understood that this buoyancy came from the thousands of years of living and dying that had occurred beneath her feet. A delicate ring of pink sorrel caught her attention, and next to it she saw an enormous snail slithering across a toppled fir. A cluster of sword ferns shone in the dim light ahead; the fronds, three or four feet long, glowed with a soft radiance.

Aunt Melanie, while working her way through the trees, pointed out some of the herbs and flowers springing up from the soil, from between roots, or sometimes straight from the ragged bark of the trees. Eschewing their tongue-twisting Latin names as "more for show than anything else," she used only the more expressive common names. Kate liked especially the ones called bleeding heart, sugar scoop, fairy lantern, scarlet paintbrush, and glade anemone.

Like the crater filling with fog, Kate's heart began to fill with a sense of unaccustomed peace. Everything here seemed to fit somehow, to belong just where it was. She turned slowly around, discovering new seedlings sprouting from almost every surface. Sinuous vines of purple and brown wound around trunks, making little rope ladders for small animals to climb. One tree, long dead, was covered completely with a leotard of light green lichen. Across fallen logs marched dozens of colorful mushrooms, some no bigger than ants, some shaped like luscious red lips, some round and wrinkled like exposed brains. From virtually every cavity in the trees something surprising appeared. Ferns and fungi, conifers and broadleafs, each one unique in dress and design, each one part of the common community. Life of all kinds was here wholly at home.

Despite the accumulating clouds above, sometimes a stray shaft of light would penetrate the intricate mesh of branches to reach the forest floor far below. One of these, stretching like a fiery filament, fell upon a moss-covered rock by Kate's feet. She leaned closer to study it.

To her amazement, the rock had some lines deeply etched on its surface. Many of the lines had been filled with moss, and she had to trace their pattern with her finger to feel where they ran. When she found one line encircling the others, she realized they were too deep and regular to be accidental. There could be no doubt. They had been carved.

She stepped back a pace to get a better perspective. Then she saw the unmistakable design of the lines. It was a face. A human face. With wide, deep-set eyes, the face glared at her, across time beyond memory. Its open mouth seemed to be shouting something, a warning perhaps, in a tongue Kate could not comprehend.

"Hey, look at this," she said, pointing.

No answer. She whipped around to see where Aunt Melanie had gone. But she was nowhere to be found. Kate ran a few steps ahead, suddenly finding herself at the edge of a clearing. Not again, she thought. Where could she have gone this time? A pang of fear shot through her, and she noticed her aching hand. For the first time, the forest began to feel somehow perilous.

"Aunt Melanie!" she called.

No sound but the swishing of branches.

Kate ran deeper into the forest. Again she shouted.

No answer.

Then she saw them. Arrayed before her were the most awesome trees she had ever seen. As solemn as a group of pilgrims gathered to pray, they stood together in silence. Drawing in a deep breath, Kate gazed at the uplifted boughs arching three hundred feet above her head, their lacy branches permeated with light. At the base of the trees, heavy burls hung like jowls, bordered by fibrous bark as delicate as strands of hair. Powerful roots clenched the soil firmly, as they had for centuries upon centuries.

Redwoods.

Then, in the center of the grove, she saw the most majestic tree of all. It stood taller and broader than the rest, older than anything else in the forest. It rose straight out of the earth with all the strength and grace of a monarch.

Kate moved closer, laying her hand respectfully on the tree's gnarled trunk. So thick was its base that she guessed it would take five or six grown men holding hands to encircle it but once. She craned her neck backward, following the narrowing girth higher and higher, through successive canopies of mossy boughs.

Lowering her eyes, she discovered a hollow cavern within the folds of the massive trunk. Although it was only as high as her waist, it seemed to be quite deep. Something about its dark interior frightened her, yet tugged at her as well, so she approached it cautiously. Stooping to peer inside, she suddenly froze. Staring at her from the blackness of the cavern were two gleaming eyes.

The eyes regarded her intently. Then, in a flash, she recognized them.

"It's you," sighed Kate. "I called and called and when you didn't answer I got scared."

"No need to be scared, dear." A hand reached out from the cavern and, taking Kate's arm, drew her inside. "I didn't hear you calling. As it happens, I was listening to something else."

"Aunt Melanie, you're impossible."

Her heart still beating with excitement, Kate slipped the day pack off her shoulders and sat beside her great-aunt within the hollow of the tree. Slowly, her eyes adjusted to the dark, and she perceived the subtle gradations of colors around them. Rising from the earthen floor, the ribbed wooden walls of the inner trunk were streaked with black, charred by some forest fire perhaps a thousand years before. She looked at the wood bordering the cavern's entrance and saw that it was only four or five inches thick, yet she knew it must be supporting considerable weight.

As she leaned back against the wood, her body relaxed. She felt safe. As if this tree would hold her, protect her against anything that could possibly happen. She looked through the entrance to the grove outside. The scattered shafts of light and wispy streaks of mist made the scene look more like an impressionist painting than a real stand of redwoods. It was cooler here amidst the trees than it had been near the lake, and she folded her arms against her chest to stay warm.

"We beat the loggers here," said Aunt Melanie. "Let's be glad of that. I wanted you to feel the power of this place, when everything's quiet, at least for a minute or two. Before we head up to where their road comes into the crater, how about a quick taste of hot chocolate?"

Kate nodded at the suggestion. Swiftly, she unzipped the pack and poured out two cups of the steaming liquid. The smell was as delicious as the taste, and she held the cup close to her nose. Stretching out her legs, she realized that she had not sat down since emerging from the Jeep before dawn.

"I saw a face back there," she said, her voice echoing dully within the hollow. "A face carved in a rock."

"You mean a petroglyph," corrected Aunt Melanie. "You must have found one of the Halami warning stones."

Kate took another sip of hot chocolate, warming her hands against the cup. "Warning stones? What were they warning about?"

Aunt Melanie answered in a near whisper. "This redwood grove was the most sacred of all places for the Halamis. They believed that spirits would gather here, among the redwoods, sometimes even coming and going through the trees themselves. Anyone who enters this grove does so at his own risk."

Kate fidgeted on the earthen floor of the hollow. "Spirits who live with these redwoods couldn't be evil," she said. "This feels like a place for good spirits."

The elder nodded. "*To the trees that touch the sky, Blessed by spirits ever nigh.* I feel that way too. But even good spirits can do strange and frightening things sometimes." She tilted her head in her usual way. "This grove is in the heart of the oldest forest you or I will ever see."

"And this tree is in the heart of the grove."

"Yes," replied Aunt Melanie. "I call this tree the Ancient One."

The Ancient One, repeated Kate to herself. Older than old. The very center of the Hidden Forest. As she reached to touch the inner wall of the tree, her thoughts drifted from the hollow to the grove to the great woods itself. From the first moment she stepped across its green border, she had been struck by the diversity of life around her. Yet now she sensed something else, something even more remarkable. This forest not only had diversity, it had unity. Just as the branches overhead intertwined in a complex pattern, so did the living beings of the ancient forest intertwine in a way she could scarcely begin to comprehend. Perhaps that was what made her feel so peaceful here. Connected, part of this place, in a way she had never felt before.

Lightly touching Aunt Melanie's thigh, she said, "I'm

so glad to be here, with you. I could never be here alone, though. It wouldn't be the same."

"Even if I weren't here," replied the elder, "you wouldn't be alone."

Kate nodded, absently reaching for the delicate frond of a fern that had sprouted near the entrance.

"Maidenhair fern," said Aunt Melanie reflectively. "See how black the stems are? The Halamis used it for making their baskets. Down lower, the color isn't so strong, so they used to get it from the highest places they could find. And when it grows near redwoods, the tops are good for making tea that helps to ease a fever. That may be what first tempted them to find a way into the crater, looking for plants like maidenhair."

Stirring, Kate bumped her bandaged hand against the wall of the hollow. It throbbed, aching. She thought of the bubbling green pool, and the ghastly wormlike creatures it harbored. "Do evil spirits live by the Circle of Stones?"

"Not spirits," replied Aunt Melanie. "Not exactly." She cleared her throat.

Kate looked at her uncomfortably, remembering her uneasy feeling about the stones. "What then?"

"It's best we discuss it later, dear," she said, her voice again almost a whisper. She scanned the shaft of her walking stick, leaning against the wall of the hollow. The yellow eyes of the carved owl's head seemed to be observing them. "Some other time."

"Can't you tell me just a little?"

Aunt Melanie's tongue pushed against her cheek. She seemed to be on the edge of answering, searching for the right words. *"Azanna,"* she said at last. "The Halamis called the Circle of Stones *Azanna.* What it means is—"

Just then they heard something new. Distant, yet still jarring. Kate, like Aunt Melanie, held her breath, straining to hear. The sound grew steadily louder, until there could be no mistaking its source.

"Loggers," said Kate. "They're in the crater."

9

the walking stick

"COME on," replied Aunt Melanie, already on her way out of the hollow. "I want to meet them before they reach the redwoods."

"But what will you do then?"

"I'm going to confront them. Face to face. I'm going to count on the fact they all know me. Heavens, I taught most of them how to read and write! And if Frank's with them, I know he'll listen to reason. He knows that cutting down these trees won't do anything to solve our real problem. Not really. It just postpones things." She halted, hearing the distant revving of a chain saw. "They're up by the road cut, trying out their saws. Let's go."

"What about Billy?" asked Kate. "He's not going to listen to reason."

The dark eyes hardened. "He'll have to hurt me before he hurts this tree."

Aunt Melanie strode across the redwood grove, heading the opposite direction from the way they had entered. Grabbing the day pack, Kate followed, her moment of peace now shattered. The noise of the chain saw buzzed through the forest like an angry hornet, searing her ears. She wished they could go faster, wished they could fly over the forest and descend on the intruders like a pair of eagles.

Soon the great trees grew thinner, and they sloshed through a swampy section where the air was alive with mosquitoes. Sometimes they could keep their feet on small stones sprouting from the water, but more often they had to trudge straight through the muck. At last, brushing away a cloud of insects, Kate could see the misty cliffs ahead.

Higher they scrambled, until finally they left the woods and were moving across the rock-strewn rim of the crater. Aunt Melanie turned to the right, traversing just above the trees. The fog grew thicker, covering the cliffs and flowing over the forest. Kate could hear the distant lapping of lake water on the shore below, but saw only a vaguely blue shadow beneath the clouds. Once she caught a glimpse of the dark island through the gathering mist; it seemed closer to the shore than she remembered.

Aunt Melanie stopped suddenly. More chain saws revved from somewhere nearby. "Their road cut is just above us," she said, breathing heavily. "Thirty yards, maybe. But since the road stops at the hole they blasted in the cliff wall, they'll have to carry their gear down inside, and that will take some time. A few of them may already be down in the forest, I'm afraid. With this fog, they could have passed us without our knowing it. But judging from the sounds, I think most of them are still up there. And they'll have to pass by here if they want to—"

She stiffened, her eyes widening in sudden dread. "My stick!" she exclaimed. "I left it in the redwood grove—in the tree."

The distraught woman started back across the rocks when Kate caught her by the arm. "What are you doing?" she asked in disbelief. "You can't go back for it now."

"I must," panted Aunt Melanie. "It mustn't fall into their hands. It mustn't."

Kate studied her in consternation. "But we can't leave

here now. Not if you want to stop them before they're all in the forest."

Aunt Melanie shook loose from her grip. "I don't know what else to do."

"Wait," said Kate. "Let me run back for the stick. I can run a whole lot faster than you can. With any luck I'll be back here before you have to face any of them."

For a few seconds, Aunt Melanie's eyes searched hers. "All right," she said at last. "But be careful. As important as the walking stick is, you are more important to me."

"I'll be careful," Kate promised.

Nervously, the white-haired woman squeezed Kate's unbandaged hand. "Then run like the wind. And stay as quiet as a Halami, in case some loggers are already down there. *Halma-dru*, my child."

Throwing her braid over her shoulder, Kate turned and ran back across the crumbled pumice they had just traversed. She could not see more than a few feet ahead in the fog, so she had to judge distance solely by instinct. After a few moments, she left the rocky rim and veered into the forest.

Before long the rocks were swathed in ferns and mosses. She found herself in the swampy place again, but without any landmarks it was difficult to know where to cross. She felt a twinge of fear that she could easily get lost in this dark forest, full of strange places and, she suspected, still stranger beings. A mosquito stung the back of her neck and she slapped herself.

She plunged forward, stepping through the thick mud, avoiding the deeper parts by staying near the shoots of bright green grasses that sprouted on all sides like miniature bamboo forests. Squelching rapidly through the marsh, she tripped on a branch and landed with a splash on her hands, immersed up to her elbows in cold, murky water. Regaining her feet, she sloshed ahead, not bothering to brush the mud from her legs, arms, and chin.

Finally she reached more solid ground, a grassy meadow much like the one they had met when first they entered the forest. Leaping across a rippling rivulet, she scanned the trees ahead for any signs that might guide her to the redwood grove, but saw none. She entered the mist-filled woods, padding across the springy terrain in the hope of seeing something familiar. But for her own breathing and the crunching of needles underfoot, she heard no sounds. The forest was eerily silent.

Then she heard voices. She ducked behind a moss-covered boulder. There were two people not ten feet from her when she again raised her head from a spray of ferns. To her surprise, they were not loggers, but boys. She recognized them immediately: Jody, who had stolen Aunt Melanie's envelope, and Sly, Billy's younger brother. She scowled at the very sight of them. Sly wore a .22-caliber rifle over his shoulder. He was poking Jody with his finger, goading him about something. Kate pushed apart the ferns, straining to hear what they were saying.

"C'mon, Jody," urged the older boy with the rifle. "This is your big chance."

"My chance for what?" replied the other, taking an awkward step backward.

"To prove you're not a chicken heart."

"I don't have to prove anything," Jody replied. "I just don't like killing things when there's no reason. C'mon, Sly, let's go find the others."

"Chicken heart."

"I am not," protested Jody, pushing a lock of red hair back from his forehead. "Killing them is bad luck, and besides, it's just too easy."

"Show me," demanded Sly, taking the rifle off his shoulder and inserting a bullet. "Show me how easy it is, or I'll make sure everybody knows what a chicken heart you really are. They already know how you botched getting the envelope."

Jody said nothing, but glanced over his shoulder at a low branch of a broken-topped Douglas fir towering above them. Following his line of vision, Kate saw nothing but a brownish hump rising vertically from the branch. Then, astonishingly, the hump rotated its head, revealing two perfectly round brown eyes. They studied the scene below with unmistakable curiosity, unaware of any danger.

It was an owl. Not twenty feet above the ground, the bird rested regally on its perch, its chocolate-colored plumage dotted with white spots. Kate sucked in her breath. She knew she should not take any more time here than she had already. But she could not bear to leave now.

"Jody Chicken Heart O'Leary," recited the barrel-chested boy. "That's gonna be your name for the rest of your days."

Jody gave him a sharp look. "Gimme that gun," he said, reaching out for the rifle.

With a smirk, Sly handed it to him. "Good. Now let's see you blast that owl over hell's half acre."

He won't do it, thought Kate. It's just sitting there, innocently sitting there. Though it was larger and lacked the same red color, it reminded her of the owl who had saved her life at the green pool.

Her mind raced to find some way to stop the shooting without giving herself away. Then she spied a small rock by her feet, tangled in the roots of a fallen sapling.

Jody stood still, rifle by his side. Slowly, he raised it, planting the butt of the gun against his shoulder. Motionless, he held that position for several seconds. Perspiration glistened on his cheek.

At the same time, Kate reached for the rock. She took careful aim at the branch supporting the owl, then wound her arm like a shortstop about to fire the ball at home plate. Meanwhile, the proud bird did not move so much as a feather. It simply stared at the people below, watching them with huge round eyes.

"Chicken heart, chicken heart," taunted Sly.

"Back off," Jody retorted.

"Chicken heart!"

Kate released the rock just as the boy squeezed the trigger. The gun exploded, shattering the stillness of the forest. The rock whizzed past the owl's perch, but it was too late. As she watched helplessly, the bird tumbled backward off the branch and fell with a thud to the forest floor. It landed in a craggy bed of downed branches and dead needles.

"Took you long enough," said Sly roughly as he took back his rifle. He strapped it over his shoulder. "I'll try to find another one so you can get some more practice." Grinning at his own joke, he started off into the forest.

Jody didn't answer. His eyes were fixed on the place where the owl had fallen. As Kate watched from her hiding place, he slowly approached the spot, pushing aside the stiff branches that hid the bird's body from view.

Bending down, he looked at the creature, whose enormous eyes were now closed. Absently, he stroked the bird's round chest. Then, as if he were performing a small act of repentance, he lifted a large slab of moss from the wet soil at the base of the fir and started to lay it over the body of the owl when a soft hooting sound echoed out of the forest mist. *Hooo-hooo. Hooo-hooo.*

Jody straightened himself, his expression grim. Then his face seemed to tighten. "Aw, who cares, anyway?" he said. "It's just a stupid old bird." Without looking at the owl again, he walked off in the direction of a whining chain saw.

Taking care to avoid Jody, Kate sprang into the forest. Swerving around massive trees and leaping over fallen logs, she moved as fast as she could. The sound of the chain saw drew nearer, leading her, she knew, to the redwood grove. Some of the loggers must have passed them in the fog, as Aunt Melanie had feared. *There's no way to stop them now,* she lamented. *All I can possibly do is get the walking stick.*

Concentrating on following the sound, Kate did not notice the steady darkening of the forest. The fog itself grew thicker, while less light fell from the sky above the trees. Nor did she feel the forceful sweep of the wind that leaned ever more heavily against the trunks and boughs around her.

Suddenly, she burst into the redwood grove. Just to her left was a logger sitting on a downed limb, struggling to repair his chain saw. "Mother-killing saw blade," he grumbled, removing his hard hat and wiping his brow with the

sleeve of his red plaid shirt. "I didn't carry you all this way
just so you could break down on me."

Kate then focused on another logger, tall and wiry, who
had buried his chain saw deep into the trunk of one of the
redwoods. He was sliding it up and down, back and forth,
gunning the engine as sawdust sprayed in all directions.
Then he pulled out the saw, set it idling on the ground, and
reached his arms upward to stretch his back.

"Hey, Dick," he called to the man working on his saw.
"Sure beats having a desk job, doesn't it?"

"Uh-huh," grunted the other. "And sure beats unem-
ployment checks."

"You can say that again," agreed the first, picking up his
saw once more.

Standing deeper in the grove was Billy, wearing a red
T-shirt with the Blade fire department emblem. Kate froze
as she saw him yank the starter rope of his chain saw, then
lift it into the air, preparing to slice into the Ancient One
itself, home of the hollow where she and Aunt Melanie
had quietly rested only minutes before. The chain saw
screamed as he lowered it to rip into the tree's midsection.

At that instant, the sky flashed with an explosion of
lightning. Kate looked up to see black clouds condensing
above the branches. She realized the forest had grown
much darker, as the tall trees started to sway under gale-
like winds.

One by one, the chain saws went silent, as lightning
flashes grew more frequent. The howling wind brought an
enormous limb crashing to the ground near Kate, and one
man cried out in pain as another falling branch clipped
his leg.

"Make a run for it," shouted one logger.

"Let's dust this place," called another. "Get back to the
trucks and we'll wait out the storm."

Lightning sizzled across the sky, punctuated by earsplitting blasts of thunder. Branches waved wildly, and some
splintered off and came tearing down from the higher
canopies. Hail the size of golf balls pounded the trees and

the forest floor. The great redwoods swayed back and forth in the wind, creaking and groaning like wrathful beasts.

For a moment, Kate stood paralyzed. Then she dashed toward the Ancient One and threw herself into the shelter of its hollow. Hailstones pounded the trunk, and some rolled harmlessly through the entrance. She sighed, knowing she was safe, as were the trees, at least for the moment. She spotted Aunt Melanie's walking stick, leaning against the inner wall of the hollow.

A person moving outside the entrance caught her attention. It was Jody, loping past in an effort to escape the raging storm. Just then, a branch as broad as an anvil came crashing down directly on his shoulder. He was flattened by the weight, his jacket torn open. He lay motionless on the ground outside the hollow.

Without thinking, Kate bolted out and rushed to his side. With a heave, she managed to pry the heavy limb off of him. Hailstones bounced off her head, arms, and back as she worked to lift him to his feet. He was semiconscious, but too limp to stand. Pummeled by hail, she grabbed him under his armpits and dragged him over the ground and into the hollow of the great tree.

She propped him up against the wall, trying her best to make him comfortable. His shoulder was bloody, but there was no way to tell if any bones had been broken. He leaned his head back against the cavern wall and moaned painfully.

Jody then opened his eyes. A look of confusion and fear filled his face as he saw Kate bending over him in the dark cavern. He rolled to the side and tried to wriggle away from her. Before she could restrain him, he was already halfway out of the hollow. Hailstones pounded him, but still he tried to crawl away.

"Let me go," he cried, half delirious. He kicked his legs wildly to break free of her grip.

"I'm just trying to help you," protested Kate, struggling to pull him back inside.

"Let me go," he shouted. At that instant, he caught sight

of two loggers running past the tree. "Harry," he called to one of them. "Harry!"

Kate's mind raced. If the loggers found him they would find her as well. And if they found her, they would also find the walking stick. With great effort, she caught hold of his leg and dragged him back into the hollow.

Desperately, she tried to pin him to the earthen floor. Yet despite his wounded shoulder, he was too strong for her and soon wriggled free. She jumped him again, trying to clasp both her arms around his waist. Jody grabbed her left arm above the elbow and rolled over, throwing her to the ground. He crawled madly toward the entrance, but before he reached it Kate reared back with both feet and kicked him as hard as she could in the ribs.

He flipped over, smacking his head full force against the wall of the hollow. With a groan, he slumped into unconsciousness and lay limp on the earthen floor.

Meanwhile the logger, hearing Jody call his name, stopped in his tracks and wheeled around. He seized the other man by the sleeve and gestured toward the tree. "It's the orphan kid," he declared, raising his voice to be heard over the clattering hailstones and crashing thunder. "He's in some kind of trouble."

"Let's get him before this mother-killing storm kills us all," shouted his companion.

The two loggers approached the redwood. Her sore hand throbbing, Kate pulled Jody's body back into the far extreme of the hollow. She cowered there in the darkness, trying desperately to breathe quietly. She could see the leather boots of one of the men planted just inches away from the entrance.

"Where the hell is he?" demanded a husky voice. "I know I heard him calling."

"Maybe you just thought you heard him," answered the other man. "He ain't here now, that's for sure."

A bright flash of lightning illuminated the grove, and for an instant, the inside of the hollow. The first logger laid his hand against the entrance, wrapping his callused fingers around the edge.

"Just let's check out this little cave," he called as he bent lower to look inside.

Kate scanned the hollow cavern for something—anything—she could use as a weapon. Her eyes fell upon the walking stick. The intricately carved markings on the shaft seemed to be glowing dimly, apparently reflecting the lightning outside. Strangely, the stick was vibrating, twitching, as it leaned against the wall.

Must be the vibration from the storm, thought Kate, as she reached to grasp it. Just then the face of the logger came into view. He searched the interior, his eyes adjusting to the dark.

Suddenly, a powerful energy flowed into Kate's hand holding the walking stick. It coursed through her whole body, a rising river of electricity. Without willing herself to do so, she struck the head of the stick hard against the wall of the cavern. The sound reverberated as though she were inside a bass drum. Then she struck it a second time, and a third.

A burst of white light filled the hollow. Pulsing bands of electricity leaped outward from the trunk, encircling it with fire, as if the tree had been struck by lightning. The logger fell back, stunned.

When the afterglow had faded away, both Kate and Jody had vanished. No sign of them remained, but for a small stain of blood mixing with the soil and hailstones at the base of the Ancient One.

PART TWO

Into the Island

10

maidenhair

KATE awoke in darkness. Was it all just a dream, a terrible dream? Had she never left the comfortable bed in the cottage?

She rolled to one side and felt a piercing pain in her left hand. Pulling the hand to her chest, she could see the dark ribbing of the hollow trunk surrounding her. Opposite, still unconscious, lay the boy Jody, blood smeared over the shoulder of his jacket. He looked more pitiful than hateful right now, but still Kate detested him. Then she felt the shaft of the walking stick resting against her thigh.

It was no dream. She struggled to kneel, grabbing the stick. At least it's safe, she congratulated herself. Aunt Melanie will be relieved. Then she noticed something curious about the cavern. It seemed smaller, more cramped somehow than she remembered.

In a flash, she thought of the logger who had almost found her—and the stick as well. Thank heaven lightning had struck the tree at just that moment. She chuckled at the memory of the big man, wide-eyed and fearful at the sudden flash of light. Peering out the entrance, she could see no sign of him or his companions. Scared off by the storm, probably. Her grin evaporated as she realized they would soon be coming back.

She looked again at Jody, slumped against the cavern wall. He'll survive, she told herself. That shoulder will be plenty sore, but he deserves it, every bit. He didn't really want to shoot that poor owl, that was clear. So why did he do it? A stupid dare, that's why. Probably stole the envelope on a dare too.

Dutifully, she reached over and wrapped the torn edge of his jacket over his injured shoulder, arranging his arm in the most comfortable position. Then she crawled out of the hollow.

She was surprised to see no hailstones on the ground. It seemed very odd, until she realized that she must have been unconscious for quite a while. Maybe the loggers had given up and gone back to town. In that case, Aunt Melanie might be somewhere near.

She called Aunt Melanie's name, but heard no answer. She must be back at the loggers' new road. It might take some time to find her again in the fog, but now that Kate had the stick it didn't really matter. She stretched stiffly, reaching first to the sky and then to her feet, then headed for the far side of the redwood grove. As she walked, she couldn't banish the feeling that something about the grove felt different than before. What exactly had changed, she didn't know, but the strange feeling nagged at her nonetheless. She stepped across a fallen branch and into the thick forest beyond the grove.

Soon her worries disappeared, as the Hidden Forest felt as dense and alive as ever. Nothing here had changed. In fact, it hadn't changed for thousands and thousands of years. It must have been her imagination, or the shock of the lightning bolt.

Hopping over a tangle of ferns growing from a long, cylindrical mound of earth that she guessed was the remains of a decomposed trunk, she tried to recall how Aunt Melanie had led her out to the rim. Fog shrouded everything as before, even obscuring the lower branches of the mammoth firs and cedars and hemlocks that surrounded her.

For the moment, she put the loggers out of her mind and moved silently through the misty woods. *Stay as quiet as a Halami,* Aunt Melanie had said. Kate began to pretend she was a young Halami, padding across the soft forest floor, stalking an elk or a deer. The walking stick became a spear, her sneakers disappeared, and she was barefoot. The land around her felt full of life, awesome, mystical, sacred.

Then she heard a voice, a small, lilting voice. Someone was singing, not far ahead. She knew at once it was Aunt Melanie, singing to guide her through the fog. All must be well, or she would not be making such lovely music.

Still the Halami, Kate resisted the urge to cry out and run to her. No, she would steal even closer, silent as the flowing fog. She would surprise her, leaping out from behind a tree at the last possible instant.

Stealthily, Kate approached. The singing grew clearer, stronger. She recognized it as one of the old Halami chants that Aunt Melanie often sang while working in her garden. A woodpecker battered against the trunk above, almost in time to the rhythm.

The music was now just a few feet away, behind a curtain of fog. Kate moved slowly, placing her feet with great care so as not to make any sound. Then her arm brushed against a protruding branch and a twig snapped sharply. The singing stopped.

Kate strode forward, holding the walking stick high. A diminutive figure, bending over a clump of maidenhair fern, stood up to greet her. Two dark eyes opened wide when she stepped into view.

Kate's eyes, too, opened wide. She was standing face to face not with Aunt Melanie, but with a girl dressed like no one she had ever met before.

The girl, high cheeked and round faced, looked at Kate fearfully, as if she were confronting a ghost. Three vertical black lines marked her chin. Upon her head rested

a bowl-shaped hat, woven from reeds like a basket, decorated with a geometric design. Her black hair, tied in two
ropes with simple strands of cedar bark wrapped around
the ends, fell over her shoulders and almost to her waist.
One hand clutched a small, straight-sided basket without a
handle that was filled with fronds and stems of maidenhair.
A square leather bib hung over her chest, dangling above
the loose skirt made from strips of reddish-brown bark.
She wore nothing on her feet.

With a shriek, the girl dropped her basket of ferns and
ran like a frightened deer into the forest. Kate hesitated for
a moment, then ran after her.

"Hey, come back!" she shouted, leaping over fallen limbs
and dodging trees. "I won't hurt you. Come back."

But the girl didn't stop. She tore through the forest, leaving Kate farther and farther behind. Soon the gap was great
enough that she could no longer be seen or heard through
the fog, and Kate slowed her pace. Giving up the chase at
last, she was preparing to halt when, without warning, the
ground gave way beneath her.

She screamed, plunging downward, until she landed with
a thud on a floor of packed dirt. Her hand throbbed painfully,
and the back of her neck stung when she lifted her head.
Clambering to her feet, she brushed a chunk of mud off her
jeans and anxiously surveyed her surroundings.

A pit, she realized in disbelief. *I've fallen into a pit.*
Despite the pain in her neck, she craned her head upward.
The pit was about ten feet deep, vertically walled, with a
steep overhang near the top to prevent anyone who was
trapped from climbing out. Above, she saw the fog filtering
through canopies of branches. Escape was impossible
without help.

"Aunt Melanie," she cried, mortified. "I'm in this pit. Can
you hear me? Aunt Melanie, please hear me!"

No answer came but the gentle swishing of branches in
a light wind. Again she tried calling, again without success. Dejectedly, she sat down on the dirt floor of the pit,

arms around her knees, her head bowed. She kicked the walking stick away from her foot.

Then she heard a snarling sound above her. Looking up with a start, she saw the face of what looked like a coyote, brown ears erect, peering down on her. Teeth bared, the animal growled viciously as though getting ready to spring.

Kate's heart pounded. She scuttled to the far side of the pit, but the snarling beast could still see her. Leaping to her feet, she grabbed the walking stick and held it like a baseball bat.

"Stay away from me, you," she said fiercely. "Or I'll make a home run out of you."

At the sight of the stick, the animal ceased growling, dropped back its ears, then retreated out of sight. An instant later, another face appeared in the same place. It belonged to the girl. She studied Kate apprehensively, her brow beneath the basketry hat wrinkled in fear.

There was a bark, then the girl turned and said something unintelligible. Another bark, this time softer. The girl again stared into the pit. At once, Kate realized that the coyote-like creature must be her pet, a scruffy sort of dog.

"Help me out," said Kate. "Please. I won't hurt you, I promise."

Consternation showed in the girl's dark eyes. She drew back from the edge of the pit.

"Please," Kate called after her. "Please help me out." Then, on a sudden intuition, she shouted, *"Halma-dru."*

Tentatively, the girl's face reappeared.

"Halma-dru," repeated Kate in a quieter voice.

At that, the girl clenched her jaw and pulled back out of sight again, leaving Kate shaking her head despondently. It was no use. She could be stuck in this pit until the end of her days.

Suddenly the end of a large branch appeared at the edge of the pit. With a groan, the girl heaved it over the lip. It crashed onto the earthen floor by Kate's feet, showering her with broken twigs and strands of moss.

The girl pointed to the branch, saying, *"Ai-ya, ai-ya."* The dog's face appeared by hers, and it barked excitedly. Without hesitating, Kate started to ascend the makeshift ladder. Placing her feet in the notches where smaller branches protruded, she climbed higher, holding the walking stick between her teeth. Occasionally the notches would break, sending her sliding backward again. Gradually, however, she made progress. When she had climbed as far as she dared without breaking the branch, she raised her arms skyward. Her hands reached barely above the opening.

The girl clasped Kate's wrists and heaved, pulling her upward. For a moment she hung there, suspended, her legs kicking freely. A clod of dirt from the edge of the pit dropped onto her head, stinging her eyes. Then the girl pulled again, this time hard enough to lift Kate's head and shoulders above the hole. Swinging her legs to the side, she caught the edge with one foot and hauled herself out of the pit.

She lay on her back on the bed of needles, exhausted. Rolling to her side, she found herself eyeball to eyeball with the carved owl's head of the walking stick. The yellow eyes gleamed at her, and she rolled back quickly.

She heard the girl also panting heavily, and sat up just as she did. Seated on the verdant forest floor, they observed each other warily. Kate dared not move, lest she frighten her again.

Cautiously, the brown dog approached Kate, fluffy tail curled up high over his back. Forcing herself to remain still, she nevertheless glanced at the walking stick on the ground by her side. The dog nudged her shoulder roughly, then sniffed her sweatshirt with a thin, pointed nose. Suddenly, he licked her on the side of the neck.

"Monga," said the girl sharply, but the laughter in her eyes betrayed her true feelings. *"Monga ha-lei shluntah."*

The dog padded to her side, nuzzling her cheek. The girl giggled, grinning bashfully at Kate.

"Halma-dru," said Kate slowly, her brain refusing to accept what her heart told her must be true. "Do you speak English?"

The girl's face went blank. Tentatively, she said, *"Yiteh neh chi wiltu."* She studied Kate searchingly, as if expecting an answer.

Kate could only shake her head. Looking from the girl to the walking stick and back again, she patted herself on the chest and said softly, "Kate."

A light of understanding kindled in the strange girl's eyes and she patted her own chest. *"Laioni."*

"Lai-oni," repeated Kate.

The girl smiled again. Indicating the dog, she said, *"Monga."* In response, it pawed her playfully.

Keeping her gaze locked on Laioni's, Kate reached up and touched her own head. "Nice hat," she said, pointing toward the basketry cap.

Laioni didn't seem to register the compliment. Instead, her attention focused on the long blond braid drooping over Kate's shoulder. Seeing this, Kate lifted the braid. "You like this?" she asked, somewhat puzzled. "It's just plain old hair, like yours."

As Kate lifted her braid, Laioni lifted her own two ropes and giggled again. *"Hunneh,"* she said carefully.

"Hunneh," repeated Kate, knowing she had just learned another word for *hair.*

Laioni, however, was not yet finished. She pointed at the braid and said something Kate couldn't catch. Sensing she hadn't communicated, the girl looked around for something to help her express the new thought. At last she noticed the walking stick. Taking care not to touch it directly with her hand, she indicated the owl's head handle.

"The stick?" muttered Kate. "What does that have to do with—" Then suddenly she understood. Laioni did not mean the handle itself, but rather the eyes. The yellow eyes. "Yellow," declared Kate. "You mean my hair is yellow." She paused, then lifted her braid again. *"Hunneh* yellow."

Laioni's eyes glittered. *"Hunneh* yell-ow," she replied, laughing.

Guess she doesn't see too much yellow hair where she

comes from, thought Kate, laughing herself. Then she wondered: Where does she come from, anyway?

At that moment, Laioni rose to her feet with effortless grace. Pointing at Kate, she said, "Ka-teh." Then she beckoned, apparently asking her to come. She walked backward a few steps, Monga dancing about her feet, before turning into the forest.

Full of uncertainty, Kate took the walking stick, stood up, and started to follow. There was something distinctly familiar about this utterly unfamiliar girl. Yet what could it be? Where was Aunt Melanie when she needed her? She would know where this girl came from, maybe even speak some of her language. Perhaps she was one of those modern descendants of the Halami who lived somewhere in the region, keeping the old ways alive. But was it possible that included not learning to speak English? In any case, she knew enough of the old ways to have figured out how to get into the crater.

Kate shrugged, deciding to save her questions for later. As they strode through the forest, she spotted a moss-covered boulder she had seen near the place where she had first met the girl. Sure enough, a few steps later Laioni picked up her basket of ferns, hardly slackening her pace. She continued to lead Kate into the forest, Monga at her heels, moving confidently despite the heavy mist. It was clear she knew these woods well.

Some distance farther, Laioni stopped. Kate came up to her side and saw, to her surprise, that they had arrived at the redwood grove. Laioni lowered her head briefly, indicating Kate should go forward.

Hesitantly, Kate stepped into the clearing. Once again she felt the indefinable difference in the great trees. Her gaze fell to the Ancient One, and with a start she realized that it looked smaller than before. Or were the other trees in the grove larger?

She glanced at Laioni, standing at the edge of the clearing. Kate motioned for her to come, but she remained there, both wonderment and fear written on her round face. Monga sat expectantly by her side, tail wagging.

What does she think I am, some kind of tree spirit? Kate grinned morbidly at her own humor, trying to dispel the queasiness in her stomach. Something about this place was just not right. She turned again to the Ancient One and approached it gingerly, her sneakers crunching on the needles.

Placing her left palm on the gnarled trunk, she lowered her head to look inside. She realized that she had not thought about Jody since leaving the tree. It took a few seconds for her eyes to adjust to the dark, but when they did, the scene stunned her.

Jody was gone.

Whirling around, she scanned the grove for any tracks, any signs. There were none to be seen. He couldn't have gone far, she reasoned. He wasn't even in shape to walk.

Uneasiness swelling steadily inside her, Kate walked back across the grove toward Laioni. As she came near, she spied a small, rounded boulder at the edge of the clearing. Her spine tingled. It was the same warning stone she had seen before, or one just like it. Yet something had changed. Not the expression on the face, still screaming some silent admonition. Not the depth of the lines carved into the surface. Not the position of the stone, warning anyone who might dare to pass too near.

Then in a flash she knew. The stone bore no moss. The lines seemed freshly cut, as if carved only yesterday.

Catching her breath, she looked to Laioni. Who was this girl dressed in Native American clothing who spoke no English and watched her with eyes as alert as an eagle's? At once, the answer came clear. She did not want to believe it, but the trees and the warning stone and the girl herself told her she must.

She darted back across the redwood grove and dove headlong into the Ancient One's hollow. Biting her lip, she lifted the walking stick and struck it hard against the wooden wall. Once, twice, three times.

Nothing happened.

She held the owl's head in front of her face, but no illumination glowed within the yellow eyes. It was merely a shaft of lifeless wood. "Take me back," she pleaded, her voice trembling. "I don't belong here."

After waiting for an endless moment, she lowered the stick reluctantly. Outside, Monga gave two sharp barks. Kate leaned toward the light. Through the shifting mist she saw the dog sitting, as before, next to Laioni, a living member of the Halami tribe.

And she knew that she had traveled back in time.

ebony eyes

NOT knowing what else to do, Kate rejoined Laioni and Monga, whose foxlike tail wagged energetically as she approached. For her part, Laioni seemed surprised at first that Kate had not simply vanished altogether into the redwood grove. After a few seconds, however, she beckoned shyly for Kate to follow her into the forest, apparently concluding that this visiting spirit had decided to stay with her for a while. Reading her expressions, Kate solemnly trudged after her.

Laioni led her purposefully through the woods, without any visible signs of a trail to guide her. Monga, meanwhile, ran around them in wide circles, returning occasionally to brush Laioni's leg with his tail before darting off again. The fog seemed to be lifting, and soon Kate could see shreds of deep blue through the branches ahead. The trees soon thinned and they passed into a verdant meadow, much like the one where Kate had almost lost her sneaker with Aunt Melanie . . . was it just this morning? Or several centuries in the future? Kate noticed little of her surroundings this time, stepping mechanically over fragrant flowers and brightly flowing rivulets. All she could think of was the white-haired woman who was anxiously waiting for her to return with the walking stick. She hoped Aunt Melanie was all right.

As they neared the shore of the blue lake, Kate's lingering doubts that she had indeed traveled back in time disappeared. For there by the lake she saw what could only be an encampment of Halamis. Seated beside a fire pit were two women, one much older than the other. They seemed to be preparing food, singing softly as they worked. They were dressed much the same as Laioni, wearing woven hats, loose leather tops, shredded bark skirts, and three lines on their chins.

Near the younger of the two, a shallow cradle made from woven willow shoots held a sleeping infant, laced into the cradle with a long strip of deer hide. A few paces farther from the lapping waters of the lake stood a brush hut, appearing rather temporary, conical in shape with a dense covering of grasses and tree limbs. Tools of all descriptions lay scattered on the ground: a pouch made from some kind of bladder, a scraping implement carved from an antler, a gouging tool that had what looked like a beaver's tooth for the blade, a comb and a sewing awl that gleamed like polished bone, a gray stone dish holding some oily substance, a spoon sculpted from a seashell, and other implements.

When Laioni and Kate came within ten feet, the two women halted their singing. Seeing Kate, they dropped their work and leaped to their feet, fear clearly visible on their faces. The younger woman, probably Laioni's mother, barked some stern words at the girl that caused her to frown. Laioni then stepped nearer and engaged in an animated exchange during which she pantomimed Kate's rescue from the pit. Grimly, her mother took Laioni by the wrist and placed herself between Kate and the girl. She faced Kate, scowling, and spoke sharply, motioning with her hands for Kate to go away and leave them alone.

"Believe me, I'd go if I could," muttered Kate. "Do you have any bus tickets to the twentieth century?"

Suddenly, the woman's eyes focused on the walking stick. At the sight of it, she cried out and took a quick step backward. The older woman behind her, who was rubbing her hands together nervously, released a long, low moaning sound.

It struck Kate that somehow they seemed to recognize the walking stick. Perhaps they might even know enough about it to show her how to tap its strange power so it could take her home again. She tried to think of some way, any way, to win their trust.

She scanned the camp, racking her brain. Her eyes fell on the fire pit, ashes glowing orange, and an idea flashed into her head. Moving slowly and deliberately, she took off her day pack and removed the thermos. Then, as the three Halamis watched with a mixture of dread and curiosity, she unscrewed the top, poured half a cup of steaming hot chocolate, and drank a sip herself. Then, bending down, she placed the cup of brown liquid on a flat stone near her feet. Backing up a few paces, she pointed to the cup and said, *"Halma-dru."*

Monga scampered over to the cup, sniffed it for a few seconds, then reached his long tongue into the hot chocolate. Lapping it into his mouth, he shook his bushy tail vigorously and barked twice.

With that, Laioni darted out from behind her mother, evading the woman's grasp. Ignoring her worried chattering, Laioni reached for the cup. No sooner did she touch it than she swiftly drew back her hand, yelping as if something had bit her. Turning to her mother, she said in amazement, *"Chu. Chu tkho."*

"Chu," echoed Kate, guessing she had just heard the Halami word for *hot*.

Waving her mother back, Laioni cautiously picked up the cup and sniffed its contents. After a moment of deliberation, she took a small sip. As she swallowed, her face burst into a broad smile. She turned to her mother and said something in an excited voice.

Laioni then carried the cup to her mother, who refused to

try it. After repeated urgings, all of which were rejected, Laioni brought the cup over to the elder woman. With unsteady hands, the old Halami raised the cup, then faltered as Laioni's mother spoke to her harshly. She answered back in a gruff voice, then brought the cup to her face. She inhaled once, chirped in surprise, and took a small taste. Like Laioni before her, the old woman smiled from one high cheekbone to the other. She took another swallow, smiled again, then held the cup out to Laioni's mother.

Hesitantly, the woman took the cup, glanced doubtfully at Kate, then inserted her index finger into the cup. Fear melted into wonder as she felt the liquid, warm without the aid of fire. With another glance at Kate, she brought the cup to her lips and, after smelling its contents, swallowed the remaining hot chocolate. The creases on her forehead relaxed and she nodded at Kate, her eyes still afraid but somewhat accepting.

The rest of the day was spent around the encampment. The two women resumed their work, singing together, pausing only when the infant needed to be nursed or cleaned. The men of this group, Kate learned through Laioni's energetic pantomimes, were away for some time, perhaps on a hunting expedition. Laioni seemed to be concerned for them, almost afraid, though she gave no indication why.

Using her own pantomimes, Kate kept the conversation going, hoping she might eventually learn something useful. She tried to find out whether the Halamis hunted with arrows, with spears, or by digging pits like the one she herself had fallen into. Then she tried to learn whether their prey was elk, deer, rabbit, or squirrel. But she succeeded only in making Laioni laugh.

"So you've never seen a rabbit that looked like that?" Kate asked, giggling herself. "How about like this?" She hopped around the campfire, doing her best imitation of a kangaroo. Laioni laughed again, while the two Halami women glanced worriedly at each other.

Deciding to try another line of questioning, Kate pointed across the lake toward the wall of sheer cliffs surrounding

the crater. "Is that where your father went?" she asked
Laioni. "Past the cliffs and down into the forest?"

The Halami girl's expression swiftly darkened. She
looked toward the cliffs, frowning, as if some grave danger
lurked beyond them. She said a few sentences and then
kicked angrily at a clump of grass.

Kate did not need to understand her words to know that
something was wrong in the forest outside the crater.
Yet she had no clue what it might be. Aunt Melanie, she
felt sure, would know. But Aunt Melanie was somewhere
very, very far away.

Then Laioni gestured toward the walking stick, a look
of awe on her face. She asked Kate something in a soft
voice, but Kate could not make sense of her words. Yet the
impression was clear: Laioni, like her mother, knew something about the stick. With luck, if she waited for the right
moment, Kate might learn something from them about its
secrets.

Later that afternoon, Laioni showed Kate a simple game
of throwing polished sticks at a stake planted in the ground.
Since Kate had often played horseshoes with Grandfather,
her aim was impressive, though not as good as Laioni's.
Whenever Kate missed a throw, Laioni would look at her
strangely, as if she thought Kate was not playing as well as
she could.

Next, Laioni led her to the confluence of two bubbling
rivulets that emptied into the lake not far from camp.
Revealing three miniature carved canoes resting in the hollow of a nearby rock, she carried them to the flowing water
and placed them in a small whirlpool formed by the mesh-
ing currents. The canoes, shaped with pointed bow and box-
like stern, were each carved from a single block of wood.
They reminded Kate of the dugout canoe she had seen
once with Aunt Melanie in a museum close to the airport.

Airport, mused Kate. She had never thought about life
without one within an hour's drive. Cars, too, she had
taken for granted all her years. She doubted she could ever
explain to Laioni that people, ordinary people, would one

day cruise faster than the swiftest deer and fly higher than the soaring eagle. And she wondered whether Laioni's intimate knowledge of this place, her place, would be possible in the age of automobiles and airplanes. Motion and speed were so addictive, crowding out the calmness and focus needed to know one special place well. Then, with a pang, she wished she could simply board some time-traveling airplane that could bring her back to Aunt Melanie.

Laioni took three pebbles from the swirling streams of water—one buff, one black, one slightly crimson—and placed one into each of the toy canoes. Released into the whirlpool, the little boats floated in small circles, sometimes spinning rapidly, sometimes gliding into choppier waters, where they inevitably capsized.

Kate was soon captivated by the miniature canoes. She laughed with Laioni whenever one tipped over, dumping the pebble occupant into the water. By vigorous gestures, Laioni indicated that the same thing had happened to her once or twice. Monga, having positioned himself by the edge, batted at the boats with one of his paws.

What a far cry, Kate reflected, this was from the television and high-tech video games of her own world. Not since she had played Pooh Sticks as a small child down by the river with Aunt Melanie had she had such a good time with so few props.

As she bent low to take a drink from one of the rivulets, Kate viewed the fragmented reflection of Laioni's face in the water. She watched the Halami girl slowly cock her head to one side. Strange. For an instant, she saw not Laioni—but Aunt Melanie. Sitting up with a start, she gazed at the girl seated next to her and all at once realized why she had seemed so familiar from the first moment they met. Laioni's eyes were the eyes of Aunt Melanie, black as ebony, with a few flecks of hazel green around the edges. Kate thought about the crumpled photograph she had seen at the cottage of two youngsters on the Isle of Skye. The dark-eyed girl in the picture taken fifty years ago (or four hundred fifty years from now, depending on how one counted) looked so much like Laioni it was uncanny. Of course, the very notion that they could be related was absurd, yet Kate couldn't banish the feeling entirely.

Abruptly, Kate noticed that Laioni was also staring at her. Not at her face, though: She was examining her green cotton sweatshirt with keen interest. Kate raised her forearm so that Laioni could feel the material. As the Halami girl rubbed the cloth between her thumb and forefinger, her face assumed the wondrous expression of someone encountering silk or satin for the very first time. "Mmmmmmm," she said, closing her eyes.

Kate reached to touch the strips of cedar bark constituting Laioni's skirt, and the Halami girl started to giggle. Kate smiled at her and said, "Pretty different, huh?" Laioni seemed to understand, and giggled again.

At that moment, a strange but lovely smell, almost like almonds roasting, came wafting through the air to them. With the ease of a springing fawn, Laioni jumped to her feet. Monga at once sprinted to her side, his tail swishing expectantly. She pointed to her mouth and patted her abdomen, indicating the time had come for a meal. Kate suddenly observed the slanting light crossing the cliff wall of the crater, and realized that it was late afternoon already. She was hungry, powerfully hungry, having eaten nothing more substantial all day than hot chocolate.

As Kate stood, Laioni plucked the three small boats from the water and returned them to their resting place on the rock. Meanwhile, Kate happened to glance toward the reflectionless blue lake. Beyond the rising mist floated the same sinister island, as unnerving now as it had been the first time she had seen it with Aunt Melanie. Eerie in its utter blackness, it seemed to slide slowly across the surface. With a slight shiver, she turned away.

Laioni led her back to the fire pit, where her mother continued to chant as she worked. At that moment, she was parching some type of seeds on a flat rock next to the hot coals. Kate could not keep herself from investigating the source of the rich aroma. Drawing closer, she watched the woman skillfully moving the seeds around with a wooden stick, taking care to heat each one evenly. It reminded Kate of making popcorn over an open fire, and she felt a sudden sense of loss amidst her swelling hunger. The last time she had made popcorn was with Aunt Melanie.

Just then, the Halami woman put down the stick and directed her daughter to do something. Laioni quickly picked up a round, broad-bottomed basket with straight sides and very tight weave. Taking care to avoid the walking stick that Kate had leaned against a rock, she carried the basket to the nearest rivulet flowing into the lake. Dipping it into the water until its pattern of repeating parallelograms was submerged, she then brought it back to her mother.

Kate turned to see the older woman pounding some seeds into meal on a flat stone between her legs. Every so often she put down her cylindrical pestle and sifted, lightly tapping a shallow basket of meal with her finger to make the finest meal fall into a woven hopper. All the while she watched Kate with a mixture of curiosity and suspicion.

By now, Kate's hunger was almost unbearable. She watched expectantly as Laioni's mother, using wooden tongs, placed two round stones from the fire pit into the water-filled basket. Why is she cooking stones? Kate wondered. Then the woman added a bowl of rootlike tubers to the basket. Methodically, she began removing cooler stones and replacing them with freshly heated ones from the fire pit. Soon the water began to boil, and a new smell overpowered the aroma of the parched seeds. The baby, hungry as well, started to cry.

At last, Laioni's mother nodded to Kate to sit down. She said something to the older woman and to Laioni, and the meal was served. In addition to the freshly cooked tubers, Laioni produced a basket filled with red berries, seeds, and strips of some unknown vegetable. Her mother retrieved from the brush hut a tray of dried fish, as tasty as the smoked salmon Kate had eaten in Scotland once on a trip with Grandfather.

For her own part, Kate contributed what little hot chocolate remained in the thermos, complementing the herbal tea brewing by the fire. Everyone ate ravenously, including Monga, who tore into a generous clump of fish meat by Laioni's side. Lifting her baby from the cradle, Laioni's mother began to nurse the child, who squeaked and squealed like a rusty wheel while drinking.

As they ate together, the sun dropped below the line of cliffs to the west. The air grew a touch colder, though heat from the steaming lake and the fire pit kept them warm. In the distance, a lone owl called *hooo-hooo, hooo-hooo.*

Kate surveyed the various tools and utensils scattered on the ground. They seemed so different here, freshly used and lit by the glow of fire coals, than they would hundreds of years later in some natural history museum or art gallery. Each one was made with such care and grace and pride that it was really a work of art. Yet they were made to be used, not shown. That, she suddenly realized, was the point: In this time, art and life were still the same.

Soon Laioni's mother replaced the now-sleeping baby in the cradle, lacing the strip of deer hide carefully across the tiny body. Kate could see no moon above them, and she shuddered to think that soon they would have no light at all but the campfire. The crater swiftly filled with darkness, the sort of deep impenetrable darkness that always made her feel uneasy. She wondered what might have happened to Jody.

Then the Halami women began to chant, singing to the vanishing light ringing the rim of the crater. Laioni's mother tapped lightly on the bottom of a large basket, while the old woman shook a rattle made from a deer's hoof. Laioni hummed in the background, climbing a scale and then dropping back, joined on occasion by Monga's high whining howl. Kate gazed into the glowing coals and listened, her eyelids growing heavier with each repetition.

> *Ayah-ho ayah-ho*
> *Tlah hontseh na hoh-ah*

Ayah-ho Ayah-ho
Heyowe halma-dru.

Gradually, gradually, her cares melted into the mist and she thought only of the present, of glowing cliffs encircling her, of blue waters gently lapping, of voices strange and sonorous. The night-sky eyes of Laioni saw her nodding off, and she quietly came to guide Kate to her bed of soft grass in the brush hut.

Kate felt like someone both dreaming and waking at once. It seemed almost as if Aunt Melanie had appeared in a younger form to put her to sleep, to tuck her in gently and whisper good-night, just as she had done so often when Kate was a child.

12

the time tunnel

A chain saw buzzed, quite near her head. Kate woke up with a start.

She found herself sandwiched inside the brush hut, with Laioni on one side and the old woman on the other. Laioni's mother was nowhere to be seen. Monga lay curled up outside the entrance. Then the buzzing noise came again, and Kate realized that it was only the elder Halami snoring.

All at once, her worldly concerns came crashing back. She reached for the walking stick, lying at the entrance to the hut, and pulled it to her chest. How stupid to have tried to fetch this stick alone! Aunt Melanie should have warned her, though most likely she didn't know herself of the danger. And now she was here, thrown back five hundred years in time. Worse yet, she had not even a clue how to get home.

She gazed at the indecipherable etchings carved deep into the wooden shaft. The owl's head on the handle gazed back at her, unwilling to reveal its secrets. There must be some way to make it come alive again, Kate told herself. Less for her own sake than for Aunt Melanie's. She needed help, and soon. Kate could feel it, as vividly as she could feel the chain saws about to rip into the trunk of the Ancient One.

Then, like a slap in the face, she realized the true depth of her dilemma. She had traveled back in time inside of the great redwood, whose life reached from this time all the way to her own. If that tree were cut and killed, could she still get back at all? Even if she could solve the riddle of the walking stick's power, if the medium connecting her to the future did not exist anymore, she would be stranded. She struggled to remember the theory about time tunnels. Something about places where living things can grow undisturbed for a very long time . . . So if one of those places is suddenly disturbed, let alone demolished, what happens to the time tunnel?

She lowered the stick, knowing well the answer. Her thoughts then turned again to Jody. Troublesome as he was, he was lost in this strange time just like herself. She pondered what could have happened to him. Perhaps he had somehow wandered off, only to end up at the bottom of some Halami pit. Perhaps he had been removed from the tree by force. There was no way to know.

Stretching, she crawled out of the brush hut onto the stony ground. Although the sun had not yet topped the ridge of cliffs, a diffuse early morning light filled the crater. Across the meadow, birds fluttered and chirped in the branches of the mighty trees. The lake sent up wispy trails of mist, obscuring the black island completely. She heard the sound of footsteps and turned to see Laioni's mother emerging from the forest with a handful of skunk cabbage and a sprig of wild iris, the flower Aunt Melanie liked to call blue flag.

Yesterday's fear still written on her face, the woman glanced nervously at the walking stick, then acknowledged Kate with a nod of her head. Her eyes, not so dark as Laioni's, looked at the purple kerchief tied around Kate's hand, stained with blood from the day before. *"H'ona tuwan teh,"* she said in a low voice.

Kate did not understand, but instinctively pulled her hand to her side. She sat on a nearby rock, watching the woman clean the broad cabbage leaves and the root of the flower in the stream, singing softly as she worked. Then she dangled them over the hot coals of the fire pit for a minute, warming them, before crushing them between two stones. At last, she scraped the moist mass onto her hand and carried it over to Kate.

Keeping an eye on the walking stick, the Halami woman gently lifted Kate's bandaged hand. Ever so delicately, she unwound the kerchief, exposing the tender skin to the air. As Kate winced, she applied the poultice to the spot, chanting some rhythmic words.

Almost instantly, Kate felt a soothing sensation. Despite its pungent smell, the healing substance dulled the pain while sinking into her raw skin. Laioni's mother quickly doused the purple kerchief in the water, then wrapped it again around her hand, weaving the ends together securely. She ceased chanting just as the sun edged above the cliffs.

Laioni emerged from the tent. She eyed Kate mischievously and did an imitation of the old woman's snore before bursting into a giggle. Kate laughed as well, for the moment forgetting her troubles. Monga pranced around the fire pit, bouncing on his scruffy brown legs.

Laioni and her mother then exchanged some sentences, indicating the wounded hand as they spoke. Laioni's mother, clearly concerned about something, tried to ask Kate a question, pointing first to the hand and then to the walking stick. Not comprehending, Kate could only shake her head. More than ever, she longed to return to her own time.

Then Laioni decided to try. She gestured toward the stick, then staggered back a few steps as though she had encountered something of great power. Next she touched her own left hand, wincing as though in pain. She brought the hand nearer to the stick, whereupon her expression changed to satisfaction.

At last, Kate understood. They could not fathom why, possessing the special strength of the walking stick, she had not healed her own hand. How could she explain to them she didn't know how to use it? Then an idea took shape in her mind.

Holding the stick in both hands so they might see the many intricate carvings on the shaft, Kate twirled it slowly in her palms. Finally, she laid it across her lap and began making various faces and gestures designed to show ignorance, confusion, uncertainty. Between each pantomime, she pointed to the stick.

Only bewilderment registered on the Halamis' faces. Determined, Kate tried again, running through any expression she could think of that could possibly convey her problem.

Still there was no communication. Exasperated, Kate pointed to the confused faces of Laioni and her mother, exclaiming, "That's how I feel. Don't you see?"

A light seemed to kindle in Laioni's eyes. She chattered something to her mother, who grew suddenly somber. The woman pointed to the stick, indicating the full length of the shaft, then turned her gaze back to Kate. The look of fear in her face had deepened.

"That's right," blurted Kate, her vision growing misty. "I don't know how to use it." She looked to the sky and raised her hands in despair. "Who can help me?" she cried. "Who can help me?"

The Halami woman stared at her for a long moment. Then she uttered a single word, so softly Kate could barely hear it. *"Azanna,"* she said. *"Azanna."* Then she stepped quickly away to the other side of the fire pit, dragging Laioni by the arm.

Azanna, repeated Kate to herself. The word sounded vaguely familiar. She knew she had heard it before, but where? It doesn't matter, she shrugged sadly. Just another Halami word.

Dejectedly, she lifted herself from the rock. Laioni was arguing with her mother about something, but Kate was not interested. She swung the walking stick angrily. With a sharp crack, its base whacked against the stone.

All at once, she remembered. Kate could hear Aunt Melanie's voice telling her the meaning of *Azanna,* speaking hesitantly in the hollow of the tree. To learn more about the stick, to have even a chance of going home, she knew she must return to the Circle of Stones.

13

the circle of stones

STRIDING around the foggy perimeter of the lake, Kate tightened the knot of the kerchief around her hand. Fear of the deadly green pool rose within her as she stepped over rivulets running down from the cliffs. Aunt Melanie had said that its spell would work only once. Yet Kate now existed in an earlier time, so perhaps the pool's curse would call her still more strongly. She grasped the walking stick tightly, as a climber grasps a safety rope. Almost as dreadful as the green pool, in her mind, were those seven stones themselves. Something about them haunted her, something more than their sheer size. They had seemed eerily aware of her presence, almost as if they were alive.

Before turning to ascend the rocky slope, she stooped to pick up a small piece of pumice and hurled it into the lake. Though fog obscured its landing place, she heard a distant splash. Somewhere across the water was the Halami camp she had left so abruptly, not even staying to have some breakfast. She recalled the faces of Laioni and her mother, one crestfallen to see her go, the other clearly relieved. She picked up another of the light stones and threw it in the same direction. To her surprise, this time there was no splash. All she could hear was the sound of waves lapping against the shore.

She did not linger to learn what had happened. Perhaps it had landed on the island, although that begged the question of why the first stone had hit water instead. Unless the island really could move . . . No, that was impossible. Looking up the slope to her right, she could see the misty outline of the ribbed formation that rose out of the cliff wall behind the Circle of Stones. But the Circle itself remained invisible.

Turning her back to the lake, she started clambering up the rocky incline. As before, she was forced to use her hands to pull herself higher. Suddenly, she heard a clatter of rocks falling not far behind her. She whirled around.

"Laioni!"

The Halami girl struggled up the slope to meet her. Just behind, pouncing from rock to rock, Kate could see a familiar shaggy, brown shape. Stretching below them, a curling cloud rolled across the lake. At length the pair arrived, panting heavily.

Kate shook her head. "You shouldn't come," she said sternly, waving Laioni back.

The girl set her jaw firmly and looked straight at Kate. It was clear she did not want to go back.

"But it's dangerous up there," insisted Kate. "Go back now, while you can."

Laioni didn't budge. Instead, she held out her hand, which was full of dried seeds. She took a mouthful, then offered the rest to Kate.

She not only looks like Aunt Melanie, thought Kate. She's just as stubborn. Frowning, she took a swallow of the seeds but didn't taste them. Then she continued climbing the slope, motioning to Laioni to stay behind her.

As the ground at last began to level off, Kate caught a glimpse of the great boulders. Their cracked and blistered surfaces loomed ominously, half hidden by the swirling mist. They seemed to change constantly as she approached them, like huge faces moving back and forth between light and shadow. Kate eyed the spot, at the base of the smallest of the enormous stones, where she knew she would find the bubbling green pool. Sucking in her breath, she prepared to confront it.

To her astonishment, the pool was bubbling, but not green. Cautiously, Kate drew nearer to see only a natural bowl of boiling water, fed by the same small rivulet where Aunt Melanie had scrubbed her hand so relentlessly. The pool bubbled and splattered like the clearest of hot springs, devoid of any aroma but the faint smell of sulfur. Somehow, the evil spell had vanished. Or, Kate realized all of a sudden, it had not yet arrived.

Straightening herself, she scanned the collection of giant stones. Mist moved slowly over their deeply lined surfaces. Behind the bubbling pool, she saw a narrow passageway between the smallest boulder, which was roughly the size of a pickup truck, and the boulder next to it, which was as broad and bulky as a barn. She knew that the passageway would lead her into the center of the Circle, but she hesitated. *They're watching you,* said the voice of Aunt Melanie in her memory, and the hair on the back of her neck prickled. She stood there, motionless as stone herself, searching for the strength to step into the passageway. Just then, she heard someone breathing beside her.

It was Laioni, her face full of awe to stand before *Azanna,* the Circle of Stones. Without turning from the boulders, she slipped her hand into Kate's. This gesture by the girl with Aunt Melanie's eyes gave Kate an unexpected surge of courage. Yet she also found herself all the more keenly aware that the true Aunt Melanie was far, far away. And, she knew in her bones, Aunt Melanie needed her help.

Side by side and hand in hand, they walked past the pool and between the two great cracked boulders. His head low to the ground, Monga followed at their heels. On their left, the gray wall of the larger boulder rose high above their heads, while on their right, the surface of the smaller boulder was coated with an undulating skin of mist. They spoke not a word, nor did Monga make a sound, as they passed through the channel.

Finally, they emerged and stepped into the middle of the Circle. Standing together, their clothing as unlike as their worlds, Kate and Laioni slowly pivoted as if greeting all seven of the stones. Each of them had a distinct shape, though all shared the same blistered gray texture. The shifting mist swirled thickly around them, making the giant boulders seem like one enormous unbroken ring of rock.

When the visitors had turned a complete circle, they stopped. Not knowing what else to do, Kate let go of Laioni's hand and said aloud, "I am—we are—here, Great Circle. For your help. If you really are watching like my Aunt Melanie said, if you can hear me somehow, then won't you do something to show us? Please. See, you're my only hope."

They waited for several minutes, but no response came. More fog flowed into the ring until all they could see of the boulders were dark shadows hovering behind a cloudy curtain. Kate felt sheepish for trying to communicate with, of all things, rocks. Even gigantic rocks. Things were different here in Lost Crater, but not that different. She shrugged, looking sadly toward Laioni, whose eyes showed only empathy.

Kate started to leave, when her foot tripped on a small stone that had been obscured by the fog. Although she caught herself before falling, the walking stick slipped from her hand and fell with a smack against the ground. As she reached to pick it up, she heard a strange sound, like a faraway echo of the stick's impact.

Slowly, the sound swelled into a distant drumbeat that reverberated around them. Monga whimpered worriedly, and Laioni reached down to stroke his furry back. The sound grew louder, fuller, just the opposite of a normal echo, until it reached the volume of cannons blasting nearby. The cannons erupted faster and faster on all sides until Kate and Laioni both covered their ears with their hands.

The ground beneath them started to shake, clearing the

mist with its vibrations. Kate was knocked to her knees by a powerful tremor, and she feared suddenly that the old volcano had come to life. She and Laioni and Monga would all perish, along with any chance to see Aunt Melanie again. The violent heaving continued, throwing them together in one ungainly heap.

Then, as swiftly as they had begun, the tremors began to fade. The great reverberations slowed and grew quieter by degrees. The mist continued to dissipate, flowing from the Circle like water from a lake whose dam has burst.

Then Kate realized with horror that the giant stones themselves were changing. Before her eyes, as though the fleeting mist were peeling away layers of crusty skin, the boulders began to metamorphose. Laioni let out a little scream and covered her mouth, while Monga crawled quickly into her lap. Kate grabbed the shaft of the walking stick and drew it protectively to herself.

Over the tops and backs of the great boulders grew gnarled and scraggly black hair, thick as tree limbs and curly as uncombed wool. Bent and bulbous noses formed from shafts of protruding rock, some narrow and twisted, others flat and globular. Kate shuddered to see a pair of deep indentations open behind each nose, where burned light as intense as newborn stars. Above these gleaming eyes, heavy ledges of rock transformed into burly brows, sprouting the same unruly hair that now covered most of the surface of the boulders. Wide mouths opened, lined with lips that burgeoned and swelled like streams of lava. Pointed chins jutted almost to the feet of the visitors. Kate suddenly understood that the cracks she had seen covering the boulders were in fact deep lines, wrinkles on the skin of these strange beings.

"You are welcome," an infinitely deep voice rumbled. It came from one of the largest of the stone creatures, directly to Kate's left.

"Yes, welcome," echoed another, smaller one to the right.

"No they are not," objected a third voice, sounding like rocks grinding together. "We don't know them yet."

"T-t-tellll usss whooo youuu arrrre," crackled the biggest of the boulder-beings in a slow, difficult manner.

Kate slowly stood and drew in a deep breath. "I am Kaitlyn Prancer Gordon," she said, her voice unsteady as she scanned the craggy creatures. No arms or legs could be seen beneath the masses of scraggly hair. Only faces, chiseled by time, were visible. And all seven of them were scrutinizing her carefully. "I come from—ah, the future. Blade . . . Blade, Oregon. This is Laioni. She's a Halami, from here, well almost here, and that's her dog, Monga."

After a period of silence, the first creature, whose face bore more wrinkles than any of the others, stirred. "That will do for now. We ourselves have many names, among them *Azanna*, the Ones Beyond Age, although of course we really do age like anything else."

"Speak for yourself," interjected another, less wrinkled creature.

"Silence," thundered the first angrily, as two nearly identical boulders behind Kate started giggling together, making a sound like a couple of bubbling streams. The deeply wrinkled being frowned, then added, "With age, however, comes wisdom."

"So you must be very wise," said the two tittering creatures in unison.

At this, the Circle erupted into a chorus of wheezes, guffaws, and other forms of crude laughter. Only the eldest creature refrained, shifting slightly from side to side with her eyes closed.

At length, the raucous laughter subsided, and the creature's eyes again opened. "You may call us the Stonehags," she said, a trace of disgust in her voice. "We will now tell you our names, in order of seniority. I am Untla, the oldest. I can tell you much, for I have seen many, many years."

"If you don't fall asleep while you're talking," muttered the young Stonehag on her left.

Another chorus of laughter ensued. The two like-shaped creatures rocked so hard in mirth that they bumped into each other with a crash, breaking off some brittle hairs, which tumbled to the ground in a cloud of dust.

Emboldened by these antics, Kate turned back to Untla and asked, "But how do you speak English? I mean, I can understand you perfectly."

"To you I speak English, to your friend I speak Halami, and to the dog I speak Canine," answered the Stonehag. "My sisters and I have the gift of universal communication, which comes from living so long and watching so many different kinds of creatures. Now Gruntla, it's your turn."

The largest of the Stonehags, as big as a brontosaurus, made a low grinding sound as if she were clearing her throat. After a long pause, she said in a voice like an earthquake, "I ammmm Grrruntla. I ammmm the biggggest annd the c-c-closessst to ssstone, ssso heeeed whaaaatever I sssay, lllest I g-get aaangrrry annd—"

"Quit threatening them," chided the smallest Stonehag, seated to the right of Untla. "You should be ashamed, spouting off like that just because they're so tiny." Blinking her deep-set eyes, she continued, "I am Nyla. And I have to put up with this all the time."

Gruntla shook with rage and started to speak again, but Untla gave her a sharp look and commanded, "Enough. Now who's next?"

"I am," grumbled a voice on the other side of the Circle. "But I don't trust these intruders, and I won't tell them my name. Might put a curse on it, they might."

"That's Jbina, trusting everybody as usual," blurted one of the two nearly identical Stonehags. The other one, to her right, started to titter, but she kept right on speaking. "I'm Yogula, twin sister of Bogula."

"And just as stupid," threw in Jbina.

"Now it's my turn," cut in a lighter, thinner voice, belonging to the least wrinkled of the Stonehags. "We always save the best for last, but I hate all the waiting. I am Zletna, the youngest. But tell me," she asked, pushing her pointed chin practically into Kate's chest, "which of us do you think is the most beautiful?"

"Not you, that's for sure," called Jbina.

At that, a raging argument broke out between the two Stonehags. Howling, cursing, squabbling, screeching, and thumping filled the air.

"Wait!" shouted Kate at the top of her lungs. "Stop your fighting." The quarreling Stonehags relented, although Jbina continued to grumble to herself while rocking back and forth. "Please," Kate pleaded. "There isn't time for this."

"What's the hurry?" snapped Jbina. "Our kind of time we count in thousands of years."

"Hear her out," grumbled Nyla.

"Tell us what brought you to us," commanded Untla, her wrinkled face contorting into an enormous yawn.

"I need your help," began Kate. "This stick—it brought me here, but I belong five hundred years from now. And I've got to get back right away."

"Why the rush?" Jbina demanded suspiciously.

"Aunt Melanie's in trouble. And the loggers, they're going to cut down the redwoods any minute now. She'll try to stop them, I know, and anything could happen to her."

Untla, eyes closed, said, "This person is known to us."

Kate's heart skipped a beat. "Aunt Melanie? You know her?"

"Yes," answered Untla. "She has visited us before."

"Yyyyou're wrrrrong," replied Gruntla, speaking in her agonizingly slow manner. "Thaaat waaas annnotherrr p-p-perrrsonnn."

Untla's eyes opened. "No," she declared. "The same. She came with the very walking stick that this girl used just now to summon us."

"That's just it," Kate fretted. "I don't know how to use it. If it called you, that was by accident. I need you to tell me how to make it take me home. Do it for Aunt Melanie's sake, since you know her, not for mine."

"Melanie. Hmmm, I remember her now," said Zletna. "I quite liked her."

"You're such an easy mark," derided Bogula. "You just liked her because she called you 'dear.'"

"So what?" retorted Zletna. "I like being treated with some respect for a change."

"Silence," bellowed Untla. Concentrating her gaze on Kate, she continued, "You indeed have a serious problem, if what you say is true. For there is only one being alive who can tell you how to use that stick, and it is not one of us."

"But who is it?" demanded Kate. "Who can tell me?"

"Wait," interjected Jbina. "How do we know she didn't steal the stick from its rightful owner?" Narrowing her eyes, she added, "None of these two-legged creatures can be trusted. They only arrived here a century or two ago, and they already act like they're the only ones around."

"Some are like that," said Nyla, "but some are not. They're different from each other, just like we are."

"Except for us," piped Yogula, leaning to one side to nudge Bogula, who sniggered noisily.

Stepping nearer to Untla, Kate held the walking stick before her craggy face. "You know I'm telling the truth," she implored.

Untla lifted her knobby nose into the air and looked skyward, deliberating.

"Please," said Kate.

The nose descended. She peered at Kate for a long while, then finally spoke. "The ruler of the Tinnanis. If you want to learn the ways of your stick of power, you must go to him."

Laioni cried out suddenly, startling Kate. With consternation on her face, the Halami girl pointed in the direction of the lake beyond the boulders. She babbled some words Kate could not comprehend.

"What she is telling you," spoke Nyla sympathetically, "is that the Tinnani Chieftain can only be found by voyaging across the blue water to the island called Ho Shantero."

"The black island?" asked Kate in disbelief as a cold shiver slid down her spine.

"Yes," replied the Stonehag. "The one whose name means Island That Moves."

"And the Tinnanis—I thought they were just a myth. Are you sure that's right?"

"The Tinnanis are no myth," answered Untla firmly. "They are merely seldom seen, or are seen only in disguise, like the Stonehags. The stick you carry was made by the Tinnanis many generations ago. It is possible that even the Chieftain does not remember how it can be used."

At that moment, the ancient Untla yawned widely, exposing several rows of blackened teeth. "He is very unpredictable," she continued. "As changeable as the weather, just like his father and grandfather before him. But hear me well: Hold tightly to your stick of power. The world outside this Circle is already fraught with danger, and the power of evil grows steadily stronger."

Kate's mouth went dry and she asked, "Isn't there anything you can tell me about how to get to him safely? That island scares me half to death."

Untla yawned once more, this time making a deep, dull groan, so low in pitch it nearly fell below Kate's range of hearing. "The stick will show you the way, if you pay attention." She then closed her eyes and started immediately to snore, making a sound like a crashing landslide.

Shaking her head, Kate merely stared at the sleeping Stonehag. Then another voice called to her.

It was Nyla, smallest of the Stonehags. "There is one more thing we can tell you," she said in her gentlest rumble. "Show me the walking stick, and I will read you the words carved on its shaft."

Kate lifted the object near to Nyla's wrinkled face. The creature concentrated for a moment, crinkling her bulbous nose. At last, she spoke: "These words are written in the Tinnani Old Tongue, a speech so ancient I have not seen it for many ages. I am not sure I can still remember how to read it."

"Try," pleaded Kate. "It might help."

Nyla's deeply recessed eyes studied the shaft for a long moment. At irregular intervals, she made strange guttural sounds that seemed to indicate puzzlement, discovery, or simply effort. Finally, she spoke again, rumbling with satisfaction: "There. I am not so forgetful as I thought. These words are some sort of prophecy." And she read:

> *Fire of greed shall destroy;*
> *Fire of love shall create.*

"But what does it mean?" asked Kate. "What does fire have to do with anything?"

"That," answered the Stonehag, "only you can discover." She furrowed her already wrinkled brow. "But beware. Fire can strengthen and sustain you, but it also can consume you. Your enemies are near, and many. Your path home will be more difficult than you ever imagined." She eyed Kate tenderly for a moment and the edges of her swelling lips lifted slightly. "If you ever make it back to your own time, I want you to come visit me again."

Kate gazed into Nyla's deeply recessed eyes, seeing the bright bowls of light within. "I don't think I'll get the chance."

The Stonehag quivered. "If you can somehow learn the true meaning of the prophecy, then you may find your way home. And, I suspect, you may find something else as well." Nyla heaved a heavy sigh, full of ancient longing. "At least you have a purpose, a calling, something you must do with your life. That is a blessing, a true blessing. Some of us can only wait and watch as life moves past."

"I'll trade you," Kate said flatly, turning to go.

"Wait," commanded the voice of Untla, awake once more. She yawned again, groaning deeply, before continuing. "There is one thing more. We have a gift for you, a gift that might help you on your journey."

Jbina grumbled something to herself, and Nyla glared at her. But Untla paid no heed. The wrinkled being heaved her massive body to one side with a thunderous grunt. Kate drew closer to see what she had uncovered, and discovered a spring of purest water gurgling out of the ground.

"Drink," said Untla.

Kate bent lower when a flash of memory halted her. "There was another pool," she said worriedly, "a poison pool. It was just outside your Circle."

"Then it is no concern of ours," replied Untla. "The water at your feet will enable you, for a time, to share the Stonehags' gift of communication. You will understand all that you hear, whatever the tongue, and you will answer back and be understood. It is a gift you already possess in part, as does the one you call Aunt Melanie, for you have already shown that you can walk the bridges of time and place."

"I only want to walk back," said Kate quietly as she bent low. Placing her cupped right hand in the water, she drew some out and drank it. The water chilled her teeth, it was so cold. It cascaded down her throat, seeming to linger there for an instant, leaving behind a bracing taste of freshness and purity. She took another drink, then regained her feet.

"You too," said Untla to Laioni. "And also your dog. Drink."

Obediently, Laioni knelt beside the spring. One rope of black hair dropped into the water as she bent down to the bracing fountain. Monga, by her side as always, lapped eagerly, swishing his tail as he drank.

Laioni rose. Before she could even straighten her spine, the distant drumbeat echoed again. Faster and louder it grew, until the sound of booming cannons surrounded them. The earth shook so mightily that Kate kept her feet only with the aid of the walking stick.

Abruptly, the tremors ceased. The Stonehags, enormous boulders once again, sat immobile and ageless as fog flowed into the center of their ring. No more voices rumbled; no more spring bubbled. The Circle had returned to stone. All that remained of the great beings were their words of warning, still sounding in Kate's ears.

14

fallen brethren

MONGA kept his head low to the ground as he padded behind Laioni and Kate through the channel between the two great boulders. Mist swept across their surfaces, obscuring all but the deepest cracks. The dog nudged Laioni's leg, urging her to go faster, his bushy brown tail curled tightly over his back like the mainspring of a clock.

Kate, preoccupied with thoughts of the sinister island, did not pause to study the massive stones as she passed between them. Already she wondered if the Stonehags were right about the Tinnanis. Maybe they didn't really exist. And even if they did, maybe there was some way to communicate with the Tinnani Chieftain without actually going to the island. Perhaps he or his people came ashore regularly. Surely they must. How else could they have become so deeply ingrained in Halami legend if they didn't appear from time to time?

"It will not be easy to get there," Laioni muttered to herself as they neared the other side of the passageway.

Kate spun around. "I was just thinking the same—" She

caught herself in mid-sentence. "I understood you," she said in wonderment. "I mean, you spoke Halami and I understood you."

The other girl brightened. "And I understood you. It's the gift of the Stonehags."

But Kate had no time for celebration. "The Tinnanis— are they real? Have you ever actually seen one?"

Laioni hesitated. "No one has ever seen one, at least no one I know. But we all know what they look like."

"That's not too convincing," replied Kate. "Well, then, tell me about the island. Is there any safe way to get there?"

Laioni lowered her eyes. "It is bad, very bad. People should not go there at all." She sighed. "The few who have dared to try either have turned up later, wandering aimlessly in the forest with no memory of anything about the island, or have disappeared completely. Some time ago, the son of our eldest, a boy named Toru, dreamed he should go there on a vision quest. I knew him well. We were the same age. We all knew it was too dangerous, and we tried to persuade him to change his mind, but he refused. He left the village—it's by the coast, a day's walk from here—and no one has heard from him since." She pursed her lips angrily. "I think it was the work of Gashra."

"Gashra?" Kate knew she had heard the name, but she couldn't remember where.

"The most evil being alive," replied Laioni venomously. "He lives in the steaming mountain, whose name we never speak lest it increase his power. He can reach into people's minds and twist their thinking in terrible ways. If they are too good to be useful to him, like my friend Toru, he poisons their dreams to make them chase after death. If they are already evil, he draws them into his service, like he did with Sanbu."

"Who is Sanbu?"

"One of my people," Laioni said sadly. "He grew tired of hunting for his food and started stealing from other villages. That was bad enough, but then he joined forces with

Gashra and now no one is safe. His band mutilates animals, trees, and people without care. They've made the forest outside the crater a dangerous place. That is why I am worried for my father and his hunting party—and for all the Halamis."

Kate scanned the great gray boulders on either side of them, then turned back to Laioni. "You don't have to come with me, you know."

"I know," she answered in a low voice. "I don't even know exactly why I followed you here to the Circle, except that something made me feel like—like I was supposed to help you. Monga felt that too, I could tell, from the moment you fell into the hunting pit." She surveyed the carved handle of the walking stick, barely visible in the dim light between the boulders. "When I was born, it was foretold that I would make a long and perilous journey for the sake of my people. And that in that journey, my guide would be an owl. My name, Laioni, means She Who Follows the Owl."

Raising the carved handle, Kate asked, "And you think this is the owl?"

"I don't know," whispered Laioni, bending to scratch the top of Monga's head. "I don't even know the true meaning of my name, for the owl symbolizes two very different things to my people. To some, it is a symbol of the forest world that supports us, something to be cherished. To others, it is a symbol of death, something to be feared."

Kate glanced uncertainly at the walking stick. "That's another reason not to come with me."

"No," replied Laioni. "By coming with you, I will learn my true fate. I believe that you did not arrive here when you did by accident. There must be a reason."

Frowning, Kate lowered the stick. "That's where you're wrong. It's just bad luck, that's all." She paused, reflecting. "You don't think I'm some kind of spirit, do you?"

Laioni smiled. "You come through one of the great trees, you heat tea without a fire, you summon the Stonehags, and you carry a stick of power. That's enough for me."

"But I'm just a girl, like you."

"Then you wouldn't have feet like that," objected Laioni, pointing to her bright green shoelaces. "They're as green as new leaves."

Shaking her head, Kate repeated, "I'm just a girl."

"Whatever you are, I think you are here to help my people."

Kate bristled. "What do you mean?"

"These are dangerous times, as the Stonehag said. The power of Gashra grows stronger by the day. His mountain has come alive, rumbles with anger, and spouts burning clouds. Sanbu and his warriors steal and waste whatever they want. Parts of the forest where my people have lived for generations are dying, changing from green to brown, rivers are turning to fire, and our brothers and sisters the creatures of the forest are growing scarcer. Even the fish that once were so plentiful we could walk across the streams on their backs are now hard to find. If I am ever going to make a journey for my people, as the prophecy said, it must be soon." She swallowed with some difficulty. "There is something else. That boy, Toru, my friend—he was, he was the one I hoped would father my children someday. I have to find out what happened to him."

"You may be better off looking by yourself."

"I think we're both better off staying together."

"You're an optimist," replied Kate. "Like me. And also like someone else I know, who has eyes just like yours."

"The one you call Aunt Lemony?"

"Aunt Melanie," corrected Kate. "But I think she'd like your way of saying it." Her expression clouded again. "I hope I get to tell her someday."

She turned back to the curling clouds of mist that faced them at the other side of the passageway. The time had come to leave the protection of the boulders, to seek out the Tinnanis, if indeed they existed. She glanced at the smaller boulder to her left that she knew to be Nyla, wishing she could hear again the Stonehag's rumbling voice. But there was no time for that now. Kate started walking again, disregarding the renewed throbbing on the back of her left hand.

At the instant she passed beyond the boulders, she stopped suddenly in her tracks. She blinked her eyes, certain the fog was playing a trick with her vision. Yet she saw what she saw.

Not five paces in front of her, next to the boiling pool of clear liquid that she knew in later times would bear an evil spell, stood an upright figure. His skin, dark green in color, was covered with rows of reptilian scales that rippled as he breathed. Clad with only a brown leather loincloth, two metallic orange bands around each bicep, and another orange band around his forehead to hold his straight black hair in place, the figure stood no higher than Kate's waist. In one hand he held a spear, taller than himself, blade up. His eyes, dull yellow in color, scrutinized her with deep suspicion.

Monga, just out of the channel, barked sharply. Laioni gasped and stood immobile by Kate's side. Just then, the small green figure raised his spear and brought its base down forcefully on the rocks by his feet. The sound reverberated off the cliffs behind the boulders.

At once, Kate was knocked to the ground. Another green warrior, who had leaped onto her back from one of the boulders, tried to pull the walking stick out of her hand. She grappled with him, rolling on the pumice-strewn terrain, amazed to find that his tiny body possessed the strength of someone twice his size.

A new attacker jumped on her back and wrapped his arms around her neck, squeezing hard. She kicked the first attacker in the chest so hard that he released his hold on the stick and fell backward with a thud. But the grip of the second one tightened on her neck and she coughed, sputtering for air.

"Laioni," she croaked desperately.

But Laioni had also been jumped, and was wrestling with one of the green beings at that very moment. Monga, snarling ferociously, bit him on the leg, making him squeal in pain and start beating the dog brutally with his fists. Monga would not let go, however, sinking his teeth deeper into the scaly flesh and shaking his head fiercely from side to side.

Kate fell over backward, landing on the rocks with such force that the warrior groaned and slipped to the side of her neck, loosening his grip just enough to allow her to pull him around her shoulder. With her bandaged hand, she punched him hard in the stomach several times until he finally released his hold. Before she could roll away, though, he kicked her under the chin and sent her sprawling backward.

The walking stick flew out of her grasp and clattered against the ground. Kate lunged for it, but the attacker who had kicked her got there first. He grabbed the stick and, before Kate could stop him, hurled it up to the warrior with the orange arm bands, who had climbed on top of the boulder directly behind the boiling pool—the boulder that only moments before, as Nyla, had warned her: *Beware . . . your enemies are near.*

"The stick!" cried Kate, as she reached for a handhold and started climbing upward. Struggling to ascend, she did not see that the warrior was waiting for her.

Yellow eyes gleaming, he raised his spear above his head. Positioning himself at the extreme edge of the boulder, he prepared to thrust the blade deep into Kate's back. He paused for the barest instant, spear held high, to savor his moment of triumph.

Just then, the boulder shifted underneath him. Merely a slight slip to the side, it was not a major movement like the jolt of an earthquake. Yet it was just enough to throw the warrior off balance. He struggled to stay on his feet, but tumbled headlong over the edge, whizzing over Kate's head to land in the boiling pool below.

Hearing the splash and the blood-curdling scream, Kate pulled herself up to the top of the boulder. There, lying on the cracked gray surface, was the walking stick. She closed her hand around the shaft, just as she heard Laioni cry out below.

She leaped to the ground next to the three other attackers, two of whom were rolling on the rocks with Laioni. Another, splattered with black blood, was trying desperately to pry Monga from his leg. With a flying tackle, she landed on one of Laioni's assailants, pulling him from her side. They rolled to the edge of the boiling pool.

Kate stood and faced the figure vengefully. She could hear the pool bubbling just behind her. His eyes met hers and narrowed to knifelike slits. Then, to her astonishment, he began swiftly to metamorphose. His legs fused together into a single powerful tail covered with green scales, tearing the loincloth to pieces. His arms suddenly shrunk inward and new, stubby legs sprouted from under his hips. Elongating to a point, his head stretched toward his nose, pushing his thin eyes to the sides of his face. The warrior had been transformed into a large green lizard.

Before Kate could move, the creature fell forward onto its belly and began to crawl toward her. She prepared to kick it back, but it swerved around her and crawled to one side. Whirling around, she saw for the first time that the boiling pool had turned green, the same frothing green that had nearly lured her to her death. Her left hand throbbed painfully, but the pool had no power over her. She watched in horror as the giant lizard, captivated by the spell, slithered over the rocks and into the cauldron.

She turned back to the others to see that the two remaining attackers also had changed to reptilian form. They began crawling toward the pool, including one who carried Monga clinging to a torn hind leg. Kate leaped at the dog, grabbed him by the belly, and tore him away from the slithering beast, who continued to crawl undeterred. Holding the dog in one arm, she suddenly saw that Laioni, her eyes wide and entranced, was walking in the direction of the pool.

"Stop!" shouted Kate. "Laioni, stop!"

The Halami girl paid no attention. She continued to stride toward the bubbling pool. Kate threw herself at her, just managing to catch her by the heel with an outstretched hand. She wrenched the foot sideways, pulling Laioni to the ground with a thud.

Laioni sat up, shaking her head in bewilderment. She watched, horrified, as the tail of the last attacker slipped into the frothing pool.

"I—I almost went in there myself," she said weakly.

Kate rose, still clutching the wriggling Monga. With her free hand, she picked up the walking stick. "Let's get out of here," she said. "Are you all right?"

"A little bruised, that's all."

Together, they stumbled down the steep slope. Kate continued to hold Monga tightly, for fear he, too, might be drawn by the deadly spell. Only after descending quite a distance did she finally set the dog free. To her relief, he did not try to run back toward the pool. Instead, he scampered over to a rivulet of water running down from the cliffs and plunged his face into the cold stream.

"He didn't like the taste," said Laioni wryly.

"I don't blame him," answered Kate, with a glance at the Circle of Stones above them. "They almost got the stick. And me, too, if it hadn't been for Nyla."

Then, recalling her first experience with the pool, she thought again of the small red owl that had knocked her aside just in time. Had that been Nyla's doing as well? Turning back to Laioni, she said, "If that's what we have to expect from the Tinnanis, I don't see how we'll ever get any help from their Chieftain."

Laioni grimaced. "Those were not Tinnanis. They were Slimnis, the Tinnanis' fallen brethren. Once they lived freely, like other beings of the forest, but now they serve Gashra. The Tinnanis are their sworn enemy."

Monga lifted his head at last and vigorously shook the water from himself. Watching him, Laioni rubbed her sore right forearm. "It is a bad sign, very bad, that they've entered the crater. This place is the greatest stronghold of the Tinnanis, the very home of their Chieftain. I am glad we defeated them, but I'm afraid more will come after."

"The leader, the one with the arm bands, must have laid

a curse on the pool when he fell in," said Kate. "His way of getting revenge, I guess."

"But he caught only his own warriors," added Laioni.

Kate pulled her bandaged hand close to her chest. "So far."

15

the blue lake

WORDLESSLY, they scrambled down the slippery slope. Kate's legs, whether tugged by gravity alone or by some new inexorable force as well, pulled her downward toward the lake at a rapid clip. Her thigh muscles strained at the steep descent, and several times rocks slid from under her feet, causing her to leap to safety before twisting an ankle or a knee.

At one point she turned to see Laioni, moving down the slope with the ease of mist rolling across the rocks. Though shoeless, she stepped over the jumbled and jagged terrain with confident ease. Monga bounced along behind, stopping every so often to thrust his long nose into a small crevice where some tiny newt or beetle had scurried to safety.

Arriving at the edge of the lake, Kate peered into the fog. No island could be seen, only splotches of shimmering blue through occasional windows in the whirling mist. Bending down, she touched the water with one finger. It felt warm, like a steaming bath. As she stood again, her

vision roamed the shoreline for anything that might con-
ceivably be used as a boat. She really didn't want to cross
the shoreline of this mysterious lake at all, but if she had
to do so, she certainly did not want to swim in its waters
unprotected.

A dark cylindrical shape bobbing near the shore
caught her eye. Moving closer, she saw that it was a log,
perhaps eight feet long, that must have blown down from
the upper reaches of a great fir or cedar and drifted across
the lake. The wood, darkened by dampness, was nearly
black.

Laioni joined her at the water's edge. "Our canoe?"

"I think so," answered Kate as she grabbed one of the
protruding branches and pulled the log closer to shore. "I'd
rather ride in something shaped like your little toys, but we
don't have much choice."

Surveying the reflectionless blue water, Laioni added
doubtfully, "I just hope we can do better than my pebbles."
She cocked her head. "Wait, I have an idea. Would you
give me the little drum you carry? I saw it when you gave
us the sweet brown tea."

Kate slipped off the blue day pack, unzipped it, and
handed the tiny painted drum to Laioni. Immediately, the
Halami girl squatted down on the pumice, placed the drum
between her legs, and closed her eyes for several seconds.
When she opened them, she looked neither at the drum nor
at Kate, but into the mist rising from the lake.

Gently, her fingers began to tap the stretched hide of the
drum, seeking their true rhythm just as Kate had seen Aunt
Melanie do at the mouth of Kahona Falls. She began
slowly to sing, as her hands alternately slid and swished
and pounded. Once again, Kate marveled at the likeness of
Laioni to her own beloved great-aunt. Although her intel-
lect dismissed the possibility of a real connection between
them as ridiculous, as mere fantasy, she remembered what
Grandfather used to say: *Wait long enough, and fantasy
becomes reality.*

Laioni continued to chant, just as Kate had heard in

another time and another place. This time, however, she
understood the lilting words:

> *Hear me O spirits*
> *My small walking words:*
> *All time in the sunrise*
> *All life in the seed.*
>
> *Our days may be short*
> *Our reach may be long*
> *We touch both our elders*
> *And children unborn.*
>
> *My struggles are yours*
> *Your mystery mine.*
> *I ask you for guidance*
> *And know you will say:*
>
> *Your spirit is one*
> *With the spirits around you.*
> *Your spirit is one*
> *With the spirits around you.*

As her last *halma-dru* melted into the mist, Laioni rose
silently to her feet. She handed the drum to Kate, who
replaced it in the day pack. Together, they waded into the
water and straddled the log, positioning themselves between
the stubby ends of broken branches that ran its full length.
Monga jumped into the water and started paddling vigorously alongside.

Kate, seated in front, pushed off from the shore. The
ground beneath her sneakers fell away swiftly; in no more
than a yard from the water's edge she could no longer
touch bottom. She had no way to measure the depth of this
lake, but all her instincts told her it was unfathomably
deep.

The log sank slightly under their weight, submerging
everything below their hips in the warm water. Fog soon

enveloped them, and the cliffs around the rim disappeared from view. Ahead and behind, Kate could see nothing but curls of mist spiraling out of the blue water. She leaned slightly forward and began to paddle, while Laioni did the same. Monga, meanwhile, splashed along beside them. Holding her bandaged hand under the water at one point, Kate noted how clear the water seemed, even as it imbued her forearm, fingers, and kerchief with a vibrant blue color. She had never seen water like this before.

But for the sound of their paddling and the constant lapping of little waves against the log, the lake was still. Gradually, however, Kate grew aware of a slight chill in the air, of a shadow in the mist she could not really see.

Suddenly, the island burst from behind a curtain of fog not fifty yards ahead. Blacker than charcoal, the spindly spires and pinnacles rose like the turrets of an abandoned castle. Then Kate saw what she most dreaded to see: the gleaming black surface of the island seemed to be moving, quivering like living skin. *Like it was crawling or something,* the Forest Service man had said.

At that instant something solid brushed against her foot. She cried out, wrenching up her leg just as Monga started barking furiously. Then the front end of the log rose high out of the water, throwing her backward into Laioni.

With an explosion of spray, the makeshift boat capsized. A great wave lifted and crashed down over the flailing voyagers, drowning their screams in the swell of a powerful whirlpool that dragged them downward.

Soon the eerie stillness returned to the lake. Except for a lone log drifting unattended, nothing but mist moved on the surface.

16

thika the guardian

KATE felt a scratchy tongue licking her face. She sat up with a start.

"Hey, Monga, that's enough," she sputtered, pushing the affectionate dog away. In response, he shook his shaggy body vigorously, splattering her with water.

She looked around to see Laioni and Monga, like herself, dripping wet on a dark stone floor. Though her clothes were drenched, she felt uncomfortably warm. Laioni had lost her woven basketry cap; her twin ropes of black hair were draped, glistening, over her shoulders.

Over their heads swept a great transparent dome. At first Kate thought it had been fashioned from glass or quartz, but then she saw it flex and bend with a gentle undulation, moved by some powerful current. She marveled at the clear membrane, arching above them like an enormous half bubble. Outside, the world was entirely blue, but for the thin shafts of light penetrating from far above and some curious white shapes that encircled the dome. Tall and slender, they waved slowly like great windblown branches. The stone floor was unadorned except for a square silver plank in the center, possibly a trapdoor of some kind.

"Where are we?" asked Laioni, scanning the shifting blue light filtering through the dome.

"Beats me. It's almost like we're under the lake somehow. Everything is so blue up there, except for those big white things. They look almost like trees."

Observing the square plank, Kate said, "I wonder if this is the way out." Crawling nearer, she inspected it closely. Wrought of gleaming silver, with inlaid patterns of interwoven branches, it fit perfectly into the smooth floor. Pulling from her jeans pocket the Swiss army knife she always carried, she tried to pry it open, but with no success. The trapdoor, if indeed it was a trapdoor, would not budge.

"You carry strange tools," said Laioni, staring in wonder at the knife.

"Still doesn't do any good," grumbled Kate. Then she spied something unusual stuck into the slit between the silver door and the floor. Pinching the object between her thumb and forefinger, she pulled it free. "It's a feather," she observed, more mystified than ever. "A pure white feather. An owl maybe?"

"Maybe," answered Laioni in a noncommittal tone.

"But how could an owl get in here? It doesn't—"

Just then a spindly shadow fell across the silver square. Kate jerked her head upward to see one of the white treelike figures moving closer to the dome. It was tall, perhaps ten times as tall as Kate and twice as high as the dome, covered with knuckle-shaped lumps like a branch of coral. As it bent closer to them, it laid a bony appendage on the surface of the dome itself with a sound like fingers rubbing against an inflated balloon. Now Kate could see that the appendage was not pure white as it had appeared from a distance, but rather ribbed with veins of very light yellow. Then, with shock, she realized that the knuckle-shaped lumps each contained a single round, blue eye. Hundreds and hundreds of them covered the knobby skeleton.

"You, hsh-whshhh, dare to enter the realm of Ho Shh-hantero," boomed a watery voice that echoed inside the dome. "What is your name, shwshhh, and your purpose?"

Kate clambered to her feet and attempted to address the many-eyed creature. "Kaitlyn Prancer Gordon is my name, and this is Laioni and Monga. We are here to meet with the Chieftain of the Tinnanis."

"Tell me, shwshhh, why you want to see him," commanded the watery voice, sounding like liquid sloshing through a pipe. "I am Thika, First Guardian of Ho Shh-hantero, and no one may pass beyond here without my permission. Speak quickly, hshh-swshh, for I have very little time."

Kate answered cautiously, "We have something urgent to discuss with him."

Thika's knobby limb moved slightly on the transparent dome. "How do I know, shhhhwshh, you are telling the truth? You might be, hshh, hshh, really an agent of the Wicked One, or just another Halami, shwshhhh, following some deluded dream."

At this, Laioni glanced anxiously at Kate. Monga, sensing her distress, paced around her feet.

"Because I carry this," answered Kate, waving the walking stick.

"That, shhhwsh, is not good enough," gurgled the voice of the Guardian. "I already know you carry a stick of power. Hshhwshhh. That is the only reason I did not banish you immediately, hshhh, through the Tinnanis' tunnels, shhwsh, as I have done with every other intruder who has dared to approach Ho Shhhantero. By now you would be returned to the forest below, ssswhshh, with no memory at all of our meeting. But you could have stolen the stick, hhshh-whhshh, or won it through treachery. No, if you are to pass by me, shhwsh, you must tell me more of your mission."

"All right," Kate said reluctantly. "I need the Chieftain to tell me how to make the stick work, so it can take me back to my own time."

"Shhhwshh," sloshed Thika. "You say, hshhh, you are from another time?"

"Yes."

"Then I, shhhwsh, will let you pass."

Kate and Laioni exchanged relieved glances.

"After," continued Thika, "you have said, shhwwwsh, the password."

"Password?" asked Kate. "But, but—I don't know what you mean."

"Any language, hshhh, will do," declared the coral-like creature, its multiple blue eyes concentrating on Kate. "I am old enough, shhwshh, to remember even the Old Tongue. Now hurry, hurry, hshh-whshh. Choose well your words. For you will have, sshhwsh, only one chance."

A lump expanded in Kate's throat, swelling so much that speaking would have been difficult even if she did know the Guardian's password. She felt a rush of despair, overwhelming her like the waters of the blue lake had overwhelmed her not long before. What could she do now? If she had but one chance as Thika said, then she had already lost it. She would never see the Tinnani Chieftain, never see Aunt Melanie. How could she possibly know some long-forgotten password, as ancient as the Tinnani Old Tongue?

Then, like the subtlest rays of dawn emerging over the horizon, an idea glimmered at the farthest edge of her consciousness. She furrowed her brow in a desperate effort to remember some words she had heard but once, words etched into the shaft of the walking stick, words written in the ancient Old Tongue.

She cleared her throat. Slowly, haltingly, she recited them:

Fire of greed shall destroy;
Fire of love shall create.

With a sudden tearing sound, like the ripping of heavy cloth, the knobby appendage of Thika the Guardian reached through the transparent dome. More supple than it seemed, it wrapped itself around the waists of all three companions, even as they wriggled and kicked to break away.

"Let go!" shouted Kate, fighting in vain to free herself. "You can't send us away."

Thika did not relent. As the appendage tightened around Kate's waist, several of its deep-socketed eyes probed her with curiosity. "You, shhhwhshhh, are an odd creature," it said disapprovingly.

As the Guardian lifted them up through the dome, Kate saw that the transparent membrane instantly sealed itself, like a bubble that could be punctured but not burst. Still struggling to break free, she barely managed to suck in a last breath of air before she was totally submerged in water.

Upward they swam through the omnipresent blue, higher and higher until Kate finally stopped struggling. Below her she saw the shrinking circle of the dome, the silver square clearly visible in the center of its dark floor. Around it stood more than a dozen treelike creatures, each of them studded with eyes identical to Thika's. Above, she saw nothing but a dark shadow growing rapidly larger.

Just at the point she could hold her breath no longer, she heard again the same tearing sound. Air suddenly replaced water, and she could breathe again. The grip around her waist relaxed, and she found herself sprawled on another stone floor, gasping. Beside her lay Laioni and Monga, looking as bewildered as they were drenched.

A smoldering torch, fastened to the wall with a lacy metal band, burned unsteadily above their heads, sputtering as it flickered. It appeared to be consuming some sort of incandescent gas. Dark stone surrounded them. The chamber was featureless but for a single stone stairway beneath the torch leading up into darkness. Kate noticed at once that the perfectly carved steps were very small, half the normal size, just like the ones in the tunnel behind Kahona Falls.

Thika's appendage, rising through a hole in the stone floor that was covered with the same transparent membrane as the dome, studied them with its many round eyes.

"Welcome, hhhsh, to Ho Shhhantero," the now-familiar voice sloshed.

Kate, still grasping the walking stick, leaped to her feet, as did Laioni. "Ho Shantero?" they asked in unison.

"Yessshhwsh," answered the Guardian, twisting and undulating like a snake as it spoke. "You knew the ancient password, shh-wshh, so I have brought you here as I am commanded. Hshhhh. But at times, shwshh, I doubt the wisdom of the commands. You should feel most privileged, hhhshwsh, for you are the only ones of your kind ever to enter here, sshwsh, unaccompanied by a Tinnani."

Reflecting on Thika's words, Kate wondered what humans had ever been admitted here in the company of a Tinnani. And had they ever left? Before she could speak, however, Laioni asked her own version of the same question.

"The boy Toru, one of my people," she began timidly. "He came to the lake as we did, not long ago. What happened to him?"

"I seem, hhhsshhh, to remember him," replied the Guardian, whose movements beneath the torch cast coiling shadows upon the stone walls and floor. "He was driven by a dream, shhwshh, a false dream. It was the work, whhshh, of the Wicked One."

"What did you do with him?" Laioni, water still dripping from her body, stepped a bit closer. "Tell me, please."

"I sent him away, shhhwshh, through the tunnels, whhhshh, escorted by a Tinnani who made him forget all he had seen. Swshhh. He was left in the forest somewhere quite distant, hhhsh-whshh, but he should have returned to your people by now."

Laioni's gaze fell. "He has not."

"It could be, shhwshh, he was captured by the Wicked One," said Thika.

"You mean Ga—" began Kate.

"Hhssswshh! Never say that name," interrupted the sinuous creature, its blue eyes focused squarely on her. "It is forbidden here. If you must speak of him, hhsh-whhsh, you may call him the Wicked One."

"He's growing stronger, isn't he?" asked Kate in a quiet voice.

The blue eyes scanned her with pained intensity. "By the day, shhwshhh. We measure his strength, hshhwsh, by the warmth of the lake. For as it grows warmer, the Guardians grow weaker. Hhhssshh-swhshh. Already some of our very best have died from the heat, sshwshh, a terrible slow death that saps our strength and turns us whiter than skeletons. Soon the rest of us will follow, hwshhhh, unless something changes."

The many-eyed being made a low gurgling sound, like a dog growling underwater. "But the Wicked One, hwshh, cares not about us, nor about any living thing but himself. He thinks the whole world, shwshh, and everything in it, shw-shh, exists solely for his benefit, to be consumed or destroyed as he chooses. The Guardians he knows only because we stand in the way, hwsswss, of his true desire."

"What is that?"

"To invade Ho Shhhantero and make it his own. Yesshh-hwsh! He does not even care if he destroys it in the process, so long as he controls it at last. Whssshhh, for time beyond memory, since the Great Battle long ago, the cool waters of this lake prevented him and his molten warriors from reaching the floating island, hsh-whshh, for they must stay as hot as their realm underground or perish. And none of his servants above the ground—like the Slimnis—have dared to enter the crater either, hswshh, rightfully fearing the wrath of the Guardians. But those days, whhshhh, are numbered. Hssshhhh. The Guardians are nearly no more."

Kate glanced at Laioni, then addressed Thika. "We saw some of his servants in the crater. The ones you call Slimnis."

Thika's limb lifted with a jerk. "Slimnis? In the crater? Are you sure?"

"I'm sure," answered Kate. She squeezed the knotted kerchief in her left hand, causing more water to drip onto the floor. "We fought them, and we won. But I'm afraid more will follow."

"Those are terrible tidings indeed," replied the Guardian. "Hwhssshh. If the Chieftain ever was going to help you, shhwsh-shhwsh, he will not be in the mood now. He has, hhhswshh, greater problems of his own."

"The waters of the lake are warm in my time, too," said Kate somberly.

"Then, hshwshh, I pity you," spoke the watery voice. The creature straightened itself, observing Kate closely one more time. Then it slipped swiftly down the hole in the stone floor. The sound of ripping fiber rent the air, followed by a distinct pop, followed by silence.

Kate pivoted to face the narrow stairway. The light from the flickering torch danced mysteriously upon the carved steps, making them seem more like water than stone. She stepped closer, drew in a deep breath, and started to climb.

the black island
of ho shantero

LEAVING a trail of water behind her, Kate ascended the darkened stairway, followed by her equally wet companions. She wondered at the skilled hands that had carved these small steps out of the solid rock. Unlike the buff-colored pumice she had seen elsewhere in the crater, this rock was utterly black, perhaps charred in the final fiery gasp of the volcano that created the crater long ago. As in the pumice outside, small holes permeated every surface, lessening the weight of the rock and making it at least conceivable that beings of great intelligence could have somehow caused this island to float. Still, if she had not seen so much to convince her that Ho Shantero did indeed ride upon the waters of the lake, she would never have believed it possible.

The stairway spiraled up, up, and up. At each complete turn of the spiral, another torch flickered, casting its wavering light for several more steps. Beneath each torch, Kate saw the outlines of petroglyphs cut deep into the blackened stone. Faces of all descriptions, winged creatures soaring

high above the trees, long-tailed lizards, stick figures that
seemed to represent humans, cones and needles, roots and
branches, all crowded the dimly lit walls. As she continued
to climb, taking the miniature steps three or four at a time,
Kate guessed that the petroglyphs told a single connected
story. If only the stairway were better lit, its walls would be
a continuous mural of Tinnani history, twisting and turning
like the cycles of time.

At length, the stairs came to an end. Before them ran a
long hallway with a rounded ceiling, itself dimly lit by two
of the same sputtering torches. Kate, Laioni, and Monga,
ears thrust forward in alert position, started to walk down the
hallway, the clattering sound of the walking stick echoing
and re-echoing within the walls of stone. Soon they heard a
new sound as well: the steady drip-dripping of water not far
ahead.

"I wonder where that sound is coming from," said Laioni.

"There, look," observed Kate, pointing to a raised circle
in the middle of the floor, barely visible in the dim light. "It
looks like a fountain of some kind, except there's so little
water."

"And look," added Laioni, leaning close to the tiny
spout of water gushing out of a hole in the center of the circle. "This water has colors in it. Can you see?"

As Kate bent lower, she discovered several subtle, shimmering rainbows within the spray. "You're right, but in this
light it's hard to tell if it's the torches making those colors
or the water itself."

Just then Monga started barking loudly. Kate and Laioni
straightened to see—or, more accurately, to sense—they
were surrounded by eight or ten nearly invisible beings. A
vague white glow hovered in the spot where each of the
beings stood, as much a lessening of shadow as a presence
of light. Though it was difficult to tell, the figures appeared
to be quite compact, no higher than Kate's waist. They
were each rather round in shape, and if she wasn't mistaken, Kate thought she glimpsed the barest flash of yellow
near the top of each form.

Without a sound, the ring of glowing beings opened in the direction of the hallway, then moved closer to Kate, Laioni, and Monga. They came very near, paused, then as soon as any of the three companions moved down the hallway, moved closer again. Kate realized they were being herded, like sheep, by the vaguely visible creatures.

Monga continued barking until Laioni reached down and stroked his scruffy coat along his neck. "It's all right," she whispered. "They're not going to hurt us."

"What makes you so sure?" asked Kate, her brow furrowed.

"Because," announced Laioni, "they are Tinnanis."

Kate stopped short. "You mean these white glowing shapes? The Tinnanis don't have real bodies?"

At that, a stirring sound filled the hallway, accompanied by a muffled sort of clucking, almost like the stifled laughter of great birds.

"They have bodies," replied Laioni. "Just like the Slimnis can change from their basic lizard forms into manlike shapes, their brothers the Tinnanis can change from their basic forms into invisible puffs of wind. Right now they're not quite invisible so we can see them enough to be herded."

"And what is their basic form, when they're not invisible?"

Laioni did not answer. Her eyes focused on something down the hallway. Kate turned from her to look, and saw that a new and brighter light had come into view. As they drew nearer, the light expanded, until finally it opened into a wide and high room.

As they entered the chamber, Kate thought of the great hall of the grand Scottish castle she had once visited with Grandfather. Glowing balls of white whom she now knew to be Tinnanis lined the walls on both sides. Overhead, a dozen sputtering torches flamed, suspended from a circular chandelier made of heavy metal chains. Though the torches were no brighter than those lining the hallway and the spiraling stairs, because so many of them hung from the chandelier a brighter light filled the room. Darkness still clung

to the walls and corners, but at least Kate could see Laioni
and Monga more easily.

At the farthest end of the room, Kate spied three grand
high-backed thrones. The middle one, tallest of the three,
was delicately wrought of white whalebone, studded with
stones of all colors and descriptions. Purple amethyst, yellow sulfur, red jasper, green-and-silver agate, and black
obsidian rimmed its edges. At the very top, the whalebone
curved as if to support something shaped like a sphere, but
the cup-shaped space was empty. In a flash of irreverence,
Kate imagined that one of her softballs would fit perfectly
there. The two thrones on either side, carved from huge
transparent crystals of quartz, were identical. They shimmered in the wavering torchlight like two gigantic blocks
of ice, clear and cold.

In the central throne, as well as in the transparent seat to
its left, round balls of white glimmered. Then, as Kate and
Laioni stood transfixed, the two forms started to solidify.
The glowing masses grew whiter, even as they grew more
defined. Kate glanced to one side to see that the same thing
was happening to the rows of Tinnanis lining the walls of
the chamber. When she turned back, the true form of the
Tinnani Chieftain had nearly materialized.

She gasped, for the owl's head handle of the walking
stick had seemingly sprung to life. The Chieftain's eyes,
perfectly round and yellow, were those of an owl, but the
rest of his face seemed more human. Instead of a beak, a
long hooked nose hung low above his small mouth. His
eyebrows, made of dozens of tiny feathers, protruded from
his forehead like tufts of white cotton. Fluffy white feathers
covered his round body, and two great white wings pressed
close to his shoulders. Beneath his cloaklike wings, two
arms sprouted, now resting across his ample white belly,
which was adorned with a wide belt bearing an amethyst
crystal in its buckle.

Both legs, like both arms, were covered completely with
white feathers. His feet, shaped like those of a man, looked
tough and callused. From each of his fingers and toes grew

talons, curved and sharp, though Kate suspected they could be retracted for everyday uses like walking. He wore a gleaming silver band around his brow, tilted slightly to one side. But for his face, hands, and feet, he looked like an enormous white owl, glowering at both Kate and the walking stick.

To the Tinnani Chieftain's left, another owl-like person solidified in the crystalline throne. Equally tall but less rotund, this Tinnani had softer facial features, a shorter nose, and even larger yellow eyes, which radiated both wisdom and suffering. In the talons of one hand, she held a long staff like a scepter, dotted with red rubies. Around her neck was draped a string of glistening pearls, no less white than her feathers. Studying the visitors with care, she snapped her jaws together sharply, making a sharp clicking sound.

The Chieftain stirred impatiently, then called to one of his aides in a hooting voice much like that of the owl Kate had heard in the forest. "Oysters!" he commanded. "Bring me some oysters." Then he added irritably to his wife, "Will they ever learn to have them ready as soon as I materialize?"

Her yellow eyes blinked. She hooted softly, "Nobody knows when you're going to materialize, dear, so it takes them a moment."

"Well, *I* know when," grumbled the plump Chieftain. "That ought to be enough." His head turned on his neck a full one hundred and eighty degrees, and he called to the scurrying aide: "And get me some pickled mousetails while you're at it." He smacked his lips and again turned to his wife. "Don't tell me they're bad for me, I know it already. But today is a special occasion."

"So was yesterday," she said calmly.

"And so may tomorrow be," thundered the Tinnani from his throne. "I can eat mousetails anytime I like. It's part of being Chieftain, about the only part I enjoy. I wish I could chuck all the rest."

His yellow eyes concentrated on Kate. "Now, as to you," he hooted, "the one who tells my First Guardian she comes from the future and calls herself Kaitlyn. How dare you enter Ho Shantero spreading false rumors of warriors and assassins inside the crater? You have already caused me and my council no end of heartburn on the subject. Tell us now, finally and forever, that this rumor is a lie."

Kate started to speak when a Tinnani wearing a wide-brimmed hat made of blue feathers stepped forward. "Begging your pardon, Your Wingedness, but shouldn't we introduce you first?"

The Chieftain ruffled his wings annoyedly. "Formalities, formalities. I know who I am, so what does it matter if they do? Oh, all right, but be quick about it." He sat back, tapping his belt buckle with one sharp talon.

The hatted aide spread his wings wide. From the back of the chamber came a chorus of deep horns, with a slight flourish of flutes at the finish. "I present to you Hockeltock de Notnot, Fourteenth Chieftain of the Tinnanis." Again the horns sounded. "And Chieftess Hufter Blefoninni, who rules at his side." The Tinnani closed his wings, bowed to the enthroned couple, and withdrew.

"Now, your answer," commanded the Chieftain, still tapping his belt buckle.

"The rumor you spoke of," began Kate, speaking as firmly as she could manage, "is not a lie. It is true. We met four of the creatures you call Slimnis near the Circle of Stones. They attacked us and we fought with them." After a pause, she added, "They won't bother anyone again."

"Liar," sputtered the Chieftain, turning to his wife. "Hear how she persists?" The Chieftess sat impassively, following Kate's slightest movement with her wide yellow eyes. "It's enough to give me indigestion," muttered the Chieftain. "Oysters! Where are those oysters?"

At that instant, a pair of Tinnanis wearing long capes of woven grasses flew to the throne from the back of the hall, one bearing a low-rimmed basket piled high with delicacies, the other a narrow container made of shiny purple stone. Laying the bounty on a low table brought by another aide, they bowed and backed slowly away.

"It's about time," snapped the rotund Tinnani, stuffing raw oysters and pickled mousetails into his little mouth. "Mmmmmff, dere id nodding ataw wike ekfewend dafood," he said while chomping.

After swallowing three such mouthfuls, the Chieftain reached for the narrow container, brought it to his mouth, and washed it all down. A brief look of satisfaction, almost mirth, crossed his face, then abruptly turned into a scowl. "Your story is clearly false. What would the Slimnis want with you, two humans and a mangy little dog?"

Monga growled quietly. Laioni reached to him and stroked his head until he grew silent again.

Kate stepped forward, displaying the walking stick. "They attacked us," she declared, "because they wanted this stick."

A fluttering of wings filled the chamber. Several of the Tinnanis drew nearer, hoping to get a better view of the intricately carved object. The Chieftess in particular stretched forward to examine it closely. Then the Chieftain waved them all back with one of his hands and spoke sternly to Kate.

"Do you think you can fool me so easily? That is no stick of power. It is nothing but a fake."

"It is not," objected Kate. "It's the real thing. It brought me here from the future. Through a time tunnel. All I need is for you to tell me how to make it take me back. And soon, before they cut down the Ancient One, or I won't get back at all."

The Chieftain scowled at her. "Even if you speak the truth, why should I help you? All your kind has ever done is torment my people."

Laioni stepped forward. "That's not so, Your Wingedness. The Halamis live with your people and the rest of the forest beings in peace. A few of our number have turned bad, it is true, but most of us take only what we need, honor the land, and cherish its fruits."

"She speaks the truth," spoke the Chieftess gently.

"Oh, she does, does she?" demanded the Tinnani by her

side. Facing Kate, he asked bluntly, "Can you say the same for the humans of your time?"

Kate blanched. "Well, ah, I guess—no, not really. I'm afraid the people in my time have forgotten most of what the Halamis knew." She stiffened her spine. "But some haven't forgotten. Aunt Melanie, the one who—"

"Enough," bellowed the Chieftain, reaching for another handful of mousetails. "We already know what the humans of your time are like. We have even learned to speak their language." He sniffed the delicacy appreciatively. "For we have met one of them."

Kate's heart leaped. "So you know Aunt Melanie?"

The Chieftain leaned forward, dangling the uneaten mousetails from his hand. "I will tell you about the humans of your time. They are thankless, grasping, and unconnected. To themselves, to the land, to their fellow beings. They know no wonderment. Their memory is short and their vision is shorter. They believe the world is nothing more than a bundle of firewood for their use, to be burned and the coals discarded."

"Much like another in our own time," muttered the Chieftess.

"Aunt Melanie's not like that," objected Kate. "And the others—well, they can still learn. They just need help. That's why Aunt Melanie's so important to the future. And she's in big trouble. I know she is. Won't you please help me get back to her?"

"Absolutely not," said the Chieftain. He plunged the mousetails into his mouth, chewed briefly, and swallowed them with a gulp. Then, with a gleam in his yellow eyes, he said, "I will, however, do something better."

He hooted to an aide standing next to the entrance of one of the side tunnels ringing the room. "Bring me the visitor from the future."

Kate gaped at the Chieftain, then at Laioni. "Aunt Melanie? Here?"

They heard a scuffling sound from the side tunnel. Two

Tinnanis emerged escorting someone who alternately kicked and cursed at them.

"Hey, let me go, you stupid owls," shouted the visitor as they entered the great hall. His injured shoulder had been bandaged, and one arm hung in a sling beneath his repaired yellow rain jacket. But his mood was clearly not one of gratitude.

"Jody," said Kate disappointedly.

"Bring him closer," commanded the Chieftain.

As soon as the boy came near, his eyes met Kate's. "You!" he exclaimed angrily. "You're the one who did this. You lousy . . . Where in hell's half acre am I? What did you do with all my friends?"

Kate's eyes narrowed spitefully. "Like the one who dared you to shoot the owl?"

Jody suddenly fell back, as if he had been hit with a two-by-four. He looked at Kate with an expression of real remorse, then suddenly his eyes grew wide with fear. Looking around at the dozens of owl-shaped figures surrounding him, he whispered, "Is this—is this my—my punishment?"

Kate could not help but grin. "Yes, and you'd better behave or they'll do to you what you did to their friend."

The boy shuddered, ran a hand through his red hair. "I've got to be dreaming," he muttered.

The Chieftain spun his head toward Kate. "And you want to go back to people like that?"

Gripping the shaft firmly, she replied, "They're not all like that." Then a question came to her. "Why did you bring him here, since I'm sure you found out what he's like right away? Why didn't you just leave him in the redwood grove?"

"To learn more about the future," snapped the Chieftain, dropping a raw oyster into his mouth. "And we learned more than we wanted to know."

"You could have done that without bringing him here," pressed Kate, "and saved yourself a lot of trouble. I think you had another reason."

The ruler of the Tinnanis did not reply. Then the Chieftess snapped her jaws and spoke: "You are right. It was the prophecy."

"Prophecy? What prophecy?"

"Silence!" boomed the Chieftain. "I will have no talk of prophecies in front of these unworthies. Now go away, all of you."

"Wait," pleaded Kate. "Won't you tell me anything about this walking stick? I came all this way for your help."

The Chieftess started to speak, but the voice of Hockeltock de Notnot cut her off. "No," he insisted. "We have no more time for strangers. Now, leave. I have other matters to deal with."

Kate could see Laioni's crestfallen face from the corner of her eye, even as her gaze fell to the ground. She thrust her hands sadly into her pockets. Unthinkingly, one hand closed around her Swiss army knife and the other around— something else. Half curious what the small round object could be, she pulled it out to view it. At once, she had an idea.

"Wait," she said, stepping nearer to the throne. "Wait a minute. I have something here you will like." She extended her hand, displaying a single, plastic-wrapped peppermint candy, the one she had found in the tunnel behind Kahona Falls.

The Tinnani ruffled his wings and eyed her suspiciously. "How do I know it's not some kind of poison?"

"It's not. I'll prove it." Kate removed the wrapping and crammed it back into her pocket. Then she took an exaggerated lick of the peppermint, smiling broadly. "It tastes great."

The aide with the feather hat rushed up, waving his hands excitedly. "Don't do it, Your Wingedness. It's a trick."

"Here," said Kate as she dropped the item into the Chieftain's hand. "I promise it's safe."

Casting an imperial glare at the aide, the enthroned Tinnani turned to his wife. "Does she tell the truth?"

The Chieftess spun her head slowly toward her husband, then blinked. "She does."

The Tinnani brought the strange object to his nose and

sniffed. Nothing on his facial expression changed for a long moment. Then all at once, he smiled. "Nothing that smells this good could be poison," he said, plunking the sweet into his mouth.

His eyes widened with pleasure. "Ooooooh," he said giddily. "This is like nothing I've ever tasted before. It is exquisite, fantastic." He leaned forward. "Tell me, where did you get it?"

Kate's eyes twinkled. "It is a great and rare delicacy, Your Wingedness, called peppermint. It is found only in my own time, five hundred years from now."

"Huh?" said Jody, who had been growing increasingly bewildered. Among the various speakers, he could understand only Kate's language. Yet hearing her words did not make them intelligible. "What do you mean, five hundred years from now?"

Kate scowled at him, waving threateningly in his direction the owl's head handle that so resembled the Chieftain. "This is going to get you, if you say another word."

Immediately, the boy stepped back a pace. He stared at her warily.

Kate turned back to the Chieftain, who continued to suck delightedly. "It is an exotic fruit from my time," she said. Then, judging her moment, she added, "If you tell me how to get back there, I promise that if I ever return I'll bring you more."

"How many more?" asked the Tinnani, straightening the silver band on his head.

Kate deliberated. "How many would you like?"

The Chieftain's tufted eyebrows lifted. His voice, cracking with anticipation, replied, "Fifty. A hundred. No, a thousand!"

"A thousand it is," agreed Kate.

"Ten thousand."

"Okay, but that's my limit."

"How soon can you come back?"

"I don't know," she answered cautiously. "But I promise it'll be as soon as I'm able."

Turning to his wife, the Chieftain asked, "Will she keep her word?"

Her yellow eyes scanning Kate as if they could see straight through her, the Chieftess nodded in assent.

Hockeltock de Notnot raised his great wings. "All right then. We will tell you. But I warn you, the answer to your question is easier to say than to do. Go ahead, my Chieftess, tell this human what she needs to know to make the stick of power do her bidding."

And the slender Tinnani by his side raised her scepter, the signal she was about to speak.

18

the tale of the
broken touchstone

BENEATH the flickering light from the torches, the
assembled Tinnanis drew nearer, embracing their rulers in
a wide semicircle. Their eyes, plus all other eyes except
Jody's, fell to the feathered creature seated on the crystalline throne. Her gaze, like Jody's, remained on Kate.

The Chieftess stretched herself upward, pressing her
plumage close to her body, so that she seemed nearly as tall
as her throne. At length, she lowered the scepter. In a deep,
gentle voice, she began to speak:

"The walking stick in your possession is indeed a stick of
power. And it is old, very old indeed. Its memory stretches
far beyond my own, beyond the Chieftain's, beyond that of
any living being save the Stonehags, into an earlier time
when our world felt not the heat of the Wicked One's breath.
Like its makers the Tinnanis, it can render its holder or
someone nearby completely invisible." She paused. "I can
see by your expression you already know of this power."

Kate, recalling the chase through the muddy streets of
Blade, nodded.

"It was given other powers as well," she continued, "many of them long forgotten. It is named the Stick of Fire, and it is said that it will burst into flames when so commanded by its rightful owner. That is not a command to be used lightly, however, for it will destroy the stick and all its powers. Carved on its handle is the likeness of the great-great-grandfather of my husband, the Chieftain Solosing de Notnot. It was he who caused the Stick of Fire to be made and these words to be carved into its shaft:

> *Fire of greed shall destroy;*
> *Fire of love shall create.*

The Stick of Fire possesses other powers, too, but the most important of these by far is the ability to travel through time."

"Yes," said Kate impulsively. "But tell me, how do I make it take me back?"

The yellow eyes of the Chieftess regarded her thoughtfully, with a hint of sadness brewing behind them. "Patience, Kaitlyn, patience. The powers of the stick you carry are more subtle than you think. For in the world that now exists, the Stick of Fire possesses a will of its own, uncontrollable by any creature. Its decisions about who to take through time and when are its own, and there is no predicting what it might do next."

Kate felt suddenly weak in her knees. "You, you mean there's no way to make it take me home?"

"I did not say that," answered the gentle-voiced Tinnani. "There is one possible way to control the power of the Stick of Fire, and only one. That is to do the single deed that would give you even greater power than the stick itself."

"What's that?"

The white wings stirred softly. "Healing the Broken Touchstone."

A muffled chorus of hooting sounds filled the chamber as the Tinnanis whispered among themselves. Again Kate addressed the Chieftess: "What does that mean? Healing the—whatever. Tell me."

"I shall," she replied. "For if you can heal the Broken Touchstone, the Stick of Fire will bend to your will."

The Chieftess paused, closing her round eyes for a long moment. She rotated her round head from side to side, snapping her jaws rhythmically as she did so. Then slowly her eyes reopened, and she began: "The Great One, creator of all that exists, made in the earliest days of this world a single object that would harbor all the glorious powers of creation. It was a single sphere, of purest red obsidian, light as a bubble and powerful as a galaxy of stars. The Great One called it by a simple name: the Touchstone. It was entrusted to the Tinnanis for their safekeeping, and it was installed upon the throne of their Chieftain."

Kate's vision roamed to the empty cup on top of the throne. She noticed that the Chieftain, still sucking on his peppermint, was also gazing at the spot, a look of longing in his eyes.

"For time beyond measure," continued the Chieftess with a slight ruffling of her wings, "the Touchstone rested safely on the throne deep within the walls of Ho Shantero. In exchange for their protection, the Touchstone gave the Tinnanis wonderful powers, and the most important of these was the power to connect living beings of all kinds to one another. So the Tinnanis became friends and stewards to all. They forged connections so that one group's desire did not mean another group's destruction. And because of this, their forest world thrived."

Here she stopped momentarily, squeezing the scepter with her sharp talons. "Then, in the reign of Solosing de Notnot, everything changed. The Wicked One, whose strength had been rising unnoticed for a long time, craved secretly to own the Touchstone, to turn its great power to his own ends. He dared even to enter Ho Shantero itself with the aid of his warriors, mounting a fierce attack. The Tinnanis, peace-loving and trusting, had underestimated his lust for power, and were caught completely unprepared.

Still they managed to beat him back, to win the Great Battle in the end, but only through tapping the Touchstone's own power—and only at enormous cost. Many brave lives were lost in that battle, and one thing more: The Touchstone cracked during the course of the fighting. A fragment of the sphere fell out, and its power decreased dramatically.

"After the battle, the Chieftain Solosing de Notnot decreed that the Broken Touchstone should not be healed, unless at some time in the future its full power was required to nurture the forest lands below—or to save the Tinnanis from total destruction." She lifted her white wings and sighed deeply. "We have reached such a time today. But now, at our moment of greatest need, both pieces of the Touchstone are lost to us."

"Lost?"

"Yes," replied the Chieftess. "As I said, Solosing de Notnot believed it was better for the Tinnanis to live without the Touchstone's full power than to risk its falling into the hands of the Wicked One again. So the sphere was not repaired. The Chieftain replaced the Broken Touchstone on his throne, and he hid the Fragment away in the most distant and difficult place he could find. So much time has now passed that its whereabouts are utterly lost from memory, known only to the spirit of Solosing de Notnot himself. The Wicked One he banished underground forever for his treachery, plus all of his servants with only one exception. To the Slimnis the Chieftain gave a second chance, both because they are the Tinnanis' brothers and because he believed they would never allow themselves to be manipulated again by the Wicked One."

"He was wrong," muttered the Chieftain, bobbing his head angrily. He bit down hard on the remnant of the peppermint.

"Yes," agreed the Tinnani at his side, her eyes increasingly sad. "For a time, the forest thrived again. Living things flourished everywhere and the blue lake cooled to a comfortable temperature. Even with only the partial power of the Broken Touchstone, the world lived in harmony and peace. Then, inexorably, the power of the Wicked One rose once again. He won over the Slimnis, who helped him find further recruits, above the ground. One of them, a man called Sanbu, is the most dangerous of all, for he is both very strong and very clever."

Kate glanced at Laioni. "Is he the same one you told me about?"

The Halami girl grimaced, then said, "The same."

"Gradually the Wicked One developed enough strength to reach into others' minds, even within the very walls of Ho Shantero. One of those minds, sadly, was the Counsellor to the Chieftain, a man named Zinzin. Harshnaga Zinzin."

As she mentioned that name, several Tinnanis screeched angrily in the background. Some scraped their talons against the stone floor. Kate looked at Jody, who stood paralyzed with fear. He clearly believed they were preparing to devour him.

"Zinzin," the Chieftess went on, "heard the whisperings of the Wicked One but lacked the strength to banish him from his mind. The Wicked One promised him wealth beyond measure and power beyond his dreams. One day not long ago came the moment of truth: The Wicked One commanded him to deliver the Broken Touchstone as a gesture of loyalty. He obeyed, and during a holiday feast when no one was watching, he stole the Broken Touchstone and escaped from Ho Shantero. With the help of Sanbu, the traitor delivered it to the Wicked One in his mountain lair. But Sanbu then killed him, perhaps out of jealousy, perhaps thinking his master would reward him for his show of strength. So in the end Zinzin's treachery got him nothing more precious than an early death.

"Since the theft of the Broken Touchstone, our forest has fared poorly. The power of the Wicked One has swollen, and he has tempted many new creatures to join his cause. Sanbu now commands a small but growing band of warriors. Like the Wicked One himself, they see the other beings of the forest not as friends but as adversaries. They use whatever they like with no thought of the future, burning great trees to make bonfires, catching more fish than they can eat and wasting the rest, hunting any animals that get in their way or killing them just for pleasure, fouling the streams with their excrement. The Wicked One has grown so confident that he has climbed steadily upward, almost to the surface, sending fire to the forest below and heat to the waters of our own lake.

The Chieftess raised her wings and gestured toward the assembled Tinnanis. "At the same time, our own power has diminished. No longer can we nurture and strengthen the life of the forest as we have for so long. Without the Touchstone, even our ability to keep the island of Ho Shantero afloat will come to an end, forcing us to abandon our ancestral home before it sinks and is lost forever."

"The island is still floating in my time, five hundred years from now," said Kate hopefully.

The Chieftess remained somber. "Even after we have been forced to leave, the island will stay afloat for a while solely through the lingering enchantment of the Touchstone. So your glimpse of the future tells me nothing about its fate, or ours."

Turning her soulful eyes toward the Chieftain, she concluded her tale with these words: "And amidst all this suffering that we have borne, there is one wound greater than all the rest."

With a wave of her wing she indicated a bench of black stone near the vacant throne. A torch flamed above, illuminating the bench, but Kate could see nothing resting there. Then, by looking slightly askance, she discovered a faint, frail glow of white light upon its seat. The light seemed to pulse, quivering with every breath of some unseen being.

"There," said the Chieftess, "lies our daughter, our only child. Not so many years ago, I held her as a newborn in the curl of my wing, singing her the songs that hold all the history of the Tinnanis. Then, before long, she, too, was singing, in a voice of such beauty that none who heard her could ever forget it. That is why we named her Fanona,

which in the Old Tongue means Song That Never Dies."
She lowered her voice. "It is a bitter irony now."

"It is indeed," agreed the Chieftain, who reached out a
hand to clasp that of his wife.

A heavy silence filled the chamber, and for a long
moment the Chieftess did not move except to blink her yellow eyes several times. Finally, she continued: "When our
little Fanona was born, it was prophesied that in some mysterious way her life would be bound up with the Broken
Touchstone. We took that to mean that somehow, during
her reign far in the future, the missing Fragment would be
found and the Touchstone healed at last. We imagined her
armed with the Touchstone's full power, power she could
use both to nurture the forest and to protect our people
against the Wicked One. Yet when the sphere vanished
from this hall, she grew weaker and frailer by the day, until
she has now not even the strength to show her feathers.
Now we see that the prophecy may have had another
meaning, that she may never rule at all from her throne of
clear crystal. For unless the Broken Touchstone is returned
soon, she surely will die."

She blinked again, then slowly spun her head back
toward Kate. "There is one more prophecy you should
know, though I cannot tell what it might mean for you. It
concerns the lost Fragment:

> *Fragment, object of desire,*
> *Shall be found anew.*
> *One who bears the Stick of Fire*
> *Holds the power true.*

Those are the words of the prophecy, as translated from the
Old Tongue, but hear me well: It could have two quite different meanings. Some believe it means that the Stick of
Fire has the power to find the Fragment. The Wicked One,
as he showed by sending his agents to attack you, believes
that is the true interpretation. He craves nothing more than

the Fragment, for then he could heal the Broken Touchstone and all things would bend to his desires."

"What is the other meaning?"

"That not the stick itself, but the one who bears it, holds the power to find the Fragment. So someone from another time, someone who traveled here through the power of the stick, might be the one to find it."

"Now I understand why you brought him here," said Kate with a nod toward Jody. "You thought maybe he was the person from another time."

"Proof of our desperation," lamented the Chieftain. "Only the prospect of saving both our forest world and our daughter made it worth the effort to bring him to Ho Shantero. We tried to fix his broken arm, but he has deeper injuries beyond our power to repair."

Jody, mustering his courage, stepped forward again. Facing the Chieftain, he declared, "You've got no right to keep me prisoner this way. Even if I did shoot that owl." He turned to Kate. "This has to be a dream, a terrible bad dream. But if it's not, if it's really happening to me, what do I have to do to get out of here?"

"The same thing I have to do," she snapped. "You see this stick? It can take us back to our own time. But only if we can find the Fragment."

"The what?" he asked.

"And also the Broken Touchstone," added Laioni. "You'll need both pieces to heal it."

Kate winced. "That means going—"

"To the lair of the Wicked One," completed the Chieftess, shaking her broad wings. "No task could be more difficult." She glanced at the fragile glow hovering above the bench of stone. "Or more important."

Jody stepped closer to Kate, watching the owl-headed stick warily. "Let me get this right. You're saying that's some kind of magic stick?"

"You could call it that."

"But it won't take us home unless we can find something else?"

Kate nodded. "Two things."

Jody scratched his tangled head of hair. "And finding them means leaving this owls' nest."

"Yes, but it's going to be dangerous."

"I'm coming with you."

"I mean really dangerous," repeated Kate. "You should stay here and wait."

"You just wanna get rid of me! Well, it's not that easy. Where that stick goes, I go." He looked spitefully at the Chieftain. "I won't miss this place one bit."

"The feeling's mutual," said the Chieftain, although to Jody it sounded like nothing more than the hoot of an angry owl.

"What about you?" Kate asked Laioni. "Shouldn't you go back to your people? The chances, they're so slim."

The dark eyes flashed. "What are my chances if I go back? My people are doomed unless the Broken Touchstone is taken back. The Wicked One is destroying our lives, our forest, our home. Unless he is stopped, we will all end up like Toru." She clenched her fists. "If you go to the Wicked One's mountain, then I go too. I am She Who Follows the Owl."

Kate's mind churned. It was likely she would perish in the attempt to find both pieces of the Touchstone, that much was clear. In that case she wouldn't be much use to Aunt Melanie or anybody else, ever again. But if she chose to do nothing, then she and Laioni would be safe, at least for now. Yet that meant she would never even have a chance to help Aunt Melanie in her time of need. Nor would she ever see her again.

She looked for a moment into the yellow eyes of the carved handle. "All right," she announced. "I'm going to try." Casting a harsh glare at Jody, she said, "Why don't you just stay here? You'll only get in the way."

"No way," he replied. "I told you, I go with that stick. If this isn't just a bad dream, I'm not gonna miss my chance."

"He can't stay here," declared the Chieftain. "Gives me heartburn just to look at him."

Kate frowned and faced the ruling couple. "Before we go, then, isn't there anything else you can tell us about where to find the Fragment?"

"Nothing," answered the Chieftess solemnly, spinning her head one way and then the other. "Just remember what you have heard. It may prove useful."

"Then I think," said Kate to Laioni, "we should go first to the lair of the Wicked One. At least we know the Broken Touchstone is there. The Fragment—who knows where it might be? Maybe it doesn't even still exist."

"It exists," declared the Chieftess firmly.

Just then Monga placed his front paws on the table by the Chieftain's side. In one swift gulp, he swallowed all the remaining oysters.

"Monga," exclaimed Laioni in dismay, pulling him away. "Monga, no."

The Chieftain glowered at the dog, who wagged his tail gleefully. Then he turned to Kate. "Make it twenty thousand peppermints."

Kate sighed. "All right, but it's all irrelevant if I get killed trying to get back."

"No getting killed until you deliver the peppermints," commanded the Chieftain. "It is forbidden." Seeing the look of consternation on his wife's face, he quickly proposed, "Now then, let us give you something to sustain you on your journey." Tapping his claws on his belt buckle, he hooted, "Bring me three bags of *minarni.*"

Immediately, one of the grass-caped aides flew to the thrones, bearing three brown leather pouches with long straps meant to be tied around the waist. One he gave to Kate, one to Laioni, and one, reluctantly, to Jody.

Peering into the pouch, Jody lamented, "Bird food! Are we supposed to eat this?"

"Quiet," ordered Kate. "I still haven't decided to let you come."

"You will find it both nourishing and filling," said the Chieftain, adding under his breath, "even if the taste is unremarkable." He stirred his wings. "And before you go, I have one more thing to offer you. It might not be any help, but then again it might." He clapped his hands and spoke a strange word: "Kandeldandel."

From the rear of the crowd of Tinnanis stepped a scrawny-looking figure. His white feathers stuck out unevenly, less orderly even than Monga's fur. In one hand he held a manila-colored wooden flute. His small mouth twisted slightly up to one side, giving the impression of a permanent grin. Upon his left shoulder rested a small, rust-colored owl with large brown eyes. He stepped before the thrones of the Chieftain and Chieftess and bowed awkwardly, nearly losing the creature perched on his shoulder.

Jody's brow furrowed. "I don't like the looks of this one."

"I present to you," announced the Chieftain, "Kandeldandel, third flutist in my orchestra."

"At your service," hooted Kandeldandel in a deep bass voice that seemed permeated with humor, like a cross between a foghorn and a belly laugh.

At that, the small brown-eyed owl flapped his wings and whistled angrily. Kandeldandel cleared his throat and added, "And my friend Arc, Your Wingedness. He is at your service too."

"Mmm, yes," muttered the Chieftain. "I forgot you two go everywhere together." With a note of defensiveness, he continued, "Kandeldandel is one of the few people I can spare right now. When the Broken Touchstone disappeared, he wasn't around to join in the search. Probably off someplace playing his flute—which he does quite well, by the way. Only trouble is, when he plays, it has the unfortunate effect of putting out fires. So he can't play for you at your fire pit. Maybe, though, his music can lighten your hearts while you travel to the Wicked One's mountain." Eyeing the musician, the Chieftain added skeptically, "If he sticks around that long."

The Chieftess nodded in agreement. "It is right that Kandeldandel should go. An excellent choice."

Kandeldandel shifted his weight uncomfortably, dropped his flute with a clatter, bent over to pick it up and dropped

Arc off his shoulder, retrieved the flute, helped the small owl settle back on his perch, then dropped the flute again.

"Gee, thanks," said Kate dismally.

"How do we get out of here?" demanded Jody.

"My, my, he won't like the answer to that question," said the Chieftain to himself. He leaned toward Kate and smacked his lips. "Don't forget your promise, now, if you succeed."

"If I succeed," repeated Kate weakly.

The wise eyes of the Chieftess connected one last time with hers. Raising her wings slightly, she said, "Hold fast to your stick of power. It is your only hope, and ours as well. *Halma-dru* to you all."

It was Laioni who answered. "And to you as well."

The Chieftain clapped his hands three times. Suddenly, Kate heard a fluttering of wings. Before she knew what was happening, a pair of strong talons wrapped around each of her arms, just below the armpit. In an instant, she was airborne, carried vertically as if she were standing on an aerial escalator, rising toward the top of the great room. With a metallic creak, a circular door slid open in the middle of the ceiling, beyond which she saw clouds of white vapor.

She cast a final glance below. White-winged Tinnanis ringed the three thrones, one of which sat empty. The last thing she heard before rising through the door was a voice calling, "Oysters! Bring me more oysters."

19

airborne

As she sailed through the opening, borne by two Tinnanis pumping their broad wings in constant rhythm, Kate saw the island of Ho Shantero from a new vantage point. Blacker than coal it remained, but it seemed somehow less sinister. Water flowed over most of its surface, draining down from the spindly spires to run in broad streams across the island's main bulk. She wondered if this water, pumped to the tops of the spires by some strange mechanism, could be part of the system that kept Ho Shantero afloat.

At once she realized that these very streams, rippling and shifting over the surface, were the source of the impression of movement, of crawling, that had so frightened her. She grinned at her own gullibility, then found herself wishing that some of her fears of Gashra, the Wicked One, might prove to be so unfounded. Yet her heart held little hope.

The island disappeared in a sea of white vapor as the Tinnanis carried the companions ever higher. Kate caught passing glimpses of Laioni, smiling as another pair of white-winged Tinnanis lifted her through the clouds. She saw Jody only once, hoisted by his belt and uninjured arm, his usual downtrodden look replaced with one of sheer amazement. Monga she heard barking through the mist, but never viewed; she imagined the spirited dog was probably enjoying his first taste of flight. Once she spotted Kandeldandel, flute in hand, flying erratically with the small reddish owl by his side.

Kate soon relaxed her body, trusting herself to the hearty creatures whose wings beat so powerfully above her. Their talons squeezed her upper arms tightly, but not hard enough to stop her circulation. She felt the fluffy leggings of their trouser feathers above each of her shoulders, and sometimes the quivering plumage tickled the edges of her ears. To her surprise, she heard virtually no sound as the Tinnanis flew, only the vaguest whoosh of air at the start of each downstroke.

In her mind's eye, Kate tried to fathom what lay below, as if she were drawing her own version of Aunt Melanie's map on the impervious clouds beneath her. She imagined the deep blue lake, two Halami women and a baby in a cradle still camped on its shore. The women sang softly while preparing their next meal, although the younger one regularly lifted her head, listening for a sound she had waited too long to hear. By a field of rushing water at one end of the lake, the green spires of the Hidden Forest rose skyward. Near its center, the great grove of redwood trees towered in stately grace, and in the center of the grove stood the Ancient One. Beyond, toward the ridge of cliffs, a small green pool frothed ominously. Next to it rested a ring of great boulders, silently waiting and watching.

Suddenly the mist melted into trailing wisps that hung in the air like the breath of dragons. Gray sky appeared overhead. The ragged ridge of gray-brown cliffs loomed out of the clouds, encircling the entire crater. From this bird's-eye view, it resembled an enormous bowl of steaming soup. Sunlight scattered in the swirling masses of mist, illuminating their upper reaches. Kate felt suddenly cold, for the first time since crawling through the tunnel behind the waterfall.

Over the rim the Tinnanis carried her, so close she felt she could almost kick the rocks with her feet. No longer protected by the crater, she was buffeted by cold winds. Her teeth started to chatter, and her dangling body swayed within the grip of the talons. Her upper arms and neck began to ache.

Passing across the high cliffs, Kate understood clearly why Lost Crater would remain undisturbed for the next five hundred years. No one, without the aid of wings either natural or man-made, could surmount those steep and slick walls. *The Back of Beyond,* Aunt Melanie had called this place.

As they cleared the rim, the view took her breath away, and for a moment she forgot about the cold. Forest, ancient and sprawling, stretched as far as she could see under the overcast sky. From this height the differences from her own time leaped out boldly: No dusty brown squares splattered the ridges, no mud-filled canyons crawled toward the sea. Not all looked well with the forest, however. Some sections, scorched by fire, still smoldered. Thick, black smoke clung to some of the valleys, and strange clouds of steam rose from the more distant rivers.

Then, on the horizon, Kate spotted an unfamiliar, rounded mountain that was belching steam from its summit. In a flash, she realized it was in the same location as the jagged, fang-shaped peak she had seen from Kahona Falls, the one known in later times as Brimstone Peak. And she knew she was viewing the fortress of Gashra, the Wicked One.

A thunderous, crashing sound filled the air. She looked down to see Kahona Falls, pouring endlessly out of the vertical wall of the crater. The Tinnanis then started to descend, carrying her straight into the billowing spray of the waterfall. As they drew nearer to the trees below, Kate glimpsed a delicate brown rope bridge stretching across the crevasse she had crossed using Aunt Melanie's rickety wooden ladder. Some means of transportation, she thought, had not improved in the last five hundred years.

In seconds, she was dropping into the tops of the trees. The wind died down until it scarcely whispered in her ears. She felt steadily warmer, though not as warm as inside the crater. Burly branches rose around her, and her feet brushed against several lacy canopies. With a whooshing of wings, the two Tinnanis lowered her gently to the forest floor, potent in its fragrance of needles, cones, and resins. Her feet touched down on the spongy ground just as the talons released their grip around her aching arms.

Holding the walking stick in one hand, she craned her stiff neck to see the creatures hovering above her. One of them called good luck in a low hooting voice. Before she could answer, they lifted swiftly toward the sky, white wings beating in unison.

20

call of the owl

SECONDS later, Laioni and Monga joined Kate on the needle-strewn floor of the forest. Tall trees, straight as stalks of corn, pushed skyward on all sides. Their gnarled trunks, though not so covered with moss as their cousins inside the fog-filled crater, rose equally impressively into the air. Delicate fronds of fern sprouted from twisted roots and broken branches, while limbs low to the two girls' heads supported a panoply of birds and squirrels, butterflies, and beetles. Monga leaped at one squirrel, nipping at the tail almost as bushy as his own.

"How was your ride?" asked Kate, already knowing the answer.

Laioni smiled slowly, still savoring the experience. "For a moment, I had wings."

The aroma of some June blossom, sweet and fresh, wafted to Kate's nose. She listened to the branches swishing high above her head. Intermittently, when the wind quieted, she could hear the distant rumbling of Kahona Falls. Then came a loud cracking of twigs.

Jody stepped into view from behind a stately Douglas fir, rubbing the back of his neck with the hand not bound in a sling. "Some ride," he said derisively. "But it was worth it to get away from those owl-people."

"I hope you appreciate what they did for you," said Kate testily.

"What's to appreciate?" he shot back.

"They fixed your shoulder, for one thing."

"And gave you flight," added Laioni sternly.

Jody stared in surprise at the Halami girl, then turned back to Kate. "What did she say?"

"She said you got a chance to fly, and that's something else to appreciate."

Glancing upward, he allowed, "It was pretty amazing, I'll say that. Once you got used to it."

Laioni's expression softened slightly, but she said nothing.

"One thing's for sure," Jody went on, "I don't think I'm dreaming anymore. My neck wouldn't hurt like this if I was dreaming." He contemplated Kate suspiciously. "You just made up all that stuff about their getting revenge for that owl I killed, didn't you?"

Kate merely grinned.

"Hey, how come you understand all these weird languages? You talk to owl-people and Indians, too."

Her hazel eyes narrowed. "Because I listen to people like Aunt Melanie, instead of stealing their mail."

Jody's face reddened. "You're just like her. Think you're the smartest person in the world! Well, you can't fool me. I know you just want to leave me here, wherever this place is. Well, forget about it, because I'm sticking to you like glue till I get home."

"This *is* your home," replied Kate. "Just five centuries earlier."

"You expect me to believe that?"

"I don't care if you do or not. Just keep out of my way. If this walking stick is ever going to get us back, we've got lots of hard work to do."

"No harder than working in the sawmill," said Jody, pushing a scraggly lock of hair off his forehead. "And I've done that for five summers." He scanned the Douglas fir by his side. "Sure are some mothers around here. I couldn't believe it from the air. Never saw anything like it, so many trees. This place would keep the mill busy for years. Got any idea how many houses you could make out of just one tree like this?"

Kate looked at him frostily. "And how many houses would it take to make one of these trees?"

Just then a long, low hooting sound floated through the forest, like the call of an owl but subtler, gentler. It was accompanied by several slightly higher voices from the trees saying *hooo-hooo, hooo-hooo*. The initial owl-like sound grew louder and clearer until a lone Tinnani, flute at his lips, came walking toward them from behind a yew tree. Kandeldandel.

Jody squinted at the Tinnani. "Aw, no. I thought we left all you buzzards behind."

Kandeldandel, whose head reached only as high as the boy's waist, flashed him a vengeful glance. Then he trilled a few high notes on his flute. Immediately, the small red owl Arc swooped down from the branches above. With a loud whistle, the owl veered directly at Jody.

"Hey!" the boy exclaimed, ducking his head just as Arc sailed past. "He tried to dive-bomb me."

Kandeldandel ruffled his feathers and turned his back on him, while Arc whistled again happily and landed on the Tinnani's shoulder. Stepping closer to Kate, Kandeldandel lowered his flute and said in his deep, laughing voice, "Seems your friend doesn't appreciate good music."

Before Kate could respond, Jody picked up a spruce cone and threw it at Arc. It missed by a wide margin, prompting a new round of amused whistles.

"Too bad you're such a lousy shot," Kate lamented.

Jody glared at her. "And what kind of shot are you?"

"Better than you, that's for sure."

He stooped, picked up a cone and tossed it to her. "Let's see."

Kate hefted the cone in her hand. "You see that tree over there leaning to the side?"

Jody's face widened into a grin. "No way you can hit that. Too far away."

"And about ten feet up, you see that white fungus?"

"Give me a break. You're all talk. Besides, you're a—"

"A girl?" Kate's eyes flashed angrily. She turned to the fungus, a white mound not much bigger than a catcher's mitt, sprouting from the side of the trunk. Biting her lip, she concentrated on its position.

"This I've got to see," said Jody derisively.

Rearing back as if she were about to fire one to home plate, she paused, her weight entirely on one foot. Then she flung herself forward as her arm released, snapping like a whip. The cone whizzed through the air, slicing past a heavily laden branch. It glanced off the bottom edge of the fungus, causing a shower of white particles to fall to the forest floor.

The boy gaped in amazement.

Trying to remain nonchalant, Kate resisted the urge to smile. Pointing to the bulldog wielding a baseball bat emblazoned on her sweatshirt, she said simply, "Girls can throw too."

Jody gazed at her with new respect. "Hey, you've got an arm like Luis Aparicio's."

Kate's eyes gleamed. "That's some compliment. He could throw like anything. Made more double plays than any other shortstop in history."

"And stole bases like crazy too."

"Took me two whole years to get his rookie card for my collection."

Jody nodded. "My favorite's Honus Wagner. The Flying Dutchman. Stole seven hundred bases and played every position except catcher for the Pirates."

"But he was best at shortstop," Kate reminded him.

Jody indicated her bright green shoelaces. "Wouldn't even have made the team with laces like that, though," he teased. "They're like a neon sign."

Despite herself, Kate grinned.

Laioni tugged on her sleeve, looking positively bewildered. "I hear your words, but they mean nothing."

"Don't worry," Kate replied, "it's just baseball talk." Her expression hardened again. "Nothing to do with Gashra."

"What's Gashra?" Jody asked.

"He's the one we're up against. He's got the Broken Touchstone, and we'll have to be faster than Honus Wagner to steal it from him. Let's get going."

"We should follow the river to make the best time," said Laioni. "But the canyon is very wide and that will make us easy to spot. Gashra's allies are everywhere."

"Then we should stay more hidden, in the trees. Can you find a way? We'll follow you." Kate suddenly remembered Kandeldandel, who was nowhere in sight. "Where did that Tinnani go?"

"Someplace far away, I hope," muttered Jody. "And his pet owl too."

Just then, an ear-splitting blast as loud as a train whistle sounded right between Jody's feet. He screamed and jumped nearly half his height into the air. Upon landing he whipped around to see what had made the terrifying noise.

Facing him, grinning blithely, stood Kandeldandel. Arc, who had released the whistle, sat innocently upon his shoulder. Kandeldandel bobbed his head in owl-like fashion, then hooted, "Just thought we'd say hello."

Jody could not understand his words, but the mocking tone was clear. He grimaced and lunged at them. Arc lifted off into the branches, while the Tinnani stepped sideways and raised his full-feathered wings. His half grin broadened into a smile. Then, without warning, he brought the wings down and disappeared in a puff of white light. Not even the flute remained visible.

"You scared them," scolded Kate.

"Scared *them?*" blurted Jody. "Didn't you see what they did to me? First they dive-bomb me, then they nearly blast a hole in my backside."

Kate and Laioni exchanged grins before starting to stride into the forest. After a few steps, Kate said, "I guess Kandeldandel can get Arc to do anything."

Laioni cast her a knowing glance. "Tinnanis have a special way with owls. Not only with their close friends like Arc, either. Owls follow them everywhere they go, day or night."

"I thought owls slept all day."

"They do," answered Laioni as she ducked beneath a branch, "unless a Tinnani is around. Tinnanis love to call them into action, hooting just like owls but with deeper voices. Kandeldandel does it with his flute too. So if you ever see an owl in flight during the day, you can be sure it's the work of Tinnanis."

Kate recalled the mysterious owl who had saved her from the spell of the deadly green pool. It even looked a bit like Arc, come to think of it. Could Tinnanis have been responsible for that? No, she told herself. Not possible. Besides, Tinnanis may not even be around in five hundred years—especially if Gashra had his way.

Monga, who was prancing immediately behind them, suddenly turned his head at a sound. Ears alert, he bounded off after some small, scurrying animal. Meanwhile, Jody reluctantly fell in behind, still grumbling to himself about the sneak attacks. He stopped every few steps to check under his legs for any new sign of trouble.

For the next several hours, they trekked through the thick forest. The terrain, hilly and rolling, reminded Kate of the up-and-down trail that ran near her hometown. Of course, there were significant differences: New England had no great trees like this, for one. But what about five hundred years ago? Hadn't her mother once told her that the land in her part of Massachusetts once supported enormous forests of hemlock and chestnut, now replaced with subdivisions and shopping malls? She wondered, and found herself feeling some sympathy for Jody. It wasn't his fault that he happened to grow up in a time and place where the livelihood people thought would continue forever was finally coming to an end. He was just unlucky enough to be born at the hardest moment in the history of his hometown.

Kate spotted an especially juicy clump of huckleberries and stopped to eat a few. The taste brought back instantly the tart flavor of Aunt Melanie's homemade pie. Wistfully, she reached her hand into the pouch provided by the Chieftain. The *minarni* contained some kind of spindly roots that tasted like burned toast, as well as some reddish leaves, soaked in sauces and dried, with a flavor like vanilla pudding. As the Chieftain had promised, the food gave an unexpected surge of strength. Its stiff, chewy texture also made it seem more filling than its appearance warranted. She started walking again, then glanced behind at Jody, wondering whether he had decided to try any. No doubt if he had, he wouldn't admit it.

Suddenly, she halted in her tracks. A wave of nausea passed through her. Dozens of deer, including several does and fawns, lay stacked haphazardly in piles beneath a tall Douglas fir. Arrows still protruded from some of their bloody hides. Several decapitated heads hung mutilated from the tree's lower branches. Many of the carcasses, their meat rotting and spoiled, bore armies of flies and squirming brown maggots. Laioni knelt weeping before the tree, whose bark had been brutally slashed and gouged by knives. Monga lay beside her, his tail drooping.

Quietly, Kate approached and knelt beside her friend. She laid her arm across Laioni's bare shoulders and waited until her sobs eventually ceased. Then she asked simply, "Who?"

Laioni turned a tearstained face toward her. "Sanbu," she whispered.

"But why?"

"Who can tell? Maybe—maybe he just thought it was fun. Maybe he wanted to get them before anyone else. Hunters like my father also stalk deer."

Kate shook her head. "But your father would have taken only what he needed."

"And thanked the deer for the gift," added the Halami girl, staring blankly at the slaughtered animals beneath the tree.

Rising, Kate turned away from the gruesome sight and slowly walked the perimeter of the area. She saw a discarded knife carved from flint embedded in the branches of a bush, but no other sign of Sanbu's band.

Jody joined her. "Who did this?" he asked, surveying the gory scene.

"Sanbu," answered Kate. "One of Gashra's men. Can you believe this mess?"

Jody pushed back a dangling lock of red hair. "Reminds me of a war movie I saw once."

Without looking at him, Kate replied, "Reminds me of a clear-cut I saw once."

Jody stiffened, but said nothing.

Laioni, trailed by Monga, walked up to them. "We should go," she said, her voice hoarse. "Sanbu might still be near."

21

the crossing

OFF they strode into the forest, with Laioni leading the way as before. She took them rapidly higher, ascending the spine of a ridge that they followed for a great distance until it dropped down into a steep-walled valley. The forest grew even thicker, with young trees seeming to sprout from the very roots of their elders. Yet despite the changing landscape and the increasing distance from Sanbu's slaughter, the carnage remained fresh in Kate's mind.

Frequently, they crossed clear pathways through the undergrowth, winding between the towering trees. Animal trails, Kate surmised, though she could not be certain. Some of them Laioni chose to follow for significant distances. Others, perhaps traveled more by people than by four-legged wanderers, she avoided. Kate wished she had studied Aunt Melanie's hand-drawn map more closely. She seemed to recall something near Brimstone Peak, a section of the map that was veiled in darkness. But she could not be sure.

At one point she heard a low whistling above her head.

She looked up to discover Arc descending slowly toward her, his rusty red wings spread wide. The huge brown eyes of the owl studied her intently from the middle of his wide facial disc. For the first time, Kate noticed his little ear tufts and the long white feathers sprouting from both sides of his silvery beak, giving the impression of well-combed whiskers. With a gentle whistle, the diminutive owl settled on her left shoulder.

"So you'd like a ride?" asked Kate, enjoying the feeling of his soft plumage against her cheek.

Arc ruffled his feathers contentedly.

"I wonder where your friend Kandeldandel is," mused Kate.

The owl raised his wings slightly, as if to say, *How should I know?*

"Do you think he'll turn up again?"

Arc merely repeated the gesture.

"Nothing predictable about him," said Kate with a smile.

The owl whistled softly and shook his long whiskers.

Kate realized at that moment how much Arc combined elements of other animals: the wide eyes of a cat, the round shape of a bear, the talons and wings of a hawk. Right now, at rest, he seemed as harmless as a down pillow. Yet in an instant he could become a skillful hunter, sailing soundlessly through the air in search of prey. A creature of many contrasts, she thought—much like human beings.

They entered an area more verdant than anyplace they had seen since leaving Lost Crater. Walking on the stretches of soft, spongy moss felt like stepping across a mattress. Presently the sound of splashing water reached them. They came upon a narrow canyon with dark rock walls covered with thousands upon thousands of lushly layered ferns. High as houses rose the richly decorated rocks on both sides. Kate counted five small waterfalls streaming down through the ferns, looking like marble columns in a temple of green. Arc moved to the edge of her shoulder and released an ascending whistle that reverberated within the walls. Then he listened to the echo, bobbing his head rhythmically.

Ahead, the canyon opened into a grassy clearing where the water from the waterfalls combined to form a surging stream. As they approached the clearing, the continual rushing of the stream grew louder. Gurgling over rounded rocks, the water cascaded steadily through the wide channel. Monga started barking, and Laioni called to him sharply. Stepping closer, Kate saw the immense form of a black bear standing near the opposite bank, her hind legs submerged in the stream. Nearby two identical cubs rolled on the grass together, wrestling playfully.

Using her forepaws for bats, the bear took several swipes at the stream, spraying water on the bank and her cubs. Finally, she knocked a substantial silver-colored fish out of the water, which lay flapping in the grass for no more than two seconds before the bear cubs reached it. One of them grabbed it and held it between two black paws. Then, like a child eating a Popsicle, the bear sniffed the wriggling fish and took one enormous bite out of the fleshy midsection. The other cub tried to take a bite of his own, causing the fish to fall on the grass. They rolled over each other trying to get it, finally tumbling over the edge of the bank into the rushing water. The mother, meanwhile, ignored them and continued to smack the water in search of more fish.

Suddenly a white-winged creature materialized in the air just above the bear and settled on her massive shoulders. The bear roared and reared up, spinning on her feet like a dancer.

"Kandeldandel!" exclaimed both Kate and Laioni at once. Arc flapped his wings and whistled in greeting.

The playful Tinnani waved to them, flute in hand. He rode the jumping, twisting bear with the moxie of a cowboy riding a bucking bronco. Every time the bear swatted at him, Kandeldandel evaded the blow just in time, losing not so much as a feather. Kate and Laioni were laughing heartily as Jody came up from behind. Seeing the cause of the commotion, the boy merely glowered.

At last Kandeldandel lifted off and landed on the far bank. Grasping the still-flailing fish with his talons, he took flight again just as the bear and both of her cubs came charging at him. He rose barely out of arm's reach as the mother bear swatted and roared angrily. With perfect accuracy, the Tinnani dropped the fish with a splat precisely on her long, black nose. He then flew off into the trees.

"That was some show," said Kate with a smile.

"Too bad the bear didn't get him," grumbled Jody. He eyed the little owl on her shoulder with scorn. "Or his pet owl."

Arc flapped his wings and whistled angrily.

"Kandeldandel's a trickster," Kate replied. "He just likes a good laugh." Turning to Laioni, she added, "I don't know what else he's good for, though. He's here and then he's not here. We sure can't count on him to help us against Gashra."

Laioni indicated Arc with a tilt of her head. "Even his owl friend can't depend on him for a good ride. That's probably why he decided to perch on you for a while."

"At least I'm better than a wild bear," agreed Kate.

"Let's go," said Laioni, giving a pull on one of Monga's ears. "That bear's so mad now she might decide to chase us instead of him."

As Kate started to follow, Arc stretched his wings, then opened his beak wide in a yawn. He gave a long, low whistle, apparently announcing it was time for a nap, before closing his eyes tightly. They hiked along the bank for many miles, climbing successive inclines and declines, wading through stretches of marsh grass, jumping across small side channels and muddy ravines. Throughout, Arc slept peacefully upon his perch.

At last the group entered a valley so pristine that if the allies of Gashra had already entered it, no one could tell. The forest here felt peaceful and harmonious. Although Laioni regularly scanned the bubbling stream and waving branches for any signs of disturbance, Kate grew gradually more relaxed. Danger seemed as distant as Gashra's steaming mountain lair, at least another day's walk away. Even the memory of Sanbu's slain deer began to fade.

At one point, Laioni halted and turned to Kate. "We should cross the stream here." Seeing the sleeping creature on her shoulder, she added, "He looks very comfortable there. I think you've made a new friend."

Kate grinned. "He's kind of cute, don't you think?"

Arc suddenly opened his eyes and bobbed his squat head from side to side, as if he were embarrassed.

"I especially like his whiskers," said Laioni, stepping into the stream.

The small red owl blinked, ruffling his wings proudly. Then, with a chirplike whistle, he lifted off from his perch. His whisker-feathers seemed to flap just as vigorously as his wings as he flew across the stream and vanished into the tall trees.

Kate watched him until he disappeared, then decided to use this opportunity to take a drink. She lowered her head into the rushing water, feeling its coldness cleanse her face. Monga joined her at the water's edge, lapping eagerly. Jody, with some awkwardness due to his sling, bent down to do the same.

"Ahhh," said the boy, raising his face from the stream. "Tastes good." He took another several swallows. "Clear too. I've never seen a stream so clear. You could catch fish here no trouble."

Kate, her face also dripping, lifted herself to her feet. "That bear back there was having some trouble," she said wryly.

"Yeah," answered the boy, raising himself to stand. "Bet she feels the same way I do about pesty owl-people."

Laioni, who had crossed over while they were drinking, called to them from the opposite bank. Monga obediently marched into the stream. Using the walking stick to give her balance in the fast-moving water, Kate followed.

Step by step, she pushed across the channel. About halfway across, she briefly paused to glance back at Jody, who was just entering the stream. Then, without warning, the earth shifted under her feet. She cried out, fighting to keep herself upright.

With a grinding heave, the stream bed lurched to one side, opening a long chasm that snaked from the trees by the far bank over the grassy meadow and into the stream itself. Kate fell into the water, managed to raise herself, then tumbled backward again as the earthquake shook the ground again, this time more intensely. Her lower back struck a pointed rock jutting up from the stream bed and she shouted in pain.

Then fear flooded her veins. The walking stick was gone! Battling to regain her feet, she saw it floating swiftly down the stream. She struggled toward it, but another series of tremors knocked her face first into the churning water.

"The stick!" she sputtered, toiling to stand. But no one could hear her over the thunderous roar that swelled in the air, drowning out any other sound.

At that instant, she felt a shock of heat on her hand. A new, sizzling sound hissed in her ears and she realized that the water just upstream was steaming like a boiling pot. Fiery fingers of orange lava poured out of the chasm and into the water, sending thunderheads of vapor into the sky. Lava rolled along the stream bottom, consuming anything in its path. Through the rising steam Kate saw the oncoming river of orange only a few feet away.

A set of long talons wrapped around her left armpit and lifted her barely out of the water, just as the molten fluid rolled across the spot. Kandeldandel, flapping furiously, carried her over the stream bank, across the grass, and into the shelter of the trees. He dropped her on a tangle of brush with a splintering of broken branches. Laioni and Monga bounded to them.

"The stick!" she exclaimed. "It's in the stream."

Laioni's jaw fell open and she turned downstream.

Kandeldandel hooted, his yellow eyes widening. Not hesitating another second, he flew off into the billowing steam.

Laioni yanked Kate by the arm to help her stand again. They stumbled together along the bank, searching for any sign of the walking stick. Despite the fact that the tremors had grown milder, they could see nothing in the water but sizzling columns of steam, writhing like wrathful spirits.

"It happened so fast," moaned Kate.

"Gashra," said Laioni hatefully. "I should never have taken us back into the open."

"It wasn't your fault," said Kate, wiping the water from her forehead and eyes. "You couldn't have known."

"I should have known. You depended on me and I failed you. And failed my people as well. If the stick is lost—"

"There!" shouted Kate, seeing a winged figure burst forth from the mist with a familiar shape clutched in his talons. As the Tinnani settled on the ground next to them, Kate grasped the walking stick again and hugged Kandeldandel. "Thank you, oh thank you," she said.

"Don't make a fuss, now," he hooted gruffly, pushing her away with his arms. "I just happened to be in the neighborhood."

"I'm still grateful," breathed Kate happily, running her finger along the shaft. "That was too close. Without this we'd be sunk."

Kandeldandel's permanent grin twitched slightly. "You needed a bath, anyway."

"Hey," said Kate. "Where's Jody?"

The grin expanded. "Now comes the fun part."

Spinning his head atop his neck, the Tinnani turned his gaze toward the opposite bank and flapped off into the steaming waterway. Kate and Laioni barely had a chance to look at each other in puzzlement when suddenly he emerged again from the billowing clouds, this time bearing an ungainly package in his talons. Jody, clasped by the back of his belt, was hanging upside down, kicking his legs wildly and cursing the beast who had kidnapped him.

"Put me down," he shouted, his face nearly purple with rage. "Put me down, you big birdbrain."

As soon as they had crossed over the edge of the bank, Kandeldandel obliged. He dropped Jody squarely into a waist-high tangle of skunk cabbage and ferns bordering the stream. With an aerial bow to the boy's flailing feet, he flew off into the trees, playing a rippling tune on his flute.

Kate and Laioni approached, standing with their backs to the forest. They couldn't help snickering as Jody's scraggly red head popped up from amidst the skunk cabbage. He spat out several torn bits of fern. "Bluck. This tastes awful! I'm gonna get even with him yet."

"Don't be too hard on him," said Kate. "He did save me, and also the stick. Now he's just having a few laughs."

"So are we," Laioni whispered in her ear, bringing on another fit of giggles.

Jody tried to stand, but his good arm slid on a mat of slippery stalks and leaves and he tumbled backward in a helpless heap. "Quit laughing and give me a hand, will you?" he pleaded.

Kate laid her walking stick on the grass and stepped forward to help pull him out. Laioni moved in the same direction, when a violent jolt from behind sent her sprawling forward. She crashed into Kate, bowling her over. They both landed on Jody, who fell back again into the mass of greenery.

"What kind of a joke—" Kate's words evaporated as she saw a huge man lifting the walking stick from the grass. "Hey, put that down!"

The man who had plowed into Laioni from behind stood, holding his heavy flint-tipped spear in one hand and the walking stick in the other. His hair, tied on top of his head in a knot skewered by a sharp bone, was as black as Laioni's. Two diagonal slashes of black paint cut across each of his cheeks. But for a simple deerskin loincloth, he wore nothing.

"Sanbu!" shouted Laioni, clambering to her feet.

The muscular man started toward her, when Monga snarled ferociously and charged at his leg. Sanbu whirled around, fury in his eyes, and kicked the dog forcefully in the ribs. Monga flew through the air and landed with a bone-crunching thud on the edge of the stream. Pawing frantically at the loose soil, he slid over the edge and into the still-steaming water.

Laioni screamed, throwing herself in the direction of the yapping dog.

"Put that down," cried Kate, pointing at the walking stick.

The big Halami raised his spear over his head with his other arm, preparing to thrust it into Kate. As he lifted the weapon into the air, a sudden whooshing sound, like concentrated wind, emerged from the forest. Just before he brought it down, six or seven large spotted owls soared out of the trees and directly at him, talons extended.

"Aaaarghh," groaned the warrior as the pack of owls descended on him, screeching angrily.

With amazing agility, Sanbu leaped to one side and swung both the spear and the walking stick wildly over his head, causing the owls to change course and dodge him. They soared past without inflicting any harm. Spear still held high, the warrior took aim once again at Kate. He leaned back, gathering his strength for the kill.

Just then a lone rust-colored owl, much smaller than the others, came sailing out of the woods, whistling wrathfully. It was Arc. His brown eyes, disproportionately large for his small body, focused on Sanbu and sized up the situation. With all the speed he could muster, Arc lowered his head and flew straight into Sanbu's chest.

Sanbu cried out in surprise as the small missile made contact. The force of the impact knocked him back a step and caused him to drop the spear, while Arc fell to the ground, momentarily stunned. Before his fellow creatures could regroup for another attack, Sanbu whipped the walking stick around and brought its heavy handle down with all his might on the helpless owl, crushing the bird's feathery chest.

"Arc!" screamed Kate, eyeing the lifeless owl as she rose to her feet.

She dove at Sanbu, trying to grab the stick. Simultaneously, Jody leaped onto Sanbu's back, wrapping his good arm around the warrior's neck.

Sanbu shrieked and snapped forward at the waist, sending Jody hurtling to the ground. He then easily twisted free of Kate's grip. Stepping back, he swung the stick at her viciously.

Kate ducked as the shaft whizzed just over her head. As Sanbu raised it for another attempt, the screeching pack of owls descended again. This time they circled close, talons scraping and scratching him wherever possible, trying to get near his head.

As one talon gouged deeply into the flesh of his forehead, Sanbu cried out in pain. He spun around and retreated into the forest, with the owls in close pursuit. Kate watched him vanish into the dense growth, her stomach clenching. For in his hand he held the Stick of Fire.

22

the burial

𝒜 somber rain began to fall as the bedraggled group moved away from the exposed stream bank to find protection under the tall trees. Wordlessly, they gathered at the base of a mighty Douglas fir. From somewhere out of sight, Kandeldandel played long, low notes of mourning on his flute, notes that sounded vaguely like the call of an owl, but mellower, deeper. The slow lament filtered through the trees, one note following the next like a funeral procession.

Kate, feeling drained of hope, stood leaning against the trunk of the tree. Her right hand felt strangely naked now with no shaft to grasp. Moving stiffly, Jody sat down on a root near her feet.

"You all right?" he asked, looking up at her. "I mean, are you hurt?"

Kate shook her head and managed to say, "I wish I'd picked up his spear when he dropped it. We'll never get another chance like that." She glanced at him, adding, "Thanks for trying to help."

Jody frowned. "I wasn't really helping you. I was just trying to get the stick back."

Laioni approached them, followed by Monga, who was limping slightly. In her hands, she carried the body of the dead owl. Carefully, she laid it in the fold between two wet roots. Arc's reddish feathers, still fluffy and soft, nestled easily within the wooden cavity.

As Laioni knelt by the owl's side, Kandeldandel's music ceased. The final flair of his flute melted into the continual patter of rain on the branches. With sagging wings, he emerged from the forest and strode solemnly to the grave of his friend. His crooked mouth twisted lopsidedly, no longer seeming to smile.

"I'm going to miss that little guy," said Kate.

"He's been on my shoulder since he was just an owlet," said Kandeldandel, the laughter gone out of his voice. "His whistling wasn't like real talking, but I never mistook his meaning. He was always there whenever I needed him. But the one time he needed me—where was I? Off playing my flute."

Kate nodded despondently.

The rain grew heavier, splattering the earth with large droplets, as though the air of the forest itself had condensed into tears. Then Kandeldandel lifted his deep bass voice in gentle song. Lost in her own thoughts, Kate did not listen carefully to his words of mourning, but heard only one small part:

> *Farewell old friend*
> *I will miss your song*
> *Your laughing voice*
> *Is now so still*
> *As quiet as I feel*
> *As quiet as death.*

In time the song came to an end. Kandeldandel bent low and ran his finger slowly over the length of the fallen owl's whisker feathers. Finally he stood up again, rigid as a tree. He remained there, motionless, eyes fixed upon the grave.

Meanwhile, Laioni rose and walked purposefully toward a cedar nearby. A few minutes later, she returned with a handful of green needles, which she rubbed briskly between her palms until they gave off a strong scent of cedar. She spread the crushed needles over Arc's plumage, taking care to distribute them evenly.

Laioni then stroked the feathers of the owl's chest, lightly and lovingly—once, twice, three times. Lifting a large section of moss from the earth at the base of the fir, she laid it gently over the body like a blanket.

Jody gave a muffled gasp, and Kate turned to see him watching the ceremony intently. He seemed deeply moved, touched by this ritual whose ancient origins made it feel no less familiar. His mind, Kate knew, bore the image of another fallen owl.

Spotting a few stems of maidenhair fern, Laioni walked over and bowed her head in gratitude to the plant. Then she picked some shafts and carried them over to the tangle of roots next to Jody. Positioning herself on one of the larger roots, she plucked off the fronds and began to bite along the full length of each stem, moving each one methodically through her mouth. When the stems were pliable she laid them lengthwise beside her.

Monga approached, limping. He watched her working with melancholy eyes, then curled into a compressed brown ball by her feet. Kate followed her motions absently, as did Jody. Meanwhile, Kandeldandel paid no attention to her, continuing to gaze at the final resting place of his friend.

Carefully, Laioni ran her fingernail along each black stem. The pressure flattened the fibers and created a slit running the full length. She separated the sections, then began to twine them together, using her teeth as well as her fingers to hold them in position.

Kate, watching her work, grew gradually more curious. "What are you making?" she asked at last.

Laioni answered without raising her head. "Something for Arc."

Before long, the object took enough shape that Kate recognized it: a miniature version of the round basketry cap that Laioni had been wearing when they first met. Biting off the uneven ends, Laioni held the small woven circle in the palm of one hand. She examined the little black moon thoughtfully. Then she carried it to the owl's resting place and laid the gift gently on top of the blanket of moss.

The rain slackened, falling more as mist than as droplets. Laioni stepped again to the cedar and reached for one of the burly branches protruding from its trunk. From the underside of the branch she pulled a small section of fibrous bark and stretched it apart until it was a mass of thin threads in her hands. Then she snapped two sticks, one thinner than the other, from a dead limb overhead. Swiftly, using her fingernails, she peeled the bark from the thicker stick. When she tried to do the same with the thinner one, however, she caught a sharp sliver under her fingernail.

"Eh!" she cried, shaking her hand.

"Here, I'll do that," said Jody, taking the stick from her. Pulling a small knife out of his pocket, he opened the blade and sliced off the bark in a few swift strokes.

"That is a beautiful tool," said Laioni gratefully as she took back the stick.

"What did she say?" Jody asked.

"She said she likes your knife."

Jody closed it and replaced it in his pocket. "It's my granddad's. He let me borrow it." He wrinkled his brow. "Hope I get to give it back someday." Glancing at Laioni, he asked, "What's she doing now?"

"Making a fire, I think."

"Good idea," he replied. "I'd sure like to warm my hands."

"I'd like to warm my everything," said Kate. "This rain is making me really cold."

"You took a swim too," added Jody.

Laioni, having bitten a small notch in the thicker stick, placed it on top of the shredded cedar bark. Bending over to keep the rain off, she placed one end of the thinner stick in the notch and started rapidly rolling it between her palms. As the stick twirled, glowing hot dust fell onto the cedar bark tinder.

As Kate and Jody watched expectantly, a thin trail of smoke started to rise from the shredded bark. Laioni then ceased twirling the stick and lifted the tinder, blowing on it gently. Nothing happened. She replaced the pieces and resumed the operation until the tinder again began to smoke. Once more, she blew lightly across it until, at length, it burst into flames. She dropped it to the ground and placed a few small dry twigs on top.

"I'll get some bigger sticks," said Jody.

As he moved away, Kate whispered to Laioni, "Guess he's not as bad as I thought."

"I feel pain in him," she replied. "Great pain."

Blowing over the growing flames, Kate tried to recall what Aunt Melanie had said about his past. Something about losing his parents . . . and about Frank, his grandfather. Before long, the fire crackled vigorously on the forest floor, and she stood up to warm herself.

"Come over here," she said to Kandeldandel, still standing dejectedly beside Arc's grave. "Come on," she repeated with a wave of her hand. "It feels good to get warm."

Monga, who had already shifted his location to be nearer the fire, sighed contentedly.

"Good idea," said Jody, emerging from the trees with as many dry sticks as his one arm could hold.

As he dropped the pile of sticks, Kate reached for a downed limb nearby. She snapped it in two and tossed both halves into the flames.

Kandeldandel approached, ruffling his wings, and settled himself by the fire next to Kate. Jody stepped warily aside but the Tinnani did not even look at him. Lifting his wooden flute to his lips, he began to play a slow and simple melody, permeated with sadness.

Eyeing the winged creature cautiously, Jody stretched his free hand toward the fire. Suddenly, the flames extinguished, dying out completely. Only a few smoldering coals remained where an instant before fire had burned strongly.

"What the heck happened?" the boy moaned. "I didn't even get near enough to feel it."

"I don't know," answered Kate. "There wasn't any wind."

Kandeldandel's eyes widened, and he quickly put down his flute. The music ended in mid-note, but the fire instantly burst back to life.

Laioni smiled. "That was a clever trick."

"Not so clever," lamented Kandeldandel. "Happens to me all the time, whenever I play near a fire."

Jody, who could not comprehend any of the Tinnani's words, said, "Don't be surprised if my being here puts it out again. I'm just a jinx."

"Why do you say that?" asked Kate.

The boy shook his head dismally. "Because every time I start feeling a little comfortable—not even happy, really, just comfortable—something always happens to spoil it."

Kate sighed heavily. "Same thing happens to me."

Jody glanced at her skeptically.

"What do you mean?" asked Laioni.

Kate gazed for a while into the orange flames before responding. "Every time," she started, then swallowed her words. "Every time I get close to somebody, anybody—I lose them. Anybody important to me. First it happened to Grandfather, and now it's happened to Aunt Melanie too. I'll never see her again, or Mom and Dad either." She turned toward Laioni as tears began to cloud her vision. "Just when Aunt Melanie needs me most, we get separated."

Laioni reached for Kate's unbandaged hand and brought it to the leather bib covering her chest. Placing the hand over her heart, she said quietly, "You won't lose me. I promise."

Kate studied her, then replied, "I hope you're right."

Releasing her hand, Laioni added, "You're not the only one who has lost someone you love."

Kate glanced toward Kandeldandel, whose yellow eyes merely stared at her blankly. Turning back to Laioni, she said, "You mean your friend Toru. Do you really think he's dead?"

Laioni's gaze fell. "I don't know."

"The hardest part for me is not even saying good-bye," said Kate.

"I know what you mean," agreed Jody. He shook his dangling locks. "My folks just went out for an errand. Back in two hours, they said. Ha. Some joke."

Kate felt a surge of empathy. "That's the worst, no warning at all. At least when I lost Grandfather, I knew it was coming."

"The same with Toru," said Laioni.

"How did you know?" asked Kate.

"Monga told me." Laioni turned to the dog peacefully curled up by the fire. "He spoke to me."

"You mean the way he acted?"

"No," she answered firmly. "I mean he spoke to me." She looked again at Kate. "My people know that when an animal speaks with a human voice, then someone's death is near. Just before Toru left our village to follow his dream, Monga barked—but instead of a barking sound, he spoke words. Real words. I was standing right beside him, so I know. No one else heard him, so as hard as I tried I couldn't persuade Toru to stay."

"What did Monga say?"

"He said, *It is time.*" Laioni threw another chunk of wood on the fire, sending sparks into the air. She motioned to Jody. "The boy, did he say he lost both his parents at once?"

"Yes," replied Kate.

Laioni moved to Jody's side. "I am sorry for you," she said, her voice so filled with sympathy that he seemed to understand. He looked at her for a moment with both sadness and gratitude, then turned away, embarrassed.

As the fire continued to warm the companions, Kate lifted her head to scan the trees rising like steeples on every side. The rain had stopped. Gray sky above the treetops glowed dusky peach with hints of purple. The forest, darkening toward the end of the day, creaked and stirred with new sounds. She saw the shadowy shape of a small animal scooting between two massive trunks, beginning its evening prowlings. Monga must have caught its scent, for he suddenly raised his head, ears alert, sniffing.

"What do we do now?" asked Kate, not sure whether she was speaking to anyone in particular. "Maybe there's nothing left to do, now that the stick is gone."

"You mean we're stuck here for good?" questioned Jody.

"Looks that way."

"I have an idea," said Laioni softly. "It won't return the ones we have lost, and it won't bring back the Stick of Fire, but it might help somehow."

Stooping low, she retrieved a broken cedar bough from the ground, its needles wet from rain. Carefully, she placed it on the fire, creating a thick column of smoke that smelled of cedar. She cocked her head, then said, "I need just one more thing."

"What?"

Slowly, Laioni's head swung toward Kandeldandel, still holding his flute. "A feather."

"Now, hold on," protested the musician, covering his chest with his wings as he backed away. "Just because I put out your fire doesn't mean you can pluck one of my feathers."

"I wasn't going to pluck one," she replied. "I thought you might have one that's ready to drop."

Kandeldandel's fluffy brows came together. "Oh, all right," he hooted. "But you should face it, you're finished. Whatever chance you had to find the Touchstone, let alone the missing piece, it's gone now. And without Arc . . . well, all the fun's gone for me. So I'm leaving." He pulled a white feather from under one of his wings, twirled it once, then handed it to Laioni. Spinning his head toward Kate, he added, "This is the last you'll ever see of me. Good-bye."

He vanished in a puff of white light.

Kate gazed sadly at the spot. "Just when I thought he was maybe going to stay with us for a while, he disappears."

"Count your blessings," muttered Jody.

Laioni raised the feather, as big as her hand, high above her head. Then she lowered it to the flaming cedar bough and said, "Cedar, rain, and feather. Earth, water, air. Join with our fire to call the four directions."

She waved a puff of scented smoke toward the stream. In a low voice, she chanted, *"North, origin of weather, color of white, we ask you for wisdom."* Again she swept the feather through the rising smoke, this time toward the forest, singing as she did, *"South, birthplace of new life, color of green, we ask you for wonder."* Then, waving in another direction, *"West, source of our dreams, color of blue, we ask you for vision."* And, last of all, to the opposite side, *"East, home of the sun, color of yellow, we ask you for strength."*

As her words hung above the crackling fire, mixing with the aromatic smoke, Laioni lifted the feather and drew a large circle above her head. Then, lowering her arm, she waved it gracefully at Kate, then at Jody, then at Monga, sending each the power of the four directions. She then dropped the feather into the flames.

After a long silence, Kate said, "That was beautiful." She studied her empty right hand. "Too bad it won't help us get the stick back."

"Maybe we could help ourselves," suggested Jody meekly.

Kate turned to him. "What do you mean?"

"I mean," said the red-haired boy, speaking a little louder this time, "maybe it's still worth a try to get it back."

"Sanbu's halfway to the mountain by now," Kate replied dismissively. Then, facing Laioni, she asked, "He'll take it straight to Gashra, won't he?"

The Halami girl contemplated for a moment before answering. "Sanbu's camp is on the way to the mountain. It's too far to go the whole way before nightfall, so he'll probably stay at his camp tonight, celebrating with his men, then leave for the mountain in the morning."

"What did she say?" questioned Jody.

"That he'll probably stay at his camp tonight and deliver the stick in the morning."

"Then why don't we go after him now?" he suggested.

"Are you crazy? Track him through the night?"

"At least then we'd have a chance to get the stick back," urged Jody. "A surprise attack."

Kate muttered, "I don't know. For one thing, how could we find his camp at night? For another, do you think we could stand even half a chance against his band of warriors?"

Jody stepped closer. "If we don't get the stick back, we're stuck here forever. Right?"

Kate said nothing.

"So we've got nothing to lose. At least it's worth a try."

"I know where his camp is supposed to be hidden," offered Laioni. Then, regarding Kate thoughtfully, she added, "There's something else, isn't there?"

"Why do you say that?"

The Halami girl studied her tenderly. "What is it?"

"Well, it's—it's," she stammered, "it's just that, well, I really don't—don't like the dark."

Jody started to smirk, then caught himself. "That's okay," he said. "I used to hate being out in the woods at night too. Especially with big trees like this around. But now I know it's no big deal."

Kate drew in a deep breath. She scanned the swiftly darkening boughs above them. "I don't know."

"Hey," said Jody. "You remember that story about Babe Ruth, the one where he stands at home plate after two strikes and points to the stands?"

"Sure," grumbled Kate. "Everybody knows that one. He pointed to the center-field bleachers, then hit a homer right there. What's that have to do with anything?"

"Well, you see," began Jody, "I never thought the best part about that story was the homer. Lots of guys hit homers. Even I've hit two or three. The best part was he had the guts to stand up there and say he was gonna try. To take a risk. In front of everybody. That took real courage."

Kate looked into the flickering fire. She heard again the words of the Chieftess: *Hold fast to your stick of power. It is your only hope, and ours as well.* The fire coals crackled, and she saw deep within the flames the remains of Kandeldandel's feather. Now nothing but a burnt shaft, it still held itself as straight as the stick she once had carried.

"All right," she said at last. "Let's give it a try."

PART THREE

Into the Tree

23

night vision

BEFORE starting off, Kate and Jody separated the burning sticks, threw dirt over them, and stamped out the remaining flames. Seeing Laioni watching them with fascination, Kate realized that it must never have occurred to her to put out a fire with one's foot. Kate smiled to herself, appreciating anew the advantages of sneakers—even ones with bright green laces.

As the last lick of flame withdrew from the embers, Kate's eyes fell to the cradle of roots holding the small bundle of feathers that once was Arc. How similar they were, cold embers and lifeless body, both deprived of the fire that made them something so utterly different.

Laioni squeezed her arm gently. "We should go now."

"Where exactly do we have to go?" asked Kate, feeling the same queasiness she always felt when no light burned nearby.

"We will stay in this part of the forest for several more hours," answered Laioni. "I know this area well, so even without any moon, we should not lose our way." She hesitated before going on. "Then we will descend into a valley that is always dark, even in the daytime. No Halami goes there, not even my father when he is hunting, because there the power of Gashra is very strong."

Kate squirmed. "Isn't there another way?"

"No," Laioni replied. "Not if we want to reach Sanbu's camp before dawn. The Dark Valley lies between us and Gashra's steaming mountain. We must cross the Dark Valley, then climb the ridge until we are above the trees, to reach Sanbu's camp."

"I really don't like this idea."

"Neither do I," said Laioni. "I have never set foot in the Dark Valley. But going that way is our only hope to catch him before he delivers the stick to Gashra, if he hasn't already."

At that moment, Monga passed close to Laioni's legs, brushing his tail against her. She reached down and rubbed his head, whispering, "I know you'll be with me." The dog then nuzzled against Kate's jeans. Grinning, Laioni added, "And with Kate too."

Laioni then turned and started into the forest. Jody tramped along stiffly behind her. Monga hung back, waiting for Kate to start walking. When at last she did, the dog stayed just ahead of her, still limping slightly.

As they entered the deep woods, darkness pressed still closer. Kate could barely see the shadowy shapes of trunks and fallen branches in the swiftly departing light, and with every step the forest grew thicker and darker. Unseen branches stretched out long arms to scratch her face and poke her chest, sudden puddles of water swallowed up her sneakers without warning, slippery logs tripped her more than once. She could tell by the crashes and cursing ahead that Jody was doing little better. By contrast, Laioni seemed to move through the trees with the ease of a strutting deer.

Each time Kate stumbled or bumped into something, Monga trotted to her side within seconds. He seemed genuinely concerned for her well-being, whimpering sympathetically or tugging on her pant leg with his teeth to help

her find a better route. Kate began to feel like a toddler trying to walk, constantly thwarted by too-little legs that buckled without mercy. Frustration and anger swelled inside
her, shoving aside fear, and even Monga's concern started
to irritate her.

"Leave me alone," she grumbled, pushing the dog away
as he tried to lick her neck after she walked into a mossy
boulder. "I can do just f—Ohh!"

In her impatience to back away, she thrust her head
directly into a jagged limb. Laioni, hearing her shout,
strode back and quickly joined her.

"Are you all right?"

"Fine," snapped Kate, rubbing the back of her head.
"Except that I'm stuck in the wrong time and stumbling
around like a two-year-old in the middle of the night." She
studied the outline of Laioni, whose black hair and eyes
blended thoroughly into the background, and added quietly, "It's hopeless. I can't keep on like this."

"I have an idea," said the other girl. "It might help."

Without a sound, she knelt beside Kate's feet and began
fumbling with the tops of her sneakers. At first Kate stepped
backward in surprise. Then, weighed down by a growing
sense of despair, she merely stood passively, certain that
whatever wild idea Laioni had would make no difference
anyway. After quite a bit of tugging, pulling, and twisting,
Laioni removed Kate's green-laced sneakers and her socks
as well.

"What are you doing?" Kate demanded.

Laioni rose, pushing the socks and sneakers at Kate.
"Put these in the basket on your back. I want you to try
walking without them."

"What?" exclaimed Kate. "Are you kidding? It'll be ten
times worse."

"Try it."

"All right, but it's stupid." She slipped her arms out of
the day pack, unzipped it, and threw in the footgear. "Totally
stupid."

"The ground is soft, even though your feet are like my

baby brother's. Touching the earth with your feet will help you see."

"That's ridiculous," grumbled Kate. "How can my feet help me see?"

"Try it," repeated Laioni.

She stepped away, picking her route with special care through the growing blackness of the woods. Monga, tail held high, padded close behind. Awkwardly, Kate started to trudge after them.

Immediately, the newly barefoot girl felt a flood of sensations from her feet. Protected as they had been for most of their existence, they seemed more aware to touch than her fingertips. Kate's amazement at their sensitivity did not last long, however, soon giving way to an overwhelming sense of discomfort. Sticks and roots jabbed into her arches, slimy puddle water seeped between her toes, and unidentified insects wriggled across the tops of her feet. Still, trying to be brave, she stifled her groans and pushed slowly ahead.

To her dismay, the forest grew steadily darker with each passing minute. As the last lingering remnant of light faded from the cloudy sky above, the towering trees and mounting mist seemed to soak up any stray sources of illumination. No moon shone through the darkening boughs; no stars glittered overhead. Night had come to the ancient forest, and with night came true and total darkness.

Then, to Kate's astonishment, a subtle change began to occur. Perhaps because there was now no light left to trick her vision, perhaps because she was forced to rely only on her other senses, she began to feel gradually more secure in her movements. Her feet pained her less, though they remained uncomfortably sensitive. Stepping somewhat more easily on the spongy turf, she seemed to have sprouted special antennae that could perceive the shadowy shapes surrounding her, at first only barely, but with time more and more fully. She could almost reach out with this new sense, or combination of senses, to touch and see in ways that required neither hands nor eyes.

With slightly more confidence, Kate moved through the lightless forest. Soon she grew comfortable enough to close her eyes for a brief moment, just to feel whether it would slow her down. It did, but much less than she expected. She somehow *knew* where a low branch loomed or a log rose out of the earth. Her senses were saturated by the subtle slopes and contours of the forest floor underfoot and the swishing sound of Monga's tail brushing ferns and flowers just ahead. She understood that to her five senses a new one had been added, one that she had never known before: a kind of quiet hearing, a vision of the night.

Just then, a bat flew quite close to her face, brushing her cheek with its wing. She froze, cowering, as several more bats swooped near. All at once, her momentary calm disappeared. She dreaded again the dangers lurking in this place.

She recalled a description by Aunt Melanie of a night stroll she had once taken, in woods far removed not in distance but in time from the woods where Kate now walked. Aunt Melanie described proceeding through a dark and moonless forest, a prospect that made Kate shiver at the time, only to discover a strange beam of light cutting across her path. It seemed shockingly bright to Aunt Melanie, utterly out of place in the deep darkness. The beam sliced through the thick web of snags and branches to fall like a spotlight on a large brown-winged moth resting on the trunk of an aging fir. The light, Aunt Melanie said, hung in the air like an incandescent rope reaching from one end of the forest to the other. She wondered what could possibly cause such a thing, when all at once she discovered its source: It was the light of the rising moon.

Kate sighed, wishing the moon might send a shaft of bright light into this forest on this night. What she would give to see its silvery sphere swim into view above the treetops! Now that she had experienced night vision, she desired the moon's light less for guidance than for comfort. More bats swished past her head. The darkness of this place felt increasingly menacing. Yet no moon appeared. Instead, the forest seemed to grow ever blacker, ever more perilous.

The ground sloped downward, and Kate knew that they were descending into some kind of valley. She wondered whether this could be the Dark Valley that Laioni had described. She stepped on a stick that suddenly hissed and slithered out from under her foot. With a start, she jumped back. Her intelligence told her it was only a snake, yet that did little to calm the rapid beating of her heart.

Trees creaked and groaned on all sides as she moved past. The air smelled smoky here, as if the earth had been singed by fire not long ago. Perhaps because of the smoke, Kate's eyes started to sting, causing her to blink frequently. Bushes and ferns held more and more gleaming eyes, some of them round and black, some slanted and yellow. Most frightening of all, however, was the darkness itself. As she dropped deeper into the valley, the darkness grew thicker and heavier, submerging everything around her in impenetrable ink.

Something heavy stepped on her toe. She gasped and quickly backed away, then jabbed her neck on the broken branch of a tree. As she cried out in pain, Monga pawed her leg, whimpering.

"Who's there?" she asked.

"It's me," answered the voice of Jody. "I walked— walked right into this tree. Almost knocked me flat on my can."

"You klutz, you really scared me. Can you believe how dark it is? I'm getting the jitters about this place."

A scream pierced the night. It came from not far away. Monga barked, then dashed into the darkness.

"Laioni," exclaimed Kate. "That's her voice, I know it." She tried calling her name, but no answer came.

The crunch of needles told her Jody had stepped nearer. "This doesn't feel like regular night." He crunched still closer. "And all this smoke in the air . . . Makes it hard to breathe."

"Jody, I'm really worried." She cupped her hands to her mouth and called again: "Laaaiooo-ni."

Still no answer.

Then, from the blackness, they heard a strange, heavy breathing. It was accompanied by a new crunching sound, coming closer. Yet this crunching did not sound like feet, at least not like human feet. It sounded more like a body sliding, dragging, over the ground. Kate stood utterly still, while Jody moved so close that his shoulder rubbed against hers. The breathing and crunching grew steadily louder.

Suddenly a hand grabbed Kate's ankle. "Hey," she cried, yanking her leg free. "Let go!"

"Don't be frightened," whispered a voice by her knees.

"Laioni! What are you doing down there?"

"I'm crawling," she replied weakly. "Feeling my way. Here, help me up."

Both Kate and Jody bent low to pull the Halami girl upright. She struggled to stand, as if she were dazed, then leaned against Kate for support. Monga whimpered, moving around them in a slow circle.

"What happened?" asked Kate as she wrapped her arm around Laioni's shoulder. Feeling something wet against her hand, she exclaimed, "Hey, you're bleeding."

"It's all right, just a scrape," Laioni said, her voice still barely audible.

"Why didn't you answer when I called?"

"I couldn't," came the whispered reply. "Something strange happened to my voice. I can't—can't talk any louder than this." She rubbed her neck. "But I'm lucky to be here at all. A hunting pit, over there somewhere. I almost fell in. Only saved myself by grabbing onto a root."

"Like the one I fell into," said Kate.

"Yes, but you'd probably never have found me. This smoke, it's so thick." She coughed, sounding not much different from the grating and rasping of the branches overhead. From faraway, some unseen animal shrieked in a long, high-pitched wail. Then, with chilling certainty, Laioni added, "There's something more than smoke here."

"The Dark Valley," said Kate, her own voice feeling weak.

"The whole place feels haunted," whispered Jody.

"How are we ever going to find Sanbu's camp if we keep bumping into trees and falling into pits?" Kate's eyes, already watery from the pervasive smoke, brimmed still more. "Now we're never going to get the stick back."

"Ask your Indian friend if she can lead us out of here," said Jody.

"She's already cut up from trying," answered Kate. "She can't see any better than we can."

Laioni whispered somberly, "I've never felt like this before in the forest. I don't know where to go, don't know what's ahead. The trees do not speak to me. Even Monga doesn't know what to do." A distant screeching sound rose up like raucous laughter. "It is the work of the Wicked One."

"But what do we do now? How do we get out of here?"

Laioni gave no answer. Instinctively, the three voyagers moved closer together, standing like three small islands in a swirling sea of darkness. Monga, too, drew nearer, his tail curled tightly over his back. They listened to the gnashing and scraping limbs, the creaking and groaning trunks, the howling and screaming of invisible beings surrounding them.

Then, from the dark reaches of the forest, a new sound joined the others. It was warmer, fuller, flowing out of the trees like a sweet fragrance. A low, continuous sound. Like the call of an owl, but mellower, deeper.

"Kandeldandel," said all three at once. Monga barked excitedly.

"It's his flute, for sure," cried Kate. "Maybe it can lead us out of here."

"Let's find him," whispered Laioni.

As Kate started forward, Jody grabbed her by the arm. "Wait. Are you sure this isn't just one of his tricks? He could be leading us over a cliff for all we know."

"We'll have to take the chance," replied Kate. "It's our only way out of here. Let's go, before he stops playing."

With Laioni in front, the three proceeded cautiously into the forest. Though the mysterious groanings of trees and beasts continued, the call of Kandeldandel's flute filtered through to them. Whenever they seemed to be approaching its source, the music moved farther away, leading them onward.

Soon the terrain began to change. Instead of going down, they were climbing upward. Gradually, the smoky smell began to dissipate, and Kate began to see the shadowy outlines of trees and branches once again. Though no moon shone, the sky radiated a diffuse light, perhaps from the stars shining behind the curtain of clouds overhead. As they pushed higher, not pausing even to catch their breath, the gentle illumination from the sky grew stronger. She noticed that the trees were getting sparser, their trunks thinner.

She paused to study one of the spindly shapes, her eyes no longer irritated by smoke. "The trees," she panted, "they're getting shorter."

"We're climbing above the tree line," huffed Jody. "Pretty soon there won't be any trees at all."

"Hush," urged Laioni, her voice returning. "I think I know where we are now, and we must be quiet."

Higher, ever higher, the hooting flute led them. Before long the needle-strewn ground evolved into broken bits of moss-covered rock. Large round boulders appeared more frequently, dotting the terrain. Forest noises no longer permeated the night air. As small shrubs and grasses replaced the gnarled and twisted trees, Kate's vision improved still more and she began to perceive even subtle shapes like Monga's pointed ears.

As the terrain grew more rocky, she leaned her back against a boulder and put her socks and sneakers on again. Jody looked at her in amazement as he passed by, realizing for the first time that she had been walking barefoot in the forest.

The music beckoned to them, drawing them still farther up the slope. This time, however, the flute did not seem to depart as they came near. As Kate stepped over the increasingly stony surface, she saw Laioni stop at a large boulder at the crest of the ridge no more than twenty yards ahead. As the owl-like music swelled in volume, she moved swiftly up the incline, reaching the boulder at the same time as Jody.

There, leaning casually against the opposite side of the boulder, was the Tinnani. His enormous round eyes flickered in Kate's direction as she topped the rise, but otherwise he gave no sign of noticing that he had company. He trilled a few lilting notes on the flute, then lowered it from his half-grinning lips.

"Thank you," said Laioni very softly.

Kandeldandel swiveled his head in her direction. "Thank you for what?" he asked, also in a quiet voice.

"For leading us out of that valley," whispered Kate.

"Valley? What valley? I was just playing my flute, that's all."

"Come on," replied Kate. "You know what you did."

"Still don't know what you're talking about," hooted Kandeldandel quietly. "I just happened to be in the neighborhood again."

"And we just happen to be glad you were," said Kate, smiling.

The Tinnani's yellow eyes met hers, connecting for an instant. Kate saw in them an unmistakable gleam of satisfaction, and she suspected, despite the protestations, that he was pleased.

Jody stepped forward and nudged Kate's elbow. "Man, am I glad to get out of there." Then he added, without looking at Kandeldandel, "Since you know how to talk to him, why don't you tell him thanks from me too?"

The Tinnani lifted his tufted brows. "His manners are improving."

"In a big way," answered Kate.

"Too bad," replied the flute player, sounding disappointed. "He was much more fun the other way."

At that moment, Laioni gasped. Kate turned to see her staring at a ridge that ran parallel to their own, slightly higher and to the left. Like theirs, it climbed ever more steeply into the clouds, ultimately to join the massive shoulder of a mountain summit. Mountain, Kate realized with a jolt. This must be Gashra's mountain.

Then she saw what Laioni had seen. Near the top of the visible flank of the ridge burned a single campfire. Three or four figures, dimly lit by the golden glow, danced slowly in front of the flames. Listening very carefully, she caught the barest hint of human voices chanting in unison.

"Sanbu's camp?" she whispered.

Laioni viewed her gravely. "That is where we will find our hope—or meet our death."

At that moment, Monga stepped deliberately between the two of them. He shook himself once vigorously, as if he had just emerged from a swim. Then, turning toward Kate, he barked. But instead of a dog's bark, he spoke three unmistakable words.

"It is time," said the dog.

24

attack

KATE'S anxious eyes met Laioni's. "Did you hear that?"

"I heard it."

"But who—"

"We will know soon enough," the Halami girl whispered. "Let's go. Sunrise is near, and it will take some time to get up there."

Then Jody spoke, his gaze fixed on the distant campfire. "They must have some guards around here someplace. But where?"

"No way to tell from here," said Kate.

"We can't just walk right into them," countered Jody.

"Do you have a better idea?" Kate demanded, trying hard not to raise her voice.

Before the boy could reply, Kandeldandel took off with a flapping of his wide wings. Flute clutched in one hand, he rose into the air and glided into a billowing bank of clouds.

"Guess that's the last we're gonna see of him," said Jody.

Kate followed the white-winged figure until it disappeared from sight. "Don't be so sure."

"We should go," said Laioni, glancing at each of the others.

"I wish we had stopped Sanbu when he was alone," said Kate.

Jody shook his head. "It's not like we didn't try. This time, though, we have surprise on our side."

"Hope we have some luck too," added Kate.

Monga pawed the ground uneasily. Then, suddenly, he lifted his head with a jerk.

Above them, a familiar white figure emerged from the gray clouds. Down Kandeldandel plummeted like a meteor. Then at the last possible instant, he veered up before landing on top of the boulder. He folded his wings behind his back and said simply, "There is only one guard."

"What did he say?" asked Jody.

"One guard," answered Kate. "He must have checked it out from above." Then, facing the Tinnani, she asked, "Where is he?"

"Never mind," said Kandeldandel. "I'll take care of him." He considered the idea briefly, then added with a smirk, "It will be a pleasure."

"Don't take any chances," warned Laioni. "Someone is going to die before this is over."

"It won't be me," replied Kandeldandel briskly. Then his permanent grin faded. "I have a score to settle with Sanbu."

"A score?" Kate scrutinized him. "You mean what he did to Arc?"

The Tinnani fiddled with his flute for a moment. "That, and something else. Something big enough that I want to do a lot more than just put out his fire." He faced Kate squarely. "You see," he said slowly, "my full name is Kandeldandel Zinzin."

"Zinzin . . ." Kate furrowed her brow. "Wasn't that the name of—"

"The traitor who stole the Broken Touchstone," finished the Tinnani. "The one who was murdered by Sanbu." His round yellow eyes narrowed. "He was my father."

"I understand," said Kate.

"No you don't," retorted Kandeldandel. "How could you? How could anyone? But it doesn't matter, as long as the lowly musician who happens to be his son can avenge his death, and Arc's too. And maybe restore a tiny bit of honor to an old family name in the process."

"All right," declared Kate. "You can take the guard if that's what you want. But let's get one thing straight, here and now. You're more than just some lowly musician. You're one of us."

Kandeldandel fluttered his wings uncomfortably. "Fine," he said, "but just don't try to depend on me. That's the one thing I can't stand, someone depending on me."

"Okay, then. We won't depend on you to nail that guard. We'll just hope like the dickens you do it."

The Tinnani nodded. "That's better."

"Hey, check this out," said Jody, forgetting to keep his voice quiet.

"Shhhhh," admonished Kate. Then she saw what he had discovered: a long flint-tipped spear resting on the ground by the boulder. "That looks like Sanbu's," she whispered in surprise.

"It is," hooted Kandeldandel. "I brought it with me, just in case."

Jody hefted the heavy spear, struggling to hold it with his one good arm. But it clearly required two hands—or one the size of Sanbu's—to carry it.

"That won't work," said Kate. "Let me take it."

"Well, all right," agreed the boy reluctantly. "Guess I'll have to stick with my knife."

"We must go," whispered Laioni in earnest. "The sun will rise soon."

Kate gripped the spear firmly, hoping she might once again hold the Stick of Fire. "Let's go."

At that the Tinnani took flight, rising silently and swiftly into the clouds. Kate, Jody, and Laioni, Monga at her heels, began to traverse the rugged, rock-littered terrain to the parallel ridge. They descended into a steep-walled canyon carved by successive rock slides from the higher elevations. Crammed with broken boulders, the canyon required jumping from rock to rock, always gauging one's weight carefully to avoid slipping. Even without his limp, the usually sure-footed Monga would have found the crossing difficult.

Finally they left the boulder field and started to scale the neighboring ridge. The terrain was steep, but at least they could walk again. They pushed upward, panting from exertion, even as the eastern sky began to lighten above them. Kate felt the temperature drop noticeably as they ascended, drawing closer to the lumbering clouds that obscured the sky. Then, for no apparent reason, her bandaged hand began to ache.

Suddenly, a triangular green head lifted above a large boulder not far ahead. Two thin yellow eyes focused directly on Kate. Then the lizardlike being reared up on his hind legs. He raised his hands to his mouth and readied to call out a warning.

Kate seized Laioni's arm and pointed at the Slimni. Just then, a winged figure rocketed down from the clouds, talons extended. As the Slimni started to shout, Kandeldandel attacked from behind, digging his talons deep into the green scales of the creature's back. With a squeal of pain, the Slimni dropped his hands and twisted violently to free himself. Kandeldandel rolled sideways off the boulder, pulling the reptile with him. They fell out of sight.

The group clambered as fast as they could up to the boulder. Monga, first to arrive, froze at the spot. He stood still, growling barely audibly, until the others joined him.

There, standing over the body of the slain Slimni, stood Kandeldandel. Black blood was splattered on his talons and once-white abdominal feathers. The lizardlike being, though nearly decapitated, still grasped one of his legs. Finally the Tinnani succeeded in pulling frcc, thcn said in a low voice to Monga, "You can stop growling now." Spinning his head toward Kate, he added, "One down, five to go."

"That's how many you saw?" questioned Kate, placing her throbbing left hand protectively under her right armpit.

Kandeldandel, still clutching his flute, tried to shake the black blood from his leg feathers. "That's all. There might have been more inside one of the huts, but I don't think so. They were celebrating, and no scoundrel likes to miss a party."

"We're in luck, then," whispered Laioni. "The rest must be off hunting."

"Or pillaging," threw in Kandeldandel.

"Is Sanbu there?" asked Kate.

"He is."

"Did you see the walking stick?"

The Tinnani's gaze fell. "No. Either he's already given it to the Wicked One, or it's in one of the huts. My eyesight is good enough I'm sure I didn't miss it."

"Pretty good spying for a lowly musician," said Kate, tossing her braid over her shoulder. "I sure hope they still have it. Otherwise all this is for nothing." She paused. "Hey, listen."

From far up the ridge came the chanting of husky voices, wafting on the wind. A single drum pounded relentlessly in the background.

"A victory chant," observed Laioni.

"Come on," said Kate. "Let's spoil their party."

Stealthily, the attackers crept forward across the rocks. Monga led the way, though still hobbled from his last encounter with Sanbu. The brave dog pushed himself to go first, for he, too, had some business to settle at the camp. Laioni followed him closely, hunching her back to keep low. Next came Kate, carrying the spear parallel to the ground so it would not be seen by Sanbu or his men. Just behind came Kandeldandel and Jody, allies for the moment at least.

As they advanced, the chanting voices grew gradually louder. Finally, Monga stopped at the side of a large boulder covered with orange lichen, wagging his prodigious tail. As Kate and the others joined him, crouching behind the boulder, they could see the camp just ahead. Five men, one larger than the rest, sat on stones beside the flames, poking the fire with sticks and singing. All wore deerskin loincloths and black streaks painted across their cheekbones. The warriors seemed unprepared for battle, their black hair falling loose to their shoulders.

In contrast to the encampment of Laioni's mother, no tools decorated the ground. Instead, Kate saw three spears, all with the same gray head as Sanbu's, a stone hatchet, several knives, a large pile of firewood, and a bow with two flint-tipped arrows leaning against a stone nearby. The half-eaten carcass of a mutilated deer lay discarded near the fire, covered with flies.

The larger man turned to say something to one of the others, who laughed boisterously in response. As the big man rose to his feet, Kate sucked in her breath, for she could see he was indeed Sanbu. He stepped over to the other warrior and pushed him backward off his stone. The smaller man sprung to his feet and said something in an angry voice, whereupon Sanbu struck him in the jaw with a brutal blow. The warrior fell backward onto the rocky terrain, groaning as he rolled to one side.

Sanbu strutted back to his place and sat down again. He grabbed a slice of dried meat from the man seated next to him, then uttered a command. The warriors resumed their chanting. One of them pounded heavily on a drum of stretched deerskin. Sanbu's victim rejoined the group, rubbing his tender jaw. Meanwhile, the first reddish rays of sunrise struck the camp, bathing the men and their two brush huts with rubescent light.

"If Monga could jump one of them, that would distract the others," Kate whispered to Laioni. "Then we could search the huts for the stick."

Laioni whispered into Monga's ear, which stood rigid and alert on his head. The bushy tail swished from side to side until she had finished. For an instant his dark eyes connected with Laioni's, then he bounded off toward the campfire.

Suddenly, he halted, sniffing the air. Laioni turned to Kate and said anxiously, "Something's wrong."

Monga abruptly changed his course. Instead of pouncing on one of the men seated by the fire, he veered sharply to the side and bolted for one of the brush huts. At that instant, a shaggy brown dog, a full head taller than Monga, emerged from the entrance. With a ferocious bark, the dog sprang at Monga, who met him in midair just outside the hut. They dropped to the ground, rolling over each other and snarling viciously.

Kate, Laioni, and Jody dashed into the camp, as Kandeldandel took flight. The five warriors leaped to their feet, reaching for their weapons. Sanbu saw Kate running toward him, carrying his own spear, and he let loose an earsplitting cry of vengeance. The powerful Halami picked up a spear, reared back, and hurled it at Kate.

Just as Sanbu released it, something knocked against his arm, throwing his aim askew. The spear clattered against the rocks as Kandeldandel, talons extended, descended on top of him. Screeching like twenty owls, the Tinnani swiped across his shoulder, cutting deep into the flesh. Sanbu whirled around, grabbing one feathered leg with both of his burly hands. He threw Kandeldandel to the ground and bent to grab the stone hatchet.

At that instant, Kate plowed into his side with the spear, throwing all her weight into the charge. Sanbu roared in pain, dropped the hatchet, and staggered backward. He tripped over one of the sitting stones and fell into the fire. With a shriek, he rolled out of the coals and struggled to pull the spear from his ribs.

At the sight of Sanbu tumbling into the fire, the man he had struck only a few moments before cried out in fear and ran down the ridge as fast as he could. Meanwhile, Laioni and Jody battled together against another warrior, their three arms against his two, wrestling with him on the rocky terrain. Kandeldandel, having regained his feet, danced just out of reach of a stocky, muscular man who now wielded the hatchet. Nearby, Monga fought desperately with the bigger dog. They rolled across the ground in a snarling tangle of brown fur.

Kate seized the opportunity to search for the walking stick. She turned toward one of the two brush huts and dashed to the entrance. Kneeling, she peered inside the dimly lit enclosure, searching for the Stick of Fire.

As she knelt down, another warrior appeared from his hiding place behind a lichen-streaked boulder. He raised his bow, drew back the string, and shot an arrow directly at Kate's back. His aim was good, and the arrow whizzed straight toward the unsuspecting target. It plunged into the blue day pack and smacked against the metal thermos still within, knocking Kate on her face with the force.

Saved by the thermos, she rose unharmed. She pulled the arrow out of the pack and stared at it, aghast. Silently, she thanked Aunt Melanie for packing the hot chocolate. She peered out the entrance, but could not see the marksman.

Mustering her courage, she darted over to the other brush hut. This time she threw herself inside before anyone could attack from behind. Scanning the interior, she spied a familiar shape in the shadows. She lunged for it, grasping the shaft in her hand—only to discover it was just another spear. She threw it aside, heart pounding like the warrior's drum. Where is that stick? She hoped it was not already in Gashra's hands.

In a gesture of hopelessness, she threw back her head and took a deep breath. Two yellow dots gleamed at her from the ceiling of the hut. The walking stick! Hidden in the brush above her head, it was nearly invisible but for the carved owl's head handle. Kate reached upward and yanked it free, just as a powerful hand grasped her ankle and dragged her violently out of the hut.

The warrior whose arrow had missed its mark stood above her, glowering. Now brandishing a knife instead of a bow, he suddenly kicked hard at her head. Kate dodged the blow and jumped to her feet, still holding the walking stick. As the man spun around to face her, she swung the stick with all the force of a home run hitter, connecting with a thud on his left eye. The blow sent him reeling backward.

But before Kate could recover her balance, another hand grasped the shaft.

"Sanbu!" she cried, as the warrior's angry eyes, roiling with rage, met her own.

He tried to jerk the stick away, but Kate held fast. Then she did the only thing she could think of doing: She bit, and hard. Sinking her teeth into Sanbu's sweaty wrist, she closed her jaw with all her strength.

"Eeaaaah!" he shouted, smashing his fist against Kate's shoulder.

Pain seared her upper back, but still she hung on. Again Sanbu struck, this time on the back of her neck. She bit with all her energy, translating her pain into force.

Sanbu suddenly abandoned his grip on the shaft and pulled back his hand, wrenching her neck sideways. As Kate toppled to the ground, he reached to pick up a spear, blood streaming from the wound in his side. Lifting the spear high, he screamed vengefully as he prepared to end her life.

Just then, Laioni hurled herself directly into his chest. "Run!" she cried to Kate. "Escape while you can."

Sanbu threw Laioni to the ground and stabbed fiercely at her with his spear. Before Kate could even rise to her feet, he sliced into Laioni's thigh, cutting her deeply. Again he raised the spear, cursing wrathfully at this Halami girl who dared to challenge him.

At that moment, Monga released his death grip on the throat of the large dog. He backed away, staggered, and fell, then lifted himself weakly. One ear hung badly torn, while his right front leg dragged useless along the ground. Seeing Laioni's peril, he forced himself to bound across the camp. Just as Sanbu was about to drive the spear into her chest, he leaped at the warrior with his last particle of strength.

As Sanbu shrieked, Monga clamped his jaws around the man's neck. Sanbu fell backward, struggling to pull the dog away. But Monga held firm.

Kate glanced in the direction where she had last seen Jody and Kandeldandel, but saw no sign of them. She stepped to Laioni's side and helped her to stand, though her leg bled profusely. Together, they stumbled away from the camp, climbing higher on the ridge. Using the walking stick as it was meant to be used, she steadied herself against the increasing weight of Laioni's body.

"Leave me," rasped Laioni. "Leave me or they'll catch us. I'm too weak to go on."

"I'm not leaving you," declared Kate, leaning her against an angular boulder. Ripping the purple kerchief from her hand, she wrapped it tightly around the slashed leg to slow the bleeding.

Laioni whispered, "Go on, please. They'll kill you too."

"You're not going to die," retorted Kate. Gazing at the camp below, she saw Sanbu and Monga still rolling on the ground, locked in deadly combat. Yet she could see no one else. Where were Jody and Kandeldandel? And the other warriors?

All at once, the pale early-morning light swiftly dimmed. Kate turned toward the sky to see legions of dark clouds gathering overhead. A stiff breeze, cold as ice on her face, swept across the ridge. The few shrubs and grasses sprouting from between the scattered rocks bent savagely under the weight of the wind. Then came the first rumble of thunder, echoing ominously over the face of the mountain.

Laioni suddenly started to slump forward. Barely catching her before she fell, Kate draped the unconscious body across her own shoulders, grabbed Laioni's dangling arm, and lifted her in a fireman's carry. She straightened up with difficulty, feeling the weight in her knees and lower back. But where to go? She could not carry such a burden very far. She only knew she needed to find some sort of shelter, away from the oncoming storm and any of Sanbu's men who might try to track them.

Straining to see in the limited light, Kate's eyes roamed past the camp, across the rocky scree, and into the high reaches of the forest. There the shrunken and twisted trees, though deformed by endless winds, might offer some protection. Farther down the slope stretched the forest itself, visible now only as a sweeping sea of deep green, but for one nearby valley that was utterly dark. Beyond the forest, she could barely make out the towering cliffs of Lost Crater.

A blast of lightning sizzled across the sky. In the momentary light, Kate glimpsed two men, one carrying a spear, standing amidst the boulders just above the camp. They surveyed the ridge, searching for something.

Immediately, Kate turned to climb. Height was now her only hope for escape. Even with the help of the walking stick, Laioni's weight made progress very difficult. Yet she forced herself, laboring mightily, to ascend the rocky ridge. It did not occur to her that every step brought her closer to the lair of the Wicked One.

25

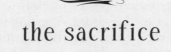

the sacrifice

HIGHER Kate climbed, step by arduous step. Laioni's body sagged heavily on her shoulders, causing her to stop regularly to catch her breath. After resting only a few seconds, she continued up the slope, panting in the thin air.

She constantly craned her neck, scanning the ridge for any sort of hiding place that might shield them from the sharp eyes of Sanbu's warriors, let alone Sanbu himself if he survived Monga's attack. Yet she saw no sign of shelter, only an increasingly jagged jumble of gray granite and white quartz. Even the shriveled shrubs grew fewer and fewer, requiring something more receptive than solid stone to sink their roots.

A clap of thunder exploded, and with it came the first splattering of sleet upon the rocks. Kate positioned herself on a flat, oblong stone and swung around to view the camp below. But heavy gray clouds now rolled across the ridge, and she could see nothing beyond the approaching storm.

As she turned back toward the high shoulders of the mountain, a sudden flash of lightning burst against the boulders just to her right. She leaped instinctively to the side and, in doing so, lost her footing. She tumbled with Laioni onto the rocks, her shout overwhelmed by a new pounding of thunder.

As she rolled to her knees, the dark clouds opened fully, showering the slope with a freezing downpour of sleet and hail. By the time she could crawl to Laioni's side, hailstones dotted her twin ropes of black hair. It took all of Kate's strength to lift her again. Standing unsteadily, she straightened her back against the frigid gusts of wind.

Another simultaneous blast of lightning and thunder crashed across the slope, nearly knocking her down again. In the wavering light she spied a shallow overhang of rock nearby. It looked barely big enough to cover the two of them, but she knew there was no other choice. Tottering across the slippery slope with the help of the walking stick, she carried Laioni to the overhang. Kneeling, she wedged Laioni into the deepest recess under the gray stone slab and slid herself, exhausted, beside her.

The hail gathered swiftly on the stones outside their shelter. Soon the rocky expanse of the ridge was transformed into a sheet of white ice. The air grew bitter cold, and Kate realized that she could see the puffs of her own breath. Laioni's breathing, though, she could not see at all. Placing her hand against the Halami girl's mouth, she felt just the barest hint of warmth, and that only at irregular intervals.

"Laioni," she cried, shaking her friend by the shoulders. "Laioni, don't die. Please don't die."

She laid her hand against Laioni's leather bib, on the same spot where she felt a heart beating strongly not long before. "You promised," she pleaded. "Remember? You promised."

Tears brimmed in Kate's eyes, even as she started to shiver from the cold. Feeling her fingers going numb, she thrust them under her armpits for warmth. Her neck and shoulders ached, both from Sanbu's blows and from the weight of the burden they had carried so far up the rocky ridge. She examined the blood-soaked kerchief tied around Laioni's thigh. The bleeding had halted at last, but that meant nothing if now she died from exposure to the elements.

Kate touched Laioni's pale cheek with two throbbing fingers. To her shock, she discovered that the cheek felt even colder. As the wind whipped across the slope, driving the hail into wavelike drifts, she pulled off the day pack and removed her sweatshirt. Frantically, she tried to wrap it like a blanket around Laioni. Yet she knew it would do little to slow the deadly process. She remembered Aunt Melanie telling her the tragic story of a young couple, married not yet one week, who froze to death in a sudden storm on Brimstone Peak. Rescuers found them several days later, huddled together, inseparable in death as in life.

Laioni shivered all at once as if having a seizure, which caused her head to fall forward. Kate, herself shivering in her T-shirt, raised the heavy head again. She noticed once more how much this girl from another time looked like Aunt Melanie, even with her eyes closed. Was this how Laioni's life would end? Frozen to death on the side of a mountain?

Kate bit her lip at the thought. *It's so cold—cold. She's going to d-die unless I can do something. Sh-she's going to d-d-die.*

The storm swirled across the ridge with increasing fury. Kate listened in vain for some slackening in the wintry wind. But the wind howled incessantly, stealing what flickering flame of life remained in the girl by her side.

Monga knew, thought Kate. He knew that someone's death was near. But did he know it was Laioni's? She struck her knee angrily with her fist. It's too soon for her to die. Too soon!

She observed Laioni's face, now frosted with hundreds of tiny hairs of ice. Her lips looked like gray-blue granite, her skin like shadowy storm clouds. *If only I could build a fire. Then at least she'd have a chance.* Glancing at her own sneakers, Kate wondered whether they might burn.

No, too wet. And besides, she had no matches. She didn't even have a pair of sticks to rub together, as Laioni had done in the forest.

Another series of shivers rattled Laioni. Kate moved still closer to her chilled body, enveloping her with her own bare arms. Her eyes, blurring with tears of pain and helplessness, fell to the walking stick. Frost partially covered the shaft, obscuring the symbols carved into the wood. The eyes of the handle stared icily back at her. So this is Laioni's fate, she said to herself bitterly. This is what happens to She Who Follows the Owl. She wanted to learn the true meaning of her name, and it is Death. *If only I could make a fire. If only . . .*

She blinked, focusing again on the stick. The Stick of Fire. What was it the Chieftess believed? Something to do with the name. Then she remembered: *It will burst into flames when so commanded by its rightful owner.*

No, she told herself. Forget it. Forget the whole idea. Besides, the rightful owner was Aunt Melanie, and she was as far away as ever. Even if Kate herself were the rightful owner, burning the stick would throw away her sole chance of ever seeing her great-aunt again.

Yet, could it be that some small part of Aunt Melanie might reside right here in this Halami girl? Whether or not a traceable connection between them existed, Kate knew that wasn't the point. She had begun to feel that all living things are linked, often in ways impossible to see. Perhaps in some mysterious way she herself was more connected than she could ever know to Laioni, somehow tied to an unknown people from an unremembered time.

She reached for the walking stick, then caught herself. *Hold fast to your stick of power,* the Chieftess said at their parting. *It is your only hope, and ours as well.* Her only hope of returning to her own time. Her only hope of helping Aunt Melanie. Her only hope of saving the Ancient One.

Filled with uncertainty, she touched the stick with the tip of one finger. *Do not do this lightly,* rang the voice of the Chieftess, *for it will destroy the stick and all its powers.*

Again Laioni's frame convulsed in a sudden shiver.

Kate seized the stick and brought it close to her face. "Burn," she said in a low voice. "Burn if you can, Stick of Fire."

Nothing happened. The icy wind screamed across the frigid ridge, mocking her act of desperation. Kate listened, then realizing the futility of her attempt, threw the stick to the ground. It clattered on the hail-coated rocks by her feet.

Then, so slowly as to be almost imperceptible, the yellow eyes of the handle began to glow strangely. A thin plume of smoke started to curl upward from the middle of the shaft, and the hailstones beneath the stick hissed in contact with some new source of heat. Soon, an ellipse of melting ice formed around the walking stick, while water dripped along the edges of the stones.

Kate watched with a mixture of hope and grief as the Stick of Fire ignited. With growing intensity, strange white flames flickered along its length, licking the wood eagerly, burning away the ancient images of the Tinnani Old Tongue. As fiercely as the blizzard blew beyond the overhang, it could not snuff out this crackling fire.

The walking stick burned vigorously, swelling in strength, until Kate's feet and legs began to feel progressively warmer. She leaned Laioni closer, so that she would be warmed but not singed by the heat. So brilliant were the flames, as if their source were not a stick but a star, she could not look directly into them without scalding her eyes.

Gently, very gently, she lay Laioni's head upon her shoulder so that she might hear her breathe above the continual wailing of the wind. And then she waited.

26

dying flames

FOR several hours, the tempest raged. Hail and sleet surged across the mountainside. But for the circle of bare rock surrounding the overhang where a small fire burned brightly, the entire ridge wore a cloak of white ice. Kate, exhausted from the long trek and fierce battle, basked in the warmth of the flaming stick until at last she dropped off into a fitful sleep.

She woke with a start. Laioni's head now lay on her lap, the Stick of Fire still burning at their feet. Her heart leaped to see the ruddiness returned to Laioni's complexion. Touching her cheek gently, Kate felt again the warmth and life of her loyal friend. Amidst all that she had lost, all that she had left behind, at least this one thing had been saved.

She's alive. Kate savored the words, leaning her head back against the rock. *Laioni is alive.*

Yes, her sober inner voice replied, but what good will it do? Laioni would survive the storm, and even now slumbered peacefully on her lap. Yet the powers of Gashra continued undiminished. Aided by the Broken Touchstone, he would surely press ahead with his plans to devour the forest and destroy any creatures who dared to stand in his way. Her sacrifice, quite probably, was in vain. Most likely Laioni was spared only to fall some other day.

At least, Kate assured herself, there was this silver lining: The Stick of Fire will not fall into the hands of Gashra. He can never use it to find the missing Fragment. He can never heal the Broken Touchstone, augmenting his already terrible power. That much, at least, Kate had denied him, even if she had denied herself in the process.

Looking into the dancing white flames, Kate marveled at how evenly and strongly the stick blazed, yet with only a tiny trace of smoke. Never had she seen any light so intense, except perhaps in the eyes of Nyla, smallest of the Stonehags. Even in its final act of self-destruction the stick displayed deep power. Although the shaft lay largely disintegrated, the coals burned on with vigor. She knew they would continue to flame for some time. The carved handle, though completely charred, burned more slowly than the rest, so that the head of Chieftain Solosing de Notnot, creator of the Stick of Fire, remained recognizable. That's appropriate, thought Kate. The Chieftain's image will be the last part of the stick reduced to cinders, his yellow eyes aglow to the very last.

She sighed, remembering the warm glow from the fireplace in Aunt Melanie's living room. She would never know the comfortable feeling of that room again, its damp cedar smell, its many hideaways for Atha, its stockpile of quilts. She recognized that she would spend the rest of her days imagining but not tasting Aunt Melanie's homemade spice tea. With everything else from her own time that she would miss—Mom and Dad, Cumberland, her favorite shortstop glove, baseball cards, extra-thick mocha shakes— nothing exceeded the longing she felt to see again the old cottage and the elflike woman who lived there. Most of all, she hoped that Aunt Melanie was safe, though doubt loomed larger than hope in her heart.

She surveyed the landscape beyond the overhang. The

storm, its anger finally spent, was at last beginning to disperse. Scattered shafts of sunlight broke through the parting clouds and swept across the ridge, illuminating patches of ice-crusted rocks. The wind slackened, and she could now make out most of the mighty shoulder of the mountain, although the summit remained hidden by clouds.

Then she remembered. This was Gashra's mountain. Somewhere up there beyond the vapors encircling the summit lay the very lair of the Wicked One. She glanced again at Laioni, sleeping deeply in the healing warmth of the Stick of Fire. Soon she would wake to find the stick destroyed, along with her people's last hope of halting the growth of Gashra's power. Perhaps she would resent Kate for valuing her life above everything else.

Whatever she might think, the deed was done. It could not be reversed. While the stick continued to burn vigorously, it moved inexorably closer to becoming nothing more than a heap of ashes, its power consumed, spent, used up.

The same could be said, Kate realized sadly, about her own brief life. With no hope left of returning to her own time, there was nothing left for her to do but to live out the rest of her days with the Halamis, waiting for the inevitable time when Gashra would crush them completely. In losing the walking stick she had lost any chance to do something significant in the struggle against him. Saving Laioni was the last act of real worth she would ever accomplish. And though it might not mean much in the grand scheme of things, she knew that she could not have done differently.

Feeling the aching stiffness in her back, Kate decided to stand. Carefully, she slid her legs out from under Laioni, laying her head gently upon the flat stone. The girl snorted and her arm twitched as if she were about to wake up, but soon she drifted back into slumber.

Slowly, Kate rose to her feet. She stepped around the crackling fire and away from the overhanging rock that had shielded them from the storm. Out of reach from the heat of the fire, she felt the brush of brisk wind against her chest. She grabbed her green sweatshirt, which now lay on the rocks by Laioni's side, and pulled it on. Then, cautiously, she crept around the side of the rock and peered at Sanbu's camp a few hundred feet below. She saw no sign of any life there.

Questions tugged at her mind. Had Monga survived the attack? His bravery was so much bigger than his body, yet courage alone was no match for Sanbu's strength. If indeed he lived, did that mean Sanbu did not? That the little dog had not followed her trail, had not found his way to Laioni's side during the storm, worried Kate deeply. She wondered for the first time whether the death he had fore-seen was in fact his own. And what of Jody? Despite him-self, the boy from her own time had begun to win her grudging respect, if not her friendship. And Kandeldandel? What she would give right now to hear the soothing strains of his owl-like flute, or to see that mischievous grin again. She dreaded the thought that he might have been injured or that he was now, like Arc, a lifeless bundle of feathers.

Sadly, her eyes roamed across the great forest world stretching endlessly before her. In very little time all of it, including the sheer volcanic cone she could see rising in the distance, would fall under the domination of the Wicked One. And she had seen enough of his work to know that he would destroy whatever was not useful to him and devour the rest. Not only did that mean many individuals would die, from Laioni to her mother, from a certain Tinnani flute player to Fanona, stricken daughter of the Chieftain and Chieftess, it also meant that the forest itself, the living, breathing community that Kate was only beginning to com-prehend, would ultimately perish. What that might mean for Lost Crater, and for the Hidden Forest deep within its walls, she shuddered to think. And the Ancient One: If Gashra had his way, it would not be there for Aunt Melanie to encounter five hundred years from now. The loggers' work would have been accomplished long before their time.

She bent down to touch her toes, stretching the sore muscles of her legs and back. Then she straightened her-self, again scanning Sanbu's camp below. Gradually, a new feeling of resolve took hold. Maybe her own usefulness was not yet exhausted after all. If Sanbu lurked down there somewhere, perhaps she could use whatever energy she had left to inflict a small but painful sting in his, and therefore Gashra's, hide. There was no reason left to be cautious. Her days were numbered just as surely as Fanona's.

Yet she knew deep inside herself that such thinking was folly. What could she possibly do to harm Sanbu, let alone Gashra? At the first opportunity they would finish her off. Only the storm had granted her any protection, and its fury had now passed. She possessed no weapons, no warriors, no chance. Nothing would be stupider than to walk into a waiting ambush at Sanbu's camp, except perhaps strolling unarmed into Gashra's own lair. Even a ruse was impossible, for she had no way to fool them. She didn't even have the one thing they still thought she had: the Stick of Fire.

Regretfully, she watched the white flames consuming the remains of the stick. *The one thing they still thought she had . . .*

Suddenly an idea dawned. Possibly, just possibly, she could use Gashra's desire to find the Fragment to trick him into giving up the Broken Touchstone. Such a plan, she realized, was more than risky. It was impossible. Almost certainly it would spell her own death. Yet if she had to die in this strange time and place, perhaps it would be better to die in pursuit of something important. Rather than wait passively for the enemy to strike her down, she would take the battle to the enemy. Her stomach churned uneasily, for she knew this meant searching not for Sanbu, nor for any other agents of Gashra—but for Gashra himself.

Kate swung her eyes toward the cloud-covered summit. Knowing she faced certain defeat somehow liberated her deepest reserves of courage. If through some miracle she could lure Gashra into parting with the Broken Touchstone, his power to damage the forest and all its inhabitants would shrink drastically. If she failed, they would be no worse off for her effort. Either way, she would not die without having lived with some purpose. For if she could not protect Aunt

Melanie herself, at least she could try to protect the Halami girl who shared with her great-aunt more than just eye color. And if she could not save the Ancient One from destruction in her own time, at least she could try to save it in another.

She cast one more glance toward the sleeping form by the blazing coals. Laioni was safe for now, at least. Kate swallowed, knowing she would almost certainly never see her friend again. Then, from somewhere in her memory, she heard the words of the Stonehag Nyla: *At least you have a purpose, a calling, something you must do with your life. That is a blessing, a true blessing.*

Grabbing her blue day pack, she slipped her arms through the straps. Then she stepped away from the over-hang onto the icy rocks of the ridge, starting for the sum-mit. She did not know whether she would succeed in her quest, but only that, like Babe Ruth, she would try.

27

alone

STRUGGLING to ascend the frosted ridge, Kate nearly slipped several times, tottering momentarily on the edge of an icy rock before regaining her balance. Even when her sneakers seemed firmly planted, they were dangerously unstable. Pausing once to catch her breath, she turned to discover a distinct trail of her own footprints across the whitened slope. If Sanbu or his warriors wanted to pursue her, they now would have no trouble. She pushed on, wishing she could simply rise into the air with a few beats of her wings like Kandeldandel, avoiding the laborious climb.

Gradually, she crossed beyond the reach of the hailstorm. The rocks, while still wet, no longer glistened with ice. Stepping more confidently, Kate continued to climb higher, stopping intermittently to check to the rear for any followers. As she gained altitude, the sweeping wind swelled steadily in volume. Soon it sounded as loud as Kahona Falls, roaring ceaselessly. At the same time, fog swirled about her again. She felt increasingly warm, though she assumed this feeling came from her own exertion.

Then, all at once, she discovered the source of both the sound and the heat. Scores of deep cracks ran down the ridge from the summit, reaching toward her like elongated fingers, shooting walls of steam skyward. A city of geysers confronted her, hissing incessantly. She halted, staring in amazement at this inferno. Reaching the summit meant finding a path between the roaring plumes of steam, if such a path even existed.

Biting her lip, she strode forward into a narrow channel between two of the long cracks. The rushing of steam filled her ears, just as the billowing clouds of white vapor filled the air above her head. On either side, dozens of fumaroles rose from the ground, painted brilliant shades of orange, rust, yellow, and blue. Acidic gases sputtered from small craters beside the steam vents, while murky pools bubbled and churned.

Perspiring from the heat, Kate started to run through this gauntlet of steaming crevasses. The deep cracks drew nearer together, and steam clouds smothered her completely. The air reeked of foul-smelling sulfur, burning her throat and scalding her eyes. She choked, gasping for air.

Stumbling forward, she finally reached what seemed to be a gap between the crevasses, a narrow space less than an arm's length wide. She hesitated for an instant, not knowing what lay on the other side. Then she threw herself across the gap and fell to her knees on the rocks.

Panting, she drank in the cooler air, wiping her streaming eyes on her sweatshirt. Fog no longer swirled around her and she could see the darkening late-afternoon sky above the ridge. Behind, curling columns of seething gases poured out of the crevasses. Ahead, the summit loomed starkly, ringed with craggy cliffs and cinder cones.

The wind whipped across the desolate mountaintop, bitter cold against her face. No one but Gashra could feel at home in this tormented landscape. Everywhere, rocks bore the scars of excessive heat and force, whether singed until they turned black or baked until they burst apart. The ridge resembled the inside of a cauldron whose contents had long since boiled away, leaving behind a residue of incinerated rubble.

Rising to her feet, Kate spotted a small pool of clear water not far away. Unlike the other pools on the summit, it did not froth and bubble darkly. Instead, it stood perfectly still, clear as a crystal. Something about this pool called to Kate, beckoned to her softly and compellingly. She was too weak to resist its pull, too tired to remember the attraction of another enchanted pool, near the Circle of Stones.

How strange, she thought, to find a place of such beauty and purity amidst such devastation. If the rest of the mountaintop was designed to frighten away intruders, this transparent pool seemed a stunning exception. It sparkled invitingly, reflecting the slanting light of the setting sun.

She bent lower to examine the lovely little pool. The roaring steam vents still sounded in her ears, but she felt a renewed peacefulness gazing into this water. Although she hadn't expected to see her reflection, her own face looked up at her, tinged with gold from the sunset. So clear and still was the water that she could even see the hazel green hue of her eyes. She turned her head, and the mirrorlike surface revealed the loose, haphazard knotting of her braid, as well as the caked dirt on her neck and lower jaw.

Captivated by the perfect image, Kate smiled in satisfaction. As she did, she watched her own lips part to reveal a row of pearly white teeth. Then, unaccountably, the teeth in the reflection started to darken, to take on the color of her tongue, until finally they disappeared. Her mouth, oddly misshapen, grew redder and redder, as if it overflowed with her own blood. Her eyes sank drastically inward and her cheekbones suddenly hollowed, stretching her face into ghoulish proportions. At the same time, all her hair fell away, while her nose hooked cruelly downward. A deep gash appeared, slashing across her face.

She cried out, putting her hands to her cheeks. Though she felt the living skin still there, she staggered backward, almost falling into the steaming crevasse behind her. She caught herself just before tumbling into the scalding gases.

Then she ran past the clear pool, up the rock-strewn slope toward the summit. Like a terrified animal fleeing from a deadly predator, she ran without sense or direction, trying only to get as far away as possible.

At length, she leaned against a charred boulder twice her own height, panting for breath, her heart beating rapidly from both exertion and fright. So this was how Gashra welcomed his guests, she told herself, still seeing the haunted image. She shook her head, trying to dispel it forever. Throwing her braid over her shoulder, she drew herself up straight. *Well, he can't scare me so easily. No way. I won't let him.*

Even as she felt that sudden surge of resolve, the sun dropped below the shoulder of the mountain. The sky grew instantly darker. Her confidence departed as well, dissolving into the starless night.

In the last lingering light, she noticed some deep indentations in the surface of the boulder. Backing away, she could see the design more clearly. It was a face, an enlarged version of the Halami warning stone in the Hidden Forest. The carved face glared at her, mouth open wide, exuding panic. Despite herself, Kate shivered at the sight.

Then, as the light grew still dimmer, the mouth began to move. At first the lips quivered ever so slightly. Then they drew closer together, before suddenly stretching apart in an effort to shout.

"You will die!" screamed the face on the rock. "You will die!"

Kate lurched backward, then tripped over a jagged rock just behind her. She fell on her back with a thud, then rolled to one side. Fighting to keep some semblance of calm in the deepening darkness, she crawled quickly away from the boulder. Glancing back at the carved face, she could no longer discern its outline, nor even see the boulder against the night sky. Nothing but blackness filled her eyes; nothing but wailing wind filled her ears. She held her breath, paralyzed, half expecting the very rocks beneath her hands to come alive.

Then she saw three rounded rocks beginning to gleam with a vague reddish light. Instinctively, she jumped to her feet, but some hypnotic power within the light forced her to halt and sit down again. The glow within the rocks deepened, turning them into pulsing points of luminous red. All at once a spindly column of wavering light started to rise slowly out of each. The three glowing red columns swayed and twirled, growing taller all the time, until they condensed into the shapes of thin, wispy women. Halami women. They wore loose stringy skirts, chest bibs, and hair tied into twin ropes by their shoulders, though they were no more solid than shredded clouds. Silently, the ghostly trio turned to face Kate, red eyes gleaming wrathfully. They released a chorus of ear-splitting screams that made her cover her ears and bury her head between her knees.

At length the screams ceased and she raised her head again. At that moment the three ghostly figures began dancing around her, baying and howling, encircling her in a ring of shimmering red light. As though reliving the agony of their own tortured deaths, the spirits wailed hideously, flailing their arms and tossing their heads wildly from side to side.

"Stop," Kate cried in desperation. "Leave me alone!"

But the spirit-women did not stop. Long into the night, for hours that weighed on Kate like centuries, they wove their shrieking circle ever more tightly around her. At one point she picked up a rock and hurled it at one of them. It passed harmlessly through the vaporous head, landing in the darkened distance.

As the deathly dance wore on, Kate's eyelids drooped heavily. She fought to keep them open, knowing she must remain alert, despite her exhaustion. Anything could happen if she fell asleep. She slapped herself on the cheek so hard it hurt. Then she continued to watch the writhing spirits, waiting for the dawn she feared might never come.

28

in the lair
of the wicked one

THE ground suddenly shook violently, jolting Kate awake. Rocks leaped into the air around her, and she could hear nothing but a deafening roar welling up from deep inside the mountain. She tried to stand, bracing herself against an oblong rock, but the terrible tremors knocked her back to her knees.

Then, with one final heave, the earth ceased shaking. Kate pushed herself slowly to her feet. She stood there, watching the first rays of dawn's light touch the crest of the peak. Far away, she heard the rumble of a distant rock slide set off by the earthquake. She knew that Gashra must be preparing a great onslaught against those who resisted his control. And she also knew that, somehow, she had survived the night alone on his haunted mountain.

Feeling hungry, she thrust her hand into the leather pouch still tied around her waist. Cramming the remainder of the *minarni* into her mouth, she tasted again the deep history and knowledge of the Tinnanis, whose very existence now hung in the balance. The food, dry and chewy, renewed her strength, even though she wished she could find some water to wash it down. She was not about to drink from any of the pools on this mountainside.

Slowly, she started trudging up the slope. The entrance to Gashra's lair had to be somewhere near, although she could only guess what it might look like. Then, sensing something following her, she whirled around, heart pounding. She saw nothing but the clouds of steam rising from the crevasses below and the blackened debris of the rocky ridge. She shivered involuntarily, recalling the ghostly apparitions of the past night. Perhaps they were still stalking her, even in daylight.

She felt the entrance before she saw it. A powerful gust of heated air, like a blast from an open furnace, struck her face. Turning toward the heat, she spotted a triangular cave among the charred boulders, descending into the dark depths of the mountain. Two pools of lava bubbled and steamed at either side of the entrance, casting a wavering orange light into the mouth of the cave.

As she stepped closer, the heated air blew more strongly in her face, smelling like sulfur, drying her eyes and forcing her to squint. Then the hot wind slackened, only to resume a few moments later, as if the mountain itself were breathing through this passageway. The large scab on the back of her left hand began to throb again, just as it had before whenever Slimnis lurked nearby. She swallowed, certain that this was the entrance to the lair of the Wicked One.

She scanned the dimly lit cave. What chance could she possibly have to outwit Gashra, to steal the Broken Touchstone? Next to none, probably. But she knew the odds against her were no worse than those against Aunt Melanie, five hundred years later, struggling to save a cherished stand of redwoods.

Waiting until the fiery breath slackened, Kate entered the mouth of the cave. Long rows of lava pools lined the passageway like torches, throwing their eerie light upon the rock walls. As she walked, her sneakers sometimes slid across slick puddles of mud or crunched on crumbling bits of pumice. Her elbow brushed against a knifelike protrusion, ripping her sleeve and gashing her skin.

At that instant she heard a loud hiss, followed by the sound of slithering bodies ahead of her in the cave. She froze, until the sounds melted into the steady gurgling of the pots of lava. She placed her aching left hand protectively under her sweatshirt, but the throbbing pain only grew more intense. Then, feeling something moving behind her, she turned to the rear. But she saw nothing except the dimly lit cave.

Creeping forward again, she began to notice the varieties of colors and formations sprouting from the rock walls. Hundreds of lavender crystals, spun fine as hairs, drooped down like scraggly beards. One formation puffed outward like a cluster of silver balloons, expanding and contracting with the underground wind. From the ceiling hung mineralized tendrils and jagged stalactites, sometimes merging into columns with the sharp stalagmites thrusting upward from the floor.

The passageway wound downward, descending into the abdomen of the mountain. With every step, the air grew warmer. Kate frequently mopped her dripping brow with the sleeve of her sweatshirt, but perspiration continued to sting her eyes.

Then, mysteriously, the chain of lava pools came abruptly to an end. Inching ahead, she perceived in the darkness before her the slightest glimmer of orange light. As she drew closer, the glimmer brightened into a strong glow, while the floor of the cave sloped much more steeply downward. Soon the drop became so sharp that she could not help but run, across loose rocks and broken bits of crystal, toward the source of the light.

Suddenly she found herself standing in a mammoth chamber. Frothing orange lava filled most of its floor. Only the polished shelf of stone on which she stood and a steeple-shaped island of black rock rising out of the bubbling lake of lava were not submerged. High above her head, giant red stalactites hung down like pointed fangs, casting fearsome shadows on the ceiling.

At that moment the surface of the lake began to swirl in a powerful whirlpool. Slowly, accompanied by a clamorous slurping sound, a colossal figure started to emerge out of the froth. Dripping in superheated lava, the creature rose out of the lake as if riding on an invisible escalator, then strode onto the wide stone ledge only a few yards from Kate.

A towering red beast, with the head and body of a *Tyrannosaurus rex* and the enlarged arms and legs of a human, glowered down at her. Standing more than twenty feet tall, the creature swished his massive tail angrily on the stone floor, spraying lava globules around the room. Armorlike red scales covered his entire body, though often obscured by the layers of caked lava. Only the bulbous black eyes, each one the size of Kate's whole head, and the deep purple lips that ran the length of his teeth-studded jaws did not carry scales. As the beast raised one of his huge arms, she could see a row of fleshy suction cups embedded in the scales underneath, running from the armpit all the way down to the palm of his hand. A foot-long slab of meat, all that remained of some unfortunate being, dangled from the center of one suction cup near his wrist.

Part dinosaur, part man, and part octopus, the great carnivorous creature snorted furiously, sending from his nostrils a poisonous cloud of red vapor. As he did so, dozens of gemstones and skulls and glittering baubles hanging from bands around his neck jiggled and clattered. Simultaneously, several lizardlike Slimnis emerged from the shadows at the edge of the floor and slithered toward darkened tunnels in the rock near the cave entrance. With lightning speed, a long arm lashed out and slapped its suction cups across the back of one escaping Slimni. Roaring thunderously, the red beast lifted the squirming creature into the air and took a single dinosaur-size bite out of the midsection, then snapped up the green head and tail with another enormous swallow.

A thousand-tooth grin spread across his face, and he bellowed, "Hmmmmm, breakfast." With that, he released a single titanic belch that rattled the great stalactites on the cciling. Lowering his gigantic head toward Kate, the monster then rumbled, "What, you come to Gashra with no offerings?" His swollen eyes scanned her closely. "Hmmmmm . . . What is hidden in your sack?"

Feeling the heat from his body as well as his sulfurous breath, Kate backed away. Slipping one arm out of the day pack, she unzipped it and pulled out the small painted drum. She held it in front of herself with both hands and said nervously, "An offering. For you."

"Rubbish," roared the gigantic beast, swatting the drum with a swipe of his huge hand. It skidded across the stone floor and landed beside a vast hoard of accumulated treasures, including piles of sparkling jewels, spears, knives, Halami baskets, assorted tools, carved statuettes of Gashra himsclf, and several large red stones twisted into strange shapes. "But," he added, "I'll keep it anyway." He bent closer. "Hmmmmm . . . what else do you have?"

Kate reached into the pack and retrieved the last of its contents: Aunt Melanie's metal thermos. Slinging the now-empty sack over her shoulder again, she displayed the thermos to Gashra, more uncertain than ever about her goal. It would be difficult enough even to learn the location of the Broken Touchstone, let alone steal it. She needed to stall for time. But how? He clearly didn't like the drum, and was even less likely to appreciate a beaten-up old thermos.

To her surprise, another many-toothed grin wrapped around the face of the Wicked One. He slapped the thermos with the palm of one hand, attaching it to a suction cup. Bringing it closer to his jaws, he bit ferociously into the middle. "Hmmmmm," he said, emitting a sound like gurgling lava that could only be a laugh. "Good ore."

Clapping his hands together, he bent the thermos in half. Then, with a distinct air of self-satisfaction, he slung it over one of his necklaces and pinched the two ends together to affix its position. Eyeing Kate again, he rumbled,

"Nice. Very nice." His eyes suddenly narrowed and he thundered, "But it doesn't make up for all the trouble you've caused me."

Kate cleared her throat. "What trouble do you mean?"

Gashra glared at her. "You killed my servant Sanbu."

The news hit Kate like a bucket of cold water. If Sanbu was really dead, then maybe Monga . . .

"I will miss him," continued Gashra, gnashing his teeth savagely. "He was, hmmmmm, useful to me. Very useful."

Planting her feet firmly on the stone floor, Kate declared, "He tried to steal the Stick of Fire from me."

"Did he?" growled the beast, feigning surprise. "Hmmmmm, how clumsy of him." Then Gashra bent low and said in his most soothing voice, "The last thing I would want is for a servant of mine to cause you any harm! Oh, no. You are far too important. I wouldn't want you getting hurt. Not even a little bit bruised." The purple lips stretched into a gargantuan smile. "By the way, where is the stick now? Hmmmmm?"

Kate, perspiring from more than the heat of the chamber, answered, "I destroyed it."

The Wicked One reared up and waved his tentacle-like arms. "You *what?*" he roared, so forcefully that one giant stalactite broke loose from the ceiling and plunged into the frothing lake of lava. "Don't you know that stick is the only way to find the Fragment? Hmmmmm?"

"I know," answered Kate, maintaining her calm. Then she added, trying her best to sound truthful, "I already found it."

The oversized eyes of Gashra swelled still larger. "You did? You have it?" His tail waved excitedly. "Show it to me."

"It's hidden," she replied. "Why should I show it to you?"

Gashra snorted angrily, releasing a cloud of red vapor. "Because," he snarled, "I will kill you if you don't."

Forcing herself to remain stationary, Kate declared, "Then you'll never find the Fragment."

Gashra paced back and forth, contemplating. "Hmmmmm. I hope it's not too hot in here for you," he said, again using his most soothing voice. "Like all underground beings, I require a certain amount of heat." He flashed a few dozen teeth, adding, "But not for long. With every minute, my power is building, thanks to the Broken Touchstone. Soon I will be strong enough to stride freely on the surface. And a great moment that will be! But now, back to you. Tell me your name. Your short name, the one your friends call you."

"Kate."

"Kate," repeated Gashra. "Such a nice name, hmmmmm. Yes, very nice. Now, Kate, consider this thought. Have you ever imagined what we could accomplish together?" He waved his tail again. "If you help me, your greatest dreams will come true. Just think of it! We will control everything, you and I. The whole world will be ours. Every last needle on every last tree, every last feather on every last wing. Nothing can stop us."

Kate fidgeted. Then, judging her moment, she asked, "How do I know you really have the Broken Touchstone?"

"I have it," rumbled Gashra cautiously.

"Where?"

The bulbous eyes surveyed her with suspicion. "Somewhere."

"Then how do I know you really have it?"

"How do I know you have the Fragment?"

"I wouldn't be foolish enough to come here unless I did," answered Kate.

Gashra lifted his long arm and licked the row of suction cups. "If you don't cooperate, I could boil you in lava. You'd end up like the rest of my souvenirs." He waved a hand toward his hoard of treasures.

Kate gasped, for she suddenly recognized the origin of the twisted red stones scattered throughout the jumbled pile. Bodies. Bodies of all kinds of animals: deer, owls, Slimnis, serpents, squirrels, and at least one Tinnani that she could see.

Powered by renewed rage, Kate turned back to Gashra, who continued to lick his suction cups with evident pleasure.

"You can't threaten me," she said firmly. "I know how much you want that Fragment."

Gashra lowered his arm and examined her thoughtfully. "It's a pity, hmmmmm. You look like such a tasty little morsel. But you're right. I do want that Fragment. And I will grant you your deepest wish if you will just give it to me."

Taken aback, Kate asked, "What wish?"

The dinosaur's eyes closed for a moment, then reopened. "I will reunite you with the one you call Aunt Melanie."

Kate shuddered. "How did—how did you know that?"

"The forest has many ears loyal to me," rumbled the reply. "Even if you don't really have the Fragment, for I can feel a great capacity for treachery in you, I think you could still help me find it. Hmmmmm, yes, I'm sure that's right. After all, the Stick of Fire chose you for a reason. Here is my promise to you: If you help me find it, I will send you back to your Aunt Melanie."

Her resolve disintegrating, Kate asked hesitantly, "You would really do that?"

"Of course," roared the Wicked One. "In a flash." He scooped up a handful of lava in his hand from the lake, then rubbed the hot liquid against the back of his neck. "Good for the skin," he explained, grinning broadly. "Unless of course you're made of mere flesh."

At once Kate remembered her scalded left hand. She cringed at the memory of the deadly green pool, of Aunt Melanie scrubbing the hand so furiously in the rivulet. In her mind's eye she followed that small stream as it flowed down over the rocks of the crater and into the depths of the Hidden Forest, ultimately to empty into the blue lake and finally to join the crashing cascade of Kahona Falls. She wanted to see Aunt Melanie again more than anything else in the world.

"If I'm going to join with you," she said slowly, "you've first got to tell me your plan."

"My plan is to conquer," bellowed the beast. "To own everything I can, hmmmmm, and destroy whatever I cannot. And my first great assault is only minutes away." He shrugged his head toward the bubbling lake of lava. "Even without the whole Touchstone, my power is swelling rapidly. Soon it will be great enough to drown most of the forest in a sea of fire. That will take care of those miserable Tinnanis, and their friends the Halamis, for good. Ha! They'll regret ever trying to stop me. In just a few minutes, the pressure of this lava will be so great that it will burst free at last, blasting away the top of this mountain and everything else in its path."

Kate then noticed that the level of the frothing lake had risen steadily since she first arrived. Now it slopped over the edge of the stone floor, consuming more of the ledge every second, nearing the dark tunnels through which the Slimnis had escaped. Lava lapped still higher on the steeple-shaped island, while Gashra's tail now swam in the scalding fluid.

"Are you with me or not?" roared the Wicked One.

Stepping back from the rising lava, Kate found herself standing near the entrance to the cave through which she had fallen. Looking down at her feet, she kicked a loose rock into the orange liquid. It hissed as it was swallowed by lava. "All right," she said at last. "I'm with you. But first show me the Broken Touchstone."

"Hmmmmm, gladly," gurgled Gashra triumphantly, as he opened his massive jaws to the widest. He reached inside his mouth and removed from under his tongue a glowing red sphere no bigger than a softball. Holding the sphere high above his head, Gashra savored its deep radiance for a moment. "Here," he announced proudly, "is the Broken Touchstone."

"I still can't see it," said Kate. "I want to see the place where the Fragment fits."

Hesitating for a moment, Gashra lowered his hand to the level of Kate's head, keeping it just beyond her reach. Resting comfortably between two of his enormous fingers sat the ruby red sphere.

She looked at the glittering stone, captivated by its inner luminescence. A jagged crack cut diagonally across its surface, leaving a gap no more than three inches long and half an inch wide. Perhaps, she thought, by joining forces with Gashra, she could possibly tame him, moderating his greed enough that all the beings of the forest could again live together in peace. After all, anything was possible with the restored Touchstone. Yet, even as she nursed this idea, it felt strangely foreign somehow, almost as if it came from outside of herself rather than from within. Again her thoughts turned to Aunt Melanie. Kate could see her face, even hear her voice. But the words sounded blurred; she could not quite make out what her great-aunt was saying.

At that moment the mountain shook violently. The walls of the chamber swayed and buckled as if made from mere paper. Several of the huge stalactites on the ceiling broke loose and came crashing down into the lava in a series of splashes. Large stones tumbled from the island, as the lake surrounding it bubbled with new ferocity. Molten rock surged higher, lapping against the base of the treasure hoard and reaching almost to Kate's feet. She struggled to keep her balance so that she would not fall into the lava, but she felt its heat singe the hairs of her legs under her jeans.

Gashra, waving his tail with anticipation, turned his head away from Kate to see the frothing lake just behind him. At that instant, a small globule of lava flew off his tail and landed with a loud hiss on Kate's right sneaker. She jumped back, her foot sizzling with pain.

Shaking the orange substance from her sneaker, she saw the charred remains of her once bright green laces, now black as charcoal. *Like new green leaves on the first day of spring,* Aunt Melanie had said of them. *As green as new leaves,* in Laioni's words. How would new leaves fare under Gashra's domination? She tried to imagine the next first day of spring in this land, and saw nothing. She listened for the call of an owl in the forest, and heard nothing.

Just then, her eyes fell upon one especially contorted red stone that lay at the very top of the treasure hoard. It was larger than the others, twisted almost beyond recognition. Yet Kate knew instantaneously that this was the body of a young human being. A boy or a girl—perhaps even Laioni's lost friend Toru—had joined the Wicked One's list of victims, a list that would soon grow much longer.

Seizing the moment before Gashra turned around, she lunged for the Broken Touchstone resting lightly on his fingers. Grasping it in one hand, she started to scramble up the pile of rocks leading to the cave. In an instant she was within a few feet of the entrance. Struggling to reach it, she could see the flickering light of the lava torches just ahead.

Then, with a thunderous blow, Gashra's tail smashed against the wall of the chamber right above the entrance. Rocks and dust and stalactites tumbled down, blocking the cave and sealing it forever. Kate tumbled backward and rolled down the rocky slope, dropping the sphere. She stretched out her arm, reaching to retrieve it, but Gashra moved more quickly. He scooped up the sphere, breathing heavily as if the few seconds out of its contact had weakened him significantly.

"How dare you?" he roared, his full strength returning along with the fiery color of his scales. "Treacherous human! I should never have listened to you."

Bruised and scraped, Kate rose to her feet and declared, "I will never help you. Never."

"Then you shall die, like all the other forest creatures," raged Gashra. "I already have enough power to rule the world from here to the ocean. Hmmmmm! I don't need you or the Fragment to destroy my enemies once and for all."

Squeezing the glowing sphere in his enormous hand, Gashra waded into the lava lake. Whipping his massive tail back and forth so rapidly it propelled him across the churning surface, he stepped onto the steeple-shaped island. With three great bounds, he ascended the black rocks and stood atop the pinnacle. There he stood, laughing, looking down upon Kate.

Holding the Broken Touchstone in his outstretched hand, Gashra leaned back his head and cried, "The time has come, O mountain of wrath. Break your bonds, free your power. Explode in triumph!"

Again the mountain rumbled and shook, though this time it vibrated down to its deepest roots. The lava lake seethed with new energy, spitting fire high into the air, as hot winds swept around the chamber. Powerful explosions under the earth rocked the walls arching overhead, drowning out every sound but the gurgling laughter of Gashra.

In that instant, Kate did the only thing left to do. She picked up a fist-size stone. There was no time to take proper aim. Her legs wobbled from the vibrations and her eyes stung from perspiration, but she knew she would never make a more important throw. Rearing back like a practiced shortstop, she hurled the stone at the small sphere resting on Gashra's hand. She watched expectantly as it sailed through the air, straight at its target.

But it missed. The stone passed just above the Broken Touchstone, striking a giant stalactite hanging down from the ceiling. With a plop, the stone fell harmlessly into the bubbling lake of lava.

Seeing this, Gashra laughed still louder. Kate was crestfallen. She knew that she had lost her last chance to separate the sphere from its greedy master. Then, as she backed nearer to the rock wall to escape the surging lava, she saw the stalactite swaying precariously.

Dislodged by her stone, the huge formation broke loose from the ceiling with an ear-piercing crack. Gashra looked up just as the stalactite crashed down onto his outstretched arm, knocking the sphere from his hand. It fell, bounced off the rocks at the base of the island, and landed in the frothing lake. With a shriek of terror, he leaped down from the pinnacle and swung his long arm toward the precious object.

Suddenly, from the shadows behind the treasure hoard a white-winged creature appeared. Soaring like an arrow, it flew toward the floating sphere, clasping it in its talons only an instant before Gashra's hand reached the spot.

"Kandeldandel!" cried Kate, her voice mingling with the violent rumbling of the mountain.

"Take it," called the Tinnani as he flew over her head and dropped the Broken Touchstone into her hands. He then landed on the narrow ledge beside her and pulled on her arm. "Follow me," he cried, ducking into one of the dark tunnels.

Kate darted after him, even as the volcano erupted with a deafening roar.

29

torrent of fire

GUIDED by Kandeldandel's wide owl eyes, which could sense contour and shadow where Kate saw only blackness, the pair hurried through the lightless tunnel. Knowing that Kate could not run in such darkness, the Tinnani walked as briskly as he could without leaving her behind. Staying no more than a few steps behind him, she clasped the sphere in both hands, aware of nothing but her desire to escape and the insistent throbbing of her left hand. Kandeldandel hooted frequently, perhaps to keep her aware of his exact location, perhaps to frighten any Slimnis lurking ahead in the dark passage.

The tunnel, narrower than the cave by which she had entered Gashra's lair, sloped gradually downward. Soon Kate discovered a smooth trail running along the middle of the tunnel floor, scraped away by countless Slimnis slithering over the rocks. Feeling more confident, Kate accelerated her pace, keeping her feet within the bounds of the smooth trail, so that she was striding almost on Kandeldandel's heels.

A powerful tremor rocked the mountain, knocking loose some rocks from the roof of the tunnel. One of them grazed Kandeldandel's wing, causing him to step suddenly to the side. Kate, following closely, moved likewise. Her foot caught on something protruding from the floor and she fell forward, plowing into the rock wall.

"Uhhh," she exclaimed, sprawling on the tunnel floor. "The Touchstone! I dropped it."

"I don't see it anywhere," panted Kandeldandel, scanning the darkness for any sign of the sphere. "It can't be lost."

"All I feel are rocks," said Kate as she groped with both hands in the debris. "Where is it?"

At that moment, a dim illumination began to fill the tunnel. From somewhere behind them, a gentle glow expanded, casting a few flickering rays of light on the pair and their surroundings. Kandeldandel stood bolt upright, facing the source of the strange light, but before he could speak Kate spied a familiar round object hidden behind a rectangular rock.

"There," she cried, seizing the Broken Touchstone once again. She lifted it into the air to show Kandeldandel, but his attention was focused on the tunnel behind them.

"Lava," declared the Tinnani, his yellow eyes swelling. He grabbed Kate's shoulder with the talons of one hand and jerked hard to make her stand. "Let's get out of here."

They dashed through the tunnel with all the speed they could muster. Darkness posed no problem now, since the orange glow behind them grew stronger and stronger. Hurtling down the jagged-walled corridor, they started to hear the sizzling of lava pressing closer, destroying anything it touched. Even as she ran, Kate noticed that the back of her neck felt increasingly warm.

"The way out," hooted Kandeldandel, pointing to a pinpoint of gray light far ahead.

Running still faster, the pair practically flew down the tunnel, leaping over dislodged rocks every few steps. Kate held tightly to the sphere, while the gurgling and hissing behind her grew steadily louder. She huffed for breath, her throat burning from the caustic taste of sulfur.

Just as he reached the narrow crack in the rocks that was the exit, Kandeldandel stopped suddenly and whirled around. Kate bumped squarely into his feathery chest. Then, seeing the bright illumination on his face, she turned around herself. What she saw made her gasp and nearly drop the sphere. Not ten feet away flowed a thick tongue of incandescent lava, filling the entire tunnel with sizzling igneous fluid, bearing down on them fast.

"Let's go," cried Kate, pushing the Tinnani toward the opening.

Kandeldandel slid through the narrow exit, his fluffy plumage pressing close to his body. "Come on," he shouted from the other side.

"I'm coming," answered Kate, glancing back at the moving wall of fire.

She ducked her head, since the opening had not been made with humans in mind, and turned sideways to pass through more easily. Sliding into the crack, she felt the scorching heat of approaching lava on the hand that held the Broken Touchstone. Even the rocks around her were growing warmer, reflecting the volcanic heat.

The passage was narrower than she thought. Squirming, she edged still deeper, but the rocks pressed ever more tightly upon her chest and back. She dug in her feet and pushed as hard as she could, succeeding only in wedging herself more firmly. She pushed again. No motion. She tried to back up, but could not move. Her heart pounded and perspiration rolled down her brow and stung her eyes. But she could not lift her arm to wipe her sweaty face.

She was stuck.

"Come on," called Kandeldandel. "What's taking you so long?"

"I'm stuck," moaned Kate. "Can't move! And the lava—it's like fire. Help me!"

The wall of molten rock moved steadily closer. All she could see was the orange light dancing on the rocks next to her face. She drew in her legs as far as possible, but the simmering lava advanced irresistibly. Hotter than a blazing furnace, the fluid flowed nearer. In another few seconds it would incinerate her, drowning her quest forever in a river of fire.

Then, above the lava's spitting and crackling, Kate heard a new sound. Low, mellifluous notes flowed into the opening, like the call of an owl but somehow mellower. She recognized it at once.

"Hey," she cried to Kandeldandel, "are you crazy? I need your help, not your music!" The leading edge of the lava advanced toward her sneakers, and the treads on her soles started to melt. "Please," she pleaded, feeling the heat on the bottoms of her feet. "Help me."

The Tinnani merely continued to play on his flute, filling the air with cheerful song.

"Kandeldandel," gasped Kate. "This is no time for games. I'm going to die!"

All at once the orange light around Kate faded. The heat of the rocks swiftly diminished, while the treads of her sneakers stopped burning. The lava in the tunnel grew quickly colder and harder, congealing within seconds into solid rock.

"What—what happened?" she asked, her heart still racing.

Kandeldandel, having lowered his flute, replied, "I never thought my little flute could come in so handy."

"You did that?"

"Guess so," the Tinnani answered in his laughing voice. "You gave me the idea when you said the lava was like fire."

"I'm still stuck, though. Even your magic flute isn't going to pry me out of this crack."

"Try this," suggested Kandeldandel. "Take as deep a breath as you can, then when I say, blow out all the air. And hurry, before the lava heats up again."

Inhaling as instructed, Kate waited for the command, then exhaled completely. At that instant, powerful talons clutched her forward arm and pulled. She felt herself move, but only slightly. Again Kandeldandel tugged, budging her only a fraction of an inch. The rocks around her face and hands grew steadily warmer, reflecting the first flickers of orange light. Just as she was about to gasp for air, the Tinnani pulled a third time. She slid forward and tumbled out of the opening, landing right on top of him.

"You did it!" she shouted, hugging Kandeldandel no less tightly than she clutched the sphere of red obsidian in her hand.

"Owww," he screeched, pushing her away. "You hurt my wing."

"Sorry," said Kate, rolling away. She sat on the rock-strewn ridge, drinking in the cool mountain air. "I never thought I'd be glad to see this place again, but I sure am."

"I'm not," answered Kandeldandel, struggling to his feet. He tried to move his left wing, then winced in pain. "I think something's broken."

"Gosh, I'm—"

A loud rumbling filled the air, cutting short Kate's apology. She looked up, noticing for the first time the heavy black clouds darkening the sky above them. Yet she knew they were not clouds of rain or snow, just as the rumbling was not thunder. Turning toward the summit, she realized they had exited below the hissing steam vents, still pouring clouds of hot vapor into the air. Beyond the steaming crevasses she saw a gargantuan pillar of smoking, smoldering ash rising out of the top of the peak, lifting its billowing burden skyward.

The rumbling expanded to an ear-splitting roar. Suddenly the mountain shook with an explosion so violent it knocked both Kate and Kandeldandel to the ground. Struggling to regain their feet, they saw the entire summit above the steam vents rip itself apart in a catastrophic burst of orange flame. Bubbling lava surged out of the gaping crater, while incandescent globs rained down on the ridge like a torrent of fire.

"Let's get out of here," cried Kate.

Hurtling down the slope as fast as they could, the pair raced to outrun the lava flowing out of the seething summit. Disregarding the danger of slipping on the jagged and slippery stones, they ran with one thought and one thought only: to escape. More explosions rocked the mountainside above them, flinging lava high into the darkened sky, fueling the outpouring of molten rock.

They dashed ahead of the all-consuming avalanche, but it gained on them rapidly. The ridge line began to level out, and soon they reached the upper edge of the forest. Kate scanned the twisted trees, survivors of countless brutal storms, knowing that in no time they would perish in a flood of fire. As they continued downward, the jumbled rocks of the ridge were replaced by a soft mat of mosses and ferns. Before long, mighty trees towered over their heads, their branches laden with nests and cones and needles.

The air grew thick and smoky, and Kate realized they were entering the Dark Valley. Though her step faltered for an instant, she quickly picked up speed again. She had no choice.

The ground shook again, as the rumbling to the rear grew ever louder. Kate glanced over her shoulder to see a tidal wave of superheated lava descending on the forest, snapping tall trees like toothpicks, instantly cremating trunks and branches. In a matter of seconds, the wave would be upon them. She held the Broken Touchstone close to her chest, consoling herself that at least she had robbed Gashra of his greatest prize.

Just ahead, Kandeldandel halted at the base of an especially grand fir tree. He moved close to the trunk, whose girth almost equaled that of the Ancient One, and laid the hand that held his flute against its gnarled bark. Kate ran over to him, sensing that the Tinnani had chosen this tree as his place to die.

He turned a solemn face toward her and reached out his other hand. Kate took it wordlessly, stepping close to his side. They stood together by the trunk of the great tree, their feet upon its massive roots, as the hot wind of the onrushing lava blew against their faces. Trees cracked and swayed and burst into flames all around them.

Kandeldandel released a long, low hooting sound. The earth under them started to quiver and quake. Closing her eyes, Kate whispered some words of good-bye to Aunt Melanie, hoping that somehow, some way, she might one day hear them. As she started to say the same parting words to Laioni, the roots of the tree suddenly buckled and spread apart.

30

torchlight

THEY dropped swiftly down, landing with an echoing thud on the earthen floor of an underground cavern. Gnarled roots lined the walls around them. Kate looked up just in time to see the fir tree consumed by a rolling wave of flames, barely an instant before the roots above her head closed tight again. She turned to Kandeldandel, sitting beside her on the dirt floor, his face illuminated by the light of a torch affixed to the wall. The playful half grin had returned.

"Thought I'd keep you in suspense," he hooted casually.

"You did that all right," declared Kate. "Where in the world are we?"

"Can't you guess?"

As she scanned the hollow cavern around them, Kate's first thought was that this was yet another underground tunnel leading to the mountain. But if that were so, why wasn't it already filled with lava? No orange glow in here. The only light came from the slender torch suspended high above them.

Then Kate peered directly at the torch itself. It seemed

familiar in some way. It burned some sort of incandescent gas, but bore no markings at all except the lacy metal band that held it to the wall. Suddenly she remembered where she had seen torches like this before.

"Ho Shantero!" she exclaimed. "This must be one of your Tinnani tunnels."

"Indeed," answered Kandeldandel. "If you hadn't broken my wing back there, I could have taken you back by an easier route."

"You mean by the seat of my pants, like you did Jody."

The half grin broadened into a smile. "With you, I thought I could hoist you by your braid."

"No way." Kate beamed. "I'd pluck out all your feathers first."

The Tinnani's round eyes widened. "You wouldn't dare."

"Don't tempt me."

"Don't worry, I won't." Kandeldandel waved a hand toward the gleaming sphere. "Anybody who could get that away from the Wicked One is too much for just one little Tinnani."

Gazing into the luminous Touchstone, Kate hefted it in her hand. It felt remarkably light for an object of such unfathomable power. She caught Kandeldandel's eye. "Nobody's more surprised than me," she confessed. "Besides, I couldn't have done it without you." Nudging his leg, she added, "Guess I'll let you keep your feathers. For now, anyway."

Kandeldandel hooted happily.

Then Kate furrowed her brow. "What do you think happened to Gashra? Is he dead?"

"I doubt it," answered her friend. "He's been defeated before, only to rise again later. His plans are ruined, and he'll need some time to regain his strength, but he'll be back someday. You can count on it."

Kate, thinking of a time far in the future, nodded sadly. "Then let's go back to Ho Shantero. At least the Broken Touchstone can help your people repair the forest after the eruption."

Kandeldandel bobbed his head thoughtfully. "I hope

there's some forest left to repair." He indicated the sphere, and his voice brightened. "Don't get me wrong, though. There will be plenty of happy people when you march in with that little item in your hand."

"Especially the Chieftess—if, like she said, the Touchstone will make her daughter well again."

"That's right," agreed Kandeldandel. "Just to hear Fanona sing again . . . Believe me, that would be worth all our trouble."

"So what are we waiting for?" asked Kate, jumping to her feet.

Kandeldandel, wincing slightly from his injured wing, followed suit. "Let's go," he said, his deep voice echoing inside the cavern.

Since the tunnel had been designed to accommodate many Tinannis, both in flight and on foot, Kate could easily stand with ample headroom. Holding the sphere in the palm of her right hand, she passed beneath the glimmering torch. Suddenly, it flamed much stronger and brighter than before. Seeing this, Kandeldandel half grinned at her.

Kate returned the favor. "For someone who calls himself 'just one little Tinnani,' you sure managed to do your part for your old family name back there."

For an instant, the half grin disappeared and Kandeldandel regarded her intently. "You really think so?"

"Absolutely," replied Kate as she passed beneath another torch. It too swelled in strength, illuminating them both. They continued walking side by side, listening only to the reverberations of their footsteps in the tunnel. At length, Kate asked, "By the way, how did you ever get inside the mountain?"

"Same way you did. I just followed you, after turning invisible of course. Those Slimnis were so eager to avoid getting eaten, they didn't even notice."

"I thought something was following me back there in the cave. I'm glad it was you and not one of those ghosts." She stared ahead into the long tunnel, lit by a series of identically wrought torches. "How far is it to Ho Shantero, anyway?"

The Tinnani ruffled his feathers. "A good day's walk, I'm afraid. It's quicker than going overland, but not as fast as flying."

Kate teased, "At least with your broken wing I know you'll stick around for a while."

"Sad but true," answered Kandeldandel.

Suddenly Kate remembered Jody's injured arm. "What about the others?" she asked. "Jody and Monga—and Laioni. Are they all right?"

Kandeldandel fiddled nervously with his flute as he walked. "Jody's fine. He was fighting for his life, and doing pretty well for having only one arm. But then he got into some big trouble. He'd have been killed for sure if I hadn't carried him off."

"So that's why I couldn't find either of you when Laioni and I were escaping."

"And when I returned, you were gone." He clucked with satisfaction. "But I got back in time to help Monga finish off Sanbu."

"So he's really dead."

"Really."

Kate pulled on Kandeldandel's feathered arm, slowing him to a stop. "You're not telling me something."

The yellow eyes lowered. "Monga's dead too. Died with his jaws clamped around Sanbu's neck. The little fighter, he gave it everything he had."

"And more," added Kate somberly.

The Tinnani sighed. "He had more courage than a whole army of Slimnis."

Leaning toward him, Kate said, "Like another little fighter I remember."

Kandeldandel raised his eyes to meet hers. "I can't believe Arc is gone."

They started walking again, neither wanting to speak. Only after several minutes did Kate raise her voice again. "Do you think you might find yourself another owl someday? That spot on your shoulder looks kind of bare."

The Tinnani spun his head halfway around, then back again. "Haven't thought about it."

Kate reflected for a moment. "Thanks to that little owl, I'm here today."

"And thanks to you, Laioni is too. She told us what you did."

"You found her?" asked Kate as another torch sprang to life above her head.

"It took a little looking, but finally I saw the circle of melted ice from the air. When Jody and I got there, Laioni was just trying to make herself walk so she could follow you. But she couldn't have gone more than a few paces, she was so weak. She told us everything, though she didn't have to. The burned stick said it all. Jody stayed to help her get down off the mountain while I left to find you."

"I'm glad she's alive," said Kate quietly. "Even though the stick was my only chance to get back, I really had no choice."

"You had a choice," replied Kandeldandel. Then he added lightly, "Besides, your way of starting a fire was a lot easier than her way."

Kate nodded. "But now I know why Aunt Melanie always likes to pack matches." She shifted the blue day pack on her back. "It's hard to believe I'll never see her again."

Kandeldandel lifted his good wing and stretched it toward her. "You've made some other friends, though. Friends you will see again."

Together they strode down the tunnel. Many miles lay between them and the floating island of Ho Shantero, but they had much to discuss. Kandeldandel was particularly keen to learn the rules of modern baseball, though he soon proved himself a forgetful student. Kate, for her part, received her first instruction in how to hoot like an owl. As they moved past each successive torch, its power would instantly increase, flooding the tunnel in new and potent light.

31

the fire of love

ALTHOUGH they passed dozens of intersecting tunnels along the way, Kandeldandel guided them effortlessly
through each and every turn. At last, they approached a
circular terminus illuminated by a ring of torches. As the
Tinnani indicated the ceiling, Kate lifted her eyes to see a
small square of silver embedded in the stone high above them.

"The trapdoor," she said. "We must be under the lake."

Kandeldandel hooted lightheartedly, then suddenly
stopped. "I forgot about something."

"What?"

"These tunnels—we made them without stairs so that
no intruders could pass out of them if they somehow got
inside. The only way to go through that silver door is to
fly." He hunched his injured wing. "And that's impossible."

Kate looked from him to the trapdoor and back to him
again. "This is terrible," she moaned. "We come all this
way, and now we can't get through the front door."

"It could be weeks before anybody comes along to give
us a lift," muttered the Tinnani.

Kate squeezed the Broken Touchstone in frustration. "This is one of those times I wish I could fly."

At that, an infinitesimal glimmer of light flashed deep within the sphere. Before Kate could take another breath, she found herself rising slowly into the air. Too amazed to utter a sound, she rose to a height of approximately three feet off the ground, then drifted to one side until she hung suspended directly above Kandeldandel's head.

"Guess it's my chance to give you a ride," she said in amazement. "Grab onto my feet."

The astonished Tinnani did as he was instructed. With no effort whatsoever, Kate lifted him straight up into the air above the torches. Upon reaching the silver door, she pushed on its surface and felt it swing open with unexpected ease. She passed through the hole, carrying her passenger as well. After setting him down safely on the dark stone floor, she landed by his side and closed the trapdoor.

A sudden tearing sound ripped the air. A tall, treelike figure studded with knobby blue eyes reached through the transparent dome above them. As the appendage approached, Kate noticed that sunny yellow now replaced its former bone white color.

"Thika," said Kate, gazing into as many of the round blue eyes as she could.

"Kaitlyn," the watery voice replied. "This time, hsssh-whshhh, I have no need to ask you for the password."

"You sound stronger than before."

"Indeed I am," sloshed the many-eyed creature. "As are the other Guardians. Though we are told much of the forest land outside the crater has been destroyed, shwshhh, the Wicked One's power is spent. Already our lake grows cooler. And all this, whhshhh, thanks to you." Thika swayed back and forth with a series of quick undulations. "I only wish the temperature would never rise again."

"Yes, I know," answered Kate solemnly. "I can't do anything about that now."

"You have already done, hhsssh, more than you know," gurgled the Guardian. "For by saving our world in this time you have given the creatures of that later time a chance to save themselves. Hsh-whshh. Let us hope they are wise enough to do it."

Kate made no reply.

"Hey," piped up Kandeldandel, tapping his flute impatiently on his leg. "Can't you talk some other time? We have some important business up there."

"Whshhh, I see doing battle has not cured you of cheekiness," said Thika sharply. "But this time you are forgiven. I see you are injured, shhhwhsh, and the Chieftain and Chieftess await."

"And besides," added Kandeldandel, "I'm hungry."

The knobby appendage wrapped itself around the waists of the two travelers, avoiding the Tinnani's drooping wing. Instinctively, Kate pulled the sphere close to her chest. She barely had a chance to inhale before she was being transported through the deep blue waters of the lake. Upward Thika carried them, until the dome seemed nothing more than a distant bubble below them surrounded by several gangling yellow creatures.

She heard the tearing sound once more, then suddenly she could breathe again. As she turned to Kandeldandel, sitting in a puddle beside her own at the base of the narrow stone stairway, Thika the Guardian bent low before her in what could only be a bow.

"Thank you, shhwsh," the familiar voice sloshed. "Though you have only two eyes, hssshhwsh, you are now an honorary Guardian."

"You're welcome," said Kate, electing to take the words as a compliment.

With a rip and a pop, the many eyes of Thika disappeared down the hole in the middle of the stone floor. As Kate, dripping wet, rose to her feet, the torch lighting the stairway immediately swelled in luminosity. Kandeldandel stood and shook his feathers like a wet dog, then gestured to Kate to lead the way.

Up the spiraling stairs she climbed, Kandeldandel on her heels. He began to hum a playful tune, no less melodious than that of a meadowlark but with the deeper resonance of an owl. As the ascending torches flamed more brightly, Kate could see the enormously detailed carvings in the black stone of the stairwell. A pictorial history of the Tinnanis since the beginning of time unfolded before her eyes, a tale of mountains rising and forests blooming, of creatures birthing and living and dying, of struggle and harmony, of great migrations, of simple homes under the roots of trees, of loyalty and betrayal, of season following season time and time again.

Nearing the top of the stairs, she heard a faint tapping sound. As she rounded the final spiral, it grew steadily louder, until with a start she discovered its source. A lone Tinnani, shorter and plumper than Kandeldandel, was at work carving a new scene into the stone. He stood upon wooden scaffolding, one chisel in each hand and a sharp-tipped implement held between his teeth. Turning briefly to Kate he grunted in greeting before returning to his painstaking labor.

Peering over his folded wings, Kate examined the new petroglyph. She saw a huge mountain exploding, with the unmistakable image of Gashra raising his arms wrathfully deep inside the volcano. Animals, birds, and people fled from the fiery outpouring of lava, while towering trees collapsed and burned all around. Then, to her surprise, she spotted a small human figure, joined by a flute-bearing Tinnani, scurrying to escape the cataclysm. In the human figure's hands rested a radiant sphere, drawn larger than life, bearing a jagged crack across its surface.

"Can't you make me taller?" asked Kandeldandel, scrutinizing the scene from below the scaffolding.

The craftsman scowled at him, then went back to work. Kate grinned at Kandeldandel before continuing up the last few stairs. As she topped the stairway she confronted the entrance to the great chamber. She realized instantly how little of it she had seen on her first visit.

Lit by powerful torches, the rounded ceiling revealed an intricate engraving of a single majestic tree, whose many branches bore fruits and flowers of all sizes and descriptions. Its stature reminded Kate of the Ancient One, although she had never heard of any tree bearing such a wide variety of fruits. Then at once, she understood. Instead of bearing the normal fruits of the forest, this gargantuan tree supported all the living beings ever found in this world. Thousands upon thousands of creatures, from a tiny ant to a great woolly mammoth rested upon the branches. Elk and spider, butterfly and bear, mushroom and hornet, fern and salmon, Tinnani and human, each held a particular place in the pattern. Each stood as a separate individual, each stood as a member of the whole. The numberless branches of this tree wove back and forth in a complex interlocking design, bristling with energy and vitality. For this was the Tree of Life.

As she proceeded toward the chamber, she walked beside the circular stone fountain in the center of the floor. Its meager trickle instantly shot skyward in the form of an energetic geyser. Instead of clear water, however, the splashing fountain radiated a spectrum of intense colors. Flashing prismatic hues in every droplet, it shimmered like a cascade of liquid light.

"The Rainbow Fountain is restored," said Kandeldandel approvingly.

Kate nodded, but already her attention was caught by the assemblage of white-feathered figures she could see through the nearby archway of inlaid yellow and black stone. Passing beneath the archway, she entered a high-ceilinged chamber whose walls displayed a repeating motif of tall trees tended by soaring Tinnanis. As she entered, the flickering torches suspended from the chandelier flamed strongly, revealing the careful craftsmanship of the walls as well as the recessed stone ceiling, a vaulting dome of glittering concentric circles. After long absence, bright light again graced the central chamber of Ho Shantero.

Tinnanis filled the chamber, many more than the last time Kate stood within its walls. Some wore streaks of gray or red on their white plumage, some stood slightly taller than the rest of the crowd, some carried infants not much bigger than Arc upon their shoulders. All of them hushed with a brief fluttering of feathers when Kate stepped into the room. Kandeldandel, strutting behind her, puffed out his chest and held his head high. Watching the pair with wide owl eyes, the Tinnanis parted as they approached, clearing a pathway that led to the three carved thrones at the far end of the room.

The rounded body of the Chieftain filled the central throne of white whalebone, while the more slender Chieftess sat erect in the transparent throne to his left. The crystalline seat to the right remained empty, but next to it a frail white form lay on the bench of polished black stone.

As Kate drew nearer, the reclining form seemed to solidify, to harden before her eyes. Fanona. She was tall, like the Chieftess, with the same large, knowing eyes, and two small silvery tufts protruding from the top of her head. The Chieftess glanced in the direction of her daughter, whereupon a slow smile crossed her face.

Kate stood before the Chieftain and Chieftess, bowed slightly, then held in her outstretched arms the glowing red sphere. The Chieftain, dangling several mousetails from his mouth, reached his own hands toward it, quivering with anticipation.

"The Broken Touchstone," announced Kate.

"Dewiffud mby Kootwyn, mmmff, da Conquawa, mmmff," replied the Chieftain.

"It's best not to make pronouncements with your mouth full, dear," chided the Chieftess gently.

Glancing at her sharply, the Chieftain swallowed with all the subtlety of a croaking bullfrog. Then he wriggled in his throne and repeated, "Delivered by Kaitlyn the Conqueror."

"Call me Kate, please," she said as she handed him the sphere.

The Chieftain took it carefully in his hands, talons retracted so as not to scratch its surface, and studied it momentarily. Then he lifted it into position at the top of his throne. As it came into contact with the cup-shaped pedestal, the Broken Touchstone flashed brilliantly, causing the assembled Tinnanis in the chamber to cluck and hoot in admiration.

"Guests," bellowed the Chieftain. "Bring in the guests." Pausing for a second, he added, "And bring some more oysters while you're at it." Turning to Kate, he said, "We are most grateful to you."

"And to you," declared the Chieftess, looking straight at Kandeldandel.

At her words, Kandeldandel shifted nervously, dropping his flute with a clatter on the stone floor. Seeing this, the Chieftain closed his eyes and shook his white head in dismay.

At length he peered again at Kate. "You have saved our realm from destruction," he continued. "The Wicked One is defeated, the Touchstone is returned, and most precious of all," he said with a wave toward the black stone bench, "our daughter Fanona is nearly revived." Shifting his gaze to Kandeldandel, he studied the musician for a moment, his face showing both amazement and pride. Then he declared, "And you, Kandeldandel Zinzin, have brought honor both to yourself and your proud family."

The musician straightened his back and stood as tall as he could manage. This time he did not drop the flute. He bowed to the enthroned Tinnanis and hooted softly, "I was glad to be of service, Your Wingedness."

The chamber instantly echoed with a loud chorus of cheers, hoots, and hurrahs that shook the chandelier. Tinnanis bellowed and screeched, celebrating their great victory. They danced together in small circles, tossing loose feathers into the air. Then the Chieftess, who had been pensively fingering the string of gleaming pearls around her neck, snapped her jaw and raised her ruby-studded scepter. Silence descended.

"We are joyous," said the Chieftess in her clear, ringing voice, "for all the reasons you have heard. Yet we cannot forget that our joy is also mixed with sadness." She gazed again about the room, with the expression of someone who knows both triumph and tragedy. "While we cherish our victory, it came only at great cost. Much of the lowland forest beyond the walls of our crater is now lost, buried beneath a blanket of molten stone. Regeneration will require many lifetimes, and our friends who died cannot ever be returned. Many of our favorite places are wiped away forever."

She sighed, as her round eyes scanned the many faces filling the room. "And we have also lost something else. None of you, not even the youngest, will ever live to see the final healing of the Touchstone. The missing Fragment will never be found, for the only clues to its whereabouts were destroyed with the Stick of Fire."

The Chieftess focused on Kate, who averted her eyes. "Your sacrifice was great, but it was even greater than you know. For with the loss of the Fragment, the Touchstone must remain forever diminished. Though our daughter Fanona grows stronger by the minute, and will one day assume her place on the throne, she will never nurture the forest with the power that was prophesied."

She glanced toward the Touchstone. "But saddest of all is the glimpse of the future that I have seen in my dreams. Though the Halamis who survived will leave, seeking new lands to the south, other humans will eventually arrive. They will exist here, yet not live here. The forest to them will be only a tool, a meal to be consumed. They will not know it as a friend."

Ruffling her white wings, the Chieftess turned once again to Kate. "As the people without wonder arrive, I am afraid that the Tinnanis will be forced to leave. For, just like the trees, we cannot survive very long in such a world. Though I do not know with certainty that we will need to depart, my heart has little hope that we can stay.

"All that will remain are a few tokens of our past, such as this island, which will stay afloat for a while after we have abandoned it. Yet when the power of the Wicked One rises again several centuries from now, do not expect to

find any Tinnanis residing in the realm of Ho Shantero."
She hooted once softly. "Though I have lived now for many
thousands of years, I never have known a time of such
grief."

Kate, along with the rest of the room, stood in stony
silence. A grass-caped Tinnani flew to the throne of the
Chieftain bearing a tray of raw oysters. Uncharacteristically, he pushed them aside, grumbling something about
indigestion. At that moment, two familiar faces appeared
in the crowd, pushing their way toward the front.

"Laioni!" Kate cried, reaching to hug her friend tightly.

"You're safe," bubbled Laioni. "I thought I'd never see
you again."

Kate looked deep into her smiling eyes, then at the bandage around her thigh. "I thought I'd never see *you* again."

"You should not have burned the stick."

"I did what I did," answered Kate.

Then the joy in Laioni's face evaporated, and she pulled
back from the embrace. "Most of my people, you know,
were killed in the eruption."

"And your mother?"

Laioni's eyes grew misty. "My mother too. And my
grandmother and baby brother. They should have stayed
here in the crater instead of trying to return to the village.
My father, they say, has survived, but he is busy organizing
the few others who lived so we can find a new home.
Almost everyone I knew is gone."

Kate said softly, "They have joined Toru."

The Halami girl stiffened. "Did you see him?"

"I—I don't know, for sure."

"Then," said Laioni, "I will keep hoping he is alive. Perhaps we will find each other again, even if it's a long time
from now."

Kate viewed her lovingly. "I guess anything is possible."

Laioni's head drooped. "It's not possible to bring
Monga back to life. I wish he didn't have to die."

Hugging her again, Kate could only say, "I know."

"He loved me not like a dog, but like a brother."

"Or," whispered Kate, "like a sister."

Though her vision was clouded, Kate then caught sight of Jody, standing uncomfortably in a sea of Tinnanis. He no longer wore an arm sling, but his face was lined with pain. Without letting go of Laioni, she said, "You were great up there."

The boy shrugged, pushing the stray locks of red hair off his forehead. "A whole lot of good it did. Without that stick of yours, we'll never get back to where we belong. Now we're stuck forever in this crazy owls' nest."

The Chieftain glared at him.

"Sorry," said Kate, tugged herself by the thought of home.

Jody, seeing her consternation, said, "Look, don't be too hard on yourself, okay? You did it to save somebody's life, and that's important. More important than anything Honus Wagner ever did."

Kate almost smiled. She released Laioni and stepped toward him. "Thanks," she said quietly.

"Sure," he replied, his eyes fixed on hers.

Feeling a sudden surge of gratitude, Kate gave him an awkward hug. "You're a real friend," she said, then backed away again.

"Oh, I don't know." Blushing, he thrust his hands into the pockets of his jeans. "Oh, yeah," he said, clearly hoping to change the subject. "I thought you might want this." He pulled out a charred, jagged object. "It was all that was left of the stick when the fire went out. From inside the handle, I think. Thought you might want to keep it, though I'm not sure why."

As she took the object in her hand, Kate noticed a tiny glint of red beneath its blackened exterior. She rubbed it against her sweatshirt, revealing more of the true color. Suddenly, she gasped, closing her hand around it. Rushing toward the Chieftain's throne, she darted to its base and reached for the Broken Touchstone.

"What in the world?" sputtered the Chieftain. "Put that back!"

"Just a minute," answered Kate. Holding the Touchstone in one hand and the charred remains of the handle in the other, she brought them together, fitting the object into the crack in the sphere's surface. It slid inside perfectly.

A burst of bright red light and the sound of a distant explosion filled the chamber as the two pieces fused into one. Lifting the sphere above her head for all to see, Kate declared, "The Touchstone is healed."

A simultaneous exclamation of awe arose from the Tinnanis, like the breath of a unified being. Then from somewhere at the back of the room, several deep horns blew triumphantly. "The Touchstone is healed," chanted many voices at once. "The Touchstone is healed."

As Kate replaced the glowing sphere atop the throne, her eyes met those of the Chieftess, whose countenance now bore a new lightness. "So it was in the stick all the time," said the Tinnani in wonderment. Softly, she recited the words of the ancient prophecy:

Fragment, object of desire,
Shall be found anew.
One who bears the Stick of Fire
Holds the power true.

"This is a day to remember," announced the Chieftain. "Let there be a feast! A feast like none ever seen before in the history of my people." Above the cheers from the crowd, he commanded, "Break out my entire storehouse of delicacies!"

"Yes, Your Wingedness," replied the Tinnani wearing a long cape, before flying off toward one of the side tunnels.

Yet despite the rising tide of joy around her, Kate stood alone and detached. For although this place and time now bathed in the light of the unified Touchstone, her longing for her own place and time only increased.

Laioni, perceiving her sadness, came closer. "We have lost many, you and I." Then, taking Kate's hand in her own, she suggested, "Come with me, as one of my people. Join the Halamis—the few that are left—and help us find our new home."

Kate looked at her soulfully. "I will come with you," she said at last. "But my home will never be here, now. My true home I'll never see again."

"It is a pity," spoke the Chieftess, who had been listening. "The very act which found the Fragment, lost for so many ages, is the same act which denies you the ability to return to your own time. For when you destroyed the Stick of Fire, you destroyed its power to travel through time. There is no other way."

"No," declared another voice, resonant and melodic. "There is another way."

Kate turned to see Fanona, her strength now fully restored, standing atop the bench of black stone. She spread her wings to their fullest, her feathers gleaming whiter than purest quartz. The two silvery tufts atop her head made her height, already considerable for a Tinnani, even more dramatic. Her wide yellow eyes, deeply thoughtful, roamed from her mother to her father to the Touchstone and finally to Kate.

"You are right," said Fanona, "to say that the Stick of Fire is no more. Yet because it was destroyed in an act of love, new power has been created. As the words carved into its shaft foretold:

> *Fire of greed shall destroy;*
> *Fire of love shall create.*"

She lowered her wings. "The power that once resided in the stick now dwells in the Touchstone itself."

"Really?" asked Kate. "You mean I can go home?"

"You can?" demanded Jody. "How? When?"

"The Touchstone," answered Kate, indicating the luminous sphere. "She says it has the power."

"And she is right," declared the Chieftess, looking proudly

at her daughter. "Yes, just as the prophecy at her birth was right. She saw what I failed to see, that the fire of love can create."

"How do we get back?" asked Jody.

The Chieftain, eyeing the boy with disdain, raised his voice. "Tell us now, Fanona, how can the Touchstone send these people home?"

Fanona emitted a flowing, rippling sound, more like the gurgle of a brook than the call of an owl. "All it requires is the help of one being whose life stretches unbroken from this time into the future." She contemplated for a moment, then asked Kate, "Do you know any such being?"

"The Ancient One," she replied. "The redwood tree that brought us here."

"And so shall it take you home," declared Fanona.

Suddenly remembering the tree's imminent peril, Kate blurted, "But what if it's cut—killed, before we get back?"

"Then you will be stranded in a timeless prison, a shadow land cut off from time as you know it." Fanona concentrated her round eyes on Kate. "It is a serious risk. Are you sure you are willing to take it?"

"Stay here," whispered Laioni. "Stay here with me."

Kate shook her head. "I can't, Laioni. I want to go back, and I'll take my chances."

"Me too," said Jody.

"Then let us fly to the redwoods," urged Fanona. "There is no time to waste."

32

Iaioni's promise

LAST to arrive at the redwood grove was the Chieftain. Flapping his white wings vigorously, he landed beside the small bonfire built by some of his attendants, who had already started roasting a variety of delicacies over the hot coals.

"Don't forget the chives," he ordered as he folded his wings and straightened the silver band on his head. Then, facing his wife, he said, "Sorry to keep you waiting. Had to check on the preparations for tonight's feast."

"You're forgiven," replied the Chieftess. "Never let it be said that Chieftain Hockeltock de Notnot ever neglected his culinary duties."

Kate detected a note of resignation in her remark, but the Chieftain did not seem to notice. He stepped over to Fanona, who was seated on one of the burly roots of the Ancient One, gazing into the radiant Touchstone.

"It is good to see you well again," he hooted softly.

Fanona looked up and smiled at him. "It is good to be well, even though I do not yet have enough strength to bear the thought of leaving Ho Shantero."

"Don't trouble yourself with such thoughts now," answered the Chieftain. "You won't have to do that for a while yet."

"It is still too soon," said Fanona, ruffling her white wings. "I can only hope that the new people, the ones in my mother's dreams, might somehow come to change their ways. Then perhaps we will not have to leave at all."

Turning to Kate, the Chieftain asked, "Well? Are you ready to begin your voyage?"

"I'm ready," she declared. Then she faced Jody, who stood listlessly by the trunk of the great redwood, and called, "Are you set to go?"

He nodded his head, but did not look at her.

"He is going, isn't he?" asked the Chieftain.

"He's going," said Kate. "Something's bugging him, though."

"Perhaps he wishes he could stay for the feast," chuckled the Chieftain, tapping his belt buckle with his finger talons.

"Sorry we'll have to miss it. I'm sure it'll be great."

"That's all right," replied the plump Tinnani. "Leaves more food for the rest of us."

"I'm afraid I won't be bringing you any more peppermints," Kate said. "I mean, without the stick, I'm not going to be doing much time traveling."

The Chieftain frowned. "I hadn't thought about that."

"You might be surprised," said the Chieftess, stepping closer to Kate. "You might find another way to visit us. There is more than one way to travel through time. In any case, if you should ever return, you know you are always welcome."

"With peppermints, of course," added her husband hopefully.

Kate turned to face Kandeldandel, whose injured wing was thoroughly wrapped in bandages. "I wish you could come with me. You'd love some of the flute music that gets written in the next few centuries."

The half grin broadened slightly. "I'm sure. But I wish

you didn't have to go at all. I mean, what happens when I start to forget all those baseball rules you explained while we were walking in the tunnel?"

"That's another reason to find a new little owl for your shoulder," answered Kate. "He'll help you remember." She paused. "And when I forget how to make those owl calls you taught me, what do I do then?"

"That's easy," Kandeldandel answered. "Just practice them. The way I practice my flute."

He lifted his flute to his lips and started to play a sweet, prancing melody. Without any warning, a loud commotion arose from the Chieftain's attendants preparing the roasted delicacies. Kandeldandel, oblivious to any sounds other than his own music, continued to play jauntily.

Then the voice of one of the attendant Tinnanis rose above the clamor: "But how could the fire go out? There isn't even any wind!"

Kandeldandel's eyes widened and he shot a remorseful glance at Kate. He quickly lowered his flute, and the bonfire sprang to life once again. Cries of amazement came from the attendants.

"What luck," said the musician disgustedly.

Laughing, Kate whispered to him, "Don't worry. The Chieftain will get enough to eat tonight."

Kandeldandel grinned at her, bobbing his head from side to side. Then he stopped, his expression suddenly serious. "I'm going to miss you," he said. "Never thought I'd feel this way about, of all things, a human being. And it looks like this is our last conversation. Even though I hope to still be around in five hundred years, all the Tinnanis will probably have left the crater by then."

"Maybe you can sign up for some sort of special duty that would keep you here after everyone else," she suggested, trying to maintain a lighthearted tone.

"Doubtful," answered Kandeldandel. He moved nearer, then touched her arm lightly with his good wing. "No hugs, now," he cautioned sternly. "You're likely to break my other wing."

Kate, unable to find any words, merely ran a finger over the soft feathers of his shoulder.

At that, Kandeldandel turned and walked over to Jody, still standing off to the side. The Tinnani extended a hand, saying in his bass voice, "You did all right."

To Jody, his words sounded only like deep hooting. Yet the boy lifted his head and studied Kandeldandel thoughtfully. Slowly, reluctantly, he, too, extended a hand. They clasped, boy and Tinnani, and shook briefly.

Kate joined them as their hands separated. She looked quizzically at Jody. "Something's on your mind, I can tell."

Pushing back the loose locks of red hair, Jody said, "I just, well, I just . . ."

"Yes?"

"I just want you to know something."

"What's that?"

"I know you're gonna try to stop them from cutting down these redwoods."

"If they're still standing," Kate replied.

"Well," continued Jody, "I just hope you don't expect me to help."

"No, I don't expect that. All I ask is that you stay out of my way."

Jody gazed down at his feet, saying nothing.

"We'd better get going," said Kate. "If the Ancient One gets cut before we get back, the time tunnel will shut and this whole conversation's pointless."

"Before you go," spoke a familiar voice, "I want to say good-bye."

Kate spun around to face a dark-eyed Halami girl. They studied each other for a long moment. Finally, Kate reached into her pocket and pulled out her well-worn Swiss army knife. "Here. This is for you. It might come in handy."

Laioni hesitated, but when Kate pushed the knife toward her, she finally accepted it. "Your special tool," she said gratefully. Then, in a hopeful voice, she added, "Perhaps you can use the one carried by Aunt Lemony."

Kate smiled, choosing not to correct her.

"I have no gift for you," Laioni said somberly. "Only a promise."

"A promise?"

Laioni's features hardened with determination. "I promise to teach all the Halami ways I know to any children who survived the eruption. They will learn our songs, our stories, and our blessings. They will teach their own children, who will teach their children, forever into the future. That way, perhaps, in your world many, many years from now, there might be a few small reminders of the Halamis left to greet you."

"I won't need any reminders," said Kate. "But I know you'll do as you say. And I'll think of you often, even though I'll never get to see you again."

Laioni cocked her head to one side. She gazed intently at Kate for several seconds. "You cannot be certain of that."

At that moment, a lilting song filled the air. Its source was Fanona, still seated upon a massive root. As she lifted her resonant voice, all conversation ceased. Even the wind seemed to hold its breath, listening to the young Tinnani whose name meant Song That Never Dies.

The feather falls
drifting down through the clouds
hoping to fly
Away . . . under moon under sun

Touching the boughs
reaching upward like arms
seeking to fly
Afar . . . over trees over peaks

To find the ground
landing soft as a seed
again to fly
Above . . . beyond years beyond stars.

As her last note melted away, Fanona gracefully rose from her seat. Bearing the glowing Touchstone in her hands, she positioned herself just outside the hollow of the Ancient One. "It is time," she declared.

Then Kate heard a chorus of gentle hooting above her head. She looked up to see a dozen or more owls, of several different sizes and colorings, resting in the lower branches of the great redwood. Some of the owls ruffled their wings and bobbed their heads, while others sat motionless on their perches. All of them watched the scene below with wide, understanding eyes.

She turned for the last time to Laioni. "Good-bye," she said, her voice barely audible above the calls of the assembled owls.

"Halma-dru," came the reply.

Kate stepped to the base of the massive tree. As she passed in front of the Chieftain, he tugged her sleeve and whispered, "Don't forget what to bring, if you ever come back."

Nodding, she ducked into the hollow. She sat there, smelling once again the tree's moist resins, as Jody entered. He glanced at her doubtfully before squeezing in beside her. She paid no attention, concentrating instead on her echoing memory of Laioni's final word.

The owls' hooting abruptly ceased. A sudden flash of red light filled the hollow. Kate felt herself whirling, whirling impossibly fast, before she lost consciousness.

33

deep roots

Kate awoke, yet her body slept on. Her conscious mind swelled with strange new sensations, alert and aware, while her skin and bones and muscles felt numb, or worse than numb. Her body felt nothing at all, not even the absence of feeling. It was detached. Departed. Gone.

"Where am I?" she cried, and her words rang emptily in the airy darkness.

"What happened?" she called again.

No answer came. She felt as if she were floating somehow. Blackness surrounded her. She could see nothing, hear nothing, feel nothing. Not even the pulse of her own heartbeat broke the omnipresent silence.

Then, a scent. Barely present, neither far away nor near at hand. Elusive. Subtle. Tingling her, tickling her. Fresh and potent, fragrant as crushed pine needles. A wet smell, ripe with resins. Flowing through and around her, holding her essence like water in a cup. The scent of the forest, so strong that it seemed alive.

"Where am I?"

Still no answer. No sound at all.

And then, echoing out of the fragrant air itself, she heard a voice. Deeper than the deepest double bass, the voice vibrated from both above and below.

"I hold you, small friend. I hold you and protect you."

It was the voice of the Ancient One.

Kate's consciousness whirled. Could it be true? Was her mind, or whatever was left of her mind, just playing tricks?

"Tell me your wish," reverberated the voice. The smell of moist resins grew stronger.

"I—I want to go home," she answered. "To my own time. To the twentieth century."

The air around her shuddered, as if a powerful wind had shaken the redwood down to the roots. "Are you certain? That is a time of great sadness, great pain."

"It's my time," she answered, "and I want to go there."

Silence ensued, tense and uneasy, until the Ancient One spoke again. "Not all creatures who stand upright and vertical know they are connected to everything else. Some of your kind know only their loneliness. They have lost their own roots, drifting aimlessly as fireweed seeds. They are angry, and might hurt you if you go there."

"I know," she answered. "But they might hurt Aunt Melanie, too, and I've got to stop them. I've got to." She felt a piercing, knifelike pain slice through her being. "And they'll hurt you too. They'll try to cut you down! You've got to take me back. Now. Before it's too late."

The tree seemed to sigh deeply, and she could almost feel lacelike branches stirring around her. "Perhaps. Perhaps. Perhaps. But first you must go deeper within me. You must understand things you never understood before. It will be hard for you, very hard. For you are of a race that has forgotten how to stand still. To stop all running, all racing, all searching—to sink instead your roots in a single place, to watch seasons roll past by the thousands. And to stand tall and straight, anchored equally in earth and sky, to bend with the wind but not to break, to bear your own weight gladly."

As she listened to the low, richly toned voice, Kate began to hear something else, something even deeper than the voice itself. It was a coursing sound, like the surging of several rivers. She realized with a start that it must be the sound of resins moving through the trunk and limbs of the tree. And, strangely, through her own self as well.

Then she heard something more. With all her concentration, she listened to a distant gurgling sound. It came from far below her, rising from the deepest roots of the tree. They were drinking, drawing sustenance from the soil.

Another sound joined with the rest, completing the pattern, making music both rhythmic and delicate. Like an intricate fugue, it ran from the tips of the remotest needles all the way down the massive column of heartwood and through the fibrous filament of bark embracing the body of the redwood. Back and forth, in and out, always changing, always the same. This was the sound, Kate realized at last, of the tree itself breathing. The sound of air being cleansed and purified for all the creatures of the forest. The sound of life being exchanged for life, breath for breath.

"Great tree," spoke Kate in wonder. "I feel so young, and you are so very, very old."

A full, resonant laughter filled the air, stirring even the sturdiest branches. "I am not so young as you, perhaps, but old I surely am not. The mountains, they are old. The oceans, they are old. The sun is older still, as are the stars. And how old is the cloud, whose body is made from the vapors of an earlier cloud that once watered the soil, then flowed to the river, then rose again into the sky? I am part of the very first seed, planted in the light of the earliest dawn. And so are you. So perhaps we are neither older nor younger, but truly the same age."

As she listened to the rhythmic breathing of the tree, Kate felt herself beginning to breathe in unison. A sense of her body was slowly returning, a body that bent and swayed with the fragrant wind. Every element of her being stretched upward and downward, pulling taller and straighter without end. Her arms became supple, sinewy limbs; her feet drove deeply into the soil and anchored there. She stood enormously tall and strong, while humility and peace flowed through her veins. Centered and surrounded, sturdy and whole, she felt content beyond human experience.

A sweep of time swirled past, seconds into hours, days into seasons, years into centuries. Spring: azaleas blossoming and pink sorrel flowering. Summer: bright light scattering through the morning mist, scents of wild ginger and licorice fern. Autumn: harsh winds shaking branches, gentle winds bearing geese. Winter: ceaseless rains, frosty gales, more rains brewing. Again and again, again and again. Seasons without end, years beyond count.

Fire! Flames scar her outer bark, charring even her heartwood. But she survives, standing tall, saddened by the loss of a few less sturdy friends. Winds, powerful winds. Healing the scar, she grows new girth above the burn to balance better her colossal weight. Near to the ground, a radial crack develops, very small at first, becoming a home for generations of insects and a restaurant for generations of birds. Young redwoods sprout at her base, yearning for life, full of green vitality.

White rot infects her, stinging with pain, lasting many cycles of seasons. Winds and rain. Winds and rain. Hail as big as spruce cones. Internal stresses creep into the body of a large lower branch until, with the next wild wind, it splinters and breaks apart, rocking her very roots. *Hooo-hooo, hooo-hooo.* Fire again! This time much more is lost—bark, sapwood, heartwood. Some of the old fire scar is obliterated by the new. Healing, waiting, balancing in the shifting soil, standing sturdy throughout. Winter, spring, summer, autumn. New growth works its way across the scar.

A lone Tinnani stands beneath her boughs, spreads his white wings in awe. Welcome, Little One. The Tinnani lowers his head sadly, departs from the grove. Gale winds, broken branches. Mist, mist, mist. An earthquake shatters the stillness one winter morning. As the earth trembles, the great roots grip tightly, feeling the strain, yet hold firm. *Hooo-hooo, hooo-hooo*. Rhododendrons, azaleas, salmonberry, huckleberry. Five-finger fern takes root at her base, mingling with mosses and maidenhair. A doe and her spotted fawn step serenely into the glade, nibbling at the ferns.

Then, suddenly: A sound unlike any other sound ever heard fills the forest. Piercing, screeching, banishing forever the centuries of stillness. A shudder, a scream of pain erupts from her whole being. Stop! Stop, please. Go away, leave in peace. The pain deepens. The sound grows louder.

It is the sound of chain saws.

34

new light
in the forest

DAZEDLY, Kate shook her head. The ridge of hard wood pushing against her back told her she possessed a human body again. Instinctively, she reached to touch her long braid, feeling the strands of hair between her fingers. In the dim light she could see Jody seated across from her, looking rather dazed himself.

The hollow. They were once again in the hollow. The gargantuan trunk of the Ancient One embraced them both. She could still feel the watery breathing of the redwood pulsing through her veins. She could, even now, hear the rumble of its deep voice echoing in her ears.

Then she heard something else. A whining, screeching, screaming sound.

"No!" she cried, leaping to her feet and springing out of the hollow.

Billy, wearing his weather-beaten hard hat, held his chain saw firmly as it tore into the flesh of the Ancient One. His red T-shirt, wet with perspiration, hung untucked around his waist. He leaned into the saw, spraying chips of bark and sawdust into the air.

Even as her eyes adjusted to the light outside the hollow, Kate instantly perceived the plight of the great tree. A huge notch had already been cut in the trunk, opposite the side where Billy now worked. Yet she hesitated, feeling helpless to stop the big man. Looking around desperately for anyone or anything that might help, she could see no more than a few half-melted hailstones on the ground, evidence that the storm had passed some time ago. But she saw no one else in the grove. No sign of Aunt Melanie, nor even another logger.

"Stop!" she cried at the top of her lungs, trying to attract Billy's attention. "Please, stop."

But he could not hear her over the roar of the chain saw. Sawdust continued to fly, as he ripped ever deeper into the trunk of the redwood.

Then she spotted a two-gallon can of gasoline, resting on an exposed root a few feet behind Billy. She lunged for it. Lifting the can with both hands, she raised it over her head. Stepping as close to Billy as she dared, she threw it at his broad back.

"Oww," cried the surprised logger. He straightened up, yanked the saw out of the tree trunk, cut the engine, and whirled around. Seeing the gasoline can at his feet, his eyes flashed with anger and immediately focused on Kate.

"What do you think you're doing?" he demanded.

"Stop cutting," pleaded Kate. "You can't cut down this tree."

"I can cut anything I want," retorted Billy. "Now get out of my way. It's dangerous this close, and you're gonna get hurt."

As he placed his heavy boot on the engine housing, preparing to start the saw again, Kate stepped closer. "Please stop. Please."

"Out of my way," the man growled. "I've got work to do. I'd still have help, too, if that old aunt of yours hadn't talked Frank into convincing the other guys to quit." He grasped the handle of the starter cord. "Never saw such a bunch of chicken hearts in my life. Those that weren't scared off by the storm—just because Harry got too close to some lightning bolt—were scared off by Frank's baloney. Can't believe they bought that line about not doing anybody any good. Even Sly fell for it." He shook his head in dismay. "Well, that leaves me, and I'm gonna get at least a few of these mothers before the day is out. Already close to finishing off this big one here."

"But—"

"Get away!" commanded Billy.

Kate stood immobile.

"I said, get away." Billy dropped the starter cord and pulled her by the arm to the other side of the grove. "Now stay here."

"I'll watch her for you," said someone walking toward them.

"Jody!" exclaimed Kate. "He's going to—"

"Shut up," said the boy with a scowl. Turning to Billy, he declared, "I'll make sure she won't bother you."

"All right," grumbled the logger. "But don't mess it up like you did last time."

Jody's face reddened. "I won't." Then, as Billy turned to go, Jody caught his arm. "But first, can I start your saw for you? I always liked that big model, and my granddad never lets me start his."

"Oh, all right," replied Billy, striding back to the tree. "Just make it quick."

"But Jody," cried Kate. "You can't!"

"Wanna bet?" replied Jody, sprinting over to the chain saw. He placed his boot against the housing for support. Then, leaving one hand in his pocket, he grabbed the handle with the other hand and started to extend the cord.

"No, don't," cried Kate, running several paces closer. Billy then turned toward her, eyeing her sternly, and she froze. Glowering at Jody, she muttered, "I should have known."

Testing the tension on the cord, Jody stretched it slowly away from the housing. Six, twelve, eighteen inches.

"C'mon, hurry," said Billy impatiently.

"Don't," Kate shouted in desperation.

At that instant Jody pulled his other hand from his pocket, clasping his pocket knife. He quickly pulled open the blade. Then, with a swift downward swipe, he slashed the starter rope in two. The cut cord snapped back into the housing.

"Hey," exclaimed Billy, staring in disbelief at the now-inoperable saw. "What the hell are you doing?"

"Just helping out," replied the red-haired boy, smirking as he stuffed the handle and most of the starter cord into his pocket.

Furious, Billy started after him. Jody leaped over a fallen branch and dashed as fast as he could into the forest with the big man on his heels.

Kate felt like cheering. Before she could utter a sound, however, Billy halted his pursuit after just a few steps. He spun to his right, stooped over, and lifted from the bushes another chain saw, evidently left behind by another logger fleeing from the storm. Cursing to himself, he stepped on the housing, yanked the starter cord, and immediately gunned the engine. Without even glancing at Kate, he strode purposefully back to the Ancient One and plunged the chain saw deep into its trunk.

As the blade tore into the body of the tree, Kate suddenly felt a searing pain in her side. Gasping, she saw that Billy had pierced the innermost core of the trunk. As he drove his saw deeper, her pain intensified, as if a serrated knife had sliced into her ribs, pulling back and forth, ripping at her abdomen. She stumbled, then tripped on a rock just behind her, twisting her knee badly as she fell.

"Ehhh," she moaned, rolling to one side. She tried to stand, but her leg buckled underneath her. "Aunt Melanie," she wailed, as the pain in both her knee and her torso grew worse. "Help me." But her words were lost in the din of the chain saw.

Oblivious to her agony, Billy pushed the saw blade farther into the heart of the tree. Sawdust spewed in all directions. The towering redwood leaned slightly in the direction of the notch in its trunk—and in the direction of Kate.

Meanwhile the pain in her abdomen swelled steadily. Writhing on the ground, she thought she would pass out. Then, all of a sudden, the pain ceased. She lay on her back, breathing heavily, utterly exhausted. But for the ongoing throbbing in her knee, she was hardly sure she was still alive. Above her she saw the majestic boughs that still felt like limbs of her own, supported by the massive trunk that linked earth to sky, past to present. With all her heart she hoped that the tree might survive this assault, just as it had survived the assaults of so many fires, storms, and earthquakes in the past. She tried to sit up, but was still too weak to move.

Slowly, the redwood began swaying from side to side. With a tremble that reached from its roots to its tallest canopy, it tottered on its base, wobbling precariously. The bulging roots, coated with sawdust, held the soil as firmly as ever, but could no longer support the weight of the great tree. Yet still it stood. This tree would not go down easily.

At last Billy pulled out his saw, cut the engine, and backed quickly away from the trunk. Only a thin shaft of hinge wood remained of the once-sturdy column. Although Kate was now much nearer to the tree than himself, he could not see her from his new position. He watched with satisfaction as the redwood tilted still farther to one side. Holding itself high to the very last, it seemed to stand suspended by the sky alone for a long and perilous moment.

Then, in slow motion, the Ancient One leaned, leaned some more, leaned even more. Billy stepped sideways to get a better view, when suddenly he caught sight of Kate, doing her best to crawl clumsily away from the tree.

"Move!" he shouted.

"I'm trying," she panted, dragging herself across the ground.

Without pausing to think, Billy ran toward her, even as the hinge wood finally shattered with an ear-splitting *crack,* as unforgiving as a backbone snapping in two. Grabbing her by the waist, he carried her out of the way just before the tree toppled to the ground with a thunderous crash. Cones and small branches rained down on them, and the entire forest shook from floor to ceiling.

Panting heavily, Billy dropped Kate on a bed of moss-covered sticks and tumbled to the ground beside her. He wiped the perspiration from his eyes with his T-shirt, then glared at the ungainly heap at his side.

"Of all the damn fool things," he said angrily. "You could've gotten us both killed."

Kate pushed herself slowly to a sitting position, wincing as she leaned against her injured knee. Her eyes met Billy's briefly, then looked past him to the fallen form in the center of the grove. She could not believe that a being so magnificent as the Ancient One was now destined to be reduced to an assortment of patio chairs, redwood decks, and hot tub sidings. More than a millennium of life— destroyed in no time at all by a single chain saw. Her gaze lifted to the gaping hole against the sky where the tree had once stood. Despite the new light now reaching the forest floor, she felt submerged in darkness.

"Don't you even say thanks?" fumed Billy. "I saved your life, for Pete's sake."

Sadly, she swung her face toward him, her eyes brimming with tears. "Thanks," she whispered, then turned away again.

For a long moment, Billy looked at her. Then, with a disgusted grunt, he rose to his feet. He stepped over to the chain saw, started to bend down to retrieve it, then caught himself. He straightened, glancing again at the mournful girl seated at the edge of the grove. A frown crossed his face and he said something under his breath. Then he turned and walked off sullenly into the forest.

A few moments later, a diminutive figure stole quietly out of the trees to Kate's side. Feeling herself suddenly embraced, she faced the person kneeling next to her. Blinking to see more clearly, she found herself looking straight into a pair of warm, ebony-colored eyes.

"Aunt Melanie," she said weakly. "It's you."

"It's me, dear," answered the white-haired woman, hugging her. At last she drew back, her shell earrings clinking softly as she moved. "I'm so glad you're all right. The walking stick kept you safe, didn't it?"

Kate could only nod.

The dark eyes studied her knowingly. "I wish I could have been with you."

"You were," answered Kate. Then she blurted, "The Ancient One. Billy—"

"I know, I know." She brushed a hand through her white curls. "But he's stopped now. Frank and I saw him heading for his truck as we were coming back here to try to find you."

"How—how could he?" Tears again filled her eyes.

Aunt Melanie looked to the ground. As she started to speak, she noticed Kate's swollen knee. "Your leg!" she exclaimed. "We should get you to the doctor."

"It hurts," sobbed Kate. "It hurts so much."

Aunt Melanie nodded, knowing full well that Kate did not mean the pain in her leg.

Just then a pair of heavy leather boots crunched toward them on the needles. A gaunt-looking man bent down to them. "Is she hurt?"

"Her knee, Frank."

"Let's take her back to town. Doc Harris can put anything back together."

Aunt Melanie glanced toward the fallen redwood. "Almost anything," she whispered.

afterword

FOR Kate, the next year flew past with the speed of a fast pitch. Her knee healed rapidly, and the Bulldogs' first-string shortstop was soon back on the field. But in contrast to prior years, softball was not Kate's sole diversion from classes. The school play, the Language Club, and the Time Travel Book Club (which she co-founded) also required lots of attention. She barely had any time to toss sticks with Cumberland in the yard, or even to write an occasional letter to Aunt Melanie.

Not that she didn't often wonder about Lost Crater, about Laioni and Kandeldandel, about the new park Aunt Melanie's letters described, about Jody and Frank and Billy. Sometimes, too, she woke up in the middle of the night, frightened by a dream about a giant tree crashing down on top of her. Yet just as often, she was overwhelmed with a craving for fresh huckleberry pie and spice tea. So it was with genuine enthusiasm that she accepted Aunt Melanie's invitation to visit her again during June. She did not need her parents' encouragement to say yes, as she had last year. This time, however, she packed her waterproof boots.

Once she arrived, she felt almost as if she had never left. The days were filled with fresh oatmeal cookies on top of homemade pie, the moist fragrance of spruce trees outside the cottage, the familiar musty smell within, the feeling of snuggling inside a soft quilt before the fire, laughter at Aunt Melanie's mischievous jokes, and of course the occasional peppermint candy. One evening Frank and Jody came by for supper, and Frank was coaxed to play his harmonica late into the night. After they left, Aunt Melanie read a poem that Jody had written about the pain of losing loved ones, a poem that Kate felt she could have written herself.

Kate and her great-aunt took walks together. They played Pooh Sticks on the bridge. They ate and ate, and ate some more. They talked freely, about the town's changes, about cooking with local herbs, about times good and bad.

And they talked about Kate's adventure. About Laioni, about Kandeldandel, about Gashra. The Touchstone. Fanona, whose voice Kate could still hear in her memory. The floating island of Ho Shantero. The Chieftain and Chieftess. Parching seeds the Halami way. The Stick of Fire. The Dark Valley. Sanbu. Monga. Nyla and her six Stonehag sisters. Whether Tinnanis still inhabited Lost Crater. The Slimnis. Arc. Thika. The Ancient One. And so much more. Although Aunt Melanie listened closely to each of Kate's descriptions, she seemed to pay special attention to any details regarding Laioni.

"You would have liked her," said Kate before slurping noisily from her mug of hot chocolate.

The white-haired woman smiled mysteriously. "I'm sure."

"I couldn't believe how much she was like you."

"We're all cut from the same cloth, you know," said Aunt Melanie. "Makes no difference whether we were born five years ago or five hundred years ago, whether we live on this side of the ocean or another." She scrutinized

Kate thoughtfully. "I imagine the same thing even holds true for tree spirits."

Suddenly Aunt Melanie tossed aside her quilt, rudely awakening Atha, who was curled up by her side. "That reminds me. I almost forgot. There's something you left behind last time you visited."

She darted out of the living room, trailed by Atha padding softly behind her. Soon the sound of boxes and furniture being slid around, plus a few angry grumbles, filled the cottage. Finally she returned, bearing two dilapidated sneakers, ragged and torn. One of them sported luminous green laces, while the other's laces were burned as black as charcoal.

"My sneakers!" exclaimed Kate. "I thought I'd lost them. I can't believe you kept them for a whole year."

"Just thought you might like to see them again." She added with a grin, "Though for the life of me I'll never understand how you could have let those nice green shoelaces get ruined."

"It's amazing, really. That the thing that brought me to my senses when Gashra was doing his best to trick me— was those stupid laces."

The elder nodded. "Now that's an impressive connection across time and space. Your grandfather would have loved to hear about it."

Kate laughed out loud. "That's for sure."

"By the way, how did your hand heal?"

"Just fine, except for this little scar."

Aunt Melanie took a peppermint from the abalone shell, popped it into her mouth, and offered one to her guest. "Here. Have one for the road."

"The road? Are we going someplace?"

She crunched down on the peppermint, then swallowed. "Yes, dear. We're going up to Lost Crater."

"Really? Is there still time today?"

"Just enough. The road's been paved. Of course, if you'd rather use the old ladder again, we could wait until tomorrow and go in that way."

Kate rolled her eyes. "Let's take the road."

Aunt Melanie smiled. "Somehow, that's what I thought you'd say. Let's go, then. There's something in the redwood grove I want you to see. A surprise." She gave Kate's hand a squeeze. "And don't worry. This time I'll remember to bring matches."

SOON Kate found herself walking with Aunt Melanie along a newly completed trail that started at the hole blasted one year ago in the wall of the crater, descended over the rocky slope and through the swamp, then wound its way deep into the Hidden Forest. Not so hidden anymore, Kate reflected, thinking of the large asphalt parking lot where Trusty sat next to a dozen other cars. Presently they came to a large painted sign saying:

> Welcome to Cronon's Crater Park, containing the northernmost stand of ancient redwood trees in existence. Please remain on the trail. Exploration of other parts of the crater is strictly prohibited until scientific studies are completed.

As they moved down the trail, Kate drank in the rich aromas, abundant sounds, and lush green growth of this forest. Mist curled through the branches above; needles padded the ground below. With every step deeper into the virgin woods, she felt embraced by the vibrant array of life around her. Embraced, it almost seemed, by friends. Yet she also felt queasy, even a little bit frightened, to confront the sawed-off tombstone of the great redwood.

At one point she heard a soft laughter beside her and turned to Aunt Melanie. "What's so funny?"

"Oh," she replied, "I was just thinking about that silly Chieftain. Imagine thinking peppermints are such a great delicacy."

"I knew you'd get a kick out of that."

Aunt Melanie nodded. "Almost as much of a kick as I

get from owning a pack with a genuine arrow hole in it."
She swiveled slightly to reveal the prominent stitches in
the material of the blue day pack. "Awfully glad it wasn't
you instead."

"So am I," Kate replied.

Abruptly Kate halted. She stood again at the edge of
the clearing, facing the towering grove of redwood trees.
Upward they climbed, like columns supporting the dome
of the sky. A rush of reverence filled her, along with a
whisper of peace she had not felt for a year. And something
more, something strange, almost like a sense of gratitude
lingering among the boughs.

Then, in the center of the grove, she saw the stump. The
rest of the massive tree had been removed, so that its
remains jutted out of the ground with unnatural severity.
As Kate moved closer, she saw several small signs affixed
to the stump. One of them, positioned to face the trail,
read: *Height: 363 feet. Circumference: 27 feet. Weight:
513 tons. Age: 1,423 years.* On the face of the stump, signs
marked particular tree rings on the cambium or heartwood.
Said one: *Charlemagne crowned Emperor, 800 A.D.* Said
another: *Norman conquest of England, 1066 A.D.* Then,
moving outward toward the bark: *Eruption of Brimstone
Peak, 1452 A.D.; Fire scar, 1583 A.D.; Declaration of
Independence signed, 1776 A.D.; Severe fire scar, 1810
A.D.; Earthquake damage, 1847 A.D.* Last of all, at the
outer edge of the trunk, was this sign: *Felled by loggers,
1992 A.D.*

Turning to face Aunt Melanie, Kate asked, "Is this what
you meant by a surprise? These signs?"

The white head moved slowly from side to side. "Look
again."

Scrutinizing the stump once more, Kate noted the intricately drawn rings, some so close together they could
barely be distinguished. She scanned the thick band of
ridged bark encircling the wood, the burly roots at the
base. Yet she could not find anything that could have
prompted Aunt Melanie's interest.

Suddenly she noticed something else. At the far edge of the stump, lifting its tiny head skyward, sprouted a single young seedling. It stood barely a foot tall, yet its branches were lined with new-growth needles, no less green than a pair of shoelaces she had once worn.

She glanced at Aunt Melanie, who smiled at her gently. Then she stepped over to the seedling and bent lower to touch it. Running her finger down its length, all the way to the delicate, hairlike roots, she could feel both sturdiness and suppleness in its fibers. The young redwood held itself with unmistakable dignity, seemingly aware of what had stood before on the same spot.

As she straightened up, Kate caught sight of a small, rust-colored owl resting on the lowest branch of a neighboring tree. He studied her with wide brown eyes above flowing whisker-feathers, looking for all the world like a great-great-great grandson of Arc. The owl fluttered his wings slightly.

Then, from another direction, Kate heard the sound of an owl hooting deeply, richly. It hung eerily in the air, like the call of a distant flute.

THE MERLIN EFFECT

PUFFIN BOOKS
Published by the Penguin Group
Penguin Group (USA) LLC
375 Hudson Street
New York, New York 10014

USA * Canada * UK * Ireland * Australia
New Zealand * India * South Africa * China

penguin.com
A Penguin Random House Company

First published in the United States of America by Philomel Books,
a division of Penguin Putnam Books for Young Readers, 1994
Published by Ace Books, a division of Penguin Group (USA) Inc., 2004
Published by Puffin Books, an imprint of Penguin Young Readers Group, 2014

THE LIBRARY OF CONGRESS HAS CATALOGED THE PHILOMEL BOOKS EDITION AS FOLLOWS:
Barron, T. A.
The Merlin Effect / by T. A. Barron.
p. cm.
Summary: When she joins her father and several others investigating a strange whirlpool and
possible sunken treasure ship off the coast of Baja California, thirteen-year-old Kate is drawn into
a centuries-old conflict between Merlin and the evil Nimue.
ISBN 978-0-399-22689-2
[1. Merlin (Legendary character)—Juvenile Fiction. 2. Buried treasure—Fiction.
3. Fathers and daughters—Fiction.] I. Title.
PZ7.B27567Me 1994 [Fic]—dc20 93-36234 CIP AC

This omnibus ISBN 978-0-14-751032-7

Printed in the United States of America

1 3 5 7 9 10 8 6 4 2

To my father,
ARCH BARRON

With special appreciation to
BROOKS,
age four, who will one day sing with the whales
and to
TERRY,
who values the empty places between stars
as well as the stars themselves

Thanks also to those who advised me on matters of
science: Eric, on genetics; Charlie, on whirlpools;
Celia, on marine flora and fauna; and a certain gray
whale off Baja California, who swam up to my kayak
and let me touch his back.

The whirlpool drowned the treasure ship
Upon that dreadful morn,
And buried it beneath the waves
Along with Merlin's Horn.

And so today the ship's at rest,
Removed from ocean gales,
Surrounded by a circle strange
Of ever-singing whales.

A prophesy clings to the ship
Like barnacles to wood.
Its origins remain unknown,
Its words not understood:

One day the sun will fail to rise,
The dead will die,
    And then
For Merlin's Horn to find its home,
The ship must sail again.

—fragments from
"The Ballad of the *Resurrección*"

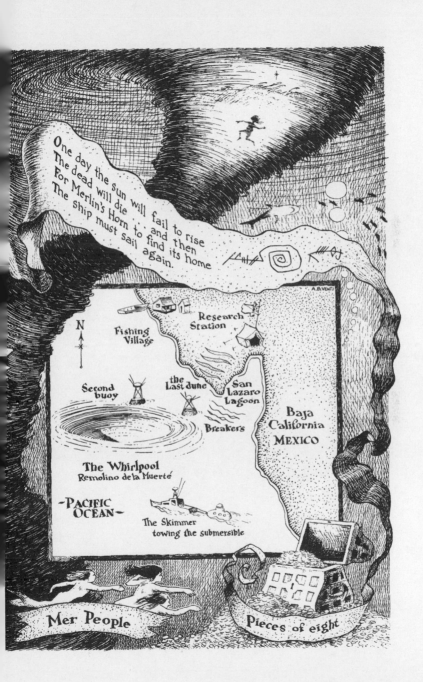

One day the sun will fail to rise
The dead will die . . . and then
For Merlin's Horn to find its home
The ship must sail again.

A.B.VENTI

N

Fishing Village

Research Station

Second buoy

the Last dune

San Lazaro Lagoon

Breakers

Baja California

MEXICO

The Whirlpool
Remolino de la Muerté

-PACIFIC OCEAN-

The Skimmer
towing the submersible

Mer People

Pieces of eight

contents

PART ONE

Beyond the Lagoon

1

at sea

FARTHER from shore, nearer to death.

With every pull of her paddle, Kate recalled the much-repeated warning about these waters. Yet today felt different. Today the sea looked tranquil, even inviting.

Her arms, brown after almost a month in the Baja California sun, churned rhythmically. The kayak cut through the water, slicing the glassy green walls that rose and fell like a heaving chest. As the protected lagoon receded behind her, open ocean stretched before her. The swollen sun drifted low on the horizon, glowing like a lump of melting gold.

A wave slapped the kayak, drenching her. She shook herself, pulled a piece of kelp off her forearm, then resumed paddling.

She glided past the forest of mangroves lining the mouth of the lagoon. Despite the low tide, she skirted within a few feet of their long, spindly roots. Planted in the mud, they resembled a family of long-legged waders. An immature heron resting on a branch watched her slide by, but Kate's attention had turned to a copper-stained mound at the end of the bay. The last dune. And beyond it, the breakers.

Never been out this far before, she thought. What a place to see the sunset! Too bad she had waited so long to venture out. Now only a few more days remained before she would have to leave all this for good.

She lay the paddle across her lap, licking the salt from her sunburned lips. As the vessel coasted quietly with the current, she listened to the trickle of water running down the ends of the paddle. Slowly, the sun ignited sea and sky with streaks of crimson. Just beneath the waves, a web of golden light shimmered.

A plover swooped past, barely a foot above her head, searching for a crab-meat supper. Meanwhile, two sand-pipers, standing one legged in the shadow of the dune, chittered noisily next to the hissing, rushing waves. Kate drew in a deep breath, feeling the warmth of the fading sun on her face. At midday, it had struck with brutal force, yet now it soothed like a gentle massage.

As the current pulled her past the last dune, she scanned the line of whitecaps ahead. The breakers splashed and sucked, a stark barrier of volcanic rock. Yet the ocean beyond looked calm, serene, almost deserving of the name Pacific. At this moment, it was hard to believe all those tales of sudden squalls, murderous shoals, and swelling tides that had made this stretch of Mexican coast a sailor's nightmare for centuries. Not to mention the legendary *Remolino de la Muerté,* the Whirlpool of Death, discussed by the local people only in whispers.

True or not, those tales—along with the harshness of the desert landscape—had kept the population of this area to a few scattered fishing villages. Almost nobody came here by choice. That is, until her father plunked his research team at San Lazaro Lagoon.

With a flick of her paddle, she spun the kayak around to face the lagoon. At the far end sat the research camp, its white canvas tents washed in the rich colors of sunset. Behind them rose the flagpole, still sporting the purple T-shirt hoisted by her father when the official colors blew away, and the wind generator, its steel propeller spinning lazily. Close to the beach, the converted trawler *Skimmer* lay anchored. Not far away bobbed the silver-colored submersible, awaiting its next deep-water dive.

She shook her head. Dad was still working on the boat. Though she could not see him, she could hear the familiar sputtering of the aging trawler's engine. It didn't make any difference that the ship was almost beyond repair, that the project's days were numbered, or that a spectacular sunset was about to happen. He probably wouldn't budge to see a sea monster taking a bubble bath in the lagoon. Or the lost ship *Resurrección,* laden with treasure, rising out of the waves as the old legend predicted.

And the others on his team were no better. Terry constantly fiddled with his scientific equipment, whether in his tent, on the *Skimmer,* or on the team's two buoys. Isabella, for her part, divided her time between her makeshift laboratory and the submersible, which she pampered as if it were her own baby. She would be down inside its hatch right now, doing her evening maintenance, if she had not agreed yesterday to work the camp's radio constantly in a last-ditch attempt to get the project's permit extended.

During the past few weeks, Kate's job as cook and dishwasher for the team had allowed her plenty of time for exploring the beach, snorkeling, scaling dunes, or taking sunset kayak rides. None of the others had ever joined her, not even her father. So much for her high hopes of spending lots of time with him in this isolated lagoon. She had seen only a little more of him than she had of her mother, who was thousands of miles away at their home in New England.

For a while, she had at least been able to share supper with him when the group assembled in the main tent at the end of each day. Lately, though, even that tradition had suffered, as everyone worked later and later into the night. The specter of the project's permit expiring, with no results to show for the entire month, hung like a dark cloud over them. Especially her father. He had given up trying to learn anything useful from the villagers, and had spent the last twenty-four hours on the *Skimmer,* trying to adapt Terry's precious equipment to his own purposes. Outside of his increasingly tense arguments with Terry, his conversations had shrunk to a distracted *thank-you* to Kate whenever she brought him some food.

Not that this so-called team had much in common to talk about anyway. Isabella was a marine biologist, Terry a graduate student in undersea geology, Kate's father a historian. He was leader of the group in name only. About the only thing they managed to do cooperatively was to tow the submersible out to sea for Isabella's deepwater dives.

Kate dipped her paddle and heaved. The kayak spun like a leaf on the water. Once more she was facing the sinking sun. Its color had gone from gold to crimson, and it seemed squashed, as if a great boot were stepping on it.

With a start, she realized she had drifted out and was almost on top of the breakers. Rough water boiled just ahead. Quickly, she paddled a few furious strokes in reverse, then started to turn the craft around. Better to watch the sunset from inside the lagoon. That way she would be sure to get back in plenty of time to prepare supper.

Suddenly she halted. The breakers didn't really look so bad. Not nearly as dangerous as the rapids at Devil's Canyon where she had kayaked last summer. Sure, Dad had firmly cautioned her never to cross them. Yet he and Terry did it every day in the *Skimmer* to check the buoys. The white water would make a thrilling ride. She might not get another chance. And besides, she was thirteen now, old enough to make her own decisions.

Surveying the line of turbulence, she picked the best point to cross. Farther out, in the calmer waters of the sea, the team's two buoys floated, decorated with brightly colored equipment. The first buoy seemed surprisingly close; the second, much farther out. In the distance, beyond the second buoy, a spiraling tower of mist hovered over the sea, swirling slowly. For an instant, the mist thinned just enough to reveal an ominous pursing of the waves, rising out of the water like an undersea volcano.

Farther from shore, nearer to . . .

Kate bit her lip. It was probably nothing more than a reef. And even if it were something more dangerous, it was too far away to pose any risk. Whatever, it seemed to taunt her, daring her to cross the breakers.

She glanced over her shoulder at the research camp. No one would miss her. Absorbed as he was, her father wouldn't even notice if supper came a little late tonight.

Just as she raised her paddle, a lone gull screeched overhead. She hesitated, looked again out to sea. The distant mist had thickened once more, concealing whatever she had seen. Sucking in her breath, she propelled herself at the breakers.

The wind gusted slightly, playing with her braid, as she drove the kayak forward. Effortless as a frigate bird soaring on the swells, she raced across the water.

"Hooeeee!" she shouted aloud as the craft plunged into the whitecaps. She paddled even faster. The narrow boat almost seemed to lift above the waves.

With a final splash, she cleared the breakers completely. The water grew calm again. Breathing hard, she placed the paddle across her lap and glided toward the sunset.

It was nearly time. Rays of peach and purple mingled with the sky's brighter flames. The rippling crests around her quivered with scarlet light. Water birds fell silent. The sun pressed lower and lower, flattening against the sea. Then, in the blink of an eye, it dropped below the horizon.

She shifted her gaze to the strange spiral of mist beyond the second buoy. Was it only her imagination, or could she hear a distant humming sound from that direction?

Absently, she drummed the shaft of the paddlc. A trick of the ocean air, perhaps? The local villagers claimed to have seen and heard many bizarre things off this coast. Isabella, who had grown up not far from here, had told Kate many of their tales during lulls in her lab work.

Too many, probably. One night last week, while paddling in the lagoon, Kate had heard what sounded like wispy voices, wailing and moaning in the distance. What was she to think? That she had heard the ghosts of the *Resurrección*'s sailors, swallowed by the whirlpool nearly five centuries ago? She was too embarrassed to tell anyone about it, or about how poorly she had slept that night. She was too old for that kind of thing.

Yet . . . her father didn't seem to be. He had spent his whole career as a historian trying to prove that some pretty far-fetched stories could actually be true.

Jim Gordon had a reputation as an accessible man, one of the most approachable people at the university. People rarely bothered to call him professor. Just Jim would do. No matter that he was one of the world's leading scholars on the legend of King Arthur, that he had done more than anyone to prove that Merlin was not merely a fictional wizard but a real person, a Druid prophet who lived long ago in what is now Wales. His book *The Life of Merlin* had become not only a classic study of the links between myth and history but a popular best-seller as well.

Many, including Kate, wondered why a Spanish

galleon wrecked off Baja California should be of any interest to him, a professor of early English history. But on that subject, he kept silent. Even to his colleagues. Even to his daughter.

Kate slapped the water angrily with her paddle. Jim this. Jim that. If he were so approachable, how come she found it so hard to get any time with him? Something had happened to the father she used to know, the father who used to enjoy nothing more than leaning back in his chair and telling a good story about ancient heroes and gallant quests.

A briny breeze blew over the water. Feeling a bit chilly, she reached under the kayak's spray skirt and took out a crumpled blue cotton shirt. As she unsnapped her life jacket to slip into the shirt, she looked back toward the camp. A band of pink shone in the sky above the tents. Although it was still light, a sprinkling of stars had started to appear overhead.

Then she saw the moon, rising out of the eastern horizon like an evening sun. At first only a wispy halo lifted above the desert hills, then a slice of gold, then a disc of dazzling orange. Higher the moon rose, climbing slowly into the twilight sky. It cast a fiery path across the water, a path that burned its way to her tiny vessel, flooding her with amber light.

Turning again out to sea, she followed the rippled path to the buoys and beyond. The waves glittered, as if paved with gold.

She took up her paddle. There was just enough time, if she hurried, for a brief sprint to the first buoy before dark. Kitchen duty could wait for once. She grinned, picturing the amazed look on her father's face when she would tell him what she had done.

She began to paddle toward the open ocean.

2

darkness

VIGOROUSLY she stroked. The kayak surged forward, bounding over the water. Even as the sky darkened overhead, the full moon brightened, lighting her way.

She raced toward the first buoy, her heart pounding more from exhilaration than from exertion. Only twenty more strokes and she would be there. A gust of wind pushed the kayak slightly off course, but with a hard pull to starboard she corrected it. Fifteen, twelve, ten. She raced a gull, skimming the waves. Five more. Three more.

Her wake washed against the first buoy. She exhaled in satisfaction and set down her paddle. From this close, she could see the full extent of the buoy's gadgetry. Cylinders, plastic cases and colorful cables dangled from its sides. Thick nylon netting covered most of its base, shielding it from dolphins and other curious marine life.

Its gleaming transmitter dish, aimed toward shore, gave it the appearance of a refugee robot from space.

Coming about, she wiped the perspiration from her brow with the sleeve of her shirt. Darkness was settling, but the camp remained visible among the dunes. Someone had switched on a light.

She glanced to the rear. The tower of mist beyond the second buoy seemed anything but threatening now, a billowy presence curling on the waves.

Then she heard the humming. The same sound she had heard before, only louder. It came from somewhere out to sea, somewhere behind the mist. Like the drone of a distant engine, it churned steadily, ceaselessly.

She tried to pinpoint its source but could see nothing. A boat out there? Unlikely. The *Skimmer* was back at camp. Fishermen didn't stay out this late. Who else might be sailing after sunset? That was a good way to end up like the *Resurrección,* dragged down by . . .

The whirlpool! So that's what that was. *Remolino de la Muerté,* considered by some to be as ancient and foreboding as the sea itself. She shivered slightly. Perhaps the sailors on board the *Resurrección* had heard that very same humming, only to drown a few moments later.

Raising her paddle, she turned back to shore. Airy fingers of fog were spreading across the lagoon. With any luck, she would return to camp with a little light to spare.

Just as she dipped her paddle in the water, another sound arrested her. At first she thought it was the kayak, creaking strangely. Then she realized it was more of a banging sound, coming from behind her.

She swung her head back out to sea, straining to hear.

Although it was hard to tell, the new sound seemed disconnected from the constant humming of the whirlpool,
and closer. Between the rhythmic pulsing of the waves
against her boat, it banged irregularly, like an off-key
bell. Now it beat furiously, now it died away, now it
came back again.

Something about this sound gave Kate the eerie feeling that it came from a living creature. Like a person
drowning, flailing, fighting for another breath. Yet she
knew well the ocean often distorted sounds. It could be
nothing more than the waves pummeling a reef.

A sudden motion caught her eye and she focused on
the second buoy, perhaps a hundred yards away. A large
object, silver in the moonlight, rose out of the waves
and smacked the buoy with terrific force. The buoy
rocked violently, almost toppling over. Something was
trapped there!

She turned again toward shore. Whether from thick-
ening fog or deepening darkness, the tents could now
barely be seen. Another light went on, flickering weakly.
She had to start back.

Then a high-pitched shriek ripped the air, lowering to
a piteous wail. It came from the second buoy. She had
no idea what kind of creature could make such a sound.
She only knew it was a creature in pain.

Biting her lip, she whirled the kayak around. Her
paddle spun in the air as she raced toward the far buoy.
Salty spray stung her eyes, but she covered the distance
in seconds.

As she approached, a hulking body lifted slightly
above the waves and took an exhausted gasp of air before

thrashing and rolling wildly in the water. A new wave drenched her, and with it came recognition. It was a whale.

Never had Kate seen a living being so large, at least three or four times her height in length. White barnacles peppered the whale's glistening skin, covering head, back and fins.

Isabella had mentioned that a small group of gray whales remained near the lagoon all year round, instead of joining the rest of their kind in the annual migration to the Arctic. Although this behavior baffled scientists, no one had ever succeeded in getting close enough to study them. All anyone knew was that the whales stayed by the whirlpool, circling and singing without rest.

Isabella had even given Kate a brief lesson in whale biology in case she should be lucky enough to see one of them during her kayak trips. She had only half listened, estimating her chances of spotting a whale at zero. Yet there could be no mistaking this huge creature that was right here before her, struggling to stay alive.

Careful to keep clear of the enormous body, Kate brought her kayak nearer to the buoy. She realized, as the whale rolled over, that she had encountered a young male. Big as he was, he had only reached half of his adult size. If, in fact, he ever made it to adulthood. For his plight was clear. His tail flukes were completely tangled in the nylon net attached to the buoy. Wires wrapped tightly, sliced deeply. Blood swirled on the water. The corner of one fluke hung loose, nearly severed.

Once more the whale flailed, knocking his tail against the instruments, blowing a blast of spray that rained down on Kate. She stowed her paddle and leaned over to the side, nearly swamping the kayak, trying to pull the net off the tail, itself almost as big as her boat. Yet as hard as she tugged, the net would not come free.

Bracing her hands on the slippery skin, she tried again, pulling with all her strength. No success.

Her fingers stiff from cold, she reached for one of the two big knots attaching the net to the buoy. At length she succeeded in untying it. Carefully, she pulled herself over to the other knot. It resisted, but finally gave way. As the net slid into the water, she felt a surge of hope. Then she realized that the net connected to the buoy in a third place, at the base of the transmitter dish.

At that instant, the great tail whipped out of the waves, smacking her hard across her left side. The kayak flipped over, plunging her into icy blackness. She swallowed water, struggling to breathe. Her arms flailed, but she could not pull herself out of the boat. Pain shot through her chest, throbbed in her head. Desperately, she punched at her spray skirt to free herself.

Suddenly she tasted air again. She gagged, coughing up sea water. The momentum of her roll had flipped the kayak upright, but the boat now rode dangerously low. Her sun hat was gone; her spray skirt was torn. Choking, she rubbed her stinging eyes, as water cascaded down from her hair and shoulders.

Even as she scolded herself for trying to rescue a whale all by herself, the injured animal abruptly ceased fighting. But for a single quivering fin, he lay motionless in the water.

She surveyed the young leviathan, lying limp by the

buoy. Resignedly, she looked toward shore. The wavering lights of camp seemed to welcome her, offering warmth and safety and dry land. Then the whale stirred, releasing a low, shivery moan, the sound of a living being preparing to die.

The whale's eye, as round and silver as the moon itself, met hers. For a long moment, they held each other's gaze.

Instinctively, she reached for the transmitter dish where the nylon net connected to the buoy. One of the two rods anchoring the dish to the buoy had already broken. Perhaps . . . She stretched herself farther, farther, waves slapping against the boat and her chest, until at last her hand grasped the remaining rod.

She hesitated. This equipment belonged to the team. Her father, she knew, was trying to use it, as was Terry. Breaking off the dish might cause some real damage.

Once more she peered into the silver eye. It watched her intently, not blinking.

Clenching her teeth, she gave a wrenching tug. The rod snapped, the transmitter dish plunged into the water.

Several seconds passed. The whale did not move. Then, suddenly, his tail lifted, yanking the net free from the buoy. His massive head bent downward. His flukes, red with blood, arched upward before smacking the water with such force that Kate nearly capsized from the wave. Then he dived into the depths, pulling behind the transmitter dish ensnared in a web of nylon.

Alone again, she retrieved her paddle. Spotting a flickering light through the mist, she started for shore, feeling exhausted but pleased with herself. Water sloshed inside the kayak, but she could do nothing about that now. A loose object bumped into her leg: her father's headlamp, stored in the kayak for evening outings. Strapping it on her forehead, she flicked it on, sending a thin white beam across the bow.

A big wave tumbled over her, soaking her again. Then another. She paddled hard, ignoring the growing ache between her shoulder blades. For some reason, the going seemed more difficult this direction. A tricky bit of current, perhaps, or the added weight of the water she had taken on. Her arms felt weaker with every stroke. Her head hummed.

At once, she realized the humming was not just in her head. Checking over her shoulder, she saw rising out of the mist a great bulge of water, coursing and crashing under the lamplike moon.

The whirlpool! The current had dragged her closer! She threw all her effort into every pull of her paddle. But *Remolino de la Muerté* tugged steadily at her slender craft. Her shoulders throbbed. As she grew more tired, the boat began to slip backward. In no time, she lost what little headway she had gained. Soon the second buoy disappeared into fog.

Again she stole a glance to the rear. Now the whirlpool jutted out of the sea like a circular tsunami. Spiraling whitecaps curled around its frothy rim, climbing steadily toward the center. Sheets of cold spray rained down on her.

Terror crowded out her thoughts, growing with the din of the whirlpool. She stroked feverishly, though waves battered the boat and she could no longer see the lights of the camp. Even the moon faded now and then from view, obscured by the rising spray.

Then, not far ahead, a dark shadow appeared. Slowly, against the swirling mist, the form grew fuller and sharper. Broad at the base and ragged at the top, it lifted above the water as precipitously as an island. But Kate, catching her breath, knew it was no island.

It was a ship.

Suddenly, a great wave swept over her, an avalanche of foam, capsizing the kayak. A few seconds later, the small boat drifted back to the surface, floating aimlessly. For now it carried no passenger.

3

the horn of merlin

SCRAMBLED eggs, coming up," announced Jim Gordon, trying for the third time to light the burner. "Just got to get this blasted thing to work. Meanwhile, you can finish off that tea in my thermos."

He struck another match, then blew gently on the gas outlet while holding the flame as close as possible. With a *whoosh,* the burner caught fire, just as the match started to singe his fingers.

"Ow! There now. We're set." He straightened his tall, lanky frame, so that his bristly brown hair grazed the ceiling of the boat's cabin. Planting a heavy cast-iron pan on the sputtering burner, he tossed in a lump of butter. As the smell of sizzling butter filled the cabin, he wiped the mist inside the window with his sleeve, scanned the dark waters outside, then observed the girl in the corner bundled under two wool blankets. Beside her on the floor lay her wet clothes in a pile.

Kate raised her head, looked into his chocolate brown eyes. "Pretty stupid, huh?" She took a sip from the mug in her hands.

Her father cocked his head and started cracking eggs into the pan. "No, I wouldn't say stupid. More like idiotic." He threw the shells into a trash bin under the steering wheel. "That was a close call for both of us. I try hard never to go out past the second buoy."

She listened to the waves lapping at the sides of the *Skimmer*. "I can see why."

"At least you had enough sense to wear your life jacket. And that headlamp. I never would have seen you otherwise."

"It was dumb luck, not sense."

Turning back to the eggs, Jim began stirring them with an old wooden spoon. "Like them plain? Or my special way, Baja Scramble?"

"Your way is fine," mumbled Kate feebly. She swallowed some more tea, her eyes roaming the boat's interior. The chipping gray paint, the shelves of food supplies, the boxes of diving equipment and spare parts, and the piles of nautical maps gave no hint that this was anything but a normal shrimp trawler. Only the counter by the burner, piled high with computer equipment, discarded printouts, and reference books on sonic imaging, revealed anything different.

"How come you were out so far in the kayak?"

"I was just, ah . . . exploring."

"Exploring!" Jim stopped stirring. "You could have been killed!"

She frowned, said nothing.

"Don't you know there's a whirlpool near here? Half a mile wide and probably just as deep?"

"Sure, but—"

"Then what ever possessed you to come out so far?"

"The second buoy." She paused, on the edge of describing her contact with the whale, then thought better of it. "I wanted to, ah, check it out."

Her father scrutinized her, then resumed cooking.

"You've got to respect the sea, Kate. It's full of surprises, often deadly. It's no place to play around. There's an old saying about this coastline. *Mas lejos de la orilla, mas cerca de la muerté.* It means *Farther from shore . . .*"

"*Nearer to death,*" she finished grimly. Trying to change the subject, she asked, "So why were you out with the *Skimmer?* You almost never sail after dark."

Jim tasted the eggs, then went back to stirring. "Well, it's like this. You know how long it's taken me to get Terry to part with his precious equipment so I could use it to take a sonic picture?"

"Ever since we got here."

"Right. Well, no sooner do I get it all set up and start to shoot the area right under the whirlpool than the screen goes blank. Completely blank! The monitor showed a malfunction at the second buoy, so I hustled out here to check."

Kate stiffened. "The second buoy?"

He glanced her way. "Don't worry, we're safe. I've

got us tied up tight to the buoy. We'll only stay here a little while longer, so I can do the repairs."

Stirring uneasily, she asked, "Repairs?"

"On the sonar gear." Pouting, he wiped the spoon on
the edge of the pan. "Some damned sea animal decided
to get playful with the transmitter dish. Broke it clean
off, though I'm sure it's still there, tangled up in the net
someplace."

Again she stirred beneath the blankets. "What if the
transmitter dish is . . . gone?"

"Sunk? No chance. I tied those knots myself."

"But—"

"Before I can repair the buoy, though, I need to see if
any data got stored before the dish broke off." Reaching
his long arm to the topmost shelf, he steadied himself
against the rocking of the waves and pulled down a jar
of salsa. As he unscrewed the cap, he nodded toward a
black cable stretching from the computer out the door of
the cabin. "I'm processing that right now. It'll take a few
minutes. The equipment here on the boat isn't as powerful as what we have back at camp."

Pouring the spicy salsa into the pan, he mixed it with
the eggs. "I'm glad you've learned your lesson. All my
life I've been around water, and I've never seen anything half as dangerous as this coast. If I didn't have to
come here to find out more about that galleon, believe
me, I'd be somewhere else."

Feeling he just might be ready to open up to her, Kate
decided to save the truth about the transmitter dish for
later. She drew in her breath. "What's so special about
that old ship, anyway?"

Dumping a heap of eggs on a plastic plate, he handed it to her. "There you go, Baja Scramble."

"Thanks," she replied, looking dubiously at the concoction. Suddenly, the aroma aroused her hunger. She took a small bite. "Hey, this is pretty good." Another bite followed, then another. "Can't believe how hungry I am."

"A swim will do that," he said wryly.

"Now can you tell me?"

He aimed a fork at the eggs in the pan. "Tell you what?"

"What's so special about that ship."

Glancing at his watch, he said, "Almost time to see what we've got. Then a few quick repairs and you'll be back at camp before you know it."

Kate surveyed the cabin, her head swaying to the rhythm of the waves. She sensed she should try a different approach. "Want to hear something crazy? When I first saw your boat, in all that mist, you'll never guess what I thought it was."

"Let me guess. The Navy? The *QE II?*"

"No," she answered. "Even crazier. I thought you were the sunken ship, sailing again like the legend says."

"The *Resurrección?*" Jim laughed. "Guess I've infected you with my own wild dreams." He grinned mysteriously. "You never know, though. Myth and reality aren't always so far apart."

"Something you've tried to show with Merlin."

"That's right," he said through a mouthful of eggs. "Merlin's life and legend are impossibly intertwined.

That's one reason a lot of people still refuse to believe he was a real person."

Kate stabbed at the remains on her plate, then asked as casually as she could manage, "Will raising the *Resurrección* help you settle something about Merlin?"

"You could say that."

"But, Dad, we're in Mexico. Halfway around the world from where Merlin lived! What could he have to do with this place?"

"More than you know," he replied, setting down his fork. "But raising the old ship isn't really necessary. Besides, there's no way, with this little manpower and time, I could ever hope to do that. Especially with the whirlpool so near. All I need to do is prove the *Resurrección* actually existed. If I can just do that, then . . ."

"Then what?"

"Then I can organize a proper expedition to salvage whatever is left of it."

"Then what?"

Jim tugged playfully on her braid. "Then maybe you'll stop asking so many questions."

"I learned that from you."

"I see your point. Historians do ask questions for a living. All right, then, here's one for you. How about some hot cocoa? I think there's some powdered milk around here someplace." He took a plastic container from the shelf and set it down with a thud. "Now all we need is the cocoa."

"Please tell me."

"All right. Tell you what?"

Straightening her back, she asked, "What could Merlin have to do with the ship? Besides, didn't he live in the
fifth or sixth century? The *Resurrección* went down—"

"In 1547," completed her father. "You remember more
of the old bedtime stories than I thought. Could it be
you're a fan of Merlin, too?"

"I *hate* Merlin," blustered Kate, surprised at the force
of her own words. "He's just a stupid magician. I couldn't
care less about him. But if I listened to your Merlin stories, I got to see you every once in a while! At least that
used to be true before you got all wrapped up with this
ship project."

Jim turned away and began prying open a canister of
cocoa. "That bad, huh?"

"That bad."

Pouring some of the powder into two green mugs on
the counter, he went on, "Some father I am. You have to
nearly drown yourself to get my attention."

"It worked, didn't it?" She managed a grin. "You used
to say the first quality of a historian is resourcefulness."

Thoughtfully, Jim mixed some powdered milk in a
pot. "Guess I don't blame you for feeling that way." He
sighed. "Too bad you didn't like the old stories, though.
Telling them to you gave me a chance to work through
my theories about Merlin."

"Well, I did sort of like the ones when he turned King
Arthur into different kinds of animals."

"You especially liked the one about Arthur becoming
a fish. You made me tell it every night for a month." He
lowered the pot of milk onto the still-sputtering burner,

then winked at her. "So I'm not a total failure as a story-teller after all?"

She eyed him for a moment. "Almost total."

"Thanks," he replied. "Do you, by any chance, remember any of the stories about the Thirteen Treasures?"

After a long pause, she replied, "The Thirteen Treasures of the Isle of Britain. Merlin had to search for years before he found all of them."

"Almost all of them."

"Whatever. Then he took them to a secret hiding place called the Glass House."

"That's right. Nobody knows where the Glass House might have been, only that Merlin planned to store the Treasures there until the prophesied return of King Arthur. He believed that Arthur would need them to win the Final Battle."

Jim checked his watch. "Hold on. I'll be right back." He stepped to the door, opened it, ducked his head and walked out on the deck. His first stop was the machinery bolted to a metal stand in the middle of the deck; his second, the buoy bobbing just off the stern. The chill, salty air of the sea flooded the cabin, as did the sound of waves sloshing against the boat. And, in the distance, another sound, humming steadily, that made Kate's stomach clench.

In a few seconds, he returned and shut the door. "I'll know pretty soon whether I got any data before the accident. Now . . . where were we?"

"The Thirteen Treasures."

"Right." He gave the milk a stir, then asked, "Can you remember which was the one Treasure Merlin wanted most? The one he thought was more powerful than all the others combined?"

Kate's brow furrowed, as she listened to the *kerslap, kerslap* of the waves on the hull. "It wasn't . . . the sword of light. Or the cauldron of knowledge. Or the knife that could heal any wound." Her eyes roamed the cabin, coming to rest on the pair of green mugs. "I remember! The thirteenth Treasure. The magical drinking horn."

His gaze seemed to peer right through her. "The Horn of Merlin."

"But what does all this have to do with the ship?"

"Everything." Sliding into his chair, he leaned back and said, "In all the years I've been studying Merlin, no element of the legend has been more fascinating—or frustrating—than the Horn. It's kept me awake for more nights than I can remember. The trail has led me to Cornwall, Normandy, Iceland, Italy, Spain, and now here. And with very little to show for it. Until recently."

He doused his finger in the pot of milk. Shaking his wet finger, he declared, "As it is, I still don't know much. But what I do know is . . . intriguing.

"The story of the Horn has two parts. The first part begins long before Merlin ever found the Horn, in a forgotten land called *the place where the sea begins*. It concerns a legendary craftsman, Emrys, his love for someone named Wintonwy, and the origin of the thirteenth Treasure. The second part is even more mysterious—the part that concerns the whirlpool and a certain Spanish ship."

"The *Resurrección?*"

"None other." He searched her face. "Care to hear a story?"

Kate half smiled. "Better be a good one."

"You can be the judge of that." He reached over and squeezed her forearm under the blankets. "Make yourself comfortable. This will be like old times."

4

the story of the thirteenth treasure

LONG ago, in a land beyond reach and a time beyond memory, a great craftsman lived alone on a mountain precipice. Only the eagles knew where to find him. Yet even they did not visit, for they, like all the creatures of this land, were not welcome.

His true name has been lost from memory, but he is known in legend as Emrys of the Mountain. So vast were his skills that he required no helpers, no messengers. Indeed, Emrys needed no one even to bring him food, for he had devised ways to make stones into loaves of bread, snow into cheese, water into wine.

Such solitude suited his purpose, for Emrys wanted no one else to understand the secrets of his craft. His knowledge was hard won, and he hoarded it greedily. He refused all offers to sell either his skills or his creations, for he held no interest in riches or titles or the ways of men.

Any visitors who, by design or chance, came near his alpine hold returned with both empty hands and empty thoughts, able to recall nothing of what they had seen.

Emrys almost never ventured forth, except when he needed to gather the few substances that he could not himself manufacture. He worked ceaselessly, since his work was his only passion. Yet he rarely felt satisfied with the fruits of his labor. He destroyed any creation that he did not deem utterly perfect.

After all his years in the mountains, only twelve creations met his standards, and only twelve did he retain. They were his Treasures. First he forged the sword of light, so powerful that a single sweep of its flashing blade could kill any creature, whether made of flesh or of spirit. Then he made the ever-bubbling cauldron of knowledge, the whetstone that could turn a strand of hair into a gleaming blade, the halter that could make an ordinary horse run like lightning, and the pan that produced the world's loveliest smells. Next came the mantle that could turn its wearer invisible and the ruby ring that could control the will of others. To these Emrys added the inexhaustible vessel of plenty, the harp that could make haunting music at the merest touch, the knife that could heal any wound, and the chessboard whose pieces could come alive on command. Finally, he designed the flaming chariot, whose fire came from the very heart of the Earth.

Yet with all his Treasures, Emrys still lacked one thing. He remained mortal. He was destined to die like all mortal beings. In time, his hands would lose all their skill, his mind would lose all its knowledge. The shadow of this fate so darkened his days that, at last, he could bear it no longer.

In desperation, he left his mountain lair to search for the secret of immortality. He had no idea whether he could find such a thing, but he knew he must try. He brought with him only two of his Treasures: the sword of light and the ruby ring that could make others do his bidding.

His quest led him to many wondrous lands, but he did not stay long in any of them. Emrys searched and searched, following every clue he encountered, but without success. Nowhere could he find the secret that he craved. No one could help him.

At last, after many years of searching, he finally gave up. He made ready to return home in despair.

Then, as he sat in the shadow of a great tree, he heard a young mother telling her child a story. She told of a mysterious realm beneath the sea called Shaa. Only mer people, half human and half fish, lived there. No one but the mer people could find their way to Shaa, though many had tried. All anyone knew was the legend that it lay in *the place where the sea begins, the womb where the waters are born.* Merwas, emperor of the mer people, had ruled the realm of Shaa with wisdom and dignity over many ages. In fact, it was said that Merwas had discovered a way to live far beyond his time, that he could remember the birth of islands that men considered older than old.

To most listeners, this tale would have been nothing more than a simple child's entertainment. Yet to Emrys, it held a seed of hope. He vowed never to rest until he discovered whether the ancient ruler Merwas still lived beneath the waves.

But where was this land of Shaa? *The place where the sea begins, the womb where the waters are born.* It was not much of a clue, but it was all that Emrys had.

With his superior skills, he fashioned a hood that allowed him to breathe underwater with the ease of a fish. He descended into the sea, full of renewed hope. Yet soon he began to realize the enormity of his challenge. The realm of Shaa, if it did exist, would be nearly impossible to find. So vast were the many seas, he would have barely begun his search before his remaining life ran out. Still, he vowed to persist.

Years passed, and although he followed many leads under the sea, he was ever disappointed. Even his ring of power and his flashing sword could not help him. He began to wonder whether he had really heard the story of Shaa at all, or whether it was only a remnant from his fevered dreams.

One day Emrys smelled the sweet aroma of an underwater plant called apple-of-the-sea. It reminded him of apple blossoms in the spring. For a moment he felt captivated by the perfume, and he strolled in memory through apple groves he would never again see on the land.

Then, out of a crevasse before him, a strange form arose. First came the head of a woman, with long black hair flowing over her shoulders. She seemed darkly beautiful, although her eyes were shadowed, almost sunken, so that they gave the impression of being bottomless. With a gasp Emrys realized that, below her shoulders, her body was nothing more than a cloud of dark vapor, curling and twisting like smoke. Two thin, wispy arms formed out of the cloud, one of them clasping a dagger in its vaporous hand.

"Who are you?" asked Emrys, his own hand on the sword of light.

"Nimue issss my name." Her voice hissed like steam vapor.

"What do you want from me?"

She pointed at his ruby ring. "It issss beautiful."

Emrys drew back.

Nimue watched him, coiling and uncoiling her vaporous arms. "It would sssseem a ssssmall pricccce to pay . . . to find the ssssecret entrancccce to the realm of Shaa."

"You know the way to Shaa?"

"An enchantressss knowssss many thingssss."

Emrys hesitated. The ring had helped him often over the years. Yet he knew also that soon he would die and the ring would then serve him no more. Although it was probably folly to trust the enchantress, what did he have to lose? Giving Nimue the ring seemed a small price to pay for a chance to achieve immortality.

So Emrys agreed to the bargain. Nimue took the ring and scrutinized it carefully with her bottomless eyes. Then, wordlessly, she beckoned to her servants, a band of enormous eels with triangular heads and massive jaws who had been hiding in the shadows. Emrys knew at once that they were sea demons, among the most feared creatures in the ocean. His blood chilled at the very sight of them.

Yet the sea demons did not attack. They merely surrounded Nimue with their slithering bodies. Cautiously, Emrys followed as they led him some distance to the mouth of a deep abyss dropping down from the bottom of the sea. Here, declared Nimue, was the entrance to the secret realm ruled by Merwas.

Then Emrys noticed that the abyss was guarded by a monstrous beast of the sea, a spidery creature with many powerful legs. Though the creature had only two narrow slits for eyes, it seemed to sense the presence of intruders. Its huge jaw opened a crack, revealing a thousand poisonous tongues.

"Treachery!" cried Emrys. "That monster will never let me pass."

But Nimue only laughed and hissed, "I ssssaid I would bring you to the door. I did not ssssay I would open it for you." With that, she turned her vaporous form and melted into the dark waters, followed by the sea demons.

Before Emrys could decide what to do, the monster stirred and suddenly attacked. Wielding the sword of light, Emrys battled bravely, but the spidery creature pinned him against an outcropping of rock. With a last thrust of the sword, Emrys cut off one of the creature's legs. As it shrieked in pain, Emrys slipped past and escaped into the abyss.

Darkest of the dark, the abyss plunged downward. Emrys, wounded and weak, followed its twists and turns, doubting he would ever reach the end. And even if he did, who could tell whether this was indeed the route to the land of Shaa? More likely, Nimue had tricked him yet again.

Then, at last, the abyss opened into an undersea cavern as wide as a valley. Water so pure it seemed to glow dripped from the high ceiling, gathering into waterfalls that tumbled radiantly into the lake filling the cavern. Fragrant winds, bearing all the smells of the sea, flowed through the cavern's airy spaces. *The place where the sea begins, the womb where the waters are born.* At the far end of the cavern rose a magnificent castle made of streaming, surging water, its turrets and walls as sturdy as glass yet as fluid as the ocean itself.

Instantly, Emrys found himself surrounded by mer people, glistening green. They appeared unafraid and rather amused by his curious form. They escorted him to the shining castle and brought him to the great hall, which was filled up to the base of the windows with water, allowing the mer people to come and go easily. There, seated upon a crystalline throne, was their ruler, a mer man whose eyes flamed brighter than lightning bolts and whose long, white beard wrapped around his waist and prodigious tail. At long last, Emrys stood before Merwas, ruler of the land of Shaa.

When Merwas demanded to know what purpose had brought Emrys there, and how he had discovered the way into Shaa, Emrys told him of his quest to find the secret of immortality. Yet Emrys chose not to reveal that he had been helped by Nimue, fearing that the mention of the enchantress would make Merwas suspicious. The ancient ruler listened carefully, then declared, "Your search, though valiant, has been in vain. I have nothing to give you except a brief rest while you heal your wounds and prepare to return to your home." Then, in a voice like waves crashing upon the cliffs, he added: "You have much yet to learn."

Despite the beauty of this land under the sea, for Emrys it seemed utterly bleak. His quest lay in ruins. He wished he could just lie down and die, rather than attempt the long journey back to his mountain lair.

Then, while wandering alone through the corridors of the castle, he chanced to meet Wintonwy, the only daughter of Merwas. The bards of that realm had long celebrated her virtues. Sang one:

> *Graceful as coral, true as the tides,*
> *Constant as currents the rising moon rides.*
> *Fresh as the foam, deep as the sea,*
> *Bright as the stars, fair Wintonwy.*

For the first time in all his years, Emrys fell in love. He set to work, crafting for Wintonwy a bracelet of gleaming bubbles and other wondrous gifts. Although Wintonwy ignored him, Emrys hoped that his attention might eventually touch her heart.

And, in time, Wintonwy took notice of him. She invited him to join her on a voyage through Shaa. They set off immediately and traveled to the farthest reaches of the realm.

One day, as they camped near a fountain of warm water, Wintonwy chose to explore alone while Emrys designed a new creation. Suddenly, he heard her screams. He leaped to her aid and found she had been attacked by a vicious shark. Seeing he could not reach her in time, he hurled the blazing sword of light with all his strength.

It struck the shark in the eye just before the ferocious jaws clamped down on Wintonwy.

She was badly injured, but alive. Emrys carried her in his arms all the way back to the castle, singing continually to ease her pain. Upon seeing them, Merwas raced to join them. Although the old emperor worried how a shark had managed to enter the realm, he chose not to dwell on such concerns, overcome with relief that his dear Wintonwy was safe. In gratitude for saving her life, he asked Emrys to make a wish—any wish.

"To spend the rest of my days at your court," answered Emrys without pause.

"Then you long no more for eternal life?"

"No, my king. I long only to live my life anew at Wintonwy's side."

Bowing his head, the emperor declared: "If my daughter agrees, your wish shall be granted."

Soon the castle came alive with the announcement of their wedding. While Wintonwy prepared for the ceremony, Emrys labored to make a wedding gift of unrivaled elegance. On the eve of their marriage, he unveiled it, a drinking horn whose beauty surpassed anything he had ever made. It was shaped like a spiraling shell, and it glimmered with the light of stars seen through the mist. And, remembering his mountain home, Emrys endowed the drinking horn with a special virtue. Anyone who held it near could smell the fragrant air of the mountaintop, even if he did so at the bottom of the sea. He named it *Serilliant,* meaning *Beginning* in the mer people's tongue.

Emrys offered it to Wintonwy. "I give you this Horn,

the most lovely of my Treasures, as a symbol of our love."

"Our love," she replied, "is all we shall ever need to drink."

The Emperor Merwas then came forward. "I have decided to give to Serilliant a special power, the greatest I have to bestow."

"What is this power, my father?" asked Wintonwy.

"It is . . . a kind of eternal life, but not the kind most mortals seek. No, I give to this Horn a power far more precious, far more mysterious."

"Can you tell us more?"

Merwas lifted the Horn high above his head. "I can tell you that the Horn's new power springs from the secret of the newly born sea, the secret we mer people have guarded for so long."

As he spoke, the Horn swiftly filled with a luminous liquid, as colorful as melted rainbows. Then Merwas declared, "Only those whose wisdom and strength of will are beyond question may drink from this Horn. For it holds the power to—"

Merwas never finished his sentence. The castle gates flew open and Nimue, leading an army of sea demons, drove down on the helpless mer people. The sea demons, growling wrathfully, slew anyone who stood before them.

As Nimue aimed her black dagger at Merwas himself, Emrys raised the sword of light in wrath and charged. But just before he could strike her down, Nimue held up one vaporous hand. On it rested the ring that Emrys himself had once worn.

"Look into thissss ring," commanded Nimue. The ring flashed with a deep ruby light.

Emrys froze.

"Now," she continued. "Drop your ssssword."

Unable to resist the power of the ring, Emrys shuddered, then dropped the sword of light.

"Good." The enchantress laughed. "I could kill you, but I will not becausssse you have been quite ussssseful to me. You wounded the sssspider monssssster, allowing me at lasssst to enter the realm of Shaa."

Emrys wanted to pounce on her, but he could not find the strength to move.

"Go," ordered Nimue.

Haltingly, Emrys turned and left the castle.

When at last the invaders departed, both Merwas and his beloved Wintonwy lay dead. The few mer people who survived fled the castle, leaving it abandoned forever. They scattered far and wide, becoming the most elusive creatures in all the sea.

Yet Nimue's triumph was not complete. The Horn somehow disappeared during the battle, and neither she nor her sea demons could discover its whereabouts.

Emrys, stricken with grief, eventually made his way back to his alpine lair. There he resumed the life of a recluse, but never again did he create any works. He did not even try. For the rest of his life he bore the pain of the love he had found and so soon lost. Worse yet, he bore the pain of knowing that but for his own folly, fair Wintonwy would still be alive.

5

the ballad

WHAT a sad story," said Kate, swaying with the rocking of the boat. "But what does it have to do with Merlin? Or the sunken ship?"

Her father poured hot milk into the mugs and handed one to her. "I told you that the story of the Horn has two parts."

"You mean . . . Serilliant . . . became the Horn of Merlin?"

"Yes! Merlin, in his search for the Thirteen Treasures, finally found it, the most precious Treasure of all. He kept it with him for a time—though for some reason he didn't take it to the Glass House with the others. And then, somehow, he lost it."

"Lost it? How?"

"Nobody knows."

Kate's eyes fastened on her father.

"Losing the Horn must have been a terrible blow. So terrible that I'm convinced it finally killed him."

She squeezed some of the water from her braid, then leaned forward. "So what happened to the Horn?"

"I've been trying to answer that question for years."

She watched his face, anxious but determined. "And you think finding the *Resurrección* will help you do that."

"That and more."

Clasping her mug with both hands, she inhaled the rich, chocolate aroma. The memory of the whirlpool's icy waters now seemed far away. "Dad," she asked quietly, "what is this all about?"

He ran a hand through his bristly hair. "I suppose there's no harm in telling you. We're almost out of time. And unless I can get a sonic picture that shows something, this whole project is as sunk as the *Resurrección*."

"Maybe Isabella can talk the government into an extension."

"I doubt it," he said dispiritedly. "She did phenomenally well to get us a permit in the first place. They have strict rules against people coming down here, you know. Whirlpools and killer shoals don't fit the tourist paradise they're trying to promote. It was only because of Isabella's stature as a scientist that they let us in at all—and then only for a month, with no extensions possible. Still, I was certain that would be enough time to find some hard evidence about the ship. Then, with the prospect of all that gold bullion, they'd be sure to change their tune and grant an extension. But here we are, with just three days left."

Jim set aside his mug and stood up, his frame almost filling the cabin. He stepped to the counter and punched a few commands onto the computer keyboard. With a scowl, he studied the screen. "Nothing yet. We'll give it just a bit longer, and if there's still nothing, we'll fix up the buoy and try again."

"After you tell me what's going on."

Returning to his chair, he said, "All right, you win. But first, you've got to promise me *never* to tell anyone what I'm about to tell you. Not even your mother, not even Isabella. The risks are too great. Do you understand?"

Kate swallowed, but not her cocoa. "Yes."

Jim stared into his mug for a moment before speaking. "For starters, if the Horn of Merlin could be recovered, it would put to rest all the doubts about whether Merlin himself really existed."

"But how?"

"There is only one Horn of Merlin, and its life was so closely intertwined with the wizard's, at least for a time, that from the standpoint of history they have become inseparable. If one existed, so did the other. And if the Horn still exists, it will be simple to recognize—not so much by its spiral shape and rainbow fluid as by its power."

"You really believe it has some sort of magical power?"

"I do."

She scrutinized him. "This is about more than just history, isn't it?"

"Right you are. We're talking about the Horn of Merlin! Many people—and many forces beyond our comprehension—would go to enormous lengths to get it if they knew it still existed."

Kate looked at him skeptically. "You mean like that enchantress Nimue?"

He nodded gravely. "They could have human forms. Or others. I'm talking about forces that thrive on pain, injustice, chaos. It makes me shudder just to think what they might do with the Horn . . . although the true nature of its power remains unclear. Merlin must have known what it was, but he never shared the secret with anyone else."

"Emperor Merwas, in your story, said the Horn's power had something to do with eternal life."

"He said it was *a kind of eternal life, but not the kind most mortals seek.*"

She frowned. "What's that supposed to mean?"

"Don't ask me. But it does give you an idea of the magnitude we're dealing with."

Swallowing some more cocoa, Kate couldn't shake the feeling that her father knew more than he was revealing. Yet she felt reluctant to press him too hard, since he was being so uncharacteristically open with her. Better to try an indirect approach.

"There are lots of legends about the Horn, aren't there?"

"Plenty," he responded. "In the centuries since it disappeared, the Horn of Merlin has popped up in all manner of folklore, all over the world. I'm up to thirty-seven languages, and I've been looking hard for only a few years. But none of the references says anything specific about the Horn's power. It's always *the mysterious Horn, the marvelous Horn, the wondrous Horn,* and the like. And none of the references talks about the Horn actually appearing again. None . . . except one."

"Which one?"

Peering straight at her hazel green eyes, he said, "That

reference came from right here. It was an old ballad, known only in the fishing villages in this part of Baja, about the wreck of the *Resurrección.* It was Isabella who first told me about it, more than three years ago. Over coffee in the faculty lounge. She thought it was just another bit of Merlin trivia, having no idea that the reference to the Horn was so unusual. But I checked her translation, and there it was."

Kate took a final slurp of cocoa. "Can you remember how it goes?"

"Can I remember? I haven't been able to get it out of my head now for years." He cleared his throat. "Starts like this:

> *An ancient ship, the pride of Spain,*
> *Embarked upon a quest*
> *To navigate the ocean vast*
> *And still survive the test.*

> *It carried treasures rich and rare*
> *Across the crashing waves*
> *Beyond the flooded fields that are*
> *So many sailors' graves.*

> *Its goal to link the Orient*
> *With distant Mexico,*
> *The ship set sail with heavy hearts*
> *And heavier cargo.*

> *The galleon brimmed with precious gems,*
> *Fine gold and silver wrought,*
> *Silk tapestries and ivories*
> *And spices dearly sought.*

From China, Burma, Borneo,
Came crates of lofty cost,
And one thing more, the rumors said:
The Horn that Merlin lost."

Kate listened, feeling the boat surging on the swells. *"The Horn that Merlin lost."*

"Yes, but note that it says *the rumors said.* Not a very reliable reference! It could mean that the Horn was on board, or that the ship was destined somehow to encounter the Horn, or something else entirely."

"The *Resurrección* has plenty of its own legends, doesn't it?"

"More than its share," he agreed. "You've got to remember, not many sunken ships are surrounded by so much controversy. Some people think that it never existed, or if it did, that it carried nothing of value. But if you ask the villagers around here, they'll swear it went down off the coast, although they can't give you any proof. And a few historians agree, saying that when it set sail from Manila it was carrying enough treasure to wipe out the entire war debt of Imperial Spain. That's more than ninety million dollars in today's currency."

"So why hasn't anybody tried to find it before?"

"I guess no one was crazy enough. First, it's hard to raise money to pay for an expedition when the very existence of the ship is in doubt. Second, the ocean bottom is deep around here, averaging half a mile. Third, there is the matter of the whirlpool. I don't need to elaborate on that."

"No," she said weakly.

"I will say this, though," he continued. "The whirlpool itself has been rather elusive. Since it's almost always covered with mist, and since these waters are so dangerous for sailing, very few people have ever actually seen it. Or have lived to tell about it."

"Let's talk about something else."

He gazed at the steamy window of the cabin. "Come to think of it, the shroud of mist is a little like Avalon. It was the mist more than anything else that made Avalon seem to King Arthur less a real place than an enchanted dream, less part of his own kingdom than the Kingdom of Faërie."

When he spoke again, his voice was barely audible. "Some of the villagers had another name for the whirlpool besides *Remolino de la Muerté.* They called it *el lugar donde empieza el viento,* which means *the place where the wind begins.*"

Despite her visceral feelings about the whirlpool, Kate found herself slightly intrigued. "That makes me think of the realm of Shaa. You know, *the place where the sea begins.*"

"Sounds similar, I admit," said her father, adopting a professorial tone. "But just because two things sound alike doesn't make them related. It's like a billion other coincidences throughout history."

"But you jumped on a coincidence when you heard Isabella's ballad," objected Kate. "You put this whole project together on the basis of one little reference to the Horn."

"Not quite," Jim answered. "The ballad was my first

clue, to be sure. But I didn't get really serious about this thing until I discovered something else."

"What else?"

"You might recall I went to Spain a couple of years ago for a conference. Well, I took the opportunity to search through the Spanish archives in Seville, hoping to find something that would help me determine whether the *Resurrección* really existed. Eventually, I did turn up something—although, strangely, it was filed in the wrong place."

"What was it?"

"Some papers that appeared to be the original ship's manifest for an unnamed galleon that sailed from Manila in 1547. When I checked through all the details, it matched to a tee the other surviving descriptions of the *Resurrección*. There was one thing odd about it, though."

A large wave splashed against the hull, jostling them both. Kate leaned closer. "Odd?"

"Yes. Along with all the other items on the list—gold and silver, jewelry and tapestries, spices and ivory—there was some kind of strange marking. Like nothing I'd ever seen before."

"What did it look like?"

He took his clipboard and drew a design. Tearing off the page, he handed it to her.

"Like this."

* * *

KATE puzzled over the mysterious marking. "Somebody's signature?"

"More like a code," her father replied. "Look at that spiral in the middle."

She looked up at his lanky form swaying with the movement of the boat. "A code for what?"

"That's what I wondered, too. I tried to find a way to decipher it, not really expecting I'd succeed. The trail got incredibly complicated, and I got involved with other projects, but something kept me from giving up completely.

"Then one day I was doing some research on a little-known language that is said to have been developed by some of the followers of Merlin in medieval times. They were a strange bunch, many of them doubling as monks, and they had some sort of secret society. Their language is related to Ogham, an ancient Druid alphabet, with some important twists. Suddenly I realized that it looked a lot like the marking on the manifest. So, for the heck of it, I tried to translate it."

She twirled the page in her hands. "And?"

Jim turned the page right side up. "It said . . . *Serilliant*."

"The Horn? So it really was on the ship?"

Jim stroked his chin. "It could be nothing more than a hoax, a medieval prank of some kind. Yet, if it's true, and if the Horn could be recovered . . ."

As his words trailed off into the sound of splashing waves, Kate felt again there was something else, something about the Horn, that he was not telling. She folded the page and slid it into the pocket of her wet cotton shirt on the floor. Still, what did it matter? He had told her more than anyone else about his dreams. Even if they were destined not to come true, he had shared them. With her.

"Dad, what did Merlin look like? Sometimes I try to picture him in my mind, but it's hard."

"How do you picture him?"

"Tall," she answered. "Even taller than you. With a bent, pointed hat that made him look even taller. Straight, white hair, flying in all directions, like hay. Probably a big wart on his nose."

"That's the archetypal form, all right. But the evidence suggests he looked different than you think."

"No pointed hat?"

"No pointed hat. The only two things he wore constantly were the Horn—for the years he had it—and the blue cape, the one decorated with stars and planets that he used to bring light to dark places."

Kate ran her finger along the rim of her mug, considering the image. "You said losing the Horn killed him in the end. How did he die, anyway?"

"He was entombed in a cave by the sea, somewhere on the British Isle of Bardsey. That's about all we know, that and the date: 547 A.D."

"Hey, that would have been exactly one thousand years before the *Resurrección* set sail."

"So it would," acknowledged the historian. "Another coincidence, no doubt."

"What happened to him?"

"Most people think he sealed himself in the cave permanently because he was so distraught at losing the Horn. Yet that's by no means clear. My own view is that he was sealed in the cave by someone else, someone who wanted him out of the way forever."

"Who?"

"His greatest rival, who tried for years to steal his power, and finally, the Horn."

"Who was he?"

"She."

"You don't mean—"

"Yes. I mean Nimue."

"But . . . couldn't he stop her?"

Jim turned toward the window and the moonlit waters beyond. "Apparently not. Perhaps Merlin was so angry at himself for losing the Horn and jeopardizing Arthur's return that he allowed Nimue to finish him off, as the ultimate punishment. Perhaps he had grown arrogant while he had the Horn and underestimated her strength. Or perhaps . . . she had some help."

"Help?"

"Some sources indicate that Garlon, a legendary seaman of the time who seemed to have had a personal grudge against Merlin—I have no idea why—teamed up with Nimue."

Kate sighed heavily. "She and Merlin must have really hated each other."

"That's an understatement. I imagine, though, that beneath their bitter rivalry, there was some mutual respect.

Maybe, even, a kind of admiration. After all, they did
share some things in common, like their fascination for
the sea."

"Sounds like that's about all they shared."

"I wish I knew! You have no idea how many conflict-
ing theories there are surrounding Merlin. For example,
there's a mountain of good evidence that he died in the
cave. Yet there are some people who still maintain that
he descended into the sea at the end of his life. They
point to an old ballad:

> *He that made the wode and lond*
> *So long before in Engelonde*
> *So too made the steormy sea*
> *And the place where Merlyn be*
> *Searching still in mystery."*

"Searching still in mystery," repeated Kate. "For the
Horn, I guess."

"I guess."

"You said Merlin was fascinated by the sea."

"That's right. He spent a good deal of time there. The
name Merlin itself comes from the old Welsh word
Myrrdin, meaning 'Sea Fortress.' "

A vague recollection stirred in her. "And wasn't the
first name of Britain something that meant 'Merlin's
Isle'?"

Jim's eyes gleamed. *"Clas Myrrdin."*

Placing her mug on the counter next to a pile of printouts, Kate thought of the others, probably still hard at
work back at camp. "How did you get Isabella and Terry

to come along on this project? They're not interested in Merlin."

"Not in the least! It's a marriage of convenience, that's all. Our interests don't overlap one bit. Isabella is studying one fish in particular that was supposed to be long extinct, but was found recently in the catch of a local fisherman."

"And Terry?"

"I didn't really know him when I asked him to join us, which was risky. But I knew he is a leader in sonic imaging technology, even if he is only in his twenties. He was the first person to merge sonar, much like whales use to communicate underwater, with the same thermal sensing devices used by satellites. I thought, naively, that getting him meant getting to use his equipment. Was I ever wrong. He's been using it to study the unusual volcanic activity off this coast. And he's—"

"A total jerk." She touched the black cable with her bare foot. "Too bad you can't just get Isabella to take you down in the submersible. Then you wouldn't need to use Terry's stuff to get a picture."

"She guards the submersible with her life! Being the director of the Institute's deep-water research program is not nearly as important to her as being the submersible's chief pilot. And she's reluctant to take it down anywhere near the whirlpool, for fear it might be damaged. So unless I can come up with something very convincing, she won't risk it."

Giving the counter a pat, Jim rose from his chair. "It's time." He punched the commands into the computer once again, then waited.

Nothing.

Lips pinched, he shrugged. "Looks like I struck out." He turned toward the door.

"Look," exclaimed Kate, pointing to the screen. Slowly, a hazy image was beginning to form.

He whirled around. Instantly, he activated the printer. For several agonizing seconds, they waited for the hard copy to emerge. At length, a single sheet of paper edged its way out of the printer.

He snatched it up, his face alight, and studied the hazy image. "It's there!" he announced buoyantly.

Kate took the paper, and her heart sank. "It doesn't look like anything," she lamented. "Just a weird gray blob."

"You could call it that," agreed her father. "Or you could call it an underexposed picture of the area below the whirlpool. Here, look closely. Imagine it with five times the resolution, if I had been able to make a complete image. Can you see those three lines? Could be masts. See? Mizzenmast, mainmast, and foremast, with the mainmast broken. And maybe, just maybe, the hull of a ship, viewed from an angle of about forty-five degrees."

She shook her head.

"And look here," the historian went on. "That patch, could it be . . . sails?" Poring over the picture, he muttered, "No . . . no. They couldn't still be intact after four hundred fifty years! The pressure alone down there would have ripped them to shreds." He focused again on Kate. "Forget the cocoa, we should be drinking champagne! There's something down there, no doubt about it."

"If you say so," she answered uncertainly. "Are you sure it's not just a smudge?"

"I admit it's not clear enough to prove anything. It does fire the imagination, though. Even this quality isn't bad for three thousand feet down! I'll give Terry this much. He knows his stuff." His expression darkened. "But he didn't count on the fact that the buoys' sonic beams seem to attract the local whales. It was probably one of them who wreaked havoc on the buoy."

Kate cleared her throat. "Dad, there's something—"

"I still can't believe it," he interrupted, tossing the page on the counter. "By itself, this picture is worthless. Just a smudge, as you said. But a longer shot is going to show us something. Maybe something amazing. I just need to hook up the transmitter dish, and we'll find out."

As he started for the door, she caught him by the pant leg. "Dad, I've got to tell you something."

"Tell me after I reconnect the dish."

Rising under the shroud of blankets, she stood before him. "The dish isn't there."

He grunted as if he had been punched in the chest. "Not there?"

"That's right," she said tentatively. "I saw it . . . dragged off by a whale."

"What? Are you sure?"

"I'm sure."

"No whale could have done that. Not unless he had hands to untie the net."

He reached for the door handle, when Kate placed her own hand on his.

"The whale didn't untie it," she confessed. "I did."

He stared at her in amazement. "You what?"

"And I broke the dish, too. Trying to rescue the whale! He was all tangled up in the net, and I thought he would die for sure unless I did something."

"Did something!" roared Jim. "Kate, how could you be so stupid?"

He flung open the door and pushed past her. She watched helplessly as he strode to the stern, almost tripping on the mass of cables dangling from the metal stand in the middle of the deck.

He leaned over the railing by the buoy and began fishing for any sign of the nylon net or the lost transmitter dish. The splashes grew louder, as did his cursing.

Kate turned away, unwilling to watch. Angrily, she threw her wet braid over her back. She was certain that her father's cherished project was dead. As dead as their brief moment of closeness. And she was certain that she had killed them both.

6

piece of eight

GROUNDED from using the kayak, Kate found her only solace exploring the shoreline along the promontory, especially when low tide unveiled a band of beach, a hundred feet wide, stretching between the black lava rocks and the rim of the sea. On one such foray, she pulled off her sandals and loped along the sand, her feet slapping into puddles and sinking into soft depressions.

Her eye caught a tidal pool, and she kneeled to examine this miniature ocean, frightening an orange crab who skittered away sideways. Shoots of eel grass waved in the water, undulating, sheltering the tiny blue fish who zipped in and out of the comely groves. Snail tracks flowed like ski trails down the sloping stones.

Spying a gnarled barnacle as big as her fist, Kate reached into the pool to grasp it when a small explosion burst in the water. She jerked back her hand as a sting ray lifted off the sandy bottom and floated to the far end of the pool. With a mixture of fear and fascination, she watched it move, flapping in slow motion like an underwater bird.

Then, from beyond the mouth of the lagoon, from behind the bank of fog resting on the water, she heard distant voices wailing. Eerily strange, yet hauntingly familiar, the songs of the whales filled the air for a few seconds, then died away.

Kate thought back to when she and her father had returned to camp in the *Skimmer* two days ago. No sooner had they dropped anchor than Isabella had met them on the beach and informed Jim that, despite all her pleas, the government had rejected her request for an extension. In three short days, she had said, they would have to leave the lagoon.

An explosion of activity, and of tempers, had ensued. After much ranting on both sides, Jim had finally convinced Terry to help him attempt to take one more picture. The young geologist had agreed, although he had expressed serious doubts it would be possible without the missing transmitter dish, and even more serious doubts they would find anything at all below the whirlpool. He had made it clear that he would cooperate only because the group's sole hope of remaining past the deadline would be to produce a recognizable picture of the sunken ship. As they had set to work, Isabella had sequestered herself in her makeshift lab, trying to complete her own experiments.

For the past two days, none of them had stopped working, leaving Kate to explore the beach on her own. She moved on, roaming among the rocks, watching striped lizards scurry through the pickle weed and cardon cactus. Spying some water spurting from a siphon hole in the sand, she dug furiously until she uncovered a plump, white Venus clam. She considered digging up the whole colony and preparing the tasty clams for supper, but she quickly discarded the idea, knowing that no one would pay any attention.

As she continued down the beach, she found herself seeing less of her natural surroundings and more of the discarded debris of civilization that had floated ashore even in this isolated lagoon. The beach seemed to be littered with plastic oil containers, stray bottles, beer cans.

"Looking for a message in a bottle?" asked a voice behind her.

She spun around to face a pale-skinned man, heavy in the shoulders and chest, squinting at her from behind his thick glasses. His sandy hair lay twisted in all directions, apparently uncombed for several days.

"Terry," she said in surprise. "What are you doing here?"

He continued to squint at her. "Decided to take a walk on the beach. Do you mind?"

"No, of course not. It's just that I've never seen you take a walk before."

"That's because this is my first. Thought I'd better take at least one before we leave. Tomorrow's our last day, you know."

She kicked at a crab shell protruding from the sand. "I know. I guess that means you and Dad haven't made much progress."

"Only a little. You have no idea what we're up against, technically speaking." Thrusting his hands deep into the pockets of his flaming orange Bermuda shorts, he added in a cutting tone, "We had a bit of vandalism to the equipment."

Her cheeks grew hot. "Look, I apologized already! Three or four times. Isn't that enough?"

"No," he answered crisply, trying to shield his eyes from the sun. "You can't imagine what I put into developing those devices. Both on the boat and on the buoys. To have you come by and rip it all apart . . . well, it's beyond asinine."

"I was just trying to—"

"Save a whale, I know. How sweet. Maybe that will qualify you for the Vandal of the Year award."

"Get lost."

"Is that what you said to my transmitter dish?"

Kate could only stare at him, feeling pain more than anger, regret more than rage. To her consternation, her eyes grew quite misty.

As Terry watched her, rubbing the two-day stubble on his chin, his expression softened slightly. "Consider it over and done with, all right? At least you waited until the end of the month to do it. The truth is, my work wasn't going anywhere anyway. I really need another six months to analyze the weird volcanism of this region."

"Weird?" she asked, grateful for the change of subject.

He wiped some perspiration from his pallid brow. "Suffice it to say that some rather strange things are happening off this coast. Things that can't be explained by plate tectonics and continental drift."

"You mean like the *Resurrección?*"

Terry guffawed. "I'm talking about *real* things. Things you can see, measure, and record. Like the unexplained surges in temperature I've detected on the ocean floor. Not phantom ships that exist for no one but wishful historians."

Again her cheeks felt hot. "You can't say for sure it's not down there."

"I'll grant you, there might be some old fishing boat down there, or something that looks enough like one to pull the wool over the bureaucrats' eyes. That's why we're working like mad to try for another picture. But a Spanish galleon from five hundred years ago? Complete with masts and sails and a load of treasure? Give me a break."

"How can you be so sure? You haven't been down to check."

"Because I believe in the fundamentals of science, that's why! Not in rumors or legends or whatever."

Squaring her shoulders, Kate shot back, "My Dad's proved plenty of legends are true."

"Sure," he replied. "As true as nursery rhymes."

"If he says the ship exists, then that's enough for me."

"That's why you're not a scientist."

"What's the difference?" she demanded. "You take theories and try to find out if they're true. He takes myths and does the same thing."

"Theories you can prove. Myths you can't. That's the difference." He narrowed his eyes still further. "Tell me the truth. Do *you* honestly believe in this Merlin character?"

"My dad thinks—"

"Not your dad. You."

"Well, I . . ."

"Do you believe it or not?"

"Well, no," she said quietly. "But that doesn't mean he didn't exist."

Terry nodded in satisfaction. "At least you're more of a realist than your father. He seems to think that wizards and treasure ships are all over the place, just waiting to be found."

"That's not fair," objected Kate. "Sure, he gets caught up in his dreams every once in a while. Doesn't everybody?" Stooping, she picked up a fragment of a sand dollar. "Didn't you ever want to find buried treasure when you were a kid? To hold in your hand something kings and queens and pirates fought over . . . like a real piece of eight?"

"Not really."

"Too bad." She threw the sand dollar into the rocks. "You missed a lot."

"A lot of bedtime stories." Without another word he turned and started striding back to camp.

7

an ancient ship,
the pride of spain

THAT afternoon, Kate stood outside the main tent watching the wind generator twirling slowly in the hot sun. She kicked a clump of sand, spraying it into the air. Several grains flew into her eye.

I couldn't have wrecked things more for Dad if I'd tried, she lamented, rubbing the sore eye.

The roar of an engine arrested her thoughts. She recognized the battered brown van as it chugged into camp, coughed, then lurched to a stop by Isabella's tent. It was Thursday, and that meant fish market day. The last fish market day.

Isabella, her slight frame made a bit taller by the bun of brown hair piled on her head, emerged from the tent. She looked tired, but not as thoroughly disheveled as Terry. Kate ambled over just as the van's door slid open and an elderly man with sun-baked skin jumped out. In one of his leathery hands, he clasped a net full of fish.

"Buenos dias," he said cheerily to both of them.

"Buenos dias," they answered simultaneously.

That was the last of the ensuing conversation that Kate could understand. Despite her efforts to learn Spanish in school, the real thing went so much faster. She listened to the syncopated rhythms of their speech and the rising inflection at the end of each sentence, trying to catch a word or a phrase.

The old man, moving with surprising agility, spread out the net on the sand. Isabella began examining the fish, peppering him with questions. He answered readily, tugging nervously on his bushy black mustache whenever she paused to inspect the catch.

Finally she pushed aside a larger fish to reveal a rather pathetic, spiny creature with goggle eyes. Catching her breath, she arched her thick eyebrows. Slowly, she said a few words Kate took to mean, "I'll take that one."

Visibly disappointed, the fisherman waved a plumper specimen before Isabella's eyes. But she shook her head and pressed a large clump of pesos into his hand. He quit protesting at once. Then, with the vigor of a much younger man, he packed up the remaining fish, tossed them into the van, and saluted Isabella and Kate.

As the van roared off in a swirl of dust, Isabella studied the fish in her hands. "Amazing," she muttered.

"Pretty ugly," observed Kate.

"No doubt about that, eh?" answered Isabella, still studying the fish.

"You don't expect me to cook it, do you? It wouldn't feed one person, let alone four."

"No," she responded as she pried open the fish's mouth and examined its teeth. "This one is not for cooking."

"What's it for, then?"

"Come see."

As they entered the tent, Isabella brought the fish over to her wash basin and scrubbed it under the rainwater tap. She pulled open each fin and counted the spines before laying it carefully in a pan. Then she dried her hands on her white T-shirt, pulled a fat textbook off the shelf, and began thumbing through the pages.

Kate watched with interest as the marine biologist checked various passages, glancing from time to time at the fish in the pan. At last she turned to a two-page chart showing the evolution of a particular genus of fish. Her slender finger pointed to an illustration of a gaunt-looking fish with oversized eyes. "There," she announced. "Remarkable, eh?"

"That's it, all right," agreed Kate. "Could be the ugliest fish in the book."

"Could be," said Isabella, closing the book. She turned to Kate, her gray eyes dancing with excitement. "More important, though, it's a museum piece. Until recently, everybody, including me, thought this species went extinct several hundred years ago."

Kate looked at the fish with new interest. "So this is the fish you've been studying."

"Hoping to study is more like it. I've been waiting to get my hands on a fresh specimen so I could run a genetic analysis."

"That's what you've been looking for in the submersible?"

"That and other things. As long as I don't go too near the whirlpool, or too close to the bottom because of the recent volcanic activity, there are enough interesting things around here to keep me going for a lifetime."

She reached for her small camera and took several pictures of the fish, top, bottom, both sides. Then she handed Kate a sterilized mask and put one on herself. Next she donned a pair of rubber gloves.

With a thin scalpel, she slit open the fish, found the spleen, extracted a blood sample and inserted it in a centrifuge. While the machine whirred, she carefully wrapped the fish and packed it into her small propane freezer. A few minutes later, she removed a tiny vial from the centrifuge and carefully transferred the liquid to a petri dish which she placed inside a compact incubator.

Peeling off her mask and gloves, she sat down at her desktop computer and punched in a few lines of information. Then she turned and said, "Fun, isn't it? Like waiting to open a Christmas present."

Kate found the analogy mystifying. "Hard to picture that goggle-eyed thing under a Christmas tree."

Isabella laughed. "The truth is, I feel that way about everything in the sea. That's what comes of growing up in a Mexican fishing village, I suppose. As a child I could hear the sounds of the sea everywhere, all the time, even in my dreams." She waved a hand at her little laboratory. "Seawater covers three fourths of our planet, spawned the very first life, even flows through our veins—yet we know almost nothing about it. Did you know that less than five percent of the ocean floor has ever been mapped, that we know more about the dark side of the moon than we do about the bottom of the sea?"

"No, but I know all I want to know, after meeting that whirlpool."

"Ah, *Remolino de la Muerté,*" replied Isabella in her gentle voice. "You are lucky to be alive."

"I suppose so," answered Kate. "Sometimes being alive doesn't feel so great, though." She tapped the top of the incubator. "Did you always want to study sea animals?"

She laughed again. "Always. That is, after I got over wanting to be a pearl diver. The sea has so many mysteries! Maybe if I live to be three hundred, like some of the folks around here claim to be, I could answer all my questions."

"Do they really say that?"

"Sure, that's what they say. It's a local tradition, eh? Claiming you're older than the sea. No one outside the fishing villages believes it, mind you. But there's no way to prove they're lying, since nobody keeps birth records."

Kate cocked her head toward the tent flap. "How about that guy who brought you the fish? He seems pretty spry for an old man."

"Manuel?" Isabella brushed back a stray strand of hair from her bun. "I don't know how old he is, but that's another curious thing about the villagers here. The old ones, even the ones who say they've lived for centuries, have the energy of youngsters. My mother used to say it's something in the water."

"That would be great if it's true."

Smiling, Isabella recalled, "I used to dream about living to be a thousand." She waited a moment, then asked softly, "And where, I wonder, do your dreams take you?"

Kate started to answer, then caught herself. She walked over to Isabella's little wooden altar by the tent window, bordered by six hand-painted carvings of saints. Beneath the altar sat a long table laden with vials of chemicals, beakers, meters, glass columns, a large microscope, and several more petri dishes. Without facing Isabella, she said, "Someplace where I won't cause any trouble."

"That's not much of a goal."

Kate leaned over the microscope for a few seconds. "It's the best I can do right now."

"Haven't you ever thought about what you'd like to do with your life?"

"I guess so."

Isabella lifted one petri dish to the light and examined it. "And?"

"Well, sometimes when I play softball I think about what it might be like to play shortstop for a real major league team."

"That's a good goal. Any others?"

"No."

"Come, now. Tell me."

Kate thought for a moment. "I suppose sometimes I've thought about . . . about *creating* something, like a book or a symphony or something." Her shoulders drooped. "Right now, though, all I create is trouble. Even when I try to do the right thing, like rescuing that whale, I mess things up royally."

Brushing back some loose hairs from the bun on her head, Isabella said, "I've been meaning to ask you about that, but with everything else going on I haven't had a chance. You're quite sure it was a gray whale?"

"Sure as could be. A young male."

"How was he caught?"

"By the tail, in the net. One of his flukes was almost completely cut off. Blood was everywhere."

"Oooh, that sounds bad. Was he able to swim after you set him free?"

"Hard to tell. He dove out of sight as soon as he could."

"I don't blame him."

Hesitantly, Kate asked, "Do you think he survived?"

Isabella frowned. "No way to know. It's possible. It's also possible that he bled to death, or wound up as food for sharks." Almost as an afterthought, she added, "One thing is certain, though. If you hadn't come along, he would have surely died. You gave him a chance, albeit a small one."

"A lot of good that does for Dad's project."

"You did what you had to do, Kate." She replaced the petri dish on the table. "And who knows? Perhaps what you did had some hidden virtue to it."

"What could be good about destroying the buoy?"

The woman drew in her breath. "For one thing, you

made close contact with one of the gray whales who stay here year round. In fact, it may be the first time that's happened since the whalers came here and nearly wiped them out a century ago. The grays who migrate to the Arctic seem to have forgiven, or at least forgotten, those days, but the year-round group has avoided human contact entirely. And since they never seem to stray from the whirlpool, it's been impossible to observe them. All anyone has been able to do is photograph them from a distance and, sometimes, record their mournful songs."

"He did sound awfully sad. But I thought that was because he was dying."

"No, they're always like that. I've never heard anything like it. So sad, beyond what words can explain."

Biting her lip, Kate said, "The worst part is, I really wanted to help Dad on this trip. More than just cooking and doing dishes. I wanted . . . to be his assistant or something. He's always pulling me out of trouble, like he did at the whirlpool. And look what I've done! I've ruined everything."

"That remains to be seen," answered Isabella, examining the collection of petri dishes. "What feels like an ending might turn into a beginning."

"That sounds nice, but life doesn't really work that way."

Isabella's mind seemed to drift somewhere else for a moment. After a while she said, "Maybe you're right. Our sorrows and our joys do stick with us. Especially our sorrows, it seems." She shook her head, as if trying to banish some unwanted memory.

Then, motioning for Kate to come nearer, she pointed to one of the petri dishes. "There is another side, though. Do you see this little dish? Only yesterday, I put a single cell in it. Now look at it. Multiplied into thousands of new cells already. All from that first microscopic dot."

With a shrug, Kate said, "I don't get it."

Isabella pondered the petri dish for a moment, then tried again. "Something that has always fascinated me about evolutionary biology is that the process never ends. Life keeps growing, changing. Every spiral of DNA is part of the greater spiral of life, a spiral that goes on and on forever. Have you ever thought about that?"

"No."

"Well, to put it another way, you might say *all the future lies within the present*. In other words, the very first single-celled creatures that appeared in the ocean held in themselves all the possibilities of evolution. They were the simplest life you could imagine, more water than organism. I call them *water spirits*. And yet they contained the seeds of fish, dinosaurs, and even humans. Small as they were, they had all the power of creation."

Kate waved at the little wooden altar. "I thought you believed God created everything."

"I do," she replied. "Like a good Catholic. And I believe in evolution, too. It's just one of God's tools to keep life from getting stagnant. Creation is an ongoing process, as I said. And the best part is, you and I are part of it. You still have in yourself all the possibilities of the water spirit."

Kate stared at her blankly, then moved to the window. "You're not ready yet to hear this, are you?"

"I'm ready," she responded. "I just don't believe you, that's all."

Isabella moved to the microscope and began sorting through some slides. Finally she came to one that she studied for some time. At length, she exhaled wistfully.

"What is it?" asked Kate, her curiosity aroused.

"Come see."

Kate peered into the lens, adjusted the focus. "Stars!" she exclaimed. "Stars in a night sky."

"Remarkable, isn't it?" grinned the scientist. "They're microbes, found in a single drop of seawater. Yet from this perspective, they look as big as a galaxy."

Raising her head, Kate said quietly, "You know what I like best about looking at the stars?"

"Hmmm. How many stars there are?"

"No. How many *spaces* there are. All those empty spaces between the stars. That's where I can imagine traveling for ever and ever. That's where I can imagine infinity."

Isabella gazed thoughtfully at the microscope. "Just as every star is part of creation, so are all the empty spaces between the stars."

With a nod, Kate turned toward the window flap. She looked beyond the main tent and the wind generator, to the slate blue bay beyond. Numberless rows of gray waves crisscrossed the expanse, broken only by the occasional burst of white where currents collided. "I'll never forget the sight of that whale's tail, all ripped and bloody." She watched the water again. "I read someplace

that the whalers used to harpoon baby whales, but not
kill them, so their screams would bring their parents
close enough to get harpooned. Is that true?"

"I'm afraid so. That's when some gray whales would
go wild and try to sink the ships. So whalers called them
devilfish and the slaughter began. It was a sorry end to a
friendship that started out so nicely."

"Nicely?"

"When the first sailors arrived here on the galleons,
the whales were still friendly. Not frightened. The crew
of the *Resurrección* was even saved, according to legend, by whales who were swimming nearby."

"You're kidding."

"That's the legend. There's the old ballad that I translated for your father. It talks about that, and a few other
things just as strange."

Kate moved closer. "Isabella, would you sing it for
me? The whole thing?"

She glanced at the timer on the incubator. "I suppose
so. We still have a few minutes left, eh?" She waved
away some rebellious hairs. "It goes on forever, but
lucky for you, I can't remember it all."

An ancient ship, the pride of Spain, she began, her
lilting voice describing the ship's fateful journey. Only
occasionally did she pause, muttering a few Spanish
phrases to herself before continuing. All the while Kate
listened, engrossed.

As the tale concluded, Isabella intoned:

> *And so today the ship's at rest,*
> *Removed from ocean gales,*

Surrounded by a circle strange
Of ever-singing whales.

A prophesy clings to the ship
Like barnacles to wood.
Its origins remain unknown,
Its words not understood:

One day the sun will fail to rise,
The dead will die,
  And then
For Merlin's Horn to find its home,
The ship must sail again.

"*Magnifico!*" Kate clapped heartily. "*Magnifico!*"
Isabella bowed in return.

"Can you do that last part again? The part with the prophesy."

She obliged.

One day the sun will fail to rise,
The dead will die,
  And then
For Merlin's Horn to find its home,
The ship must sail again.

"Thanks," said Kate. "Leaves you wondering, doesn't it?"

"A good ballad can do that." Isabella turned to the incubator. "Time to check on our little Christmas present."

"It couldn't look any worse than that fish itself."

On went the sterilized masks and rubber gloves. Carefully removing the petri dish from the incubator, Isabella took a small sample and heated it in a water solution. She then carefully mixed it with a substance labeled *radioactive precursor.* Allowing the mixture to cool, she started draining it through a glass column, injecting new chemicals from time to time.

Seeing Kate's puzzled expression, Isabella explained, "Controlling the ion concentration."

"That helps a lot."

At last, she connected a small meter attached to a photoelectric cell to the glass column. Instantly, the arm of the meter began to quiver, pulsing with a subtle rhythm.

"What does that mean?" asked Kate through her mask.

Isabella did not answer. Seemingly oblivious to everything else, she drew a diagram of a spiraling strand of DNA in her journal, making several notations beside it. Then, meticulously, she cleaned and sterilized her equipment. After that she repeated the entire procedure.

When the meter began bouncing again, recording its invisible quarry, Isabella inspected it closely. Shaking her head, she declared, "This can't be right."

As Kate looked on, the woman cleaned every piece of equipment once more. Methodically, she retraced her steps. For the third time, she connected the meter.

It bounced again.

Isabella grabbed her journal and moved to the computer. There she started entering data until the screen filled with letters, numbers, and symbols Kate could not recognize. Her concentration unshakable, Isabella manipulated the information for some time.

At length, she turned an expressionless face toward Kate. Her voice as calm as the lagoon at dawn, she said simply, "That fish is even more amazing than I thought."

8

one out of three billion

CAN'T this wait, Isabella?" Jim rubbed his unshaven cheek. "We're almost ready to try another picture. With any luck at all—"

"Luck has nothing to do with it," interrupted Terry, standing in a wilderness of cables sprouting from the back of his computer terminal. He glanced toward the tent flap and pushed his thick glasses higher on his nose. "But we'll never finish if people insist on interrupting us."

Undaunted, Isabella raised the flap to the tent. "If you won't come to the meeting, the meeting comes to you," she declared. She strode inside, followed by Kate, who avoided her father's gaze.

Terry ignored them. "You talk to her, Jim, while I keep working." He continued to tinker with the circuitry.

"Isabella," pleaded Jim, waving a sheaf of printouts in his hand. "Can't you save it for later?"

"No," she replied firmly. "This could be a lot more important than your picture. Believe me, Jim, it's worth your time." She cocked her head at Terry. "And if he wants to miss out on something this big, well, that's his business."

The young geologist looked at her doubtfully. "How big?"

"Big."

"All right," he grumbled, setting down a pair of tweezers holding a microchip. "This better be good."

"Five minutes, no more." Jim stretched his stiff back, dropped the printouts on his desk, and fell into his chair. Leaning back, he propped one foot on the desk, knocking off a barnacle-encrusted shell that had served as a paperweight.

As Isabella started to speak, Kate heard the crash of a wave on the shore and the grinding of sand being sucked down into the lagoon. She would miss this place, its many sounds and smells.

"You know that fish I've been looking for? Well, today I found one, a good adult specimen."

"So?" demanded Terry impatiently.

Isabella paid him no heed. "I did a genetic analysis. Did it three times to make sure there was no error. And I found something truly bizarre."

She sucked in her breath, weighing her words. "The fish has found *a kind of eternal life*."

Kate glanced at her father, but his eyes were fixed on Isabella.

"What do you mean by that?"

"I mean . . . it would never have died of old age.

Sure, it could still be killed, as it was when it was taken out of the water. But that's different."

"Wait a minute," protested Terry. "You said it was an adult. How could it have grown to be an adult without growing old?"

Isabella blew some dangling hairs out of her eyes. "It's rather strange, I admit. The fish looks like an adult . . . except at the genetic level. I can't explain it, but something must have happened to make its genetic structure stop deteriorating. Its DNA shows none of the normal decay that occurs over a lifetime. On top of that, it looks exactly like DNA from fish that lived in this area long ago. It's almost as if the fish . . . became *young* somehow. And stayed that way."

Like the villagers, thought Kate, though she dared not say it aloud.

"That's hard to believe," said Jim.

"It's absurd," declared Terry.

Isabella faced him. "Any more absurd than gene splicing was before somebody did it? Or X rays? Or television?"

"Or continental drift," added Kate.

"Give me a break," snarled the young man. "I don't need geology lessons from you."

"Maybe you need something else, then."

Jim raised his hand. "Quiet, you two." He turned to Isabella. "Let me get this straight. You're saying that this fish of yours is not just a modern-day descendant of some ancient species. You're saying that it's ancient *as an individual.* That it has found some way to live on and on, perhaps forever. Is that right?"

Isabella nodded, as a pair of gulls passed over the tent, screeching loudly. "It's more than that. This fish is not just frozen in time, stretching its life across centuries without decay. It seems to be constantly renewed. Recreated. Reborn."

"But how could that be?" demanded Jim.

"We're all ears," said Terry, fingering a cable.

"Let me give you a theory. It's nothing more than a guess at this stage, mind you, but maybe it will help. Have you ever heard of a disease called progeria?"

No one responded.

"All right, then. Progeria is a rare genetic disorder that causes premature aging in children. It's horrible to see. Kids grow old so fast that by the time they're nine or ten years old, they look like they're eighty. They develop arthritis, hair loss, bone deterioration, everything. By the time they reach eleven or twelve, they die. And all this happens because one tiny little gene on Chromosome Eight—that's *one gene out of three billion*—happens to be in the wrong position."

Terry checked his watch. "What's this got to do with your fish?"

"Now, it's been proven that some viruses can carry a gene that can change the regulatory system of the host being. So it's possible there is some sort of virus or other substance in the water that can rearrange the genetic material of the sea life around here."

"In the water?" asked Jim.

"Why not?" Isabella replied. "We're only beginning to learn about the strange things that inhabit the sea. You've heard about the undersea volcanic vents—smokers. They breed forms of life that can exist at temperatures above three hundred degrees Fahrenheit, that can live off of sulphur instead of light and air. Like nothing else on Earth."

"So you're saying," pressed Jim, "that something in the water here is altering the genes, causing the aging process to slow down."

"Or even stop."

"But that would mean that creatures could go on living . . . indefinitely."

"That's right," said Isabella calmly. "Think about it logically. Germ cells and cancer cells can reproduce endlessly, making them practically immortal. So might it not be possible, just possible, that the right genetic formula could do the same for us?"

Terry frowned skeptically. "This is ridiculous."

"Is it? In some ways, the fish I examined is not so different from you or me. Our own bodies are constantly replacing themselves, aren't they? Over a seven-year period, every cell in our bodies is replaced. So I suppose you could say that we have some of the same power of renewal. Maybe we just have to learn how to use it better."

Jim considered the notion, like a gourmet savoring a rare delicacy. "You know, legend has it that Merlin somehow learned how to stay the same age. He even figured out how to live backwards, growing younger instead of older with time. The bards called him *oldest at birth, youngest at death.*"

"Hey," piped Kate. "Maybe you should call this thing *the Merlin effect.*"

For the first time in two days, Jim Gordon smiled at his daughter. He then asked Isabella, "Could this—this

Merlin effect of yours also slow down the deterioration of things that aren't alive, things like wood and cloth and rope?"

"Perhaps, if they're made of organic materials."

"Now look here," said Terry, his normally pallid skin flushed with color. "I've had about enough of this. Are we talking about science—or hocus-pocus?"

Isabella studied him with something like pity in her eyes. "For some of us, the more we learn the less we know."

"Come on, Isabella! You're a scientist. This doesn't stand to reason."

"Reason isn't always enough," she answered. "As a scientist named Einstein once said, *Subtle is the Lord.*"

"Let's get back to the facts," insisted Terry. "Couldn't this fish be just some kind of mutant? A random, isolated case that will never happen again?"

"Sure," answered Isabella. "But it's possible something more is going on here." She scanned the faces inside the tent, listening to the sloshing and splashing of waves in the lagoon. "Have you ever wondered why this area is so rich in species found nowhere else, or thought to be extinct? Not just fish but crustaceans and porpoises and other things, too. No one, as far as I know, has analyzed their DNA structures, but there is no question now that we should."

Kate stopped twirling her braid. "Are you saying," she asked hesitantly, "that the whales who stay here year round might have been here for ages?"

"Could be. That whale you saved might even have been around when the *Resurrección* went down."

"Sure," said Terry, "and maybe he's also the whale who swallowed Jonah."

Isabella locked into his gaze. "Maybe."

"Nonsense! I suppose the next thing you'll tell us is that Jim's lost ship will rise again, as the legend says."

"Its name is *Resurrección*," said Isabella softly.

"This is absurd," declared Terry. "Do you really expect us to believe that there is some sort of fountain of youth down there?"

"Not a fountain of youth. Not exactly. More like a fountain of . . . creation. A place that breeds new life in things."

"Enough." He retrieved his tweezers. "I'm going back to work. You people can waste your time if you want to." He dove again into the mass of cables and circuitry attached to the terminal.

Jim, deep in thought, lifted his foot off the desk. "Creation," he muttered, rubbing his beard. "Do you really think that's possible?"

"Theoretically, yes," replied Isabella.

Focusing on a point somewhere beyond the walls of the tent, he said in a hushed voice, "Imagine . . . a power like that. What it could do. What it could mean."

For a time, they were silent. The tent flap fluttered in the salty breeze, snapping like a flag in a storm.

A moment later Terry tugged on Jim's sleeve. "Give me a hand here, will you? Hold these two cables in place while I check the current."

The historian jolted, then rose from his chair. As Isabella and Kate looked on, Jim and Terry labored to make the final adjustments and connections. They tossed questions and commands back and forth as latches clicked, hinges squealed, keys tapped.

At last, Terry straightened up, walked over to the computer, and announced, "Now or never."

He flicked a switch on a jerry-rigged control panel and pressed *Enter* on the keyboard. The computer hummed steadily but gave no other indication that anything was happening. Then, with a subtle flash, an image started to appear on the screen.

At first a hazy patch coalesced near the bottom of the screen, looking like nothing in particular. A few wavy lines formed above, tilting at steep angles. Numberless dots appeared, then receded, along the left side, as though something was moving in and out of focus.

As the group watched, the image on the screen wavered. It seemed to grow less, rather than more, recognizable.

"What is it?" asked Kate, perplexed.

"Whatever it is, it's useless to us," observed Terry. "Something is malfunctioning."

"And we don't have time to find it and fix it," added Jim in a somber tone. "If only we . . . wait a minute. What's *that?*"

Terry started to adjust the controls, then froze, staring at the screen.

Collectively, they held their breath as the resolution on the screen swiftly deepened. The patch near the bottom took on the dense, curved shape of a great hull. The wavy lines solidified into three masts, two straight, one broken near the base. The dots grouped themselves to the left of the masts, drooping like tattered sails.

"My God."

"It's . . . the *Resurrección*."

Then, inexplicably, the picture began to shimmer, like a reflection in a quiet pool that is disturbed by a stone. All at once, the lines grew fuzzier, the solid places grew lighter.

Terry immediately banged several commands on the keyboard. "What the devil?" he cursed, pounding ever more vigorously.

To no avail. The image of the ship slipped steadily away. Within seconds, it melted to a ghostly shadow, then abruptly disappeared. The screen stared at its viewers, completely blank.

"How could that happen?" demanded Jim. "Is something disconnected?"

Terry shook his head slowly. "Can't be. The terminal is still operating."

"Then what's wrong?"

"Don't know," muttered the geologist, activating the computer printer. "Maybe what we saw was captured in the memory."

After a long pause, a page emerged from the printer. It too was blank.

Terry snatched the page and crumpled it. "I can't believe it," he stewed. "It was almost as if . . ." His words faded away, much as the picture had done.

"Yes?"

"As if . . . something *erased* it."

Jim shook his head. "I don't follow."

Terry eyed him uncertainly. "The only way it could happen is if another set of sonic waves, from another source, canceled out the signals. And there's nothing around here that could do that."

"Oh, yes there is." Isabella stepped forward. "Whales. Gray whales."

"Don't be absurd," said Terry. "Their echolocation isn't nearly as powerful as my equipment."

"What if a group of whales were to project a certain frequency together, in concert? That could do it."

"But that would require a level of intelligence that's never been proven."

"Or disproven."

"You're saying they might be *deliberately* interfering with my sonar?"

"I'm saying it's possible, eh?"

As Terry and Jim traded glances, Kate asked, "Why, though? Why would the whales want to eliminate the picture of the ship?"

"Only they could answer that," Isabella replied.

Jim gazed unhappily at the blank screen. "And we won't be around to ask them. The picture was our last chance."

"We may have one more chance," said a gentle voice. Everyone turned to Isabella.

"We can try . . . the submersible."

"But I thought you were worried about the whirlpool."

"I am, believe me! We're talking about *Remolino de la Muerté.*" She searched Jim's eyes. "I saw the ship. So did you. We can't leave here without trying."

"How long will it take to get the submersible ready?"

"Several hours," she answered. "We'll need to check

everything. Thrusters, fuel tanks, oxygen tanks, pressure housings, the works. And I'll need to insulate the battery pack so the pressure from the whirlpool doesn't cause seawater to short the electrical system. We'll work through the night if we have to."

"I'll be your copilot," volunteered Jim.

"Wait," cautioned Terry. "Are you sure about this? I'd like to stay and complete my work as much as either of you, but I don't want anyone to get killed because of it."

Kate felt a sudden surge of gratitude, a feeling she had not before associated with Terry. "He's right," she declared. "I've seen the whirlpool. You don't want to risk going anywhere near it. Even for the ship. Even for the—"

Her father coughed loudly, cutting her off.

"We'll avoid the vortex—the spinning wall of water—and try to slip underneath." Isabella gathered in her arms a stack of nautical maps. "If the whirlpool doesn't reach all the way down to the bottom, we might be able to hug the sea floor and avoid it entirely."

"Not so fast." Terry pointed at the maps. "The sea floor in this area is spotted with volcanic activity. And my seismograph has been acting strangely. There could be an eruption building. Maybe a major one. I wouldn't want to be anywhere in the area."

Jim pondered his warning. "What would an eruption do to the ship we saw?"

"If it's sitting near the epicenter? Wipe it out, most likely." Terry toyed with the rim of his glasses. "As it would anything nearby. Might even destroy the whirlpool itself, or do some strange things to it."

Jim faced Isabella squarely. "It's your call."

She considered the blank computer screen for a moment. Then she planted her small hand on top of it. "Come. We have much to do before we sail."

9

the eye of light

BY dawn, they were nearly ready.

As amber light streamed from the east, singeing the peaks of the waves in the lagoon, the ocean breeze blew stronger. Kate stood on the deck of the *Skimmer*. She leaned against the railing, watching Isabella and her father crawl in and out of the silver submersible that floated beside the old trawler. One by one, each item on Isabella's checklist was inspected, tested, adjusted, approved.

Navigation instruments. Depth sounder. Cable winch. Mechanical arm. Hoisting bitt. Batteries.

Watching the process under the steadily lightening sky, Kate knew she could do little to help other than load the odd case or find the occasional replacement part. Terry, meanwhile, had no need for her at all, or at least no faith in her abilities, as he labored to transfer much of his equipment to the metal stand on the *Skimmer*'s deck.

She felt deeply torn about this voyage. She wanted her father's project to succeed. She wanted him to find the ship, to recover the lost Horn of Merlin, to put to rest forever the doubts of those who refused to believe that Merlin truly existed. In a way, his life's work was at stake. Yet . . . so was his life. To imagine him and Isabella willingly flinging themselves into the waters around *Remolino de la Muerté* . . . She frowned, observing the heavy clouds to the south.

Scanning sonar. Camera forward. Camera aft. Viewing ports. Batteries, again.

Kate marveled at how much equipment was crammed into the submersible. Shaped like a bulbous fish, or as Isabella liked to joke, a fat football, it was no bigger than a standard minivan. Yet it held enough gear and supplies to support two people for five days at a maximum depth of seven thousand feet.

Emergency tether. Strobe lights. Floodlights. Titanium sphere. Hatch.

"That's it," pronounced Isabella, pulling herself out of the submersible's hatch and onto the *Skimmer*. She moved to the railing and gently placed her arm around Kate's waist. "Try not to worry," she whispered.

"I'm trying."

At that point, Jim's head lifted out of the hatch. Wedging his shoulders through the narrow opening, he grumbled to Isabella, "Why do you have to drive a subcompact?"

The marine biologist watched him with amusement. "Next you will be knocking my choice of color."

"Silver is fine," he replied, clambering aboard the *Skimmer*. "I'd just like a little more legroom."

Terry joined them. "All set."

Eyeing the conglomeration of hardware Terry had assembled on the deck, Jim said, "You've made my old trawler look more like an oil rig."

The stocky geologist pushed back his glasses. "I'll strike oil before you do."

Isabella regarded him quizzically. "What are you up to? Those are some of your most specialized instruments, aren't they?"

Terry waved proudly at the metal stand. "I'm trying something completely new. Revolutionary, even. If it works, I'll get a better fix on the volcanic activity on the ocean floor than we have ever had. Than *anyone* has ever had."

"Let's hope it's calm down there today," said Jim.

"Up here, too." Isabella scanned the bank of dark clouds moving in. "I don't like the looks of those clouds."

"Nor do I," agreed Jim. He tugged lightly on Kate's braid. "See you by sunset. Let's have Baja Scramble for supper."

"Be careful," was all she could manage to say.

He turned to Terry. "Turn us loose anywhere near the second buoy. Then hold tight to the steering wheel! I don't have to tell you about the wicked currents out there by the whirlpool."

"No, you don't." Suddenly Terry's face fell. "Damn."

"What?"

"I can't stay at the wheel. After I release the submersible, I've got to operate my instruments."

"But you can't! Someone's got to steer."

"Someone else, then. Maybe you should ride on the boat instead of the submersible."

Jim scowled. "Now wait a minute. This is my opportunity."

"Mine, too."

"You can't do this."

Terry folded his arms.

"Wait a minute, Dad." Kate's own voice surprised her. "I can do it."

"Do what?"

"Steer the boat. I've done it before."

He caught his breath. For a moment he stared at her, swaying to the rhythm of the rocking vessel, then slowly shook his head. "I can't ask you to do that. We'll be out there near the . . . No, Kate, no."

"You didn't ask. I volunteered."

"Sounds like she's willing," said Isabella.

Jim observed his daughter, then touched her nose with his finger. "I'm tempted to say thanks."

"Hold it," said Terry. "What if the water gets rough? I've got my best instruments on board. Are you sure she can handle it?"

Kate's torso stiffened. "I can handle it."

"I believe you," declared Jim. "Let's get going. You take the wheel when Terry goes to release the cable. Got it?"

She nodded.

"And if the waves get heavy, turn into them. That way you won't capsize."

She nodded again.

"And don't forget to put on your life jacket."

"All right," growled Terry. He faced Kate. "Just keep away from my instruments."

"Let's go." Isabella raised her voice above a gust of wind. "The weather's looking meaner."

She scampered over the side and down the hatch of the submersible. Jim followed, more awkwardly. An instant later, his hand reached up and pulled the hatch closed with a *clank*.

Without a word to Kate, Terry raised the anchor, checked the cable connecting the two crafts, and stepped into the cabin. As he turned on the engine, she cast her eyes toward the rising waves beyond the breakers and the heavy bank of mist beyond. She remembered her life jacket, then realized it was in the cabin with Terry. She grasped the railing securely, even as the first drops of rain struck her face.

Slowly, the trawler and its gleaming silver cargo slid into the lagoon. On a good day, with a favorable wind, the *Skimmer* could cruise at seven or eight knots. With a heavy load like this, Kate knew, it would be lucky to make half that speed, although that was still faster than the submersible could move under its own power. As she listened to the straining, sputtering engine, she wondered how long it would take before that noise would be joined by the ominous humming she had heard once before.

The water grew increasingly rough as they reached the mangroves. Submerged in high tide, the trees seemed now less a forest than a green labyrinth concealing many dark mysteries. A massive wave slapped the boat, jostling

Kate. She staggered to one side, wrapping her hands more tightly around the railing.

Regaining her balance, she saw the last dune come into view. Soon would come the breakers. And beyond . . . She did not want to think about it. But she could not help herself. Her body tensed, just as another wave flooded the deck, spraying water into the air, soaking her jeans and cotton shirt.

She tried to distract herself by focusing on the submersible, bobbing along behind. How bad was the ride for its passengers? They couldn't be comfortable in there. What would it be like for them to travel below the surface, way below, where light never shines? Someday, perhaps, she would find out. In another ocean, another time.

The boat shook violently as they entered the breakers, twisting her stomach into knots. Feeling nauseous, she looked toward the lagoon. Shreds of swirling fog had started to consume everything, making the camp less and less visible. The rain pelted harder. Before long she could see only the top of the flagpole above the mist, then nothing.

As the *Skimmer* chugged past the first buoy, a brown pelican dropped out of the darkened sky. The bird plunged into the frothy waves, surfacing an instant later with a struggling, squirming fish.

Farther from shore, nearer to death. The words echoed in her head to the cadence of the wheezing engine. *Farther from shore . . .*

Waves of water, waves of fear. The boat pitched wildly from side to side. Wind roared. Lightning exploded in the air, followed by the rumble of thunder, booming between sea and sky, melding with the humming sound that drifted over the sea.

Terry threw open the cabin door. "It's time!" he shouted above the storm.

Kate stepped toward him but slipped on the deck, careening some distance before she could catch herself on the railing. She righted herself awkwardly, then stumbled to the doorway.

"Get the wheel," he commanded. Without closing the door, he hurled himself onto the deck.

Grabbing the steering wheel, Kate twisted the boat into an immense wave just as it swallowed the bow. Glancing over her shoulder, she could see Terry crawling the last few feet to the lever mounted at the stern where the cable attached. Once he released it, Isabella could retract the cable and descend.

Bracing herself, she held tight to the wheel despite the violent swaying. Wave after wave crashed against the hull. Yet she remained firmly planted, holding the boat on course.

It's been more than two minutes, she realized with a start. Swinging her head toward the stern, she could see Terry struggling to move the lever. He was straining, throwing all his weight into the task. A wave washed over him. He strained still harder. Yet the lever did not budge.

He started to pound at it with the heel of his hand. Then, seeing Kate through the doorway, he called to her.

"The hammer! Bring me the hammer!"

She began letting loose of the helm, when she realized

that to do so was to risk a disaster. Grasping the wheel firmly with one hand, she shoved the cabin chair underneath as a brace, scraping her knuckles in the process. She stepped back. It would hold, but not for long.

Pulling her father's old hammer from the box of tools in the corner, she worked her way across the deck, fighting to stay on her feet. At last she reached the stern and handed Terry the hammer. He smashed the lever several times, to no avail.

Just then a great wave collided with the port side. The metal stand bearing Terry's instruments slid perilously close to the railing. He leaped to it, hauled it back, then staggered over to Kate.

Mist wrapped around them, so tightly that they could no longer even see the submersible at the other end of the cable. The swells heaved, the *Skimmer* tossed.

Terry raised the hammer to swat again at the jammed lever.

Then a strange thing happened. The cable to the submersible suddenly went slack—from the submersible side. Kate and Terry stared at each other, thunderstruck, knowing there was no way to release the cable from that end.

Kate leaned over the railing, peering into the impenetrable fog. At that instant, a huge wave hit the hull. The boat lurched sharply. She pitched over the side, though one hand somehow held on to the railing. She hung there, dangling above the raging sea.

"Hellllp!" she wailed. Water sucked at her legs, hauling her downward.

Terry reached his hand toward her, stretching to grab

hold. Suddenly he caught sight of his instruments tottering near the edge of the deck. He hesitated for a fraction of a second.

Another wave arched and toppled over the stern. Kate's grip tore loose, and she tumbled into the sea.

She groped madly for the surface, gasping for air. The pounding in her head merged with a clamorous humming sound that swelled steadily.

Panicked, she tried desperately to swim away from the sound. Away from the whirlpool! More waves tumbled over her, sapping her energy. Her limbs weighed like anchors. The *Skimmer* had vanished in the fog and spray.

Without warning, the water grew calmer. An enormous wave seemed to carry her upward, higher than the ragged surface of the sea. Instead of pounding her, the water swirled past, racing around and around in a great circle. Then, to her horror, she saw that below her a dark, yawning chasm was opening: a huge hole in the middle of the ocean.

The hole drew her nearer. She fought to get away, but the dark center expanded, reaching toward her, pulling her down.

The world started spinning. The gray sky above shrank into a vanishing eye of light, shimmering with the moving mist. Everything whirled faster and faster. A wall of blue rose above her, high as she could see.

Then, all at once, the sky disappeared.

PART TWO

Beyond the Whirlpool

10

mist

A twisted train of dreams besieged Kate as she floated in and out of consciousness. Swirling, undulating images swam into view and then burst apart, scattering into grains of sand. Falling! She was falling downward, ever downward . . . Curling, crashing waves. *Help! I need to breathe!* Falling, spinning, falling, spinning. A family of gray whales, all pouring blood from their severed tails. Someone else, someone she knew. *Dad! Dad, I'm here!* But he could not hear, hidden behind the steel walls of the submersible. Then another figure. Terry. *Reach! Just reach for me!* Still falling . . . Wispy sails. A sunken ship. Waves, more waves, surging and subsiding, pounding her, twisting her back to the point of breaking. Sudden calm. Dead quiet. Sand on her tongue.

Drenched and bruised, she opened her eyes.

She spat out some sand. With effort, she tried to

make herself stand. But the dreadful dizziness returned and she fell back, her head whirling.

For some time she merely lay there, her face in the wet sand, waves gently lapping at her sneakers. When at last the spinning slowed enough, she resolved to try again. More slowly this time. She slid one arm forward and planted her hand on the sodden ground. Despite the throbbing in her neck, she rolled to her side.

Fog. Fog everywhere.

She rested, gathering her strength, before daring to try to lift her head again. With a groan, .she pushed herself to her knees. The dizziness flowed into her brain like water into a broken boat, yet she held her body rigid, unwilling to relinquish her gains. Then the sand started to sway and slide beneath her and she toppled once more.

She turned slowly onto her back. The world continued to swirl, and the ceaseless spinning seemed to exist as much within her mind as without. Again, she perceived the heavy mist surrounding her. And a salty taste on her lips. Or was that, too, just a dream? Fog curled and billowed, wrapping around her, covering the surface of this little island where she now lay. If indeed it was an island.

Gazing upward at the shifting clouds, she became conscious of a sound. Humming like an army of engines, it seemed omnipresent, coming from everywhere and yet nowhere in particular. It reminded her of the whirlpool's dreadful droning, while at the same time it was somehow different. Then the clouds grew thicker, racing around with increasing speed. Everything she could see began to rotate, whirling endlessly, as if she were stranded in the middle of a cyclone.

Dizzy again, she grasped the ground with both hands, squeezing the sand in her fists. Sheets of mist flowed past, shielding her from the twisting clouds above. All the while the humming sound persisted, vibrating in her ears.

Concentrating on every movement, no matter how small, she rolled to one side and clambered to a kneeling position. *As long as I don't move too fast, maybe . . .* She rested awhile, then gradually, painfully, lifted herself to her feet.

She took a wobbly step, surveyed her surroundings. The rolling fog obscured all beyond a few yards. This island seemed to be nothing but a low, sandy mound, without much color and without a single tree, bush, or blade of grass. The only vegetation she could see was a purplish algae that rimmed the shore, glistening in the watery light.

Something shiny, half buried in the sand, caught her eye. She stooped to retrieve it, when suddenly the entire island shook with a violent tremor. The ground buckled savagely, knocking her off her feet.

Then, as abruptly as it had struck, the tremor ceased. Kate lay there, tears welling in her eyes. *Am I that weak?* Or did the ground really shake? She tugged lightly on her braid, the way her father so often did.

A deep desire rose within her, a desire to find him, to be with him again. Someplace where the ground didn't shake, or seem to shake. Someplace out of danger.

Out of danger. Those final moments on board the

Skimmer were so compressed, so cloudy. She could only remember the storm, and Terry starting to reach for her—then letting her fall. Yet there was something else, something about her father, that nagged at the edges of her memory. She knew it was important. But what could it be? All she could recall was the vague feeling that something had gone awry. That he was in trouble.

She shook her head, pushing aside such worries. In not very long he and Isabella would surface in the submersible and make their way back to camp, with or without any help from Terry, with or without some evidence of the sunken ship. *At least the weather is calmer,* she told herself. *The fog may be thick, but that storm seems to be over.*

Haltingly, she forced herself to rise. Dizziness swept through her again, and she placed both palms on the sand for support. Her right hand brushed against a hard object. Seeing the shiny glint again, she closed her fingers around it and pulled.

For an instant the sand held firmly, as though unwilling to part with its prize. Then, with a slurping noise, the object came free, leaving behind a little tomb that filled swiftly with water. She wiped off the wet sand, then held the object before her.

She blinked in surprise. It was a finely wrought comb, carved from white ivory. Upon its back, embellished in gold, shone the face of a woman. With the hint of a smile and sad, loving eyes, she looked almost sublime. *The Virgin Mary? Isabella might know.*

Mystified but exhilarated, she twirled the comb in the luminous mist. Then she slipped it into one of the pockets of her wet jeans. Though her back ached and her knees trembled, she rose once again and cautiously stepped forward. Her feet sank into the soft sand.

But for the undulating mist, nothing stirred. This island seemed totally uninhabited. Not even a solitary crab scurried over the ground. She felt utterly alone.

Cupping her hands, she called into the mist. "Hello! Can anybody hear me?"

No response. She tried again with the same result. It might be ages before anyone found her in fog like this. She could barely see beyond the water's edge. She kicked a clump of sand, wishing it were the face of a certain young geologist.

She rolled up the sleeves of her blue cotton shirt. The humid mist felt warm, like the inside of a kiln. *Strange it's so hot on such a cloudy day.* She trudged into the fog, leaving a string of gray footprints behind.

A new sound knifed the air. Kate halted, listening. Beyond the continuous humming, a distant scream wavered. Slowly it deepened into a mournful wailing, a wailing she had heard before. Louder it swelled, until joined by other voices, creaking and whistling like winds of pain. Soon it seemed that the sea had found a voice of its own, raised in unending sorrow.

Whales. They were out there, somewhere beyond the fog. *So sad, beyond what words can explain.* That was how Isabella had described their songs.

Then, as she walked, the mist before her shifted, darkened. At first she thought it was nothing more than the same swirling vapors, restless as ever, playing tricks with her vision. But as she watched, the fog seemed to pull apart, to separate, unveiling a hulking form just ahead on the beach.

She stepped backward. The shape grew more distinct, gathering in fullness as the clouds dissipated. She caught her breath, staring in disbelief.

11

at anchor

MIST swirled around the hull of the old wooden ship, draping the ragged sails like layers of translucent silk. It rested, tilted to one side, in the sand. The mizzenmast leaned precariously toward the bow, pointing directly at Kate. The mainmast still towered above her head, though it ended abruptly in a tangle of rigging.

Cautiously, she moved closer, examining the red-painted hull carefully. One section near the rudder had been smashed apart, exposing a dark cavern at the base of the hull where barrels and crates of many sizes and shapes rested, together with heaps of ballast stones. Dozens of round clay jars hung overhead, lashed to the rigging. Cannons, tapered in the muzzle, protruded from notches. Numerous rope ladders ascended to the sails, covering even the captain's quarters above the stern, giving the impression that the whole ship lay covered with cobwebs.

Approaching the hull, she spied an enormous anchor, planted on the beach. Cast in the shape of a pointed fishhook with double barbs, it looked massive, unmovable. Kate bent to touch the heavy black chain, twisted into knots and curls. She tried to lift one of the links from the sand. It was impossible.

Straightening herself, she surveyed the wreck. It looked eerily like the phantom ship on the computer screen. Yet she knew that was the one thing it could not possibly be. So how did it get here? And when? Her heart told her one thing, her head another.

Her gaze fell to the shaft of the anchor. Some sort of symbol marked it, raised from the iron in bold relief. She threw aside the broken plank that partially covered the spot. There, before her, was a rough circle and within it, *the letter R.*

She glanced upward into the churning mist, lit so eerily from above. *No way. It can't be.*

Using her sleeve, she wiped the salty dew from her face. Hesitantly, she approached the gaping hole in the hull, stepping over ballast stones, splintered timbers, and shards of pottery. She spied a capstan, the rotating wooden drum sailors used to raise anchor before the invention of the mechanical winch, lying on its side on the sand. Next to it sat the top half of a huge earthenware vessel, the kind used centuries ago to store water for long ocean voyages.

Only a few shafts of light entered the hold, leaving most of it in shadows. She paused at the opening, letting her eyes adjust. An odd smell, spicy and potent, wafted from somewhere nearby.

She kicked aside a small bundle at her feet, which clanged against the floor. Curious, she peeled back the dusty cloth to find that it covered an ornamented pitcher. As she held it up to a shaft of light, it shone brightly, and she realized it was made of solid gold, intricately carved with images of a shepherd tending his flock. A fearsome face was carved into the spout. Once in a museum she had seen a gold ewer like this, raised from a wreck in the Caribbean, never dreaming she might hold one in her hands one day. Carefully, she placed it on a wooden crate and moved deeper into the hold.

Boxes, bundles and chests crammed the odd-cornered room. The air smelled damp, musty, with a hint of the strange spicy aroma. Wedged together along the walls, hung from the ceiling, piled on the floor, they seemed too numerous to count. Spying one chest that had been split apart, she drew nearer. From it she pulled a delicate silk cloth of azure blue embroidered with threads of silver that glittered like Himalayan rivers.

Stepping over a pile of ballast, she noticed a group of rectangular stones visible through a hole in the floorboards. She stooped to look more closely. The stones gleamed only dully, but there could be no mistake. Gold. Gold ingots. Dozens, perhaps hundreds, of them. Right under her feet.

Then something flashed by her sneaker. Kate knew what it was before she touched it, before her hand curled around its rough-hewn edge. Lifting it to the light, the silver object glistened. *A piece of eight.*

She hefted the old coin, surprised at how heavy it felt. On one side she saw a Hapsburg shield, displaying the mint mark next to the denomination, a Roman numeral VIII. On the other side, a bold cross. Within its quarters, she could make out two standing lions and two castles. Much of the inscription was illegible, but the words *Carlos I, Rex* were plain to see. As was the date: 1547.

She squeezed the coin in her hand, as hard as she could, feeling it gouge into her fingers. This had to be a dream. Had to be.

Carefully, she placed the coin in one of her pockets. She spied a thin wooden ladder tied to a trunklike column that appeared to be the bottom of the mainmast. Her heart racing, she ascended the ladder, rung by rung, passing through two more decks as full of shadows and cargo as the hold.

Her head bumped into a trapdoor. Heavy though it was, she managed to raise it by pushing with her shoulder. The door fell open with a clunk. She climbed through the hold to find herself standing on the main deck of the ship. Cannons, six to each side, lined the wall. Beside one rested a case of black iron balls.

Kate drew nearer and, with effort, lifted one of the cannonballs. She remembered reading, in one of her father's reference books about galleons, a vivid account of warfare at sea. She imagined sailors heating cannonballs to red hot before firing them at enemy ships, hoping to set fire to wooden decks or blow up powder magazines. Then she spotted another case, this one containing bar shot for ripping sails and rigging. Next to it lay a rammer, a wad hook, a powder ladle, and other tools of cannonry. All this equipment lay idle, useless against whatever force had grounded the ship.

The spicy smell, much stronger than before, tickled her nose. It seemed to emanate from the captain's quarters. Cautiously, she approached. Before lifting the door's polished brass latch, she glanced skyward, through the web of rigging, luminous in the mist.

The door swung open. She had to stoop to pass through it, entering a room much less cluttered than the hold. Much lighter as well, thanks to a glassless window at the stern. The air practically vibrated with the spicy aroma. An elaborate tapestry, depicting a Chinese harbor, hung from one wall. A thin bed, blankets rolled in a mound, lay beside a polished desk made from exotic woods. On the desk sat a quill pen, a jar of black ink, a bronze astrolabe and a sextant for navigation, a double-handled gold cup etched with rows of snakes biting their tails, a candle holder wrought of gleaming jade, and one slender volume bound in red leather.

She touched the book's flaking leather cover. It was old, very old. As old as the piece of eight. As old as the ship named . . .

Shaking her head, she moved further into the chamber. The floorboards, dotted with small stones the size of date pits, creaked underfoot. She ran her finger along the desk's smooth rim. *The captain's quarters.* Noticing a roll of papers leaning against the desk, she unfurled it, finding a collection of intricate maps. She studied them one by one, turning each of them sideways and upside down. Yet she could not recognize any of the images or decipher any of the script.

Baffled, she tossed the roll onto a bulky pile of brown rags stuffed in the corner. The spicy smell struck her again, and she turned to a black cooking pot resting on an upturned barrel by the rags. Leaning over the pot, she saw it contained a thick brown liquid. She sniffed. Cinnamon. Ginger. Clove. And something else, subtle and mysterious.

Just then, she felt an odd sensation. As if something, somewhere were watching her. She straightened up, scanned the chamber. Nothing stirred. But for the omnipresent mist circling outside the window, she discerned no motion, no life at all.

Yet . . . she could not shake that feeling.

She took a deep breath, but her heart continued to beat rapidly. Turning back to the desk, she decided to examine the ancient volume. Maybe it held some clue to all this. She reached to touch it.

Something rustled behind her. She whirled around, then froze.

The pile of rags was moving.

12

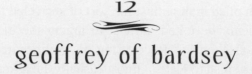

geoffrey of bardsey

SLOWLY, a wrinkled hand emerged from the rags. Another hand followed, then a grizzly gray beard, a hawk-like nose, and two coal black eyes beneath wild, scraggly brows.

Both hands lifted high into the air, as the dark eyes regarded Kate solemnly, without emotion. At that instant the beard parted, revealing a wide mouth holding very few teeth, while those it held hung blackened and askew.

Kate started to back away, fearing the old man beneath the rags was preparing to pounce on her. Then he released a bizarre, bellowing noise, one that sounded something like an antique car horn.

He's yawning, she realized in amazement. Anxiety swiftly gave way to curiosity. She watched the man stretch his arms, scratch his bedraggled hair, and pull vigorously on his beard, all the while continuing to yawn.

At length, he ceased. "Drat this infernal heat," he muttered in a rolling, hefty accent. "Makes a man sleepy. A nap's a luxury, I say, but not necessarily for the living." He struggled to stand while reaching for a delicate porcelain dish piled high with some sort of shriveled fruit.

Suddenly he jolted, almost dropping the dish. "My goodness! A guest." Recovering his composure, he extended the dish to Kate. Almost casually, he asked, "Care for a date?"

"Uhh, no thanks," she replied uncertainly.

The old man popped a date in his mouth. "Delicious," he pronounced, spitting the pit onto the floor. "Fresh as could be." A sudden anguish filled his face. "Have we been introduced? I've quite forgotten."

Tentatively, Kate extended her hand. "I'm . . . I'm Kate. Kate Gordon."

The hawklike nose twitched. "Gordon. A Scotswoman, eh?"

"Well, my grandfather came—"

"Delighted," he continued, scratching savagely behind one ear. "Cursed sea lice! Now, where were we? Ah, yes. You were saying where in Scotland you hail from."

"Oh, not me. No."

"A new province, I take it. *O'Naughtmeno*. Fine alliteration. Declared your independence already, have you?"

"No, no. I mean—"

"To learn who I am, I know." The old man scratched again, shaking his unruly hair. Then, to Kate's surprise, he crumpled into a kneeling position, took her hand, and gave it an awkward kiss. "Geoffrey of Bardsey, at your service."

Before she could reply, he let out a piteous groan. "*Ehhh!* Now I've done it."

"Done what?"

"The knee. Old riding mishap. From before I gave up horses—and most everything else, mind you—to become a monk. Would you mind terribly . . . *ehhh,* helping me, *ehhh,* up?"

Kate grabbed him by the arm and hoisted. The old man struggled to stand, nearly toppling them both. He pulled anxiously on his beard, then staggered to the chair by the desk and collapsed, breathing heavily.

"Are you all right?"

"Right? Oh, yes. Couldn't be better. Nothing a good nap can't fix." His eyes narrowed, and he seemed confused. "Could have sworn . . . Wasn't I just taking a nap?" He scratched, this time the other ear. "Yes, now I remember. A good nap in the corner. Then someone came in."

"Me," offered Kate.

"You?" He fought to lift himself from the chair. "Have we been properly introduced?"

"Yes," she answered, half amused and half exasperated. She eased him back in the chair. "I'm Kate. You're Geoffrey of something."

"Bardsey. So we have."

"Bardsey," she repeated. "Wasn't that the name of the island where Merlin died?"

Geoffrey nodded. "Entombed. By Nimue." His eyes grew moist. "A miserable way to go, that." He stretched his arm toward the porcelain dish, took another date. Chewing it slowly, he turned toward the window, then back to Kate, as if she had reminded him of something deep in his past. At length, he asked, "You know of Merlin?"

"A few of the stories. My dad knows a lot more." She leaned against the desk, her expression grave. "Where are we, anyway?"

The wild eyebrows lifted. "You don't know?"

"How could I know?" she retorted. "It's all such a blur."

"I take your meaning," Geoffrey replied dispiritedly. "And it grows worse with each passing century."

Kate stiffened. "Century?"

The old man's eyes fixed on hers. "You are my first guest in . . ." He paused, trying to count on his fingers, then gave up in frustration. "In many years. Not many people care to pay a visit to the *Resurrección.*"

The name rang in Kate's ears. "That can't be true!"

Geoffrey spat out a pit, wiping his mouth with his ragged sleeve. "Forgive my manners. I've forgotten most of the little I knew."

She seized his sleeve. "But the *Resurrección* got swallowed by the whirlpool ages ago!"

The brown rags stirred uncomfortably. "Ah, yes. A dreadful experience, let me assure you. One I don't plan to live through again." He swept his eyes over the chamber. "Not that I object to these quarters, mind you. Far better than Wytham Abbey, I should say! And well stocked. I could last another half millennium with a bit of rationing. All the best spices, including cardamom from

India, to make my tea and freshen the air. Fine tapestries to look at, sea biscuits and garlic to eat, sweetmeats and honey for dessert whenever I please. Not to mention the fresh fish that wash up on shore. And let us not forget the dates! I do love them. The ship's wine I finished off about a century ago, I'm afraid, but I still get plenty of clean water from this vaporous air. I could hardly want more, but for an occasional idle conversation like this."

"This isn't idle," protested Kate. "This is serious! And I still don't believe you. If you went down with the ship, how come you're still alive?"

Geoffrey's mouth gaped wide with another yawn. When finally he finished, he replied, "Oh, I do my best to keep occupied. It does get a bit tedious at times, of course. I keep reminding myself that the word *monk* comes from the Greek *monos,* for *alone.* So perhaps it is my fate to be here. Still, there's not much to do except eat and sleep, pray and count combs."

"Combs?"

The haggard head nodded. "It was the twenty-sixth of May—I remember it so clearly—when the *Resurrección* set sail from Manila, bound for Mexico. We were heavy with cargo, including a big shipment of ivory combs. Lovely ones, carved with Our Lady's image. Thirty-one thousand, eight hundred and forty-three, to be precise." He frowned. "Though for some reason I've been able to find only thirty-one thousand, eight hundred and forty-two."

Feeling the bulge in one of her pockets, Kate's stomach clenched. "So we really are . . . at the bottom of the whirlpool?"

"The very bottom."

"And the light and air down here—"

"Is carried down the funnel, of course. It's often a bit dusky, I admit, but the light is quite sufficient, unless perhaps you are practicing calligraphy."

Kate swallowed. "You're pulling my leg."

Geoffrey looked puzzled. "Pulling your leg? How could I? I'm nowhere near your leg."

"I mean you're fooling me."

"Not at all," he replied. "If you were to step a mere forty paces from this ship in any direction—not that I would advise it, mind you—you would meet the spinning wall of the whirlpool. And beyond that, the sea."

"Half a mile down," added Kate. "It's a lot to swallow."

"Yes," laughed Geoffrey. "Even a large whale would have difficulty swallowing so much."

"I didn't mean . . . oh, forget it."

"Don't worry, though. After eighty or ninety more years you will come to accept living inside a maelstrom as a fact of life, as I have. Even your memories of blue sky will fade." He glanced up wistfully. "I should have liked to see it once more, though. Just once."

"But it's not a fact of life!" objected Kate. "I want to see my dad again! And my mom. And Isabella. I'm not going to just sit around here eating dates forever!" Then a new realization dawned. "Didn't you feel that tremor a while ago? There could be an eruption down here. Maybe a big one! It could wipe out the ship, the whirlpool, everything."

Geoffrey yawned once more, this time for nearly

a minute. "Quite so," he said drowsily. "I feel another nap coming on."

"No," she insisted. "Not now."

The old man's eyelids closed. "Curious things, eruptions," he murmured. "Most unpredictable."

"Wait!" She shook him by the shoulders. "You can't sleep now. Listen. I think my father's down here someplace. In the submersible. Maybe, if we can find some way to contact him, he could help us get out of here."

Geoffrey's eyes opened a crack, regarding her suspiciously. "What would your father be doing down here?"

Kate started to speak, then hesitated. "He's, ah, looking for the ship."

"He wants the gold and silver aboard?"

"Well . . . not exactly."

"Something else, then?"

She said nothing, remembering her promise not to reveal anything about the Horn. Yet . . . what harm could it possibly do to tell this old monk? It might even elicit his help. On an impulse, she pulled from her shirt pocket a soggy piece of paper bearing a strange design. She unfolded it carefully, then held it before his face. "If you know what this means, then maybe I can trust you."

GEOFFREY studied the design, exhaling slowly. *"Benedicite,"* he said in a quiet voice. "So you know about Serilliant."

13

the order of the horn

I know a little," answered Kate.

"Are you," Geoffrey asked, his eyes suddenly alight, "one of *the Order?*"

"The what?"

"The Order of the Horn." Geoffrey pushed himself out of the chair. He clasped Kate in an enthusiastic embrace, surrounding her with rags whose odor overpowered even the pot of fragrant spices. "I thought I was the last!" he exclaimed, his voice cracking. "I am overjoyed, overjoyed indeed."

"But—" began Kate, cringing at the potent smell.

"And we haven't had a woman join the Order since, my goodness! Since Katherine of Monmouth, ages ago."

Kate finally wriggled away. "What are you talking about?"

"You know, the Order of the Horn! The secret society dedicated to finding Merlin's Horn and delivering it to the Glass House, where it truly belongs."

She stared at him blankly.

"You have not heard of it?"

"And I'm not a member of it, either."

Geoffrey's bushy brows pinched together. "How cruel of you to mislead me."

"I didn't. You just assumed."

"If you didn't come here in search of the Horn, why did you come?"

She blinked. "By accident. I got thrown overboard."

Geoffrey observed her, toying with his beard. "And yet you know about the Horn."

"Not much, really. Just that lots of people have wanted it, for whatever reason. And whenever they find it, they lose it again."

Light returned to the deep-set eyes. "That is truer than you know. Merlin is only one of many who have sought it and been disappointed. Even that sorceress Nimue, for all her cleverness, has been frustrated."

"Nimue!"

The old man grimaced. "So you have heard of her. Let us hope that neither of us should ever have to meet her."

"You mean she's still around?"

"She is searching for the Horn, and nothing will stop her."

Sadly, Kate nodded. "My dad's in the same boat."

Geoffrey, looking perplexed, scratched the point of his nose. "But Nimue doesn't use a boat."

She rolled her eyes. "I mean, Dad's searching, too." Another wave of longing washed over her. "I wish I knew how to reach him. I'm sure he could help us."

"It is far easier to come here than it is to leave, I'm afraid. In fact, it's impossible as long as the whirlpool lasts. Yet if he is seeking the Horn, perhaps he will come here on his own."

"Before this whole place erupts, I hope." She considered what Geoffrey had said. "So the Horn . . . is really here?"

Geoffrey chewed some hairs for a moment, then said only, "It is near."

Kate edged a bit closer. "Is it the Horn that has kept you alive?"

"I cannot say for sure."

"You must have a theory," she pressed. "You've had five centuries to think about it."

"Well," he replied, "I have just a guess, nothing more."

"And?"

"My guess is that . . . the Horn keeps me from dying. Just as it keeps the whirlpool from collapsing and this ship from crumbling. Perhaps its power circulates with the swirling vapors here, passing into the very timbers and sails above our heads." He smacked his lips. "That would also explain why my dates remain so delightfully fresh."

Kate backed up a step. "And it would also explain Isabella's fish."

Confused again, Geoffrey asked, "Whose fish?"

"My friend Isabella's. The ugly old fish she found, the

one with the wacky DNA chromosome. It should have been extinct."

Geoffrey studied her worriedly. "You're babbling, my dear. It's all been a bit much for you, hasn't it? You clearly need a nap."

"I'm fine," she replied tersely. "What else do you know about the Horn's power?"

At that instant a tremor rocked the ship, sending both of them sprawling. The walls swayed violently, creaking and popping. The tapestry tore loose and fell. With a crash, the porcelain dish shattered on the floor.

Then, silence. Plumes of dust swirled around the room. Geoffrey groaned painfully as he crawled to the chair.

Kate clambered to her feet. "Are you all right?"

"Barely," he replied. "Blast these tremors! Just look at my dates. Ruined! Covered with soot."

Kate squeezed the thin arm beneath the tattered clothes. "Listen to me. We've got to get out of here before a really big one hits."

"That could be centuries from now," groused Geoffrey. He plucked a date from the floor, blew the dust off it, and took a bite. "Right now I'm worried about more pressing matters."

"Like your dates," said Kate in disgust.

"Not wholly ruined," he observed, chewing slowly. "Pity about the dish, though."

"At least you could answer my question."

Geoffrey kept chewing. "Question?"

"Can you tell me anything else about the Horn's

power? And is there some way we can use it to get out of here?"

Seemingly oblivious, Geoffrey inserted the rest of the date into his mouth. He removed the pit and threw it over his shoulder, but it caught on his tangle of hair and remained there, dangling.

"Delectable," he pronounced.

Kate demanded, "Come on. Tell me."

He gave her a sidelong glance. "Tell you what?"

"About the Horn!"

"Persistent, aren't you?" He crinkled his nose. "You remind me of another headstrong youth, one I understand Merlin found extremely difficult at times. His name was Arthur."

She drew a deep breath. "I don't care," she replied. "Answer me."

"Such stubbornness he had," mused Geoffrey. "Imagine, thinking he could civilize the Saxons! The very idea he could teach them how to farm, convince them to join hands with other peoples instead of vanquishing them. Why, it's a wonder Merlin was able to keep him alive as long as he did. If that scoundrel Mordred hadn't . . ." The old man suddenly looked much older. "I do hope Merlin was right, though."

Caught off guard, Kate asked, "Right about what?"

"About Arthur," came the wistful reply. "That he will one day return."

His wrinkled hand reached under the chair for another date. Seeing this, Kate snatched it up and held it directly in front of his nose.

"Tell me," she demanded.

He reached for the date, but she yanked it away.

"It looks delicious," she said, twirling the sweet fruit in her fingers. "Soft, tender, juicy . . ."

"Please," he protested. "This is highly unfair."

"Tell me."

Geoffrey pulled anxiously at his beard. "I cannot! Not because I don't want to, but because I really don't know. No one knows. The precise nature of the Horn's power has remained a mystery, except to a few mer people—and the great Merlin himself, although that knowledge could not save him from his terrible end."

"Why all this secrecy?"

"Its power must be very great. Too great, perhaps." He started to stretch his hand toward the date.

Holding the precious item just out of reach, she queried, "Isn't there anything you *can* tell me?"

He shook his head, knocking the clinging date pit to the floor. "Only the riddle," he muttered.

"What riddle?"

"Merlin's own concoction. But it won't help, I can assure you. No one, not even a member of the Order of the Horn, has ever solved it. The only way to discover the power of the Horn is to drink from it! And that honor, as the Emperor Merwas long ago commanded, is reserved only for those with extraordinary wisdom and strength of will."

She tossed the date into the folds of his habit. "Tell me the riddle."

Geoffrey scooped it up, plunked it in his mouth, threw

away the pit. Then he reached under his rags and
scratched his chest vigorously. At length, he relented,
and began to recite:

> *Ye who drink from Merlin's Horn*
> *May for dying not be mourned,*
> *May grow younger with the years,*
> *May remember ageless fears.*
>
> *Never doubt the spiral Horn*
> *Holds a power newly born,*
> *Holds a power truly great,*
> *Holds a power ye create.*

"*Holds a power,*" repeated Kate, deep in thought. She
paced around the captain's quarters. "Holds a power *you*
create? That doesn't make any sense."

Releasing another cacophonous yawn, Geoffrey slid
lower in the chair. "You might try taking a nap. It might
come to you while you sleep." He yawned again, his
blackened teeth rattling. "Might just join you myself."

Without facing him, Kate said, "Merwas supposedly
said the Horn's power had something to do with eternal
life. Is that true?"

Only a sputtering snore arose from the bundle of rags
in the chair.

Ignoring him, she continued to pace, saying over and
over what lines from the riddle she could remember. Yet
the more she struggled, the more contradictory they
seemed. Like pieces in a faulty jigsaw puzzle, they simply did not fit.

Glancing toward the snoring Geoffrey, she realized that she felt a bit drowsy herself. Maybe he was right, after all. Maybe a little rest would help. She would not allow herself to sleep, but at least she might be able to think more clearly.

Rounding the polished desk, she approached the thin bed by the wall. She pushed aside the roll of blankets and stretched out her body. Her sore back relaxed. She stared at the ancient timbers, working the riddle in her mind.

Soon she was breathing in time to Geoffrey.

14

uninvited guest

COLD. Blood chilling, bone-freezing cold. Biting enough to make Kate shiver. Aching enough to make her cry out in pain.

She awoke, shivering.

She grabbed the worn blanket at the base of the bed and pulled it over herself. It did no good. The bitter wind seemed to pass straight through the cover. Where did all that warm humidity go so suddenly?

Glancing at Geoffrey, she could see him snoring peacefully in the chair, apparently unaware of the extreme chill. Teeth chattering, she started to call to the old monk. But before she could utter a sound, something halted her.

A small shred of mist was forming in the window, curling over the sill like a sinewy finger. Yet this mist was darker, heavier, than any Kate had seen before. Through the window it snaked, stretching toward her.

Slowly, the dark finger flowed through the air to the edge of the desk. It oozed across the bronze astrolabe, through the twin handles of the gold cup, and around the slender red volume. Onward it moved, gradually approaching the bed where she clung to her blanket, transfixed.

She tried to scream, but she had no voice. She tried to rush from the bed to wake Geoffrey, but she had no strength. She felt helpless, caught in the icy grip of an irresistible power.

The flowing finger of mist stopped above the bed, hovering before her face. As she watched, it began to metamorphose. The mist condensed into the body of an infant, round and chubby, with an almost cherubic face. Clad in a graceful, silken robe, the infant hung in the air with no apparent effort. His full cheeks and gentle nose gave him a comforting, jovial appearance. Only the eyes, bright but deeply recessed, seemed oddly out of place.

As Kate stared in disbelief, the infant smiled at her kindly. Despite her shivering, she felt herself relax ever so slightly. At that moment a low, melodic laughter filled the room, and the infant's body shook with humor.

"You look cold," he purred. "Here, let me help you."

With that the infant blew upon Kate, and his breath was as warm as the desert sun. Her skin tingled, her muscles loosened, her heart expanded. Soon the chill wind had vanished. Cautiously, she allowed the blanket to slip from her shoulders.

"Thanks," she said hesitantly. "How did you do that?"

"It matters not," he replied in a soothing tone. "All you need to know is that I have come to protect you."

"And," she asked, dropping the blanket completely, "who are you?"

Again the infant smiled. "I am your friend. My magic is strong, and I am here to help you."

"Can you—can you help me get out of here?"

"If that is your desire."

"It is!" shouted Kate, so loud she was sure her cry would wake Geoffrey. Yet he slumbered on, slumped in the chair.

"Good." The hovering infant laughed, swaying with pleasure. "I will be happy to return you home."

"You can really do that?"

"With ease." The cherubic face beamed. "I need ask only one small favor in return."

"What favor?"

"I would like you to help me get . . . the Horn."

Astonished, Kate leaned closer. "The Horn of Merlin?"

"It does not belong to Merlin," said the infant, a hint of raspiness creeping into his voice. "It never did."

"But I don't have any idea where it is."

"You will." The soothing tone had returned. "I am sure you will."

She cocked her head. "If your magic is so strong, why can't you get it yourself?"

For a split second, the deep-set eyes glinted with something resembling anger. Then, just as swiftly, it passed. "I could, of course. But before I can help you, you must prove your worth."

"And what would you do with it?"

"I would simply . . . enjoy its power."

"Which is?"

"The power to live forever, of course."

Something about that definition did not seem quite right to Kate, but she was not sure what. "I don't think Geoffrey would like this idea."

"That old fool? You can disregard him. He is of no consequence." Floating in the air, the infant started circling the bed, as if tying a noose around her. "It is a simple matter, really. All you need to do is await my instructions."

Something about the way he said the word *instructions* made Kate feel a bit chilly again. She drew a deep breath and said, "I'm not sure. I'll have to think about it."

"Think about it?" snarled the infant. Then an aroma, sweet as apple blossoms, filled the room. The infant's eyes flamed once more, then began to sink deeper and deeper until finally they disappeared altogether, leaving only two holes, vacant as the void. At the same time, the cherubic face swelled into the face of a woman, whose long black hair fell over her shoulders. The rest of her body returned to mist, dark as smoke, with two wispy arms curling like tentacles. One of her vaporous hands brandished a blackened dagger.

Kate shrank back on the bed. A single word came to her, a word that chilled her anew. "Nimue."

"Yesssss," said the enchantress, her voice like a jet of steam. "It issss I, or more precisssssely, my image. For my body cannot yet passss through the wallsssss of the whirlpool. Not yet, but ssssoon. Very ssssoon."

"What d-d-do you m-mean?" asked Kate, clutching the blanket again.

Nimue hissed in satisfaction. "You will ssssee. And if you do not help me, you will regret it."

"I w-won't," she said with effort.

"Then you will ssssuffer."

"Geoffrey!" she shrieked, shaking with cold. "Geoffrey, wak-ke up!"

The old man did not stir.

"He cannot hear you," declared Nimue, swimming lazily in the air above her. "Sssso lissssten. I sssseek only one thing, and that issss the Horn. Whether you help me or not, I will get it. Of that I am ccccertain! For ssssome reasssson, though, I feel mercccciful today, enough to give you a ssssecond chancccce. If you assisssst me, I will sssspare your life."

Kate tried, without success, to stop shivering. "I w-w-will n-never help y-you."

"True?" spat Nimue. "I ssssuspect not. Here issss ssssomeone I shall sssssoon desssstroy, unless you change your mind."

The enchantress waved a misty hand. Another image, wavering in the dim light of the room, appeared beside her own. It was a face, one Kate recognized instantly.

"Dad!"

"Sssso you know him, do you? Then mark my wordsssss. He issss my prissssoner."

"Let him go!" she wailed.

Nimue's mouth curled. "Hissss fate issss in your handssss."

The face of her father cringed, as if he were in pain. Kate herself cringed at the sight.

"All r-right," she answered in torment. "I will h-help you, if you p-p-promise not to harm him."

"Good choicccce," pronounced Nimue. "I will not harm him."

"P-promise?"

"I promisssse," said the enchantress, twirling her smokelike form. "Now here issss what I assssk of you."

Raising one of her hands, Nimue swept it before Kate's face. A ring on one thin finger flashed with ruby light, so bright that it hurt her eyes.

"Look into my ring," Nimue commanded.

Kate averted her gaze, unwilling to do as she said.

Then the enchantress bellowed, "Look into my ring, or I will kill your father."

Biting her lip, Kate slowly lifted her head. The ruby light exploded in her eyes, but this time she did not turn away. All she could see was the powerful pulsing of the ring. All she could feel was its light burning into every corner of her brain.

"Very good," echoed the voice of the enchantress through the red fog that clouded Kate's vision. "That issss much better. I will give you no instructionssss now, but for thissss one command. Whenever you hear my voicccce, wherever you may be, you will do only what I ssssay. Issss that undersssstood?"

"Yes, Nimue," replied Kate slowly.

"Then let ussss tessssst your loyalty," the enchantress continued. "Raisssse your right arm, near to your mouth."

With stilted movements, Kate obeyed.

"Now bite your wrisssst. Hard."

Unable to resist, she clamped down her teeth on her own skin.

"Harder," ordered Nimue.

Kate bit fiercely, until a drop of blood swelled on her wrist and trickled down her arm.

"You may ceasssse," said Nimue, satisfied at last. As Kate lowered her arm, the enchantress declared, "You will not remember any of our meeting, nor any of our converssssation. You will only remember my voicccce, whenever you hear it. And that will be ssssoon. Very ssssoon."

Ruby light burst before Kate's eyes. Nimue disappeared, and with her, the cold.

15

the red volume

KATE awoke, more tired than when she had lain down to rest. Her mouth tasted strangely rancid, despite a lingering sweetness in the air. She stared at the glassless window, watching the vapors swirling outside, trying to recall a vague memory. Something about the window . . .

She rolled over, exhausted. It must be the constant half-light down here. How could Geoffrey ever sleep well, let alone keep track of the months and years? He had no sunrises and sunsets to guide him, no waxing and waning moon, no stars swimming overhead.

Besides, it was hot. Uncomfortably hot. Why did she have any need for a blanket? She threw aside her cover, then felt a piercing pain in her wrist.

Seeing the bloody wound on her skin, she gasped. Tearing a strip of cloth from the tail of her blue cotton shirt, she gingerly wrapped the injured arm. *Such a deep cut! Strange I don't remember getting it.* She paused before tying the bandage. Something else was odd about this cut, though she couldn't quite put her finger on it. It looked almost like . . . teeth marks. But of course that was impossible.

At that moment, Geoffrey yawned with the subtlety of a fog horn. Stretching his bony arms skyward, he shook his wild mane, scratched behind his neck, and, only then, opened his eyes.

"Yes," he crowed, "nothing like a good nap." He glanced her way. "Good morning to you, Miss Gordon."

"Call me Kate, all right?"

"Would you prefer Maid Kate?"

"Kate is fine."

The hawklike nose grew slightly pink. "My, such familiarity! As you wish, then. Good morning to you, Kate." With sudden concern, he added, "Why, you're wounded."

"I'm fine," she replied, trying the knot. "Just a scratch."

"Happens to me at least once a fortnight," consoled Geoffrey. "Did you find any success with the riddle?"

Kate merely frowned.

"Have a date, then." He picked one off the floor himself. "We shall eat something more substantial later. But first, I must practice my lessons."

"Lessons?"

Sliding the chair closer to the desk, he reached for the leather book. "A few of Merlin's gems, that's all. After centuries of practice, I have mastered only a few. Still, progress is progress."

Kate eyed the battered volume. "What is it, a magician's handbook?"

"You might call it that. It is a compendium of some of my mentor's wisdom, which I collected from learned sources over many years, then recorded in my own hand. Otherwise I could never remember any of it."

Cracking open the book, he paused at the first page, greeting it like an old friend. To Kate's surprise, the page was covered with slashes, curves, and crosses—the same secret language her father had spoken about. All except for six lines at the top, which were written in letters, but not words, she could recognize.

"What language is that?" she asked, pointing to the first six lines.

"Why, it's Latin, of course." Geoffrey looked at her askance. "Did you never go to school?"

"Sure," she answered. "I just, ah, missed Latin. What does it say?"

"Well," he sniggered, "it's my personal inscription. Books are precious, you know, so such things are customary."

"But what does it say?"

Geoffrey held the book closer. "My, such abominable handwriting," he muttered. "Even if it is my own."

Then he read:

> *The man who dares to steal this book*
> *Shall soon be hanged upon a hook,*
> *His entrails pulled, his liver cooked,*
> *His eyes gouged out, his backbone crook'd.*
> *For I would rather lose my purse,*
> *And he would rather die in curse.*

Lowering the book, he observed, "Rather makes the point, doesn't it?"

Kate gulped. "Rather."

He flipped through the pages, each one decorated with a small illustration at the top. After a time, he came to one showing a spoon with feathered wings.

"What's that?" asked Kate, pointing to the picture.

"Oh, that is the charm for levitation. One of the least useful but most entertaining ones in the book."

"Can you do it?"

"I can try," agreed the monk. "Let me see." He studied the page, mouthing some mysterious words to himself. Then he set down the book, pointed a long finger at the cooking pot of spices resting on the upturned barrel, and cleared his throat.

"Arzemy barzemy yangelo igg lom," he chanted.

Nothing happened.

Geoffrey pulled up his sleeve, cleared his throat again, and tried once more. *"Arzemy barzemy yangelo igg lom,"* he intoned. Quickly, he added, *"Abra cadabra."* Turning to Kate, he whispered, "That sometimes helps."

At that moment, the cooking pot quivered slightly. It slid toward the rim of the barrel. Then, with a slight crackling sound, it slowly lifted into the air, hovering a few inches above the barrel.

"You did it," said Kate in wonderment.

Geoffrey lowered his finger. The pot clattered back to its place, with a small amount of liquid sloshing over the top. He sighed wearily, but his dark eyes gleamed. "Just a little parlor trick, really."

"That's amazing! What else can you do?"

Geoffrey thumbed through the book, stopping at a page displaying an ant strolling beside an elephant. Underneath was a strange, convoluted design, surrounded by dozens of pictures of animals, plants, and constellations. "This is one of my favorites, the charm to change your shape. All you need to do is imagine very clearly what you want to become and say the proper words. Or, if you prefer, you can say nothing but concentrate deeply on this page, and something will happen."

His mouth twisted doubtfully. "Of course, it might not be what you *want* to happen." He slapped the side of his head. "Drat those sea lice! As I was saying, these things can be tricky. The first time I tried to change myself into a robin, it was a bit too close to mealtime. My poor stomach rumbled just as I was concentrating, and I came out a rather spindly worm. Took me three whole days just to climb back up to the desk. Then I had to open the book again, which was no small feat for a worm."

Ignoring Kate's stifled laugh, he went on, "Still, it remains one of my most handy charms, as it was for Merlin himself. Do you know all the creatures he turned Arthur into? A fish, a hawk, a butterfly, a unicorn, and more. I find it oddly comforting to know that I can change myself into a totally different being any time I choose. Like starting life over, in a way." He sighed. "The difficult part is deciding just what I want to become."

He flipped to a page embroidered with intricate green-and-gold vines. "This one allows you to learn the languages of animals and plants. It has its pitfalls as well—Boar is perilously close to Camel, and Mosquito quite frankly gives me a headache—but it has proved invaluable to me. I have even used it to communicate with the whales."

"The gray whales?" asked Kate.

Geoffrey blinked his eyes slowly. "The ever-singing whales."

Kate spun her head toward the window. Somewhere out there, beyond the mist, beyond the whirling wall of water, swam those elusive creatures. She thought, with a pang, of the young whale she had tried to help. How long could he have survived with that severed tail? She would never know. Just as she would never know where and how her father was right now, although she could not suppress the uneasy feeling that something was wrong.

Without warning, the brass latch lifted and the door to the captain's quarters swung open. A large figure shadowed the doorway.

"Where the hell am I?" demanded a husky voice.

16

magma

KATE'S mouth went dry. "How did you get here?"

Turning sideways to fit through the door, Terry stepped inside. A swollen bruise marked his forehead, his glasses were gone, his Bermuda shorts hung ripped, and his entire body was smeared with wet sand.

"I'm the last one to answer that question," he muttered, leaning against the wall for support. "The boat, that storm . . . It happened so fast." He squinted at her. "I thought you were dead."

"No thanks to you, I'm not."

Terry looked down at his feet, started to say something, then caught himself. He thrust his chin at her. "You can't blame me because you fell overboard."

"I can blame you for not grabbing me when you had the chance," she retorted.

"I did what I could."

"Right."

Patting the bruise on his head, he winced. "I suppose you also blame me for what happened to the submersible."

The submersible. Suddenly it all came back to Kate. The hammer. The jammed lever. The cable releasing at last—from the wrong end.

"How could that happen?" she demanded.

Terry shrugged. "I have no idea. It wasn't supposed to happen, just as we weren't supposed to get thrown into the sea."

"But Dad and Isabella might be in danger! The submersible might be damaged or something."

"I doubt it. That thing is built to withstand a tidal wave. Probably has, more than once. Isabella must have had some way to release the cable from her side."

"Then why didn't she ever use it before? That doesn't add up."

"Look, quit the interrogation, will you? I know only as much as you do. They could be dead, for all I know."

"They're not!"

The geologist moved toward her, but clipped his thigh against the corner of the desk. "Ow! Where are my glasses?" Bending nearer, he asked hoarsely, "Are we the ones who are dead? I mean, this ship and all. It's ancient! A real museum piece. And, what's more, it's loaded to the gills with—"

"Treasure," completed the pile of brown rags on the chair.

Terry jolted. "What, er, who . . . are you?"

Creakily, the old man rose and extended a hand.

"Geoffrey of Bardsey, at your service." He paused, looking confused, then asked, "Have we already been introduced?"

"And this is Terry Graham," said Kate, stepping to Geoffrey's side. "No need to kneel on his account."

"I'm hallucinating," moaned the broad-shouldered young man. "Or dead."

"You're not dead," declared Kate. "Not yet, anyway."

"Then where am I? Who is he?"

Facing him squarely, Kate replied, "You're on the *Resurrección*. Remember? The ship you said wasn't real. At the bottom of the whirlpool. And Geoffrey here is a survivor, kept alive somehow by a magical Horn. Is that enough for you?"

"Enough to convince me I'm crazy," said Terry uncertainly. "Wait. Did you say we're at the bottom of the whirlpool?"

Kate nodded.

"So that sand out there is really the ocean floor, three thousand feet down?"

Again she nodded.

"But . . . that isn't possible! Look, be rational. It's so warm here. Too warm for that far down. Unless . . ." His eyes bulged. "Have you felt any tremors?"

"More than one."

Terry went pale. "Then, if this is the ocean floor, magma must be pushing closer! There could be an eruption any moment." He waved at the air. "And we're stuck down here. Hopelessly stuck."

Sensing his anxiety, she felt an unexpected touch of sympathy. "Maybe not."

"Hopeless is an unfortunate state of mind," offered Geoffrey. "It is very difficult, while feeling hopeless, to remain at all, well, hopeful."

Kate and Terry traded perplexed looks. Then Kate asked the monk, "Are you absolutely sure there is no way the Horn could help us?"

"Not unless you can solve the riddle."

"Tell me what else you know about the Horn," she insisted. "Maybe it will give me a clue."

Geoffrey regarded her doubtfully. "I suppose I could tell you a story I learned during my time in the Order of the Horn—the story of how the Horn came to be found, and then lost, by Merlin. Beyond that, all I can tell you is how, long after Merlin's demise, I came to find it again."

"Go ahead," she pleaded.

"I really would rather—"

"Please."

Geoffrey cracked his withered knuckles. "I never could say no to the ladies," he muttered. "All right. It is, I admit, an intriguing tale. One of hope and promise."

He reached for the red volume, tucked it under his arm, then started hobbling toward the door. As he passed Kate, he remarked, "The deck is the place to do it, though. Out with the sails and the fresh air."

Reluctantly, Kate and Terry followed.

Geoffrey led them onto the deck, past the rows of cannons and the cases of cannonballs and bar shot. Near the trapdoor, he stopped and lifted a rammer off the deck. Reaching as high as he could, he used the rammer to tip over a round clay jar lashed to the rigging above his head.

A brief cascade of water, collected from the constant vapors of the whirlpool, poured onto his upturned face. Then he shook himself, cast the rammer aside, and tottered onward.

His version of a shower, thought Kate. All he needs now is some shampoo. Strong enough to kill lice.

At the base of the snapped mainmast, the monk stepped over a tangle of rigging and sat down on a broken barrel. Motioning to the others to join him, he looked up into the swirling clouds of mist, as if searching for a glimpse of the blue sky he had not seen for half a millennium.

Kate sat on the dark wood of the deck before him, leaning her back against the side of a crate. As Terry joined her, he grumbled, "Do you really expect to learn anything useful from this character?"

"Got any better ideas?" she replied.

"No." He gingerly wiped the salty dew from his brow. "But every minute we sit here the eruption gets closer."

Geoffrey tilted his haggard face toward them. He scratched behind his knee and between two toes, then intoned, "Our story begins in the age of Merlin, long after Arthur perished at the hands of Mordred."

Terry released a painful groan, causing Kate to elbow him.

"Merlin learned of a legendary craftsman, whose life was steeped in tragedy. He lived all alone, high on a mountain precipice. His true name had been lost from memory, but he was known as—"

"Emrys," finished Kate.

Geoffrey and Terry both looked at her with surprise, though the elder's expression showed a touch of admiration, as well.

"You are correct," said Geoffrey. "Now may I continue?"

"Yes."

"Oh, by the way. When I come to the part concerning me—how I came to find the Horn—I will speak of myself as Geoffrey. That is because . . . this is how, long after my time has passed, I hope the story will be told."

He squared his shoulders. "Now listen well, for you shall learn how Serilliant came to be . . . the Horn of Merlin."

17

the story of the whirlpool's birth

WHEN King Arthur died, the wizard Merlin's hopes for peace and justice in *Clas Myrddin* died as well. His only scant comfort came from the prophesy that one day, under certain conditions, Arthur might return. The prophesy told of a Final Battle that would follow where Arthur would fight against all the assembled forces of wickedness. If Arthur won, the world would be liberated, but if he lost, the world would sink into chaos and despair.

Merlin believed that the Thirteen Treasures created by Emrys would be essential to Arthur in that colossal battle. Merlin's friends, the elusive mer people, had told him enough about the Horn named Serilliant to convince him that it was the most valuable of all the Treasures. Yet they would not reveal, even to Merlin, the secret of its power. They warned him that the Horn must never fall into the hands of Arthur's enemies, or his cause would surely be doomed.

After years of searching, Merlin finally discovered the mountain hideaway of Emrys. Merlin found the craftsman on the verge of death, still tormenting himself for the loss of his one true love, the mermaid Wintonwy. Although Merlin could do nothing to relieve Emrys' pain, he convinced him to contribute the Treasures to the cause of Arthur. So Emrys gave Merlin the flaming chariot, the cauldron of knowledge, the mantle of invisibility, the knife that could heal any wound, and the other Treasures in his possession. But he could not deliver the three that had been lost: the sword of light, the ruby ring that could control the will of others, and— most precious of all—the mysterious Horn.

Guided by the directions Emrys provided, Merlin made his way to the realm of Shaa. At last he came to the entrance. There he found a fearsome monster of the deep, a spidery creature with a thousand poisonous tongues. By the monster's side lay the sword of light. Merlin hid himself and waited until the moment the monster began to doze. Then, changing his own form into a small crab, Merlin managed to spirit away the sword of light.

After passing through an abyss, darkest of the dark, Merlin entered the realm of Shaa. It lay, as legend described, in *the place where the sea begins, the womb where the waters are born.* No mer people remained there, having abandoned the realm after Nimue's brutal attack. And, as Merlin had hoped, Nimue and her army of sea demons had also left, having found nothing more in

Shaa to steal or destroy. Even the ancient castle of Mer-was stood vacant, its great hall drained of water and of life.

Merlin searched relentlessly for the two Treasures still missing. Yet he could find no clue to their whereabouts. Finally, near the forgotten castle, the wizard happened upon an enormous pile of discarded conch shells. All were spiral in shape, all were empty—but for one, which seemed to glisten strangely. Out of curiosity, Merlin retrieved it, only to realize that it brimmed with a rainbow-colored fluid. He knew in a flash that he had recovered the lost Serilliant. Triumphant, he returned to the land above the sea.

Only those whose wisdom and strength of will are beyond question may drink from this Horn. Merlin knew well this command, yet he found himself increasingly consumed by his desire to experience the Horn's power. He believed that his vast wisdom would surely pass the test, and would no doubt make up for any deficiencies in his strength of will. In time, he ignored his own better judgment and decided that Arthur would want him to take a drink from the Horn.

And then he drank. His eyes flamed with a newfound brightness. Yet because he had not waited to drink from the Horn until his strength of will was greater, he began to grow possessive and arrogant, more so with each passing day.

Telling himself that no one but himself, perhaps not even Arthur, could fully appreciate the Horn's power, Merlin carried it with him wherever he went. Before long he stopped calling it Serilliant and started referring to it as the Horn of Merlin. Though it came to be no less part of his garb than his fabled blue cloak, he steadfastly refused to divulge to anyone, even his closest friends, the nature of its power.

While under the sea, Merlin had discovered an ideal place to store the Treasures until the return of Arthur. This place was far from Britain, deep beyond imagining, and almost impossible to find. Merlin called it the Glass House. He kept its location secret, although from time to time he hinted that it lay hidden beneath the waves. In time, he brought all the Treasures to the Glass House for safekeeping. All, that is, except the ruby ring, which he had not yet found, and the Horn itself, which he could not bear to leave behind.

Merlin traveled widely, with the Horn ever at his side. In his arrogance, he flaunted it, believing that the Horn was destined to remain with him always. No one, he told himself, would be so foolish as to try to steal it.

He was wrong. The sorceress Nimue had long envied Merlin. She had often tried, with limited results, to trick him into parting with his secrets. Realizing that the Horn could confer unrivaled power, she vowed that she would one day possess it. Then, at last, she would be greater than Merlin, greater than anyone who might dare to challenge her.

Carefully, Nimue crafted a plot. It was founded on the belief that, one day, Merlin would choose to return to the Glass House under the sea to inspect the Treasures hidden there. To succeed, she knew she would need an ally, one who would not shy away from a great battle on the open ocean.

She sought out a certain sea captain, a man named Garlon. Such great distances had he sailed that it was said that neither war nor weather could sink a ship if Garlon the Seaworthy stood at the helm. For some reason known to no one but Garlon himself, he seethed with contempt for Merlin. Nimue knew not the origins of his hatred, but she knew well how to fan its embers into flames. She approached Garlon aboard his ship one day, enticing him with her sweet perfume and her promises of wealth beyond measure. But these meant less to him than the chance he had longed for, the chance to humble Merlin at last. He agreed to help.

For a long time, Nimue waited. At length, the desired day arrived. Disguised as a cloud of mist upon the water, she watched as Merlin readied a barge drawn by a great whale. The wizard boarded the barge, then commanded the whale to take him to *the place where the sea begins, the womb where the waters are born.*

As the barge drew farther away from Britain, mysterious winds seemed to gather around it, driving it toward a faraway destination. Unnoticed, the sorceress followed at a distance. Hidden behind her curtain of mist, Garlon sailed his own ship, propelled by the same winds that drove Merlin.

Finally, the winds ceased. Merlin released the whale and prepared to plunge beneath the waves. At that instant, Nimue cast aside her disguise. She attacked the lone wizard, joined by her band of sea demons and the vengeful Garlon.

Although he had no army to defend him, Merlin held his own for some time. The battle raged on for weeks, turning night into day and water into fire. But in time, the combined forces against him proved too strong. Merlin realized that he could not prevail. In that bitter moment, he also understood his own colossal folly. He had broken the command of Merwas; he had wasted his opportunity to protect the Horn; he had betrayed the very cause of his king.

As Nimue and Garlon bore down on him, Merlin tried to think of some way to save the Horn, even if he could not save himself. In desperation, he hurled the Horn as far as he could from the attackers.

Nimue merely laughed, gloating in triumph. "Do you think you can sssstop me sssso eassssily?"

Then, as the Horn hit the water, something remarkable occurred. As it started spiraling downward into the depths, the Horn caused the water to start spinning around it. Soon the ocean itself began whirling with ever-greater force, and a dark hole opened on the surface of the sea.

A great whirlpool was born.

Seizing his chance, Merlin mustered all his remaining power. He cast a protective spell over the whirlpool, so that only those who were friends of King Arthur—or Arthur himself—could enter the whirlpool and survive.

Nimue tried to force her way into the mouth of the whirlpool but could not. She exploded in rage. Merlin had denied her the Horn! She swooped down on the exhausted wizard and carried him away, dropping him into a deep cave on the Isle of Bardsey, which she sealed forever.

Yet, so great was Nimue's desire for the Horn, she could not accept defeat. She returned to the whirlpool, determined to wait until it finally slowed and collapsed, no matter how long that might take. After all, there was now no risk of being menaced by Merlin. In exploring the area below the whirlpool, she discovered Merlin's Glass House. She claimed it for her own, although its store of Treasures held no interest for her. The one Treasure she most wanted lay beyond her reach . . . for the moment.

Nimue took Garlon, against his will, to the Glass House under the sea. Although he had no desire for the Horn, he had been useful to her once, and might be so again. Yet he resisted serving as her underling, even as he resisted living deep under the waves. Once he tried to escape to the surface and was apprehended by her sea demons.

Though the sea demons wanted to tear Garlon to shreds, Nimue halted them. Instead, she raised her vaporous hand and laid on him a terrible curse. *If Garlon should ever again go above the surface of the sea, he would instantly disintegrate and perish—unless he had first taken a drink from the Horn.* Thus Garlon's loyalty was ensured, for unless he could somehow recover the Horn, he would never again feel the touch of sunlight on his skin.

Years passed, turning into decades, then into centuries. Still the whirlpool persisted, surrounded in time by a group of whales, singing and circling without end. All this time Nimue waited, with Garlon at her side, kept alive by the power of the Horn that seeped through the whirlpool into the surrounding waters. Yet she had not counted on the fact that the Horn would also nourish the whirlpool and keep it spinning strongly—so strongly that it showed no sign of ever collapsing. While she suspected that the whirlpool's strength would prevent any friend of Arthur who might get in from ever getting out again, she also began to fear that her vigil might be prolonged forever.

Unknown to Nimue, on the one thousandth anniversary of Merlin's demise, the spirit of the great wizard appeared in the dream of Geoffrey of Bardsey, the last surviving member of the Order of the Horn.

"Last of the faithful," the spirit of Merlin declared, "I come to you with a command."

"Are you sure?" asked Geoffrey in protest. "I am rather weak and frail."

The spirit examined the aging monk with evident disappointment. "You are the only one I have left. For one thousand years I have slept in constant torment, not knowing whether the Horn could still be saved for Arthur. Yet now, through the whispering of mer folk who come near my cave, I have learned that there is indeed a thin strand of hope. But I need your assistance."

The spirit of Merlin then told Geoffrey all that had befallen the Horn. He concluded with this command: "Go now to the distant port of Manila. There you will find, preparing to sail, a ship known as *Resurrección*. You must smuggle yourself aboard, then ride with the ship, wherever it may go. For its route will take you close to the mighty whirlpool where the Horn lies to this very day."

Geoffrey scratched his neck nervously. "Surely you are not expecting me to sail into the mouth of a whirlpool."

The spirit scowled at him, then said only, "The ship will lead you to the Horn."

With that, the spirit disappeared and Geoffrey of Bardsey awoke. Despite his fears, not to mention his tender feet, he made his way across Asia to Manila. He arrived just as the ship was being loaded with priceless treasures. He boarded and hid himself away, but not before he made a small coded entry in the ship's manifest, on the remote chance that it might one day alert an ally who could somehow provide assistance.

Soon after the ship was launched, Geoffrey discovered its generous stores of food. Finding himself eating better than ever before in his life, he began to conclude that his original fears had been misplaced. Surely Merlin would never reward his loyalty by causing him to plunge into a deadly whirlpool!

Months passed at sea, and Geoffrey began to wonder whether he would ever see the hills of his home again. Then came a morning when the ship suddenly changed course, spinning in ever tighter circles. Sailors started cursing and howling like wounded beasts. Geoffrey rushed out to the deck to discover that the ship was, indeed, being swallowed by the whirlpool. Men screamed in fright and leaped overboard into the churning waves, even as wind tore at the sails and the mainmast snapped in two.

Just as he uttered his final prayers, Geoffrey heard the men crying that they were being devoured by whales. Then, to his astonishment, he saw that they were in truth being saved, carried to shore before they could drown.

Alas, the whales did not seem at all interested in saving Geoffrey. Though he called to them, waved his arms wildly, and begged to be taken in their jaws, they paid no attention to him. So one man, and one man alone, went down with the doomed ship.

18

ageless fears

GEOFFREY hung his head dejectedly. "And here I have stayed."

"I wish my dad could have heard that," said Kate. "But I thought you were going to tell a story of hope and promise."

The old man pouted. "I suppose I exaggerated a bit."

"A bit! I feel more hopeless than ever."

"Enough sitting around," announced Terry, pushing to his feet. "I'm going out there to see if I can learn anything useful."

"Be careful," warned Kate.

"Don't go too far," added Geoffrey.

"Do I have any choice?" The young man gestured at the whirling wall of water surrounding the ship. He strode off, stumbled on a warped timber, then lifted the trapdoor and descended.

Watching him, Geoffrey sighed. "Impatient youth! Though I can't suppose I blame him for wanting to try to find a way out of here. But with the whirlpool's strength intensified by the Horn, no one—not even a great magician—could escape."

"How did he get in, anyway? You said that only a friend of Arthur could enter the whirlpool."

Thoughtfully, Geoffrey tugged his beard. "I cannot say. Perhaps time will tell."

"I wish I could talk to Dad," Kate said wistfully. "He'd have an idea . . . unless he's in too much trouble himself right now."

"Tell me," probed the monk. "Just what would your father do if he were here?"

"He'd think. About where we might find a clue. The way he did with the ballad."

"Ballad?"

Kate pursed her lips. "It's an old ballad about the ship, the whirlpool, the whales. I can't remember much, but it ends in the weirdest way:

> *One day the sun will fail to rise,*
> *The dead will die,*
> *And then*
> *For Merlin's Horn to find its home,*
> *The ship must sail again."*

"Weird, indeed," agreed Geoffrey, studying her with keen interest. "Especially that part about Merlin's Horn finding its home." He swatted at a strand of rigging dangling by his head. "Can't make hide nor hair of it, I'm afraid."

"Maybe the Horn's home is wherever it is now." She returned his scrutiny. "You do know where it is, don't you? How did you find it, anyway?"

"Stubbed my toe on it, to be precise. It was practically buried in the sand near the anchor."

"Have you ever . . . taken a drink from it?" asked Kate, her voice a whisper.

"No," he replied. "You recall what happened to Merlin when he took a drink before he had passed the test of Merwas, don't you? He lost whatever good sense he had! And before long, he lost everything else as well. That's not to say that I haven't been tempted. I have. Often."

"You must have plenty of willpower to resist."

"Not really. I'm as weak as any mortal being. Weaker, no doubt. But I do have one advantage that poor Merlin never had. The whirlpool surrounding this ship seems to coax out the essence of the Horn, and I breathe some of it in these swirling vapors every day. That has to ease my thirst a bit, although it is not the same as drinking from it directly."

A bit guiltily, he added, "On top of that, I sometimes allow myself to sniff the Horn's aroma, just to smell that fragrance of the mountaintop that Emrys gave to it."

"Do you do that often?"

The hint of a grin touched Geoffrey's face. "Only on Feast Days and Holy Days. Of course, there are dozens and dozens of those! Last time was the Sunday after Saint Vitus' Day."

Staring into the mist off the bow, Kate said darkly, "If your story is true, while we're trying to find some way to pass through the whirlpool, so is Nimue."

At the mention of that name, Kate felt a cold wind blow over the deck of the *Resurreccíon*. She shivered and turned to Geoffrey. Oddly, he did not seem to have noticed anything. Her chill soon passed, yet it left her with the uncomfortable feeling that she had felt it before, and would, before long, feel it again.

The old man patted her arm. "That wretched sorceress craves nothing more than the chance to drink from the Horn. But for several centuries now, we've had something of a stalemate, she and I. She can't get into the whirlpool, and I can't get out! The wall that divides us is utterly impermeable. So you needn't worry. Nimue and her sea demons, along with Garlon, have been trying for ages to get in here, with no luck. Why should anything be different now?"

"She must be getting awfully impatient."

He angled his face upward. "If it makes you feel any better, on top of Merlin's protective spell, we have the whales."

"The gray whales?"

Geoffrey nodded. "They seem to work very hard at keeping intruders away from the whirlpool. And, similarly, the ship."

Kate reflected on this. Could the whales, as Isabella suspected, have purposely tried to erase the sonic image of the sunken ship? Could the whale who was so badly tangled at the buoy have been trying to interfere with the equipment?

"Why would they do that?" she demanded.

"At first, perhaps, it was their old loyalty to Merlin. But in more recent times, they mainly want to keep people away from themselves."

"What makes you say that?"

He scratched vigorously inside each of his nostrils, then lifted the slender red volume. "They told me so themselves. I can listen to them whenever I like, with this."

Kate slid closer. "Your little red book?"

"Haven't done it much lately," he continued, trying to stifle a yawn. "This infernal heat, you know. Makes me sleep more than usual. But in times past I have listened to the whales for hours on end. Because their hearing is so good, they have become the ocean's eavesdroppers. I have even listened to the songs of the whales who don't stay by the whirlpool year after year, who swim every year to the far north. From them I have learned about the coldness of currents, the size of newborns, the passage of seasons, the taste of krill, the motions of stars."

"You were saying that the whales want to keep people away."

A cloud passed over Geoffrey's face. "Once, long ago, the whales befriended everyone, just as they did Merlin. They were as helpful to him as the mer people—more so, because they were not so difficult to find. Ever since the fall of the realm of Shaa, mer folk have lived in the shadows, appearing only rarely. Not so the whales. In Merlin's day, and even in mine, they felt no reason to hide. So they had no hesitation about showing themselves to save the sailors from the *Resurrección*. I am sorry to say they paid dearly for that mistake."

"How?"

"Word spread. Hunters came in droves. Soon only a few whales remained alive. Some of the survivors simply swam away, never to return. Others chose to stay in these waters near the whirlpool, circling endlessly, grieving for their lost mothers and fathers, sisters and brothers. Still others chose to swim to the far north, hoping to evade more hunters by moving always, never resting. They are the lucky ones, because they have grown old and died, making room for new generations who are not burdened by such painful memories."

At once, Kate understood. "So that is why the songs of the whales who stay around here are so sad."

"Right. The nearness of the Horn sustains them somehow, as it does the ship, the whirlpool, and myself. But for them, continuing to live means continuing to suffer. Their fate is most cruel. They cannot forget, cannot move on.

> *Ye who drink from Merlin's Horn*
> *May for dying not be mourned*
> *May grow younger with the years*
> *May remember ageless fears."*

Kate thought again of the young whale ensnared in the net. Had he been more afraid of drowning, or of her? She ran her hand along a length of rigging, sturdy as it was when it left Manila centuries ago.

Geoffrey looked at the vapors swimming about the

sails. "It is said, by the whales themselves, that their agony will not be over until the whirlpool itself comes to an end."

At that, the trapdoor flew open. Terry squeezed through the opening up to his armpits. "A steam vent!" he exclaimed, his voice full of fear. "Opened up right by my feet, not far from the hull."

"Steam, eh?" asked Geoffrey calmly. "No wonder it's so beastly hot."

"Don't you see?" the geologist cried. "The eruption is going to happen any time now! We're all going to be burned to ashes, including your precious Horn."

Geoffrey's wrinkles deepened. "My, my! That *is* rather worrisome."

"Worrisome! Can't you understand, old man? This isn't going to be just another tremor. This is going to be a full-scale eruption!"

Geoffrey shook his head. "But I don't understand how such a thing could happen. The Horn ought to be protecting us, as it has these many years. Something must have changed! I only wish I knew what."

Kate seized him by the shoulder. "The whales might know! You said they hear all kinds of things. Try listening to them!"

"An excellent idea," agreed the monk.

"A ridiculous idea," countered Terry.

"Come on," said Kate, taking Geoffrey's arm to help him stand. "Let's try it."

Opening the book to the page decorated with green-and-gold vines, Geoffrey inhaled deeply, then began to concentrate on the page. At once, the continuous humming of the whirlpool reduced to a mere whisper. All other sounds, including their own breathing, diminished. At the same time, one sound grew steadily louder, until it seemed to spring from only inches away.

The wailing rose and fell like the surging waves. Kate could not tell just how many whales were singing, only that some of the voices sounded young and vibrant, others old and thin. All of them exuded sorrow.

She glanced at Geoffrey, who was scratching his ear anxiously. All of a sudden, he stopped. His hand fell to his side. For a long moment he stood as still as a wax figure.

Finally, the ragged robes stirred. At the same time, the mournful cries of the whales receded until, at last, they could no longer be heard.

Geoffrey grasped a line of rigging to steady himself. His face a mixture of fear and confusion, he mumbled, "It can't be so."

"What did they say?" pressed Kate.

"They said," he replied, almost choking on the words, "that Nimue has finally lost her patience. That she has set out . . . to destroy the whirlpool."

"But how?"

From the corner of her eye, Kate saw Terry lean forward to hear better.

"She has found some way to make the rock beneath the ocean floor buckle and boil. Until . . . until it explodes like a volcano."

"The eruption," whispered Terry.

Kate tugged Geoffrey's robe. "Where is Nimue now?"

"Still in the Glass House, not far from here."

"But wouldn't the eruption destroy that, too? And all the Treasures there?"

"Nimue cares not! If somehow she can shatter the whirlpool and escape with the one thing she craves more than any other, that is her only goal."

"Wait a minute," objected Terry. "I'm the first to agree we're on the edge of an eruption. But . . . this is *geological force* we're talking about. Primal. Uncontrollable. Even if you accept the idea of a sorceress and her sea demons, which I don't, they couldn't control volcanic energy. Nothing can! And besides, why would anyone want to do something like that?"

Geoffrey examined him grimly. Then he reached one hand deep into the folds of his habit. He seemed to be searching for something, or possibly scratching again. Then, slowly, he pulled out his hand—and a gleaming object, suspended from a necklace of scarlet coral beads. Shaped like a curling conch shell, it glistened with a sheen of blue and silver. Within its mouth brimmed fluid no less radiant than a rainbow.

"This is why," he announced.

Kate stared in awe at the Horn.

Terry pulled himself through the trapdoor and came over for a closer look. Like Kate, he kept looking at the wondrous object, which glowed with an opalescent luster.

She reached to stroke its smooth surface with one finger. Quietly, she said, "They're all the same shape, aren't they?"

"What are?" asked Geoffrey.

"The Horn, the secret code, the whirlpool. They're all a spiral."

"Yes," agreed the monk, a curious gleam in his eye. "So they are."

"Let me get this straight," said Terry. "You're saying this—this sorceress of yours is trying to cause an eruption just so she can get that thing."

"Precisely."

"Are you sure you heard the whales say that?"

"Quite sure," Geoffrey answered. "They were perfectly clear." He replaced the Horn under his garment. "The only questionable part came at the end."

"What was that?"

"I hesitate to tell you, since I might have misunderstood."

"Tell us," Kate insisted.

"All right. It seems Nimue has taken some unfortunate souls as her prisoners." He swatted the side of his neck. "That may or may not be true, but the puzzling part is that the whales described the prisoners' ship as, well, an enormous bubble."

"A what?"

"Quite absurd, I agree. Imagine a ship built like a bubble."

"I can! It's my dad!"

The wooly eyebrows lifted. "Your father? Are you sure?"

"Yes!"

"I am sorry to hear that. Dreadfully sorry."

Looking from Geoffrey to Terry, Kate cried, "We've got to do something!" She grabbed the monk by the shoulders. "Isn't there any way we can get out of here while the whirlpool is still going?"

His dark eyes seemed to darken even more. "No. I told you, the whirlpool is impermeable. No creature of flesh could survive the passage."

"But *something* must be able to pass through it!" She glanced at the whirling spiral of water. "You said yourself the power of the Horn seeps through somehow. How else could it affect the whales?"

Geoffrey jolted as if he had been struck with a hammer. "You might . . . be onto something. Yes, yes . . . you just might." Pensively, he combed his beard with his fingers. "I am not sure it will work, but . . . there could, in fact, be a way. I am stunned that in all the time I've been here I never thought of it before."

"What is it?"

"It will be risky. Very risky. I would not try it at all, except that the Horn, and all the other Treasures, are in such grave danger. Everything Merlin worked so hard to achieve, everything he did to aid Arthur, is at stake."

"Dad's *life* is at stake!" Kate shook him fiercely. "You've got to take me with you."

He pulled free. "I am sorry," he said firmly. "It will be dangerous enough for one person to go. As it is, I have no idea how to stop Nimue. I only know I must try."

"I can help you," she pleaded.

"I may be a fool," he replied, shaking his head, "but I am not that much of a fool. As unsafe as you may be here, you are safer here than going with me. Even if I can somehow survive the whirlpool, the route to the Glass House, which I know only from the whales, is fraught with dangers and darkness." His furrowed face filled with compassion. "I will do what I can to help your father."

"Take me with you. Please."

A sudden tremor rocked the ship. Geoffrey shouted, tumbling backward into a maze of rigging. Terry skidded across the deck, smashing a row of clay jars. As timbers splintered and buckled, the floorboards under Kate gave way. She fell through a hole, landing on a mound of bundles in the darkened deck below.

With a final shudder, the violent quaking ceased.

Struggling to gain her bearings, Kate rubbed her sore neck. She crawled over the bundles to the wooden ladder and rapidly scaled the rungs. Seconds later, she burst out of the trapdoor onto the main deck.

Pulling Terry loose from a web of torn rigging, she helped him to his feet. Then, as if one, their eyes trained on the spot where Geoffrey had stood only a moment before.

He had vanished.

19

swirling vapors

WHERE did he go?" asked Kate.

"Beats me," Terry muttered.

She ran over to the mainmast. The old man was nowhere to be seen. Picking up a cannonball at her feet, she hefted it like a shot-put.

Where had he gone? Her neck stung, her back ached. Yet those things did not trouble her nearly as much as the disappearance of her prime companion in this strange undersea world. Despite his bizarre manner, she had found herself almost liking Geoffrey. He reminded her a little of her own grandfather, eccentric and vulnerable, or maybe of someone she had known in a story, or a dream. No matter. He was gone.

In frustration, she hurled the cannonball into the mass of rigging at the base of the broken mast. Then an idea drifted into her thoughts. Maybe he, too, had fallen through the floor! Maybe even now he lay sprawled on some stack of crates on a lower deck. She started shoving the rigging aside, searching for another hole in the deck.

Without a word, Terry came over and started helping. Although he was a bit clumsy without his glasses, he was strong enough to heave aside cases and timbers that she could barely budge.

After several minutes of furious searching, she concluded it was useless. Panting, she crumpled onto a barrel and sat there, her head in her hands.

Terry straightened up stiffly. Delicately wiping his sore brow, he said, "No sign of him."

Kate lifted her head. "No. Thanks for helping, anyway."

"Sure." He leaned against the mast. "Don't know where he could have gone."

Her gaze fell on the jumble of rigging, and suddenly it came to her. "I do. He's gone to stop Nimue."

"But how?"

"He said there was a way."

Terry kicked away a piece of bar shot. "He must be part fish, then. And even so, he couldn't survive the whirlpool. Can you imagine the pressure of that water, with the strength to hold back half a mile of ocean? It's probably several thousand pounds per square inch." He studied the swirling vapors. "No, not unless the whirlpool slowed way down, for whatever reason, could anything pass through it and survive."

Stubbornly, Kate threw her braid over her shoulder. "Then where is Geoffrey? He found a way."

"I'll give him this," said Terry. "If he did find a way, he's plenty ingenious. Not to mention self-sacrificing." His shoulders drooped a notch. "I guess you already found out how self-sacrificing I am."

She turned to him, saw the regret in his eyes. "Up there on the *Skimmer?* Look, you wanted to grab me. You just didn't move fast enough."

"No way. I was more concerned about my equipment than anything else. I might not have saved you, but at least I could have tried. Really tried."

Kate scrutinized him. "If that's an apology, I accept. Now let's get back to finding some way out of here. Maybe the whirlpool has a weak point."

"Don't kid yourself. Lousy as it is, our only sane option is to stay put. There's a tiny chance we could survive an eruption. But there's zero chance we could survive the whirlpool."

"It's not the eruption I'm worried about. It's my dad! And Isabella! I can't just sit here and do nothing."

Terry shook his head. "Keep your wits, will you? This is real, not just a story in some book."

Kate sat upright. "That's it. The little red book!"

She rushed to the mainmast and retrieved the slender volume lying at its base. "He used this!"

"Come off it," scoffed Terry. "Talking with animals is one thing. Disappearing into thin air is another."

Madly, she flipped the pages to the one displaying an elephant and an ant. "This must be it! What did Geoffrey say to do? Either say all the magic words, or just look at the design and . . . concentrate. Hard."

Clenching her jaw, she started to imagine herself as

a deep-water fish. Like the one Isabella bought from the fisherman. She stared at the page, then suddenly halted herself.

That wouldn't work. Terry was right. No fish could withstand the pressure of the whirlpool wall. What had Geoffrey said? *No creature of flesh could survive.* Even a piece of eight would probably not last.

She chewed her lip. What was it she had said that gave Geoffrey his idea? That the power of the Horn, somehow, gets through . . .

"Give up," advised Terry.

"There has to be a way!"

Following the curling clouds of vapor with her eyes, she considered the puzzle. She tried to recall Isabella's theory of how *the Merlin effect* might work. Some kind of particle that circulates in the water, altering the genes. Circulating. Water.

Water! That was the answer. Something more like water than like flesh might be able to get through. How had Isabella described those early single-celled creatures? *More water than organism.*

She closed her eyes, fixing her thoughts on the idea of water, vaporous and elusive, without shape or substance, rising softly through the air. Then, opening her eyes, she did her best to hold the image in her mind and stare at the page without blinking.

Nothing. She concentrated harder, holding the book before her face. Water being. Water creature. *Water spirit.*

Just then, Terry snatched the book from her hands.

"Give that back," she cried, wrestling with him. "I need it!"

Holding the book just beyond her reach, he crooned, "When in doubt, try hocus pocus." He gestured wildly and said in his deepest voice, "I am Ali Baba Heebee Jeebee, the great magician."

"Give it back!" she bellowed, finally getting her hand on the volume. She tried to pull it away from him. "I've almost got it right."

"Have you tried this?" he asked, pretending to sweep a cape across his shoulders. *"Abra cadabra!"*

There was a nearly inaudible *pop*, just as the book dropped to the deck. No one picked it up again.

20

water spirit

BEFORE feeling came memory.

Vague as reflections in a pool, wispy as visions in the mist, the first memories drifted to Kate. The many forms of water flowed in and around her. She remembered all she had been and might yet become. She yearned to begin again.

I am rain. Showering, sprinkling, misting, pouring. Rolling with thunder, pulsing with light. I scatter the sun, each droplet a prism, connecting soil and sky with archways of color. To soak, to fill, that is what I am about. To find every last thirsty thing and give it new life. I sparkle as I weep. For I am made to dance, even as I cry.

I am stream. Bright and bouncy rivulet, born of mountain snows, cascading through a meadow. Cold on the tongue. Brimming with sunshine. Splash, trickle, lap, gurgle. Over the rock, under the spout, down the channel.

Call me *creek* in Colorado, *burn* in Scotland, *wadi* in Egypt, *arroyo* in Spain, *billabong* in Australia. I link summits to seas, freshets to rivers. I seek, I surge, I murmur and purl. And I never rest, I never stop.

I am ice. Smooth and sharp, gripping and binding. Ever so slowly I spread and harden, over lakes, over leaves, over windows and roads. As an icicle I stretch to the tallest, as a sheet to the thinnest, as a floe to the widest. As a glacier I grow heavy, squashing the land, gouging valleys out of mountains, ponds out of pinnacles. I seize, I freeze. That is my way.

I am snow. Part water, part crystal, part miniature star. Feather and diamond bonded as one. My life is a flight, twirling and gliding. Though I am distinct from all my trillions of cousins, we are so alike in our luminous hearts that we can coat canyons and cities and make them seem one. I whiten the land, brighten the air. I bring frosted galaxies down to the ground.

I am cloud. Rumbling, gathering, steaming, stretching. Vapors are my body, thin as a breath, yet thick enough to stop the sun. Finer than filigree, broader than basins. Cumulus, nimbus, cirrus and stratus. Whatever I yield shall float back to me. My gifts to the world are always returned.

I am ocean. Raging and bitter, glassy and great. I move with the moon, I ride with the tides. Smelling of brine, brimming with life, tasting like salty kelp stew. No roads cross my surface, no sun shines below. I am the edges of continents, the bottoms of chasms, the peaks of tsunamis. Though my waters lie deep, my mysteries lie deeper still.

And with time, Kate understood that she held within her all these forms. She could swim with the wave, sail with the mist. Her body wrapped around her like a flowing tail, transparent as dew and subtly gleaming. Liquid as the sea itself, she swept into the swirling vapors above the old ship, gracefully rising.

For now she was a water spirit.

Soon the mist deepened into fog, the fog into droplets, the droplets into heaving waves. The current whirled her around, faster and faster. Immense waves pressed into her, flattening her to nothingness.

For an age she spun through these reeling waters. Then, gradually, the pressure reduced. Though she had no need to breathe, she felt her body expand, and she drank of the wide ocean again.

Darkness surrounded her, except for some strange and shadowy lights that circled and flickered. She could no longer see the ship. In every direction, deep currents throbbed, flowing into underwater canyons and around the roots of islands. She had passed through the whirlpool.

PART THREE

Beyond the Abyss

21

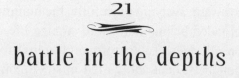

battle in the depths

KATE soon discovered she could swim in an entirely new way, without stroking or kicking. Such motions were impossible anyway, since her new body, which had expanded in size once she emerged from the whirlpool, bore no arms and no legs. Something of a cross between a transparent jellyfish and a slender frond of kelp, she possessed a lithe, ribbonlike form. She was, in fact, little more than a long and lacy tail. She needed only to sway herself from side to side, undulating with the currents, to move in any direction, including up and down.

A group of thin fish swam past, their tails and jaws radiating blue phosphorescent light. Twisted black smokers jutted off the sea floor like shrunken volcanoes, venting bright clouds of chemicals that illuminated the water while making it taste of rotten eggs. Giant white clams, so large they made the Venus clams of the lagoon look like mere infants, clung to the base of the smoking vents. Kate flowed past one of them, feeling its intense heat. She knew that it spewed superheated gases, boiling bile from the center of the Earth.

As she swam, swaying gracefully, the humming of the whirlpool faded behind her. More strange life forms appeared on all sides. Tube worms, clustered together in bizarre bouquets, bent and curled in slow motion. Their tops opened in scarlet plumes, possibly a kind of mouth for drinking the chemicals billowing from the smokers. A ghostly crab bolted away as she approached, sliding into a narrow crevasse. Tiny blue limpets, oversized snails, and wormlike larvae congregated on the rocks.

Then, in the dim light, she perceived another shape. Huge, streamlined, and gray, it floated just above the bottom, completely motionless. It possessed an enormous tail, wider than she was long. Just behind its jaw, a great eye regarded her cautiously.

A whale.

Almost imperceptibly, she wafted nearer. The whale, an adult male, did not stir, following her movements with his unblinking eye. Before long, she could see the cluster of barnacles on his belly and tail, the knobs of his vertebrae, the twin blowholes.

Suddenly, the massive back arched and snapped, sending the whale gliding away into the shadowy depths. The current washed over Kate, rolling her backward. She brushed against a cluster of tube worms, felt them tickle the full length of her body.

As the whale departed, he began to whistle in a low, haunting voice. Soon other invisible singers joined him, wailing and weeping, reliving their sorrows. Kate listened quietly, feeling her own longings. Dad . . . a prisoner of Nimue. *I've got to find him.* But how? He could be anywhere.

At once she sensed that something apart from herself had frightened the whale. Curious, she whirled around.

Swimming awkwardly, a most unusual creature approached. Although shaped somewhat like herself, this figure looked spindly, even shriveled. It resembled more a twisted root than a graceful tail. Jerkily, it swam toward her, evidently eager to communicate.

The creature blinked its single swollen eye, the color of blue-tinted ice. Then it spoke to Kate telepathically, in a voice she recognized with a twinge.

"Where the devil are we?" asked Terry. "And *what* are we?"

"I was hoping you had stayed behind."

"So had I. Guess, ah, you were right about the book. You're full of surprises."

Kate felt a surge of both pleasure and embarrassment. In her old body, she would have blushed.

"So tell me. What are we?"

"We're some kind of water creatures, I guess." A laugh bubbled up. "You look a little on the skinny side, though."

"Incredible," said Terry, curling his transparent tail so he could see it. "I still can't believe this is real."

"As real as the ship and the whirlpool." She spun slowly in the water. "Why did you decide to follow me?"

"I didn't. I just found myself here." The bulbous eye blinked. "How do we get our old bodies back?"

"Maybe Geoffrey can do that, if we ever find him

again." She resumed swimming. "That won't be easy, though. He had a good head start. You can bet he's on his way to the Glass House, wherever that is."

Struggling to stay with her, Terry called, "Listen, are you crazy? We've got to get out of here before the eruption happens. As far away as possible, while we still have time."

"You do what you want," she replied, waving her tail more rapidly. "But I'm going to try to find my dad, if I can."

Terry hesitated, then tried to keep pace with her. "You're not getting rid of me that easily," he grumbled. "I'll stay with you, at least until we can figure out how to get our old bodies back. Hey, what's that?"

Both of them stopped short, staring at the cloud pouring from a smoker straight ahead. They watched the cloud slowly rising into the water, pulsing with reddish light.

"Did you see that?"

"I'm not sure," she replied. "It was there, beside that cloud. Then it vanished."

"It looked like something out of a fable," he said, a touch of awe in his voice.

Kate, studying the smoking vent, did not answer for some time. "It could have been the weird light down here, playing tricks."

"Could have been. But I'm sure I saw it. And it looked just like . . ." He paused, unable to say the word. "Like a *mermaid*."

Together they floated, silently waiting, hoping to glimpse it again. But they saw nothing beyond the glowing fumes.

"Let's go," said Kate at last. She slid through the water, waving her gossamery form. Despite her fears, she still could not help but enjoy the feeling of weightlessness, of being so insubstantial that she was almost part of the water itself. Then, with a sharp pang, she thought of her father and Isabella. Even if she could possibly find them, would it be in time? And what could she hope to do to help them? Seeing a house-size boulder covered with a thick mat of yellow vegetation, she drifted toward it, occupied with her thoughts.

At once, the boulder stirred. From under its hulking form, more than a dozen burly legs extended, groping on the rocks. The vegetation, so soft and swaying from a distance, hardened into murderous spikes, each one as long as a lance. The monster, with narrow slits where eyes might once have been, lifted itself from its lair and opened its gargantuan mouth, where an army of tongues rippled like a nest of blood red worms.

"Look out!"

The pair turned and whipped through the water. But the spidery creature pursued them relentlessly, crashing over fuming vents and rock outcroppings. The faster they swam, the nearer it drew, legs churning, snarling angrily. Beads of brown sludge oozed from the edges of its mouth.

Glancing to the rear, Kate could see the monster pulling nearer. Terry, swimming clumsily, had fallen so far behind her that the beast was almost on top of him.

"Hellllp!" he cried. "It's going to—"

As his words disappeared in an avalanche of snarling, Kate spotted a shallow cave about equidistant between them. Without thinking, she reversed her direction and raced back toward it, throwing herself directly into Terry and driving them both into the mouth of the cave. They wriggled inside just as the monster arrived.

Protected by a ledge of overhanging rock, they pressed against the back of the cave. The cries of the creature echoed around them, rising in repeating crescendos. Then, inexplicably, the noise ceased.

For several minutes they waited, not daring to move. Still as stone, they could only hope that the monster had finally given up and departed.

"There!" screamed Kate.

A long, leathery leg reached into the cave, slithering toward them. They shrank still deeper into their burrow, even as the leg lashed out at them. It grazed Kate's flank, but could not quite reach her.

For an instant the leg seemed to hesitate. Then it planted itself against the rock ledge directly above them. The snarling resumed, as the leg began pulling on the roof of the cave, trying to tear it away.

A jagged piece of rock broke loose. Kate grabbed it in the folds of her tail and stabbed at the leg. The creature roared wrathfully, but kept its leg in place. Harder and harder it pulled. The water in the cave grew murky with crumbling rock.

All at once, the rock ledge buckled. Before Kate or Terry knew what had happened, the slab flew off, exposing the cave. There, gaping at them, was the cavernous mouth. The squirming tongues stretched toward them.

Then, in a shriek of pain, the monster jerked backward. A titanic tail wrapped around its body, squeezing mercilessly. The yellow spikes snapped off like stalactites as the beast writhed and kicked, trying to free itself from its attacker, a great blue scorpion with a poisonous barb and slashing fangs.

Great clouds of sediment rose all around as the two leviathans wrestled, battling in the depths. The scorpion's fangs ripped at the flesh of its opponent, even as powerful legs tried to break its back. On and on they fought, screaming and roaring, pounding themselves against the sea floor.

Kate and Terry could do no more than cower in the small hollow that once had been a cave. They waited for some chance to escape, knowing it would probably never come. Meanwhile, the battle grew ever more violent. The monsters thrashed and tumbled, battering each other's bodies, unwilling to stop until one lay vanquished.

Finally, the legs of the spiderlike beast hung limp. The blue scorpion lifted its head and bellowed a cry of victory.

"Don't move," whispered Kate. "Maybe it will go away."

"Don't bet on it," Terry replied nervously.

Using its great barb, the scorpion butted the corpse fiercely, making sure its adversary would not rise and strike again. Finally, coiling its tail, it seemed to prepare to crawl away, when suddenly it halted. Spotting the two gleaming forms in the hollow, it stretched its neck toward them.

The colossal head lowered until it hung only a few feet above Kate and Terry. Darkly, the scorpion's indigo eyes examined them. Then it opened its jaws, baring the horrible fangs.

22

the passage

Λs the deadly fangs draped over them, the two water spirits huddled tightly together.

"You shouldn't have come back for me," grumbled Terry. "That was stupid."

"Guess so," Kate said sullenly.

"I suppose I should say thanks."

"I suppose I should say you're welcome."

Just then, something odd happened. The fangs began to melt into seawater, along with the rest of the scorpion's head. The blue armor covering the length of its body grew steadily lighter in color, fading to the point of transparency. The indigo eyes flashed for the last time. Then, with a slight *pop,* the scorpion disappeared completely.

Floating in its place, barely as large as one of the fangs, was a grotesque little fish with a beaklike nose. The entire body was covered with scraggly white hairs, while the dorsal fin wriggled energetically, as if trying to scratch. Then, to the astonishment of Kate and Terry, the fish spoke.

"I never should have shown you the book."

"Geoffrey!" whooped Kate. "It's you."

The fish opened his jaws to the widest, much as the scorpion had done, then gurgled noisily before snapping them shut. "Pardon my yawning," he said grumpily. Swimming closer to Terry, the fish eyed him suspiciously. "And what, may I ask, is this?"

"The same could be asked of you," answered Terry. "I never thought I'd owe my life to a scrawny old fish."

"Delighted to be of service," came the reply. "Actually, before you arrived I was searching for some way to slip past the many-legged creature." His thin mouth pinched as he fought to hold back a yawn. "Thanks to you, I was able to mount a surprise attack."

"Where," asked Kate as quietly as she could, "is the Horn?"

The fish looked at her slyly, then uncurled a small fin under his tail just enough to reveal a gleaming object tucked inside. "Reduced in size, but safe enough." The fin closed tight again. "Well now, if you're going to accompany me—"

"Yes!" exclaimed Kate, her whole transparent body vibrating. Then she fell still. "Was that creature you killed related to the spider monster who guarded the entrance to the land of Shaa?"

The old fish blew a bubble, which expanded to the size of his head before popping. "No doubt."

"Does that mean the entrance to Shaa is near?"

"Nearer than you know." The fish's white mane quivered. "The land of Shaa lies at the bottom of a great abyss. *Darkest of the dark,* as it is known in legend."

"That's the only way I want to know it," said Kate.

"You may not wish to accompany me, then."

"You mean—?"

His dorsal fin wriggling, the old fish said grimly, "That is the way, the only way, to the Glass House. For the Glass House and the land of Shaa lie on the same path. If you are going to join me, you must travel down the same dark passage as Emrys and Merlin did long ago."

Kate felt suddenly limp.

"You can go back to the ship in the way you came, if you choose. I shall do my best to send word."

Her single-celled form tensed. "I'm coming with you."

The old fish studied her. "Are you quite sure?"

"Quite sure."

"Well then, as I was saying, if you're going to accompany me, you will need to dress more appropriately. A disguise, what? As you are, you'll soon end up as salad for one of Nimue's sea demons."

Terry swung his silver-blue eye toward the monstrous corpse, whose mouth gaped wide, its tongues hanging limp. "Whatever sea demons are, they can't be as bad as that thing over there."

Shaking himself, the old fish said to Kate, "He doesn't know very much, does he?"

"No," she replied. "But he's learning."

"Don't count on it." Terry turned to Geoffrey. "I won't delay you any longer. Would you mind changing me so I can get out of here?"

"It will be a pleasure," replied the fish. He burbled some syllables and waved his fin awkwardly.

Pop. Terry's watery shape vanished. In its place swam an ugly fish with goggle eyes, the same kind of fish that Isabella had analyzed in her makeshift laboratory.

"Hey, what's going on?" sputtered Terry. "I meant change me into a person. Not a fish version of Frankenstein! Change me back. Right now!"

"That might be risky," answered Geoffrey. "In the first place, people don't survive very long at the bottom of the sea. In the second place, I am not sure I can do it. Going from human to animal is much easier than the other way around. You might end up as a peacock or a giraffe."

Kate could not suppress a giggle. "That might be an improvement."

Pop. She found herself as an elegant fish with emerald green scales and a phosphorescent stripe down both sides. Elegant, but for the fact that in her nose she sported a large brass ring.

"What's this?" she exclaimed. "There's a ring in my nose."

"A nice touch," pronounced Terry.

"My apologies," said Geoffrey. "It's happened to me before. I must work on that charm."

"Can't you make it disappear?"

"Unfortunately not," he sighed. "A quirky business, this. At least I got the luminous stripes right. You can be our torch. There is no light where we are going."

With a quick jackknife he darted away, followed a few seconds later by Kate and Terry, muttering to themselves about their new forms. The white-haired fish led them across the ocean floor, offering a running commentary about how to swim like a fish.

"Your head is sagging," coached Geoffrey. "Look dead ahead."

"Easy for you to say," huffed Kate. "I've got this stupid ring in my nose."

She tried again.

"Not like that! You're weaving like a drunkard. Use your spine. Your whole spine."

"Here, I'll show you," offered Terry. "It's easy once you get the hang of it." He gave a sharp jerk of his tail and promptly flipped over backward.

"Gee, thanks," moaned Kate.

After several false starts, however, she started to move with some confidence. Before long she and the others reached the very spot where they had encountered the spidery creature. As they approached, a black chasm loomed before them. Wider than a whale, it looked impossibly deep and utterly dark, illuminated only by the faint glow of a smoking vent nearby.

"Is that it?" asked Kate doubtfully.

Geoffrey eyed the chasm. "The abyss."

"You're joking," said Terry as he cautiously approached the edge. "Magma is pushing higher all the time! Going down there would be like swimming straight into the eruption."

"You can wait for us here if you prefer," offered Geoffrey, circling slowly above the entrance. "Of course, you might have to deal with the mother of your many-legged friend. And she might not be in a very jolly mood when she returns."

With that, Geoffrey dived into the abyss. Not far behind came Kate, whose phosphorescent stripes cast a pale blue light on the jagged rock walls, and behind her, a reluctant Terry.

Suddenly, a fissure opened in the rock just ahead of them. Molten lava bubbled out, sizzling like hot coals doused with water. The walls of the abyss trembled as the space filled with a distant rumbling. Gradually, the fiery lava dimmed, hardening into stone before their eyes.

"As if it weren't hot enough in here already," said Geoffrey, jackknifing past the fissure.

"This is insane," objected Terry, starting to retreat.

Kate beckoned to him with her fin.

"But we'll be fried fish fillets if we go any deeper."

"It's our only chance," she replied, darting past the smoldering stone. She did not look back, but waited to hear him swim again before she continued.

Downward they swam, plunging into the chasm. Despite the uncomfortable warmth of the water, Kate felt increasingly gripped by a strange chill, a chill she had felt somewhere before. The vague, half-formed memory of a nightmare swelled inside her. It was not a matter of temperature, or of anything physical. Something about this place blew biting cold on her innermost self. The chill only deepened as they descended.

"Douse the torch!" ordered Geoffrey.

Kate obeyed. The abyss fell raven black. Although she could not see, she still could feel. The icy feeling grew stronger, working into her bones, her brain, her blood. *Darkest of the dark.* She wanted to shriek. At that instant a shadowed figure swept by, rising out of the depths. It brushed her with its frozen breath as it passed.

In time, she dared speak again. "What was that?"

"I don't want to know," said Terry, shaken.

"A sea demon." Geoffrey's tail twitched nervously. "We must be doubly careful now. We should proceed without any light."

Terry frowned. "But I can't do that. I'll swim straight into a wall."

"Not advisable," the elder fish replied crisply. "Stay right with me, close as you can."

Following his suggestion, Kate positioned herself immediately behind Geoffrey, while Terry trailed her closely. Sometimes, especially rounding bends, they would bump into one another, jamming faces into tails. As they continued, though, they swam with increasing coordination. Kate gradually became aware of a new sense guiding her motions, that ancient instinct that binds a school of fish together as they swim in unison. In time their three bodies moved almost as one.

For what might have been hours they voyaged downward. At last, ever so slowly, Kate discerned a subtle light ahead. For a while she thought it was merely her own wishful thinking. Yet the passage was indeed growing less dark. The abyss began to widen and to dive less steeply, even as it brightened. Finally they entered a great cavern, wider and taller than they could tell.

Geoffrey angled upward, leading the others. With a trio of splashes, they broke through the surface of what appeared to be a lake, set inside the expansive cavern.

"Air," puzzled Kate, keeping her gills underwater. "How did air get down here?"

"The sea holds many surprises," answered Geoffrey. He swished his tail, then said, "If you look up, you will see another."

23

sea stars

RAISING her eyes to the ceiling of the cavern, Kate saw the one thing she least expected to find, far beneath the stormy surface of the ocean.

Stars. Hundreds of them, thousands of them. Shimmering with an eerie undersea light, beaming down upon the little band. Like an endless procession of candles, the stars vaulted overhead, illuminating the immense chamber.

She could see none of the familiar constellations she had come to know during her evenings at the research station, when the dome of night had risen over San Lazaro Lagoon. Yet here she found a myriad of new patterns and shapes, clusters and swirls. Galaxies upon galaxies adorned the cavern, floating in fairylike reflection on the water. And, as ever, the spaces between the stars spoke to her of wonder and infinity.

Then a familiar wailing echoed, a song of loss and longing. The three companions listened in silence.

Geoffrey swayed his dorsal fin. "Whales may wander far and wide, seeking some way to ease their pain, but it does them no good. Even such a flowering of undersea stars cannot soothe them."

"I remember," said Kate wistfully, "my dad's stories about Merlin."

Geoffrey's fin stopped moving. "Yes?"

"He told me how sometimes Merlin would enter a cave, someplace blacker than night, and take off his cape that was studded with stars. Then he would flick his cape in such a way that the stars would float up and stick to the ceiling of the cave. So when anyone else came, it would be light instead of dark. My dad said that if you ever found a cave like that, you could tell that Merlin had been there."

"Hmmmm," said Geoffrey. "I rather like that story. Perhaps it is true."

"And perhaps it is just a story," replied Terry.

Geoffrey examined him with reptile eyes. "So you don't believe in Merlin?"

"Believe he really existed? No, I'm afraid not. He makes a fine legend, I'll give you that much. I don't expect to run into him on the street, though."

"You might run into someone who knew him," cautioned Geoffrey.

"Meaning Nimue?" asked Kate.

The white mane bristled. "Do not speak that name. We are close. Too close."

At that moment a fragrant wind, full of the smells of

the sea, swept over them. Kate suddenly noticed that, on every wall of the cavern, waterfalls gathered and tumbled into the lake. The water within them sparkled with such purity that the cascades seemed to glow with liquid light.

Here we are, she thought, in the realm of Shaa. *The place where the sea begins, the womb where the waters are born.* Then, in a hushed voice, she asked, "Where is the castle of Merwas?"

Geoffrey simply plunged downward, leaving her question unanswered.

They swam just deep enough in the warm currents to coast along the border between light and dark. Below, all was black. Above, the horizon stretched over them like a shining circle, perfectly round. Within this circle danced the stars, seeming to belong first to water and only second to air.

Once Kate glimpsed a solitary form swimming above them. Its shape was blurred, but it appeared to possess the tail of a fish and the upper body of a man. She turned to Geoffrey to catch his attention, but by the time she looked back, it had disappeared.

Before long, the lake began to smell richer, like the scent of deep woods in autumn. A few trunks of kelp rose from the bottom, with fronds so intricate and plentiful that Kate had to swim carefully to avoid entangling her brass ring. Prickly sea urchins clung to rocks. Eels drifted lazily past.

Fish of all sorts wove their ways through the sparkling water. Some, as slim as snakes, encircled the swaying trunks of kelp that climbed upward from the bottom.

Others, brightly painted, inhabited the colonies of pink and purple coral shaped like lacy fans, bulbous horns, or grooved brains. Passing nearby, Kate could hear hungry fish biting the corals with their teeth, crunching and scraping in search of food. Towering sponges, splashed with colors, sprouted on all sides. And from dens under ledges, shadowed eyes watched with interest.

Surrounded by the jungle of coral and its many inhabitants, Geoffrey slowed his pace. He swam almost leisurely, hardly bending his back. At length, he surfaced again. The others followed.

Kate gasped. Facing them stood a glorious castle with walls made of streaming, spraying waterfalls. Thundering and crashing, it lifted high out of the lake, glittering in the starlight, a tower of sculpted water. Columns of cascading liquid supported its turrets and buttresses. Archways made of rainbows ran along the rims of its battlements. Stairs of lavender coral spiraled into its rampways and towers, leading to halls and chambers hidden behind crystalline curtains.

"The Glass House," she said in wonderment.

"Known in other times," added Geoffrey, "as the castle of Merwas."

Kate fluttered her fins. "So they are the same!"

"One and the same."

Viewing the magnificent castle, she said, "What a place to hide the Treasures."

"Yes," agreed the white-haired fish. "It made good sense at the time. Remember that when Merlin found his way here, the entire realm of Shaa, including this castle, was deserted. Not only had the mer people fled, but . . . the sorceress, having searched fruitlessly for the Horn, had abandoned the cavern as well. And so Merlin believed," Geoffrey added dismally, "that it would stay that way. He simply did not count on the fact that one day she would return here and discover the hidden Treasures. Or that she would willingly destroy the Glass House and everything in it, not to mention the whirlpool and the ship and much else besides, just to get the Horn."

"That N—"

"Hush!" commanded Geoffrey, looking around fearfully.

"Sorry," she replied. "I won't slip again. I promise."

Focusing again on the Glass House, she followed the contours of its flowing walls. Then she gasped again. For at the base of one of the battlements, partially concealed by a fountain, she spied a large silver shape. *The submersible.*

She had no chance to cry out. In an instant, the castle vanished and the stars eclipsed. The world went dark, dark as the abyss.

24

prisoners

KATE awoke, shivering. *The water here is so cold I feel numb.* She reached to rub her sore head. Reached, she realized all of a sudden, with her own hand.

She sat bolt upright. Though this place was very dark, she could still make out the shape of her hand. She closed it into a fist, then reopened it. She touched her face, her hair, her arms. *No more brass ring.* She took a deep breath. *No more gills.* Her head still throbbed. All she could see in the dim light was water, running and rushing from all directions. And all she could feel was wet and cold.

A strong hand reached out of the shadows and clasped her by the forearm.

"Terry?"

"Glad you're back with the living. I was getting worried there." Glancing over his shoulder, he said,

"Especially when old Geoffrey had you looking like a partridge."

"An unavoidable detour," grumbled the old man, emerging from the shadows. He scratched the tip of his pointed nose. "I had to do it to get rid of the ring."

"That's not what you said when it happened," Terry reminded him. "But you got it right in the end, as you did with me."

"You mean to tell me," queried Geoffrey innocently, "you didn't like being a donkey?"

"Not in the least."

"Once an ass, always an ass."

"All right, you two," interjected Kate, clambering to her feet. She sloshed a few steps across the wet floor. "Where are we, anyway?"

"We are in the dungeon." Geoffrey's morose face came closer. "Somewhere under the Glass House."

"The dungeon! How did we get here?"

"We were captured. By the sea demons. For some reason they didn't kill us on the spot, but merely rendered us senseless and threw us in here."

"Have you looked around for a way to escape?"

Geoffrey eyed her somberly. "Since regaining our human forms, that is *all* we have been doing. But although these walls and this floor are made only of water, they are as sturdy as iron."

"Dad and Isabella are somewhere around here, too! I saw the submersible."

"Yes," answered the monk. "Though I cannot tell you where they might be, or in what condition."

"We have to find them." She flapped her arms to

warm herself. "Why is it so c-cold in here? It's been getting hotter and hotter as the eruption gets nearer. But now I'm f-f-freezing."

"I will show you," answered Geoffrey. He led her over to a squarish hole in the wall where no water flowed.

"A window," she marveled, shivering again.

"Come nearer. You can see the lake. And something more."

"Are you sure she's strong enough?" asked Terry.

"I'm f-fine," said Kate, not really feeling that way. She approached the window, peering out at the starlit cavern and the still water below. "It's darker in here than out there," she observed.

Geoffrey nodded. "These walls—see how thick they are?—keep out much of the light from the stars. And Nimue has not equipped her dungeon with a torch."

"You never answered my question. About the c-cold."

"The truth is," Geoffrey explained, "it is quite warm in here."

"But I feel—"

"You feel cold. You feel chilled to the bone. That is because you were touched."

"Touched? By what?"

Geoffrey raised his arm and pointed his knobby finger out the window. "By one of them."

Kate turned again to the glistening surface of the lake, just as a whitecap appeared. From beneath it came a dark form, rising slowly to the surface. At first she thought it was an enormous eel, but the intense chill in her chest told her otherwise. She watched, transfixed, as it lifted its huge, triangular head above the water.

The sea demon spun a half rotation, growled fiercely, then fell back with a colossal splash. In two seconds it was gone, yet that was all she needed to view the massive body covered with purple scales, the savage jaw, the teeth sharp as knives. The sight seemed to fill her whole body with ice.

Then a hand, larger than hers, slid into her own. It was Terry, standing beside her. As she turned to him in thanks, the chill seemed to lessen a bit. Little by little, she felt her lungs breathing and her heart pumping, with growing strength and growing warmth.

"Do you think," she asked quietly, "we still have a chance? If not to stop Nimue, at least to save Dad and Isabella?"

Terry stroked the cleft of his chin. "That depends on how soon the eruption hits. With these tremors and vents bursting open . . . my guess is we have only a few minutes left, at the most." He observed her thoughtfully. "But whatever we have, I suppose it's something."

Lightly, she squeezed his hand.

Geoffrey approached, the breeze from the window ruffling his unruly hair. "It is a bleak moment," he confessed. "Bleaker because I must share it with both of you."

"We came by our own choice," said Kate.

"By your own folly," corrected Geoffrey. "And by my folly as well. I fear we have arrived too late to stop Nimue from destroying everything. And even if we did have enough time, what could we do?" He shrugged disspiritedly. "The days of the Glass House, and Arthur's final hope, are ended."

"You don't know that yet," insisted Kate.

The old man locked into her gaze. Somewhere behind his eyes, a frail fire kindled. "Perhaps." He patted the folds of cloth over his chest where the last of the Treasures lay hidden. "You remind me that we still possess the one thing Nimue most craves. And she will not get it easily."

"Couldn't we take a drink from the Horn? Maybe its power could help us."

Geoffrey shook his head. "Whatever the Horn's power truly is, no one who has not first met the test of the Emperor Merwas may drink from it. Merlin learned that painful lesson! In any case, I doubt that taking a drink would help us stop Nimue. The Horn's power is of a . . . different nature." He scratched behind his neck. "Yet you do make me wonder. Perhaps—"

At that moment, a blinding light flashed. When Kate's vision cleared, she could see that a door had opened in the liquid wall of the dungeon.

"Oh no," she said.

"Good Lord," muttered Geoffrey, placing his hand over his chest.

first loyalty

A stout, square-shouldered man stood in the doorway, sizing up the group. In one burly hand he held a torch, but its light burned dimly compared to the glowing sword he held in the other. His face looked weathered and wrinkled, though less from outer storms than from inner ones. A torn oilskin shirt hung over his chest, the sleeves long ago removed. The hair on his head, blond and curly, matched that sprouting from his close-cropped beard as well as his biceps. His nose was swollen and inflamed, but the rest of his skin was white, like someone who has not seen the sun for many years.

Kate glanced at Geoffrey. He could not take his eyes off the shining sword of light. For her, however, it was the man's eyes that caught her curiosity. They were dark as night, much like the monk's, but with a difference. While Geoffrey's eyes seemed younger than the rest of him, this man's eyes seemed considerably older, as if his body had remained frozen in time while his eyes had continued to age.

"Welcome to my castle," he declared with a rolling accent that was made more pronounced by his stuffy nose.

Geoffrey started to speak, caught himself, then stuffed the end of his beard into his mouth and chewed vigorously.

"I am Garl-a-a-ah-ah-*choooo!*" He unceremoniously wiped his nose on his shirt, then cursed, "Damn this cold." With a loud sniff, he began again. "I am Garlon the Seaworthy, master of this house."

Geoffrey chewed still harder.

"I should have sent my servants to fetch you, but they are, ah, busy just now."

Apparently no longer able to stand it, Geoffrey tore the beard from his mouth and said, "If you mean Nimue and her sea demons, it is they who are the masters and you who are the servant."

Flame kindled in Garlon's eyes, and he raised the brilliant sword. "Who are you, who dares to speak to me this way?"

"I am Geoffrey of Bardsey, of the Order of the Horn."

Garlon pounced to Geoffrey's side. Thrusting the blade at the old man's throat, he said, "Geoffrey of Bardsey. Ah, yes. I understand you have a little a-a-ah-*choo!* . . . a little something I have long awaited."

Geoffrey tried to back away, but found himself pressed against a coursing wall of water.

"Leave him alone," shouted Kate. "Can't you see he has no weapons?"

Garlon whirled around. "His sharp tongue is weapon enough! He is nothing but a slimy old bag of bones, better off dead."

"Now, now," said Geoffrey, his eyes focused on the point of the sword and his whole body quivering, "I really didn't mean to offend you."

Garlon wiped his nose again. "Then why did you insult me?"

Still staring at the sword, Geoffrey laughed nervously. "I didn't think you would take it so personally."

Garlon jabbed the sword closer to his throat.

"It was just a spot of humor," said Geoffrey, squirming at the sword point.

"Well, I have no time for humor." He jerked the weapon away from Geoffrey, who nearly collapsed with relief. "I should kill you now, but Nimue wants to do it herself." Waving the sword toward the door, he commanded with the authority of a sea captain, "Go now. The whole crew of you."

Terry led the way out of the dungeon, stumbling in the dim light. He was followed by Kate and, last of all, Geoffrey. Garlon, torch held high, marched them down a hallway and up a long, spiraling staircase of lavender coral. The stairs seemed to twirl upward without end, climbing inside a curtain of crashing water. Geoffrey, tiring, dragged himself more and more slowly. Occasionally, Garlon prodded him with the sharp tip of the radiant sword.

At last the stairway peaked, opening into a room as spacious as any Kate had ever seen. On every side, powerful fountains formed rows of arches, one flowing into the next. The walls of water splashed and bubbled cease-lessly. Overhead, gushing jets of water merged into a vaulted ceiling.

"The great hall," panted Geoffrey, looking exhausted but awestruck.

Kate nodded, but her attention was directed not to the vast room, drained of water as Merlin had found it long ago. Nor was it directed to the array of objects near the glistening throne in the center of the floor. Instead she felt drawn to a large cage at the far edge of the great hall. Within its liquid bars, dark shapes moved.

"Dad!" she cried, running to the cage.

"Kate! Is that you?"

"It's me!" She sprinted past the empty throne. "Are you all right?"

"A little wet, but yes," her father replied.

"A lot wet." Isabella shook herself. "But at least we are alive, eh?"

"I'm so glad. I thought maybe . . ." Tears brimming, Kate held his hand through the watery bars. It felt strong. And alive. And Dad. "We've got to get you out of here."

"I've tried," he answered. "Believe me, I have. It's impossible. Until that sorceress comes back."

"Nimue," said Kate bitterly. She could almost picture the enchantress, her smoky body, her bottomless eyes . . . almost as if she had seen her somewhere before. But of course she had not. Kate released her father's grip and shook the bars with rage. "She's going to wipe out this whole place, and all of us, just to get—"

"The Horn," completed Garlon, standing behind her. He sneezed, spraying all of them. "That's right. Only Nimue and I can let them out. And she ordered—er, asked—me not to do that."

Jim wiped his face on his sleeve and shook his head in disgust. "Remind me, if I ever get out of this, to revise the accounts of Garlon the brave and heroic seaman." Then, spying Terry and Geoffrey across the room, he asked, "Is that Terry? And who is with him?"

"Yes, Terry," answered Kate, watching him help the old man hobble slowly toward them. "He's not so bad, you know. And that's Geoffrey. He's a monk. We found him on the *Resurrección*."

"The *Resurrección!*" exclaimed her father. "You've *been* there?"

Kate nodded.

"And the old man was there?"

"Went down with the ship. He stayed alive thanks to—" She caught herself, seeing Garlon listening closely. "I'll tell you later."

Her father reached his hand out of the cage and brushed her braid. "As much as I wanted to see you again, I had hoped it wouldn't be here."

She bit her lip.

"And as much as I dreamed of one day seeing the Treasures," he went on, "I never thought I'd see them through the bars of a cage."

"They're about to be destroyed, if Nimue has her way."

"I know. She thinks that she can cause some kind of disturbance—an earthquake or something—that will wreck the Glass House, as well as the whirlpool. She was boasting, just before you came, that when the whirlpool collapses, she can make off with the Horn. Unless of course, as she put it, she can lure someone into bringing her the Horn first."

Kate winced, then turned to the throne, which seemed to be made of millions of crystalline water droplets. *The throne of Merwas.* And surrounding it, the Treasures. Placed on one of its wide arms was the chessboard, with several wooden pieces sitting on it, awaiting someone's next move. Some distance away sat the flaming chariot, burning with such intense heat that it made the castle floor steam around its base.

Nearby, many other legendary objects were gathered. She spotted the knife, the pan, and the whetstone, all resting on top of a glassy table. The mantle of invisibility, copper-red in hue, leaned against a towering column of water, along with the halter and the harp. On the floor by the throne sat the ever-bubbling cauldron of knowledge, black, wide-mouthed, and nearly as tall as Kate herself. At its base lay the vessel of plenty, spilling forth a feast of fruits, cheeses, and dried venison, plus a large goblet of red wine.

The Treasures of the Isle of Britain. They represented all that humankind might need to live comfortably, and all that Arthur might need to triumph in his final battle.

She counted them. Ten were by the throne. The sword of light made eleven. The Horn was twelve. What was missing? Oh, yes—the ring. Now what was it that happened to the ring? Somehow she could not remember.

Just then Geoffrey and Terry veered off course and headed straight for the vessel of plenty. Garlon, seeing this, ran to intercept them. He leaped in front of them just as Geoffrey bent toward the goblet of wine.

"Just hoping for a swallow or two," grumbled the old man, eyeing the goblet.

"No," ordered Garlon. "I a-a-ah-*choooo!*" He wiped his nose. "I will tell you what you can touch and what you cannot."

"You know," said Geoffrey innocently, "that cold sounds positively *abysmal*. No humor intended, you understand. I know just the thing to cure it."

Garlon's eyebrows raised. "What?"

"What you need," explained Geoffrey with the barest hint of a smirk, "is a good dose of sunshine."

"Impudent swine!" fumed Garlon. He started to rush at Geoffrey, then held himself back. "I will kill you later," he promised. "After Nimue is done with you." A slow smile spread over his face. "And then I will drink from the Horn."

Kate drew near. "Do you really think Nimue will let you do that?"

"Who are you, girl?" demanded Garlon. "Tell me your name."

"Kate Gordon."

"A girl," said Garlon contemptuously. "And do you also belong to the Order of the Horn?"

"No," she replied. Then, with a glance at Geoffrey, she added, "But I'd like to."

Garlon laughed raucously, then rubbed his tender

nose. "So that is the best the enemies of Garlon and Nimue can do? To send an old man and a girl?" Again he laughed, pointing the torch at Terry. "And a coward."

Terry stepped forward in a huff, but Geoffrey grabbed his shirt.

"Careful," whispered the old man. "The sword of light can cut you to pieces in the blink of an eye."

"Don't you see what you're doing?" pleaded Kate. "You're going to ruin all of Merlin's work."

Garlon scowled. "Merlin. Bah! Don't speak that name! I am only sorry he is already dead, so I cannot kill him myself." He threw the torch at the flaming chariot, which instantly consumed it. "My gift to Merlin is to destroy the Glass House. Forever!"

Geoffrey scratched behind his neck. "Now I understand. Nimue must have tapped the power of the chariot to make the rocks under the sea seethe with fire until they erupt."

Garlon started to nod before stopping to contain a sneeze.

"I don't believe it," sneered Terry. "How can some chariot cause a volcanic eruption?"

"What are you, an alchemist?" shot back Garlon. "I will show you what the chariot can do." He planted both feet firmly, then pointed his sword at the flaming vehicle.

"No!" cried Geoffrey.

At once, the flames leaped higher, almost to the ceiling of the great hall. From the chariot came a blast of heat like a mammoth furnace, so strong it knocked Geoffrey over backward and made the others stagger, hands over their faces. A distant roar gathered, swelling in volume until it drowned out the cascading walls of the castle. Then the Glass House itself shook, swaying violently from side to side, throwing Kate and Terry to the floor.

Satisfied, Garlon lowered the luminous sword. The flames fell back to their previous level, and the castle walls stopped swaying. Surveying his prisoners as they scrambled to regain their feet, he grunted in satisfaction.

Geoffrey leaned toward Terry and asked, "Do you believe it now?"

He did not answer, but glared at Garlon.

As Kate stood, something fell out of her pocket and slapped the floor. It was the ivory comb she had found near the *Resurrección*.

She reached down and closed her hand around it. Suddenly Garlon barked, "What is that?"

"It's just a . . ." Kate's words trailed off as she felt herself gripped by an idea. A desperate, wild idea.

"It's nothing," she said, cramming the comb back in her pocket. "Nothing at all."

"Let me see it," he commanded.

"No."

Garlon lifted the sword again. "Let me see it."

She glanced at Geoffrey, still struggling to stand, and Terry, who was trying to help him, then over her shoulder at the cage holding her father and Isabella. Reluctantly, she removed the lustrous comb from her pocket.

"You can't have it," she declared.

"I will decide that," retorted the seaman, grabbing it from her. He held it before his face. "What is so special about a comb?"

For an instant, Kate hesitated. She cleared her throat, as if she were about to reveal a precious secret. Then she announced, her voice full of drama, "You are holding . . . the greatest of all the Treasures. The Comb of Power."

Garlon cocked his head. "Go on."

"Didn't Nimue ever tell you about it? This is the one Treasure that has more power than all the others combined."

Garlon looked doubtful. "More than the Horn?"

"Much more."

He moved closer. "How does it work?"

"I will tell you," she promised. "But first you must agree to free the people in the cage."

"I could just kill you and keep it."

"If you kill me you'll never find out how to use it."

Garlon lowered his voice. "Would this make me more powerful than . . . *her?*"

She nodded. "You could tell her what to do for a change."

Still doubtful, he eyed Kate uncertainly. "Tell me how it works."

"First let them out of the cage. Before Nimue comes back."

Clutching the comb, Garlon debated what to do. He rubbed his nose distractedly.

Just then Geoffrey, who had finally righted himself, rushed over to his side. "You found it!" crowed the monk. "My missing comb! How good of you."

Garlon's nostrils flared. "Your comb?"

Oblivious to Kate's stricken look, Geoffrey went on,

"This is number thirty-one thousand, eight hundred and forty-three."

"Treachery!" roared Garlon. Grabbing Kate by the shoulder, he shook her wrathfully. "It will be a pleasure to kill you." He raised the gleaming sword.

"Don't," cried Geoffrey, stepping between them.

"Get away, old man."

Geoffrey drew himself up, a mixture of scorn and pity in his eyes. "So is this what has become of Garlon the Seaworthy? Reduced to striking down an unarmed girl?"

Garlon faltered, then snarled, "Whatever I am is because of Nimue. And that miserable Merlin."

"Merlin had nothing to do with your troubles! And if you hadn't listened to Nimue in the first place, you would never have been cursed by her."

"Bah! You are wrong."

"Even after what you did, Merlin might have found it in his heart to forgive you, from the depths of his tomb."

"You lie. Merlin hated me as much as I hated him."

"Ignored you, perhaps. But never hated you. If Merlin cast you aside, that was only because he was consumed with his desire to help Arthur."

A strange, smoldering fire shone in Garlon's eyes. "So you are saying that Merlin cared more for Arthur than he cared for his own brother?"

"Yes," answered Geoffrey. "You may have been Merlin's brother, but his first loyalty was to his king."

"Merlin's *brother?*" exclaimed Kate.

"It is true," Geoffrey went on. "Garlon is the lost brother of Merlin. Lost, in more ways than one."

"Enough of this." Garlon aimed his sword at Geoffrey's throat. "I am tired of waiting for Nimue. You will give me the Horn. Now!"

"No," hissed a voice behind him. "That will not be necessssary."

26

oldest at birth

KATE reeled with a rush of cold that clutched at her spine and clawed at her brain. Even the sweetness of apple blossoms in the air could not lessen her revulsion when she turned to see the sorceress.

Nimue stretched her gaseous arms toward Kate, twisting them like tentacles. Then she cocked her head, the only solid part of her form, and fluttered a misty finger. "You shall remember."

Suddenly their meeting came back to Kate. She remembered the blackened eyes, the steamlike voice—and the terrible bargain she had made to protect the life of her father. She knew that Nimue would not easily free her from whatever form of servitude she had in mind. And though Kate could not tell what that might be, the prospect filled her with dread.

"Sssso we meet again." Slowly, Nimue coiled her

vaporous arms around Kate's waist and pulled her near. "I am pleassssed you remember me."

No words came to Kate, but a powerful shiver ran through her whole body.

"You have assissssted me, whether you like it or not," said Nimue, speaking directly in Kate's ear. "Tell me, now. Am I correct that the old fool over there hassss brought me the Horn?"

"No!" cried Geoffrey. "Don't answer her!"

Kate tried to resist, but a powerful force made her speak. "Y-yes. He h-has it."

"Exccccellent."

Nimue uncoiled her arms, leaving Kate trembling. With a low laugh that rippled up and down her smokelike form, the enchantress floated over to the throne in the center of the great hall and settled into it. Resting her head against the throne's back, she lifted her dagger and began casually twirling it in her long black hair. Finally, she swung her gaze toward Garlon and addressed him as if the former sea captain were nothing but a lackey.

"You. Fetch me the prisonerssss."

Garlon winced, then turned and strode across the room to the cage. With a blazing sweep of the sword of light, he sliced through a row of bars. A hole opened in the cage and through it crawled Isabella and Jim.

Kate and her father ran to each other and embraced. The feel of his arms, so warm and strong, melted the lingering chill of Nimue's touch. A surge of hope, small but tenacious, began to rise inside her.

Garlon shoved Jim roughly. "Get going."

Kate separated from her father. Isabella took her arm as they walked past Nimue's throne to rejoin Geoffrey and Terry. The enchantress, still twirling her hair with the dagger, observed them. Then she spat out another command.

"Now fetch me the Horn."

Garlon advanced toward Geoffrey. Sword gleaming at his side, he ordered, "Give it to me."

Geoffrey tried to hold his bent body upright. "I'd rather not."

The sword of light lifted. "Give it to me, old man, before I smite you with this."

For several seconds, no one moved. A drop of perspiration rolled down Geoffrey's long nose, hovering at the very tip before falling into his beard. At last, he cleared his throat and uttered a single word.

"No."

Rage sparked in Garlon's eyes and he stepped closer. "One more time. Give it to me or I will take it."

His hands twitching at his side, Geoffrey stared defiantly at Garlon. Then, without warning, he spat in the ruffian's face.

"*Aaaargh!*" Garlon started to bring down the sword on Geoffrey's head.

"Sssstop," barked Nimue.

Garlon froze, his blade only inches from the white mane. He looked anxiously at the enchantress.

"You brainlessss bungler."

Garlon cringed, but held his tongue. He lowered the sword.

"I ssssee now that I musssst do it myssssself." With

a gruesome grin, Nimue raised the blackened dagger, watching it glint with the fire of the flaming chariot. Almost casually, she pointed it at Geoffrey.

A bolt of white lightning exploded from the dagger and struck Geoffrey full force in the chest. The old man shrieked and flew backward, landing in a heap on the other side of the room.

"Geoffrey!" cried Kate, sprinting to him.

She grabbed his robe and shook him. Nothing. She listened for his breath, for his heartbeat. Nothing. She called out his name again, hoping for some sign of life. Nothing.

Tears welling in her eyes, she stroked his haggard head for the last time. Then she stood and faced Nimue.

"You killed him."

"Of coursssse," replied Nimue calmly. "And now you will bring me the Horn."

Kate stiffened. "I will not."

At that, Nimue lifted her hand not holding the dagger. No one but Kate saw the flash of ruby light from one of her fingers.

"Pleasssse reconsssssider. I assssked you to bring me the Horn."

Without willing herself to do so, Kate knelt by the body of her slain companion. Haltingly, she reached under the folds of his robe, slipped the coral necklace over his head, and removed the glistening Horn. As she stood, light shimmered across its curves.

Seeing the Horn, her father caught his breath. He watched, frozen in place, as Kate began walking with a mechanical gait toward the enthroned enchantress, sloshing her feet across the watery floor.

Without warning, he stepped in front of her, blocking her path. "Don't do it," he told her. "Don't give her the Horn."

Kate looked up at him. She wanted badly, so badly, to do as he wished. Yet another, stronger power commanded her to do otherwise. For a moment she hesitated, then continued walking straight ahead, as though her father did not exist.

As she bumped up against him, he gazed at her, dumbfounded. "What's the matter with you, Kate? I told you to stop."

"And I told her to come," replied Nimue, giving another low, guttural laugh. "Now you can ssssee where your daughter'ssss true loyalty liessss."

Jim tried to seize the Horn from her hands, but she dodged him. Whirling to face Nimue, he shouted, "What have you done to her?"

"Sssso," hissed the enchantress. "The protective father returnssss. Or issss it the greedy father, who would like the Horn all to himsssself? One never knowssss." She waved one of her smoky fingers at Garlon. "Go to him, will you? But do not sssssmite him until I ssssay."

Garlon bounded to Jim's side and held the sword of light at his chest.

Kate, still holding the Horn, shook herself. "Wait!" she called to Nimue, speaking groggily. "You promised . . . promised you would . . . not harm him."

Nimue twirled her hair relaxedly for a while. "Yessss, I ssssuppose I did." She peered at Kate. "But it doessss not matter, ssssince I have a better idea."

The enchantress coiled the lower part of herself

around the arm of the throne, basking in the heat of the flaming chariot. "Garlon," she instructed, "I want you to take the Horn from the girl. But do not take a drink for yoursssself! Not until I ssssay. Or what happened to that old fool will happen to you."

His hand quivering with excitement, Garlon snatched the Horn from Kate, all the while keeping his sword aimed at Jim. He brought the prize toward his face, then lowered it when he heard Nimue hiss angrily.

"Now Garlon," commanded Nimue. "Give the sssssword of light to the girl."

The seaman's jaw dropped. "Give her what?"

"The ssssword of light." Speaking to Kate, she declared, "I want you to hold the ssssword, but harm no one."

Kate nodded, as Garlon hesitantly gave her the weapon. Grasping the hilt with both hands, she could feel it vibrating with energy. The thought half formed in her mind to strike down both Garlon and Nimue, but it was swiftly overpowered by a desire to do exactly as the enchantress had commanded. She stood as still as stone, holding the bright sword.

"Exccccellent. Now we shall tesssst both the sssstrength of your will and the sssstrength of my ring." Nimue purred with delight before issuing her next order. "I want you to raisssse the ssssword above your head."

Kate did as she said.

"And now . . . I want you to kill your father."

A jolt of revulsion struck Kate. Yet, despite everything she felt, she found herself bracing to bring down the sword. She could hear the cries of Isabella and Terry, could see the horror in her father's face, could feel her stomach churning in torment. *I can't,* she told herself with great effort. *I can't do it.*

Even so, her hands tightened around the hilt, preparing to deal a powerful blow. Then, dimly at first, another idea surfaced in her mind.

"You . . . promised you wouldn't . . . harm him."

Nimue grinned broadly. "Yessss, but I made no promisssse about what *you* might do."

Kate shuddered, fighting back the power of Nimue's desire. *I can't. I w-w-wo* . . . She tried with all her concentration to say the word. *Won't. I won't.*

She lowered the sword ever so slightly, feeling stronger by the second. *I won't.* Shaking with strain, she began to take control of herself once more.

Nimue thrust out her hand. The ring flashed ruby red, blinding Kate's vision and assaulting her will.

"I ssssaid, kill your father."

"But—"

"Kill your father."

Kate looked from the void of Nimue's eyes to the terror of her father's. The stench of vomit seared her throat. Perspiration stung her eyes.

At that instant, a sudden trembling shook the floor of the great hall. Kate caught sight of the pile of brown rags that once was Geoffrey. His robe seemed to flutter in a wind that she could not feel. As she watched, the edges of his garment began to glitter, as if touched by the rays of a distant sunrise.

Then, miraculously, the robe deepened in color to azure blue, while silvery stars and planets sprouted along its borders. Geoffrey himself sat up with a start, even as his body began to transform. As he rose to his feet he grew markedly broader, until he was almost as stout and square-shouldered as Garlon. The hair on his head and beard lengthened and developed flecks of red amidst the white. The curve of his cheekbones lifted, and his hawk-like nose twisted and developed a hairy wart on one side. Wrinkles far deeper than Geoffrey's lined his brow, although the coal black eyes remained the same.

Nimue released a long, shrill hiss but remained motionless.

The man raised his prominent eyebrows, and a brief blast of wind knocked the sword of light from Kate's hands. As it slapped the coursing surface of the floor, she staggered backward. For the first time since seeing Nimue again, she felt like her own self.

"Merlin," she whispered, astonished. She traded glances with her father.

"Oldest at birth, youngest at death," quoted Jim, studying the wizard's profile like a piece of long-lost parchment.

Without taking his eyes off Nimue, Merlin spoke to the historian in a resonant voice. "An exceptional ballad, that. My only regret was that Saint Godric never got around to arranging it for troubadours."

Garlon started to speak, but choked on the words. He took a small step backward, cradling the Horn in his arms.

Merlin bowed slightly, still watching the throne. "It has been a long time, brother." His voice echoed in the chamber.

"I thought, I thought you were dead," stammered Garlon.

"You and many others." His jaw clenched. "Do you regret your treachery?"

"No! You brought it on yourself, by thinking you were so much better than everyone else."

Merlin's eyes bored into his brother's. "I have made my mistakes, just like you. I have paid a hefty price, just like you. Now I ask you, can you look to the future and not to the past? Can you cast aside petty jealousy and take my hand?"

Garlon grimaced. "Only to slice it off."

"Fool! You have not changed one bit! You were stupid to join the likes of Nimue."

"You are the stupid one if you think you can stop us now."

"I can stop you," answered Merlin. "I can stop you both."

"That," rasped the enchantress, "issss where you are wrong."

27

checkmate

IT wassss clever of you to essssscape from the cave," declared Nimue, her vaporous arms slashing the air. "You desssserve credit. But it will not change the outcome. It will merely ssssweeten my victory."

Merlin studied her with regret. "Once . . . you were so much more than this. You were . . . magnificent."

Nimue's face tightened.

"You valued knowledge more than power, beauty more than gain. I recall a time—was it so long ago?—when you turned the sands of a parched desert into a newborn sea, flowering with sea anemones. You even told me that sometimes you wished you had been born a sea anemone, so graceful and beautiful, so free from the tragedy and remorse that fill our lives."

"Ssssentimental fool! Who would want to be a lowly

ssssea anemone, fixed to ssssome rock, unable to move, even when attacked by a sssslimy sssslug?" The enchantress coiled and uncoiled her vaporous arms. "I ssssee you have learned nothing from your yearssss of confinement."

"And what have you learned?"

"That I have only one dessssire, the Horn. You denied me it oncccce. You shall not again!"

With that, Nimue aimed her dagger straight at Merlin.

Just as a bolt of lightning burst from the blade, the wizard leaped away. The bolt missed him narrowly but grazed his beard, scorching several hairs. Merlin flew into Garlon, knocking him over and sending the Horn skidding across the wet floor.

Landing near the glassy table laden with Treasures, Merlin plucked one of his own hairs and touched it to the whetstone.

"Blade!" he cried.

Instantly, the hair sizzled and exploded in a cloud of smoke. In its place Merlin held a gleaming sword with the hilt cupped over his hand. Shaking the rapier at Nimue, he declared, "If it is fire you want, then fire you shall get."

He advanced toward the enchantress. Suddenly he stopped. His cape had caught on the corner of the table.

"Look out!" shouted Kate.

The wizard spun backward as another bolt of lightning crashed past, shattering the table to shards. Treasures sprayed in all directions. At the same time Garlon took up the sword of light and slashed at Merlin's head.

The two bright swords clashed, throwing sparks in all directions. Between thrusts and parries, Merlin glanced repeatedly at the Horn lying on the floor. Yet every time he attempted to edge closer to it, Garlon fought him off, trying to do the same.

The two burly men fought furiously, working their way around the burning chariot. Fire from the chariot as well as their swords leaped at their clothing. For a split second Kate lost sight of them behind a blast of orange flames. Then Merlin reappeared, running to fetch the Horn.

But Nimue, seeing her opportunity, moved faster. Trails of mist flowing behind, she lifted off the throne and flew toward the shell-shaped Treasure.

In desperation, Merlin threw his sword like a lance at the Horn. It struck its target full force, sending the Horn sliding toward Jim.

"Throw it to me!" called Merlin.

Jim gathered up the Horn and started to hurl it to Merlin, when he abruptly caught himself. Gazing with wonder at the shimmering object, he held it before his face. All at once he seemed overcome with desire, and lifted the Horn to take a drink.

"Throw it!" Merlin cried.

Isabella tugged on Jim's arm. "Come on, throw it!"

Jim hesitated, giving Nimue just enough time to pluck the Horn from his grasp. With a savage swipe of her arm, she knocked him backward. Then she announced, "I shall be the one to tassssste itssss power."

"No!" bellowed Merlin, charging at her.

Just then Garlon careened around the chariot and collided into Nimue. The Horn flew into the air, bounced off the throne, and rolled to a far corner of the room.

"Sssstupid fool," cursed the enchantress, starting after the Horn.

Merlin changed course, hoping to get there first. But Garlon, seeing him, wheeled around and intercepted him. Panting, he prepared to strike down his brother with the sword of light.

"Garlon," pleaded Kate. "Don't!"

"I've got you now," crowed the seaman, swinging his weapon.

Merlin drew a quick breath, then lunged—not at Garlon, but at the chessboard sitting on the arm of the throne. He grabbed one of the wooden chess pieces and tumbled aside, chanting, "Arise now. Arise!"

Nothing happened. Merlin closed his eyes and squeezed the chess piece in his fist. Garlon, sensing his opportunity, advanced boldly. Across the room, Nimue raced toward the Horn.

Kate anxiously asked her father, "What was the chessboard supposed to do?"

"The pieces," he replied, "were able to—"

Just then, a series of loud reports filled the great hall. The chess pieces suddenly swelled to enormous size. Thirty-two stern figures, each one twice as tall as a man, surrounded the throne, motionless as statues. Beside Merlin, a red knight with the head of a huge horse stood glowering at Garlon.

"Come alive," finished Jim, awestruck.

Merlin regained his feet and raised his eyes to the towering knight. Then he turned to Garlon and declared, "I shall be red."

In response, Garlon pointed to a black knight of equal size. "I shall be black."

As if on cue, the two knights reared back, whinnied and charged headlong into each other. They crashed together with such impact that they flew backward, skidding across the slippery floor. The black knight plowed into Nimue before she could reach the Horn. Enraged, Nimue spat out a curse that sent him flying right into the flaming chariot. As fire devoured his wooden body, shrieks of pain echoed among the arches.

Giant chess pieces all around joined in the fray. They collided into one another and slammed into arches and walls. Hammering and pounding, they attacked one another fiercely.

Garlon mounted another black knight and rode into combat. Brandishing the sword of light, he chopped mercilessly at two red pawns and a rook. He had nearly gained the upper hand when Nimue, who was being pursued by a pair of huge bishops, yanked the sword from him, leaving him to fend for himself.

Meanwhile, as Merlin retrieved his own sword, a black rook charged full speed at him, intent on running him down. A split second before the collision, the red queen cast herself in the rook's path, bowling him over sideways.

In gratitude, Merlin turned to the red queen, bowed, and said, "Lovely move."

The queen curtsied, then replied, "Queen takes rook. One of my best."

Kate turned to her father. "In chess, if you knock out the other side's king . . . don't you win?"

His eyes ignited. "It's worth a try."

The two of them plunged into the battle, dodging several chess pieces until they found the enemy king. As the king bent to catch them, they started running circles around him until the giant warrior started to teeter dizzily. Then, in unison, they hurled themselves bodily at him. He fell over with a crash.

Swiftly, Kate and her father rolled the king through a gaping hole that had opened in the wall. As they heard the splash below, all the other black chess pieces instantly froze in place, unable to move.

"We won!"

Kate's cry was joined by the cheers of the red chess pieces, as well as Jim, Terry, and Isabella.

At that moment, Merlin spied a cloud of dark vapor drawing near to the Horn. "Stop her," he shouted above the din. "Before she gets it!"

Terry, who was standing near the Horn, scooped it up, even as Nimue bore down on him. He threw it to Merlin.

"I have it!" trumpeted the wizard, holding the Horn above his head.

In a flash, Nimue changed tactics. Instead of flinging herself at Merlin, she braced her wispy form and pointed the sword of light straight at the fiery chariot.

"Checkmate!" she cried, as a violent tremor rattled the great hall. A seething, thundering roar, coming from far below the castle's foundations, swelled to deafening volume. The Glass House rocked so wildly that everyone, including Nimue, tumbled to the floor. Merlin pitched to one side, dropping the Horn, while the chariot spouted flames all the way to the vaulted ceiling.

The crystal throne fell on its back, splitting in two. Scorched by the blazing chariot, its once-transparent frame turned to blackened coals. As the fire burned hotter, the throne melted into a simmering puddle, then began to evaporate. Soon not a trace of it remained.

As Kate labored to regain her feet, another convulsion hit. More powerful than the first, it did not merely bend the castle walls. It broke them, burst them, splitting apart the flowing beams and buttresses. The force of the tremor hurled Kate like a missile into the cauldron of knowledge, which teetered briefly then fell to the floor with a resounding thud.

"The cauldron," called Merlin from across the room. "Set it right again!"

Before Kate could do anything, however, a deep crack opened in the aqueous floor. All the bubbling yellow liquid in the cauldron poured out and vanished down the dark fissure. All, that is, but a single drop, which spattered onto her wrist, stinging like a dart.

At once, an idea dawned in her mind. Spotting the copper-red mantle lying next to a fallen column, she crawled hurriedly toward it. From the edge of her eye she saw Merlin and Nimue attack each other with renewed ferocity. Between them, lying on the floor, rested the Horn. Their clashing swords rang out, barely audible above the tumult of the castle collapsing around them.

Grasping the mantle, Kate flung it over her shoulder like a cloak. It smelled of dried autumn leaves and rustled noisily. She started to buckle its golden clasps, when her hands disappeared before her face. *Invisible,* she said to herself in disbelief. *I'm invisible.*

Struggling to keep her balance, she did her best to dash across the vibrating hall to the place where Merlin and Nimue battled. As she approached, the wizard lost his footing and lurched to the floor. Nimue, seizing the advantage, bent to retrieve the Horn. At the same time, Kate hurled herself at it. Barely an instant before the hand of the enchantress closed on the spot, Kate grabbed the Horn and spun away.

Nimue froze. "The Horn," she rasped. "It dissssappeared!"

Merlin, looking equally perplexed, clambered to his feet. Then a strange light flickered in his eyes. He backed away, in the direction of the chariot, taunting Nimue to follow him.

Simultaneously, Kate stood, holding the Horn. She could see her father and Isabella running to escape from a toppling column. As the column smashed to bits behind them, she cried out.

Hearing her voice, Jim stopped abruptly, followed by Isabella. "Kate," he called. "Where are you?"

"Here," she shouted back. Then, remembering her invisibility, she tore off the mantle. "Right here!"

"I see you now," he answered. "Let's get out of here before—"

A great crack appeared, snaking across the floor with dreadful speed. It cut directly beneath the feet of Jim and Isabella, widening into a chasm. As Kate watched helplessly, it swallowed them whole.

"No!" she screamed as they dropped out of sight. She sprinted toward the chasm, but before she reached the edge a strong hand grabbed her by the chin and wrenched her down. The Horn fell from her grasp.

Garlon stood above her, frowning. Without a word, he lifted his sword to kill her.

Suddenly a figure jumped Garlon in a flying tackle. The seaman stumbled, twisting violently under the weight of his assailant.

"Leave her alone," ordered the man clinging to his back.

"Terry!" cried Kate, pushing to her feet.

She had barely spoken his name when Garlon jerked forward, throwing Terry to the floor. Garlon swung the sword, but Terry deftly dodged the blow and grabbed him by the ankle. As Garlon fell, Terry pounced on top of him. The two men grappled, rolling one on top of the other.

Kate stood by helplessly, not knowing what to do. She had no weapon, but even if she had one, how could she use it against Garlon without injuring Terry?

They rolled to the very edge of the chasm, fighting to control the sword. Bloodstains streaked their arms and legs as well as the slick floor. Terry's youth and added weight seemed an equal match for Garlon's brawn and experience, for every time one gained an advantage, the other would reverse it.

At length Garlon kicked Terry off of him. He stumbled to his feet, grasping the sword, then raised it wrathfully.

Terry lay on his back, helpless, as the sea captain reared back to strike.

Suddenly Garlon pitched backward as one foot slipped into the chasm. An expression of horror on his face, he swung the sword frantically to keep his balance.

"He's going to fall!" cried Kate.

Then, even as he tumbled over the edge, he whipped his arm and threw the sword straight into Terry's chest. With a cry of anguish that mingled with his victim's, Garlon the Seaworthy plunged into the dark waters below.

Kate ran to Terry's side and pulled out the sword. He groaned as blood spurted from the wound.

Laying a hand on his forehead, she looked around frantically for Merlin. For help. But Merlin was nowhere to be found. All she could see was the collapsing castle and the inferno in the center of the great hall.

She turned back to Terry. He squinted up at her, trying to form some words with his lips.

"Don't talk," she whispered.

He grimaced, then forced himself to speak. "This time . . . I tried."

Her eyes clouded. Now it was she who could not speak. She felt his body grow relaxed and still.

Slowly, she stood, her heart aching. She had lost everyone. Dad, who loved her no less than she loved him. Isabella, who showed her the stars in a single drop of seawater. And now Terry, who mattered more than she would ever have guessed. She shuffled aimlessly toward the flaming chariot, half hoping that another chasm would open up and swallow her, too.

Then she saw an enormous chunk of the ceiling

break loose and smash to the floor on the other side of the chariot. Along with the impact, however, she heard familiar voices shriek in pain.

She sprinted to the spot. There she found both Merlin and Nimue, pinned beneath the weighty chunk, which was sliding into a large hole in the floor. The head of the enchantress and the chest of the wizard were held completely immobile. Meanwhile, their arms groped madly for the sword of light, which lay just beyond their reach. In a matter of seconds, the chunk would tumble into the chasm, taking both of them with it.

Crawling as near as she dared, Kate grasped the sword of light. She started to hand it to Merlin, who was struggling so hard he had not yet seen her, when suddenly a ruby light flashed in her eyes.

"Give the ssssword to me," hissed a voice.

She jerked back her hand holding the sword. Hesitantly, she began to reach not toward Merlin but toward the thin, vaporous arm that beckoned to her.

"Clossssser. Come clossssser."

She stretched to give the sword to Nimue, even as the chunk slid deeper into the hole, dragging down the enchantress. Farther Kate reached, and farther.

Then, as Nimue's fingers nearly closed on the hilt, Kate caught a glimpse of the bottomless eyes. For a fraction of a second, she recoiled. *Nimue! I'm saving Nimue.*

"Clossssser! You are wassssting time."

Hesitantly, Kate moved nearer. Her stomach knotted. *Nimue . . . those eyes. Those horrible eyes! I ca . . . can't.*

The ruby light flashed again, blinding her. But unlike

before, she fought to see through it, to see with her own eyes.

"Give it to me," ordered Nimue, sounding desperate. *"Give it to me now."*

"No," said Kate aloud. In that instant, she swept her arm toward Merlin and placed the sword of light in his hand.

The wizard, seeing her at last, grabbed the sword and immediately started hacking away at the heavy chunk, even as it dropped lower. Finally he freed himself and crawled to safety.

Seething with rage, he pointed the sword of light at Nimue. He readied to run her through, knowing the powerful weapon would destroy her. Then, to Kate's surprise, he hesitated.

Nimue eyed him savagely. "You ssssentimental fool! Kill me while you have the chancccce."

"No," said Merlin. He flung the sword aside. "I will do better."

The anger melted from his face, replaced with steely calm. He raised his hand and pointed a single outstretched finger at the enchantress.

In a flash, Nimue vanished. In her place lay a simple sea anemone, its black tentacles as long and flowing as her hair had once been. Fixed to a rock, unable to move, it was swept downward into the chasm as the chunk gave way completely.

No sign of Nimue remained, not even a scream.

28

unending spiral

HOLDING tight to Kate's wrist, Merlin pulled her away from the hole. His cape torn, his hair disheveled, he looked more like Geoffrey than the great wizard.

He gazed at her solemnly before speaking. "You resisted the ring. That took enormous strength of will, enough to break Nimue's hold on you. I am grateful."

She bowed her head. "It won't bring back my dad, though. Or the others."

Placing his hand upon her shoulder, he said, "You did your best."

"It wasn't enough."

"It was enough to keep the Horn from Nimue." Merlin then turned and walked, a bit shakily, past the flaming chariot to what remained of the throne of Merwas. There, amidst the rubble, rested the Horn itself. He carefully picked it up, watching it reflect the firelight. Then he said, with the sadness of centuries, "I have lost so much, so very much. But once again, for a brief moment at least, I hold you, Serilliant."

And he recited:

> *Never doubt the spiral Horn*
> *Holds a power newly born,*
> *Holds a power truly great,*
> *Holds a power ye create.*

He pivoted to face Kate. "It may make little difference to you now, but you are, from this day forward, a member of the Order of the Horn."

"This day is probably my last," she said somberly.

"All the more important, then, that you receive your due." He offered her the Horn of Merlin. "Drink."

"Me?" she sputtered.

He slipped the coral necklace over her head. "Merwas decreed, *Only those whose wisdom and strength of will are beyond question may drink from this Horn.*"

"I—I don't know if I should."

"Perhaps you would like first to smell its special fragrance. Then you can better decide whether you want to drink."

Hesitantly, Kate lifted the Horn's gleaming rim to her nose. She sniffed gingerly at first, then closed her eyes and inhaled deeply.

Strange sensations swirled through her. A meadowlark singing. A book opening. First morning light. Tasting fresh melon, tart and tangy. Joining hands! Pearls of dew in a lupine leaf. A winged creature, emerging from its cocoon. Warm hearth. Cold lemonade. A baby colt, struggling to stand. An infant garbling his first words. Practicing piano, finally getting it right. Tossing the pitch, starting the game. Subtle sunrise, setting fire to fields of snow. Fresh water, chilling tongue and teeth. Diving in, *splash!* Blueberry muffins, still steaming, oozing butter. A first kiss. An inspiration. A young sapling, shading the stump of a fallen elder. Shooting stars. A dream to start the day. And, underlying all, the fragrant air of the mountaintop.

Kate opened her eyes.

"Well?"

"It's . . . wonderful."

A spare smile appeared on Merlin's face. "Drinking will be even better."

"I have the feeling that, when I take a drink, it will be as if my life is . . . starting over somehow."

"Easier said than done," cautioned the wizard. "But, yes, that's the idea. After you drink, your grief will be no less than before. But your ability to make choices may be a bit greater. And if you can choose, you can create."

Kate looked again at the gleaming Treasure. A magical Horn, a whirlpool, a strand of DNA. It seemed right that they should all possess the same spiral shape. She pondered Merlin's words. *If you can choose, you can create.* In a way, creation itself was shaped like a spiral. A vast, continuing, unending spiral.

She moved a step nearer. "I think I understand."

Merlin trained his eyes on her. "Understand what?"

"The power of the Horn. It's not about living forever, stretching your life on and on like a rubber band. It's about living *young*. Starting your life over, all the time."

Showing no expression, Merlin said, "Go on."

"That's why the ship, the fish, the whirlpool, even Geoffrey—I mean you—all stay so young." She twirled her braid, thinking. "It's almost like a kind of . . . creation. The power to create your own life, to make new choices, to begin again."

"Serilliant. Beginning." Merlin gazed into the curling Horn. "The Emperor Merwas knew that renewed life is the most precious kind of eternal life. For despite all the sorrows and losses of living, each new day is freshly born."

Then the wizard gestured at the once-magnificent castle. "Come now. Take your drink, while you still can."

Feeling the pull of the Horn's power, Kate pursed her lips to take her first swallow. But even as she smelled its fragrance again, something made her stop.

The power to create your own life . . . She remembered being a water spirit, so full of possibilities. How had Isabella put it? *All the future lies within the present.* She remembered that every cell in her body can replace itself over time. And she remembered Nimue's ring, which would not let her make choices, would not let her be human.

She lowered the Horn.

Merlin scrutinized her. "You don't want to drink?"

"No. Not exactly. I don't *need* to drink." Seeing his puzzlement, she fumbled for some way to explain. "I, well, I don't really need the power . . . from somewhere else. I . . . already have it."

Merlin observed her, as he played with his beard.

"Wise you are, Kate. Drinking from the Horn will renew your body, but not necessarily your soul. That part is up to you. And you possess that power, here and now." Somberly, he reflected for a moment. "But . . . tell me. Wouldn't you like to live forever?"

"Sure I would. But even more, I guess, I'd like to grow. And change. Maybe the Horn, by making your body stop growing old, makes it easy to stop growing in other ways, too. Like . . . Nimue. Or Garlon. Or the whales."

The wizard nodded sadly. "I feel for the whales. Their pain is as great as the ocean itself! They need something more, something beyond the power of the Horn to provide. They need . . . hope. That is my wish for them. It might come from any number of sources, even something as small as an isolated act of kindness. Or it might never come at all. Time will tell."

Hearing his voice, so much like Geoffrey's, Kate could not resist asking a question. "All that time you were in the whirlpool, did you look like yourself or like Geoffrey?"

"Like Geoffrey, to be sure! The last thing I wanted to do was to alert Nimue that Merlin had returned. That is why, when I finally escaped from the cave, I arranged the elaborate ruse of smuggling myself on board the *Resurrección*. The ship, I knew, would pass near the whirlpool. So after ensuring the sailors would be saved by the whales, I sank down to the bottom—hoping, perhaps, that someday a friend of Arthur's cause might find my clue on the ship's manifest and follow me."

Despite herself, Kate blushed.

Merlin straightened up proudly. "All Nimue ever

suspected was that a bumbling old monk had been sucked down the whirlpool. Knowing that she watched me constantly, I remained disguised as Geoffrey so she wouldn't get alarmed and try something . . . drastic. As it was, she ran out of patience before I expected."

Kate cringed as a chunk of the ceiling slammed to the floor, spraying her with water. "So for all those years she couldn't get in, and you couldn't get out."

"Not until you gave me the idea." He smacked his lips as if remembering something tasty. "Fortunately, the ship was loaded with a good supply of . . . necessities."

"As well as your little red book."

At that moment, another tremor tore at the castle, ripping away an entire wall so that the gleaming stars of the cavern shone down on them directly. Kate, like Merlin, barely kept her balance. As the tremor subsided, she drank in the sight of the stars.

She thought of the world above the waves she would not see again. Of the people whose voices she would not hear again. Viewing the chasm where her father and Isabella had disappeared, not far from Terry's bloody body, she shook her head. "I only wish your little red book had some way to bring the dead back to life."

Merlin started. "How stupid of me!"

Before she could ask what he was doing, he pawed through some rubble and snatched up the knife that had rested on the glassy table. Then he ran to Terry's side and bent low. Ever so gently, he touched its tip to the wound in Terry's chest.

"The knife that can heal any wound!" exclaimed Kate, comprehending at last.

"It may be too late to help," warned Merlin. "If he has but a flicker of life still within him, the knife may revive him. But if he is gone, there is nothing more I can do."

Kate watched Terry's face for any sign of life, but saw none. "How long," she asked hoarsely, "before we know?"

"It may take some time." His expression grave, he added, "More time than we have left." With his free hand he scratched the point of his nose in the way Geoffrey often did. Then he declared, "Escape is still possible."

Dumbfounded, she scanned the crumbling walls of the castle. "Escape?"

"Before the eruption. But you must hurry! I would guess it is only seconds away."

"What do we do about Terry?"

"I will stay with him."

She realized that he meant her to go alone. "Forget it. I'm not going anywhere without you."

"You must," the wizard insisted. "And take with you the Horn." He glanced toward the shattered table of Treasures. "I would like to go with you. *Benedicite,* I would. But I cannot. Whether or not I can heal this young man, I might yet be able to find some way to shield the Treasures from being completely destroyed. If Arthur is ever to return, he will need them."

She turned the Horn in her hand. "But this is one of the Treasures, too."

Merlin shook his white head. "That may be true, but I have learned one thing in finding it, losing it, and finding it again. The Horn Serilliant deserves a life of its own. Its power is too great to be locked away, hidden from all the world. If it is to be one of Arthur's Treasures, then Arthur must one day find it himself."

"It should be kept somewhere safe. So someone like Nimue—or her sea demons—doesn't get it."

"It should go with you."

She looked from the Horn to Terry's still-motionless body. "I'm not leaving without you!"

Merlin gazed at her soulfully. "You must try to save yourself. That is what your father would want." He lowered his eyes. "And what I want."

"No."

"I will miss you, Kate Gordon."

"But I wouldn't have any idea what to do with the Horn!"

A low rumble shook the floor, almost drowning out Merlin's reply. "It is up to you to choose its rightful home."

He reached, it seemed, to touch her cheek, but never did. A jagged hole opened in the floor beneath her. She dropped into darkness.

29

the jaws of death

WITH a splash, she plunged into the water.

The lake felt both warmer and darker than before. It stung her eyes. Murky spirals of sediment swirled around her like miniature maelstroms. Fighting her way back up, she wished she could still swim like a fish, moving with her spine instead of her limbs, breathing with gills instead of lungs, craving only water instead of air.

Bursting above the surface, she gasped for breath. The air reeked of sulphur, burning her throat. Clouds of mist obscured any view of the castle, let alone the starry cavern. Rumbling surrounded her, growing louder by the second, punctuated by the sound of the castle collapsing. Every few seconds, pieces of its structure dropped into the lake.

She wondered whether she would die by drowning or

by boiling in the lava that she knew would soon spew forth, turning this undersea lake into a pot of boiling stew. *I'd rather drown,* she thought dismally. *It's quicker.* A sudden chill gripped her. Like an eclipse passing over the sun, the chill extinguished her own light and warmth. She shivered, doubly so, for she knew what had caused the change. And she knew that there was one way to die even worse than boiling in lava.

She whirled around to face the sea demon.

Murderous teeth exposed, the huge sea demon drew nearer. Slithering through the water, it approached steadily, but relaxedly, as if savoring its moment of final revenge.

The Horn. It wants the Horn. Anger flared inside her, pushing back the chill. The Horn belonged to the world, as Merlin had said. Not to a demon.

She flipped a splash of water. "Try and get it," she taunted. "Just try."

The sea demon halted its advance, a look of sudden doubt on its face. Kate thought at first that her spurt of defiance had worked. Then she realized that another creature, even larger than the sea demon, was approaching from the opposite side.

Spinning her head, she found herself staring straight into a massive face. A face she had seen only once before, at equally close range.

It was the face of a whale.

The great creature spouted, spraying her with humid breath. Abruptly, he rolled to one side, sending a wave washing over her and his own barnacled back. Waving his pectoral fins aggressively, he made a sharp clicking that echoed and reechoed in the underwater cavern.

Great, thought Kate, blinking the stinging salt from her eyes. *A sea demon on one side, an angry whale on the other.*

Then the whale fell still. He watched her intently, his round eye not wavering. Although Kate could not be sure, he seemed to regard her with something other than malice. Something more like . . . recognition.

At that moment the sea demon released a deep, fierce growl. She felt cold again, colder than before. She turned to see the sea demon swimming toward her again.

Another wave rolled over her as the whale, bending his enormous back, dived into the lake. As he submerged, he raised his tail high into the air—a tail whose fluke had been recently severed.

Kate bit her lip, as a rush of memory flooded her. She saw once more the helpless animal, golden in the moonlight, struggling to stay alive. She heard his mournful cry of death, felt his flailing tail. *So he did survive, after all.*

Facing the sea demon once more, her brief sense of celebration vanished as quickly as it had appeared. Worse, she could no longer summon her courage, or even her anger. All she felt was fear. Fear as cold and deep as the eyes of Nimue.

Fast approaching, the sea demon growled vengefully. Its immense jaws opened, ready to devour its prey and claim its prize.

At that instant, a wave lifted around Kate. Then she

realized with a shock that it was no wave. A gigantic mouth rose above the surface, and she was in its center. As swiftly as it carried her upward, the mouth closed around her.

Everything went black.

Her first impulse was to fight. Against the lack of light and air, against the fringes of baleen that pushed at her from all sides, against the fear of being eaten alive.

Futilely, she struggled. Countless rows of baleen, like the bristles of vast brushes, pressed tightly against her. She could hardly move, hardly breathe. She had been swallowed, like Jonah. Swallowed by a whale.

Then, all at once, it came clear. Like the sailors of an ancient ship, she was being borne by a whale who wanted to save her. Yet this time no land was near. And this time something else would pursue them. She ceased struggling, working her way into a small pocket of air above the whale's tongue. For now, at least, she could breathe, though the air stank of undigested krill. Her feeling of dread only deepened.

The whale's angle changed sharply from vertical to horizontal. He dropped back to the water with a loud splash. In another instant he was diving again, bearing his human passenger.

A desperate race ensued, one that Kate could see only in her mind's eye. Beyond the powerful thumping of the whale's heart, beyond the constant whipping of his tail, she could hear the enraged growling of the sea demon, and beyond that, the ever-increasing rumble of the impending eruption.

For minutes that seemed like hours, the whale sped onward, swimming on a level keel. Then, unmistakably, the growling drew nearer, even as the chill in Kate's bones grew stronger. A wrenching turn threw her hard against the whale's jaws. The growling receded slightly.

The whale raced through the depths. More and more often, the pumping of his tail would slow for several strokes before speeding up again. Kate could almost feel his growing exhaustion. She wondered how long he could keep this up, how long before the sea demon's own jaws would tear into them both.

She tried to picture where they might be, recalling visions of the cavern, the coral jungle, the undersea stars, the ruins of the watery castle. All the while, the volcanic rumbling around them swelled louder.

All of a sudden, the whale veered upward. Kate slid further down his titanic tongue, moist and reeking of krill. She realized they must be climbing back up through the abyss. She could only hope that no spiderlike monster would be waiting for them at the entrance. To the rear, the sea demon's growling grew louder. Faster and faster beat the heart of the whale. Faster and faster beat Kate's own.

Was he going to try to carry her all the way to the surface? Even if they made it, how could they possibly stop the sea demon from getting them as well as the Horn? Fears rolled through her mind, one following the next, like waves on the beach.

Then came a new fear, more potent than all the rest. Her air was running out! She gasped, or tried to gasp.

Panic seared her brain. She needed more air, needed it *now*. She could not breathe!

Her head started throbbing. Silently, she screamed. Her limbs and chest began to go numb. A shadow darkened her consciousness, made it hard to think. Hard to remember. Anything.

The shadow consumed her. She lay still.

Her head drooped a little, only as much as the fringes of baleen would allow. Yet that was just enough to bring her face near the curling Horn hanging from her neck.

The fragrance, the feeling, surged through her once more. She opened her eyes. She breathed again.

Her father's first description of Serilliant came back to her, as though he were speaking right in her ear. *Emrys endowed it with a virtue. Anyone who held it near could smell the fragrant air of the mountaintop, even if he did so at the bottom of the sea.* She brought the Horn closer, inhaling gratefully.

With a lurch, the young whale swung sideways. He was swimming horizontally again, his tail working frantically. He was not heading for the surface after all. Where then was he going?

The rumbling rose to a crescendo. Though she could no longer hear the wrathful growling, she still could feel the creeping chill. She knew the sea demon was almost on top of them.

The whale changed course again. Now he was turning in tighter and tighter circles. He seemed to be spiraling downward. As though he were entering the whirling wall of . . .

In an ear-shattering blast, the sea floor erupted. The force of the explosion knocked the whale savagely, tossing him about like a tiny seed in a gale.

Then, with terrible suddenness, his jaws opened. Out spilled Kate.

30

an unexpected twist

SHE landed, dizzy and disoriented, on a hard surface. She could feel the Horn, still tied around her neck.

Half stunned, she stretched out her arms. A wooden deck! Could it be? She sat bolt upright. Her eyes viewed the ragged sails, the iron cannons, the weblike rigging. Her lungs drank the misty, sulphurous air.

In the next instant, several things happened at once. Things that convinced her that she had indeed returned to the *Resurrección*, that she was indeed alive.

The ocean floor shuddered, heaved and broke apart. Streams of molten lava and superheated gases burst into the water, hissing and roaring like thousands of turbines. The *Resurrección* rocked and pitched as if caught in a ferocious storm, forcing her to cling to the rigging to keep from flying overboard.

At the same time, the whirlpool slowed dramatically

and contracted, bringing the whirling wall within a few
feet of the ship. Curtains of water rained down on the
deck.

As the whirlpool contracted, Kate caught sight of a
gray streak circling in the vortex. The whale! Suddenly
she understood the final few seconds of her wild ride. In
those sharp, successive turns he had entered the
whirlpool; in that downward spiral he had moved into its
spinning core. Then, to keep her out of the sea demon's
reach, the whale had hurled her onto the deck.

With a pang, she recalled Terry's prediction that no living creature could survive the whirlpool unless it slowed
down significantly. She wished she could tell him that he
had been right. And, with deeper regret, she thought of
how much her father would have loved to see this very
ship. Even lashed by such a raging storm. Even for an instant. Even if the slowing whirlpool would soon collapse
on itself, drowning the ship and anyone aboard under an
ocean of water.

Then she glimpsed, near to the whale in the spinning
wall of water, the blurred, twisted form of the sea demon.
The sight made her cringe. She had eluded those jaws, at
least for now. But what of the whale, who had given his
all for the small chance she might be spared? There was
no way she could possibly help him. She could only
clutch the rigging and watch, water pouring down on top
of her.

At that moment a cluster of new shapes in the
whirlpool caught her attention. She could not be sure
what they were, or whether she had really seen them spin
past. Yet they seemed to be there, grappling with the sea

demon, where they had not been only a split second before. And the sea demon seemed to be locked in battle,
lashing out at these strange creatures that combined the
bodies of people with the bodies of fish.

An enormous wave struck the hull, pitching the ship
to one side. Water flowed under the ship, dislodging it
from the sandy bottom. Simultaneously, the whirlpool
slowed substantially, and then—for the briefest fragment of a heartbeat—it stopped spinning altogether.

In that instant, time itself froze. The whirlpool did
not move, the ship did not pitch, Kate did not breathe.
Her only sensation was the certainty of imminent death.

Then, just before the sea came crashing down upon
her, the whirlpool started rotating again. Yet this time,
something was different. At first she could not pinpoint
precisely what had changed.

In a flash she comprehended. The whirlpool was
turning *in the opposite direction*. Wrenched by the force
of the volcanic eruption, the whirlpool's torque had reversed itself.

More water flooded underneath the ship, surging,
pushing, lifting. And then a strange phenomenon
occurred.

The ship began to rise.

Like a corkscrew that reverses and lifts upward, the
whirlpool twisted toward the sky rather than the ocean
floor. Higher and higher it carried the ship, in a slow and
stately spiral, climbing gradually to the surface.

Kate's heart leaped. Might she actually see land
again? Might she actually bear Merlin's Horn to safety?
She craned her neck to look at the swelling circle of

light above. Pastel pink and gold painted the sky. A new day was dawning.

Without warning, a burly arm reached out and tore the Horn from her neck, snapping the coral necklace in two. She stared, aghast, refusing to believe what she saw.

"So," sneered Garlon, standing before her on the deck. "Did you think you could escape me that easily?"

"Give it back!" she demanded, releasing her hold on the rigging. "It doesn't belong to you."

The sea captain laughed raucously. "The Horn belongs to whoever has it! And I intend to keep it for a long, long time."

"Don't, please. King Arthur will—"

"Never see it!" He laughed again, wiping his nose on his shirt. "Nor will my brother, the great Merlin. He is the stupid one, after all! So stupid he won't even leave a castle that is falling in."

"Merlin's not stupid," retorted Kate. "He just cares about others."

"Better to be alive," answered Garlon. With that, he lifted the Treasure toward his face. He gazed at it in satisfaction, twirling it in his hands. He seemed captivated by the golden light playing on its surface, light that grew stronger with every turn of the spiraling ship.

Suddenly he lurched violently, tackled from behind. The Horn slipped from his grasp and skated across the deck, coming to rest by a case of cannonballs.

Kate rolled out of her tackle and crawled madly toward it. But Garlon grabbed her by the calf and yanked her backward. Raging, he picked her up and shook her as though she were a rag doll.

"I should have broken your neck long ago," he fumed.

Just then the first fragile ray of sunlight, reflected off the brass door latch to the captain's quarters, touched his brow. Though a more gentle blow could not be devised, it seemed to strike him like a hammer. He staggered under the impact.

Nimue's curse, realized Kate, though she could not tell whether Garlon had felt the effect of the curse or merely his fear of it.

Frantically, Garlon threw her to the deck and ran to the Horn. He snatched it up and brought it to his face, ready to drink.

31

a day without dawn

AT that instant, the ship burst above the waves. It began to circle the rim of the whirlpool, buoyed by the water rising through the funnel.

Garlon's eyes, so like his brother's and yet so different, danced with victory. Even as he raised the Horn to his lips, he seemed poised to release a long-awaited cheer.

Then his face contorted in a spasm of uncertainty, evolving slowly into terror. He dropped the Horn as his body convulsed, falling to the deck. A subtle perfume of apple blossoms blew past. The ship's bell tolled one time, echoing eerily. Garlon looked at Kate in horror, started to cry out, then vanished into the salty air.

The dead will die . . . Kate recalled the final words of the ballad, as she stared at the spot.

She glanced toward the east. The orange sun had

barely begun to peek over the horizon. She lifted herself to her feet, only to witness a staggering sight.

Drawn upward by the reversed spiral of the whirlpool, an enormous volume of water lifted like a great wall around the *Resurrección*. This circular tsunami, spinning slowly along with the ship, raised itself to a great height. It blocked the ascending sun, covering Kate and her vessel in shadow.

For a long moment, the towering wall of water hung there, ringing the ancient ship. Kate felt sure it would collapse any second, smashing the galleon to splinters. And she hardly cared if it did, now that Garlon had been destroyed. For the briny air of the surface reminded her more of what she had lost than of what she had won.

Collapse it did, but gently, smoothly. The wall of water melted into the sea, while the whirlpool, its power spent at last, started to merge with the prevailing currents of the Pacific. As the volcanic rifts far below finally quieted, giving the ocean floor a new geography, the whirlpool itself came to rest, returning the ocean surface to its geography of old. In a matter of minutes, the waves grew calm.

Remolino de la Muerté was no more.

Kate scanned the expanse of water, deep green with flecks of gold, surrounding the ship. The sun, now well above the horizon, beamed down on her warmly. Yet, for her, this was a day without a dawn, a day when the sun did not rise, either for her or for those she had lost beneath the waves.

No longer supported by the surging water of the whirlpool, the ship floated like a stick of driftwood, jostled by every wave. Kate reached for the Horn, lying near her on the deck. Again she studied its lustrous surface, its radiant liquid, its spiral design. And again she heard the voice of Merlin, saying, *It is up to you to choose its rightful home*.

But where could that be? Someplace safe, yet not completely hidden. Someplace where the enemies of Merlin and Arthur would not find it.

Maybe Merlin meant I should keep it myself. Strangely tempted by the thought, she lifted the Horn, watching it shimmer in the sunlight. Perhaps she would change her mind and decide to drink from it one day. Or perhaps not. In any case, she would make a solemn promise to guard it for Arthur, to give it to him when he returned.

Or would she? In the presence of such power, would she eventually forget about her promise, as Merlin did long ago? And even if she could stay true, she was only one person. Those who craved the Horn would hunt for it relentlessly. She could not protect it from every conceivable threat.

Her mind drifted back to the story of the Horn. She thought of its many names, its many gifts, its many masters. She thought of its birth, inspired by the love of Emrys for Wintonwy. She thought of its connection to the mer people, ever elusive, and to the sea itself, the watery womb of all life.

As she stood on the deck of the ancient ship, an idea

came to her. It was full of risk, yet it held a hint of hope. She looked into the Horn once more, then called out as loud as she could, "Scrilliant!"

With that, she hurled it into the waves. For an instant it rested on the surface of the ocean. Then it sank out of sight.

She waited, watching, unsure what to expect.

At that moment, a ring of bubbles came to the surface, encircling the spot where the Horn had disappeared. Out of the sea rose a group of mer people, glistening green. In the middle of their circle, riding a low fountain of water, was the Horn of Merlin.

They had accepted her gift. With a single, soundless splash, they dived beneath the waves and disappeared.

Kate noticed that the *Resurrección* was listing more and more. No longer sustained by the power of the Horn, its timbers started to split and crack. A wave smashed the stern, throwing her into the rigging. The hull moaned like a living thing, then broke apart, its timbers dissolving into thousands of pieces. Into the ocean went the sails, the gold ingots, the jewels, the ivory combs, the cannons, the silks, and the thin red volume, all to be scattered on the bottom by the currents and tides.

Immersed in frigid water, Kate wrapped her arms around the remains of an old beam, hoping to stay afloat. She had no way of telling whether she would be carried out to sea, where she certainly would die, or back to the coast, where she would survive only if she could find a fishing village before falling prey to the desert sun.

A wave drenched her, nearly tearing her from the

beam. Somehow she clung on. When she opened her eyes again, she saw a strange shape rising out of the ocean. She caught her breath.

The shape surged higher. At once she recognized it. She still could not breathe, though no longer out of fear. For there, moving toward her, was no sea demon, no phantom ship. It was the submersible.

The next several minutes flowed past as quickly as a crashing wave. The opening of the hatch. The shouts. The waves. The reunion she had never believed possible.

There was her father, hugging her so hard she thought her ribs would crack, then listening with care as she described her final moments with the Horn. There was Isabella, shaking with joy to see her, explaining how they had reached the submersible only seconds before the eruption, eager to hear about the young gray whale. There was the submersible, cramped but wholly satisfactory, bobbing where not long ago a great whirlpool had churned.

As Kate described Terry's gruesome fate, the others listened in disbelief.

"Can it be so?" asked Isabella, brushing back some stray hairs. "His life should not end that way."

Jim frowned. "No one's life should end that way."

In time, the conversation turned to other matters. Kate painted vivid portraits of her last encounters with Nimue, Garlon, and Merlin himself.

Her father looked at her affectionately. "You're not a bad storyteller, you know."

Despite her wet clothes, she felt a touch warmer. "It's in my genes."

"I can just hear you now," he predicted. "Sitting by the fire, surrounded by your grandchildren. One of them asks, 'Please, Granny, tell us the one about the battle of the giant chess pieces.' "

Kate joined in the laughter. "So I'll get to tell my own stories about Merlin." Then her expression changed. "Can you forgive me for almost following Nimue's orders?"

"If you can forgive me for following my own greed for the Horn. I found out down there that my motives were less pure than I had thought. Still . . . we did manage to prove the existence of Merlin, didn't we?"

"And not just in the sixth century."

"Right you are."

"He didn't look at all like what I expected."

"At least you got the wart on his nose right." He worked his tongue, pondering something. "I think you did the right thing with the Horn."

"You really think so?"

"I do. And if Merlin could be here with us, I'm sure he would, too."

She started to smile, then caught herself. "Maybe he *will* be with us again. And maybe he'll bring Terry back with him."

"I hope so," said her father.

"Do you think he can save him?"

"Merlin is capable of many things."

Isabella leaned closer. "As is *the place where the sea begins, the womb where the waters are born*."

Jim gave her a nudge. "Not bad for a marine biologist."

Before Isabella could respond, a familiar wailing reached the submersible. Familiar, yet somehow changed. Hunched together, the trio listened to the creaking and moaning, clicking and whistling of the whales. They were all around, encircling the submersible, weaving their complex harmony.

"Something's different," said Jim after a while. "Do you hear it? Their singing isn't the same."

"Yes," answered Isabella. "There's a little less sadness."

Kate nodded, recalling Merlin's wish for the whales. "Or maybe . . . a little more hope."

Just then a gray whale, streams of water pouring from his body, launched out of the waves not far from the submersible. The whale paused, half in the water and half out, before falling back in a thunderous splash, spraying every window in the vessel.

Then he descended, lifting his severed tail into the air.

"That's him!" exclaimed Kate.

Isabella watched the whale submerge. "I have the feeling you two might meet again."

"Maybe."

"Hey," said Jim, "is anyone else hungry? I'm in the mood for a big helping of something. How about Baja Scramble?"

Isabella pouted. "I've been dreaming of pancakes."

"All right, then. We'll flip a coin."

"Here," announced Kate. "I've got one." She thrust her hand into her pocket and pulled out a silver coin, as bright as if it had been freshly minted. A piece of eight.

The submersible pitched on the swells, as a lone gull screeched overhead. Waves slapped and surged, rocking to the rhythm of the sea.

THE BALLAD OF THE *RESURRECCÍON*

An ancient ship, the pride of Spain,
Embarked upon a quest
To navigate the ocean vast
And still survive the test.

It carried treasures rich and rare
Across the crashing waves
Beyond the flooded fields that are
So many sailors' graves.

Its goal to link the Orient
With distant Mexico,
The ship set sail with heavy hearts
And heavier cargo.

The galleon brimmed with precious gems,
Fine gold and silver wrought,
Silk tapestries and ivories
And spices dearly sought.

From China, Burma, Borneo,
Came crates of lofty cost,
And one thing more, the rumors said:
The Horn that Merlin lost.

Upon its prow, the words inscribed,
God bring us safe to land,
The ship at last raised all its sails
As lovers raised their hands.

Resurrección, O mighty ship,
You bear our very best!
Resurrección, O mighty ship,
Where will you come to rest?

Prevailing winds advancing east,
Pacific storms alive,
The brave men steered for Mexico
And prayed they might arrive.

They fought against the torrents,
A plague, a great typhoon,
Pursued by monsters of the deep
And pirates seeking boon.

The sailors suffered from the sun
That cracked and baked their skin,
Yet knew, between the sea and sun,
The sea would surely win.

For seven months they eastward sailed
Adrift upon the swells
Till even men whose hearts were strong
The stench of death could smell.

All water gone, as well as hope,
They grew too weak to stand
Until a voice cried loud and clear
"Land ho! I see the land!"

A joyous cheer arose that day
From sailors nearly dead,
Yet when they steered the ship to land
Their joy gave way to dread.

Resurrección, O mighty ship,
You bear our very best!
Resurrección, O mighty ship,
Where will you come to rest?

The ship began to list and spin
As sails apart did pull
And timbers buckled under waves
That smashed against the hull.

In circles tighter than a noose
The helpless vessel sailed
And every man upon the deck
Collapsed to knees and wailed.

For though the sea's a dangerous place
With terrors great and small,
Still mariners have always feared
The whirlpool most of all.

As swirling waters swamped the boat
And snapped a mast in two,
The galleon's mates leaped overboard
Into the churning blue.

The whirlpool dragged them under waves
Where endless chasms yawn.
The noble ship sank out of sight,
Its crew and cargo gone.

Then up from waters deep and dark
A pod of whales appeared.
They grabbed the men between their jaws
As Death's own jaws drew near.

Resurrección, O mighty ship,
You bear our very best!
Resurrección, O mighty ship,
Where will you come to rest?

To shore the saviors carried them,
And lo! The men survived.
They never knew why came the whales,
Nor why they were alive.

They only knew their ship was doomed
Because of Fate's cruel hand.
So many dreams and fortunes lost
Within the sight of land!

The whirlpool drowned the treasure ship
Upon that dreadful morn,
And buried it beneath the waves
Along with Merlin's Horn.

And so today the ship's at rest,
Removed from ocean gales,
Surrounded by a circle strange
Of ever-singing whales.

A prophesy clings to the ship
Like barnacles to wood.
Its origins remain unknown,
Its words not understood:

One day the sun will fail to rise,
The dead will die,
    And then
For Merlin's Horn to find its home,
The ship must sail again.